In Leigh Anderson's normal turned crazy life journey she meets the finest men at the right time who are more than willing to keep her checking accounts loaded and willing to give her almost anything she wants...

But *everything* has its cost... Before all is said and done innocence will be shed.

After being excommunicated from the only church she's ever known when her married pastor makes advances towards her and flips the script to make her look like the bad guy and, after being viciously raped by the one person she thought she could trust, she attempts suicide.

Will Leigh accept the new path and the new unorthodox friend who has entered her life or will her lifestyle as the baby's mother of one Detroit's most paid upper class men continue to entrap her?

EVEN IF YOU DON'T...

a 3/5ths magic & kemet book

EVEN IF YOU DON'T...

This book is strictly a fictitious figment of the author's imagination.

Please do not read this novel while simultaneously trying to decipher which character is the author or this person or that person... One day, there may very well be an autobiography, however, rest assured, this is not it...

PLEASE EMAIL COMMENTS REGARDING THIS PUBLICATION TO
MIANNE@MIANNEABOOKS.COM

EVEN IF YOU DON'T...

Life Lessons

One thing I have learned,
the thing I am still learning
is that you never know what will happen
in this life you are given...

It's those unexpected things,
those unexpected gifts,
those things you do not even know you long for,
that come to you anyway and make you the happiest,

Each one of us
has a purpose, a goal
we were sent to this earth to find,
and, hopefully, before we leave this earth,
we find the trinket sent down just for us,
the trinket holding our own special dream...

Leigh

EVEN IF YOU DON'T...

Part I
In the beginning…

CHAPTER 1

I LOOKED OVER AT my son Pharaoh. Royal... African... Demanding of respect. No one had liked the name except me but I chose it anyway.

For one, I definitely wasn't going to name him Darren after his father. I don't want to call Darren trifling--he's not exactly. But he was and currently *still* is a dog.

I met him summers ago on a sweltering Saturday evening downtown at the jazz festival.

When its summertime, the only thing you're concerned about is making sure you take three showers everyday. You forget about all the negative statements and headlines Detroit undeserving and deservingly gets slashed with in Newspaper headlines. July is that one month of the year that makes every sequined-rhinestone hat, orange, pasty lipstick and stretch-pants wearing grandma in town and every guy from every hood in Detroit with a souped-up odd-colored, bass pounding, shimmering old school hooptie that just finished chiefin' on a blunt and pouring out some of his forty for tha homies—you know, the ones that'll fight if you say Tupac ain't alive?—those dudes, July makes them, the grannies and everything in between step out to mingle at Hart Plaza right down to the professional Huxtable looking husbands and wives sitting on top of the main stage's concrete stair step seating with the folding chairs they bought just for the festival; they're two seconds away from standing up and gigging to the music but, instead simply tap their feet and snap their fingers and zig-zag their heads to beats laid out in flavor that swirl around the Renaissance and the Detroit River as the musicians play.

The middle aged lonely and divorced men are too busy roaming about and gawking at all the young, 'trainable' girls they hope to sweet talk home for the night or turn into wifey #2 or 3 to be absorbed by the musicians--barely legal curves are the only jazz they're thinking about.

Puppy love couples are out again just like last night and the night before—even though they have summer jobs at the mall and need to be up early for work the next day. They think they're "so hot"—just like we did when we were their age and they try to act grown even though the boy's have mustaches as faint as spider legs barely perched above their upper lips and their girlfriend's heads wobble when they walk. In their matching throw-back jerseys you can't tell them nothing--but they know to have their behinds home by eleven o'clock. The whole time at the bus stop they talk about how much fun Cedar Point is gonna be next week but next month they won't even be going together anymore.

Mamas hiding scalp burns from relaxer touch ups and flat-ironed hairstyles promise to take the kids to the state fair if for once they just act like they have some sense. Then you've got all the little girls that had to sit on the front porch with their hair sticking up all over the place like four black poofy squares as cars drive by, enduring having their heads yanked back and forth just so they can have all those meticulously parted ponytails and intricate braid patterns designed like carvings on their head. Even if they cried the entire two hours they had to sit and wait for it to all be over, the zillions of barrettes now swinging against their shoulders that match their JC Penney outfits somehow make them forget just how painful getting your hair done can sometimes be. They struggle to keep up with their mama's who are way too preoccupied with tearing off pieces of sugary elephant's ear with acrylic nails that match their outfits to the T-- even their big toes are acrylic and airbrushed.

The police are directing traffic while smiling and signaling to each other and laughing at all the under and over dressed pedestrians. But the Africans merchants with yellow-browned eye whites don't, they never smile. Not at the sistas looking like Eryka Badu or the Fela Kuti fans buying up all the purses from the Motherland and not at the less conscious ones cleaning them out of all the knockoff Coach and Gucci bags they brought from New York...

The second Dominique, me and Sherra crossed the street all eyes were on us. Horns honked like crazy. Women with shiny feathered ponytails posted on the sides of their heads grabbed their boyfriend's arms as we walked by a line of people waiting to get what was left of Livernois's ribs. Back in the day they used to have a low budget commercial on channel 68—everybody in the store standing behind a long slab of ribs smiling real hard, with gospel music blaring in the background and the address flashing across the screen that ended with a toothless grandma in a wheelchair gumming on a rib bone. The commercial notwithstanding, nobody does ribs like Livernois. They have the best sauce, they're Black owned and they slather their ribs with tons of sauce just the way Black folks like 'em. Every year they cook at the African World, the Jazz and the Gospel Festivals.

An older brotha with locks that looked like house insulation was busy shouting frankincense oil and Nag Champa incense "end of the night specials" stopped to offer Dominique a free bootlegged CD in exchange for her number when we walked passed him.

She stopped and, of course, turned around with three CD's in her hand. "I gave him a fake number!" she protested before Sherra could get started.

Lyrics blasted against each other from cars stuck in the stationary bumper to bumper traffic along Jefferson while Niquie did her usual and flirted with as many admiring drivers as possible. I acted nonchalant, secretly enjoying the commotion even though I wasn't worried about getting any numbers. Chasing after guys had never been my thing.

To complete our girl's night out, we were about to go for dinner, catch up on all Dominique's latest gossip and chill at Floods. In the midst of it all, Darren was on a flashy red, black and silver motorcycle that looked expensive.

Dominique tossed her long, naturally spiraled hair over her shoulders like a girl of Anglo Saxon persuasion and strutted her curvy, five foot eleven frame towards him. Just like she was always on an unnecessary diet, she was always on the prowl for men. She even had this signature 'Look At Me' walk. Sherra and I slowed down to wait for her. She had the two seconds away from desperate act down and was earning enough male admirers to start a fan club.

"See, *dis* is what gets on my nerves about hangin' wit her and I'ma let her know! Niquie pretty but da way she throws herself at men-- uugh--dat takes it all away. Most of 'em ain't worth anyway. Why she godda do dis *everywhere* we go?" Sherra exclaimed rolling her eyes and smacking her lips in disgust.

"Well. Lotsa guys try to talk to every girl *they* see and the world doesn't give *them* any grief for it," I stated as I yawned and shrugged my shoulders indifferently. Just before I finished yawning and opened my eyes, he passed Dominique and was now standing in front of me.

"The night's just begun and you're already tired? Guess I'll have to catch you another time if I wanna take you for uh ride then, hungh?" My mouth was still open as Darren's golden, green-brown speckled colored eyes peered into me. They sparkled but didn't impress me as much as that motorcycle of his.

He smiled confidently. I stared back at him blankly and everything within me went blank. He looked dangerously sexy like a beautiful flaming fire one can only admire from a distance knowing the harm in getting too close. He wasn't *that* fine but slim, muscular and with the way he was standing in that black and red leather gear with his helmet tucked in the crease of his elbow, he definitely had that GQ style.

Then again, he didn't have a mustache or a goatee and, in my book, that made him look like an oreo or a metrosexual who'd grown up in the hood but only dated skinny White girls with squeaky voices and names like Trish or Jenna who worked at Hooters or girls who looked mixed like Dominique. Being a shade some considered caramel while others considered me to be brown skinned, I certainly did not fit into either one of those categories.

"I'd really like to call you. You're fine as hell. We can do lunch, dinner--whatever you'd like." He continued flashing a brilliant smile—the kind with all the windows in place, as he handed over his business card and waited for me to give him my number in return.

"Car dealer, hungh?" Maybe it was the fact that my car was flat-out raggedy and I could only dream of a new one at the time--I don't know, but I blurted it out before I had a chance to stop myself. I would find out later that that job of his was one of the checkpoints that put him on the list as one of Detroit's most wanted, A-list bachelors. He was rolling in the dough. But I'd never get a chance to ride on that motorcycle with him.

I scribbled my cell phone number on the back of his forearm after he lifted up the sleeve of his leather jacket and handed me a black sharpie.

"I love how he put his arm out for you to write on it! Now *that* was cute—real cute!" Sherra gushed once he was out of earshot.

But Niquie couldn't stand it even though she *and* her walk had gotten at least five guy's numbers that evening and an encore of claps. "You know what, Leigh? *You need* ta stop! You be frontin' like a lil' Christian Church Mouse but then you wanna ditch the act when it's convenient!" Her Revlon, smoky kohl-rimmed eyes widened as her *Oh Baby* tinted, MAC lips twisted into a sinister smirk that did little to hide her sprouting jealousy.

"Why is it you be actin' Latino wit cho' damn Salsa lessons, half-White, half-Arabic when you at da gas station and Brazillian when you tryin' to be exotic—everything *but* Black—since you wanna stand up here and ask rude ass questions, Niquie? If yo' eyes weren't so muthafuckin' big, you'd be tryin' ta claim you was Asian so you could get in on da White boys. Can we please go *there*? You uh lil' more than confused." A couple that looked like Bill and Clair fresh off a *Cosby* set frowned at us as they walked by.

Sherra rolled her eyes at them and asked them what they were looking at before she started going back off on Niquie again. "*Get it to-ge-tha*! In America and everywhere else *you still Black*! A nig-"

"—Hold up, hold up Sherra--*ma* turn!" I interjected. "Niquie, I *know* you're not trying to start something with *me*! Just like I drove you down here, I can *leave* you! I've been a referee between you and Sherra all day, *and I've had your back* while yo' ass insist on representin' for the sluts!" I didn't feel like dealing with her inflated ego today. Hey, I wasn't even trying to hook up with the guy! He just reeked of arrogance.

"He was trying to talk to *me* before you stuck *yo' ass* all out like a donkey. Y'all darker skinned females always be hatin' on the light-skinned girls..." she mumbled just loud enough for me to make the words out. Her eyes glimmered with hate and glee, the kind of mixture that can only come from annihilating someone with choice words.

I was darker from the summer sun but worrying about skin tone wasn't anywhere on my agenda. I had always been considered cute. I didn't need to wear a ton of makeup, my lashes were so long they looked fake, my hair came down to the middle of my back and I had a body a nuns cloak couldn't hide. Dark skin, light skin, blue black—I didn't care.

But one thing Sherra couldn't stand was the color complex thing. She had the clear, smooth and very, very, dark complexion of an old world queen, kept her hair done in tasteful, complimentary styles and dressed becoming for her extra thick, five-eight, shapely figure. She didn't get *any* complaints from the fellas and she wasn't the type that apologized for her darkness by only dating lighter skinned guys. Every guy she dated was close to her complexion or darker. Back in the day it was a different story, though. She had been picked on in elementary school for being dark by the same guys who tried to hook up with her later on in high school.

Niquie, on the other hand, constantly found reasons to pull the color card and threw the light over dark subject in Sherra's face every chance she got. My guess was that it had to do with the fact that her favorite enemy, her mother, was dark skinned and the fact that Niquie was used to being rewarded solely for her mixed looks.

"You know what, Leigh? *Leavvve her.* I'm sick uh dis! You'd think after yo' stepfather, you'd be scared of men! You *already* pretty Niquie, you don't have to *fling* yourself at niggas like a *fly* on a *windshield*!" Sherra couldn't contain herself any longer. Her mouth was scrunched as tight as one of those ugly ass hair scrunchies that should have never been in style in the first place.

Niquie's round, bedroom eyes became bigger than humanly deemed possible, like a baby doll caricature.

Dominique had been sexually molested by her stepfather and emotionally abused by her mother who called Niquie "A Triflin' Ass Lil' Bitch" like it was her legal name. Her mother knew about her husband's late night ventures to her daughter's room but didn't do anything about it. Even after six years of being friends, it was clearly understood that the subject was off limits. We never discussed the picture of her Arabic father she'd stolen out of her mother's closet and carried faithfully in her wallet. Sherra and I had heard about her father during Niquie's mother's numerous yelling episodes back in the day when we went over her house and whenever she screamed about it in the background when we were on the phone with Niquie.

There was only one time Niquie ever mentioned the molestation thing—the one morning when she showed up at Sherra's house bloody from fighting with Harold. But Sherra and I had already suspected something was wrong after the one time we spent the night at her house. It was the only time she had ever invited us over. Most of the time she came up with lame excuses Sherra and I could never understand whenever we suggested hanging out at her house. Their home was a well-kept mini-mansion in Sherwood Forest and from the pictures we'd seen, it was sharp on the inside; they had every cable channel you could get in the US, two brand new cars and an older classic Thunderbird. There had to be something going on for her not to invite us over especially being the show-off she was and the way she was always coming over me and Sherra's house.

The day our suspicions were confirmed, her mother had taken us out to eat at Big Fish next to Fairlane mall and had even paid for us to get manicures while she and Niquie got fill-ins and pedicures. After we played pranks on all the guys we knew, watched *Love Jones* and *Brown Sugar* and Uncut Videos, we fell asleep when the White televangelist came on right after the end of a *Two Live Crew* video that had a dwarf in it who could shake her body in ways that just didn't seem suitable for non X-rated television.

Three hours later Harold, in his drunken stupor, trudged into her room not realizing me and Sherra were there. He started singing the chorus line of a Barry White song in a bloodcurdling tone. The three of us jumped up, grabbed our things and waited at the corner in below zero weather for my mother to pick us up. It was terrible; the type of thing you were only supposed to see on the news or *Law and Order*; you weren't supposed to actually know people in messed up situations like that for real.

Her real father had ended the affair without so much as an adieu when her mother was seven months pregnant and had never called or talked to Niquie a day in her life. When he'd hooked up with her mother who was only thirteen at the time, he was already married to an Arabic woman he had four children with. From what Niquie's mother said, she met him at the gas station he owned and he had been trying to talk to her from the time she was eleven. But Niquie was still proud of the fact that he was her father instead Harold. Past the outer demeanor of pageant-like beauty and pseudo conceit, there was an extremely insecure little girl yearning to make peace with the years of abuse she'd suffered.

I guess that's why when Niquie turned eighteen she immediately got her own apartment that was, in her words, "plushed out" with expensive furniture.

Now *that* was amazing. She had never held down a real job that I could recall. But then again, I could see Harold sending her money in efforts of keeping her mouth shut and his reputation spic and span. He was a well-respected police officer--the city chief's right hand man to be exact.

She also had a brand new red Volkswagen that was currently in the shop because she drove like a maniac and had already messed up the brakes.

"Let's go to Floods, I need to eat," Niquie demanded walking ahead of me and Sherra. I was shocked she was still hanging with us. Seemed like she would have demanded to be dropped off somewhere and ditched us.

I drove to Greek Town's Casino parking structure mainly because I didn't want to be seen hopping out of my raggedy, three different shades of teal-n-rust, car and headed to the jazz club. Secondly, because of Niquie. Even though the club was only a few blocks away, with the six inch skinny white and silver Pamela Anderson and Vivica Fox looking designer heels she was wearing, there was no way she was going to be okay with walking there.

Niquie checked herself in the rear view mirror from the back seat as I turned the corner during the one-minute drive to the Casino. This was the first time she'd ever rode in the back seat of my car. Sherra usually sat in the back since Dominique *had* to sit in the front.

"I on't wanna go home at two. There's got ta be *sumthin* open later," Sherra protested, preoccupied with changing radio stations to find a commercial for a club that would be poppin' afterhours.

"...Leigh...instead of trying to fix everybody else...you should really *fix* yo'*self*," Niquie stated plainly while admiring her french manicured acrylic nails.

"Me?" I asked dumbfounded. I hadn't even gone off on her like Sherra had!

"Yes, *yyyouu*. You godda lot ta learn about life, Leigh. Darren's *definitely not* your type. He's gonna crush yo' innocent, lil' cherry still drippin' off the tree, ass. Sherra's issue is simple: *she's* just jealous." Niquie said it all so matter of factly but the scorching sting of her words swayed in the languid midnight breeze.

Once I found a spot in the parking structure she left us behind like we were supposed to trickle in her dust as she entered the jazz club.

And it pissed me off that she remembered Darren's name! But, then again, I'd seen Niquie memorize three different guys' phone numbers even though two of them had different, not easy to remember area codes.

Funny. She could move real fast in those heels after her lil' comment. She wasn't stupid. She knew better than to stick around and possibly get whipped by Sherra. Inside Niquie'd be safe. Sherra wasn't the type to fight in front of a crowd and she wasn't about to skip hanging out or eating at Flood's because of Niquie, either. They had the best soul food and tonight it was packed and bumping.

"Girl, forget her. She's da one dat's gon' have ta learn." Sherra let Niquie's comments roll off her like rain on a waxed car as we both waited in line to give the thick-necked, Heavy D looking bouncer the five dollar cover. He flirted and let us slide thru without paying. He had already tried to talk to me four different times making tonight the fifth.

Minutes later, Niquie spotted a guy that was the type of wanna-be-gangsta you laughed off when he approached you. The type you try to get to hook you up with his older, car running, job holding and tax paying brother instead. He looked her up and down more than satisfied at what stood in front of him. The whole time his eyes were stuck on her voluptuous 'Your Paying For Dinner' breasts that sat up in the casing of her Forever 21 black and white pin striped halter-top like headlights in the front of a car.

When he hugged her he held her like a rented trophy and after they ate they left the club. As Niquie crossed the dance floor and exited she ignored us like graffiti on a freeway ramp, not even tossing an eye-roll or a pithy look our way. Sherra was too busy doing a new Hustle as the live band played their version of Stevie Wonder's song, "My Eyes Don't Cry," to notice.

From that evening forward, Niquie refused to hang out with Sherra and me period, dot--even though we were the only girlfriends she had. Not too many others females could stomach her. It took her an hour and a half just to get ready to go to a movie. Makeup had to be worn for every occasion from grocery shopping to taking the garbage out even though she was exceptionally pretty without any of it. In the summer she even put foundation on already smooth legs and arms--she called it "bronzer." Correct me if I'm wrong but I'm almost certain bronzer is what White people use to give themselves a "sun-kissed glow" or—in other words—to make themselves look darker. This was a chick that couldn't stand being in the sun so bad she'd cover her legs with a magazine in the car so she wouldn't get tanned in the summer...but she wore bronzer. Now, tell me, how backwards is that?

Other girls like her—the ones who hoped for a professional athlete but usually ended up getting with *any* guy that looked a little decent and had forty dollars in the bank and all the other females like Niquie who kept makeup on when they spent the night with a guy, didn't hang out with her either--too much competition.

Truth be told, Niquie was actually spiritually inclined--when she wanted to be. She could break down parts of the bible in such a way, she'd convince an atheist to change his or her mind on the Big Bang theory. But most people couldn't tell. She hid behind incessant chatter about the latest purse she'd purchased from the Guess store, how to get your money's worth on a good hairpiece for bad hair days from a Chinese beauty supply that could make you look like a soap star and other comparable topics. Her bills only got paid when a man offered and her credit was already shot but Niquie stayed dressed in the best and never looked like anything less. She went thru men like termites on wood and her life was simple. It seemed that everything pure and good she wilted and everything tarnished and evil she allowed to stain her heart...

Niquie masked the pain of Sherra's comment about the Harold thing by making it clear she wasn't going to continue hanging with "jealous hearted females that cock-blocked on her all the time" when I called her to try to settle everything.

And Sherra refused to apologize since she felt Dominique made us look bad with her hoe-ish ways.

"YOU KNOW WHAT? We been thru way too much wit Niquie for her ta act like dat *wit us*, Leigh. It's like a play and we all got roles. You s'posed ta be da brown skinned flunkie. I'm da pitch-black one, while she sit up there and get all da attention! She think we *jus* cute enough ta hang around--like we ain't on her level or sumthen. We s'posed ta catch all her leftovers dat be riding in da passenger seat while she get all da guys dat look like dey got dey shit together.

"She think everybody up in Detroit s'posed ta worship her ass! She been mistreated so long she on't even know ha to treat her *real* friends right! *She* the type uh female that sets da Black race and women years back a coupla decades. I'm surprised she ain't give us uh paper bag test like uh old school Black sorority before she *allowed* us ta hang out wit her ass!" Sherra hissed a week later over the phone.

"I wouldn't say all *that*, you know how Niquie is. She'll come around. She was just dealt a bad hand early in life." I tried to disagree with Sherra's theory even though I knew she was probably right.

"Yeah, I just hope she don't get hurt out in the streets! She wanna be a hoe so bad, let's hope we don't see her pop up in one of dem *Girls Gone Wild* commercials or in uh Brazilian porno suckin' on uh horse since she 'on't wanna be shit that got ta do wit Black..." that was Sherra's last comment about Niquie.

"Ugh, Sherra, now you know that's wrong..."

I felt bad our crew was falling apart. This was stupid. And it was all over a guy at that. Niquie always got too much attention for her own good as it was, why did one guy trying to holler at me matter so much?

I tried to call her a few more times before I finally just gave up. If she would've returned one of my calls I would've been willing to drop the argument.

Five years ago we met at Oakland mall in Bakers shoe store when we were all sixteen. All three of us were upset they didn't have any more of those black army-looking boots like the ones Jade used to wear. Niquie liked the airbrushing on Sher's nails and wanted the number of Sher's girl who hooked up a full set for only ten dollars and I liked Niq's eyebrow arch and hadn't ever heard of waxing before and she said she'd take me the next time she went and Sherra wanted to come to my church because she'd heard about our choir. So we all wrote our numbers down on a receipt Sher pulled out of her purse and talked on three-way that night about people at our high schools and tripped on how we knew so many of the same people. Sherra went to Renaissance, I went to King, Dom went to De Porres. And from that point on the three of us were best friends.

But not anymore, not with Dominique Erion West.

NIQUIE MIGHT NOT HAVE been calling anymore to brag or whine about her most recent date but that Darren dude sure was blowing up my phone. Everyday there'd be like four calls on my caller ID from him.

"Hey, sexy. What you doin' later on tonight? Wanna catch a movie?"

I hated it when guys assumed you didn't have anything else to do but go out with them on a last minute tip.

"Hey...umm...I'm swamped with homework. Can I call you back?"

"Aright. Take care of that and when you get a chance, hit me back." The times I didn't ignore his calls, it went like that for two weeks. He was *so* confidant I would eventually call him back it annoyed me.

ONE THURSDAY EVENING, I made the mistake of answering an unfamiliar number on my cell during break in my sociology class. Darren was so charming and persistent when I tried to decline the dinner offer, no wonder he was excellent at selling cars.

I have regretted answering that call at least a thousand times--I'd be lying if I didn't admit it upfront. Life would have definitely been different if he would have hooked-up with Niquie instead. They probably would have made the perfect match, catching and taking turns giving each other Chlamydia and other nasty people diseases. Hey, they'd probably go so far, after twenty years of having an open relationship to get married one day...maybe.

But even with all the drama and heartache Darren brought into my life, Pharaoh is one of the best blessings I've been given. But at the time I *didn't* know Pharaoh would be entering my life. And I was very apprehensive about this whole date thing. A guy like *him*, pushing up on *me*? It was weird.

Then again, it wasn't like I had a trail of hotties waiting to take me out every Saturday night. Or any other night for that matter. One date, one night wasn't going to kill anybody. The other option was going home, heating up a Michelina's frozen dinner since it was too late to cook, studying for forty minutes and hitting the sack wishing I *would have* taken him up on dinner.

We met up at a gas station in Southfield. I was so tragically embarrassed of my teal 1970-ish car that didn't go past sixty-five miles an hour that I agreed to ride in his brand new Jaguar. It was so new, it didn't even have a real license plate yet.

"Don't laugh at my car!" I tried to play it off.

"I wouldn't care if you rolled up on a horse, I'm just glad I finally got a slot on yo' schedule. I didn't wash my arm the whole night until I found my phone so I could put yo' number in it." That was nice to know. "Get in," he instructed. He walked so smoothly, it seemed as if he glided over to the passenger's side of the gleaming waxed black door.

The car had two televisions in it--one in front and one in the back, satellite radio—keep in mind this was before anyone had even heard of a personal satellite car radio *and* he had a computer navigation device right underneath the radio but it was so small you couldn't tell it was there until he touched the rectangular screen and it lit up and came on.

"Where do you wanna eat? There's a T.G.I. Friday's on—"

"—On Ten Mile and Evergreen," I interjected, finishing the sentence in unison with him. "I know, I know. That's good." As soon as I finished the sentence I felt stupid. I just couldn't shake my nervousness. I was trying so hard to be comfortable around him, everything I said came out sounding rather rude. He probably thought I was being a bitch.

I glimpsed at him from the corner of my eyes making sure not to look his way too long. Direct contact was too risky. I'd probably start shaking uncontrollably from shyness. Just like the first time when we met, he made my stomach feel shaky.

He did look better though. A nice, lined up mustache and goatee now graced his face, which erased that *Is He Bi-Sexual Or A Metrosexual?* thing he previously had going on. Now he looked more like the kind of brotha I *would* go out with. With those metrosexual brothas, you had to worry about one day finding your man in bed with another dude when you came home early from vacation or work or something. I wasn't about to be stuck with a broken heart ten years down the line after finding out my betrothed was on the D.L. Oprah did a show on it and *Essence* had done a cover article on those kinds of situations and *I* was *not* about to be the one to go down that road. Not that we were going to be together--I didn't even know if I like him or not yet. But you still had to think about stuff like that. Otherwise you'd wake up one day wondering how you had gotten yourself into such a messed up situation.

"What's your major?" he asked taking his green-brown eyes off the road and stealing a glance my way. His voice wasn't significantly deep but it was as silky as his walk.

"Nursing but I'm just doing pre-reques right now. I like dissecting animals, looking at cells under the microscope—all that stuff. I'm a nerd."

"Don't look like one ta me."

"That's why they say you shouldn't judge a book by its cover. This semester I'm taking a human body lecture course, a chemistry—"

"--Yeah, I like learning about the human body, too," he laughed. "Anyway, I went to Morehouse. That was tight," he looked my way and smiled before continuing, "But there weren't any ladies around and Spellman was kinda on lock so I switched to Clark for undergrad, then I went to Duke for my masters in business..."

"...Well...I know I wanna be a nurse. They're in high demand right now and it's a good field for me to go into. I like helping people... I'll probably be one of those nurses that cry when—"

"--Yeah, get yo'self a pair of those sexy ass black cat-eye glasses, a short lil' white skirt--um hmm, you'll be crying *every* night those patients gave it ta yo' ass." He licked his lip.

Whaat? Did he think I was a hoe or something? Somewhere along the way I must have sent him the wrong message. I didn't know *how* to respond to that one. My stomach tightened and I frowned so hard the next time he looked over at me he kept his eyes on the road the rest of the ride to the restaurant.

"...Yeah, it's all about education these days. Take Duke for example. It was *that* kinda academia that changed my whole intellectual process. I'm glad I didn't limit myself by going to all Black universities only—and not just because Duke is as top of the line as it gets curriculum wise. See, in the *real* world you have to deal with and interact with different types of people, diversity is key. In order to really make it nowadays, you have to think globally. You have to be willing to find out what's going on in Japan, what's up with Canada, India and the rest of the world. Life is about a whole lot more than just the circumference of Detroit, Leigh. Most Black muthafuckas ain't on that level. They don't know shit about Maslow's pyramid of self-actualization and that's why they stay broke."

"Hmm... We talked about self-actualization in my psych class last semester...well, since you put it out there, what do you think it'll take to help Blacks make it *to that* level?"

"Its not that simple--*life's* not that simple," he stated parking in a handicap spot in front.

"Wait." He stopped me as I reached for the door. "You can't get out yet. I have to open the door for *yo' sexy ass*. Umph, umph, umph nah *thas* uh phat ass. *Damn, girl* it's real juicy and round..."

I turned around and looked back at him and I couldn't stop giggling nervously all the way to the hostess's stand. He turned his nose and upper lip up like somebody'd just passed gas, shook his head like I had done something real wrong and nodded towards a booth tucked in a back corner of the restaurant near the restrooms. The way he walked in there with the fellas at the bar nodding all kinds of whassups and whatnot, you would have thought he owned the place.

I, on the other hand, felt like I was about to start sweating any second and, as clumsy as I was, it was only a matter of minutes before I knocked a glass of water over or did something else equally un-sexy. Every time I looked across the table at his freshly tapered haircut, that casual cream buttoned-down linen shirt that accentuated his square shoulders and muscular body, the slacks that matched perfectly with his shirt and made him look like some kind of sports star, I was reminded of just how out of my league he was. A Rolex was on the wrist of the arm I had written my number on and his fingernails were impeccably clean.

I slid my hands underneath my thighs while we waited for the waitress. My nails were straight up hit. They weren't polished and were so uneven, looked like I had ten wavy Lays potato chips hanging off my fingers. Both of my baby and ring nails were long, while the other six nails were real short. I had on a pink and white T-shirt with Black cartoon chicks standing across the front of my chest. Basically I looked like a fast adolescent with an overly developed body.

Where the heck was the waiter already? It was time to get the show on the road and end this awkward, crappy ass date!

Then again, he had been pressing me so hard to go out with him I might as well make it worthwhile. Might as well order appetizer, entrée, dessert—the whole shebang. The only reason I was here was because my stomach was growling in class. Otherwise I'd have been at home, resting peacefully in the bed and *not* sweating my armpits off. I could feel the pit stains slowly rising and about to make a debut on my shirt.

"You *do* realize that's my foot you're kicking, right? I wasn't gonna say anything but you started gettin' all *aggressive* with it." He smiled amusingly and chuckled. I had been kicking my foot against what I thought was the pole under the table. I rolled my eyes, pretended not to be embarrassed and picked up a menu raising it high enough to block him from staring me down the way he was.

The next problem was deciding what I wanted. I always had a hard time choosing something when I went out to eat. It seemed like whatever somebody else ordered always ended up tasting better than whatever it was I'd ordered.

I had a taste for the Jack Daniels wings and the potato skins but I'd look greedy if I chose both.

"I don't have anything ta hide!" he exclaimed breaking the silence, startling me and interrupting my wings versus potato skins debate. Holding both of his hands up like he was in a stick-up, he flashed that million-dollar smile of his and smacked his driver's license down on the table. "Let's see yours," he added.

"I don't think so." I shook my head no. I could feel my right eyebrow lift. He was trying to be slick.

"Nah. Ungh-uh. That's not fair. Lemme see. What? Your real name Yolanka or sumthen? You got four ponytails on yo' head with a pair of them gold earring wit cho' name written in cursive in the middle of 'em?" He said it really fast and gestured grandly, whipping his hands about in a comical fashion.

"N*oo*." I laughed.

"Let me see it then--can't be *that* bad."

I resigned and pulled the license out of my jean pocket.

"A lil' classy, hungh?" He nodded his head up and down answering his own question.

I wouldn't call a silver cardholder that came in the mail as a free gift for ordering checks by mail classy but okay. Since I didn't have any business cards I kept my bankcard, license and health insurance card in it instead.

"...Umph, you even look good on a license." His eyes darted back and forth from me to my ID. "...Birthday: July nineteenth—you just turned twenty-one last week then, hungh? Happy birthday...five-four...yeah, I know where you stay at—on the corner in those tan apartments with the green awnings?"

"Yeah," The second I answered I regretted letting him know where I lived.

"You only stay two blocks away from me." The way he licked his lips until they glistened bothered me and he kept doing it after every other sentence.

"My cribs on Seven Mile right off Ponchatrain. It's Detroit's *only* gated community," he bragged pointing a finger my way like we were on an infomercial. "I'm gonna make uh lodda dough off it when I sell it.

"I shoulda never purchased a home around the corner from my family in the first place...and you know how Detroit is—a nice neighborhood'll be right around the corner from the worst, third world lookin' spot up in America." He shook his head in contempt.

I stared at the menu and avoided saying anything on that subject. *I* stayed in a neighborhood that on any given day no matter how cold or hot it was outside you could find a couple of brothas sitting on top of a car holding those brown paper bags with forties in 'em, there were four different churches within the two block radius of my place and there were two clubs that blasted everything from house music and techno to underground rap from eight til two in the morning every weekend. I stayed in the *hood*.

He motioned for a waitress with a humongous behind to come to our table. "Hey, Darren. Wha'd up, though? I'm gitin' dat car next month, Boo-Boo, watch." She smacked her lips really hard. I didn't like the rat the instant she sidled her big butt up to the table. First of all, she had the nerve to call him Boo-Boo right in front of me like I wasn't even there and on top of that she had rodent-like teeth and big, florescent pink gums and was smiling all in his face like she was retarded.

"What's up, Latrice. We'll have the Jack Daniel wings, two shots of Tequila—matter fact make that three and--that's it for now." She soaked it up as he looked her up and down, smiled and wiggled his eyebrow at her.

Huh. One glance at her and it was clear to see Southfield was turning hood. I was surprised he didn't steal a few more double takes of her ghetto booty--somebody could sit a book on top of that boy! And if she had any shame she wouldn't have worn that mini skirt hiked all the way up her thighs—last I heard, cellulite was *not* in style. Darren didn't even look like he would speak to her type. Enough about her, I decided on the potato skins but he hadn't even asked what I wanted. The wings were cool, though. I *had* been thinking about ordering them. Definitely a good sign.

When the appetizer finally came I waited for Darren to dig in first. "Go ahead," he said sliding the plate towards me. I stabbed four with my fork onto my appetizer plate. I was starving. A grimace of disapproval crossed his face. I couldn't even look up at him after that. All I could do was used the knife and fork to cut the wings into tiny pieces—something I was sure Niquie would have done.

Damn, I should have gotten the potato skins. Some things like ribs and wings you just couldn't eat without looking flat out wrong on a first date.

"What high school did you go to?" he asked picking up another wing. It was his sixth. I still hadn't touched my second one.

"King. It was cool. I--"

"—Yeah, I went to Cranbrook for lower, middle and upper school. That's as good as it gets as far as Michigan high schools go. Not too many from the city get to reap the benefits of an education like that. See, with White kids, their parents give them the advantage early on by placing them in the best schools and making sure they go to Ivy League universities. Then they become governors and presidents and shit. But niggas from the hood don't turn inta shit but thugs or the mediocrity some call blue collar—whether they're smart or not.

"Niggas don't start savings accounts for their kids college education. They're too busy buying Cadillacs they can't afford and end up going bankrupt...I was lucky. I got the chance to have the best of both worlds—formal intellectualism *and* street smarts."

I stared at the two wings glistening on my saucer waiting to meet my stomach.

"...You and your girls--you all grow up together?"

What was up with this guy? Asking questions like that completely out of the blue. I felt like I was on an interview. First my license, then it was my hood/neighborhood. Now my friends. "Not exactly."

"Aright, aright. We're about to toast. Here's to an excellent night!" Changing subjects, he raised his shot glass and waited for me to do the same.

"I've never done Tequila before. That's okay." Truth was, I never had any kind of alcoholic drink before.

"Come on, you gotta try it. Lick the rim first, drink it and then suck the lemon," he insisted.

"I'm good." That was way too many instructions for such a tiny drink. Instead I raised a glass of water I had squirted with the lemon supposed to be for the shot.

"What school did you say you go to again?" he inquired a couple of minutes later. I stared at the plate of wings while he stared at the toothpick he was rolling back and forth between his thumb and index finger.

"Detroit Community."

"Hmm...you should register at Wayne State, if something like Central or MSU isn't for you. How can a community college *possibly* offer you the type of education you need? You look like the type thata want better."

Now I knew how the baby pig fetus I dissected last week in biology felt. And what I was really starting to see was just how much I could *not* relate to a brotha like him.

Finally, to drown out all the grandiose, pompous, 'I am lucky because I have this and I have that and my degree helped me get such-and-such,' long-winded sentences, I tried the drink. It wasn't so bad after I sucked on the lemon. He watched me swallow the shot like I was on a new reality show and cheered when I placed the empty glass on the table.

When the waitress came back to our table for our entree orders he asked for another round of drinks instead. At least the drink helped me find the courage to overcome the torture of the three wings left on my plate. I even went for a fifth one but I still used the knife and fork.

"So is your family originally from Michigan?" I had never met anyone like him and I had lived in Detroit all my life.

"Sort of," he stated matter factly then switched into a laid back, dreamy-eyed squint. "...Pretty, smooth-assed brown skin, thick in all the right places without uh ounce of fat...you gotta attractive, Black girl next door look workin' for you."

"Are you trying to call me plain looking on the sly?" I asked playfully even though I was seriously hoping that wasn't what he was implying. Sometimes a person will say something like they're joking when they actually really mean what they've said.

"Ain't shit plain about 32-24-38." He laughed. "And—wait a minute—lemme guess--I'm good at this--you've *got* to be a C."

He was right. I accepted another shot "I plead the fifth. Change of subject. How many brothers and sisters do you have?"

"My family's not that big."

"Yeah... Well, I'm an only child." At this point I knew I was sweating for real. I wiped my forehead with the napkin under my glass of water.

"Good thing. Shit, if you woulda had a sister, unless y'all was identical twins, she woulda been jealous of yo' sexy ass." He smiled. The compliments were nice but, had I not left my car behind, I would have been long gone. My stomach had a swirly, 'I'm not comfortable here, please take me home' thing going on. He looked at me a bit longer than he had before and broke into a broader grin.

"Excuse me, I've got to go to the ladies room." I rushed away from the booth. If I was lucky, that trial sized Secret was still in my purse. I always carried deodorant with me but this time I had switched purses.

There was nothing worse than being musty or wearing a cute shirt with the pit stains showing every time you lifted your arm.

To my utter horror I had bits of tissue all over my forehead. The more I wiped, the more it seemed like the pieces multiplied. After scrubbing my face with the hard, restroom brown paper towel, I used the restroom and leaned against the stall door a few minutes. I was drowsy but I managed to muster up enough courage to walk back to the table. The waitress was just leaving after smiling all up in Darren's face when I got back to where he was seated with another set of drinks placed in front of him.

"It's getting late. I'm straight on the drinks. Why didn't you tell me I had tissue all over my face?" I tried to play my embarrassment off.

"You're cute," he responded with a smile before calling the waitress over and asking for the bill. We hadn't even ordered any real food. I felt even more tortured when he told the waitress to take the remaining wings from the table. A doggy bag would have been nice. I was hungrier than I had been when we had first walked in. "Aright. Last one for the road." He lifted up his glass and chugged it down. "Go ahead." He said motioning for me to do the same. Who was I fooling? This guy didn't want to get to know me. But, then again what did I know? It was only a first date. I could be reading everything wrong.

I swallowed the shot. It burned against my throat and melted into something that tasted much better with the aid of the lemon afterwards and then we headed for the door.

"Didn't we just turn around this corner?"

"Yeah, I'm looking for this club my boy told me about...they have salsa lessons or something like that going on tonight."

I sighed. Ten minutes had past and he was still driving down Evergreen.

"It's a nice night. You mind if we sit and talk?" He caught my eyes in his as he pulled into Northland Mall's empty parking lot.

"I'd love to but I'm sleepy. Call me tomorrow after I get out of school. I need to get home." At that point I just wanted to go to sleep. I'd gotten out of class at ten and it was twelve thirty already. I had a test the next morning.

He parked, turned the television off and put some jazz on. "It's a nice night. You made me wait forever just to take you out. I'm tryin' to get to know you. You live by yourself, right? It's not like you gotta check in with your mama."

A scene flashed in my head of that time at bible camp when we had to do that stupid 'fall back and let the other person catch you' exercise.

I didn't want to participate in that crap but they kept trying to convince me to do it...

"...I have class tomorrow. I need to get home." I tilted my head against the plush leather headrest. It felt like a pillow. The headrests in my car were torn and revealed their yellow, foamy insides.

"Look. I like you. But I can tell you need to relax and learn how to have a little fun every now and then. How old are you twenty-one or seventy-one?"

"That's mean. I bet *you* studied hard when you were at Duke and weren't out getting drunk the night before an exam." I fake punched him in the arm.

"Yeah, but if I woulda seen something like you, I might nota graduated on time." He stroked his goatee slowly during the weird silence that rested over us while the music lifted and dropped its sensual notes in the breeze weaving its way out of the sunroof. Suddenly, I felt like angel cake...like there wasn't a bone left in my body. He leaned over lingering near my neck. His tongue was warm and wet as it glided over my ear, first soft and feathery, then hard and playful. I couldn't make out what he saying, the deepness and low whisper of his words blended into the silkiness of the song. And that cologne...um, um, umph...it made my neck tingle. He was gonna have to stop. All I wanted was for him to stop.... there were so many sensations...so many. He licked my nose and bit it softly. It was odd but, for some reason, it turned me on and I couldn't resist anything anymore. My lips parted just enough to receive the heat of his tongue, my head rolled back in anticipation. Our tongues became batons, twirling about sensuously and delightfully in fondling, wet softness. "Hey...can I eat yo' pussy?" He breathed heavily along my neck, staring at me with lustfully intense eyes, like that of a god to a goddess. I'd never been eaten out before. Out of curiosity, I nodded yes and within seconds he pushed my seat back, caressingly unzipped my fitted jeans and eased them past my quivering thighs. At thirty-one, his years of tongue rolling expertise made me wetter and hornier than ever before. I couldn't contain the crescendo of feverish cries of ecstasy wailing from deep inside a place I never knew existed. The more I moaned, the more intense he became. He fumbled with his pants for a few seconds before pulling out the biggest, *strongest* looking dick I'd ever seen.

Thick, reddish-brown and, at about nine inches, it was much more arousing than the ones I'd caught glimpses of at the computer lab at school when porno sites occasionally popped up on the screen. My thighs loosened with sparks of expectation. "Now it's your turn to taste *me*," he breathed in my ear. Instead, I grabbed his waist before he had a chance to slide back over to the driver's seat. He slid his slim, yet muscular and heavy body on top of mine in the seat without a condom and moved like a snake. My body sucked in his rhythmic motions. We became a beautiful, soulful tug-of-war. The more he gave, the more I wanted until I couldn't take it any longer. Gyrating firecrackers stirred inside and took me to that climatic spot.

It was passionate, it was *the bomb* and it wasn't just the liquor!

He was still breathing hard and leaning over me like he wanted me to kiss him or something. Finally he moved back to the drivers side and handed me a package of Kleenex from the glove compartment. A whole box of condoms fell out. The way every kind of Trojan ever made tumbled onto the mat next to my foot pissed me off and on top of that he didn't even try to pick them up. This whole episode was obviously nothing new to him—he did this mess all the time with different females.

I tried to ignore the various array of colors and varieties of all the condoms in his extensive Magnum Trojan collection as I wiped the sex juices off my body and the seatbelt strap. I kept wiping and wiping the seatbelt strap—it felt like it was greased up with Vaseline. While we were doing it he had held on to real tight it like holding the strap was gonna keep him from making noise but he had still ended up being louder than me.

He cleared his throat, turned the music up and pulled off the parking lot. Instead of taking me to my car he drove to some store on Ten Mile stepped out and then opened the door for me to get out. "Check this out, baby. *This* is where I shop when I have time. When I don't have time my secretary goes online for me and has everything altered before I wear it. "You see that right there?" He pointed to a cream suit with the fifteen hundred dollar price tag hanging off it. "I'm getting that tomorrow to wear to work--they tailor anything I pick up the same day."

I nodded my head and smiled. He was obviously paid out of his mind. His type could have any girl. And he liked *me*? That was a major compliment.

As we got back in the car I couldn't help but think about the rose-petal softness now lingering in my body. This felt nice. Very nice. "I like Somerset... I'm glad they added all the other stores but I think they should have put something like that downtown instead of out there. Every major city has a mall downtown except Detroit but then they say the city's coming up. Go figure."

He looked over at me like what I had just said was too stupid to respond to and he didn't say anything else the rest of the ride to my car. It felt like an invisible stonewall had been placed between the driver and passenger side. When I got out of the car he didn't even come to my side to help me get out. We exchanged distant goodbyes like two strangers passing in the night. No hug, nothing. It was like we hadn't even fucked. When I opened my car door he drove off. He didn't even wait for me to get in and start my car; the way my car looked one as intelligent as he professed to be would have at least waited to see if the thing was gonna turn on or not.

The whole drive home I felt like I was evaporating and washed in sadness. This was worse than being a hoe.

He had made sure I saw the bill that somehow totaled eighty dollars even though it was only the two of us and we hadn't ordered anything except some bullshit assed drinks! That shit wasn't worth how cheap I was feeling right now and driving past all the trannies and low budget prostitutes who were taking advantage of the summer weather only added to the pain enveloping my soul. At least they were charging!

I hadn't realized *I* was the bomb, which was why he had continuously hounded me to go out with him in the first place. I was too young in the mind to know how to play the cards right.

THREE DAYS LATER HE called and I answered with the hopes of him taking me out on a real date—one that would make up for the last one.

"Hey, Leigh."

"...Hey."

"What's up? Can I stop by?"

"...Come *over*? Look. Maybe somewhere down the line I gave you the wrong impression but I don't hook up with guys like that—I'm not a hoe or anything. Thursday night was a mistake and—"

"--You think going out with *me* was a mistake?" He was indignant.

"That came out wrong. What I meant to say was that the *sex* part? *That* was a mistake. It wasn't supposed to happen. I—um—I wouldn't mind going to the movies or something—another time, of course, but not right now. I was on the way to sleep," I offered, fumbling for the right words.

"Who said you was a hoe? Women have the right to explore their sexuality. Don't you know that? That's why they started all that Women's Lib, bra burning shit."

"Well—I'm just saying...I don't get down like that—especially not on the fist date."

"Leigh, baby? Chill out, chill out. You're a very attractive young lady. I just wanna see you. No harm in that."

"Ah...maybe tomorrow--*way* before ten o'clock at night."

"Why don't you just come outside and say what's up?"

"...That's it?"

"That's it."

Against better judgment, I agreed to meet him outside. Five minutes later he pulled up in another brand new ride. "Damn, you go to bed looking sexy as hell, huh?" He ran his fingers thru my hair—hair that only four minutes ago was rolled in them big ole pink sponge rollers.

I sunk down into the passengers seat and fidgeted with my keychain, nervously twirling and twisting the keys about. He leaned towards me nearly touching my lips. I moved my head towards the window away from him.

"Do dis dick like you doin' that keychain," he muttered, sliding that penis of his out of his track pants. "You know you want it," he continued, adding insult to injury. I got out of the car and slammed the door. From the get-go I had been so stupid, I guess he figured he might as well hang on to a young, dumb and full of cum, good thing.

The first thing I did when I went back inside my apartment was erase all the different numbers he had called me from off the caller ID. Hopefully I could erase him from my memory too. This was the last of the Darren episode--if that was even his real name. He now struck me as the type of asshole that made cards up for dumb-asses like me so he could front like he was an educated businessman. For all I knew, he could be a drug dealer.

CHAPTER 2

THREE MONTHS LATER I was sick. Something was definitely wrong. There were so many times I felt so weak all I could do was lie in bed all day. Certain smells like bleach and chlorinated pools made me throw up, the vaginal discharge smelled funny and different from before--and it was thick. I knew my body and what it was supposed to smell like and this wasn't it. But I still had regular periods every month so I knew I wasn't pregnant.

I also knew it took around six months or longer to test positive for HIV... And man-o-man was I worried. All night and day I thought about AIDS. A-I-D-S. A...I...D...S. And more AIDSAIDSAIDS. Seemed like the letters were inscribed inside my eyelids.

I looked up STD's and STI's online like a maniac, checked out books at the library, bought books from the health food and the bookstore, read and returned them so I could get the money back.

I promised God not to have sex again unless it was my future husband if He would just let me be healthy and well and without a sexually transmitted disease. Any repercussion was fine as long as it wasn't a disease. I hadn't been on birth control because I was trying to remain celibate and I had only had sex two times before this Darren cat. Although the other two guys weren't anything but a couple of shady thugs, I hadn't gotten sick like *this* from either one of them.

I lost my virginity when I was raped when I was seventeen. He hadn't worn a condom either and his name, coincidentally, was also Darren. Thank God I hadn't caught any diseases from that low life or gotten pregnant by that thing. He was twenty-two and a gang member but I stayed with him after the rape even though I never did anything sexually with him again. I found out he had another girlfriend--one more his type-- the day I took the bus to his house (or should I say his mama's house where he and his six brothers and sisters slept in the living room like a bunch of roaches on raggedy stained mattresses covered with cigarette burns that they shared) to surprise him with the love letter he'd told me to write and roll up in a pair of my panties for him.

They called her Bubbly. Bubbly wore a gel encrusted ponytail with only a centimeter of hair sticking up out of the tiny little red rubber band that was struggling to hold it up. She was standing in the middle of the street with a pair of fuzzy light green house shoes on and a tee-shirt that barely covered her behind. All I could do was walk away. And he never called back.

Okay, the second guy? Well, *I thought I liked* him. That is until I went home with him. At first he was really cool to talk to. He made me laugh the entire time we ate. The live music and buzzing ambiance of Floods made the date even more enjoyable. But being the baller-type that he was, he tried to impress me with the Jaguar he drove and discussed nothing but money during the entire date.

With him, the sex was terrible. First of all, he had an uncircumcised penis that was almost invisible. Looked like a Vienna sausage wrapped up in a blanket. What really killed it was the way he huffed and puffed the whole four minutes like he was really doing something and, on top of that, to make matters worse, he kept repeating, "I appreciate dis pussy" over and over again while he was doing it.

He was so skinny it was disgusting. But you wouldn't have known that just by looking at him. Baggy clothes are good cover-ups.

After his midget penis shrunk, he tried to convince me to become a "bikini girl" at his dance club. I had left my car at the school parking lot and was stuck at his house until he took me to get my car that time, too. Dumb wasn't even the word.

He kept coughing like he was sick with a deadly, incurable communicable disease. His voice cracked every time he tried to say something and his face looked like it belonged on top of a skeleton when he took his hat off. I kept telling myself that if I could just get my car and make it home safely, I would never do this type of one-nightstand bullshit again. Plus, I had to use the bathroom. I had a bad case of number three-- that runny kind of diarrhea that makes you feel like your bottom half is going to explode every ten minutes. The dinner I'd ordered with that strange looking and sounding Ja'harree had done a number on my stomach. But I was blessed in that scenario as well. I could have gotten hurt or something worse could have happened while I was at his house.

He tried to hook up again and even came to my school to meet me a couple of times but I was done with all of that and didn't waste my time explaining. After two weeks of ignoring him he eventually got the message. He acted like he was hurt but I didn't care. As long as he got the hint I was happy. He probably had a faithful baby mama or two somewhere anyway. Most of the time when you meet a dude they already have a girl.

After these three bad experiences and my new case of daily sickness I decided to lay off sex even if that meant not having a boyfriend for a couple of years. I was living alone and was the manager of an apartment building. I didn't have to pay rent and got a five hundred dollar check each month from the building owners along with scholarship money from the community college I had been awarded for the year due to the 4.0 grade point average I had earned from studying hard. I was doing okay on my own. I didn't need any more headaches or nightmares from bad dates-- they were starting to rack up too fast. At this point, I just wanted to stay at home on the weekends anyway. When I wasn't overloaded with homework, I cooked and invited Sherra over to watch a movie or we hit the malls and window shopped with my cousin Tamika. Life was so much easier this way. Otherwise, if I kept the bad date tab going, I was going to be bitter before I turned twenty-two.

IT WAS NOW FOUR months later and I still couldn't shake the sickness. I made an appointment with a gynecologist at Henry Ford hospital. I hadn't taken a home pregnancy test even though Sherra suggested it. It wasn't like I had gained any weight and I hadn't had any strange eating habits or cravings and my periods were still as frequent as a Black person getting pulled over by a pair of Starbucks coffee drinking, Dunkin doughnut eating White cops in Dearborn.

"Sher, what if...what if it's something I don't wanna hear?"

"You still throwin' up like you was the other day when I came over?"

"Yep."

"...Well. Why don't you go to Hutzel. I already called down there. They said if you go ta da ER somebody'uh see you today. That's better than waiting til next week to go to that appointment at Henry Ford. All you gon' do is panick yo'self into uh heart attack otherwise."

"You called?"

"Yeah! Look at how you been shakin' an' stuff."

"Aright, I'm about to get dressed."

A urine and blood tests confirmed that I *was*, in fact, *pregnant*. Thank God I didn't have any sexually transmitted diseases. At this very moment I was one of the best candidates for a testimony on prayer.

But *pregnant*? ...Ah, well. Should have been more specific.

FROM THAT POINT ON until I had the baby, life was a blur with me struggling to keep my GPA up, crying all night and feeling terrible day in and day out. I definitely didn't feel like a woman with a beautiful glow even though all the men that asked to rub my stomach for good luck repeated it like a bad pickup line.

I needed to get in touch with that Darren guy immediately but I couldn't find his number anywhere and of course he hadn't called since that night he had stopped by and pulled his dick out of his pants.

I needed to look up the dealership he claimed he worked at so I could tell him about the situation but every time I grabbed the yellow pages or looked at the phone I got scared and couldn't bring myself to do it. Maybe it was a sign; maybe God wanted me to raise this child on my own without telling that dude anything.

But one day when I was cleaning up I found his business card under the bed next to one of the laundry baskets. I mustered up the strength to call him even though it was still debatable whether or not the baby needed something like him in its life.

"Southfield Metro Dealers," a chirpy receptionist answered in the middle of the first ring.

"Ah—ah, does—does a Darren still work there?"

"Darren P or Darren D?"

I looked at the card again. "It's—it's Darren P."

"Okay. Please hold."

Elevator, easy listening music goes off. New song starts. Jazz.

"Darren speaking.

"Ah...Darren? This is Leigh. You might not remember me...we went out a while ago--in the summer?" He wasn't saying anything. "Well...I found your card...and...I needed to speak with you."

"Yeah. I remember you—go ahead. I gotta appointment in uh coupla minutes."

"Um...I'm pregnant."

"You sure?" He didn't sound upset.

"Yeah--it couldn't—it couldn't be anyone else."

Silence.

Would have been nice if that elevator music could come back on right about now to fill in these gaps.

"How far along?"

"Five months."

"Aright. Keep me posted. We'll take a paternity test. Let me know what's going on. You know how to contact me."

A paternity test wasn't a problem. I already knew how the results were gonna go down. "Let me give you my number."

"Hold on." His voice was still neutral.

Music again.

Was he going to leave me on hold or hang up? 'Cause if he did, I was gonna go up to his job and pay his stank ass a visit--coming back up to my apartment like he was gon' get some more in a car again! Hmph! Who tha fuck did he think he was?

"Yeah, my bad. What's tha number?"

"313-341-9270"

"Aright. I'll hit you up."

"Ah..."

"Look baby, I got a meeting in a minute--what's up?"

"Um...can I have your cell—your cell number?"

"Yeah. 248-412-1232"

"All right. Thanks. Bye."

"Peace."

I was shocked. He didn't try to infer that the child couldn't possibly be his and he didn't suggest an abortion--which I wouldn't have been down for anyway. Not only was I scared of having one, I didn't believe in it outside of cases of rape or unsafe labor situations.

But even though Darren was initially calm about the situation, during the pregnancy he didn't help at all.

One time I was so hungry, the box of Kleenex on my nightstand--since I kept having crying spells--reminded me of a box of doughnuts. And when I pulled my hair back into a bun, I really started craving a Krispy Kreme glazed doughnut. I was gonna go crazy if I didn't have one in the next hour. I called him thinking he would offer to go the store and pick up a box from Farmer Jack. It was right around the corner from him. And I didn't feel well enough to drive.

"Hey, Darren. It's Leigh. Could you *please* do me a favor? ...I know it's late." It was eleven o'clock but, hell, the grocery store was still open. "I *really* need a box of doughnuts in my life right about now. Think you could bring some by?"

"...I'll see. Lemme call you back."

"All right." I hung up the receiver and never heard from him again. I called him three more times on three different occasions after that but he never answered.

Since he obviously did *not* want to be a part of this, I wasn't about to beg him.

But my mother, grandmother, Sherra and my crazy, ghetto cousin Tamika were there for me. Tamika was rowdy and rough around the edges even though she looked like she'd be ultimately feminine, delicate and prissy. Usually Tamika made it a point to stay away from anything that smelled like pregnancy. Pregnancy was her idea of suicide. But I had to give her her props. She was definitely there for me. Whenever I needed an order of Taco Bell Beef Burritos and my Nachos Supremes I just had to have at two in the morning along with the Coney Island banana and kiwi smoothies, she never hesitated to drive over. And whenever that miserable 'Why Did I Get Pregnant?' feeling came over, my mother, grandma or Sherra would be at my apartment trying to make me laugh with a ton of family stories.

This was going to be my mother's first grandchild, my grandmother's first great-grand and Sherra's first godchild.

ON THE DAY OF the labor Darren did at least come to Hutzel. He tried to coach but that wasn't happening. His face would go blank like he was paralyzed when I started shouting and writhing in pain from the merciless contractions that kept ricocheting like a million canon balls. And that business suit he was wearing only made him look even more out of place.

When it was show time, the remote controlled bed turned into an operating table with silver apparatuses dropping out of the ceiling like aliens ready to grip their cold clutches all over my body.

Even with all that going on, I was okay...until I saw the baby's hairy head stuck between my legs. For some reason the nurse though it would be a nice idea to show me. Call it a naturalistic approach to labor or what have you, but I call it flat, the fuck out, wrong! A first-time mother does not need to see her coochie stretched like a funnel by a small being's cranium that'll soon be around for eighteen years plus! There's plenty of time to meet and bond afterwards. I made sure she got the message when I threw that mirror in her face and cursed her ass out.

Eight hours later, after a whole lot of sweating, yelling and pushing, the miracle happened. A new kicking and screaming body of life was brought into my world. He was six pounds even and very alert. He kept looking around, didn't cry and he didn't have a wrinkle on his face with his cute little reddish brown bald, headed self. He was adorable. The nurses called him Little Man—he had a light fuzzy brown mustache. I named him Pharaoh.

Much goes into a name. I don't get people who name a baby something off the top of their head or a name with no real significance or people who don't even have a name to place on the birth certificate until days or weeks later. How could someone carry another life for nine months without being ready to name him or her something meaningful? My child was a gift and deserved much more than an empty title.

From the minute they put him in my arms, we locked eyes and got to know each other. We were both mesmerized. The look in his clear innocent brown eyes let me know he was depending on me. His eyelashes were so long they struggled to separate whenever he blinked.

When somebody wanted to hold him I tried to pretend I didn't mind secretly wishing they'd hurry up and give him back the whole time. I didn't even mind breastfeeding him as much as I thought I would and, even though I had been the main one talking about how disgusting it was for a woman to do it in public, I fed him right in front in Darren and the nurse while Pharaoh held my finger with his tiny hand and marveled at his meticulous tiny little perfect fingers and toes.

My mother, on the other hand, sat near the window complaining. It was her first time meeting Darren but instead of going off on him for being a no call, no show the entire time I was pregnant like she promised she was gonna do if she ever met him—or, in her words, "his triflin' ass," she was upset Pharaoh hadn't inherited Darren's eyes.

"Mom! He's healthy! *Thas's what's* important," I snapped two seconds away from adding some choice curse words. I wasn't appreciating her comments or being rudely interrupted from feeding my baby over that kind of bull. This lady was seriously mad her grandson had the same color eyes she and her mother and everyone else—for that matter--in our family had. Let's be real. My mom is short, thick, brown-skinned and she sports a short, relaxed hairdo. French manicured nails and all, she is your traditional Black, middle class, Detroit mama. The way she cooks soul food she could own her own restaurant. From collard greens, black eye peas, that soft yellow corn bread that taste so good it melted on your tongue like pound cake, to the best crunchy fried chicken you ever tasted. My mom never baked fish a day in my life—always fried catfish, whiting and perch with cornmeal and flour and she ate catfish with grits for breakfast—which in my opinion was disgusting but, to each his own. If I was still living with her I'd be obese.

Here she was caught up in that House Negro Mentality of hopin' an' a wishin' the child didn't look too Black. I guess she'd have felt she had something to brag about to her friends if Pharaoh would have come out with light eyes. It shouldn't have surprised me, though. She thought Dominique was simply "*gorgeous*" and every time Niquie came over she went on and on about how pretty she was right in front of Sherra but the only thing she'd say about Sherra was that she was Godly.

Ma took it to a whole *'nother* level when she complimented Darren on how well dressed he was reminding me of all the reasons I had moved into my own place when I was nineteen and why I wasn't about to move in with her right now like she was asking me to. Here I was holding her only grandchild but she was over there falling all over Darren, the infamous Deadbeat Dad Up Until Now and acting like he was Luther Van Dross in the flesh.

They didn't list Darren as Pharaoh's father on the birth certificate that day. We took the paternity test a week later at the clinic Darren wanted it done at and the results proved that Pharaoh was his son. Darren's name and paternity information was then added to the birth certificate but I still gave my son my last name so we'd both be Andersons. Besides, I wasn't too fond of Darren's last name: Pewter, a boring, grayish color was not a good choice for a first name like Pharaoh. Yes Anderson was more of a regular last name and it was dull but it was a whole lot better than Pewter.

Just like I figured Darren adamantly objected. His mother'd told him that in some Oprah movie, she had a son named Pharaoh and that they lived in the projects. I'd never seen the movie. I had just always liked reading Egyptian history and wanted to name my son something that reflected it. Darren finally left me alone about it and quit asking me to change his name but he was clearly stressed-out. This was his first child too, but the difference between me and him was *he* didn't know how to handle it. I was happy about being a parent and I was willing to die in order to protect the small, toothless person I was now held in my arms as he yawned.

Darren held him for a little more than thirty minutes and when he did, he stared at his son with an emotionless, eyes-barely-stuck-in-the-socket look the entire time. But I have to give him credit. He did stick around until visiting hours ended. He even came back the second day and drove me home.

NOT EVEN A WEEK later Darren called to discuss child support arrangements. Now *that* shocked me and made my mother a hardcore Darren fan. It shocked me even more than the way he had acted all calm when I first told him I was pregnant! He asked if I was okay with a written agreement for four thousand dollars a month instead of taking it to the Friends of The Court. And I was fine with that! It seemed like he was real worried about having a court order issued. Darren made at least twenty-five thousand a month, which, to me, was sick. I couldn't imagine anybody making that much in one month.

That wasn't the only thing that tripped me out. I hadn't been all that excited about having a baby but now, after having him, he brought a new feeling into my life, a certain kind of joy I didn't know I could feel. He hardly ever cried unless he wasn't feeling well, went to sleep at night and only woke up to eat at the same time every night. He was a really good baby. I sang and read my homework to him and in return, he'd kick his fat lil' legs. Sometimes it looked like he was trying to wave his arms and he'd give me the biggest smile like he understood what I was saying. I even learned how to tie him to my back when I was cooking or studying. Ma said I was spoiling him but this was my baby--it was just love.

Darren, however and not surprisingly, did not start off as a candidate for the Best Dad award. I used to swear I would have chosen someone else if I could have done it all over again. He only came around once a month to try to get some, since in his words, "my body had shaped back up nicely." I didn't have a single stretch mark thanks to the shea butter I faithfully slathered on my stomach when I was pregnant. Since I refused to give it up, we barely spoke when he came over. We stayed as far as possible from each other on the couch while he sat looking at Pharaoh in my arms. He was scared to hold him even months later.

I found out Darren was engaged when we had our little escapade and, at the time, was still having a hard time breaking the baby news to his fiancee. I'd spotted a few pictures of her the first time I took Pharaoh over Darren's parent's house. She was extra thin and looked like a typical video girl–you know, the light skinned, long hair, quote unquote model type. I wondered why he had cheated on her with me. ...He hadn't even tried to get a hotel room. I was still mad about that--impregnated in a car...what a cheap ass date!

Listening to a couple of the conversations he had with his boys when he was on the phone at my house it was easy to see that Darren was a wild bachelor that only cared about getting money first and coochie second.

For that and a lot of other reasons I did not feel comfortable with Darren keeping Pharaoh on the few weekends he wanted to pick him up. Although I hated to admit it, I was glad he mostly only kept him overnight on the occasional I'm Tryin' to Impress Somebody blue mooned holidays and on Pharaoh's birthdays—Darren's family celebrated every three months until he turned one.

I figured if Darren got used to spending more time with Pharaoh, it would only be a matter of time before he'd try to inculcate his lack of morale into our baby. He wasn't anything I wanted my son to emulate. Darren's idea of being a good father was giving me a brand new SUV, designer gift cards and money so everyone could see his son and his child's mother in the finest--representing for him.

For Pharaoh's birthday when he turned one, his sisters bought him two pair of Gucci shoes--a pair of leather slip-ons and a tan pair with the logo all over them. I didn't even know they made them for feet that small. They were cute--don't get me wrong--it was just that his family went all out on the financial tip. There were so many toys and outfits, I didn't think he'd be able to play with them all and soon he wouldn't be able to fit into the clothes anyhow at the rate he was growing. It was sad that Darren and his family could hook Pharaoh up with showy birthday and holidays gifts but weren't interested in spending time with him other than that. Shallow wasn't the word for it.

CHAPTER 3

I WAS HAVING A HARD time recovering the paper I typed after the computer shut off by accident. I usually always came in to type my papers a couple of hours before my classes started but today my mother was late picking up the baby. I really needed to get a computer. I hadn't finished the paper and class was about to start in a few minutes. Mr. Clark was one of those teachers who didn't play. I needed to have something to turn in today.

"You need some help?" It was that guy that was always staring at me whenever I was in the lab.

"...Yeah--it shut off right in the middle of what I was doing. The four pages I tried to print didn't come out." This was just what I *didn't* need right now. I sighed and rolled my eyes in exasperation. "I'm about to be late."

He walked over to the printer and tinkered with it. After a few seconds the jam was fixed. Every girl in the lab watched as he walked back to my computer station. "Here you go." He smiled slyly.

"Thanks." I took the paper from his hand, ejected my CD from the drive and shoved all my stuff that was on the desk into my bag.

"You always be up in here. How many classes you takin?"

"I don't know--sixteen." He paused for a second and shook his head like he didn't understand what I had said and gave me another one of those sly grins of his. "Sixteen credits, four classes." He was irritating me and it was all in my tone. Yes, he was fine--the epitome of sexy—I had to give him that. But he was the type that knew it.

He was nicely built—not over the top muscular, not grotesquely skinny, about six-two, his eyebrows connected—which was slightly intriguing and his eyes held a certain innocence in them that was mesmerizing. He looked like some kind of light skinned, curly haired, Egyptian god and, with that five o'clock shadow going on, he looked like he'd have an accent like Fabio's or something.

His jet-black hair almost touched his broad, square shoulders and made a sista want to reach out and touch it. He was street with a capturing intellectual air about him. I even liked the way he dressed. Black casual shoes instead of gymshoes, a plaid shirt with a white tee shirt underneath it, jeans that were a little baggy but not so baggy that it looked like he had a pile of clothes clumped around his feet.

Problem was he was too fine for his own good, the type of player that had enough game to talk a couple of sistas into sharing and being faithful to *him* even though they all knew *he* was out in the streets doing his own thing.

I was *not* the one. After having sex *only* three times and each and every last experience turning out to be terrible, I didn't have time for any more bull.

On top of that, the 'big-boned', big-faced chick with gums and lips that were black as tar, whose name was something that sounded like or rhymed with Meechie, who ran the lab like a computer sergeant, had a more than obvious crush on him and denied computer access to any female she spotted trying to flirt with him the next time they tried to sign in at the lab. Or, they had problems printing their documents like I just had, even though I hadn't even looked his way; I had merely noticed him noticing me. Since this was the only open computer lab and the campus was small, I wasn't about to 'lose my privileges' and there wasn't about to be no fight over this way--she could have him. She striked me as the type that would give him money. And I had already promised God I wasn't going on another date until I had my associates in nursing and I was *not* about to have sex with another man unless it was my husband. I wasn't on the market.

I frowned at him. He was standing directly in front of me blocking me from being able to get up without stepping on his shoes. "I've got class."

"You gon' be here tomorrow?"

"No." At this point, I was frowning even harder. Matter fact, my number one goal now was to get a computer by the end of the month. This was ridiculous. All the guys around here acted like it was a pick up spot instead of college. I stood up and slid my bag in front of me. Otherwise his belt would be touching my hand. This was like that *Seinfeld* episode about personal space, the one with the guy who kept stepping closer every time Jerry stepped back and right about now this dude was violating normal stranger-to-stranger spacing. I was seriously thinking about pushing him out of my way.

"Aright." He looked in my eyes and stared for a good ten seconds before sliding over and tearing a piece of paper from a scrap on the desk in front of mine and scribbled his number on it. "Call me tanight." He tried to place it in my left hand, which was resting on the strap of my bag. I snatched the number from him like it was trash and rushed out but he still kept up with me and walked me to class.

"What's yo' name? I bet its sumen all classy an' shit." I looked at him with my lips held real tight so I wouldn't go off on him for making me loose fifteen attendance points that I needed. He *had*, after all, recovered my paper. "Aright, aright. You uh lil' bougie, I figured dat." He squished his lips and face and shook his head real fast like a bobble head, trying to make fun of me. I broke into a reluctant smile before I turned away from him and walked in the classroom.

I didn't call him that night. It took Craig two months to get my number.

WEEKS LATER, EVEN AFTER I'd bought a desktop computer, had Internet *and* a printer that faxed, scanned and did pictures better than Kodak, I still went to the computer lab.

I liked talking to him. We always had good conversations. Craig was smart and had read more books than anybody I knew.

"Here you go. Read dis one first," he said handing me two books when I walked over to where he was sitting in the study lounge that was around the corner from my class. "I'm on lunch. You wanna git something ta eat right quick?" he asked.

"I can't. I've gotta go pick my baby up."

"Aright. Call me when you make it ta da crib, den."

I smiled and looked at him without saying a word. We both knew that was a joke. I had never called him. But now that he had my number, he rung my phone faithfully every afternoon when he was at work and every night like clockwork.

"Make sure you check dose books out, fa real. Dat one is on tha Isis Papers—what I was tellin' you 'bout tha other day. Da otha one is on da scramble fa Africa an' da beginnin' uh colonization."

"Okay."

He took my bag off my shoulder. "Look at'chu. Somebody done got'chu uh new bag, hungh?" he asked walking me to the brand new black Explorer Darren had given me.

"*I* got *myself* a new book bag." That cloth lime bag ripped the other day so, since I wanted one, I had bought the Vuitton I wanted ever since I saw it two years ago at Somerset.

"Peace out. Don't fa'git ta hit me up." He shut the door after I got in. The way he was sweating me was kind of cute.

"HEY, LEIGH. WHASSUP?" Craig always sounded like he was chilling.

"Hey."

"What'chu been up to?"

"...I finished studying for that physics test I have tomorrow and my mother just brought the baby back. She said he might be coming down with something. Usually he's knocked out by eight-thirty but tonight he was kinda fussy and a lil' bit warmer than usual. That's the only thing going on over here."

"I hope he ain't sick. You takin' him ta da doctor?"

"Yeah, probably tomorrow after I take my test."

"Man, I just finished readin' dis book on da Clinton Administration. It was deep...I think I'ma checkout sumthen on all da pas American presidents... Did you know most uh da United States presidents was Masons?"

"Ungh-uh. Didn't you say it's a cult or something?"

"I ain't say it was no cult. I said da Masons stole dey shit from Egyptian beliefs. Da Egyptians colors was red, blue an' white wit stars—just like da American flag."

"...Hm. That's interesting. They're always stealing *something* from Black people then trying to claim it."

"Yep. Dat's one of da reasons I *hate* White muhfuckas."

"...Hate is a strong word. You shouldn't *hate* them. Besides, you look mixed."

"My grandmama was White. My mama mixed but she *still* Black. All she know is da Black experience an' ma grandma got it, too, 'cause she was wit uh Black man."

"So you go by that one drop rule, do you? I don't think that's fair to the other part of your heritage. Why should somebody like Mariah Carey have to consider herself completely Black if she's not? People shouldn't have to deny an entity of themselves like that."

"Ta dem I'm Black an' ta myself, I'm Black. I ain't one uh dem niggas dat be tryin' ta pass fa shit else. Most Black people don't know how rich dey history is. If dey did, dey wouldn't be tryin' ta be nothin' else. Da way thangs goin' right nah, uh whole lot uh us should hate dem--all dey do is, steal, kill an' destroy."

"...My pastor says the devil steals, kills and destroys."

"My point exactly."

"It's the Black folks that *are* mixed like you that are all Afrocentric. You ever noticed how the darkest of the darkest Black people—the ones that look like they're straight from the Motherland claim they're mixed with Indian and everything else, like being mixed is gonna make them more prestigious or something. I don't get it."

"Every race, every human came straight outta Africa. Dey even got proof in China right now dat show, point blank, that Asians came from uh group uh dwarfs dat migrated from Africa. But dey try ta keep da facts covered up...I *will* say dis 'bout White people, dough--dey smart as hell. Dere's way more people uh color on da earth but dey got us all tryin' ta be

45

like dem and dey runnin' us. Dey got dat reverse psychology thang workin' on us colored people real good. Dey make us thank we ain't shit when, actually, melanin hold uh whole lodda power. Why you thank dey be tannin' an' gittin' fake lips an' shit. Dey even gittin' fake asses."

"Yeah but all you can do is pray and let Jesus take care of the rest. This world'll never be right."

"See. Dat's part uh da problem. White folks came over ta Africa wit dey version uh da bible an' beat it inta Black folks' heads dat da only choice dey had was ta suffer, listen ta da White masters an' wait fo' uh reward in heaven. Dat's some bullshit! We livin' nah, we need ta do sumethen 'bout dis shit right nah! Don't nobody on dis earth know *what* heaven gon' be like. It could be hell fa all dey know! You cain't live in da future. Dat's one uh da main problems I got wit religion."

Whoa. I hadn't asked for all that. "Man can't change this world. The bible says man cannot direct his own step. There's nothing we're gonna be able to do to change the way the world operates."

"Leigh, Black people have da most buyin' power in America. We spend da most an' make e'rybody else rich but we still ain't got shit. Black people da ones dat can change what's goin' on in da Sudan right now but we too caught up on havin' da latest gear, listenin' ta dat whack ass shit dey playin' on da radio dat be sendin' out da wrong messages ta our generation an' dese kids out here. If we wudden't so worried 'bout all uh da bullshit White folks keep thowin' in our faces ta distract us—bling bling an' shit, we'uh be payin' attention ta Africa an' able ta get it back where it's s'posed ta be…"

"…You know what? …Never mind. *I need* ta go to bed. I've gotta be up early in the morning." Maybe he wasn't, but I was a believer and I wasn't about to sit on the phone and listen to a whole bunch of blasphemy.

"…Yeah…I got class wit Spandex tomorrow."

"With *who*?"

"Spandex. My instructor. She got uh pancake ass an' always be wearin' dem awful ass leggings."

"*That's* mean. What are you doing looking *anyway*?"

"You cain't help but ta gawk at dat shit. How you gon' be dat Black an' not have no ass? Den, she got da nerve ta wear dem little tops dat don't even be coverin' her shit up."

"*You're* mean… Well, I'm about to go to sleep."

"Aright. You gon' meet me over at Machine Gun spot after you git out?" Every time he called her that--the called the girl whose name rhymed with Meechie--I started cracking up laughing. He said her face looked like it had been shot by a sawed off shotgun. "You know I need'chu around. Yesterday Dustbowl was all up in my face smilin' an' shit—you godda save me, Leigh. She ain't makin' me look good."

"Yeah—whatever. You know you like her." Dustbowl, whose real name was Phalayna, was a hoodrat who was academically gifted but grimy looking nevertheless. Her skin was a grayish-brown tone that looked like it hadn't been touched with soap or a washcloth for years. She smoked weed in the parking lot before class and, since she sat next to me physics, I had to smell that mess on her every Monday and Wednesday and she worked in the admissions office with Craig and flirted with him every chance she got.

"Naah, you got dat twisted. I'm talkin' ta da girl I need right nah."

"I still can't believe you talked about her right in her face yesterday."

"She 'ont know who Dustbowl is."

"You better stop talking about people in front of them. They're gonna catch on sooner or later. "

"Dey some character, dough. Why Crunchy lit up da ressroom yesterday?"

"All those pork rinds."

We both busted out laughing.

"Why I catch him eating the crumbs off his desk? He licked his finger, dipped it in uh pile uh crumbs an' licked 'em off."

"Ugh. You're lying."

"No I ain't. I promise you dat muthafuka did dat shit! ...Aye, after you git outta class, stop by da job 'fore you take Pharaoh ta da hospital."

"How do you get any work done? You're always either on the phone with me or we're hanging out when I'm up there. I haven't seen you go to one class yet. You're gonna lose your job *and* flunk out. Watch."

"Ungh-uh. But stop by, dough. I wanna see you."

"This time, don't make me laugh when I'm drinking water."

"Nah dat was funny--uh classic. You snorted."

"That *wasn't* funny. I couldn't breathe and my sides were hurting."

"WHY 'ON'T YOU LEMME take you out ta dinner Saturday?" Craig asked as we sat under the stairs in the study area. I dipped the last chicken nugget and a fry in the packet of sweet and sour sauce.

It was three months into another semester and I still wasn't sure I wanted to date anyone else until I was ready to get married. "You just bought me lunch today... Yesterday you bought dinner." I concentrated on the chunky red letters sprawled across the yellow paper cup of Dr. Pepper.

"I'm talkin' 'bout uh real date outside uh school." He was leaning back in the green chair across the table, staring at me without blinking, watching my every move.

"You're gonna end up falling over in that chair and I'm gonna bust out laughing when you do." I looked up at him briefly.

"I'm serious. What time you wont me ta pick you up?"

New Rule # One: Do not ride in the date's car. "I'll meet you."

"What? You gotta man?"

"No."

"Some*body* keepin' you laced..."

"I don't have a man."

"Sugar daddy?"

"Ugh. No!"

"Homey luva friend?"

I smacked my lips slightly annoyed. "If I have one, *you'll* never know."

"I done known you fa two semesters..."

"And you're still trying to figure out if I have a man?" I laughed.

"Fa real. Les go out on Saturday."

I swallowed the rest of the pop and slurped on the rest of ice in the cup for a few seconds. My mouth was extra dry and he was still staring. "...I'm still thirsty."

"Wh*aa*t?" He was partially smiling and looking partially irritated and confused.

"...I guess."

"Where you stay at?"

"I'll meet you there."

"Where you wanna go?"

I shrugged my shoulders and traced the red letters on the empty chicken nugget carton. "Somewhere in Greektown maybe..."

"Pizza Papalis, eight uh'clock?"

I nodded.

"You still shy 'round me?"

I studied the wall near the stairs as I tried to nod a quick no but my head wouldn't cooperate. I couldn't even look at him.

"YEAH, I AIN'T EVEN mad at you even though you 'on't be talkin' ta me no more. He seem like he cool."

"I *do* call you."

"When? My caller ID must be broke, den!"

"What*ever*!"

"Don't worry, when I get uh man I'ma pay you back."

"She*rr*a! What should I wear?"

"I 'on't know."

"Why don't you come with me?"

"Huh! Yeah, right. I 'on't think so. You know you on't won't me all up in y'all mix. You jus scared. As much as I love Pizza Papalis, I ain't 'bouta be nobody third wheel."

"Well I wish you would. I didn't even like him at first. He looks like a player."

"I thought you said he was fine."

"He is. But...you know how they are when they *know* they look good. I'm not sure about him."

"Well, if you not sure, den don't go."

"But I do kinda like him."

"So what's the problem? Sometimes da ugly ones be worst dan da fine ones--you never know. But you *should* know how he is by nah, y'all always be kickin' it. Y'all sound like y'all joined by da shoulders or something—like dem twins dey just separated. Only I 'ont see y'all gettin' separated no time soon."

"Yeah, well let me get dressed. I'll call you as soon as I get in."

"Yeah, right. I'll talk to you whenever."

"Shut-up. I'll call you tonight."

"Bye. And don't do nothin' I wudden't do."

"Bye." I giggled and hung up the phone.

"SO DEN I WENT ta juvie. Dat shit wuddn't fun. I always had ta fight. Three years later I got locked up in Jackson on some bogus ass drug charges an' shit." As he looked into my eyes, I could feel the pain he normally kept to himself.

"What was that like?"

Within the next hour, over a pineapple, Hawaiian deep-dish supreme pizza, we knew each other's life stories and even with the place being packed, it felt like we were the only two in the entire restaurant.

"You wanna hang out after dis?" he asked after the waiter left the check.

"Yeah. Let me call my mom and see if she'll watch the baby a lil' bit longer—but I'm *not sleeping* with you if that's what you're trying to do."

"I ain't even comin' at'chu like dat. You should know dat by nah." He picked up the black leather thing the waiter had just placed in the middle with the bill inside.

"Make sure you tip him well. You know they think Black folks are cheap."

"I 'on't care what dey thank. I ain't givin' dat muthafuka all *ma* hard earned money. An' you see how he put it in da middle like he 'on't think I can pay?"

"*Hard earned? All you do* is talk on the phone when you're at work. And who says he doesn't think you can't pay." I smiled and pulled out my wallet.

He placed my hand in his and pushed away the tip I was about to leave the waiter. "I got dis. I been wantin' ta take you out fa uh minute." He was looking real serious.

"Well, okay but you'd better tip him."

"Dang, it's like *dat*?" he asked as I closed my wallet. His eyebrows jumped.

"What?"

"You loaded. What'chu doin' wit all *dat* money on you?"

I held my finger up and whispered, "Wait a minute." I had just called my mother. "Yeah, she'll be able to keep him. I'm sorry, what were you saying?"

A strange look swept across his face. "Neva mind." When we walked out of Pizza Papalis he reached for my hand. I followed his black Mustang to Belle Isle and parked in a spot that wasn't crowded. We walked to a bench near the water and sat, quietly taking everything in. Canada looked beautiful from here.

"You know, I wuddn't mind movin' ta Canada." The way he said it, it sounded more like a question.

"You must be reading my mind. It's so *clean*."

"I like da way dey say a-*ga*in."

"I know. It's funny. It's weird how it's right across from us and, yet, so different. So clean."

"An' not as racist."

"Um-hm."

"So what are you? ...Libertarian, a democrat, or uh republican?" he asked staring at the stars with his arms stretched out on the back of the bench. By the light of the moon, his eyes looked as though he was in a far away, intangible place that longed for something I had yet to understand.

"See. That's why I like you. You're the only Black guy in Detroit I've ever met who would ask that question on a date."

"You only *like* me?"

"Hey, don't push your luck. You've gotten far, you know."

He shook his head and chuckled.

"I'm a democrat."

"...Have you done any research on da Democratic party, lately? Do some research an' get back ta me. If you pay attention ta da laws dey tryin' ta implement right about nah, you gon' find out dey ain't no better dan Republicans. Besides, dey all related an' buddy-buddy anyway. What I'm really hopin' for is uh worldwide revolution." For the next hour he broke down political issues and Bills I never even knew existed.

"When you been in jail an' trapped in da system like I been, you make it yo' business ta know what's goin' on in da White House an' wit da po-po's--police ain't shit but organized crime."

"What makes you say that?"

While he broke down his theory, I thought about Niquie's stepfather. Maybe Craig was right. Harold was certainly crooked. Niquie said he usually kept the marijuana and all the money he confiscated from civilians.

"You should check out BBC news sometime."

"I don't have cable."

"Look it up online. Dey give you uh more realistic an' uh less propagandized version uh da news from uh worldwide perspective. You'uh be surprised how many countries hate da United States. An' when you look at U.S. history, it ain't hard ta understand why. America's one uh da biggest hypocrites on this muhfuckin' planet. Da ones runnin' dis country always tryin' ta tell other civilizations—civilizations dats been here way befoe America--how ta live. Dat shit ain't cool."

"You've got a point."

We sat in silence simply enjoying each other's company.

"…What'chu plannin' on doin' wit yo'self?" He put his arm around me and drew me into a gentle embrace.

I smiled and couldn't stop smiling. This felt good. *Real* good. "…I have a lot of plans. Finishing school is the most important one—well, no. First and foremost—my relationship with God, then being a good mother, then school." He nodded his head like he dug what I was saying and continued looking over at Canada. "You know what's funny? You don't look like you'd be this sweet. You look like—" I was about to say *a smooth player* but I caught myself. Sherra was right. Just because he looked good didn't mean he had to be a hoe. "But you *are* sweet…You kinda look like a painting of the Black Jesus—minus the locks."

"Hee*ell* naw!" He broke out of our embrace and slid to the other side of the bench. A wild and almost evil look expanded across his face and—just as quickly as it had appeared—it vanished. Something about the whole thing, that look that crossed his face and the way he just snapped scared the crap out of me. Why was he so offended? I wasn't trying to be offensive!

"My bad." My stomach started rumbling. *Calm down. You're having the best date of your life and here you are ruining it.*

"Did you register fa classes yet?" He switched the subject.

"Yeah. I always do it early."

"I'ma be takin' foe classes. I ain't never taken over three at uh time. I'ma need'chu ta help me study." He slid back over and hugged me. I smiled at him. "Let's go so we 'on't hold yo' mama up." I didn't want the night to end but it *was* time to get my lil' man. "I'm really feelin' you," he said as we held hands and walked towards my car.

I looked at him and felt like I was in another place. A place where you could travel on iridescent feathers and live on the lips of your lover. The way he kissed me, soft and playful, underneath the bright indigo sky, it felt like twenty orgasms in a row on a beach with liquid crystal waves crashing against the shore while quiet storm love songs amplified from the sky.

The three guys I had kissed before this had completely turned me off. The first guy I ever kissed was in eighth grade. He licked my whole face and missed my mouth. The second guy, Ja'harree had chain-smoked right before the kiss, which made it more like licking a filthy alley and I had to wipe my whole face off afterwards. Then there was Darren Pewter who could kiss but didn't count. With the way Craig kissed, you could just tell he was good in bed.

"Call me when you git in, aright?"

I nodded yes.

This was just what I wanted. And, no. I was not going to sleep with him. I was holding on to that promised I'd made to God. I had learned more than enough from past situations.

"HEY, I BEEN TRYIN' ta call you! Where you been at? Ma mama trippin'. Can I come over? I need ta talk."

"You okay?"

"Naw!"

"Alright. Well, come on."

"How I git dere?"

I gave him the directions. That night he asked if he could stay and ended up moving in with me. Pharaoh was one but he was used to sleeping with me. I was going to have get him used to sleeping in his own room. I moved the computer desk out of the other bedroom, put it in the living room and got Pharaoh a bedroom set.

Pharaoh might have still been adjusting to having his own room but Craig and I weren't wasting any time in our bedroom. He gave my body attention like no other man had. The fact that we were best friends only made it better. It was like finding something you didn't even know you were searching for all along. Life was much more fun with Craig around. When I didn't feel like it, he always found a way to trick me into studying. Like the time he promised to eat me out when I finished my physics homework. And that was a very good deal. The way he did it, the way he put his whole tongue around my clit and vibrated it...umm, umm, umm...

We spent most of our time together laughing and every Friday we went on a date. Movies, go-car racing, going out to eat (even though Ruby Tuesdays was one of the only places he wanted to go unless we went somewhere in the hood) and we did tons of other stuff I hadn't ever thought about doing like sitting in the park and reading and picnics at Belle Isle.

Being with Craig and having fun with him for some reason reminded me of the word frolicking... I told him that one time and he busted out laughing.

But being with him wasn't just wonderful because of the fun we had together. With someone around to help with Pharaoh things were easier--not that Pharaoh was too much to handle. And there really wasn't a problem between Darren and Craig since Darren was barely in the picture. But I *did* notice that with Craig around Darren called less and tried to pick up Pharaoh much more often so he wouldn't have to sit on the couch like an uncomfortable stick figure that was still afraid to touch his own son. Usually when Darren did get him for the day, his mother took care of Pharaoh anyway.

"HEY? HEY? YOU ARIGHT?" Craig was banging on the bathroom door. "Yo' ass threw up yestaday, too."

"I'll be out. Give me a second." Shit. Morning sickness was back. And Monthly Martha Our Friend When Sexually Active hadn't come thru on her scheduled week. After Pharaoh I kept track of these things. It was five months since Craig had moved in and I had been on birth control from the second day Craig came over. Day one we hadn't done anything--he had been so pissed about what was going down with him and his mother. He hadn't really explained but it sounded like it had something to do with her new male friend.

When it came to having another child, I didn't know how to feel. I was only twenty-two and didn't know if I could handle *two* children. Craig, on the other hand, was twenty-four and ready for a child. He was doing pretty well with Pharaoh but I was still concerned about the situation.

Getting straight to the point: he didn't have a real job. He had a work-study and went to school full time. I was used to Darren spoiling me on the monetary tip. He had started sending forty-five hundred dollars a month—five hundred more than before. Together, Craig's scholarships and mine only added up to three thousand dollars a semester. How was that going to work with two kids? It seemed like I'd be splitting the money Darren sent for Pharaoh to take care of the second child--Craig's child.

Even though his car was four years old, he had a car note, insurance and a stack of bills from past due parking tickets and credit cards. Yeah, he had been doing all right when he was at home with his mother but things were different now. Another kid meant another expensive expense. I wanted to be able to buy whatever was needed whenever I needed it for the baby without having to struggle on a tight budget.

After being so broke I had to borrow gas money from my mother every week to fill that gas guzzling, put-put I rode in back in the day before Pharaoh came along, there was no way I was about to revisit living way under the poverty line like that again. Back then going to Red Lobster was a luxury. I remember one time the utility bills got so tight, I stuck a roll of toilet paper from one of the restrooms at school in my book bag.

But in a few years Craig would be done with school and I'd be a nurse. I guess we could make it till then. Maybe I was looking at it wrong. It would be an honor to carry his child and Craig had been talking about marriage from the time he moved in. Yeah, every now and then we got into it but that was gonna to happen in any relationship. What was important was that we always made up...and the way we made up...in the bedroom...apologizing again and again...we always ended up making each other very un-mad. I was in love with Craig. He was my friend and my man. I opened the bathroom door. He was leaning against the wall. "You're looking serious." I said, playing for time to try to figure out how to tell him.

"You pregnant?"

"That's what I'm thinking."

He picked me up and was about to swing me in the air. "My bad, I ain't tryin' ta scare my baby. Evrytime I thank you cain't make me no happier, you turn around an' make me even happier."

Everything was perfect.

The only problem was getting him to go to church.

CHAPTER 4

LITTLE MAURITANIA, OR MAURI as we winded up calling her, only added to the family affair.

Even though he held out as long as he could, Craig threw up in the labor room after she came out. The placenta and all the other stuff that came along with her weirded him out but he was ecstatic nonetheless. And he was adamant about giving her his last name even though I would have preferred her to have the same name as me and Pharaoh.

She looked more like Craig than me. The only things she got from me were the long lashes that splayed like wet angel feathers when she cried and my hands and feet--thank God. Craig's toes were scary. She had his big, innocent, round eyes and you could tell she was going to have his eyebrows that, although not yet as thick as his, she sometimes furrowed up into funny faces. She was always inventing new ways to make us laugh. Sometimes she would stick her tongue out and wiggle her eyebrows at us, which was hilarious for a newborn. She had his smooth, creamy light skin that reminded me of sun kissed gold. I don't know where she inherited it from but her cheeks and lips seemed to stay pineapple-strawberry pink. When she started to fuss, all I had to do was gently trace the silky loops of champagne bronze circles on her head and she would stop or fall asleep as I watched her, in awe of God's creation. She had my grandmother's gilded brown hair color.

Mauri was two weeks old when I took her to get her ears pierced. Craig insisted on coming and started looking like he was about to trip out when a nurse with a big blonde, plastic looking hairweave put the piercing gun next to her ear. He started yelling and calling me inhumane and we had to leave because neither me, the nurse nor her big hair couldn't calm him down. A month later I took her back and even he had to admit she looked adorable with the tiny diamonds in her ears. On top of that he put bows on her head anytime we went out. She was gonna grow up conceited from all the compliments.

Then, there were the not so glamorous parts. The apartment was becoming tight. Craig seemed to evaporate when it was diaper time. It was harder to get homework done and keep up with the tenants when you had to breastfeed, fix dinner and see why the baby was crying every twenty minutes. And even though he wasn't bad, Pharaoh needed attention too. He had turned two only three months ago and was becoming inquisitive and starting to get into things. Like the time I had tightened the cap on the bleach and put it in the cabinet under the sink and went in the living room for all of two minutes. I walked back in the kitchen just in the knick of time to catch him re-opening that same bottle of bleach.

Pharaoh had been a laid kid but once Mauri was born I had to let him help with her so he wouldn't get jealous. Part of the problem had to do with Craig. Before she was born Craig spent time playing with him and took Pharaoh to the store with him when he went to pick up groceries, to the mall, the barbershop--everywhere. They used to do their own thing and leave me at home, which I didn't mind at all. A girl needed time to herself every now and then.

But now with Mauri on the scene Pharaoh was a thing of the past. Craig was crazy about Mauri, Mauri and more Mauri and left Pharaoh completely out of the equation. Even though she was his first child, I hadn't expected his feelings toward Pharaoh to change. It hurt. Every time he played favorites or showed his favoritism towards Mauri I regretted having two children by two different men because of mess like that. I tried to explain it to Craig but he still kept treating Mauri better than Pharaoh and it was making me uncomfortable as hell and becoming our regular argument.

"WELL, I GUESS *I'M* gonna have to treat him special then! This doesn't make any sense! You aren't right and you *know* it!" I shouted one morning right before stepping in the shower. The night before he came home with a gold bracelet all wrapped in a gift box for Mauri and nothing for Pharaoh, not even a toy truck from the dollar store. Pharaoh didn't say anything the rest of the night.

"Aright, aright. I'm sorry! Damn!" He pulled his wife beater and boxers off and stepped in the shower with me.

"NOPE! Get tha fuck out!" When he didn't budge I pushed him out. "Move!" His fingers were gripping the white wood trim of the bathroom door as I pushed his shoulder and tried to shove him out the bathroom.

"You got one more time ta push me!"

"Don't try me 'cause I'ma do a whole lot more than push you next!" I shouted, slamming the door on his fingers.

After that Craig wasn't allowed to punish Pharaoh. The only thing he was allowed to do when Pharaoh acted up or tried to hit Mauri was make him do push-ups.

But somehow Pharaoh got over Mauri's presence squeezing him out of the spotlight. He learned how to pick her up without dropping her and she'd get all excited when he played with her. They played games together and although Craig and I didn't understand what the games were all about at times, they seemed to. At least their brother and sister relationship was what I hoped it would be.

MY RELATIONSHIP WITH CRAIG, however, was about to change just before Mauri turned one.

One early sunny Friday evening, he took the kids to Palmer Park to play while I got dressed. We were taking them to Chucky Cheese and to the movies afterwards—some new Disney cartoon thing. The way he was all excited about it, I was thinking Craig wanted to see the movie more than the kids did.

The phone rung. I raced to get it trying to placed one of the diamond studs Craig had given me on my twenty-fourth birthday in my ear not knowing it would be the call that would tear my world apart. "Hello," I panted. "Mom, you don't have to worry about watching the kids tonight--" I hadn't checked the caller ID but I figured it was her. She kept them every Friday.

"—Ha'lo--Ha'lo? Craig dere?" a young, scratchy voiced girl asked completely talking over me.

"No he's not. Who's calling?" My heart started beating wildly. Something wasn't right. Craig didn't talk to his sister. She was not only diagnosed as mentally ill but as a threat to the family. This definitely wasn't his mother and none of his female cousins ever called.

"Dis his girl. Could'chu tell 'im ta call me back?"

I panicked. What kinda mess was this?

Just before I was about to hang up on her, Craig walked in with the kids. "Hold on, here he is." I handed him the phone and went in our bedroom to pick up the cordless.

"Hey, bae." The words flowed from her mouth as easily as he held my daughter in one arm. "I'm tryin' ta git dem tickets fa da concert. I'm 'bout ta call Ticket Masta in uh minute. You still wont me ta git some seats up in da front, right?"

"—Hold up. I think you got da wrong number--"

"—*Whad*? *Dis* Angela–"

"—Like I said, you got da wrong number--"

"--Hell *naw*! I jus tried yo' cell but it keep goin' ta voicemail. *You called me* from dis number las night, right?--whad da fuck *you on*, Craig?"

He hung up on her. He must of thought that would be the end of it. I stayed on the line and let her talk. I could tell she was one of those mouthy types. If I kept quiet and let her say what she had to say, I'd find out everything I needed to know.

"Don't tell me yo' ass livin' wid uh bitch! Dat cho' girlz house you been callin' me from?"

I didn't say shit. Craig was about to walk in the bedroom. I slammed the door and sat on the floor with my back against the bed and pressed my feet against the door underneath the doorknob. As strong as my legs were, he wasn't about to be able to open the door anytime soon.

"Oh, yo' ass wanna play dumb, nah? Fuck you B*IT*CH! You bedda not step yo' ass ta my crib no MUTHAFUCKIN' mo'! Been fuckin' wit cho' ass fa three monts, payin' *yo'* muthafukin' parkin' bills an' shit an' you ain't neva wonted ta do shit but sit around ma house an' fuck—FUCK YOU! You gon' git yours, believe dat baby." With that she slammed down the phone.

My kneecaps felt like they were made out of metal when I tried to move them off the door. I took a breath and leaned against the bottom of the bed so I wouldn't fall on my face. Everything inside me was on fire. I needed to cool off before I had a heart attack. My legs got so weak he was finally able to push the door open. He stood there like a statue staring at me waiting for a reaction.

Looking at him made a sharp pain shoot in chest. I had been with this man for two years. Two years.

In that time, I had almost lost my rent-free apartment and position as apartment manager because we were always arguing about the way he treated Pharaoh like an ape mongrel baby. But I had hung in there. He was supposed to be my man, right? People go thru shit. But I had never expected him to play me like this.

He was still watching me without blinking.

Suddenly I went into a calm frenzy. I got up, walked past where he stood in the doorway, went to the kitchen, got some garbage bags and started gathering his things up one area at a time and dumped everything of his in bags.

I couldn't even force my face into a frown. I felt blank, void, expressionless, like my hands and feet had been shipped to Alaska while my heart had been placed in a furnace. I wanted him out of my place as quickly as possible.

He put Mauri down and walked up behind me. "Baby, I o'n't know--"

"--Ungh-uh. That's okay. I don't want any weak ass excuses. Save 'em for somebody who cares." I said it so flatly, like this wasn't really happening.

"Baby? Baby. Listen. I'm sorry. Pleeeaase, baby." His eyes were starting to get all glossy.

"Un-Ac-Muthafukin'-Ceptable. I've never cheated. I've never disrespected you in any way. I cook. The place is always clean. I go to school. You *never* had to worry about me going out to a club—not one time--I haven't even gone out with my girlfriends since we've been together. You don't have to pay my bills--you don't pay for anything unless it's for the baby or when we go out. I trusted you. All I asked for in return was honesty which I really don't think was too much to ask of you. *I don't have* a problem being honest.

"*You* messed up. Not me. Hmph. I'm glad I never sucked your dick... Always said I'd save that for my husband. Guess its not you-- hunh?" I said it so calmly even though I was boiling like an overcooked, cracked egg inside.

"*BBBa*by...*pleeea*se." He put his arms around my waist as I pulled his shirts out of the closet and shook them off the hangers. "Don't...I–I love you. It wuddn't even like dat. I love you! She-she ain't shit ta me. Baby don't..."

"You might as well not even say anything else. Let's pretend I'm deaf--you *obviously* already think I'm dumb. Now. I *would* fold these shirts so they could all fit in here but I don't feel like going through the trouble. You know what? Could you go get another bag?" I asked scanning the closet trying to figure out the best way to pack the rest of his things. He didn't budge. "What? You immobile or something?"

"I just—come on nah! It wuddn't even like dat, baby! Come on, nah! You ain't even hear me out." He started talking as fast as the tears were running down his face. I had never seen him cry before. But it wasn't enough to make me change my mind. I had never been hurt like this.

"I guess I'll get it myself then." As I walked to the kitchen I saw Pharaoh with his head bent holding Mauri on his lap on the couch. Looking at his somber face and Mauri's sad round eyes that had sensed a change in circumstance, my heart twisted into knots like tiny pieces of macramae; a beautiful macramae design gone wrong because of someone who couldn't follow the simplest pattern directions!

"Don't," I warned as Craig tried to hug me. His normally smooth and manly voiced was now cracking under the pressure he had imposed upon himself.

"We–we can work it out baby. Dis won't happen again. *Baby*, please. Les git married? Tamorrow? On Monday. We can go ta da courthouse! Please–"

"—Craig! Save it." I pulled all his shoes from the front closet and put them into another bag. I wanted his ass out. As quickly as possible. At that very minute, it seemed like he had a hundred pairs of the same black casual shoes.

Pharaoh tried to comfort Mauri when she started crying.

"I'm not putting my kids through this. What happens if you bring a disease home? Then, they won't have a mother or a father. Let me tell you something right now. I am *not* the one. I'm still young. I have a whole life ahead of me. I'm sure I can make it on my own. *Without* someone that's gonna cheat on me." I had to stop before I started shouting or before I stabbed him or did something else I wouldn't want the kids to witness.

"Baby...Baby...I'll-I'ma--please! *Stop!* Look at me!" He tried to cling to my back as I rapidly finished gathering his shit.

"Help me put this stuff in your car," I demanded.

"Whad? You *crazy*!"

I looked him dead in the eyes and didn't budge.

"You know whad? I'ma—I'ma--fuck it—*fuck* it! I'ma give you yo' space fa uh minute. But we gon' talk dis thing through. Counselin'--whatever I godda do. I know I fucked up but–*baby, baby pplease*. Don't trip out on me like dis. Jus give me uh chance ta prove myself ta you. We'll be like we was. I'm you an' you me, baby, 'member dat..."

I started handing him the garbage bags one by one. He eventually gave in and put his things in his car. He must have sat there an hour before he finally drove off.

I sat at the dinning room table and watched the red lights of the back of his car slowly disappear down Ponchatrain Street and my composure broke. Scorching tears poured down my face. I had been a good woman to Craig. Best friends my ass.

Pharaoh and Mauri came into the dining room. "I love you mommy. You're a good mommy. And pretty too." His face was stern and his husky voice was much too deep for a three year old.

"I love you too, sweetie." I tried to smile between the tears. Mauri touched my face with her little pudgy hands then planted a wet and snotty kiss on my cheek.

That night Craig called every thirty minutes from his mother's house forcing me to turn the ringer off. Then my cell phone rang. I was about to turn it off but it was Darren.

"Hello." I must have sounded terrible.

"What's wrong?" he asked trading a normally dry voice for one of concern.

I shouldn't have but I told him the whole story.

"I'll be over there. Gimme fifteen minutes."

He played with the kids until they fell asleep then motioned for me to come sit next to him. I was in so much pain I fell on his chest on the couch and cried until I didn't have anything else left inside. "You're a good woman Leigh." He kissed me on the forehead and carried me to the bedroom. His hand gently stroked the back of the shirt I had planned on wearing to Chucky Cheese. After he laid me in bed he left the room. "Here you go." He came back in and handed me a towel to wipe my face with but my mascara had already dripped black spots onto my top and the cream bed sheets. "Don't worry about that, it's replaceable. Come here." For the first time, his voice was soothing. Seconds later without thought, we were kissing like passionate flames, our tongues the only means of putting the fire out. I trembled as his fingers and tongue gently traced my welcoming nipples. His feathery touches made goose bumps resonate all over my body. We begged for each other tearing off the clothes hindering us from feeling one another's electrified heat and wetness.

"You have a condom?" I whispered.

He was definitely prepared and wasted no time whipping one out. Our bodies freely slithered closer until we danced and vied riding each other like it was the rodeo show. I hadn't been with him since I was twenty-one—and only once, at that. But now? Darren at thirty-four? Oh, he had gotten even better which, was almost impossible. Even his facial expressions turned me on.

Two hours later he came on the roundness of my behind mid-air, doggy style and had no problem taking care of me again afterwards. I came and I came *hard.* Three times. Ate me out *and* licked my toes. "You got some good pussy," he muttered in my ear while he rubbed his cum into my skin.

And that was some good dick, I thought as I rested my head in the crease of his arm.

I WAS HAPPY DARREN woke up before the kids the next morning. I was about to rush him out but, although I hated to admit it, I needed his company. We got dressed and actually had a conversation about things other than clothes, cars and stock accounts for a change. "I guess this was a week bad for *everybody.* I still can't believe I walked away from that accident. I 'on't have even any scratches."

"Yeah, you were going ninety-something *and* the tail of your bike was hit by a car? You better be counting your blessings. They always say motorcycles are dangerous, I don't think you should stay in that club."

"Yeah, I'm pretty much done with that shit. It was fun back in the day but I godda lodda things I wanna do before I die." For a second I though he was a mind reader. Those were my exact thoughts about me and Craig. Fun while it lasted, over now.

"It showed me something, though. Everything can change within a second. I was driving down Jefferson and--BAM!" He pounded his fist against his the palm of his left hand. "Just like that, I was down. I didn't even have time ta blink. I fell on this arm 'cause I was blocking my head from skiddin' on the pavement." He raised his right arm in the air and looked it over before moving it towards me. "I coulda became a paraplegic," he added nodding his head as he reflected back on the incident.

I held his arm briefly. "Well, I'm glad you're still here and that you aren't paralyzed." I could tell it meant a lot to him to hear me say that. He smiled briefly.

"Enough about me and the accident. What's up Leigh? Fa real?"

I sighed a deep, heavy sigh. Just as I was about to say something the doorbell rang. I peered out the living room window trying not to move the curtains.

It was Craig. I took his keys last night before he left. He stood outside ringing the bell like a madman. I couldn't continue the disturbance. The tenants would complain to the owners.

"I'll be right back." I shook my head in disgust sighing so hard I blew my bangs off my forehead. I left Darren in the apartment and went to talk to Craig at the front door of the building.

I tried to slip outside to find out what he wanted but Craig pushed past me effortlessly. "We godda talk! I know dat muthafucka ain't up in dere wit my baby, Leigh! *Tell me* he ain't in dere!" One thing for sure, Craig hadn't missed Darren's black Benz truck parked across the street.

He walked straight in the apartment since the door was still cracked open. Darren was on the couch with Pharaoh sitting on his lap. Mauri was smiling and handing her teddy bear to Darren, which *really pissed* Craig off. He was so enraged the corners of his eyebrows touched his forehead. "Oh, you ain't wastin' no time, hungh? I 'on't need'chu over here! We got business ta take care of. Get da fuck out!" his voice cracked as he snatched Mauri away from Darren's knee. "You tryin' ta come over here ta get some pussy an' play daddy?" Craig stepped over to me like he had spotted something. He pulled my hair away from my neck and spotted passion marks Darren had no business leaving. "WHAD DA FUCK?" He yelled pushing me away from him so hard I fell flat on my face.

"If you wouldn't have *fucked up*, you'd still have it," Darren taunted and turned around to help me up. Before he could help me get up, Craig jumped over to Darren, pushed Pharaoh out of the way as Darren stood up and Craig grabbed Darren by the neck. They started attacking each other physically like two beasts each holding their own. I jumped between them but it still took a while for the blows to desist. It was crazy. Darren was built but Craig was built too and way taller and yet it was starting to look like Darren was getting the best of Craig. He swung on Craig and caught him in the left eye. Darren's fist popped so hard against Craig's socket I thought Craig's eyeball was gonna burst.

I wasn't about to watch them kill each other. "Craig, *you've got to* go!" I shouted.

"And if I godda go, ma daughter comin' wit me! Ain't no punk ass bitch gon' play *daddy* ta *ma* lil' girl!" he growled. His eyes held an intimidating shade of fiery brown that glowed from deep inside past the pupil of the eye. I'd never seen a look so evil and intense in his eyes. He snatched Mauri up as she screamed her lungs out and stormed out of the apartment shouting, "DIS SHIT AIN'T OVER YET!" behind him. I knew I couldn't stop him from taking her. He acted like his life revolved around Mauri.

I ran outside and flagged him down. "You need the car seat!"

He stopped and waited as I grabbed it out of the backseat of my truck. He snatched the seat from my hands, shoved it in his car and put her in it while she continued screaming. "Tanight dis nigga bedda be gone. Da way I see it, we even nah!" he huffed before driving off.

I ran back into the apartment only to find Darren trying to coax Pharaoh out of a corner on the kitchen floor. The boy was clearly shaken up. I was putting him through all this drama and it made me feel terrible.

"Leigh." Darren shook his head. "You need to leave *that* nigga alone. I don't give you money each month to put my son under *domestic upheaval!*"

I didn't even respond. Was he blind? Couldn't he see I already felt bad without him adding to it?

I ran over to Pharaoh. "Hey, man. Come on. I know that was scary but its okay now. Come on." I put my arms out to pick him up but he snatched away instead. I ran in my bedroom and fell on the bed in tears, the kind of long, embarrassing and disgusting tears that make your chest burn and sting like your chest is infected.

The next thing I knew Darren was asking me to hang out with him. "Allen invited me on his yacht today, why 'on't you come with me..."

"...You're off today? It's Saturday..." My head was still buried between the two pillows Craig and I used to sleep on.

"Yeah."

That was rare. Darren always worked on Saturdays.

"...That's okay... You can take Pharaoh if you want..."

"Come on Leigh. If you stay cooped up in this place you aren't gonna do shit but drive yourself crazy thinking about that dumb ass muthafucka."

"...I can't..."

"I'm not trying to leave you here by yourself like this...why 'on't you just get dressed and come with me?"

I lifted my head and looked at him. Who was this dude sitting on the other end of the bed looking all concerned, like he cared? Had to be the accident. "Um...that's okay. I'll be fine." He was still sitting on the edge of the bed. When I looked over at him his elbow was on his left knee and he was resting the left side his face on his fist. Even though his brows were furrowed, he didn't look angry but I still couldn't tell where he was coming from as he looked back at me.

"...Alright, alright. I'll go."

I put on a casual sleeveless white dress and curled my hair while he dressed Pharaoh.

"You look nice. You don't have a problem showing off yo' legs, hung?" he commented as he helped me get in the truck.

I smacked my lips at him and snapped at him, "I suppose that's because it's *summer*. Look, I can just stay here if we're not gonna do anything but aggravate each other the rest of the day."

"Leigh? It was a compliment. Come on. Get back in the truck."

I could tell Darren felt bad about everything that had happen and he was actually being momentarily nice but after we went to his place so he could shower and change clothes, the ride to Metro beach was like slow torture. I was worried about my baby--not that Craig would do anything to her, I knew he wouldn't but she still had on her pajamas for heavens sake! Soon she'd need to eat. She wasn't used to his mother. What if his mother was the type that chewed up food then feed it to my baby? He hadn't gotten her diaper bag. And what if he called up that ghetto ass Angela hoodrat and took Mauri over her house? I hated him and I wanted my baby back!

THE DAY WITH DARREN was going rather well but I hadn't heard a word from Craig even though I'd called and left three messages on his mother's answering machine.

Pharaoh, on the other hand, who enjoying being in the rare company of his father, was intrigued by the boat and kept interrupting Darren from the heated office discussion he and his coworkers were having. Darren handled it rather well and took the time to answer every question Pharaoh asked.

Darren was up for sales manager, which was second only to owner of the Ford dealership and meant mega bucks. I was slightly surprised he invited me. There were only two other Black people there. A salesman called Jim and a saleswoman named Betty and both Jim and Betty had White spouses.

I was reminded of Christmas every time Jim laughed. He sounded like a happy-go-lucky Santa Claus and had the stomach to match. The only thing missing was Santa's mustache and beard. Although Jim was big and tall, he looked very non-threatening and oreo-ish.

Betty, who preferred to be called Bet, talked out of her nose and over-enunciated each syllable as though she was trying to make up for her Blackness. She was so light she could have been considered an octoroon.

My bet on Bet was that she wore the wide brim, navy straw hat to help shield her from the sun. Even so, you could still tell she was Black. I bet she hated that fact. Betty and I didn't say two words to each other the entire time we spent on the yacht.

But the extremely skinny blonde girlfriends of the guys Darren worked with wouldn't stop talking to me, which made me slightly uncomfortable. Judging from the well-done plastic noses and plumped lips and tailored clothing, nine times out of ten they were from upper class families or something close to that. Mid-upper class is still on some other stuff. It's definitely *not* like the regular, lower middle class background I came from.

If Craig had been here he would have started talking about how White folks are paying for asses now, the same type of asses they used to whip and demean and he would have said it loud enough for them to hear and wouldn't have cared. I almost laughed out loud as I thought about how ghetto, uncouth and funny it would have been to see him do that.

Then I remembered how I had answered the phone smiling and thinking about how wonderful my life was and how irritating that girl's voice sounded and how Craig and I weren't even together anymore and how he had my daughter and I didn't even know if she was crying for me or not. And that sharp twisted pain embedded itself in my chest all over again.

"You look absolutely gorgeous. Is that Ne'am?" one of the blondies asked before taking another sip of the champagne the blonde next to her had bragged that her boyfriend bought the last time they were in Paris.

I couldn't give an answer when I didn't know what the heck we were talking about. Ne'am, Neem, *what*?

"It's Ne'am," the champagne bragger named Madison assured the girl named Hailey who asked the question I still hadn't figured out. They gave each other knowing looks.

"It's cool. You can tell us. We won't hate you for it," Lexi added.

"I tried to get one of his designs last month but he said it wouldn't be available until fall. I'm impressed—then again, you *are* a model. Just part of the perks hungh?" This came from another blonde who'd just come from the kitchen and joined the conversation.

Now I get it--and if they wanna trip off a dress from TJMaxx for thirty dollars, I don't have any problem lettin' 'em do so, I thought to myself and tried to remain polite. It wasn't that I hated them, I just did *not* want to be bothered. I should have listened to my first mind and stayed home.

"You and Darren do make a gorgeous couple. He used to talk about you all the time. Now that you two have the baby he doesn't as much but—trust me—that's how they do after you've got them." I decided this blonde haired Lexi chick was pretty. She had a smiled that looked like a well-practiced smirk.

"Really?" I asked half-heartedly and mirrored Lexi's expression. She came and sat next to me. I was still feeling like I was floating out of a chimney and into the sky and I couldn't tell if her moving closer in proximity to me was exacerbating the situation. The only thing I was sure of was that this whole thing, the yacht, yesterday, the fight, none of it seemed real.

"Oh, yeah. It was TaLia *this*, TaLia *that*. That's all we ever heard when we'd all hang out and you were on shoots... You're kind of short. How did you break into modeling? I've been toying around with the idea myself. I'm five eleven and a half, you know." Hailey smiled so I smiled back and tried to push past the smoke in my head to make sense out of all of this.

"Whatever. You've said that for years and we're too old for that sort of thing. No one breaks into modeling at twenty-two. Use your degree for a change. Anyway, we were talking about Darren and *her*—*not* her career. I-am-*so*-excited-for-you-two." Sometimes when this one talked, she sounded like she was spelling the words instead of talking and she batted her eyes a lot. I once read in a biology book that the average human blinks around ten thousand times a day. Not this chick. She could win a record for rapidity. It was almost like she had blinking Christmas lights stuck on her lashes.

"After he gets this promotion, you'd better make him get you the phattest ring in Van Cleef & Arpels!" she exclaimed after five blinks in a row. One thing for sure, for a White girl this Madison chick knew how to use herself some slang.

"We knew he was finally taken when you lost your ring and he didn't even get upset!" the girl from the kitchen added. This one liked to open her mouth really wide and raise her eyebrows like she was shocked right before she uttered a sentence.

"Oh?" the sarcasm dripped but they obviously didn't catch it. I am not the type to go around blabbing my business to people I know let alone complete strangers. This would easily turn into a low-key interrogation if I told them I wasn't TaLia, Darren's ex. How convenient for Darren my name is Leigh!

"We always tease him and ask him when's the wedding. He always smiles. After he gets this promotion he'll be more stable than ever." Hailey gave me a knowing look.

"Darren does have a very hard work ethic, doesn't he?" Lexi added.

I couldn't tell whether they were sincere or playing dumb and fishing for info. I had to do change the conversation before they had a chance to continue the barrage of questions. Lexi was Allen's girlfriend and from the looks of things, Allen was some sort of CFO for Ford's accounting sector.

"Your hair looks *hot*. Where do you go?" I asked Madison after waiting a couple of seconds to conceal my attempt at changing the subjects.

"You really like it?"

"Of course," I responded like I really cared.

"I go to this dude in Rodchester. You know the new strip they just put up next to The Lofts?"

I nodded.

"*That* place. *The Hills*. Ru'chard, he's the only person I let *touch* my hair! I like take him whenever I go out of town, too. Tim gets jealous. He says Ru'chard's at our house more than he is!" She giggled.

And for the rest of the time on the boat whenever one of them came near me, I poured on the compliments, agreed to hang out with them some time soon, bided my time and moved to a location the blondes hadn't coveted.

"YOU WANT SOMETHING TO eat before I take you home?"

"…Yeah." Now I was *not* a Darren fan. Especially after the TaLia thing but the longer I was out, the better. Sitting at home thinking about all this shit that just went down would only be depressing. I kept expecting Craig to call and ask what I was fixing for dinner in a few seconds.

Darren, Pharaoh and I went to some ritzy restaurant near Somerset Mall. Even the hostesses and servers looked like models. A bottle of water was probably like fifteen dollars in this place.

"Well I guess you finally met Bet," Darren stated smiling.

"*Oh, my God.* I'm not even gonna go there. She looks like she runs when a Black customer comes in to buy a car."

"Damn, girl--you good. Aright, aright. Jim."

"Classic Mall Santa Claus. Probably mad he's not up at the North Pole right now." We both cracked up. Pharaoh was busy playing with his fork and knife.

"*Now* I see why you used to sport that mustache-less look."

"What do you mean?"

"There aren't any real Black people at your job--you were trying to fit in. Assimilation is just another form of genocide, you know."

"I ain't godda fit in wit shit. I just decided to shave it off for a minute." He gave a quick shrug.

"Well I'm *glad* you got rid of *that* look."

He slightly rolled his eyes and grunted while he scooped at the pasta on his plate. It was fun irritating Darren. He wouldn't even look up at me. I was about to really go for the goal now. "You know, when you work around people like that you can't be a strong brotha. Then you'd be too unmistakably Black, too threatening."

"Why you always talking this Black/White shit all the time all of a sudden?"

"What do you mean?"

"You never used to talk like this."

"Oh, whatever."

Once our entrees arrived, Darren's behavior changed. I mean, the whole day—or the past two days were unusual in the first place. This was the most we *ever* talked since we'd known each other. Suddenly he got all quiet and kept glancing at my hands then his gaze would swoop up to my breasts and over my face. But his expression was distant and unreadable and whenever I looked at him, his eyes flickered away like he'd been caught in the middle of criminal activity.

"What's up with you?" I asked wondering if I really *had* pissed him off.

"I'm good. You want dessert?" He obviously wasn't going to tell me what the strange behavior was all about so I dropped it. If he was mad at me, he should just tell me.

"Um...yeah. Why not? I could go for some cheesecake right about now."

"Aright. You godda be back anytime soon?"

"No. Why?" I looked up and, once again, he looked away.

"Why 'on't you roll with me then. I've got an appointment to look at a crib in the area."

"That's fine... You know, if you acted like this a little more often, we'd probably be friends."

His eyes locked into mine for a second before he looked over the dessert menu. I was really and truly annoying him now. "You're always trying to be hard." He shook his head in disagreement and lifted his right eyebrow. "Darren, Darren, Darren. You know you like me." This time he chuckled when he shook his head no.

After dinner he drove to a posh subdivision in Rodchester Hills. "If I get that promotion, this is where I'm gonna be. Watch."

"You basically *live* for your job. You'll get it. That's one thing I'm sure of," I stated as he held the door open and let Pharaoh jump out of the truck onto the sidewalk. If there was one person that loved what he did for a living, it was Darren. He usually went in at seven, left at nine Monday thru Friday and still did six hours on Saturday. He was worse than a workaholic.

"So, what do you think so far?" he asked as we walked up the spiral staircase of a brand new brick mansion.

"It's absolutely beautiful." There was a pool, a theater, a walkout basement and every room was decorated and furnished. He said the furniture came with the house.

"Okay. I'll let you two discuss things amongst yourselves. Or do you need me?" The pleasant, anorexic, twenty-something real estate agent asked. She turned toward me and added, "I know how husbands can be—a million and one questions."

"We're good. Thanks." Darren responded.

When she left Darren grabbed my butt like it was a basketball right in front of Pharaoh and said so low he was almost whispering, "Look at what you'd have if you was with me. I'd fuck da hell outta yo' ass and make you cum back ta back every night. It'uh be uh shame ta waste pussy like dis on some broke ass muthafuka. You young and you 'on't even have no stretch marks yet. You better stop being a baby factory 'fore it's too late," he cautioned. "You can have all this—all this. All you gotta do is suck this dick *and* swallow that shit up." He made a ignorant slurping sound. "You'll get uh ring, baby. Believe that." His eyes were all squinty like he was worked up and ready to bust.

"Darren." I closed my eyes for a second. Looking at his face only made me more heated. "Darren. What's my major?"

"What?"

"My major. What is it?" He just looked at me like I was crazy. "All this time and you don't even remember, hungh? NURSING! NURSING!" My nostrils flared. "All you care about is *fuckin' tha hell outta me every night*? You don't care about me--you don't even *know* me! I guess that's how all uh y'all are—hungh? I sing in the choir, play the electric violin. The kids... I'm teaching them the books of the bible in so they can find them without fumbling during sermons. Did you know that, do you even care? And I'm a democrat. And I hope to be an activist for a coupla African countries some time soon, too." I counted the list off on my fingers. "But no man has *ever* given a shit about who I am, my goals in life or *me*! No man except Craig! And he's not even real! Feel like I've been living on some fake ass island and outta touch with reality or something. I keep believing in love and look at what I get. Look at what I get!

"Me sucking your dick? Is that all you care about, seriously?" I asked again because I just couldn't believe it.

He was unnerved by my response. His eyes got all big. "Stop tr*ipp*in'." He had the *nerve* to be irritated.

"No--no. Seriously. If that's the way it is, we should get married right now! Right now, dammit! Let's do this shit! Where's the ring? Where is it?" I waved my ring finger in his face. "And you know what? If we get married, my kids won't be illegitimates anymore. I guess that'll be a plus, too, hungh?

"You live in a bubble, Darren--your own lil' world. And you think every woman on earth is supposed to fall down and bow down to you and try to fit in Darren's Bubble. You 'on't even have a *clue*. God I *hate* you! See! This is why we'll never be together!"

After that, everything went blurry. All I remember is sleeping away the hour ride home and winding up in my bed crying for so long my tear ducts got tired and stopped producing tears.

Sometime soon it was going to be time to stop looking back and time to stop being stung over and over by all the stupid mistakes I'd made--not that I regretted Pharaoh or Mauritania but, I still regretted the guys, I couldn't bring myself to call them men.

I got up and went in the kitchen to put some water on for tea. My throat was inflamed.

Darren was on the couch wide awake while Pharaoh slept with his arms tightly wrapped around his neck. Darren had his arm on Pharaoh's back. "Watch this," Darren whispered before I had a chance to say anything. He moved his arm and tried to lay his son on the couch. Pharaoh grumbled and almost woke up and, even in his sleep, Pharaoh still managed to embrace Darren tighter each time. When Darren tried to lay him down again, he did the same thing and clung to Darren even tighter than he had before.

"How long have you been here?" I was hoarse.

"Three hours. Its almost twelve," he whispered. I shook my head and went into the kitchen, put the teakettle on stove and went back into the living room and sat next to Darren.

"He needs you... Can't you see that? Craig used to be there for him but..." I didn't want to go into the issue of Craig's favoritism. At this point I didn't want to discuss Craig at all with him.

For the first time Darren looked at me with hurt and pain so visible in his eyes I was almost ready to forgive him for what he'd said earlier and for not being there for Pharaoh. For a second it seemed like there was a real human with feelings lurking behind the superficial corporate zombie.

"Leigh, when I look at him I--I don't know what to say to him, I don't know what to tell him. He's always talking about some cartoon, 'Lions and the Zed Guy'--or whatever it's called.

"Let me tell you how it was growing up. My mother never had time to play with us, my dad was always at work and when we tried to hug them they were busy doing something or going somewhere and never had time to hug us back. I grew up like, *I have on Gucci, I go to private school, I've got a babysitter that's hot, my parents are paid, that's how I know they love me. A real man makes money. A real woman works out and looks good for her man.*

"I may not be the finest man in the world. Yeah, I have a big nose and I ain't the tallest muthafucka around but I got hazel eyes, paper in the bank, I'm top-notch *everything*, baby, and I get as much—" I gave him a look. "I can have any woman out there I want.

"Yeah, I love him. He's my son. Why do you think you don't have ta get on the bus with him? You should already know he's gonna have every opportunity I've had and more. Hell, the minute he gets his license he's gonna have a brand new car. He's already had a couple of birthdays that hit my pockets up. He's my son and that's what he deserves. Soon he'll go to Disney Land--my family wants to take him. You can come if you want." He paused. "...I already started an account for when the day comes and he goes to Yale or Harvard or Cornell or Oxford. He'll be able to become anything he wants and to get anything he wants..." his voice trailed off.

He looked down at the rug. Minutes passed before he spoke again. "I know you're a good woman. When first I met you, I ain't gon' lie, I was just tryin' ta get it. You was sexy. You weren't dressed like a freak but you had a body like a stripper and a pretty face to match—that's what I was on. But you were too young--don't get me wrong, not immature...innocent--that's a better way to say it, I guess.

"At first I thought you was down with yo' girl Geneva's click and--"

"--Geneva? Who? Who is *that*?" Those three glasses of whiskey he had had the restaurant must have done a number on him.

"Come on nah, you 'on't have to play it off like that. I could tell you weren't in on that shit our first date."

"No. I'm serious. Who are you talking about? I don't know any female named Geen--Gina, Geeka-- whatever you said."

"Yo' girl. The light skinned bust-o's bitch—I mean broad--you was hanging with when I met you. My homeboy--you know the one on the blue and silver bike? He's paid *a couple* of times for some crazy hours with *dat* bitch. She's one of Detroit's best. Niggas be choosing her over

Quiet Storm ever since The Dimes had all them dancers that was infected with AIDs. Niggas was droppin off like flies from them hoes up in Dimes, fa real. But yo' girl is cooler than uh muthafucka. She don't hang out at strip joints. Yeah, Geneva be shootin' bottles up her shit and knows how to deepthroat like a pro. I've seen her ass in action a couple of times. Some of my boys ran a train on her ass a coupla months before I met you at the Jazz Fes. Eight of 'em! I came in on the tail end of that shit when they was taping it and taking pictures. Dat bitch was so drenched in cum, she couldn't even open her eyes. She was tore up on X and drunk ass hell, I swear they made her drink piss out of a—wait a minute! You *didn't* know?" He checked himself after noticing the disgust and disappointment taking over my face.

I had to sit down to catch my balance. I knew Niquie had been a trip but I didn't know she was getting down like that!

The father of my child had originally thought I was like *Niquie*?

All he cared about was his *dick*. He didn't care about me. Not then, not now. The worse feeling in the world is when *you* play *ya self.*

I had just played myself again with Darren. After years of not sleeping with him I had given it up like it wasn't nothing.

"Damn. My bad. I thought you knew." Darren apologized. "Yeah, ya' girl is wild. She used to come up to the dealership and suck Barry off, you know my boy, the dude that always be in Black Enterprise magazine?"

I couldn't even manage a simple yes. I merely shook my head in sheer embarrassment. I couldn't believe I had hung around something like that.

"He bought her all that Ethan Allen furniture for her crib when she first got it and he made dat Bitch *work* fa dat shit," he added and chuckled before remembering he was talking to me. "I'm not gonna lie, I thought you were the new face in town, hanging out with her and all but— what was I saying…" While he tried to figure out what he was about to say I was growing more and more irate. At this rate I was gonna have permanent high blood pressure. I had to call Sherra asap to tell her about this. Dominique was trifling!

"…Oh, yeah. I realized you weren't like ole girl. See. Chicks like that? They let you know the price and how it's gonna go down, off rip. But, you didn't come at me like uh typical Detroit gold diggin' bitch. Those types only care about getting their hair and nails done every week. One look at your nails the first time we went out and I knew you wasn't on that tip." He laughed. I would have been offended by that comment but I was still stuck on Niquie's triflin' ass and the fact that he thought I was some new, barely legal wanna be high-class hooker. He probably wanted to test me out before I hit the market!

For a second—one second, I wished Craig and I were on good terms so I could tell him about this shit. But knowing him, he'd probably tell me I was too innocent for my own good, which would only make me feel more stupid.

Darren looked over at me and held my hand in his. "I'm glad we hooked up, though." His voice softened. "He's not a bad deal and you're a good mother. I knew you were seriously gonna be something from the first conversation I had on the phone with you.

"But that's not what I'm on right now... Man, even *TaLia*, was a hoe... She didn't break up with me over you getting pregnant with Pharaoh. She ended up getting back with her ex! You know, Rodrick Wilson, the linebacker for the Detroit Lions? Yeah, *that muthafucka*. Nine times outta ten it was 'cause he got that four million dollar mansion in Oakland Township." Undeniable anger shot into his voice and bounced onto the apartment ceiling.

"Darren. He needs *you*. Not just what you can do for him. When you promise to call and don't follow thru, he bugs me all day for your number and tries to call you or he makes me call over and over to try to reach you. He doesn't need excuses from your sisters and mother when you don't answer. He *needs you*. When you don't call him, I have to make up a bunch of sorry excuses so he won't be hurt. I'm the one that has to sit here and watch his heart break all because his father forgot to call him back and isn't ever around to read him a bedtime story. I'm gonna do whatever I have to do make sure he knows he's loved but I'm not you and I'm not gonna ever be able to fill your spot. I grew up without a father and I know what it's like.

"I remember the first time we went out. You went on and on about education and how White parents make sure their kids get the best. The best thing for Pharaoh, what he really wants is to spend time with you, to learn how to play baseball and basketball from you and to get that pat on the back from his father when he makes a touch down--or whatever you all call it when they score in football. You don't have to repeat the mistakes your parents made. He loves you and trust me, he doesn't care about what you have or don't have. He just wants to know you love him.

"Craig was the one that helped potty train him. That doesn't make sense--you only live five minutes away. You always manage ta find time ta party four nights uh week. That's what Madison and Hailey said. '*Oh he works so hard but he plays even harder*'," I batted my eyes and put my hands in the air like a ditz as I mimicked their voices.

It felt good to say all of this face to face instead of on his voicemail. Later for Niquie. I didn't have time to worry about a hooker that had used Sherra and me as a guise to get dollars without standing on a corner. My situation with my son's father was way more important.

"I'm living and I live a good life. I'm not one of those lovey-dovey muthafuckas that go around hugging and kissing everybody to prove a point. Do I wish I would've gotten all of that from my parents? Maybe. Maybe not. They did what they knew how to do for us and they did a damn good job.

"I respect the kind of person you are. Keep doing what you do, Leigh. I hope we can be friends. I'll always look out for you--you got my word on that." With that he got up, put Pharaoh in the top bunk in his room and waited until he went back to sleep. Pharaoh kept whining and fighting his sleepiness like he knew this would be the last time he saw Darren.

When he finally did fall asleep, Darren walked to the door and stood there with his back to me for a few seconds. He turned around and looked at me with emotion filled eyes, turned the doorknob and let himself out.

Darren's relationship with Pharaoh didn't change. Once he got that promotion the only thing that happened was a bigger monthly check. He had finally reached his idea of paradise—he was now a corporate bachelor.

CHAPTER 5

AFTER DARREN LEFT I picked up the phone and called Craig's mother's house again. I still hadn't heard from Craig and I couldn't take it--I wanted Mauri home pronto.

The phone rang and this time his mother answered. "Hello Ms. Walker, is Craig there?" If he was, I was about to call Sherra and ask her come over and stay with Pharaoh. Pharaoh was crazy about her and that way I wouldn't have to bring him along for the drama I was about to act out.

"Naw, he gone but Mauri ova here. She sleep–"

"--I'm coming to get her right now–"

"--I thank he say he was on tha way ta yo' house--"

"--Aright Ms. Walker, let me call you right back." Just as I slammed down the phone the doorbell rang. I didn't want Pharaoh to wake up. He had been through enough already. But I couldn't leave him in the place all by himself. If he woke up and couldn't find me he'd be terrified. I stepped outside. "I'll come out to your car. Give me ten minutes." He looked like he was filled with rage but he nodded and agreed to wait.

I kept getting Sherra's voice mail and I wasn't about to call my mother. She'd be all up in my business and start preaching and yelling at me and she'd hate Craig forever. Yeah, she ended up liking Darren but Craig wasn't established like Darren was and didn't wear custom designer suits. If mom ever saw Craig out somewhere after hearing about this, she was definitely good for cussing him out and using that stun gun she was itching to zap a Negro with.

I ended up calling my nosy next door neighbor Debra who agreed to stay in the apartment with Pharaoh for a couple of minutes.

"Why didn't you bring my child with you?" I huffed as I slid into the passengers seat. I was still wearing the outfit I wore on the yacht.

Craig turned the radio down. "You been out enjoyin' yo'self, hungh?" he asked rather sarcastically then, quicker than I could blink my eye, his demeanor changed. "I messed up. I know. I know dere ain't no explanation but could you just giv—"

"--Uum, let's see. What should we do, Leigh? Hmm. NO!" I retorted still looking straight ahead at the windshield.

"Look. You cheated on me wit dat muthafucka las night an' I know you was wit 'im taday. We even. How long you been fuckin' him? Is dat why he be smackin' thousands down on da table each mont? Seem like it ta me! Dat nigga be buyin' you Jimmy Hoo Hoo's, or whatever da fuck that shit is, fa yo' muthafuckin birthday! Muthafukin' foe hundred dolla shoes! What da hell is dat shit about? *Dat nigga* don't need ta be buyin' you *shit*! I'm s'posed ta be yo' man but chu 'on't be *actin' like* it!"

"EVEN? Huh, EVEN? You cheated on me for three months. There is no way in *HELL*! No way in hell, we're even! You know I've been faithful ta your ass the whole time we've been together so don't even try that shit.

"What about you--how long *have you* been cheating for real? You know what? You don't *ever* have ta tell *me* 'cause *I-don't-*care! And I'm not *trying* ta get even wit cho' ass—It's *OVER*! I'm done. How about you quit stalking me?" Oh, I was gonna be all right! Fuck him!

"Ain't nobody stalkin' shit. I came by, yo' truck was here but you was gone an' dat muthafuka truck wuddn't here. You wuddn't at yo' mama's or Sherra an' yo' grandmamma ain't know where you was at."

"You called my family and friends looking for me?" Now for sure everybody was going to be calling asking questions that weren't any of their business.

"Baby. Look. Time out. I love you. We got uh kid tagether, if I 'ont know where you at, I got da right ta try ta find you."

I was out done. "Well since you were out cheating, even though you had a woman and a kid at home, you lost your right to know my whereabouts 24/7. Those days are over. From now on, what I do and *who* I do? It's none of your business."

"Don't do me like dis. If you really got love fa me like you say you do, you'uh hear me out. Baby, look. I know I fucked up. But jus listen ta me fa uh minute."

"Correction. The operative word here is: had. I *had* love for you. You know what? You need ta say whatever it is *you claim* you need to say so bad and make it quick. I'm ready to get my child."

He paused a second before saying anything, like he was trying to choose the right words. "...You perfect. You handle yo' business, you go ta church an' you talk all proper-like an' shit." He raised his pinky finger and swayed it in the air. "I am Misses Leigh." He did an impression of my voice that sounded like a cross between an old, White, British woman and a wizard. "Shit, yo' ass cain't even yell loud enough ta scare somebody... An' I love *all* dat about chu.

"But I ain't like you—I ain't perfect. I was thugged out when I was younger an', I know dis sound fucked up but, I still had some uh dat shit in ma system. I already know, you ain't 'bouta lemme fuck you in da ass an' you ain't gon' lemme tape us fuckin'. Dat's part uh da reason I love you so much—I 'on't wont chu ta be doin' all dat shit.

"An' I know niggas be on you--you fine as hell. But jus like its niggas dat wont chu, its hoes dat be all on *my* shit. Its bitches beggin' me ta move in wit 'em right na if I wont to. Bitches know 'bout chu an' dey still be on me. Shit, dere done been so many times we'uh be out an' uh bitch'uh be tryin' ta gimme her number when you ain't lookin it ain't funny.

"...Angela? She wuddn't shit ta me. I ain't even stick my dick in her an' I sho' as hell ain't put my mouth no where near her pussy but dat bitch was willin' ta do anythang I wonted her ass ta do...

"Dis was da first time I ever even did some shit like dis since we been tagether. Look at me." He tried to grab my face and turn it towards him but I moved back so fast and jerked out of his reach, he knew not to touch me again. He shook his head like he was hurt and like I was acting immature. After a few seconds passed he started talking again. "She kept on sayin' shit an' tryin' me...one day after me an' you got into it 'bout me treatin' Mauri better than Pharaoh, I was pissed at chu an' I got real weak. She kept sayin' shit dat made uh nigga feel good.

"You was always trippin' an' wuddn't even watch no porno's wit me. It seem like you was always more worried 'bout being uh good mother an' keepin' some high ass morals, an'—like I say--dat's part uh da reason I love yo' ass... From da first day I saw you I knew you was da one I was gon' marry—from day one.

"I always said my woman was gon' be uh quiet one... You always keep ta yo'self an' you uh good girl, but sometime uh nigga need--"

"—A hoodrat bitch they can run trains on? A disease? A muthafuckin' adventure in the gutter? WHAT? Being with a good girl obviously isn't enough--"

"—Look, look, look! *Calm down!*"

I didn't like how he was talking to me, taking command of the situation like he wasn't even wrong. So many times we hadn't even needed words to communicate with each other. With just one glance, he could look at me and say exactly what I was thinking but too scared to say. We had been soulmates. That's what made this so bad. I hadn't even seen any of it coming. Now here he was talking to me like this, giving me all the details of his seedy ass, rat escapade.

"I know dere ain't no excuses fa what went down--I ain't even thank it was gon' go dat far. But, it seemed like evry time I tried ta get myself outta da mess, evry time I tried ta end it, she'uh suck my dick an' do some wild shit an' tell me ta cum all in her face, an' I'd get weak. She ain't even yell at me when I got drunk like yo' ass do.

"She accepted evrythang about me. Wit chu, it's like you always be expectin' more out uh me–more dan I be expectin' outta ma'self.

"But, baby. I've learned from dis mistake an' I'm willin'--I'm willin' ta do whatever I godda do ta git yo' trust back. Church, I'ma stop hanging wit D-Man an' da crew on Sunday's--whatever! I ain't 'bout ta let *no* nigga steal my wife!" Although there were tears, there was that fiery glow in his eyes again and it sent a tingly wave of concern trickling down my spine. He wasn't about to just leave this thing alone and go his own way like I wanted him to.

"Well, you shoulda just told me you felt like that. I'm not gonna apologize for having morals and I'm *not* gonna pretend like I woulda tried to cater to your ego if you woulda told me you wanted to be a hoe out in the streets. I haven't done anything but tried to be good to you but it obviously wasn't enough since I wasn't the kind of freak you were looking for.

"When we met, I wasn't even thinking about being with anybody. You coulda just left me alone. And you coulda been out there hoein' around without any problem. You're so fuckin' selfish, it ain't even funny. You wanna have me at home cooking and playin' the goodwife and shit while you're out doing your own thing and I ain't down for it.

"If you woulda said *all this* in the *first* place, I woulda respected that a whole lot more. You coulda left me and my kids and been in tha streets all night. But now yo' sorry ass wants to sit up here and put tha blame on her for whispering in yo' ear, trying ta make out like she wasn't shit? Apparently she meant *something* ta you when you was fuckin' her in tha ass and whatnot. And you tryin' ta blame me on the sly for not sucking yo' dick and shit? No-no sweetie, *thas* fa my husband and it ain't you." I flicked my fingers in his face. I didn't have shit else to say. Even though I wasn't, I sounded like I was together even with all this going on and I could tell it made Craig even more confused and scared. He needed some kind of pitiful emotional display so he could think I still loved him and that I'd simply just take him back but I wasn't able to give him that kind of reassurance.

He was the one that knew every detail of my life, the way my father never claimed me as his child, all the bad sexual experiences. He was the one that wasn't supposed to be like the others.

"I got two words for you. Baby-Back!" I shouted.

"She my baby too. What's wrong wit her being wit her father since he ain't at home?" His piercing ochre eyes glittered in wickedness.

So this was going to be the bait. In order to avoid some kind of custody battle that would separate Pharaoh and Mauri, he was going to try to force me to take him back.

"She didn't cheat, so why should she suffer? Besides, Mauritania still drinks breast milk for goodness sake." I acted unfazed. When the opponent knows your fear or your most sacred desire, they only use it against you. Act indifferent in order to throw them off their course of action.

"I'll give you some time. Lemme know when you ready fa us ta come back home. We love you."

Oh. He thought he was going to keep playing with me anyway? Not even hardly. This time I looked him dead in his face. "Are you *bipolar* or something? *Now* you wanna act like *ya'* crazy? Be fa real, Craig! You just showed ya' ass. You aren't the man I thought you were *or* the man I loved. Don't try to blackmail me with my daughter. If you really love me and *her*, like you *claim you do*, take me ta get my child." God I hoped that worked.

He and his mother didn't get along. Before Craig moved in with me, his mother had gone thru drastic measures to make sure he moved out. She turned her television to face the living room wall and covered it with a tablecloth that was stained in a few spots on purpose so she would know when he snuck and watched it while she was gone. She had even placed a dozen angel knick-knacks in certain spots around the house so she would know if he used the stove and microwave amongst other things.

She wasn't going to let him stay at her place for long. It was only a matter of time before she locked him out again and I wanted my child home before he started living with another Angela bitch. Just the thought of him sticking the penis I had at one time called my own into some hoe's quagmire of a mouth disgusted me and was enough for me to leave him alone forever. I'd heard on the news that Medicaid had cut off numerous dental procedures. Who knew what type of oral diseases she had going on? And on top of that, she sounded like she smoked 'Black and Mild's all day.

"You got somebody ta watch Pharaoh?" He had turned back into the man I used to know for a second. I nodded a quick yes.

"Aright." He drove to his mothers place. She lived near downtown in a decent housing project that looked more like low-budget condo's. I had only been over once before.

"Come on." He invited me inside.

His mother was watching television in the dark and smoking a cigarette as my child laid next to her on the couch. I absolutely detested cigarette smoke, let alone somebody smoking over my baby! She shook her head and rolled a pair of naturally blue eyes at Craig in disgust.

"Let me git chu her stuff," she said thru a full set of clenched dentures. The dentures accented the word 'stuff' in an odd, artificial way like some sort of weird lisp. My mother was around her age, late forties, and had all her real teeth. Even my grandma didn't wear dentures and she was in her sixties.

She left out of the living/dining room and came back with a pink baby bag. Craig'd left my place with nothing but the car seat. "Take care sweetie," she said to me after she kissed my baby in the mouth. I could never understand what gave adults the notion that they could kiss a baby in the mouth. I wanted to say something about it but she wasn't the enemy here. I made a mental note to wash Mauri off before I put her to bed.

"Bring her by moe often so I can see my lil' grandbaby," she added.

Craig had bought Mauritania some clothes, toys, baby food and diapers and although she was sleeping, she didn't look like she'd been traumatized.

"I don't advise you to try to force your way in," I stated as Craig parked into his usual spot behind the building. He helped bring her things in and put her car seat back in my truck.

"I'ma call you when I git in," he said civilly before leaving. Fifteen minutes later he called just as Debra was leaving.

I debated whether on not to answer. "Hey. I'm about to get into the shower. Call me back." He gave me exactly fifteen minutes before he called back.

"Leigh, stay on da phone wit me. I cain't sleep."

"That doesn't mean I can't."

"*Please* baby. I know I fucked up but jus stay on da phone wit me."

I sighed.

"Baby, I feel like ma life over. I'm dyin' right now—"

"--Not my fault."

"If you 'on't want me no moe, it's cool. But dat shit'uh kill me— I'uh rather be dead."

"Cut this shit out, Craig. You can play crazy and suicidal if you want but *I don't* have time for it. Bye. I'm going to sleep now." I hung the phone up and laid Mauri down next to me in the bed. It was kind of strange that she hadn't waken up when I took her out of the car seat *or* when I brought her inside and wiped her face and fingers off. She must have played all day without a nap.

The look in Craig's eyes when he took her flashed in my head. I started shaking her until she woke up. "Mauri? Mauri?"

She blinked and finally looked at me. Her eyes looked normal, no far off look like she had been drugged or anything.

"Give mommy a hug."

She reached out her hands like she usually did whenever I said that.

Okay she was all right. Now I had to listen to her cry her way back to sleep but at least she was okay.

Wait a minute. Why was I being so paranoid? ...It was stupid really.

Then again, the fact that I felt the need to be paranoid...and that my hands were still shaking and wouldn't stop.

I went into the living room and sat down. The sound of the clock hanging on the dining room wall made me even more nervous. Every time the clock clicked its hand to the next increment of time, a flash of that fire in Craig's eyes when he had snatched Mauri--the exact same look that had flashed across his face an hour ago when we were sitting in the car bolted pass me...

Who'd have thought a day would come when I'd actually be afraid of Craig?

I LOOKED OUT THE window and checked the parking lot for Craig's car before I put the kids in the truck for church. Good thing I went. I felt much better once I got there. Our congregation was medium sized and, for the most part, everybody knew each other pretty well. Most of the members had been with Pastor Ellington from the time he started his ministry twelve years ago.

My mother wasn't going to be there today since she and grandma had visited one of grandma's old friend's churches so Mauri and Pharaoh sat with Tamika while I sat on stage with the rest of the choir.

The message was excellent medicine for my soul. Pastor's sermon was on overcoming obstacles and how bad things happen to good people. He admonished us to continue walking in Jesus footsteps no matter how tired we might feel; just as the daylight came after the darkest hour, so did God's blessings. He then went into a personal experience about how the devil tried to tempt him. He kept witnessing crooked men prosper while he continued struggling on his job at the city's electric company. He had struggled but remained in God's word because he knew God had something better for him. Right after the ordeal, he was able to purchase our church.

I reflected on his words and thought about my situation with Craig. Something better was coming. Craig wasn't for me but God was trying to tell me that something better was around the corner. I couldn't let this situation depress me and stop me from doing what I needed to do. Just knowing that made me feel ten times better.

But today was special not just because of the message. I had a solo part. Just as the choir rose to sing and begin praise worship, I scanned the pews for Tamika and the kids. Right before we sung I always looked their way and waved and Pharaoh'd wave back. I still didn't see them for a second before I spotted Craig. There he was with Mauri in his lap and one arm around Pharaoh. I nearly choked as I jetted off the stage to the pew where they were seated. "Whassup, baby." He smiled. "I told you I was gonna do whatever I have ta do ta get it back ta the way it was. Whatever."

"Where is Tamika," I whispered. My heart raced.

"I 'on't know." He smirked.

"Ressroom, mommy—mom, Craig's taking us to eat after church," Pharaoh whispered way too loudly. Mauri was busy amusing herself with her Craig's mustache and goatee.

I didn't have time for this. The choir was about to start the song. I flew down the stairs on the lower level where the restrooms were. "Tamika, go back and sit with my kids!"

She was sitting downstairs with the mustached, behemoth-looking church nurse whose large face had done a good job of hiding her neck from public view. She looked like she had three people stuffed inside her shirt and a toddler in each breast and always bragged about how awful her fantastic case of "sugar" (her chosen word for diabetes) had gotten.

She couldn't stand me. Back in the day I tried to be nice to her but she always had some kind of sarcastic remark to make. Anytime she looked my way she rolled her eyes but this time they were too busy huddled up gossiping about people in the congregation to notice me standing in front of them.

Lately since Tamika had been gaining weight she'd been hanging out with this Brenda chick and her click. It wasn't like Tamika paid attention to service anyway. She only came to church to see if this guy named Sammy she'd gone with in high school was there.

"They sittin' wit Craig." Tamika's crackly voice held the telltale signs of one that smoked too much.

"Come here for a second." I pulled her to the side. "I'm mad at him. Just go sit with them!" She and I hadn't been talking as much as we had before Craig moved in. She didn't have a clue about what was going on with me and Craig.

I flew back on stage in the nick of time as the song started.

LIFE WENT ON LIKE for this two long, grueling months. Every day was like being in a heat wave and trying to survive without water.

Craig and I already went to the same college. Now he popped up everywhere I was supposed to be and introduced himself to people at church and everywhere else as my fiancé and made me stay on the phone with him all night, every night. If I hung up when he fell asleep on the line, he'd come to the apartment, ring the bell until I came to the door and then ask if I was cheating on him. Since I didn't work a job away from home, every minute I wasn't in a class had to be accounted for because he was so worried I was going to hook up with Darren, who hadn't called since that whole 'suck his dick and get married' thing. Craig gave me a daily schedule of his whereabouts, demanded mine in return and even went grocery shopping with me every week.

Let's not forget the fake 'wrong number' phone calls when I tried not to answer to get a break from his crazy ass. He was always checking to make sure I was at home. Once he came over and wouldn't leave until I opened the door because he thought he had heard a guy in the background when we were on the phone. The noise, the man he heard in the background, was from the movie I was watching on TV!

Every chance he got, he interrogated Pharaoh about what we did, where we'd gone and Darren's activities or lack thereof. And Pharaoh surprised me. To only be three, he knew not to give Craig any information. He would always shrug then give Craig an 'I don't know' answer. He even asked when all this would stop because he didn't like being questioned by Craig or the way Craig was treating me.

In the midst of it all, Craig was spoiling Mauri more and more to the point where she felt she could throw temper tantrums when she didn't get her way--it was like she was possessed. She wasn't my pineapple strawberry baby anymore and it was all because of Craig. If he was around, he wouldn't let me spank her when she tried to bite me or Pharaoh in the middle of her tantrums. His thing was, since he didn't live with us, that he had to spoil her so she would know he loved her and so she wouldn't forget he was her father. He was always laughing at her antics and her mean streak, which only edged her on. It was embarrassing. I wanted to notify the police of his strange, stalking behavior but, as much as I hated to admit it, I still loved him. And maybe I was over reacting. He was just trying to show me he was trying to right his wrongs.

THREE DAYS BEFORE MAURI'S first birthday back in August, Craig came to pick her up and, against better judgment, I let him take her. What a big fat, mistake!

It was a day before the party and I couldn't reach him. He never answered when I called his cell, when I tried to reach him at his mother's house I got constantly got a busy signal and the four times I went over there, nobody answered and it never looked like they were there. I had invited family and friends to come and I didn't even know where my baby was!

Then, on her birthday he threatened not to bring her unless I either gave him some or agreed to get over the 'incident' and gave him a move-back-in date--one he thought was reasonable which, in his own words meant, "No longer dan two weeks."

But the hurt was still too fresh for me to forgive. I already knew I'd never forget what he had done. Right now he was asking for much too much. I didn't want him.

Since giving up the coochie was out, I pretended to go along with his move-in timeline. "Two weeks at the longest," I lied the morning of Mauri's party.

Debra was the only person I spoke to about my predicament. "Girl, y'all gon' be aright. All young couples go thru stuff like dat. Uh man gon' be uh man, chile," she stated.

"Thanks, Debra." I took the pitcher of strawberry lemonade she'd made for Mauri's party from her. She was also holding a covered aluminum pan of fried chicken that was still piping hot. I didn't know how that was going to go over. My mother had cooked up a ton of food and both of them knew how to do chicken in a mean fry. Ma was going to have a problem with that.

"You didn't have to fix anything."

"Chile please. Who else gon' help me eat it? Ain't nobody but me. Dat's why I'm gettin' so fat. Ever since Paul done up an' left I 'on't even cook no mo'. I 'on't know how ta cook fa one person! Ungh-uh. Keep it. Let Craig take it wit 'em if don't nobody eat it." She came over to where I was standing in the dinning room taping the Happy Birthday words on the wall with invisible tape.

"...I don't even think Craig's mother is coming. He said something about her being upset I didn't use her apartment complex's rec room."

"Been dere, too!" She shook her thick black, freshly curled shoulder length head of hair emphatically. "I 'on't care how mad dem mamas be at dey sons, dey gon' hold uh grudge 'gainst any female dey son say ain't treatin' 'em right—even when dey know dey son da one wrong!"

"Hmph."

"Listen, sweetie. Craig is uh good man an' *han'some*, too. He still learnin'—y'all ain't even reached y'all late twenties yet. He ain't neva beat on you *an'* he try ta help take care uh yo' kids from what I see. Dat's more dan I can say fa uh lodda dese young niggas 'round here nowadays. Dey got uh drought on good men na'uh'days. Whether dey from da hood or uh CEO or uh Congressman, dey be da same--only in love wit *dey* dick or some otha nigga's dick on da low! One man might like da color blue bedder dan da color orange but, you bess believe me, dey be da same.

"Nah, as far as dis break up thang go, don't make no mistake you gon' regret later. Craig love you. I can tell you dat. You da one he gon' marry. He done tole me dat uh coupla times. Dat one time you had locked 'im out an' y'all was arguin' an' carryin' on, he came over here an' tole me. He say, 'Ms. Debra, I really love dat girl. I 'ont be tryin' ta hurt her on purpose.' Den he tole me 'bout how y'all was arguin' 'bout Pharaoh. So, den I say, 'You gon' have ta stop bein' funny t'ward dat baby if you wont her ta love you, you gon' have ta treat him like he yours else you 'on't need ta be wit his mama.' Den he say, 'I *do* love him Ms. Debra.' So I was like dis here, 'Aright! Nah *act like* it, den!' We jus laughed an' laughed after dat. Den he say he was 'bouta leave an' go get'chu uh card an' sumthen fa *his* son.

I laughed. I knew exactly what day she was talking about because he came home with a teddy bear and an oversized card for me and a truck for Pharaoh.

"See, I was hot ta trot back in da day—wuddn't no man gon' control me! An' I was 'bout as pretty you. Den, when I finally started wantin' ta settle down, wuddn't no nigga 'vailable at ma age. Nah trus me, evry woman gits lonely an' gon' start wantin' uh man sooner or later— 'less she uh bulldyger." She stopped short and looked me up and down. "An' you 'ont strike me as one uh dose." We both laughed.

"It don't matta how ole dey be, truss me...Paul way older dan Craig an' what he do? Up and left an' went back ta his wife," she said switching to a serious tone.

"He was *married*?"

"Yep. An' lissen here—don't you start tryin' ta judge no body. I'm jus talkin' ta you an' tellin' you like it is. Dis is ma point: men got dey good time girls, den dey got dey keepers. Uh nigga can be blind an' his ass still gon' find uh way ta cheat. Truss me on dat. I had one all on me. He moved in an' stayed wit me. He was *paid* an' *fine*. But he had a wife an' he ain't neva divorce her neitha. An' when he died, she got evrythang. I was da one takin' care uh him when he was sick. But dat wife got evrythang. Even dough he was livin' wit me when he passed." She looked into my eyes to see if her message was seeping in. "An' all dat mess Paul talked 'bout his wife--dat bitch dis, dat bitch dat, what he do? Went back an' straightened shit out 'tween him an' her!

"Nah I'm lucky, I git social security fa my sickle cell an' I'm able ta make it financially by da grace uh God. You lucky too. You got men in yo' life dat care 'nough 'bout *chu* and dey *kids*. Don't chu fool 'round here an' mess yo'self up! 'Cause when you lonely an' ain't gettin' shit fa Valentine' Day an' da bed be cold even in da summer even dough you got da heat on, dat 'I-can-make-it-witout-uh-man shit gon' be thrown out da window!

"I'm only tellin' you all uh dis 'cause you like uh niece ta me. You always come by when I'm sick, take care uh ma cat when I be in da hospital—an' you know KiKi uh mean ole thang. I love ha but she make me not wont no moe cats once she gone.

"You Godly *an'* you smart. You 'on't be tellin' evrybody yo' business like uh lodda dese loud mouth, ignorant lil'ole girls runnin' 'round out here. Nah. Keep ya' man an' don't tell dese jealous women out here nothin'. All dey gon' do is either smile in yo' face an' try ta hook up wit cha man da minute you turn yo' back anyhow. Else dey gon' tell you uh whole bunch uh bull ta do ta him dat ain't gon' do nothin' but make 'im leave you. An' when dey git uh lil' biddy piece of uh ole man--he can be on crack--dey gon' try ta hole on ta 'im an' parade him 'round church like he da king uh England. An' dey sho' ain't gon' have no time fa you when you call 'em either. Dey gon' be too busy caterin' ta dey crack head of uh man's evry wish—lickin' his shoes clean wit dey tongue."

The bell rung ending our conversation. Craig was finally here with my baby. The way he acted once the guests arrived you wouldn't have even known we weren't together anymore. He was definitely a charmer. He had my mother smiling and laughing at all his jokes, he spoke to Debra for a while, chilled with Tamika and taught three kids from church how to step.

Even Sherra was impressed. "Girl, I can see why you 'on't never have time fa nobody."

I simply smiled. If she only knew...

IT WAS ALMOST SEPTEMBER and it was decision time. I couldn't keep holding off. Craig was coming back home. It wasn't like he had been hanging out at strip clubs or had continued cheating on me after we separated. I loved him enough to forgive him for that incident as long as it didn't happen again. After all, I did miss him and the way he made life more fun. And he *was* still fine.

"Aright. I got sumthen planned. See if yo' mama can keep da kids. If she cain't my mama uh prob'ly be able ta keep 'em fa da weekend. Be ready in uh hour. Oh, yeah. Wear sumthen kinda casual." He was obviously happy I was coming thru on my two week promise.

"Cra*aaii*g! I've got to got to church tonight. We're rehearsing for the Praise Worship festival at Chene Park and--"

"—Baby, listen. Jus call yo' mama an' see if she gon' keep da kids. I got uh surprise fa you."

"Alright, alright." I hung up and called my mother. "Hey ma. You think you can keep the kids for the weekend. Craig's got some kind of surprise he's planned."

"I thought you was going ta rehearsal tanight?"

"I know. I was. But he wants to take me somewhere."

"Aright. That's between y'all. He *is* your fiancé nah. I'm proud of 'im. He's been coming ta church every week. I'll just tell Demetrius you'll practice with him on Sunday then, um-hm."

"Yeah, tell him I'll come in early before the sermon gets started. I can't stay afterwards. I have to study for a test on Monday."

"Aright. "

"Mom, can you come get them? He told me to be dressed in an hour."

"Yeah, I feel bad for Craig. Lord knows you always be slow gettin' dressed. I 'ont know where you got that from. I'm on the way."

I reminded Pharaoh not to tell grandmother or great-grand anything about Craig or mommy, made him and Mauri promise to be good and kissed them goodbye when my mother showed up.

Craig's face was beaming when he arrived. "Aright, baby." He was just-a-smilin'. "I hate ta do dis but I godda blind fold you." He hit his left hand with his right fist and held his fist in front of his chest.

"Ungh-uh."

"Got to."

"Why?"

"I got sumthen fa you--dis our reunion—like ma man Maxwell be singin' 'bout. Turn around so I can cover yo' eyes."

I sighed and turned around. "Don't mess up my hair."

"Y'all Black women an' y'all hair... We drivin' yo' truck, aright?"

"Um-hm."

He didn't say anything the whole ride. When you can't see what's going on, even ten minutes can seem like ten hours. I heard him get out of the truck. Then my door opened and he untied the blindfold. We were at the Detroit Opera House. "Waymond Tisdale playin' tonight. I know he one uh yo' favorites jus don't be lookin' at him too hard up on stage--we got front row seats. Jus enjoy da music," he teased as a valet guy took the keys.

"Whatever." I smiled. This was obviously just for me. Craig hated jazz.

"The concert was amazing. Thank you," I said as he held the door open as we left the Opera House.

"Dat was jus da beginning. I hate ta do it but I godda blindfold you again."

"Craig!" Now I couldn't see again. He took my hand and led the way as I walked what felt like endless blocks of eternal darkness on the lopsided sidewalk.

"My bad baby, dis da las time."

"Better be. And you'd better be glad the weather is still nice. I wouldn't be doing all this walking if it was cold." I could hear people walking past us, car zipping by, then music—jazz fusion—a French singer...Les Nubians...a couple of whispers.

This time when he uncovered my eyes we were sitting at a table inside Intermezzo in Harmony Park. I had been dying to come here. It was just as fabulous as I thought it would be.

The atmosphere buzzed with tinkering wine glasses filled with rose-colored merlots, bottom crimson lip imprints on glistening the glass rims, dimly lit chandeliers hung like diamonds over square, so dark almost black wooden tables with clippings of famous African American sports players and actors of various decades, bright cherry walls were covered with large abstract paintings...

Women seated in the dinning room varying from smooth mahogany tones to the color of the inside of a mangos wearing slick buns like ballerinas, bobs and simple yet classy outfits with neatly polished, sheer manicures and Vuitton bags. A lot of them looked like they'd gone to charm school and the men looked just as upscale with neatly parted locks or bald heads that complimented their smiles.

When the saxophone player came to our table, everything blended into a euphoric wave that made Craig's cologne tickle my thighs.

The menu was exotic. There were so many choices I'd never heard of or thought of putting together. Like the entrée of mushrooms stuffed with crabmeat and brown and yellow rice with wild yams served on the side and baby spring green salad with pear and raspberry and lime or papaya vinaigrettes. It all sounded good but I decided to try the portabella mushroom sandwich appetizer and an entrée of jerked chicken breasts, brown yellow rice mixed with a spicy peanut sauce and fried plantain instead. Craig ordered his usual—a well-done steak, a baked potato with an extra potato instead of the vegetable option.

"Baby. Look over dere." He nodded at the table behind me. "All dem chicks eattin' salads look like dem switches we used ta get whipped wit back in da day. Ain't dat what dey salads look like? Dem switches yo' mama used ta make you go outside ta git so she could beat cho' ass? Ain't none uh 'em eattin' shit but switches. Black females startin' ta get anorexic too, nah hungh?" He shook his head in disapproval.

"Bay-bee! Don't say that. Those are the dancers from the Alvin Ailey Dance Company! I just talked to the one in the purple in the restroom. She was cool. She said they're on the way to Atlanta once they finish their performance here. That's gotta be exciting--to travel like that. I *love* seeing them when they come."

"Well, damn. I guess I shoulda got tickets fa dat 'stead uh da concert."

"Bay-bee, that's not what I said. I'm enjoying this. But it's cool to actually to get to meet them—you don't just bump into entertainers like that in Detroit out and about on an everyday basis like you would in LA or New York or something."

"You sound like you worship dem muthafuckas..."

"...No I don't." I took another mouthful of chicken from my fork. "This is delicious. You wanna try some?"

"Ugh. I'm straight--you used dat fork wit dem mushrooms. I 'on't see how you eat dat shit. Mushrooms is *fungus*."

"Cra*ai*gg! It taste good. You never try anything new. And back to that little comment you made--I don't worship the Alvin Ailey dancers, I worship God. All I'm saying is that I love watching them dance. Anytime I see them perform it does something to me. I remember the first time I saw them in middle school. I talked about it so much ma took me again that Saturday--that was like the best days of my life. She got us back stage after their performance and everything... You know what? She had a friend-- Sylvie Bossey. Sylvie worked there. That's probably how she us behind stage. It left a really good impression on me—meeting people like that."

"Dere you go—like dey betta dan somebody. Dey need ta eat some real food—dat's all I'm sayin'. If dey keep on eattin' like dat, dey ain't gon' git shit but White men. Uh nigga like some meat not no boney ass bitch."

I couldn't keep myself from rolling my eyes at him. That little idea I had—sneaking him into the restroom for a quickie—he had just cancelled it. And the stalls were perfect too. The doors went all the way down to the floor and had sinks in them.

"...Dis uh nice place, dough... Seem like nowadays evrytime dey remodel sumen dey make it look like dis. Probly cheaper ta fix up uh spot real quick fa some fas bread. Back in da day wuddn't nobody be rushin' ta eat at a place where da walls ain't even finished. Dis ain't nothin' but uh warehouse. Jus look at dese high ass factory ceilings!" He laughed.

I took a deep breath. "Leave it to you to break something down. *I* personally like this place. We should eat here more often and bring the kids."

"Yeah, bae. Anything fa yo' sexy ass. But I'ma have ta get rich fas if I wanna stay wit chu. You used ta havin' the finest." He lifted my hand and kissed it.

"Oh, so there *is* a gentle side to this ex-thug." I laughed.

"TAKE EVRYTHANG OFF AN' lay on da bed." Craig stated as we walked in the door. He followed behind me with a bottle of baby oil and gave me a massage. He didn't stop after five minutes to ask for a much longer one in return like he usually did.

He lit candles, put them in the bathroom and turned on the bathwater once he finished my massage. As we bathed together, the gardenia scented candles flickered bewitchingly and welcomed the love mingled with lust lingering between us waiting to be unleashed.

Craig picked me up, held me in his arms and walked to the bedroom. Both of us were still dripping wet, there was no time to dry off. We were only about to get wet all over again. We hadn't been together since I'd put him out, which made us even more animalistic. Our bodies easily responded to the familiar touches that only we could give one another. I craved his manliness on top of me and couldn't stop moaning as he blended into me. The whole morning while we lost ourselves in each other's ecstasy, I was reminded over and over why I had fallen in love with him. Everything about Craig, from the feel of his muscular arms to the square-ness of his jaw-line drove me crazy. The sensation of his body against my bare skin made my heart flutter like a flag whipping in a Chicago windstorm. I hadn't realized just how much I missed him until now.

THE NEXT DAY WE went to see *X-Men*. Both of us loved the comic strip. After the movie we went to Fairlane. "Git whatever you wont," he stated nonchalantly and lived up to his word. Any store I went in, I picked up whatever and he bought it.

Three outfits at BeBe. Total: three hundred dollars and he didn't even blink. Didn't tell me to look on the clearance rack like he usually did, either. I got a couple of tops from Wet Seal but that only hit him up for a hundred. A pair of black skinny-heeled boots to die for. Two fifty-nine. Coach store, four hundred dollars? Yes. And, no. It wasn't any of *my* money. That was one thing I had listened to Darren about. He told me not to put anybody on my checking or saving accounts. Then we went to a boutique that only hired fragile sphinx looking, seventeen year old models that talked in choppy sopranic voices, moved like robots and were no doubt a part of the Victoria's Secrets *Love Spell* cult. From them? Two pair of jeans that clung to my hips and made me look like my name was Venus #1. Three hundred and sixty-nine denary-o.

"Hey, bae, hurry up!" He called from outside of Lord and Taylor's Misses fitting room. "We got uh appointment."

"For what?" I slid a pair of Donna Karen jeans off. Too big in the waist. I wasn't getting them. I was starting to like boutiques a lot better than regular department stores. They had more original items and I never had a problem finding pieces that fit perfectly. My favorite one, Boola's, did on the spot alterations, which was very nice. You could go somewhere and if someone did have on a similar dress, it still looked different because it was custom fitted.

"Ta take some pictures," he shouted.

"Aww. That's sweet." We had two family portraits from when Mauri was only a few months old but we didn't have any pictures of just me and Craig other than a couple of cheesy Polaroid's with airbrushed back-drops from when we'd gone to a cabaret one of Craig's boys had invited us to. Other than that, the only picture we had of just me and Craig was the one my mother had insisted on taking at Mauri's birthday party.

That evening Craig outdid himself and took me to see the Alvin Ailey Dance Company. "Damn, look at chu." He smiled once we found our seats on the balcony.

"This is like the best birthday ever—only it's not my birthday." Afterwards we ate at Fishbones, talked about the kids and acted silly. Things were back to the way they were when we first started dating--the way things were supposed to be and better than they had been between us for some time.

The next semester coming up would be Craig's last one at Detroit Community. He got hired at GM as an assistant computer analyst and was going to be taking classes for his bachelor's at U of D in the evenings.

I was already accepted into the nursing program and only had three more semesters left. As long as I kept my grades up and passed all my classes I had a job at Henry Ford in the maternity ward. I had volunteered there last fall and made such a good impression with the head nurse that she offered me an internship on her unit, which would start next semester.

Together, me and Craig's income was about to be gravy. No wonder Pastor always said light came after the darkest hour.

This time when we got home, there was no need to rush. Craig had always been able to make me cum just by licking my body from head to toe and whenever he kissed me it was always perfect. He'd tickle his tongue against mine and make his way, slowly but surely, to the most hidden, intimate parts teasing, tantalizing my other tongue just right until I shook uncontrollably over and over again...

The rest of the night we made love to our favorite three songs. Every now and then he'd change the routine from slow winding shots of ecstasy to fast thrashing waves fulfilling both our needs. Craig was the

91

only man (next to Darren—but Darren didn't count) who could give me an orgasm from just penetration alone. The way Craig moved, I could have easily mistake him for a stripper.

"BABY? ...BABY? ...LEIGH?" Craig shook me a couple of times until I was completely awake.

"Aren't you supposed to be knocked out, too? Stop. You're creeping me out. I open my eyes to one big eyeball in my face!" Instead of snoring extra loudly like he should have been doing, he'd been watching me sleep.

He sustained his gaze a bit longer before going down on me. His tongue was extra soft and made my body throb. This was like when he first moved in. Back then we were rabbits in our own rite, always locking ourselves in the bathroom and running the shower to drown out the noises Craig and mommy were making so Pharaoh wouldn't hear.

He lifted his head and gazed into my eyes holding me so close I could feel his heart thump against mine. "Damn, baby. Why dis pussy godda be so good?" he asked sliding back and forth, in and out. He bit his lip to try to stop his body from shaking. *I* started shaking just from watching *him*. We both got so carried away, he didn't pull out right before he came like I made him start doing after Mauri. This time he went deeper.

"Baby! Baby! Wait! Wait a minute! St*ooo*p!" I grabbed his dick and tried to pull it out. He was well aware of the fact that we weren't about to have any more kids. Not until I was out of school and we were married.

I don't know if it started feeling so good he didn't want to stop or what but he grabbed my wrists up over my head so hard they started tingling and he kept going.

"Baby? What da fuck! Stop!" Instead, he grabbed a handful of my hair, making it even harder for me to free myself from his grip. If I attempted to slide from him I'd probably loose the patch of hair he was gripping. "Ouch-ah-ah-ouch, Baby! My hair is caught. Stop! Pull it—"

"--I love you, Leigh. Les have another baby. I wanna marry you. We can go ta da justice uh da peace Monday—"

"--Sto-pp! Owwwch—"

"--I love you, baby. I ain't 'bouta lose you again!" He let go of my hair but his upper torso still had me pinned down. My body stiffened like rigor mortis. The steel rod moved faster and faster until he came. He sighed, rolled on his side with his arm still around my shoulder and breasts. If this was his plan, he for damn sure had accomplished it and I didn't know how to feel. Was I supposed to be happy he me wanted to have another baby with him? Was this his way of proving he didn't want anybody else? I wasn't sure of the answers to either question but what I did know was that my feet were getting colder and colder while he had me locked in his embrace and this full sized bed now seemed way too small.

"What's wrong?" he mumbled as I slid away.

"I need some water," I lied. What I *needed* to do was get in touch with Tamika. ASAP. She had taken something both times she got pregnant that left her child-free, abortion clinic-free and hospital-free. And after *this* stunt, I couldn't have another child with him—not right now. Especially with the way he was allowing Mauri to turn into a baby hellcat.

"Don't worry baby, I got it," he said finally letting me go. I tried to make sense of it all while he was in the kitchen. "Why you lookin' like dat?" he asked peculiarly as he stood sideways in the bedroom doorway.

"Look." I was just going to be real with him. "You know I don't want or *need* anymore kids right now. I'm not even done with school and we just got back together. We need to get things completely straightened out first. I-I don't think what you just did was fair. I don't feel comfortable with you trying to get me pregnant on purpose."

"So you changin' yo' mind 'bout bein' wit me?" His eyes narrowed as he walked closer to the bed and looked down at me from of the corner of his eyes.

"Craig. That's not what I said. I just—"

"--You jus what? You jus what! You ain't got no reason ta have ta go school no moe. I got uh good job. You can stay home ta take care uh da kids. In uh minute we gon' be able ta git uh house an' we'uh be straight! Ain't dat what chu wont?"

"Baby? ...I'm finishing school. Me *not* finishing is *not* an option so you can scratch that thought *right* outta ya' head! I *might even* get a masters's!" I calmed myself down, "What I'm saying is that I can't—"

"--You still fuckin' Darren?"

"What?" I was dumbfounded.

"*ARE YOU STILL FUCKIN'* DARREN?" He sounded like he was talking to a person that was a bit more slow on the comprehension scale. "Is dat where you got dat new move from?" he shouted shooting fiery glints in my direction.

Where the hell was all this coming from?

"Clapping yo' ass–stop playing dumb! You know you was *poppin'* yo' ass an' shit! You ain't neva done *no shit* like dat *bafoe*!" I shot up in the bed not liking the way he was now towering over me. "I knew it! I knew it! You still cheatin' on me. Damn!" He looked away from me and stared at the wall. He was fuming. "...You still tryin' ta pay me back, ain't chu?"

Suddenly the room became silent enough to hear someone in Canada call my name. He sat down on the bed next to me and actually started crying. He covered his eyes with his left hand. "Leigh...Leigh? I love you. You 'on't even know how much I love you. Please tell me you not cheatin' on me." His pain encompassing eyes now looked so innocent it was hard to believe he had done what he just had and I instantly felt bad for him. His conscience was gnawing at him for cheating on me.

"Craig, Sweetheart." I scooted next to him and rested my cheek on his shoulder. "There's nothing going on with me and Darren--you know I can't stand him. I only love you, Craig Walker, the finest man in the world *and* my best friend. Just thinking about you turns me on—you already know that. You're the only man that's ever made me feel like this." I smiled and wiped the teardrop from his goatee. "When I finish school, we can get married, I promise. I love you, Craig." Hopefully I had eased his fears. I wanted to add, *You make sure you consume all my time. How would I have any time to cheat on you?* But, of course, that wasn't going to help the situation.

"Aright. Jus one thing." He laid down and pulled me on top of him. "I'll wait. If you godda do school--I'll wait. But I need you ta do sumthen fa my birthday."

"Yeah, baby. Whatever you want," I whispered in his ear.

"I want you ta get my name tattooed on yo' ring finger." He gave me a look that let me know he was serious.

"Alright," I complied. His birthday wasn't until next year anyway. I wasn't the tattoo type but it was doable. "You know your whole name isn't going to fit," I joked.

Tomorrow I was going to call Tamika to find out what that stuff was she drunk when she had gotten pregnant and ended up un-pregnant.

CHAPTER 6

WE LEFT THE PREVIOUS craziness from last night alone and stayed up until 6:30 talking, deepening our bond and trying to find new solutions for our old problems.

Craig was still haunted by his childhood and the time he spent juvenile detention.

When he went into detail about it, I was finally able to understand why there were so many times I caught him muttering 'Convicted felon' over and over in his sleep.

I stroked the back of his neck and shoulders and continued listening as his back faced me.

When he grew silent, I peered over his shoulder and looked over at him. Both of his eyes held a tub of tears in them but he didn't let the tears make their way down his face. "I only saw dat nigga twice, Leigh. Twice... I was 'bout ta turn nine. We went down ta Jackson on da Greyhound bus... When da nigga got out, we ain't neva hear from his ass again."

"At least you know what your father looks like..."

"A dead beat muthafucka still uh sorry ass muthatfucka. It don't matter how you flip da dice. It wudda been bedder if I ain't neva seen him.

"I was at da grocery store las year, right. An' I'm standin' in line. Alla uh sudden, I hear somebody call out 'Rufus Walker Junior!' So, I look two lines down from where I'm at an' I see ma aunt--ma fatha sister Bernadene wavin' her hand all in da air like she crazy. So I walk over dere, right. She goin' on an' on 'bout how I look jus like him. Den she start talkin' 'bout how he done cleaned up his life, got married, got two kids by some woman he married after he got out on good behavior an' shit. So she pull out dis picture—him an' his White trash lookin' wife an' dey mixed kids.

"At dis point I'm done talkin' ta her, right. I'm feelin' like dere ain't shit else ta say. She ain't never even invited us over ta her house or nothin' an' had da nerve ta post da picture up in my face like he done turned his life 'round. Like ma an' alla us ain't shit.

"Nah, I'm walkin' away, right. So she try ta git ma number right quick--so she can give it ta 'im fa him ta call. 'He'uh wanna hear from me', dat's what she gon' say. All dis time done passed an' alla uh sudden, magically, dis nigga wanna hear from us. From me? How da hell uh phone call gon' make thangs right after twenty years? ...I ain't neva understood dat shit, how uh nigga can jus forgit about his own seeds like dat-- 'specially when he know we part uh him... He tried ta say I wudden't his one time but ma made him squash dat shit. I look jus like 'im."

"You do?" He'd never shown me a picture or even talked about his father until this morning.

"I got his square ass jawline, my eyebrows connect jus like his. But he real black an' 'bout six-four—ma always say dat's da only difference in me an' him. But I ain't tryin' ta be shit like dat muthafucka! Dat's why I'm always gon' do what I godda do ta stay in Mauri's life. I ain't 'bouta bounce like dat... Dat's part uh da problem wit Black folks nah. Dese women be out here takin' care uh kids all by deyselves talkin' 'bout dey 'on't need no man'. But kids need both dey mama an' dey fatha. Cain't no woman teach no boy how ta be uh man. An' uh girl still need her daddy—psychologists say girls git dey self-esteem from dey fatha an' where dey learn how dey s'posed ta be treated by uh man when dey older.

"One uh da pitifilest thangs I eva heard was dis commercial on da radio dis Black church had fa Fatha's Day. Dey was like 'Dis event fa fatha's an' mothers das fatha's. Nah *das* some *real* ridiculous shit right dere. Ain't no woman gon' be no fatha ta *no* man. Dat's why it take both uh man an' uh woman ta make dat seed.

"You ain't gon' neva hear no shit like dat on no White radio station. Dey got us so confused. Da day I start goin' fa some mess like dat be da day I see uh woman bring uh child in dis world wid'out fucking uh dick an' wid'out goin' ta uh clinic ta git some nut shot up in her. Den, I'll go fa it."

"Yeah, that's true. *That's* why you've got all these brothas that are almost thirty still living at their mom's house, not even thinking about marriage or anything but partying. What remnants there were of the male role model and of male responsibility have been blurred in this neo-Black culture. It seems like most brothas only care about making money and pimpin'; they aren't settling down the way they did back in the day so the family life is ceasing and our race isn't prospering. You have to have family."

"I disagree wit chu on that. Some niggas understan' what need ta be done. I was livin' wit ma mama 'cause she needed me--an' you know I wudden't neva scared ta commit ta you. *You da* one dat was all scared an' shit."

"I wasn't...I just wanted to be sure, that's all..."

"I ain't have ta be sure uh you. I knew, off rip you was da one."

"Oh, yeah?" I reached over and ran my hand down his arm and paused for a moment. The space between my hand and his body felt magnetic. My fingers tingled like I was touching pure electricity. "What happened with your father? Did you end up calling him?"

"His sister gon' write his number on da side uh da National Inquirer she was readin' an' tear it off. What made it so bad was she was holdin' uh notebook—like uh planner or sumthen—in her hand. Look like she had wrote uh grocery list on it but she ain't let me write ma number in it. She ain't even tear out uh sheet to put his number on it. Dat say uh lot right dere. She ain't even thank I was good enough ta write his number on uh decent piece uh paper. I was so heated I threw da shit ma sent me down dere ta git on the flo an' walked out dat muh'fuka."

"Well...I guess all we can both do is look at it like this: at least we were blessed enough to have good mothers to raise us well. There's lot of people out there that don't even have *that*. Black women used to at least take care of their kids if they didn't do anything else but nowdays it's not always like that. Remember back in the day, like in the eighties, when they used to always have cases on the news where they'd find a baby in a dumpster? And, *Oooh*! I *know* you remember when that one girl tried to flush her baby down the toilet while she was at school? *That* was sad."

"...Ma mama wuddn't like yours, Leigh. While you an' you mama was sittin' up watchin' *Da Love Boat, Dallas, Da Golden Girls* or whatever y'all watched afta she got off work, we was strugglin'.

"Ma mama ain't wont shit fa herself. Growin' up it was like dis: If we needed uh check up or if we got sick we had ta go ta Herman Keifer an' wait da whole day jus ta see uh doctor dat barely spoke English an' treated us like we wudden't shit.

"Ma was always up in da Welfare office beggin' fa shit 'cause dere wudden't never enough food stamps ta go around. We had ta line up at Focus Hope--evry mont we was up in dat mug. Cheese—you know dat big ass block?"

"Yeah, we got that, too. It was *good*. Macaroni and cheese? The kind you bake in the oven? Hmmph. You could hook it up with *that* cheese."

"You 'ont git it. What chu know 'bout havin' hunger pains fa two straight days in uh row? What chu know 'bout Farina?"

"*Farina?*"

"See. I told'chu--you 'on't know nothin' 'bout no Focus Hope. Yo' mama ain't have ta *rely* on dat shit..."

"So what is it?" I poked him in the back.

"Whas da one thang you 'on't eat an' hate fa me ta ask you to fix fa breakfas?"

"What? Grits?"

"Yep. Evry week ma was hustlin' wit da system tryin' ta make ends meet or waitin' fa some nigga ta get off work come Friday. Dere wudden't never uh week she was gon' go try ta git her uh GED... I *hated* dat shit... You know what?"

"Hmm?"

"My bad, baby. Do yo thang. You right. I 'ont wont'chu ta work no forty hour uh week job. I'ma man. I'm s'posed ta take care uh you. But I 'ont wont chu ta be stuck if sumthen happen ta me. Get cho' degree. If mama woulda got educated, she wouldn'uh always been struggling tryin' ta make two nickels rub halfway together.

"She always came home from dem low-paying factory jobs angry an' tired... she was too ladylike fa dem typa jobs. One time she got shot at when she was workin' uh security guard job at dat bank off Greenfield an' Grand River. She wudden't never da same after dat" His eyes were so far away it seemed like he'd gone back in time and wasn't coming back. "Growing up in our house was like growing up in uh funeral home, Leigh. No hugs, no kisses, none uh dat. Ma was always mad 'bout sumthen. She'uh move me out da way when I tried ta hug her. Lookin' back on it nah, she was real angry wit my father. She loved him. Fa real. I know she did. She kept his picture on her dresser til da day I tole her he was married ta dat piece uh trash. She had been wit him from da time she was thirteen. I see why she ain't have no more love ta give after he jus walked right up outta jail an' ain't neva say shit else ta her. He put all dem long distance collect calls on da phone an' ran up da phone bills. She had ta deal wit being po' an' on her own wit three uh his kids. An' it wudden't like she couldn'uh got wit somebody else. She was pretty, niggas in da hood used ta be all up on her. Dis doctor had tried ta talk ta her dis one time she took us ta Herman Keifer but she was stuck on my fatha, thankin' we was gon' be uh family after he got out.

"She shut down after he stopped callin'. I thank we represented da nigga dat betrayed her... Seem like she thought about it evry time she looked at us. Da only thang niggas meant ta her was money afta he got out an' played her like dat.

"Da first time I 'member gettin' uh hug an' uh kiss was in middle school. Dalaina Mitchell--my first real girlfriend. She was uh brown-skinned, thick honey... always dressed real sweet, kept her nails manicured an' got her hair done evry week--she was classy as *hell*. I ain't gon' even lie--I was geeked dan uh muthafuka when I hooked up wit her. She grew up way different from my ass... You know how we used ta git new shoes?"

"Unh-uh. How?"

"...When our shoes'uh git too raggedy ta keep on wearin' em, ma'uh take us ta K-Mart, tell us ta act like we was jus tryin' uh pair uh shoes on an' leave our old ones in da box an' we'uh all walk out. She'uh be like, 'Walk out, don't look at nobody. Look straight ahead.' Den we'uh jump inta whateva niggas car she was seein' at da time an' go home wit some new shoes." Craig chuckled and shook his head back and forth in shame. "Anyway, Dalaina liked me even dough she knew I stayed up in da Brewsters. She lived over in Indian Village an' her mother was uh principal at Cass but she ain't even care. She still was down wit me.

"Dalaina used ta fix me uh lunch evry day--dat good, homemade shit. I ain't neva tell her but I appreciated dat shit. I was used ta eattin' frozen dinners, canned vegetables an' shit like hog mogs, beef tongue an' gizzards 'cause it was on sale an' what mama could afford.

"Laina'd bring stirfry's wit jumbo shrimp in 'em, chicken salads, homemade soup—shit they had had fa dinner da night bafoe. I ain't even eat salads 'til she started bringin' 'em fa me at lunch.

"Dey make dat organic an' healthy shit too expensive fa po' folks but den dey turn 'round an' sell dat genetically modified shit dat ain't good fa nobody affordable. Me personally? I thank dat's how dey keep da population uh niggas an' po' muh'fuckas down. Po' folks good fa reproducin'—dey cain't afford ta do shit like golf. Or rugby. But dey sho' can fuck fa free." He chuckled. "It don't always cost ta fuck--s'pecially if you da type uh nigga ta run off an' leave yo' seed.

"If po' muthafukas cain't afford da shit dat's healthier fa 'em, an' dey eattin' chitlins an' flamin' hot chips an' Kool Aid all da time, eventually dey gon' git diabetes or high blood pressure an' die early an' dey gon' make da government uh whole lodda money wit all da prescriptions dey gotta take bafoe dey die. Da government da biggest thug an' drug dealer out here..."

"Hm...that's true. Never thought about it like that."

"Yeah, I'm uh hood ass nigga, but I know what da fuck I'm talkin' 'bout."

"I never said you didn't." I stroked the side of his arm.

"...Chitlins an' hog mogs. Shouldn't no human have ta eat no shit like dat. Slavery s'posed ta be over but, dis day an' age, you got niggas still eattin' hog mogs. Don't dat sound like uh code word fa pig balls uh sumthen triflin'?"

"Yep. One time my grandmother made something--what was it? It wasn't greens... Anyway, she made something and put pig's feet in it. My mother *tripped*. Tripped. We ate pork chops and stuff but she she hated pigs feet. Ma said it wasn't good for grandma's hypertension."

"Well, niggas sho' be buying dat shit up at da Arabic nigga's store... Arabic's. Nah dem some moe muh'fuckas I 'on' like. First uh all, dey git free taxation ta sell niggas rat poison ta eat. Den, Arabic niggas thank dey asses better dan da Black customers dat buy shit at dey raggedy stores. Arabic's originated from Black people an' got da nerve ta hate us. Look at uh map if you wanna know jus how close dey countries is ta da African continent.

"Dey set up shop in our hoods, hooks up wit Black girls from da hood an' turn 'em inta dey baby mamas. But dey don't do right by Black women or da kids dey have by 'em no how.

"Dey go home ta dey wives stored away up in dey suburban cribs. Dey make 'em stay covered from head ta toe so ain't nobody gon' be able ta git uh peek at 'em, an' da only thang dey 'llow dey woman ta do is shop fa shit on sale. Dey some uh da *cheapest* muthafukas you gon' find. Dat's how dey stay rich.

"Niggas so undereducated, we handin' over our money ta dem fa liquor at dey ran down corner stores. We 'on't even know dey helped sell our asses inta slavery. Ain't nobody teachin' us dat shit in uh classroom. All we gettin' is uh bunch uh bull on Christopher Columbus an' shit.

"...It's startin' ta look like Black folks ain't ever gon' come up. We still 'on't own shit. When uh Black athlete play sports, he on't even own his own body. Dey trade playas like uh neo-slave trade."

"Yeah, that's true. But the Chinese do the same thing. Just like you said before there's proof that Asians stemmed from Africa but a lot of them hate Black people and they post up beauty supplies on every corner and make money off of us too."

"Yep. Dat's how dat shit go... Wait uh minute. I got off da subject. I ain't neva finish tellin' you 'bout Dalaina. Evrythang was real cool. She was always talkin' 'bout how fine I was an' shit ta everybody, showin' me off ta her friends an' shit. The whole summer right bafoe eighth grade we'uh meet up at da mall an' chill tagetha...

"So den, she was like, 'Let's do it.' Funny as it seem nah lookin' back on it, I was scared. I really liked her an' I hadn't neva done it befoe. So, I tole her how I felt 'cause dat's how we was--I could tell her anythang. But she was like, 'So? I'm a virgin, too.' Dat's what she was *claimin'*--you know how y'all females be. Y'all uh do it ta ten niggas an' only claim three, talkin' 'bout da rest ain't count 'cause it wudden't love or some dumb shit like dat.

"Anyway, she was still pressin' me hard, right. So finally, when school started I went over ta her crib. Both uh her parents was at work an' we had uh half uh day.

"It was my first time up in dey crib an' it was off da chains. I was scared ta even be up in dere. It felt like uh palace. I ain't even know people could live like dat in da D.

"So we walk ta her room, right. It was jus like I expected it ta be—all feminine wit uh canopy bed, uh T.V., cable, uh closet full uh clothes, big ass cherry wood jewelry box filled wit shit. She had her own bathroom in her room, too. A pink an' white bathroom wit soap still wrapped up an' towels she told me not ta wipe my hands on 'cause dey was decoration.

"So finally I was like, 'Fuck it' an' we did it, right. I only lasted three minutes—pro'bly not even dat--I wudden't even sure I stuck it in all da way an' she was saltly as hell. She rushed me out da crib an' didn't even sneak ta call me dat night. Two days later all da girls in class was sayin' D said I only lasted uh second an' my dick was skinny as my body—I was real lanky back den.

"...Dat was some hurtful ass shit. Some real hurtful shit. We ain't neva talk again. I couldn't wait 'til eight grade was over. Dat was da worse year uh school fa me, an' I done had uh whole lodda bad ones but dat shit was da worse one—worse dan second grade."

"When your teacher told you you were as dumb as a doorknob and weren't gonna amount to anything?"

"Yep."

I kissed him lightly on his shoulder. I wanted so badly to tell him how wonderful he was, how much he meant to me, how much he resembled and walked like an Egyptian King. But I couldn't. You know how cottage cheese is all crumpled up and bally? That was how my heart felt at that moment listening to him and I couldn't think of any words that would make that kind of pain go away

Maybe it was better my father hadn't been in my life.

One time before, I told Craig that I wished we could switch places. He should be me and I should be him for a day so we could understand each other in every way. I guess you *do* have to be careful what you wish for. I felt like I had just experienced his life, his childhood and it was overwhelming. When you look at someone, sometimes you can see who they are; sometimes you can see their scars but you can't always see the battles they've gone thru. Craig was intelligent enough to be labeled a genius and he had the sexiest smile I'd ever seen in my life. Yeah, he looked like he had been a little thugged out back in the day but, at a first glance, he looked like he'd come from a good family and a decent neighborhood and had only rebelled and pulled a thug stunt just so he'd be able to say he'd done something.

I didn't know how to show him just how much I wished he'd never gone thru any of this. The only thing I could do was listen. He ran down a list of crimes he had committed from robbing kids at gunpoint for name brand gymshoes and herringbone necklaces to grand theft auto. All the girls he had 'hit and quit'. The gang he had been initiated in. "I'm not proud uh all dis but I feel like you need ta know. You need ta know where I'm comin' from, where I been and where I'm tryin' ta git to."

"I feel…" I was about to say *privileged* but that just didn't sound like the right thing to say. "I wanna know," I finished.

"You know I rolled backed in da day, right?"

"You said something about it once."

"… Dat shit was crazy. I'm jus glad I made it out--lotsa brothas wind up in uh box in da ground.

"When you see uh chick wit uh kid leave ha baby on da porch next ta uh cat da size uh rat so she can go git anotha rock an' git high, you know dat's some shit dat need ta be illegal.

"…We used ta make bitches suck Rottweilers dicks when dey ain't have no money or when dey owed us--some niggas made 'em fuck da dogs. Lotsa times bitches fell out from dat shit 'cause dey uh make 'em do all da dogs in da house an' dem cracked out bitches had weak ass bodies. But, shit, da niggas wudden't no betta. Dey'uh offer ta suck uh dog off, too if dey ain't have no money. For uh lodda 'em, dat rock be da only thing dat uh make 'em happy once dey git hooked.

"An' even wit all dis fucked up shit goin' on right here in America, evry other country look up ta America an' keep on tryin' ta git here ta cash in on dey dreams but, da niggas dat's born here still ain't 'lowed ta do half da shit uh foreigner can do once he move here—dey ain't even godda be citizens an' dey got moe rights dan uh nigga."

"Langston Hughes wrote about that in one of his *Simple* stories. Simple says something about how foreigners could come to America and sit anywhere on the bus they wanted, while he had been born here, him and his father's father, but he was Jim Crowed."

"Yeah. I read alla his stories when I was locked up. But when you livin' shit it's different from reading 'bout it… You need ta be glad you ain't have ta live out on da street. Da streets suck all da life out chu til' you turn callous an' cain't even bleed no moe. Yo' hands clean an' you innocent, baby. If you stay like dat, yo' life uh be bedder."

What he said made me think about all the summers I spent at my grandma's house. Her block was hot. Back in the day, the part of the eastside grandma lived on was the spot for dealers in the hood.

Grandma watched Paulina's sons, Marcus, Damon and Charlie when she was at work but when they got older and started 'slanging dem thangs,' as they called it, grandma wouldn't let them step a foot on her porch.

They drove money green and shiny purple hoopties with stereo systems that pounded bass as loud as the color of their cars up and down Van Dyke from Six Mile to Seven Mile. When they drove by, the windows in your living room shook until they turned the corner.

When their mother moved to the west side and let them have the house, houses started going up for sale or they became vacant and the bums tore all the siding off, ransacked the fixtures inside and left the already abandoned houses looking like empty, door-less ghosts with nothing but rotting air and faint memories of civillization.

Females and Rottweilers stayed on Marcus, Damon and Charlie's porch and partied until it was time for the few honest working people stuck on the street to go to work. I'd watch them from grandma's bedroom window upstairs and secretly wish I was over there with them. They were always fresh but the boys they had working for them wore the same outfits back-to-back for weeks at a time.

I wondered if Craig was a baller like Marcus and them or if he was one of the ones that wore the same clothes everyday.

Damon, Charlie and Marcus all had quiet street demeanor that commanded attention from the time they stepped out the door. Hats cocked to the side and baggy jeans that hung just right made every chick on the eastside want to be with one of them. I wasn't any different but grandma wasn't having that and they knew it. They respected her and didn't try anything even though my body was calling for attention from Charlie. He had smooth brown caramelized skin and those sexy, squinty eyes that looked like he'd just hit a Mary Jane. But he never even bothered to looked my way. No matter how many times I ran to the corner store for grandma and passed their house, they didn't say one word to me even though we grew up together. I spent a whole summer daydreaming about him in the middle of cleaning up, reading the bible and practicing my violin.

When they walked by grandma's porch they pulled up their pants, asked her how she was doing and if she needed anything. She always gave an adamant no and told them she was praying for them and, in her words, "Dey slouchy pants." Once they were out of ear shot grandma'd lean closer to me and shut her eyes. She'd nod one good time like she was putting a stamp on her words and say, "Just 'cause you live in tha hood don't mean you gotta take it everywhere you go." If it wasn't for her I probably would have ended up hanging out with the posse of hoodrats a block down from her house.

When he was nineteen, Charlie was shot in the head five times. They caught him stepping out of his brand new Benz. Two chicks from down the block were with him. One was killed, the other one, a girl named Candella, took a paralyzing bullet that made her a quadriplegic at the age of fifteen. Charlie had been smart. He had the type of instinct that made for an excellent hustler. If he would have turned legal he would have been more than alright. Being street smart is something you can't learn in school or buy; it can take you far if you use it on the right type of hustle but a lot of brothas like Charlie don't.

I still remember the funeral, his face stuffed and unnatural looking in the fancy black and silver casket. It seemed like he was supposed to raise up and come back to life. He looked like he still had so much more to say. As popular as he had been, there were only nine people there outside of his family and his daughter's mother, Twyla who was fourteen.

Marcus is locked up for life and for the last eight years Damon has been missing. Last I heard he was on his way to the mall but he never came back home. The police found his car on the freeway still running.

If Craig lived anything like they had he was blessed to still be living.

"But Craig. You know your past--the way you ended up living wasn't all your fault." He turned away from the wall and finally looked at me. I looked back into him as he reached for my hand and intertwined my fingers in his. His fingers were strong.

"Da way I grew up an' evrythang I went thru--dat shit was all part uh da plan. It started wit da G7 when dey marched dey asses ova ta Africa an' gangked da land away from kings an' queens. Dey fucked us over fa centuries ta come. Dey knew how wealthy dat land was. Gold, rubber, diamonds an' shit—dey knew. An' dey knew Black muthafukas held uh lodda power.

"Dey scared uh us, dat's why dey had ta use reverse psychology ta make us thank we godda bow down ta dey asses. It's da same tactics dey used way back den goin' on right nah. Breakin' up families, killin' muthafukas in da hood, from colonization ta slavery ta da Tuskegee experiment ta makin' niggas kill each other ova petty ass shit like uh chain. Don't none uh it mean shit but destruction fa uh nigga. It's too many uh us versus dem. People uh color—no matter where dey from—India, China, Africa—dey all eat spicey shit an' got similar cultures. What White folks got? Nothing but uh history uh takin' shit dat don't belong ta 'em! So dey turn us against each other an' keep us on lock an' dey come out on top.

"Nature versus Nurture, America ain't gon' love me eitha way. Da only thang dey ever tole me was dat I'm three fifths human."

Craig's brother was in jail serving for life. Maybe there *was* something to that theory. I couldn't place all the blame on his mother. She was a victim of environment just like his father probably was but no matter where you placed the blame, it was a cycle that kept spinning and haunting innocent people who, in a different space and time, could have been so much more. The cycle keeps spinning until its victims walk without hearts

"That's why we've got to do everything in our power to make sure our kids get everything—love, education—everything they deserve. If a Black child doesn't get nurtured at home, nine times out of ten they aren't gonna get it in the school system. It's like unless you go to an all Black college you aren't gonna learn about Malcolm X or read a Chinua Achebe book. I didn't learn anything about Egypt until I started going to Detroit Community. But all thru high school, when I had teachers that were Jewish, they made sure we knew everything about the war and Hitler and what happened to the Jews. We even had to take a class on Greek mythology in high school. But when it comes to African history, we've been taught to be embarrassed about our ancestors and a lot of us still think our people swing on trees and look like monkeys—"

"—Heeel naw! Dey 'on't want us diggin' too deep inta shit. Den, dey gon' have uh whole bunch uh angry niggas on dey heads ready ta crack 'em open! Dey goal is ta keep Black people away from dey milk an' honey. It's like dis, 'Look lil' nigga but don't let cho' dirt colored hands touch da shit yo' ass helped us get 'less you gon' be uh Uncle Tom oreo type uh nigga! If you gon' Uncle Tom foe 'em, dey'uh use yo' ass ta sell rap an' shit. But when dey thru usin' yo' ass, dey gon' sho' laugh at chu behind dey closed ass glass doors."

"I don't know why this popped up in my head but think about this: Elvis—"

"—Hol up, hol up! I ain't tryin' ta intarupt you, baby but Mos Def got uh song talkin' what chu 'bouta say. "Rock N' Roll" thas what it's called—go 'head, my bad."

"Yeah but look, Elvis got with Priscilla when she was way too young and, it's been proven that some of his songs came from Black men from the back woods down south. But what was he? The king. They make excuses for the things they do but when it's a Black person—if they even *think* a Black person did something, they're ready to hang him out to dry.

"A while ago I read this story about this Black couple. I can't remember exactly what they were accused of but, they were beaten so bad, right before they were lynched, their eyes popped out of their scull in front of a crowd of White people that watched--they even brought their kids. It's crazy when you just sit back and think about it. All the things they tell you not to do, be a good civilian, don't steal, don't kill but they didn't follow their own rules. They got this country by being thugs. But then they try to make it look like Black folks are the biggest criminals. We didn't beat and rape people for four hundred years...the thing that gets me is, so many Black people are sold on this hush-hush thing. They don't wanna talk about it and they got us convinced the situation isn't worth talking about."

"See! See, dat's why I love yo' ass! We different but we da same. I cain't be wit uh woman dat ain't on the same page wit me. We both love America but we hate it—kinda like my man Claude McKay say in dat one poem." Craig kissed my baby finger and at that very moment, laying next to him, everything was perfect. "You me, baby. An' I'm you. You my better half fa sho'. I put dat on evrythang." He squeezed my hand and placed it on his heart and drifted to sleep with his head on my chest.

Now I understand why he was always bugging me to sleep on top of him every night. When he first moved in, that was the most annoying thing about him. I toss and turn a lot but at night he always locks me in his arms. If I'm uncomfortable I'm just stuck like that for the next eight hours and he breathes real loud and snores right in my ear.

But now I feel bad for even complaining about it. He just wants to hold me. The more I think about it, I feel bad for Craig *and* Darren.

Yes, my mother pulled out belts and switches--whatever was in arm's reach when I was out of line. I still remember the time she snatched the curly part of the phone cord off the phone. My legs stung the whole night from *that* whipping. But I grew up knowing I was loved. Every morning when she'd wake me up for school she'd hug me and tell me.

Don't get me wrong--I'm not trying to say my mom was perfect. She was always reminding me to stay out of the sun so I wouldn't get blacker and to marry a fine, *light* skinned man so her grandbabies wouldn't be ugly. "I ain't gon' be carrying no ugly lil' thangs around"--that's how she felt but, even considering that, I knew ma loved me. Her and grandma bought every toy on my Christmas wish list every single year and I always got what I wanted when it came to clothes. When people at church started calling me spoiled ma would say, "Ungh-uh, sweetie. My child is *loved*. That's my the one God *blessed* me with."

Mom wasn't rich but she always put money in my bank account before I had Pharaoh. The deal was, she didn't want me to go away to school so as long as I stayed in Detroit Community she'd me help out. Occasionally she'd piss me off by trying to get all up in my business so I'd quit speaking to her. Then she'd quit putting money in my account and somehow I'd ended up feeling guilty for not speaking to her and I'd call a few days later and we'd be on speaking terms again.

Two years ago mom retired from her job as an administrative assistant for a Jewish attorney she worked for twenty-eight years. Right after she got her associates degree, she got hired at a large practice in the Penobscot building downtown. When it closed down a year later, one of the newer attorneys asked her to work with him since he was opening his own office and she'd always been on time and never missed a day of work. They treated her like family. We went camping with Isaac and his family every summer. He and his wife had talked mom into putting me in violin since their daughter Rebecca was already taking lessons. Mom said his wife offered to pay for my lessons and all the times I went to Blue Lake camp with Becky but she didn't go for it. She was a strong believer in not acting or looking poor or taking things from people when they offered no matter how bad off you were. She said they'd used it against you later or started treating you like menial help and property.

On the days grandma couldn't pick me up after school, mom would take me to the office with her. When I was in high school sometimes I'd take the bus there since King wasn't that far from downtown. I always liked going to Goldberg's place.

Detroit isn't necessarily as crowded as places like New York or Chicago but one thing about the Black people in the D: They know how to dress. (Although, even back then, you still had an occasional Ghettofied Apparel Don't). Otherwise everything about the people caught in the nine to five work shuffle reminded me of jazz. Women with sharp, bright red, navy, lime green fitted suits good enough for Sunday's sermon. Those eighties and nineties hairstyles like they were about to be on the next cover of *Black Hair* or *Jet*. Red everything, Lee Press on nails, Fashion Fair makeup—sometimes way too much pressed powder. The men had their fresh out of the box S-Curls going on. Suits that were less colorful just for work with tan or black gators on their feet, walking like they knew all the ladies came dressed just to impress them. CEO conservatives in navy suits with only a dash of color in their red ties, always making sure the Vanna White look alikes slid in the revolving doors ahead of them so they could watch.

Something about the stony mud colored buildings, the Woolworth with its ninety-nine cents items and fake leather boots with the fake fur cuffed on top, the pointy shiny black bank on the corner of Woodward and the triangular landscaped area in the middle of the street across from Kennedy Square and the Cadillac building, even downtown wasn't filled with tons of tall skyscrapers, something about it all created a certain feeling, the kind of feeling that comes from good memories. Changs Chinese egg rolls and red carpet and the individual chandeliers over each booth...

Something about the way the women going into NBC's news station on Lafayette, the men going into the Detroit Edison buildings and the city county building, something about watching all the people who looked like news columnists and journalists walking into the Detroit News building on Fort street... Simply Jazz. All of it reminded me of Nina Simone's music and Charlie Parker's jazz.

After mom started working downtown, we went from shopping at Kingsway off East Grand Boulevard to shopping strictly at Hudsons and paying full price for shoes without waiting for them to go on clearance and when Gantos opened ma and I went every month and got a new outfit complete with earrings and bracelets to match the outfit for church.

At night while mom would be up ironing and doing whatever else she did late at night when I was supposed to be asleep, I'd be listening to WJZZ. Back then it was 105.9. They played songs like "Strawberry Boy" by (I think it was) a group called Swing Out Sisters and Layla Hathaway songs along with straight up neo-jazz—the kind of music you imagined listening to in a smoky bar at a hotel as the rich and famous walked by.

Ma tried to get me to listen to the 1340 AM gospel station all day but, considering the fact that Salt-N-Pepa's "Push It" was the deal back then, she didn't trip on an eight year old having a jazz habit. Besides, Goldenberg constantly praised her for raising me so well. He and his wife had Becky on a tight schedule—they were banking on her following father's footsteps and becoming a lawyer one day, too. Whenever I came and she was there we were only allowed to watch an hour of television, which always ended up being both of our favorites—*The Beverly Hillbillies* and *The Jetsons*. After that, we'd do homework--even if it was summer. They'd have an academic activity planned or we'd go to the science center or to the DIA or read. Becky was my girl. I got along with her much better than I did with Tamika; Becky didn't mind sharing her dolls or coloring books when we were younger. But once we got older she stopped hanging out at the office. I'd sometimes make a little money working during holiday breaks filing and answering the phones. Ma didn't really want me to work so that was as good as it got for earning my own money in high school. Ma always said my job was to worry about my grades. Meanwhile Becky was at Cranbrook and was totally changing. Turning into a black headed, black lipstick wearing Goth that listened to Korn and Marilyn Manson. She had traded her violin in for a guitar and worshiping Janis Joplin and Jimmy Hendrix. Last I heard she got kicked out of Yale for growing mushrooms in her dorm. So much for all those years spent watching *Degrassi High*.

I guess those little things *had* made a difference, though. My mother didn't fight with knives and chains in the streets over men like Craig's mother had and she never had men around me. If she ever dated, I didn't know anything about it even after she moved out of grandma's house and bought her own home. All in all, mom did alright earning a living as a single mother and had set a pretty good example.

CONTEMPORARY GOSPEL MUSIC BLARED on 107.5 like a triggered smoke alarm waking me up.

"Turn that off," I mumbled to Craig who was still knocked out.

I lifted my arm over him and turned the radio off and rolled back over. "Let's *not* go to church today."

"Bet," he said, rather cheerfully, between a snore and sneeze.

"...Might as well enjoy the vacation from the kids as long as we can," I said drifting back to sleep. Funny how we can get away from the very thing we need the most, the moment we see one solitary shadow of a ray of sunshine creep its way into our world.

"Bae, we godda own our own shit. Why 'on't we check out some houses. Look at whas out on da market, see what mortgages hittin' up foe. Dat's what we need ta start thinkin' 'bout. We godda git our shit tagether-- move ta da next level," Craig suggested waking me up at twelve in the afternoon.

"Awh, b*ay*-bee. Taking our relationship to the next level? That's *sweet*." He put his hand on my stomach and rubbed my navel. "I love Detroit, but I don't wanna be here all my life. What do you think about Southfield or Farmington Hills? They've got better school systems..."

"...Naw, baby. We can save way moe money if we find sumen in da D—you godda 'member, dis *only* gon' be our first house. We got uh lodda time 'foe we hit da suburbs."

Oh, God. Another disagreement.

Farmington Hills was clean, there were shopping centers with coffee shops and bookstores on every corner...without bums with cross eyes that twitched while they begged the crap out of you for spare change and followed you to your car...and sometimes spit on your car if you didn't dig down into your purse and give them something. Why *not* Farmington Hills? "Baby, I don't want to *live* somewhere I've got to pray won't be broken into every time I pull out of the driveway."

"Come here." He pulled me back on top of him. "You ain't gon' have ta worry 'bout dat wit me in da house, aright?"

"Baby..." I had to shut down and think for a minute. ...There were two options.

A: (With hostile energy) Go off on him and tell him I didn't *have* to move *anywhere*--since he sounded like he had already made up his mind about everything.

Or B: (With a calm heart) Diffuse my anger and be peaceable.

Realizations: Some things were gonna have to change on my end if I wanted this to work. I was going to have to compromise and give in *sometime*. Otherwise, if we stayed together, I was going to be running the risk of him pushing for baby number three again and there was no way I could enjoy sex like that. Role-play and bondage weren't anywhere in our near or distant future after that stunt he'd just pulled.

"I ain't tryin' ta be 'round uh whole bunch uh White muthafukas all da time..."

"...I hear you babe." But I wasn't trying to be around a whole bunch of niggas all the time either... Got to be a middle ground somewhere.

"I was thinkin' 'bout da area 'round James Cousins an' Outer Drive on da northwest end."

"Do most of the people around there own their own homes?"

"We gon' look it up online. It's uh nice area, dough..."

"Yeah, I know where you're talking about..." I was on this new, unconventional "*compromise*" *kick*.

...But I still couldn't use the bathroom or pass gas in front of him. How was *this* shit gonna work? A house? That was a lot of commitment. A commitment I wasn't sure he was necessarily cut out for just yet. *And* a lot of money.

And... And such a grown up thing to do. A house? I wasn't so sure that was the road we needed to be walking down right now so soon. We'd just gotten back together!

A house *just sounds like* a permanent thing. Think about it: nowhere in one single, solitary fairytale do you read about an apartment. Not in The Three Bears, not in Hansel and Gretel and certainly not in Cinderella. I could go on but the point is, you don't hear tell 'bout no apartment in any of them! A house goes hand in hand with marriage stuff--something you acquire after saying "I do." To me, anyway. And I've lived in this apartment since I was nineteen. Yes, it was becoming too small. Yes, I wanted Mauri and Pharaoh to have their own rooms. And yes, doggone it! it would be nice not to have to worry about tenants—I had enough going on in my own life but I was definitely going to have to wait this one out. Until I figured out what was really going on, I might not be able to ride on the House Bandwagon just yet.

The minute Craig went to the bathroom I called Tamika to get the information I needed. I had to play it off by acting like I had heard about a dangerous side effect on the news for a tea they'd said people were taking for non-surgical abortions. "Oh. That's not the same stuff then. Just trying to look out for ya'," I said after she told me exactly what it was and which health food store to buy it from. The girl had a big mouth. This way she would forget about it and wouldn't start speculating.

"Girl! Lemme tell you. Why yo' mama had ta spank da mess outta Mauri in da bathroom during Pasta sermon taday?"

It was long overdue if you asked me. "For real? My line just clicked—hold on."

It was my mother. "I'm surprised you didn't come to service taday. Everybody asked about you. 'Specially Pastor and First Lady. You two okay?"

"Yeah, hold on, mom. Tamika's on the other line."

"Tell her ta bring some of dat cheesecake over mama made last night."

"Um-hm." I relayed the message.

"Aright. Tell auntie I'll be by dere 'round five uh clock. What chu doin' tanight?"

Oh lord. Next she was going to be asking me to hang out with her again. She's my cousin, and I love her, but we have two *totally* different ideas on what a good time is. "Girl, you know me--forever busy with something. I've got too much to do around the building today."

"Oh…"

"Hey. Lemme call you back. Mom's still on the other line."

"Aright, den."

I clicked back over. "We're fine."

"Well, you gon' have ta do *something* 'bout this lil' girl. Girlfriend need some *serious* home training—over here actin' like uh cheerleader *for tha devil*! Over here knockin' King Pharaoh in tha head wit his trucks an' whatnot. Feel sorry for tha poor King. He just sat there trying ta get her ta stop wid'out hitting her back—like he's used ta her bullying him.

"I done had ta tear Mauritania's legs up 'bout eight times since she been over here. She done lost her mind an' ain't even two yet! Tryin' ta hit me back! Usually, when they be over here she fall right asleep 'til you get come get 'em an' she be aright. But since I done had them the whole weekend? Ungh-uh. Ungh-uh. She's *too little* ta be actin' like this! She like this when she's wit y'all? Never mind. You ask me? I 'on't think you never shoulda named these kids these crazy names. I'd be cuttin' a rug too if somebody named me some craziness like that. She ain't gon' even be able ta spell her own name in kinny-garden. They had a comedian on some mess on T.V. the other day made a joke about Black kids an' they names. Ya know, I couldn't even laugh 'cause look at what you done did ta my grandbabies. What's dat comedian's name? …Lord, I cain't remember that man's name. But I know one thing! Mauri gon' be writing down Kim or M.W. 'stead of her real name on her papers when she start school an' see how long it take her to spell it. Hmph!

"Oh! Oh! Then she thought she was gon' *clown* when I took them to mama's house! Started screamin' all loud when mama tried to get her ta eat some fried okara. Nah, if you not gon' set her straight, I *will*, I *sho'* will! You hear me?

"You ain't act neva like this when you was her size. An' The King *sho'* didn't. She's the *cutest* lil' thing but some whoopin's in order on that behind! Watch. Bring her back over her next weekend, um-hmm. Um-hm. Yeah." Ma said it like it was a threat. Vondela Lorretta Anderson wasn't playing! And I didn't say one word. It was about time somebody got Mauri in line. As far as I was concerned she could keep her every weekend if she liked. I wasn't too proud of the fact that I was *forbidden* to punish my own child in front of her father. But Craig was gonna go berserk if he heard ma talk about his lil' angel even though just last night guidelines for Ms. Mauri were one of those issues we'd supposedly compromised on.

"Now. All I gotsta say ta *you*, is that you know *good an' well* that the choir is depending on you. God blessed you ta have that voice. Don't start tryin' ta play Him. Gray say you ain't even call him this morning ta say you weren't coming..."

"...I know, I kno—"

"—*I know?*" She let out a crazy sigh. "*S'cuse* me? You need ta call Gray an' talk ta him."

"I wasn't feeling good. I'm going to call him right now." She was starting to irritate me.

"You goin' ta rehearsal on Thursday, right?"

"Yeah--oh, yeah. I'm coming over there to pick up the kids around—" Craig came out of the bathroom and swooped me into the air so fast I screamed.

"Eight uh clock tamorrow," he added like he was in on the conversation.

"Craig said eight tomorrow."

"Um-hmm. I heard 'im. Tell him I said hello an' ta make sure y'all both carry y'all behinds ta church next Sunday."

"Okay."

"Mommy loves you."

"Love you too, Ms. Vee Anderson. You're something else, ma."

She started laughing. "No, I ain't either! I just don't have no time ta be playin'. Not wit the Lord! An' neither do you, baby!"

"Love you too, mama." Craig joined in right before I hung up. My mother laughed.

"Lord, bless his heart, that sho' is my son-in-law, ain't it? Wit his handsome self. Aright then. See you 'round eight. If y'all hungry I'ma be done cooked *sumthen* tamorrow night—still don't know what I'ma fix, though."

"Um-hm." If I said anything else, she was going to start a whole new conversation and I was not in the mood to hear about who stunk up the restroom today during prayer or about Sister Riles latest hideous pink and gold hat that was made out of hairweave and matched her outfit.

"Bye, baby."

"Bye mom."

"What's up?" I asked Craig as he placed the receiver back on the charger.

"Lets jus chill an' go online an' check at some houses, bae. We ain't jus sat an' talked wit out da kids around in uh while," he said, playfully twirling me around in the air a couple more times. He was all excited. And enthusiastic. His eyes were actually sparkling. I'd be that ungrateful girlfriend with that nasally cartoon voice in his head who never appreciated anything if I tried to hold off. He was trying to do something beneficial for the whole family.

It kinda made sense that we start thinking about a house...

And there were four brick houses in our price range that were exactly what we were looking for—at least according to what the listings stated. We'd only really know after going to look at them.

The colonial one was really perfect. It had a new roof and the outside was white aluminum with brick on the lower level. It had a lot of the amenities I didn't even know I wanted until we came across it. Like a dishwasher and a remote controlled garage door, four bedrooms, two and a half bathrooms, now I could get used to something like this for real.

Here the tenants' guests were always stealing my parking spot, I spent enough time hand washing dishes to not ever need a facial—steam and all... Just the thought of having more than one bathroom was enough to make me start packing immediately. I wouldn't have to worry about using the toilet in front of Craig.

"HEY BABY, WHAD UP wit chu? Why you ain't answering da phone? I got in touch wit somebody ta show us da houses. Call me when you get dis message. Love you." I replayed Craig's message two more times. What was all that noise in the background about? Didn't sound like no General Motors office workplace to me. Sounded more like an after five social affair. A ghetto one. With cackling hens running rampant all over the f-ing place.

There were too many stories about Big Three plants.

A flashback of the Angela situation popped in my head. We'd been thru a lot and we hadn't even reached our third anniversary yet.

Was our relationship gonna withstand the plant's underworld trademark? Lots of married people had girlfriends and boyfriends on the side and even had outside families from getting caught up in the plant. It was like a double life haven. Drugs, prostitutes, the number's man—you name it--you could find it all in there.

Craig was the type that kept to himself...but, if the plant lived up to its reputation, I might have a problem on my hands. *Handsome? And with* a lot going for himself? Oh, there was no way the women up in that spot were about to leave him alone.

I hadn't *ever* worried about losing him. And maybe that was the problem all alone. Whenever you aren't worry about something, you're always shocked when it disappears. Like my keys this morning. Never, ever lost 'em before! And yeah, I've got a spare set, so it's not that big of a deal. But I still want those keys. I've got money in the change purse thingy that's on the ring and plus, I've got a family picture that I don't have another wallet size print of.

Now *my man*? I don't even have a spare one tucked away. And you couldn't substitute him with any other man, anyhow. Now how am I going to feel if I *really* lose him and I can't even bare to lose a set of keys I can replace for just $3.99 at the hardware store down the corner off McNicols?

No, it was time. Time for him to marry me. We were already living together, might as well do it right. They always say a man won't buy the cow if the milk is free and it's been *real free* for *way* too long. Thank God we made up. Good thing I took Debra's advice. The next time he started talking about marriage, I wasn't going to switch subjects like I usually did after we had Mauri and he started acting funny towards Pharaoh.

After that long talk Saturday night I'd finally figured out why he was constantly bringing the marriage topic up. He was worried about whether or not I'd still want to be with him after I finished school. He knew me well. I kept a small nest egg on the side in the event a brotha wasn't right. Always think ahead 'cause you never know which way the wind might blow. Just like I planned to maintain my position as apartment manager and my place for a few months after we moved just in case things didn't work out. The one thing the cheating incident taught me was to try to be prepared for the unexpected. It was a more pessimistic way of looking at life from what I would have preferred but that's what the experience taught me. To be more realistic. Before I had held Craig on a pedestal always thinking that he would never do this or never do that. That's how I set myself up to be gravely disappointed.

Since we were altering the plans, I was going to have a real wedding at my church and a reception at a banquet hall. Forget that going to the justice of the peace crap he had talked about. One good thing about his job, we could afford something nice now.

I was mulling the plans over, trying to figure out each possible outcome as I drove to school when Darren called to check on Pharaoh. That was a serious surprise. He usually only did that around birthday time or when his family needed to borrow Pharaoh for an appearance at one of the family showings.

I waited for him to inform me as to the nature of this great unexpected phoning after we completed all the necessary and the ever formal 'hi, how are you doings' but he never stated a reason, which was weird. We hadn't talked since the House-touring-Niquie-is-a-ho-and-you-wanted-me-to-be-one-too thing had gone down. Surely something had to be up.

Since he wasn't doing anything but making small talk, I took the opportunity to let him know I wasn't ever going to ever be cool with him again like I had tried to be for those two days. Might as well. "Yeah. Well everything is good on this end. Craig and I our going to be getting married and buying a house soon." He was silent for almost two minutes. I know because I kept looking at the phone to make sure my signal hadn't faded and that we were still connected.

"...You *really* gonna marry that joker?" He was so dry, he was making me thirsty in the process.

"Ah, *yeeaah*. That's where we're headed."

"What happened to going to school?" He sounded almost dead.

"I am," I assured him. What made him think I was about to end my education?

"... ... ...You can do better, Leigh. Didn't he come from the projects?"

"Why did I even bother telling you? You do whatever you please and tell me all about your latest flavor of the week. And what do I do? Wish you the best, every time. Whatever Darren." I should have known he was only going to irk my nerves. He was pass jealous.

"Well, I won't take Pharaoh off all the insurance documents--I don't know what kind of bootleg healthcare plant shit that *one* has but, I'm sure you won't be in need of the child support anymore or the healthcare plan I got you." There was an underlying unmistakable devilish tone breaking thru in his voice.

Where was all this mess he was talking coming from? I hung up on him.

I could get health insurance thru Craig, I wasn't worried about that. But could he legally just up and stop child support payments? I knew my mother would know but as much as I hated to contact Goldberg with this ghetto shit, I called him instead.

Darren was Pharaoh's father point blank. Unless he quit his job, there was no way Darren was going to be able to get away it. We had that baby together. He had some nerve. If he didn't want to have to worry about child support, he should have used one of those condoms that fell out of his glove compartment in the first damn place! Bottom line, if I took it to court, he was going to be ordered to pay. Just a bunch of baby daddy gibberish. Note to self: no more sharing of the personal life with Darren in future settings. Even though we both knew we would *never* be in a committed relationship together outside of being Pharaoh's parents, he still felt like he owned a piece of me because of the child we shared and the financial support he was *supposed* to provide for his son. To most men, if they have a child with a woman, even if they aren't still with her, it means they're entitled to the coochie from time to time. They also think it means they can control what goes on in the woman's home regardless of how many girlfriends they themselves have.

I entered my nutrition class still upset by Darren's empty threat. It wasn't like I could complain about him to Craig. He'd be happy to hear about it. As far as he was concerned, the less Darren was involved in our lives the better--regardless of Pharaoh's needs. And Sherra acted like my life was picture perfect and problem-free. Why not keep it like that? Everything was working out one way or another.

"IT'S ABOUT TIME EV'RYBODY read the assigned chapters. It makes time go by a whole lot faster," Scott said holding the classroom door open as I walked out. We were always the last two to leave. Brickshaw knew any and every thing a person could possibly know when it came business law and she didn't mind answering questions after class.

"That's why I try to take night classes. It's an older, more mature crowd. In the daytime it's like being in middle school—probably worse. When I was their age, I took school seriously. I don't know what's up with these kids nowadays."

"Like you're that much older than them. You sound like my wife."

"I'll be twenty-five in a minute. That's different from being seventeen/eighteen. Me and my fiancé are about to buy a house. I'm not trying to be in classes with little kids throwing paper airplanes pass me and popping gum so loud I can't even hear the instructor. I'm trying to finish school so I can start working."

"Thas what's up. You don't look twenty-five, though--I thought you were like nineteen/twenty. We're the same age then.

"I hear you on the career tip. I've already got my real estate license. I've been in realty for almost three years now but I'm finishin' up my bachelors. It's cheaper to take courses here and just transfer 'em over ta Wayne.

"If you don't mind me asking, what areas are you looking at?"

"I was interested in Southfield or a surrounding suburb but he wants to stay in the city."

"The city's cool too. They're planning to have the superbowl here in 2006 so they're gonna be hooking things up. And you can get some good deals on property in Michigan right about nah."

"That's cool." I walked to the atrium in the center of the building and sat down to wait for Craig. He was still in a computer graphics class. "Any suggestions?"

"Sure. You waitin' on a ride?"

"No. My fiancé's class isn't over for another half an hour."

"Well depending on how much you want to spend, and whether or not you want a new house or an older one, there are five neighborhoods you should check out," he said sitting down across from me.

"We found a couple of good ones near James Cousins and the Lodge freeway."

"That's a real good area. Especially for a first time buyer that wants to live in and area where most people own their own homes. It's not gonna be the cheapest price range you can find but it's a neighborhood that's worth what you're gonna end up paying for it. Right now rates are prime and you can easily get one locked in for like 6.5 percent."

"From what Craig said, that's not bad."

"Yeah, let me know what's up. I'd like to meet him and work with y'all on a good deal."

"Okay."

"And don't forget those tickets for the gospel concert. Ever since I told my wife a girl in my class is gonna be in it, she's been buggin' me about it. How much are they goin' for?"

"We haven't gotten them yet but I know they said something about guests tickets so I should be able to just give you a couple. It's gonna be nice. Their covering it on channel thirty-eight and on cable. You and Chante should come to my church sometime. We're having a women's conference. She'd like it."

"Aright, yeah, she'd love that. Lemme give you my business card." Just as he stood up out of the chair and handed me his card, Craig walked up and slid my book bag off my shoulder.

"Hey babe. This is Scott--he's in my class. I was just telling him about how we're in the process of buying a house. He's a real estate agent," I said as I stood up.

Scott stuck his hand out to shake Craig's but Craig just looked at Scott's outreached hand like it was plagued with leprosy. "How's ma wife doin'?" he asked putting his arm around me and kissing me on the cheek.

"Alright, thanks Scott. See you next week."

"Yeah, no problem. Nice to meet you, man," Scott said walking ahead of us towards the parking lot unfazed.

Man, was I embarrassed! "Cra*aa*-ig! Why did you act like that? He's looking to help us get a good deal on a house."

"*Dat fagot*-ass-muh'fuka. He'uh have us up in some kinda uh pink gingerbread lookin' house an' shit."

"Craig stop. He's cool. And he's got a wife."

"He *ain't* gay? Dat's why he was all up on you den—you do look good as hell tonight. I 'on't think I want chu wearin' dese jeans outside da house no moe. Dey fit uh lil' *too* good." He slapped my butt as I got in my truck. The jeans I was wearing did do a good job at accentuating my hips and butt.

"I'm hungry but it's too late to cook. You wanna hit a restaurant before we pick up the kids?" If I waited until mom was about to go to bed, she wouldn't be trying to invite Craig in for dinner and I, in turn, I wouldn't have to watch Craig go berserk and start another world war when she started that Mauri Needs Some Home Training speech all over again like I knew she would and they'd both still like each other.

"Lets git da kids 'foe we go eat." What he meant was he wanted Mauri home pronto.

"They're probably knocked-out. They're not gonna wanna do anything but go back to sleep. Why don't we drop off one of the cars and go to eat right quick--might as well enjoy the last few minutes of adult conversation we're gonna be able to have without having to spell everything." Even then, Pharaoh was catching on to certain words.

"Aright, aright. Where you wanna go, Cheryl's Place?"

"Yeah, that's fine." Next to Floods, the neighborhood bar had some of the best soul food in town and was on the way to my mother's house on Six Mile and Evergreen. Craig and I had gone there a couple of times together. Usually on the weekends the place was crowded with city workers, bus drivers, guys from the waterboard and what Craig called "old heads," that played ZZ Hill, Johnny "Guitar" Watson, Shirley Brown, Shirley Murdock, the Delfonics, Millie Jackson, Billie Ocean, Stephanie Mills and BB King songs on the jukebox over and over, who'd get on stage and take over the karaoke machine and do every kind of hustle invented out on the dance floor. They kind of reminded me of how Sherra was gonna be when she turned forty. But tonight Cheryl's Place was so empty you could hear the dude with the fingerwaves and hair net that smiled enough to display the four teeth missing on both sides of his front teeth, bang the bell in the back every time the next order of food was up in the window.

I was having a good time listening to the Tina Marie and Sade songs they had playing but I wasn't appreciating the four glasses of whiskey Craig had gulped down back to back. I never saw him drink water. Only Faygo pop, Mountain Dew or orange juice mixed with liquor.

"Do uh lodda guys up in school be tryin' ta holla at chu?" he asked curiously right before finishing off the glass the waitress had just placed in front of him a second ago.

"Do a lot of women at work try to talk to you?" I turned the tables around. But I seriously wanted an answer.

"Jus uh inquirin' mind dat wanna ta know, dat's all. I know yo' ass fine," he replied nonchalantly.

"Well. In a minute you're gonna have a whole 'nother family with some chick from your job. Watch. One day some kid's gonna call my house and be like, '*can I speak to my daddy,*' " I mimicked in a ghetto, kiddy voice. "And I'm gonna kill yo' ass and ask Jesus ta forgive me afterwards." I smiled and nodded my head.

"Naw, yo' ass gon' be like, *I 'on't care. Next.*" he mocked my voice and snapped his fingers. "An' you gon' be wit uh some new nigga you done met up at Harvard or some shit an' y'all gon' git married da followin' week."

"Oh! Oh, so you *are* planning on living a double life then, hungh?"

"Naw, come on, nah. You know it's all 'bout chu, bae. Dem women up in dere know dat. I'ma put dat picture we took over at Sears on my desk when we git 'em back...but fa real dough, we need ta git chu dat tattoo real soon. Keep dem niggas off you."

"If you wanna keep 'em at bay, you've got to a *real* ring. I don't have a problem getting that tattoo, but I'm a lady and a lady needs a rings on at least one of her fingers.

"What about *you*, though? Looks like you need my name *stapled* in your arm. That way, the next time some girl pushes up on you, somebody'll remember they've got a *wife* at home. Oooh. Um-hmm." I smacked my lips and snapped my fingers with it.

"Aright, aright--low blow but fair. You git one, I'uh git one. Come on, bae. Les dance," he stood up and helped me slide out of the booth. Isley Brothers "Between the Sheets" had just come on. It was one of our favorite songs.

"Only if you promise you won't try to throw me when you turn!" I didn't get up until he promised not to act stupid. Craig was good at ballrooming and stepping but he played too much. One time when I was following his lead, he swung me so hard I ran into the coffee table. I still had a scar on my leg from the incident. The last time, when we were

119

dancing at home, I stopped because he almost rammed me into the entertainment center.

"I was just playing, dang. Come on." That was the problem. He was always "just playing." No wonder they say women mature faster than men.

"Um-hm. If you try something this time, I'll scream terrorist so loud—and you know how Black people do—you'll get stabbed before the police show up!" I retorted as he led me onto the empty dance floor.

"*Whad*? You would do yo' man like dat? Dat shit ain't funny." He shook his head and faked a solemn face.

"Yeah, it wasn't funny when you busted my leg open either but you were laughing awfully hard! ...And you know you look like one of those Jihads--straight up like you could be part of the Taliban. Um-hm. I bet you know where Bin Laden's been hiding out all along. Tell me. What's your real name? Sheik DaBar Aladdin?" I teased. He couldn't do anything but laugh along with me. After dancing to one more song, he paid the bill and we left to get the kids. "I'll drive. You've been working all day, baby." Actually, I wasn't too fond of the way he felt he could drive after drinking like a male mermaid. I wanted to live another twenty-four years. At least be around to see the kids graduate from college or whatever they planned on doing.

"Look at my girl, lookin' out fa her man. Nah you got sixty-five points." He gently touched my arm for a second.

"Points? For what?"

"Fa why I love yo' ass so much."

"I only have sixty-five points to make good on? Ungh-uh, I demand a recall." I joked covering up the fact that I was secretly geeked he had said that. "Hey baby—you don't have to pull into the drive way. I'm just running to the door and getting the kids. It's late and you know how ma gets ta talking," I suggested as he turned the corner.

"Aright."

"Hey mom. Thanks for keeping the kids." I grabbed Mauri and slipped her into my arms. She woke up and clung to my neck happy to see me for a change. "Come on, man. Walk with mommy to the car." I reached for Pharaoh's hand.

"Where is Craig? Never mind... You gon' be at bible study tomorrow, right?" she asked as she watched me with discriminating eyes while Pharaoh drowsily walked next to me without whining.

"Yep."

"Mmm-hm. Yeah, you gon' have ta bring them over *way* more often," She said after hugging and kissed Pharaoh goodbye. She said it like *I* was the one playing favorites. Mothers always had a way of making you feel guilty about something. "Oh, yeah. Here. I almost forgot." She handed me a tupperware dish and a paper plate covered with aluminum foil. "I saved y'all some catfish, potato salad, some of mama's fried okra and some cheesecake since you and Craig didn't get none."

"Thanks, mom." But Craig didn't eat leftovers. Only freshly cooked food.

"Um-hm." She was still looking at me incriminatingly.

"Whad'up, baby girl!" Craig shouted at the first sight of Mauritania. He turned around and started tickling her. "You aright, Man?" he inquired of Pharaoh seconds later. Pharaoh nodded his head and went back to sleep. Mauri, on the other hand, squealed in delight.

"Da*dddy*." She smiled.

By eleven-thirty the kids were fast asleep in their bunk beds. I was at the beginning of what had all the makings of a beautiful dream when I felt a surge tingle through my body jerking me awake. Craig's fingers were inside me. "Whatareyoudoing! I'm sleeping!" Was I going to have to go through this every night from now on? It might have felt wonderful--if I wasn't fast asleep...but not when you weren't expecting it...when you had to wake up early the next day...and had barely gotten any sleep the night before.

"I'm writing my name in my pussy. C-r-a-i-g." He kissed me below my navel. "Looked like you liked it ta me. Yo' body was shakin'." He laughed and copied off the sounds I made whenever I came.

To my relief, he rolled over and pulled me on top of him before dozing off. The alcohol on his breath was strong.

He had his own idiosyncrasies that I wished would change sooner than later. But yet and still, I loved him unconditionally. I could hear his heart thumping as my head rested on his chest.

I'd never loved any man like this.

CHAPTER 7

I HEADED TO THE kitchen and started breakfast while Craig showered. He kept a small radio in the bathroom so he could listen to Russ Par while he was getting ready for work. "You on't be playin' in da kitchen do you?" he complemented while he wolfed down the homemade hash browns, eggs, pancakes from scratch and sausage I fixed after he got out. "Whatchu doin' taday?"

"I have to clean apartment ten out--they just moved then, I'm going to get my hair done. I'm gonna have to go to Arnetta's house since I've got the kids...you can't bring kid's to KD's place then, bible study later--"

"--If you got kids, you got kids. Don't go ta him, den! You uh mother. You s'posed ta put yo' kids first." Craig was fond of making me take them everywhere. They were his little allies. I already knew I was going to have to check Mauri before she started *really* talking. I wasn't about to have my every move reported to Mr. Walker.

"It's a woman thing, you don't understand. That's why I said we should have just let the kids stay at my mother's until tonight—she wouldn't have had a problem with it. I love the way KD does my hair. And if I don't like the way Arnetta does it, if I change it, I have to see her at church."

"Arnetta, boy..." He started laughing and making goat noises.

"Craig, stop. She's singing for God. That's mean." I masked my own laughter.

He got up ready to leave for work. "Gimme ma kiss, bae."

When the kids woke up I fed them and left them with Debra while I cleaned the vacant apartment. They weren't going to do anything but slow me down and scare the crap out of me by getting into everything in sight. When Mauri had started crawling, she had made her way to a toilet I was about to clean and was splashing her face in the water. Thank God I turned around and caught her before she started drinking out of the toilet bowl! Just thinking about that incident irritated me. If anything happened to these kids, Craig would kill me. But he didn't seem to understand that sometimes I had things to do and that I couldn't take them everywhere. Debra had a twelve-thirty appointment and wouldn't be able to keep them so I could go to KD's—and I wasn't even mad about that. She was doing me a favor keeping them in the first place.

But there was no point in staying mad at Craig. I finished all the things I had to do around the building, got dressed, got the kids and headed to Arnetta's. Mauri sat peacefully in her car seat the whole ride, which was a first.

"Girl, les do sumen different ta yo' head dis time. Why 'on't you try some color? Look at dis. Nah, dat's you all the way," she suggested as she spiraled curled another girl's hair from church. I thumbed thru the book and looked at some of the other styles. Actually the one Arnetta picked out was hot. I had never had tried highlights.

"I got uh new package uh hair too. Yo' hair long but we can put some tracks in," she added.

"Okay...but I don't want my hair to be real stiff or fake looking." I was becoming worried. I liked classic looks. I wasn't trying to look like a stripper.

While I waited to get in Arnetta's chair a conversation started about what was going to be discussed in church tonight and the Woman's Day Conference that was coming up. Everything was fine until Arnetta started singing along with a tape of one of the choir's shows. It took everything in me not to bust out laughing. She sounded just like Craig's impersonation of her.

"Leigh, yo' man fine...I bet chu he gon' love yo' hair," Arnetta said, halting my quiet snickers.

"He *is* nice looking. You two make a cute couple," the Patricia girl added.

Oh boy here we go.

"Mauri so pretty. She sho' got some hair *on her* head. Past her shoulders already–an' it's dat curly, good hair, too. Look like it's almost strawberry blonde." Arnetta smiled at Mauri.

I hated it when people ranted on and on about Mauri right in front of Pharaoh like he was invisible even though he was just as cute. And, on top of that, I didn't believe in Good or Bad hair. As long as hair grew on top of your head, who cared? That was good enough.

"He got a deep lil' voice, and act like a man," Patricia commented pointing at Pharaoh. He smiled back.

The whole time Arnetta did my hair I checked every step of the way in the mirror. It ended up turning out better than I expected. She put two different shades of light brown highlights in my hair and the extra tracks of weave gave me a slightly longer length that reached just pass the middle of my back. I looked glamorous.

When I got home, in the middle of starting dinner, I heard my phone beep in my purse. Four missed calls from Craig.

"Hey baby, you called?"

"Yeah, how come you ain't answer yo' phone?" He demanded.

"*I-was-getting-my-hair-done.*" I responded like I was talking to someone that was slow. Hopefully this overprotection thing would wear off. He hadn't acted this bad before I kicked him out. "Probably because I was in the basement," I added.

"What da kids up to?"

"Nothing. Mauri's being good."

"Lemme speak ta her."

I motioned for her to come to me and held the phone up to her ear. "Say 'Hi, daddy!' 'Hi, daddy!'"

She looked at me like she was confused for a second. When she heard his voice, a huge smile spread across her face. "EE! Da-Da!"

"Pharaoh, here." I handed him the phone.

"Hey, Craig... Nothin'. We ate fish at grandma's. It was good. Bye." He handed me the phone back.

"Did you finish doin' dat shit 'round da apartment?"

"Yep. How's work?"

"Straight. I ain't really do shit taday... Make sure you got sumthen fa me ta eat when I git in."

"When have you *ever* come home and there wasn't something on the table or on the stove?" I sighed. He was starting to irk my nerves. "I gotta go." I was just about to tell him I had a surprise for him but he could just wait to see it when he got home.

"Baby, I'm jus askin' aright? Dang. Love you."

"Yeah...love you, too."

Mauri came back in the kitchen and grabbed my legs playfully. "Hey Ma-Ma, what's going on, hungh. What's going on?" I picked her up and smiled and played with her and Pharaoh for a while. Her chubby pink cheeks giggled back. "Mommy loves you. Yes she does. Yes she does. Let's open the stove and check on dinner. Umm. Smells good, hungh?

"Okay, Pharaoh. Guess what? *You* get to use the mixing bowl on the potatoes!"

"Yes!" The mixer was his thing.

An hour later Craig walked in the front door. "Hey baby." I walked into the living room holding Mauri. She tried to jump into his arms but he wasn't paying her any attention.

He stared at me for a good twenty seconds without uttering a word. "What da fuck you do ta yo' hair? Dat shit make you look like uh video hoe!" he declared as he tried to touch my hair. I snatched away. "*And you* got weave in yo' shit? If I wanted uh hoochie mama, I woulda got one!" His face scowled disapprovingly.

"Oh my God, Craig! I thought you'd like it. You know what? Since I look like *a video hoe*, I'm gonna skip finishing dinner and head to church early. Cut the oven off in ten minutes and take the steaks out. You can put the string beans on, too. Us video hoochies need that extra hour of God!"

"Baby, look. All *I'm* saying is I 'on't like it–"

"–So *what*! I *do*!" I went into the bedroom to grab my purse and keys still holding Mauri.

"Come on Pharaoh put your shoes on…here's your parka, honey." I went to the closet and passed him his things and zipped up the black leather jacket Craig had insisted on getting Mauri even though she wouldn't be able to fit it in a couple of months. I hated it. Every little bae bae's kid in Detroit had one in colors like hot pink or lime green and even though it was real leather it looked cheap and fake.

"*Parka*? Ugh. Why you cain't just say 'jacket'? …You goin' ta church tonight? I though I tole you I had called 'bout dat house an' made an appointment ta see–"

"—No. Ungh-uh. That's all right. The hoe look-a-like can't go!" I grabbed the bible off the end table next to the couch.

"Baby! Look Leigh. I'm jus tryin' ta let you know you look beautiful wit'out alla dat fake shit. You got class an' shit. You 'on't need all dat. Fa real. You 'on't even need makeup, bae. I 'on't know why you be insisting on wearin' dat mess. Las time you wore dat powder shit it was all over my shirt. Looked like–"

"–Bye Craig."

He grabbed my arm and tried to stop me from opening the door. "I'm not feelin' yo' hair but we on't have ta argue, baby. Come on, les eat an' go look at da house. Don't dey have sumthen goin' on at church tamorrow? I ain't got shit planned fa tamorro. I'll go wit chu."

"I'm going tonight! I haven't been to bible study the whole month—"

"—Aright, aright, baby," he interjected trying ta hush me up. "I'll go wit chu. I'ma check ta see if we can meet da lady at eight-thirty instead."

"Tell me. Why is it, that you can do or say the worse things but then you think I'm just supposed to get over it when you start all those *'Baby Come On's'*?" I copied off of his 'Lets Not Argue After I Piss You Off' voice.

Instead of answering my question, he mimicked me in an effort to make me laugh. He could never just say, "I'm sorry." By now he should have known to shut the hell up since he was supposed to be coming back on the humble!

Pharaoh ran to pick up the phone as I stood by the door still holding Mauri and debating on whether or not to leave. "Here mommy, its for you." Pharaoh eagerly handed the phone to me. It was the next big thing next to the mixer. He had just learned how to dial my mother's number and I'd just started letting him answer when people called.

"Hello?"

Craig stared at me like I had a slab of tender, barbecued ribs hanging from my mouth.

"Hey, girl. I haven't heard from you in uh minute. What's up? You aright?" It was Sherra. I really needed to catch up on a lot of things with her but I knew I couldn't go into details like I wanted to right now. I never talked on the phone past two or three minutes around Craig. The one time I did talk to Sherra when he was home, he questioned everything I said and after I got off the phone with her he said she talked too much.

"Hey. Yeah, I'm on my way to church. Lemme call you back."

"Aright—wait. *You sure* you *okay*?" she inquired.

"Yeah. Bye." Sherra was my girl. She knew when something was up.

"Who was dat?" He didn't waste any time.

"I'm gonna be nice this time, since you're trying to go to church. But, I promise you Craig, if you get on my nerves one more time...and next time, check with me before you make plans that involve *me*. Tonight is not good as far as looking at the house goes."

"So you not gon' tell me who it was, hunh?" He mumbled something that sounded like, "*Prob'ly Darren punk ass,*" under his breath, picked up the phone off the charger and checked the caller I.D.

I took my jacket off and finished fixing the mash potatoes for dinner with Pharaoh's help while Craig called the real estate agent. My hands were shaky and unsteady. The tears were hot and heavy behind my eyes but I wasn't about to cry. I hated crying in front of people. It either made the person that pissed you off or hurt you happy or it made them fictitiously sympathetic.

"You still mad?" Craig asked like he was really concerned and sorry for saying that video shit although he probably wasn't going to apologize.

"Well, *yeahhh*! *Hello*? Us video hoes get like this sometimes. By the way, what's your favorite video?" I stared at my plate not even wanting to look at his face. My head was pounding. I bet he didn't care if Angela was a video *rat* when she was giving him head.

"I read books, I on't watch dat shit," he stated, rebuffing my comment while he fed Mauri a spoonful of mash potatoes. She was busy smearing food all over her face instead of eating. Every time he'd put a spoonful up to her mouth she'd grab the spoon with her hand and put the mash potatoes everywhere on her face except in her mouth.

"Huh. You used to... Stop that!" I snapped at her and him. "I don't have time to clean her up. In ten minutes we need to leave."

"Mama be mean, don't she? Mean, mean, mean," he said to Mauri shaking his head as she giggled and spit a mouthful back into her plate. The whole thing was like deja-vu. In a minute he was going to be spoiling her and ignoring Pharaoh again and leaving at eleven o'clock at night after another argument and probably hitting Angela back up!

"At no time do you spit your food out on your plate! You wanna whip-whip? 'Cause mommy will tear those legs up! You hear me? Don't let daddy get you into trouble. You still gotta deal with mommy when daddy's gone to work! Don't try me, Mauri," I shouted picking her up from the high chair.

"Leigh, stop!" he commanded, grabbing her right out of my arm as I went to the sink to grab something to clean her face with. He must have thought I was going for the spatula on the counter and about to spank her.

"Okay. Lets *not* go look at that house tonight! Pharaoh, put your jacket back on. It's time to go to bible study, sweetie. Craig, you and Ms. Mauri going or staying?" I'd gotten myself into the same old mess. It was like he had totally forgotten our discussions over that damn 'Makeup Weekend'.

"We all goin' ta church *an'* ta check-out da house." He said it like his word was bond.

As I entered church while Craig parked his car I felt the tension of my headache ease. First Lady was reading the second chapter of tonight's lesson. As usual she was sharp. Her naturally thick brown hair was pulled away from her buttery skin and made her look like a news anchor along with her fitted pink suit. She was always together; inadvertently, sisters in the congregation tried to copy her style. Being as pretty and classy and charismatic as she was, you'd think First Lady would be stuck up but she wasn't. She always acted humble and spoke to everyone after church and was forever inviting people over to their huge home in Rosedale Park for potlucks and get-togethers.

I looked around for somewhere to sit. It was kind of crowded tonight. Once I spotted what seemed like the only pew with a few seats left, I guided Pharaoh to the row and bumped past some visiting family of five's knees to our seats. See. This is why I hate being late. They didn't even try to scoot over and then Mauri was so whiney and sleepy she wouldn't let me put her down without causing a commotion. Just as I slid her back on my lap, Brother Bronson walked over to the side of the pew I was sitting at. "Hey Sister Anderson. Can you watch Hayley? I'm ushering tonight," he asked bringing his daughter from the restrooms downstairs. The smell of his cologne was absolutely intoxicating.

"Sure." I had to smile back at him. He had the type of face and body that could do something to a woman. Next to Craig, Nabari Bronson was one of the finest men I had ever seen in real life.

Something was definitely up with him and his wife, though. She and her acrylic toenails with ten different colors of paint and polish hadn't been at church for the last month. Everybody was saying they had separated. And I could understand why.

Brother Bronson was a reformed drug dealer. Three years ago he traded in his big time baller status for a relationship with the Lord. His light skinned wife reminded me of the type of 'high-class' ghetto girl that shopped at Northland Mall on a weekly basis, who'd wear tons of low budget jewelry draped around her neck—the kind of karats that looked more like droplets of gold and the kind of Al Wassam leather coats that had dollar bills drawn all over them—the kind of leather jackets Darren called Classless Hood Confetti and Eyesores. Every time I saw her she was wearing a new hairstyle and was chewing on a wad of gum real hard like it was her only meal for the day. It's a wonder she didn't pop the gum and make bubbles while the choir was singing.

At least four-year-old Hayley hadn't been ghettofied by her mother just yet. She was cute and well-mannered.

Suddenly, I found myself unable to stop staring at the darkest thing I had ever laid my eyes on. Silky smooth, razorbump-free skin, built like a football player, even with that scar on his face from where he had been stabbed back in his Menace to Society days, he was sexy.

Brother Bronson was standing in the middle of the aisle responding emotionally as though the verses from Psalms were lyrics while First Lady read. Why couldn't Craig trade in his worldly ways and become more Godly like Nabari? At twenty-six Craig still wasn't thinking about being saved.

Verses later I realized Craig was sitting next to me and ended my Craig-turned-Brother Bronson daydream. Pharaoh was sitting on his lap whispering way too loudly. "Ssh, sweetie." I tapped him. Hayley was sitting next to me like a perfect little angel, swinging her feet back and forth without making a peep. She was even holding a bible on her lap.

Craig yawned when I passed my bible over to share with him.

Brother Bronson and I should swap mates. I bet Craig would love Myesha--if he could get some of the hoochie out of her, I thought to myself. *Now that'd be a perfectly yoked couple.* She looked like she'd prefer to stay home and paint those talon-like fingernails of hers all day long instead of going to school or working--he could have the worldly housewife of his dreams if he didn't mind paying for a maid to do the housecleaning. Ten times out of ten she wasn't about to go near a mop--Brother Bronson was probably the one that did all the cleaning.

During tonight's testimonies, Brother Bronson talked about his past lifestyle, which was perfect timing. He didn't hold back and sounded self-convicted as he reminisced about how he used to have teenagers posted in crack houses for him. When he paused for a minute his eyes filled with tears until he overcame his emotions. My eyes started watering right along with his.

Me and Nabari together? We'd be like Pastor and First Lady. There was no doubt Brother Bronson would one day be starting his own ministry.

After closing prayer I felt so refreshed--church could be like that sometimes. I wasn't even worried about Craig's comment anymore. I wasn't going to let him or anything else get in the way of my blessings and the Lord's message. This right here was why I couldn't afford to be missing service.

"Thanks, Leigh." Brother Bronson took Hayley's hand.

"Oh, it was no problem. She was good." I smiled at her beaming face. "Nabari, let me introduce you to my fiancé, Craig." God forbid I ignore him. I wouldn't hear the end of for the rest of the night, tomorrow...the rest of the month.

"You aright tanight, man?" Brother Bronson asked holding out his hand.

Instead of shaking it, Craig just nodded his head upwards once like he was a nigga on the street and gave a quick, "Yeah" before turning his back to Brother Bronson and picking Mauri up.

A few seconds later Pastor came over and started a conversation with Craig. "I might check it out--hate ta rush but we got uh appointment," Craig replied to whatever it was Pastor had said.

Walking behind Craig on the way out I spoke to a few sisters in the congregation. He spotted Arnetta when we were at the double doors. "*Ba-Ba black goat, do your own woolly-ass wool. Stop making Leigh look like three hoochie-bags full!*" he sung loud enough for the group of sisters standing next to Arnetta to almost hear and then keeled over from laughing so hard he almost tripped as he walked down the front stairs of the church to the parking lot.

"*You* are getting on my muthafuckin' nerves! Take me home—I don't wanna go house hunting with you! Got me cursin' on God's property!" I shouted after locking my seatbelt. I couldn't believe him.

He mimicked me, once again in an overly proper voice. "Maybe it's the video hair?" he added busting into laughter.

"You look for that house by yourself! Gonna wind up by yourself—keep it up! Makin' me curse an' shit. You play too damn much. You don't take anything seriously—not even God."

"So what if you cuss once evry five years, you human, too. Nope, we goin' ta look at dat house together."

"You are *soooo* disrespectful! Look at the way you basically snubbed Pastor—"

"--Pastor? We 'bouta set da record straight on yo' beloved Pastor. If I ain't come ta church wit chu, he'd be all up in yo' draws. He always be findin' uh reason ta be huggin' on you all tight an' shit—you thank I 'on't be noticin'?

"What he need ta do is write anotha one uh dem books. Only, 'stead of dis one bein' 'bout uh Godly marriage fa all da single ladies up in dere waitin' on some new niggas ta join y'all church so dey can hurry up and git marry ta some bullshit ass saved nigga, he need ta make da next one, '*Pastor: the biggest Pimp in the Black community!*' Put some moe bread in his pockets." I was seething and he knew it but he just kept on talking. "Dat lady dat always be wearin' dem bright ass leather skirts wit dem flying saucer-lookin' hats—you know da one I'm talkin' 'bout. She be standin' up ten muthafuckin times evry sermon talkin' 'bout, 'Say it, say it Pastor' like da bible got crack in it an' shit--evrybody know he hittin' dat. But dey ain't gon' do shit 'cause he *Pastor*.

"An' whad about dat buildin' fund? Three years an' ya'll still tithin' money foe it? It ain't shit but anotha hustle ta keep dem Lincolns rollin' in. Thank about it, Leigh. Y'all 'on't even need anotha building.

"Know what *else* I peep? *You* wont me ta be like dat punk ass Bronson cat. He cain't even keep his wife in check an' you all *salivatin' at da mouth over him!* unless he on some game ass shit like yo' Pastor, he uh dumb ass muhfuka. He uh brotha dat's been out here—he should know whassup--*he* oughtta know bedder!"

"First of all. *You* oughtta be *afraid*. You talking about God's anointed! Brother Bronson is saved which is more than I can say for—"

"—Oh. Oh. You gon' take it dere? You gon' take it dere? You 'on't know shit about dat muhfuka! You ain't got no right comparin' me ta uh nigga you 'on't even know. I ain't neva said no shit like dat ta you—ain't *neva* said no shit ta yo' ass like dat! But I know why you like dat, dough.

"You *an'* dat bitch ain't shit but part uh da government's plan fa Black folks. Since da beginnin' uh colonization!

"Oh, God. Here we go! Everything is the White Man's fault!"

"When dem Europeans marched dey asses over ta Africa wit dey *Christian* bibles an' colonized an' enslaved kings an' queens, dey got 'em by teachin' dem all dey beliefs was wrong an' durin' slavery dey fucked us up! It was against da law fa uh slave ta have um drum, ta speak dey native tongue--all dat shit. But one uh da only thangs dey let dem git was uh muthafukin' bible. Dey European version of it--"

"—I'm not listening to anymore of this! Take me home! NOW!" I didn't know this person in the drivers seat.

"If you *believe* like you say you do, what I'm sayin' ain't gon' shake you up," he reasoned.

"Devil or Craig, which one do you prefer? Take me home! I *don't even want you stepping a foot in my house!*"

"Why 'on't you jus listen? See, dis part uh da problem! Lemme finish!" I put my fingers in my ears. "Who actin' childish nah?" he asked calmly. Like what he was saying was normal. "Dey gave slaves one day off fa da whole week. Sunday was fa church wit da one nigga dey let preach. An' dey monitored his ass ta make sure he was feedin' dem da propaganda dey colonists asses wonted da slaves ta git. Da bible was da worse kinda shit dey coulda gave us. Respect yo' master so you can go ta heaven. Take da whippin's, be uh good lil' nigga an' after you die you gon' git ta go ta heaven.

"Nah, I ain't sayin' da bible ain't real. All I'm sayin' is dat dey done changed it up so much an' polluted it. If you drinkin' uh cup uh juice wit one drop uh poison in it, is it still good fa you? Hell naw!

"Dey done' took da Egyptians version uh da bible an' ruined it ta dey benefit. I ain't never heard yo' Pastor talk about none uh dat. Dey still got us fooled Willie Lynch style. All *I'm* sayin' is da church is powerful in da Black community. Preachers oughtta be using some uh dat power ta empower people uh color insteada smoothin' evrythang over wit talks uh heaven. We suffering now!

"Jews got money. Any foreigner dat comes ta America can git dey hands on money, mansions an' what da fuck ever dey wont *but, Black folks suffering! Ain't nobody gon' help us get no legitimate shit. Da only way foe uh nigga ta make it ta da top fast is fa him ta do some shit dats gon' have his ass up in da pen doin' time, livin' like uh animal!*

"You need ta be more of uh critical thinker--'specially since you uh Black mother, baby. Start lookin' past what somebody put in front uh you, Leigh. You smart ass hell an' I love you. But chu real naïve."

"Why do you even bother going ta church with me then, *Satan*?"

"I'ma let dat shit slide since you couldn't take dat hair joke...I go 'cause uh you. Like I said, I love you. You inta church an' one uh da many things I admire 'bout chu is dat you got morals. Uh whole lodda females lack dat.

"You want me to go, so I go. An' dat Bronson cat *ain't* getting' ma woman," he stated plainly.

I tried to speak, to shout back but it felt like straw was stuffed down my throat.

"Baby. I ain't tryin' ta scare you. If you did some research you wouldn't be callin' me Satan. You godda lodda potential. When you do yo' research, you'll see what I'm talkin' 'bout. I do thangs I don't necessarily wont ta do 'cause I love you. Unconditionally. We not always gon' agree on evrythang but I *do* believe in God, if dat's what you wonderin'--you know dat." He must have been reading my mind. I couldn't believe any of this. I wished I could go back to seven o'clock in the morning when Craig was just Craig. Not this anti-Christ person now trying to hold my hand. "Hey. Look. Why 'on't we try goin' ta uh few uh dose Afrocentric services 'round da city. Dere's one right up da street on Second. Unity or sumen like dat. Maybe we'll find uh church we both—"

"--*Hell no!* Take me to my muthafuckin' apartment! I've been going to Greater Mount Zion since I was ten. Heathen!" I pushed Craig's hand away as he tried to touch my arm and punched him so hard I heard Pharaoh gasp. Craig's cheek was as pink as Mauri's and his nostrils were flared.

Suddenly I realized we were still in the parking lot. "Go! Drive!" I shouted not wanting anybody to see us getting into it. Good thing the side windows were tinted.

He didn't budge. Everything in me wanted to punch him again. It felt good. I wanted to turn his head into a shovel and slam it against the ground again and again. Wait. That wasn't cool. That was *really* not cool.

"Gimme dem directions out da glove compartment." He finally said something. I went ahead and grabbed the papers not wanting the night to get any worse that it had. We drove onto the Lodge freeway and almost the whole ride to the house in complete, intolerable silence. "Which way I turn on James Cousin?" I didn't utter a word. He snatched the computer printouts from my lap and started reading them as he drove up onto the exit ramp.

"Cra*aiii*g! Stop! Are you trying to kill us?"

"Well, read da directions, den."

I snatched them off his lap. "Keep straight until we get to Outer Drive. Then follow the curve. The address is 15999. It's supposed to be two blocks after Seven Mile on the corner."

He parked in front of the two-story colonial brick house. "It's dark. That's cool. We need ta git uh glimpse of da neighborhood at nighttime...corner house...basement, attic... Damn, it's October an' dey still got flowers out? I guess 'cause da weather still nice. You know you gon' have ta keep 'em up, right?" He lightly tapped my arm.

"How *you* figure? Like I already told you, you *might end up* buying this house for yourself…"

"You know you love me. You love me more dan you love yo'self. Bedsides, you keep up da flowers 'round da apartment building so I know you gon' hook our crib up…Pharaoh, you like da house?"

"Yeah."

"Don't ask him shit," I muttered under my breath. "As late as it is these kids should be sleeping already," I added more audibly.

"You be havin' 'em out later dan dis when you be at church…"

"…Where *is* the lady anyway?"

"Chill, baby."

"Now, see. If Scott was our agent, I bet *he woulda* been on time!"

"Whad? You gotta crush on him or sumthen?"

"What? You gotta a crush on *this* lady who's *still* not here or something? You're so ridiculous Craig, I swear!"

"*Daang*, swearin'? Video hair really doing uh number on you, hunh?"

"Like I said, you play too much and you think everything is funny… Can't be serious about anything."

"Maybe you don't play enough…"

"…Let's go. She's not here--that's it."

"Call dat number I wrote on da bottom uh dat print-out."

"Here, you call. You picked her."

"Whas da number?" he asked as I handed him my phone.

"She had uh flat. She said she tried ta call uh few times but you musta had da phone turnt off," he said after a few okay's and alright's with the agent. "We gon' meet her at six tamorrow after I git off work."

"Can't. I've got the meeting for the Annual Woman's Day Conference. Or did you forget, *Satan!*"

"Den we uh perfect match, Video Girl. We gon' go look at da house after yo' meetin'."

"It's a sign. We don't need to get this house."

"Scared 'cause da address add up ta six?" Craig asked chuckling. That very second, Craig looked like a yellow florescent-eyed demon. The shadow of the right side of his face became wolverine gray and squished all together. I closed my eyes and prayed for enough strength not to grab the kids and jump out of the car although it seemed like a much safer bet. "You scared fa real 'cause I said dat? Look Leigh, les stop dis shit right nah. I'm tryin' ta git uh house fa ma fam'ly. Dis lady at work said Linda hooked her up wit uh good deal—evrybody at work be usin' her. I love you, baby. I ain't tryin' ta hurt cho' feelings.

"You know how many women would love ta be in yo' shoes? Half dese niggas out here ain't got enough credit ta start thinkin' 'bout uh house... Ain't I been going ta church wit chu like I said I was gon' do?" He turned my face towards him. "My bad, baby. I'ma be more respectful uh yo' beliefs." He kissed me on the forehead. "Promise me one thing," he added.

Not again. The last time I promised something it ended up being that damn tattoo. "What?"

"Dat you gon' read dese three books I'ma show you when we git ta da crib."

"...Depends." No more promises for Mr. Walker. First thing tomorrow morning I was calling First Lady for some biblical guidance on this situation.

CHAPTER 8

"SISTER ANDERSON YOU SAID you and Craig are about to get married and I applaud you. You been saved for some time now and you know y'all can't be living together without being joined in marriage by God. Nah, Craig is about to be your husband—but really he already is 'cause if you're sleeping with him, in the Lord's eyes, you are married! You're gonna have to work on listening to him as the head of your household a lot more—no matter how hard it might be. And I know it's hard! It's like the devil puts you thru a *tryin'* test jus so you *won't* want to be in subjection to your man. But the bible says that you are supposed to win him over without a word and you're getting there. This *is not* the time to throw in the towel. He *does* come to service. A good example is Brother Bronson. Jus like he said in his testimony yesterday, he used to run from God. Now look at him—he's a warrior for the Lord! Maybe we can get him to talk to Craig." Ha! After his whole Brother Bronson hateration speech that idea was out. "Both of you should come to pre-marital counseling. Read those scriptures I gave you today, do the prayer for a peaceful household and a blessed marriage--don't wait. God's gonna put that Holy Spirit to work. And you've got to put *all your* trust in Jesus. God says he won't give us more than we can bear--amen! I'm gonna to pray for you. Aright?"

"Yeah," I sighed. I wanted to tell her that I flat out did *not* want to marry an unbeliever but it was pointless. I guess I should have thought long and hard before letting Satan move back in! According to her I had already signed a contract the first time we had sex. I was positive he wouldn't be down for pre-marital counseling.

Wait. That could be my out! I could make an ultimatum. If he didn't go to the counseling sessions, as I was sure he wouldn't, I was going to put him out—this time for good.

Then again, *was* that what I really wanted? Maybe I was just afraid of the unfamiliar? I'd always considered myself to be open-minded but I certainly wasn't prepared for all that anti-Christian sounding crap that came out of his mouth last night. It was becoming even more scarily apparent to me that you could live with someone for years and still not know so many things about them.

When he talked about Black issues, I always listened. He was well read and always had his nose in The New York Times, the Free Press and BBC online regularly. He watched CNN as much as he watched ESPN. I loved that about him. I hadn't met too many brothas that could match Craig's level of intellectualism.

ANY REASONING IN HIS favor was erased as the clock continued getting later and later with Craig still not back from work.

Earlier when I talked to him he insisted I wait for him to come home before leaving for the meeting. Supposedly the excuse was so we could view the house today without any confusion since he rescheduled with the agent. All that was unnecessary—probably just a stunt of his to keep me from going to church tonight. We had two cars and it wasn't like he was gonna offer to keep the kids while I was at church. Ever since he started this new job, he needed rest after a "long, hard day of work." Hard work? Please. He didn't do a fourth of what I did in one day!

I thought about all the times sticking out in my memory like an elephant's ass of his inconsiderations of my schedule and things I had to do. It was enough to make me want to attack him when he stepped in the door. Bump what First Lady said, all this understanding headship hadn't gotten me anywhere. I was becoming way too nice, always sacrificing and never appreciated. I bet if I treated him like shit he wouldn't dare walk all over me.

"Baby! I'm glad you waited—"

"--I don't wanna hear it! I seriously *do not* want to hear it! I'm sitting here on the couch, kids are dressed, my car is out front. But instead of being on my way to the meeting, I'm up here growing more and more nervous since *I'm* the one planning the songs for the choir and scheduling the slots for the speakers! In ten minutes the last meeting for planning the Woman's Day Conference'll be starting--without me! I'm never late anywhere unless you're involved. You *don't operate on colored people time* for General Motors! You might as well stay here and keep the kids. I'm too through with you, Craig!"

He had the nerve to lift me off the couch and try to kiss me!

"Ssssh! Baby, I know, I'm late but wait—"

"—No. Keep the kids I'm out—"

"—Dat's straight but hold up uh minute!" He whispered something to Pharaoh and Mauri. For a few seconds they stood behind Craig and were unusually quiet. He nodded his head at Pharaoh who pushed the button on the stereo. D'Angelo's song "Lady" came on and everything else became a blur that ended with three huge round diamonds sitting pretty on a gold band on my left ring finger.

"I'ma be payin' uh long time for it but, you worth it, baby. You mean da world ta me, Leigh. I ain't ever lettin' you go."

"We have to go to pre-marital counseling. First Lady and Pastor conduct it on Saturdays," I wailed between tears.

"Aright. It's whatever you wont, baby--oh, yeah. Look. You said you wanted it. I got it taday, on ma lunch break." He lifted the arm of his sweater and revealed a huge tattoo on his left upper bicep--my name in calligraphy encased by a chain that curved into a heart with a lock on the side. Underneath it was Pharaoh's name on one side of the heart and Mauri's name on the other next to the lock.

"Put dis on fa me." He pulled me close for a kiss and handed me a tube of A & D ointment.

"For a minute I thought you were trying to piss me off on purpose so I *wouldn't* want to marry you!" I said laughing as I rubbed the salve on his muscle. My eyes were still blurry with tears.

"I know it ain't gon' always be easy. Hey, you ain't always easy ta deal wit, either since you wanna act like you 'on't know but, I got mad unconditional love fa you an' you done already showed me you got ma back. Dere ain't nobody else on dis earth fa me. Nobody. I love you, baby an' I'ma try ta stop pissin' you off so much—I mean dat. But I still wont chu ta read dem books...I made you uh appointment ta git yo' tattoo done Saturday mornin'. Oh, yeah, I cancelled our appointment tanight fa da house. We can do it on Friday. I 'on't want you to be stressed da next time you go ta pick out cho' future home. If it's as nice on da inside as it look outside, it ain't gon' stay on da market dat long—'specially at dat price but, if it's meant fa us, we'll git it." I had to trace Craig's face with my fingers just to make sure it wasn't some figment of my imagination.

I threw my fur poncho in my arm rushing to get in the car so I could call everyone up and tell them the news. Wait until First Lady saw the ring...this wasn't anything but prayer in action! *Thank you, Lord!*

"Um, baby. You need ta do sumthen 'bout dat shirt. Yo' nipples poppin' straight thru. Put another one 'foe you leave. I 'on't want nobody lookin' at my shit," Craig said after carefully glancing me over.

Hey, he was my man and he had just *finalized* the deal. I didn't have any problem doing that for him. I put on a pink Victoria Secret's bra that was padded and a sweater to make sure the erasers weren't poking out even though, outside of Pastor, none of the brothers would be there tonight.

I was so excited, I drove like a maniac and couldn't stop talking about how beautiful my ring was and the kind of wedding I wanted.

All of them were more than ecstatic. Sherra offered to take me out to lunch the next day so we could catch up on everything. My mother wanted to have an engagement party but I declined since we would be having a bridal shower anyway. And Tamika, *crazy Tamika,* wanted to celebrate by going to a new club that was opening on Friday night--of course, I declined. I reminded her that I already had what people were going to the club looking for so she offered to keep the kids on the weekend so we could have more alone time instead, which was nice.

When I entered the conference room in the basement, it was only a matter of seconds before all the Sister's eyes widened in shock as I stood at the podium and adjusted the microphone. The room buzzed with 'How, Where and When did he do it?' questions.

"I got a feeling Sister Anderson is gonna have a testimony at the conference." First Lady smiled. "God *is working* with *you*! How do you feel about filling in a six-minute slot on the program? Yesterday morning you were distraught and now look! You're livin' proof of His glory!" she exclaimed blasting my personal business for sixty women's open ears to soak up.

"Ah--I don't know. I mean, it happened so fast...maybe at one of the services-*maybe*." I laughed nervously. My stomach flipped at the very thought. I wasn't about to divulge *any* of my personal business *anytime* soon. God was still working with me *and* Craig. We weren't ready to have any sort of out-in-the-open testimony. We were more like a Mauri Povich talk show at the current time--we had just moved on up past our the Jerry Springer episodes.

"God gon' bless you wit anotha girl 'bout four years from nah', amen! *Amen!*" one of the older Saints prophesized walking up to me prior to speaking in tongues. Well, that was good. I guess Craig *was* going to stick to his promise and not try to get me pregnant again until I finished my bachelors in nursing. Sister Jones God-given visions of past and future hadn't gotten one bad rep yet.

"Let *me* see da ring," Mt. Zion's biggest gossip started without any real enthusiasm. I shouldn't have placed my hand in hers for her to examine but I did. "Oh," her voice dropped with disappointment. "Ma cousin had one like dis. Helzberg got it marked down ta only fourteen hund'it dollars on dey Inventory Buster page in da catalog. I'm not inta gold. Platinum look bedder *and* cost more. ...How long ya'll been tagetha?"

"A few years." I answered allowing Kaneeka to catch me off guard.

"How old is he?" Her malicious eyes darted back and forth from my hand to my face.

"Ah, he's a little older than me."

"What he do?"

"What? Oh, um, he works for GM."

"He bought cho' SUV?"

"...We both have cars. And we're blessed to be in love. And I'm happy," I rushed, trying to stop this deliberate interview that was only going to come back to haunt me in the near future. It was a sure bet that Kineeka was going to tell her gossip committee all the information I had stupidly volunteered so they could find a hundred things wrong with me and Craig. Well. They might be more lenient on him since he *was* a man.

I stood there smiling and pretending she hadn't fazed me. I knew her type well. All the chicks in her clique were just as unhappy with their lives as she was. They made themselves feel better by finding something wrong with anybody that seemed to have more than them or anyone that seemed to be somewhat happy.

I couldn't remember a time she'd *ever* brought a man to service with her. Whenever a new guy came to a service, you could count on her being all over him, offering to fix him a dinner like a desperate, egg-withering spinster. She wasn't ugly even though she put me in the mindset of a piglet. The big turnoff was the way she proudly lugged her heavy, bleak cloud around, always complaining about how terrible her life was because she was given up for adoption even though she was now in her mid twenties.

Now, if I would have told her about him cheating on me, she probably would've invited me out with the other Miserable's for a roundtable of depression and despair. And after I left, they'd all discuss how dumb I was for the rest of the night as they laughed their miserable hearts away in the happiness they attained laughing at someone else's demise.

By the end of the meeting, I wasn't feeling the Woman's Day Conference anymore. Had I known it would be like this, I wouldn't have signed up to help in the first place let alone accepted the responsibility of being the event coordinator.

Everyone felt *they* should have gotten the female part of the duet the choir director had given me. No one wanted to come early to assist in the set up. I had to practically beg the younger Sisters to help pick up women at the domestic violence shelter that the church ministered to. The keynote speaker was in the hospital with pneumonia, meaning I would have to find another speaker on short notice that was credible.

All the single Sisters had something to say about how to treat a man while the married Sisters sat quietly.

Before the meeting was even over, I came to the conclusion that, with the exception of some of the older sisters, we could've sat here and talked about being uplifting, Godly women seeking to do the Lord's will until our the hairs on all our heads lit gray fires but they'd still be the same talking behind your back, 'if I don't have it why should *you*?' 'I'm so desperate, I'm gon' try to git cho' man,' type of hoochies they were before the conference.

So much for doing God's will in the community. They couldn't even get it together in the church basement.

My official engagement day was supposed to be my time to revel in happiness but the weight of this surrounding negativity was bringing me down real quick. I didn't even want to be on the committee anymore. I was actually thinking about not even going if I could find a way to back out. I didn't have time for this kind of mess but I had already committed to doing it. I couldn't let Pastor and First Lady down.

"Hey, Sister Anderson. How's it going?" Pastor came out of nowhere as I rushed up the basement steps to leave. His arms were outreached for a hug as he stood in the empty, dimly lit stairway.

"Hey Pastor." I sighed. "I don't know. This women's conference is stressing me out." Hopefully, if I talked long enough, he'd forget about the hug. Craig's comment was making me extra leery.

"God's blessed you with the ability to withstand the dynamics of interpersonal relationships. It's gonna be alright. But how have you been outside of the Woman's Day craziness?"

"Well, we'll see how well I handle the dynamics of all *these* personalities," I laughed nervously and added, "I'm engaged." I lifted my hand and showed him the three-carat ring.

Within seconds he had me locked in a suffocating embrace. "You're going to make *a wonderful wife*. You're as beautiful inside as you are on the outside," he added in a bass filled whisper. This didn't feel right. Even with the poncho on, he pressed me against him so tightly, my breasts were pinned up against his chest and something was poking into my lower stomach. His hand lightly fondled my behind while the hardness of his penis grazed the top of my skirt.

I jerked away in repulsion. Pastor's eyebrows furrowed like he was surprised. "You okay, Leigh?" he asked innocently.

"Yeah..." I couldn't look at him. Something about his eyes looked so debased, like a predator eagerly awaiting his prey.

"Well? You wanna step into the office? You seem a bit distracted. They upset you *that* much at the meeting tonight?"

One thing I truly hated about myself was that I was blinded to a fault when it came to those I loved or admired. I had a hard time believing anything less than the best about the people I cared about, even when they were clearly wrong.

Since Craig felt Pastor was friendly beyond what his role as a man of God called for--especially since he was married--this was the perfect time to find out. For real, no ifs ands or buts.

I had been a member of this church way too long to just jump to a conclusion based on an assumption. Pastor even helped me get my job as apartment manager. So, to make sure I wasn't simply being paranoid because of Craig, I was going to take him up on his offer to talk.

"Sure. Maybe you can help. Oh, *and* I would like to start a premarital counseling session." I smiled, hoping to cover up my anxiety.

"Alright." He put a wandering hand on my back leading me into his office past the empty auditorium and closed the door. No one saw us go inside.

Pastor pulled the chair next to the bookshelf and scooted it close to the side of his desk instead of sitting behind the desk.

"Oh, just a second—I have a call coming in." I faked so I could make sure my phone was still on. I put the ringer on silent and left it in the top part of my purse for easy access in case I needed it.

"Leigh, you're a beautiful person, inside and out. Don't let anyone stress you out. Not here, not anywhere. You can handle planning this event. That's why I chose you to be the coordinator. You've dealt with so much already, you're strong and *umph...*" *He* was the one that wanted me to be Coordinator? First Lady plainly stated that she thought I was a perfect candidate when she saw my name on the volunteer committee sheet. And how did he know whether or not I had been thru a lot? If God had given him a vision about me, he should just said so instead of making an open-ended statement. I never told him or First Lady about my brief separation from Craig. Today was the first time I'd ever told her *anything* about our relationship.

My eyes traveled around the office to take inventory. I had been in here a million times but at this very moment it felt like it was the first time I'd stepped inside. Everything looked expensive from the grand leather furniture, to the plush carpet and the Lalique crystal paperweights.

Three degrees: Moody Theology school in Chicago. A bachelor's from Wayne State in business and a masters from Wayne in Social Work with a concentration in counseling graced the walls.

There were at least three pictures of him alone, one of First Lady and him posing together and one of her by herself. All her buttery, good-girled smiles looked stiff and fake the more I stared at them. Her smiles were the exact opposite of the genuine-looking one she'd given me tonight when she asked me to give a testimony.

There were no pictures of the two foster kids Jermaine and Taylor they'd taken in for over two years now and planned to adopt yet there were a couple of professionally taken pictures of their biological daughter Monica blown up and placed along the walls.

"You have to remember. Jesus didn't have it easy dealing with the many personalities of his apostles, either. I know some of those Sisters are gonna give you a hard time. But push past that, you're much more mature than most of them...."

141

My eyes rested on the shiny, expensive-looking chain with clear diamonds set in the huge cross. It was too big to completely hide under the collar of his immaculately clean white button down shirt.

He was going on and on talking, it was time to cut to the chase and get the freak up outta dodge. "Yeah. Well, we really need another keynote speaker. Any suggestions?"

"I could bring in Linda Johnson. She's a counselor at Devine Enlightenment and she's starting a radio show that'll be aired on Sunday nights. Just last week we talked about having you on there sometime soon. You know I *had* to tell her about you..." He spoke deliberate and slowly. Then, without warning, paused abruptly.

"That might be a good option. I'd like to tackle the topic of Sisterhood. Everybody preaches about Brotherhood but rarely does anyone give a sermon on the complex issues of Sisterhood. The lack of Sisterhood within our communities needs to be resolved. Black women need to be more conscious of the negativity thrown at us on a regular basis. We're constantly absorbing it without even knowing that that's what we're doing which is why I personally believe we end up attacking each other instead of working together." I was starting to sound like Craig. Add to that the fact that I was getting more nervous by the second. I always talked fast when I got nervous.

He smirked. There was a strange, forbidden longing in his eyes as he cruised across my chest and leg regions. I was wearing a skirt that cut across the top of my knees when I sat down and at that moment I wished Craig would have insisted I'd worn pants. This man I now sat in front of didn't at all seem like the Pastor I knew.

"Do you think she could use that as a theme. Maybe—maybe you could call her? Maybe you could find out? You think she's available now? Right now?"

"Now, see. *Thas* what I'm talkin' about...all that zeal, on fire for the Lord! Umph, umph, umph." If my legs would have turned into eyes, then I would be getting a hell of a lot of eye contact from him.

"The speaker's taken care of. As far as the few disgruntled choir members, don't worry about that either. I told Brother Gray that the part was solely for you. No one else can top your soprano musical tone and ability." He leaned in closer from his chair towards me. "Nobody," that bass filled whisper returned.

"Okay. Thanks. You've been a tremendous help." I jumped up out of the chair ready to leave.

"Ah, Leigh? About the pre-marital counseling? I'd like to talk to you about that."

"Ah, I'll make sure I talk to First Lady about that tomorrow. It's getting late. I'd better be getting home. The kids are—"

"—Sure, sure, sure. It won't take long. Have a seat. You have an innate love fa God and you know your place as a woman under God's arrangement—many women with *years* on you still don't understand the concept. You know…you're very, *very attractive*, Leigh and a natural leader, therefore, you shouldn't yoke yourself to a man that is NOT SAVED!" He went from cool, calm and a possible Seducer-Wanna Be', to Angry Preacher Man in nanoseconds.

"You need a good provider *as well as* a Godly man. I asked Craig about his future plans last night. All the education in the world won't make up for an apathetic heart towards the Lord Jesus! God showed me that his heart is *like stone*. There *is* a chance for God to work with him. But you don't deserve to wait around for that day to come. I've watched him. He's still got a lodda growing up to do. He's not even a baby in the eyes of the Lord yet and he's nowhere close to trying to cultivate a relationship with Jesus."

He grabbed my chin. For a second, because of the way his mouth abruptly smacked open and the way he rubbed his tongue against his top front teeth as he paused, I thought he was going to try to kiss me. "Leigh, you deserve better. Reconsider marrying him. Let me show you how a real man would treat a woman like you." His hand dropped from my face to underneath my fur overcoat as he unzipped the front of his slacks and ran his hands over my breasts like he was testing grapefruits at a grocery store. "There's nothing to worry about--the door's locked." He touched my chest again, this time like they were knobs.

That straw was stuck in my throat again. I was so heated I could feel my feet sweat as my blood blazed in Mars-like fire. All the words that wanted to come out were parched. "He is my man, my fiancé and, with all due respect, Pastor, we love each other and *do* intend on getting married. I think it's best we seek pre-marital counseling elsewhere." I found my voice after what was way too long of a pause with him still touching me and turned around ready to jet out of the room.

"Wait." He placed his hand on my shoulder while zipping his pants back up with his right hand. "Sweetheart, you're misunderstanding what I'm trying to say. I *am* willing to counsel you both. But when God gives me a message, I can't ignore it." I felt the weight of his hand grow heavy upon my shoulder. Did he really think I was dumb enough to stand here and continue talking to him after his *Will She Let Me Do it?* test failed.

I looked him dead in the eyes. "No. *That* would be a mistake. You don't believe in us or in our union. You've known me for twelve years--

maybe your feelings are tainted because of that. But God hasn't given up on Craig and neither have I. He may not be saved by *your* church's standards but that doesn't make him any less of the man for *me*. I have to go. My family is waiting for me. You're corrupt. Repent before your ass goes to hell," I stated it without shouting or stammering or sounding like the scared little girl I felt inside. As my legs wobbled away I felt like my one year old was much more fearless than her own mother was right about now.

He walked toward the door holding my hand in his. "I really care about you, Leigh. I didn't mean to offend you. He simply is *not the man* for you. His inner man is not receptive to the Lord Jesus. He doesn't even claim Jesus as *Lord*! That message is from God--not me. You can't be mad with God. Promise me you won't hold what I've said against me as your Pastor or the church. I expect to see you here, Sunday aright?"

All I could do was look straight ahead as my teeth clenched shut. Was he deaf? Was he slow? A learning disorder muthafucka? "Go to hell," I said shocking myself more than him.

God helped me make it to the parking lot.

As I pressed the button to unlock the car, I felt a glare strong enough to burn thru the fur poncho and sear my back. When I turned around, as dark as it was, I could still see her.

Sister Thomas, the 'flying saucer hat, bright leather skirt, possibly sleeping with Pastor' woman Craig talked about yesterday stood shadowy and fuzzy within the ten o'clock fall night three parking spaces away. I was positive she hadn't attended the conference meeting.

The streetlights revealed the bitter glassiness in her eyes. Had this been a movie, she'd be holding a butcher knife and walking towards me for a stabbing bloodbath right there in the lot. If Pastor hadn't locked the church doors, he might be going straight to hell tonight with her help, the way she was looking.

She had to be hurting down deep inside. I was tempted to drive over and ask if she was okay but I wasn't stupid. Her gaze said everything. Besides, the best I could do in the event of combat was the tiny bottle of mace on my key chain.

Even though she had an asymmetrical bob that went from the top of her left ear to her chin on the right side of her face and was definitely stuck in an early eighties fashion faux pas, I felt bad for her and even worse for First Lady.

Pastor and First Lady had been high school sweethearts and he had openly admitted she'd taken more than her fair share of heartache from him until he finally gave himself over to God. What a lie. He was obviously still that same cheating football player only older and with a church he was masquerading in front of like he was holy.

When would First Lady's heartache end? How could she just deal with this, like it was nothing, like it was as easy as drinking a cool glass of water? Or were women just supposed to ignore this kind of behavior?

Umh, umh, umh. Whoever coined the phrase, "If it's not one thing, it's another" never lied.

I stuck my keys in the ignition and pulled off the parking lot stealing a peripheral glance of her standing lifeless yet watching. She shook her head as I passed. It all seemed so surreal, her standing there like the scorned ghost of someone who'd been dealt with treacherously. I wonder how long she'd known the Pastor--if she had been with him before he even married First Lady or something. Something about the whole thing wasn't adding up. She'd been coming to the church for as long as I could remember but she never came to any of the events. She was quiet and kept to herself; she only came on Sundays and left right after the sermon. And she never came to bible study or anything else First Lady held.

For some reason, I felt like they'd grown up together. Maybe the Pastor was her first kiss, first everything…then he got with the captain of cheerleading squad, First Lady…but he kept seeing her…on the side…

Five minutes of trying not to think about anything that involved that Pastor passed and I was still shaking and swerving on 94. I pulled off the freeway and parked near a small playground, to think and clear my mind.

I had just gotten engaged and told my *Pastor* to go to hell--all in the same day!

The Pastor was worse than Craig. How could he consider himself a man of God if he was doing an Elijah Muhammad on his congregation-- hooking up with as many sisters in his ministry as he could? Why *me* of all people? Why *anybody* other than First Lady? She was absolutely gorgeous. *And* educated.

How could he do her like that? I'd looked up to him. He had been like a surrogate father to me. Why was First Lady giving anybody advice when her own situation was so messed up?

She'd given a sermon counseling wives to keep themselves up for their husbands. She even had an annual beautification seminar with Mary Kay cosmetics and masseurs and stylists to help the Sisters learn how to give their husbands massages and to teach them how to apply makeup. And as pretty and as Godly as she was, her shit still wasn't together *and* her man professed to be a man of God! This was the exact reason I usually never talked to anyone past Debra about my business. Debra's life wasn't perfect but at least she was real about hers.

Hopefully the kids or Craig would be waking me up within seconds and I'd realize this had all been a real, real bad dream—save the engagement part.

Memories of crowded church summer picnic's at Rouge Park with any kind of fried chicken you could possibly want—crunchy, spicey, barbequey, roasted, sweet n' sour, homemade strawberry lemonade, First Lady's baked macaroni and cheese everybody and they mama waited the whole summer for; the aesthetically red, blue and purple stained glass windows I marveled at each and every time I came to church; the youth activities the church organized--like the partnership they had with The Boys and Girls Club; volunteering for the domestic violence shelters and relief services; getting so *live* during choir practice that I felt lifted off my feet by the Holy Ghost and the heady feeling I got each time I stood with the other members of the choir and sung for open hearts and for the Lord to hear; the numerous wedding receptions in the basement where everyone pitched in to help cook dishes for the bride and groom 'cause they couldn't afford caterers, the older Sisters' seven-up pound cakes that never had icing on 'em but still tasted good--none of it could erase the debased and violated emotions seeping into the core of my very being when that Pastor had the audacity to think I'd be ready and willing to get down and dirty with him at church--like it was an honor.

Every time I asked myself if I was absolutely and positively *sure* he was trying to get with me or if I was overreacting, I cursed myself out again and again for being stupid enough to even think about rethinking what had just happened.

Honestly, I didn't want to think about it anymore.

I reached over to the dashboard, turned the heat up and closed my eyes as faces and memories flashed like a slideshow.

Almost thirteen years of being saved; Revivals that lasted all night and pulled everybody in from off the streets under the tent; community service events; biblestudies; prayer night every Tuesday at six; years of waiting to get my spot—*my* spot in the choir; Sister So and So; Brother Known Him All My Life; Little Used to Be An Ugly Baby But then He turned Handsome; the two older sisters who were more like my aunts, Sister Neilson and Sister Dewy that had gone to the church for as long as I could remember and would always give me good but unsolicited advice and bible counsel that was always on time; RayRay, Paul, Tylil—the whole crew I'd grown up with and considered family... I still remember like it was only an hour ago how they'd popped up out of nowhere and beat down the scrawny thug wannabe who had tried to rob me and Sherra when we were leaving a club on the Eastside four years ago; Marcus the dwarf who'd always ask me to dance with him at bridal showers before I hooked up with Craig; nicknaming RayRay 'Knot Head' after that house party at Therese's when he slid straight down the stairs and glided onto the basement dance floor and no one could help him up for laughing so hard even though he was angry and embarrass and his back was all scratched up from the steps; being filled with pride when the church participated in television syndicated programs at the Hart Plaza Gospel Festivals and *showed out*; buying Mary Kay each time another Sister joined and harassed me to help me "help" myself by "looking" my best; seeing who wore what every Sunday; smelling Brother Bronson's cologne and knowing when Sister Watson and Sister Henderson entered the restroom even when I was in a stall by the smell of their perfumes that reminded me of some kind of weird mix of laundry detergent, metal and roses; men with smooth heads and silky 360 waves thanks to Murray's orange tub of wax; taking all the grandmothers of the church to Old Country Buffet since it was every old lady's favorite spot to complain that the food wasn't as good as their own home cookin' and having to endure watching Sister Littleton take her teeth out each and every time without fail right there at the restaurant table; having bible spelling bee's for the kids; the plays we coordinated and held at The Masonic Theater; and my all time favorite: performing downtown, off the water at Chene Park during the summer choir concert--nothing could beat our urban contemporary star-quality performances.

Other than being a mother, a sort of wife and a student, they had been my life.

...The foundation that formed my complete moral structure, all the memories that once colored and flavored my world with the kind of comfort that comes from routine, the good and bad memories and convenient familiarity--all of it, all of it had been wiped away in less than one hour like a safety net torn to pieces.

I couldn't go back.

If this was one of those mental phrase games, it would be:

Fire is to house what Pastor is to Leigh Anderson.

But I still trusted God and whatever it was He had in store for me. No one—not even a faulty Pastor could take my Savior away from me.

CHAPTER 9

"MA'AM! MA'AM? YOU OKAY?" A policeman banged on my window with a stereotypical long nineteen sixties looking flashlight in his hand that he was currently using to shine directly in my eyes. The clock on the car stereo read five-sixteen in broken digital sticks.

I cracked my window. "Y—yes," I sputtered rubbing the crust out of my eyes.

"What are you doing out this late ma'am?"

"I'm so—I'm so sorry."

"Look. I don't know what your problem is but you need to get home! This is not a place for a young lady to be sittin' around this time of night. I could write you a ticket for loitering but I'm gonna be nice since ya' got ya' bible on ya' lap. Don't try this again—especially not in this neighborhood." He got back in the car with his partner and waited for me to pull off following me until I drove onto the freeway ramp.

"WHERE DA HELL YO' *ass* been *all night*? I said where da *FUCK* you *been*?" Craig stood in the hallway shouting without giving me a chance to answer. I hadn't even made it to the apartment door. "Alla uh sudden you 'on't know how ta answer yo' goddamn phone?!?" He snatched my purse out of my hand, threw it into the living room spilling everything in it onto the hardwood floor and slammed the door in my face leaving me locked out of the apartment and standing in the hallway.

I stood at the door for a few seconds tempted to knock for him to let me in before sliding into a corner next to the door and squatting on the floor. The way I was stooping made my feet start tingling from the heels I had on.

Half an hour later, right after a loud crash, the door flung open. "What da fuck wrong wit cho' ass, hungh?" He smacked the left side of the temple of my forehead so fast I didn't see it coming. White sparks started flashing in front of me. "Git cho' ass in here." He grabbed my arm, pushed me onto the couch and sat directly in front of me on the coffee table. "I cain't even look at chu right nah," he admitted turning his head towards the dining room. My palm pilot was laying in a pool of broken glass next to the curio.

I got up and walked to the door. "I'm not in the mood for all of this right now. I was falling asleep on the road so I pulled over. The next thing I know, the police are—"

"How da fuck you sound? You fell asleep! Don't feed me dat bul*shid*! Give yo' ass uh ring an' you forgit ha ta find yo' way home at night! You ain't even have da decency ta call! What da fuck is really goin' on? You bedda start talkin'!"

"—Craig, please! I know, I know but I can't do this right now! Please!" I leaned against the door. I couldn't even be mad at him, I wouldn't have believed me either. He sneered back at me with a half smile, half laugh. But this time when he tried to shove my head, I caught his wrist mid-air. "Try to hit me one more time and the dead wagon'll be here to haul your ass out. I've been thru enough as it is. I'm not going to school today, I don't feel like talking and I'm especially not in the mood to argue. Either I can stay here and talk to you after I go to sleep or I can leave." I picked my keys up off the floor, stepped back to the door and stared him down.

"Man, do what chu do, I 'ont even give uh fuck." He walked away shaking his head and breathing extra hard.

"I promise I'll tell you everything, I just don't wanna talk right now." I picked my purse up from the floor. It looked like Craig had called every number in my contact list and the display was cracked. My palm pilot looked like someone had stomped it to pieces and the side panel of glass on the curio was completely shattered.

I got in bed fully dressed, poncho, shoes, nasty breath and all. Craig came in the room and stood in the doorway with scornful, menacing eyes filled with disgust before he slammed the door.

I called Tamika the minute he left. "Hey, girl. I know it's a lil' bit earlier than you planned on but I need to know if you can keep the kids for me later on today? Just until five?"

"Yeah, girl. On one condition…"

"What?"

"You an' Craig don't make no more uh dem thangs taday!" She busted out laughing. "I'm just playin.' *Shid*, if I had uh man dat fine I'uh have me 'bout eleven uh 'em by nah—and you know I 'on't like no kids 'xcept Pharaoh an' Mauri," she added.

I called my mother after Tamika hung up.

"Hey, mom. I'm not bringing the kids over this evening."

"Ok…everything all right?"

"With me and Craig? Yeah."

"What chu mean '*wit you and Craig,*' something wrong wit my babies?"

"No, no it's nothing like that. All right. I'll call you a little later. Bye, mom."

"…You rushin' me off the phone, nah?"

"No, mother."

"All right. Call me back when you get a chance. Craig called here last night...um-humph, you godda a good one...bedda not loose 'em wit some foolish ungodliness..." She hung up.

"WHERE WAS *YOU* AT las night?" Tamika asked picking up Mauri who was excited to get away from me.

"*Whaat?*"

"Pharaoh, close yo' ears--I thought I was the only one smoked 'round here." She laughed. "Craig called me yestaday *tra*-rippin' 'round two uh clock in tha mornin'. Wha'*chu been* up to?" She laughed again. "But fa real girl, if I was you, I wouldn't be steppin' on out on no man like Craig—an' dis coming from *mmey*. Shid, when we rolled ta dat concert las year up at Comerica Park, he had dem White girls *and* dem foreign chicks *all up in his grill*! I thought you and me wuz gon' havta fight!" This time a cough followed her laugh. She sounded like a good case of emphysema.

I ignored her comment but I couldn't ignore her purpled lips. Her gums were black and her teeth had a sunny yellow cast to them. She look didn't look like anything nice at all.

Back in the day she was the "pretty" one with the light skin and the fine, long hair that everyone made a big fuss about whenever mom took us anywhere. Now her shape was starting to make her look like she was Sponge Bob's sister. And the way she had her hair pulled back in twists she had obviously done herself made her face look wider, square and hard. Her neck had even disappeared. She was becoming the classic example of my Overly Cute Kid, Unattractive Adult theory.

Wait, I was being mean. She *had* been there for me when I was pregnant with Pharaoh and Mauri and she was the only cousin I dealt with out of all the rest of the crazies in my family. Besides, Mauri was considered adorable and I didn't want to jinx my own child with negative thoughts about T. I needed to talk to her and find out what was going on in her life. But not right now.

"Let me stop. I can tell you need some rest, lemme go'on girl. We'll talk later. You gon' have ta fill uh sister in, dough. YouknowhadImean?"

"Whatever T. There's nothing *to* fill in."

When she finally left, I got back in bed and rolled those twenty-six minutes spent in his office over and over in my head like a scene on repeat. Every time, just like earlier, I got a ghastly feeling in my stomach and the same answer every time I asked myself if I was overreacting or jumping to conclusions.

It was well into the afternoon when I finally fell asleep. The phone rang four times in a row, like the caller was trying to let me know they knew I was at home ignoring their call. "Hello, *Sherra*." She could hear the annoyance in my voice.

"Hey. Whas up wit chu? Craig called me last night lookin' for you. I couldn't tell if he was mad or worried or *what*. You okay?"

"*Girrrllrl!* We need to talk!"

"I know!"

"I'm sleeping right now. Lemme call you back, though."

"*Allrright,* bye."

"Bye."

Two seconds later the phone rung again. "H*hhello*w." I sounded like a tired game show host.

"Leigh, you sure you aright?" Whenever Sherra used my name, it was serious.

"...Girl...why did Pastor try to hit on me? Craig's been sayin' he's been trying to hook up with me for a while."

"Umh." She remained quiet and waited for me to get down to the details. I told her everything from A to Z all the way back to when Craig got his dick sucked by Quagmire Mouth, our make up session, the anti-Christ in him, to the police knocking on my SUV window. "*Whew*, girl! *The devil is alive!* At times he makes it hard ta even *believe* in tha Lord. But, I think you and Craig'll be alright. Sometimes it takes something bad to happen before dese guys nowadays get da message and stop actin' crazy. Ya'll should go ta another church," she offered an hour later. "But dese guys out here ain't no good! I 'on't even think I wanna get married anymore. If I do, it'uh be uh miracle. I want uh man that's spiritual fa real. Too many of dese brothas out here be fakin'. The same thing happened to Belinda at her church. But look at what Jesus went thru! And he was perfect. We *ain't* perfect so you *know* we gon' have some haters and some tribulations ta deal wit before we get ta heaven. You wanna go out dis weekend? I get off work early on Friday?"

"I'll have to see what Craig has up first. We can go for lunch next week, though," I offered.

"Aright. Next Tuesday uh'll be fine for me. But I think you need to tell him what happened," Sherra advised.

"Yeah, I will when he gets home. Lemme call Tamika to see if she can keep the kids until tomorrow. I don't know how he's gonna act when I tell him. If she can't, I need to ask my mom and--girl! She's gonna be all up in the business."

"Well, I can keep 'em if you need me to—"

"—Good! I don't want to get her involved unless absolutely necessary!"

"I *know*...she gon' probably curse yo' Pastor out. But you *really* think Craig gon' trip *like that*?"

"Girl, these days who knows! I *know* he doesn't believe I fell asleep in the car. Knowing him, he's probably gonna try to check me *and* my panties."

"If you can't get them Friday evening, I'll get 'em from Tamika's. That way, you 'ont have ta worry 'bout pickin' 'em up 'til you feel better. Dina'll be here, she can watch 'em while I'm gone. You know she ain't got uh job yet and why mama ain't saying nothin'? But let that be me!"

"I know! Alright, let me give you her address and lemme get off this phone and tell her you're coming. This uh'll give me time to straighten things out. Thanks, girl."

"Unh-huh. I haven't seen my lil' Pharaoh in a *long time* and I know everybody needs a break sometimes."

After we ended our conversation I felt relieved. If I couldn't talk to Sherra, who could I talk to?

Craig entered the apartment and ignored me as I sat crying on the couch watching *Light The Red Lantern*, an Asian movie that was airing on the Canadian station. This probably wasn't a good time for me to be watching anything dealing with male chauvinism and misogyny but for some reason I couldn't stop watching it.

It was almost three in the morning. He slammed the bedroom door shut--my cue to sleep on the couch.

THE NEXT MORNING HE shook his head in disdain and silently scoffed at the pancake, sausage, turkey-bacon, hashbrowns I had shredded and the orange juice I had just squeezed. "Craig, you were right about Pastor. Last night he tried to get me to do something with him!" I blurted out jumping in front of the door before he left. He moved swiftly like a stiff soldier to the back door in the kitchen and tried to leave but I blocked him by putting my body between him and the door. "Craig! Stop being like this," I pleaded handing him a makeshift english muffin breakfast sandwich I'd made for him to take with him. "You were right!" I shouted.

"Wha'chu do?" His face was stern but unreadable.

"I wish I wouldn'ta worn that skirt!I wish I woulda listened to you the first time you said it!He's been telling First Lady to give me solo parts!He doesn't think I should marry you!He's doing something with that Eighties Hat Lady and she looked like she was gonna straight up stab me— on the-the-the um-the parking lot!He touched my—my breasts, my butt— and then he pulled out his his you know If he thought I would've slept with him, he woulda tried and--" Right there, right then, after the whiny rant, I started busted into tears. I was petrified.

"Slow down, baby. I cain't understan' wha'chu sayin'. What did dat muthafukin' Pastor try ta do ta you?" His face remained placid but his voice changed.

"Pastor...he tried to have sex with me! I—I—talked to him, left--then some police came and knocked on my window. I...I was sleeping in the truck at that park off 94 and-and--" I buried my face in his leather jacket. "You were right!" I repeated over and over pounding my fist against his arm, talking so fast I couldn't breathe. I finished relaying the story as best I could muffled in his chest.

"Calm down, baby. I godda git ta work. When I git off, I'ma go over dere an' beat his ass." He didn't yell. He didn't shout. But there was a squinty, far off look in his eyes as he cracked his knuckles and then rubbed his goatee back and forth.

"No! There has to be another way to handle it! Has to be! Twelve years...twelve years!" I shook my head adamantly still gasping for air.

"FUCK THAT! I'ma confront dat muthafuka--point blank! An' we *ain't ever steppin' back in up dat bitch*! Mt. Zion, my muthafuckin' ass! I'ma call an' check on you later. Git some rest. Nobody! Nobody gon' fuck wit'chu an' git away with it! Nobody!" The lion taunted in his own jungle took the sandwich out of my hand and slammed the door behind him. It was smushed. I should have made him another one.

I called him over and over again at work trying to convince him not to go over there. The bottom line was if I tried to stop him he'd think I was lying and had actually fucked the pastor.

THREE HOURS AND TWENTY-EIGHT minutes later than it would have normally taken Craig to get home from work, I got a call. "Baby! I need you ta come down to the seventh precinct."

"What? Where?"

"Thirty-three hundred Mack. Bring seven hundred dollars," he stated matter-of-factly.

"What *happened*?"

"I can't git inta alla dat nah! I godda git ta work tamorrow! Hurry up!" The phone went dead.

Thank God Sherra had the kids.

I thought he was going to accuse me of actually sleeping with Pastor or Brother Bronson or Darren--*somebody*! But not this.

On the way to the precinct, I tried to pray. I really did. But each time either the pastor's face popped up and erased everything in my head or I started feel guilty like I'd actually done something with that pastor. I kept wishing I wouldn't have tested him. I should have left instead of stepping a foot in that office.

Was God going to make me pay for tempting a man of God? What about the kids? I wanted both of them to grow up in church. What if this whole thing messed up their relationships with God? I didn't want Pharaoh growing up being a player just because society dictated that young men—especially young black men--were supposed to carry on like pimps, mistreating women and I certainly didn't want him out there catching all kinds of STD's. I wanted him to be spiritual, grounded and happy. How was I going to explain to him why we weren't going to church anymore? We went three times a week.

And Mauri, Lord, what was going to happen to her? Already Sherra had called and told me that the fresh scar on my little girl's forehead was due to her sudden burning desire to climb up the stove while dinner was being fixed--even after getting spanked twice for previous attempts. Mauri was to the point where I wouldn't recommend her to anybody! Not to get pregnant with a Mauri, not to baby-sit, nothing involving having something like *my* Mauri! How was she going to be later on down the road if I quit going to church? Would she turn into a butchy lesbian? Detroit was starting to have a much larger population of gays and she was pretty tough acting already. Just getting her in a dress was hard. Her little muscles would get prepared to fight when I came towards her with anything that looked like a dress. How was I gonna to be able to thwart some shit like that? On the flip side, what if she turned into the type of chick that lived off her looks and was at the mercy of some man and waited on him to pay her bills because she didn't study in school and didn't have grades good enough for college? If she did, what would happen once she got older? What if she got traded in and dumped at thirty-something and was stuck the rest of her life? She already knew how to smile and play that innocent damsel in distress role when she didn't get her way with Craig or Pharaoh and it always worked. Or maybe she'd turn into a criminal.

That was it! I was going to have to find another church.

Before I got out of the car I switched the radio from the gospel station on AM to 98 FM and took the Ce Ce Winans CD out of the player and shoved it in the glove compartment so Craig wouldn't spot it.

The police station was gray and tan and dingy and reeked of Lysol. The balding, red-faced officers at the front desk treated me like I was Black trash and I was embarrassed. Here my man was in jail all because he had tried to defend me after *I* set the whole stupid plan up in the first place!

"Dat muthafuka was uh straight up bitch," Craig stated calmly in the truck once he was released. "He wuddn't let me in his office 'til dat Bruh Louis nigga came up dere. Den da bitch gon' try ta use da bible 'gainst evrythang I said, like I was stupid an' couldn't peep his game wit his whole holy act. He was tryin' ta front like you was makin' shit up. But I could see right thru his ass--he kept dat lil' muthafukin' smile on his face da whole time.

"So I grabbed da bitch an' choked da shit out 'im—evrythang so funny, right? I got in uh good coupla blows—got 'im in his eye an' in dat cotton stuffed jaw uh his--his nose was bleedin' like uh muhfuka! He couldn't swing back on me—I was too fast on 'im. So, dis nigga git so mad, he gon' say I wudden't good 'nuff ta marry you an' dat I put'chu up ta sayin' some shit on 'im! You bedda be glad I ain't git uh hold uh D-Man fa dat gun he was s'possed ta come thru wit fa me! Dey wudda been puttin' dat muhfuka under da ground in uh coupla days!"

"Craig! A gun?"

"I ain't studder. Hell, yeah! I'm yo' man, Leigh. I'm s'posed ta protect'chu no matter what. Whatever I godda do ta protect my family, I'ma do! Ain't nobody gon' make no hoe outta ma woman! Not *again*!"

"Not *again*? He never tried anything until last night."

"Wha'chu talkin' 'bout?"

"You said *not again*."

"What?"

"Never mind…"

"…I knew where dat muhfuka was comin' from from day one. Da look in his eyes was guiltier dan uh muhfuka… Then, he gon' try ta prove he got clout—he gon' call up one uh dem officers dat be up at y'all services and--"

"--Sister Newton? Sister *Newton*!" Oh God, my mother was definitely going to find out. Hopefully I'd have a chance to tell her first!

"Yeah. Dat's her name…but Leigh, next time--you godda use yo' head. You *need* ta start listenin' ta me. Uh lodda da time when I tell you shit, it be fa yo' own good. None uh dis woulda happened if you woulda jus listened. Nah I godda worry 'bout ma job findin' out…

"I think I can git Lorraina ta let it slide if dey start checkin' inta ma shit an' find out… I might git put back on probation, dough." He sighed. "But when you said it, I believed you. You wuddn't lie on some shit like dat—'specially not on yo' preacher. Why ain't chu call me when he started dat shit?"

"I don't know. I was planning to. But everything happened so weird and…I guess I thought I could handle it myself." I busted into tears.

"Come here." He held me until I stopped crying. "You think you gon' be able ta drive?"

I nodded my head yes and wiped my face with the back of my hand. "Hey, don't turn right dere—we godda git my car… You know…it's some gaps in yo' story…"

"What? I told you! After he tried all that, I got in the car. I was shaking so bad I couldn't drive—I couldn't even think. Then I pulled over at that park—right on—well, off—I don't remember the street but it's off 94. I was tired and—and. Craig. I'm not making any of this up!"

"...Whenever you feel like it, I wanna know da whole story."

"Okay. Tonight..."

I hadn't even done him like this when *he* cheated but God forbid I bring that up! The first thing out of his mouth would have been "We s'posed ta be leavin' da pas alone." We were supposed to be "movin' foeward." He didn't like me to bring up shit he did wrong. But he did have the right to know what happened--he *had* just gone to jail because of this shit.

"Baby?"

"Yeah?" He pulled me on top of him in the bed once we got home.

"I feel so confused. There's like—all these questions. How could he be like that and still be a preacher? ...Maybe religion isn't representative of God. I don't understand it."

"It's good you breakin' evrything down like dat. But, as far as First Lady go. You 'on't really know what done went down wit dem. Maybe she got her own bedroom in da house or some shit. Fa all you know, it could be like uh business partnership or sumthen. Maybe she be kickin' it with Bronson on da low. You 'ont neva know what uh muhfuka capable of. But you way moe Godly dan dey asses—dat's fa sho'."

"I wish none of this would have happened."

"Don't chu think it's bedder ta know dan ta be hoodwinked?"

"...I guess." I was lying. No. Not when you had to find out by basically being molested.

"Ignorance ain't bliss, baby."

"I can't even see myself going to another church. But, at the same time, I feel like I need to go *somewhere* but... I just don't know if I can do it. Not right now."

"Why you godda step up in somebody's church in order ta feel like you got God? Da bible say God see all an' He in alla us—he made us in his image, right? Fuck dat. Jus give yo'self time--you'uh be aright. You got *me*, baby." As he fell asleep, I stared at the white ceiling and silently asked the plaster the same questions again and again waiting for answers that were taking way too long to show up.

Fuck a fiery furnace of Gehenna. Fuck a hell below. Life right here on earth was hell. For real.

THE NEXT DAY THE stream of calls started.

First it was my mother and grandmother on three-way. Both of them were furious and wanted an explanation for all the gossip and talk that was spreading like HIV.

"Holy Spirit tellin' me ya' *lyin'*! You was probably out doin' something else—prob'ly wit uh third baby daddy! You already got two kids *wit'out doing it tha Lord's way! An embarrassment and uh disappointment! I ain't raise you no eighteen years fa you ta turn inta no Jezebel!"*

"You only put Passa in it ta cover up fa whatever you was out dere in da streets doin'! Whatever happened, you took it da wrong way! Dat's uh man uh God you lyin' on! You ain't gon' git away wit no mess like dat!" Grandmother was making her attack as well. "Passa say Craig came up ta da church tryin' ta shoot him an' whatnot! Nah, I thank you need ta git on yo' knees an' beg da Lord fa mercy. You done messed ova *two men*! I had liked Craig up ta nah but Passa say he thank Craig done corrupted chu."

"I think it's her--out in tha streets all night like uh *hussy*! Then she couldn't come up wit uh story good enough ta cover ha ass so she had tha nerve ta lie on Passa! And I *don't* think they need ta get married neitha! She need ta get it together wit God first! Otherwise she ain't gon' do nothing but mess over Craig."

"Um-hmm, prob'ly right, Vee," grandma agreed.

"Passa called me and *told* me to talk to you. He said he was just trying ta help you coordinate everything for the Woman's Day Conference. Then you asked about marital counseling. And you left.

"Nah what chu did was dirty. *Real* dirty. He been lookin' after you like you was one uh his own fa years! Even braggin' on you up in tha choir—'bout how you sing.

"I 'on't have nothin' else ta say ta you but this: don't be messin' up them kids wit cho' unholy ways. I raised you ta be better than this. I'm ashamed. I 'ont wont no parts of this mess you up here doin'." They hung up. The dial tone was as long and sharp as the pains in my heart.

I turned the house phone ringer and the voicemail off which was pointless; the congregation members wanted answers and they wanted to make sure I heard their condemning messages. The ones that had my cell number called and left messages since they couldn't get thru on the house phone. Some said they would pray for the demons possessing Craig. Others asked if he was on drugs and reminded me that there were programs for those kinds of problems. There were those that begged me to rebuke my lie and ask for forgiveness and then there were the ones who'd come to the conclusion that I had been trying to get with Pastor all along and, since he hadn't gone for it, I was now trying to destroy him and his reputation. Nobody cared to hear my side of the story—not even my mother or grandmother. I had slapped God in the face after all the blessings he had bestowed upon me, everybody said.

"You need God! But you bedda find Him somewhere else!" Sister Watkins shouted in her message.

When Kineeka and her crew clapped on the message they left I started wishing I had the type of voicemail that let you erase a message without having to play the whole thing first. I was fake and it was about time Kineeka's gang said. That seemed to be the popular consensus. All the Greater Mount Zion members who called seemed to be applauding my long awaited downfall.

There were tons of "I told you so's, She wasn't all she was cracked up ta be, She made Craig attack Passa--he was too nice ta act like dat wit'out uh reason! An' she *claimin'* she saved!" said loud enough in the background of the voicemail messages to be audible.

Somebody even said "She gon' roast in hell like uh ham hock fa sho'!" It sounded like Sister Hickman.

It was crazy. If it wasn't for the fact that it was happening and I was witnessing it for myself *I* wouldn't have believed any of it!

DEACON FARSTON AND THE ever-effeminate Demetrius Gray, the choir director, came over to "talk" to me while Craig was at work. Before they came over they called twice and asked if Craig would be home. Before they stepped inside, they asked, again, if Craig was here and looked around before finally sitting down.

Brother Farston's squinty, jaded and loathing eyes did nothing to conceal his contempt for me while Brother Gray shook his head and talked to me the way people talk to a person that's mentally retarded or psychotic or a danger to society.

"You're ruining relationships, Leigh." Brother Farston was glancing at me sideways. "You used to *beg* to be a part of the choir..." After that I couldn't hear anything else. Everything went blank.

I shouldn't have let them come over. Craig would have killed me if he knew I let them in.

Beg?

Please believe: I hadn't begged fa shit! I had *wanted* to use my God-given talent to praise Him. And that's what I did. Beg Demetrius? Heeeeeeeeeeeel no! No sir-ee.

"You need to decide if you really want to be a part of Mt. Zion. With just one unsound decision, you can loose everything you fought so hard to get and ruin your entire life. A lie is not worth your family's salvation. I'm tryin' ta do you a favor. But I still need to tell you. I don't think what you've done is right." He paused resting his right hand under his chin and continued staring at me sideways. Looked like he was about to suggest I be admitted into a mental facility for dementia and hallucinations involving his Pastor.

From day one I had never liked Deacon Farston. I always thought he looked like a Smurf. He had an odd brown, ashy potato skin coloring, his nose curved like a bird's beak and he had a raspy voice that was uneasy on the ears. People like him who had the worst kinds of voices, they were always the ones that liked to talk too much.

And another thing about him, he had the weirdest nervous habit of zipping and unzipping his book bag during service. Every five minutes or so, he'd be bent over that old ass, worn out book bag of his, unzipping it, only to zip it back up again five minutes later. What he needed to do was go get *that* checked out instead of making a house call to try to check somebody.

And I had heard he was having an affair with a married sister at the church—Sister Clementine with the Big Behind. But he was on his high horse kicking me. I was already on the ground—why not?

Church or no church, Godly or evil, this was a world that demonized women. Pastor was the man so of course they were going to have his back.

I let Farston talk himself to death.

"You need to evaluate yourself, Leigh..." Brother Gray stated before getting up to leave. He opened his mouth and sighed long and hard. When he reached for the doorknob he hesitated then used his sleeve to open it.

Before this he had been one of my favorite people. Before being saved, he was a R & B recording artist. He *made* the choir and took his job seriously and made sure every one in the choir could sing—correction—could *sang*! If you sounded like a horse, or couldn't understand the concept of cadences and breathing techniques, there was no room for you in *his* choir. Although it made a few non-singing members uncomfortable, he put Mt. Zion on the map. We didn't sound like some of those old-school choirs that turned a lot of younger people off. We were up there with the best of the latest, urban contemporary gospel artists. There had even been talks about recording in a studio.

Before all this mess had happened, having a soprano range that was capable of hitting notes only Mariah Carey attempted and with my own, one of a kind soulful voice, I was good for singing the lead parts for at least three songs on the album—the Pastor had said so himself. That was the type of thing that could've gone farther. Might as well say sayonara to that one now.

AS IF WHAT I was going thru wasn't enough, when I was out and about, members didn't even *try* to whisper when I bumped into them. I started wearing the big seventies-eighties looking sunglasses—the ones that covered half your face for better or worse and were all the fashion rage and made humans look like ants on a close up lens. I had a pair in almost every color. But I was still an easy mark. Everywhere I went, the post office, Farmer Jack, Meijers, the mall, I always ended up running into someone from Mt. Zion. It was like I was the hood version of an infamous female villain; a Black Lorena Bobbitt, Heidi Fleisch, Anna Nicole Smith or something.

People are so stupid. They just believe everything they hear without even thinking there might be another side of the story; seems like people want to believe the worse about someone. No wonder the paparazzi make so much money.

THE NEXT DAY WHEN I went to get barbeque at the carry out place on Livernois for dinner so Craig would have something to eat when he came home from work, I spotted Sister Margaret and Sister Flowers inside sitting on the bench adjacent to the window.

I tried to wait in the truck for them to come out but they were taking too long to leave so I finally went in and stood in line to place an order. I didn't want Craig trippin' if he came home and there wasn't anything to eat.

Sister Flowers and Sister Margaret started talking extra loud right in front of the eight people waiting in line ahead of me. "*Girrrll*, she *ca-ra*-zay. You know what she did, right?" Sister Margaret started and the four people working behind the counter ears became wide open.

"*Ummm*-hum—"

"--Don't speak it! *Pray on it!* Pray on it!" The way Sister Margaret shook her head and flailed her arms violently made her look even more like a light brown monkey. She had a hanging bottom lip that always held juicy wads of spit and when she spoke, the spit popped out of her mouth like a human waterfall. Black moles covered her face like freckles and she could faithfully be found wearing a starchy, long, Wal-Mart skirt with flowers all over it.

"Help dat *Jeeee*-zus! Dat's Babylon The Great! Right dare in da flesh!" Sister Flowers chimed in frantically rocking the Frenchroll sitting on the back of her head every which way. Church talk had the power to turn a Black person into a scriptural drunk.

"*Lawwwdd*, tell me 'bout it! Dese young thangs so trifling nowadays, you cain't even try ta git 'em ta da Lawd. Dey too busy tryin' ta get money out dese po' men!"

"*Um-hum*. Dat's whud she was after, see, but da devil *IS* alive!"

"Speak it girl. She already got one dey say payin' her up da creek wit'out uh paddle from fornication already--dat's how she got dat truck! And she don't work uh lick! Naw, ungh-uh. Just set 'round da house all day waitin on uh man dat ain't even her huusssband in Lawd Jeezus' eye!"

They avoided eye contact with me as if I was capable of turning them into a pillar of salt like Lot's wife and shook their heads in disdain.

A guy with an uncomfortable to look at lazy eye, in a black hairnet with orangey brown barbeque stains all over his uniform looked me over with his good eye and shook his head. I couldn't even blame him. If two older, seemingly nice, grandmotherly kind of Christian women had all that to say, it had to be true, right?

"Me? I'm sho' glad dey gave LaNeetra *ha spot* in da choir. Now that's uh *Hooly-Hollly* young lady. She go ta Lewis College uh Business, too, um-hmm." Sister Flowers smiled, touting her face in the air.

LaNeetra was the one girl I couldn't stand. She had this irritating way of pointing her finger in the air after every other word when she sung and she had a penchant for throwing the fact that she didn't have any children in my face every chance she got. She would say shit like, "I'm saving myself for my husband, unlike *some young women* dese days," and toss fake smiles my way after her rude ass remarks. She'd been wanting to replace me in the choir for the longest.

Well. She finally got her wish.

"*Ummm-hm. Yeaaas, Lawd.* An' she got da voice of an angel--*voice of uh angel*, I say! God don't make no mistakes!"

"Say it! Say it! I'm fixin' dat seven up cake for her reception, *ummmhumph.* She sho' is glad she got dat part. Shoulda got it long time ago if ya' ask me. Some praise is s*ho'* in or*du*h!"

So, basically, they were having a party, celebrating the fact that I was ousted out of the choir *and the church*? Only a month ago I was their "favorite" young Sister.

I walked out leaving my order and money behind.

The thing about it was that Sister Margaret--even though she was now around fifty-five-- had five sons all by different fathers. None of them remotely resembled the other. And Sister Flowers...way back in the day was a heroine addict. Her daughter had been taken from her and placed in foster care. Twenty-some years later, her daughter still refused to have anything to do with her. Sister Flowers was always at church crying about her daughter not speaking to her and falling out over it whenever there was a sermon on forgiving oneself for past transgressions.

As far as I was concerned, they didn't have a right to say *shit* about my situation.

ON FOX 2 LAST week, a woman who'd been having a ten year affair with a well-known preacher from a church on the westside came out with a tell-all story that went into how she and the preacher had had threesomes that mostly involved other men and how he'd made her have four abortions from the time she was sixteen. A lot of Detroiters were upset about it. "His wife is lovely, he's got kids, he's a good preacher and his plays be tha bomb—why's she airing all her dirty laundry!" they said on TV and around town. "She shouldn'ta been layin' up wit 'im!" Preacher Davis was popular for his gospel plays that ran at the Masonic Temple every year for as long as I could remember.

Everybody thought she was a traitor since she had helped the TV station's *Problem Solvers* reveal Preacher Davis's criminal history record and, with her cooperation, they were able to do an expose' with supporting evidence proving he was swindling money from his faithful flock with claims of Holy Water from Israel and actors that faked healing testaments.

She was on the Problem Solver again this week talking about the death threats she'd received.

All of this was making me nervous. Already people were calling and shouting bible scriptures either in my ear or on the voicemail. And when I flipped to Ellington's Sunday show on channel thirty-eight he was giving a sermon about a Jezebel from Babylon the Great who'd tried to infiltrate God's flock. The way he described this young, attractive thing with a beautiful singing voice, I knew he was alluding to me. His speech was convincing—even I would have thought he was innocent. I had to turn it off so I could remember what *really* happened.

But it was that black Cadillac with the tinted windows that pulled up faithfully every night at nine o'clock the entire week that worried me.

I got the feeling it had something to do with the small section on the Greater Mt. Zion's Woman's Conference in The Detroit News I'd gotten Sherra to cover. Sherra was majoring in journalism and minoring in women's studies at Wayne State and she'd gotten a job as a clerk for the women's issues section of the paper.

Craig said Ellington was no doubt trying to make sure he didn't get 'put out on front-street' like Preacher Davis.

THEN THE HARDEST CALL finally came.

"Why would you accuse my husband of such a vile act, Leigh? Did Craig force you to do it? We have loved you and treated you like family for twelve years, Leigh! Twelve years! Why would you make an accusation like that?"

First Lady didn't want an answer, this was just protocol. And even if she really did, there was no way I could give her the answer she wanted to hear. We both already knew the real deal; her fake smiles knew the truth. But pretense, ignorance, and oblivion are so much easier to befriend when reality wears thorns.

"Well, I hope you and your family the best," she stated ending the conversation. That was my last time ever speaking to her. No matter how badly I wanted to there was no way I could ever again step foot into my favorite place to be on Sundays, Tuesday and sometimes Friday nights. I was now an outcast.

My mother also stopped speaking to me. She didn't even call and ask to speak to "That Baby King," as she called Pharaoh. Grandmother would answer whenever I called her but she wouldn't say anything so I finally just quit calling. Used to be every Sunday before church she called while she was cooking breakfast.

I had let everybody down. I was supposed to be a good girl--the kind that smiled syrupy and thick; the kind that knew how to keep sticky secrets long and quiet.

They say words don't really hurt, that they don't really matter. That only sticks and stones can break our bones. But words are powerful. If they weren't books wouldn't matter, saying and hearing "I Love You" wouldn't be a big deal, there wouldn't be any such thing as a dictionary because whether you said "Ugly" or "Sky" neither word would have a meaning...

Words might not break your bones but, in certain instances, they can certainly break your spirit.

The teacher tells us in kindergarten the color is red, and, it is therefore understood to forever be the name of the color.

They believed me to be the thing now satanic and clearly evil and now, so did I.

For hours every day I'd wonder if I had overreacted, if I *was* in fact crazy and should have just shut the hell up.

I decided to punish myself. I fasted for a week and a half, didn't go window-shopping, didn't watch T.V. and I prayed for two-hours, three times a day.

I still hadn't picked up the kids from Sherra and Dina's house. I was glad they were keeping them. I could barely make it thru the dreadful, non-ending, twenty-four hours each day and I had gotten so weak from fasting and barely drinking water, I fainted two times in one week, both times I was in the tub. I remember everything slowly fading into golden black smoke and not being able to hear anything. Craig found me one time and handed me a glass of water once I regained consciousness. He wasn't the crying sensitive type but when he'd found me like that he looked like he was about to cry.

The second time, I woke up and almost dialed 911 but changed my mind. Who had time to sit in an emergency room? Probably would have ran into more church mafia there anyway. I drunk some water from the tub faucet and eventually gained enough strength to crawl back in bed and just laid there. I couldn't go back to sleep.

CHAPTER 10

CRAIG WAS VERY UNDERSTANDING. He postponed the house-hunting thing. He didn't complain when I listened to old choir tapes and sermons or when I started leaving the television on a channel that aired sermons from various churches all day. He didn't mutter his usual, "Das some fake-ass shit," "Aw, here da hypocrites go again, 'Jee-uz an' da Nazerith put gas in ma car'--dumb ass muhfuckas!" comments under his breath like he usually did. He didn't mock the choir in his usual irritating, chirpy imitations. He didn't pester me for sex and he didn't threaten to jack off in front of me since I wasn't up to giving him any. He'd even quit pressing me to read those Afrocentric books he had suggested…

But when I decided to take him up on the Afrocentric services he'd mentioned a little while ago, he balked at the very idea. "You jus got out some shit, nah you wanna go back ta somebody tellin' you how you s'posed ta live yo' life? You gon' have ta be moe strong-minded Leigh! All dese fake ass muhfuka's don't need ta be holdin' dis much weight in yo' life.

"Dey done showed you dey true colors. All'uh 'em gon' have ta check deyselves—includin' yo' mama. If she don't, her loss. She uh victim uh mind control, too. Bible thumpers some uh da worst lame-assed bitches out here!" He let out an exasperated sigh as he pulled his car in front of the house we were about to walk thru.

"I had read sumen in uh psychology book 'bout shit like dis. When you leave uh extreme belief like what you was jus caught up in, you godda be careful what chu jump into next. You godda find da middle ground, baby, otherwise you gon' end up joinin' uh cult or sumthen. Take some time out ta figure shit out, den, go on from dere. You been wit dat church fa half yo' life. What chu rushin' inta some moe bullshit fa?" He lightly caressed my knee. "We need ta pick up da kids tonight. I know you ain't feelin' up to it but dey *our* kids. I ain't cool wit cho' girl like dat fa her ta be keepin' ma kids. At least when dey was wit Tamika, she *was* family—an' I know who she is. Da kids ain't gon' even know whas goin' on anyway. I on't want dem thankin' dey abandoned an' shit."

I sunk deeper into the passenger's seat as we drove to look at this stupid ass house we were supposed to look at two weeks ago. "Giving it time" was definitely not going to make me feel better and "giving it time" wasn't going to help me prevent Mauri from being a lost soul before she turned two!

Craig's eyes softened when he looked at me. "Come on baby, les go look at da house. She waitin' on us…I'm tryin' ta git cho' mind off dis shit."

The round faced middle-aged Mexican-looking, African American woman leaned against her white Benz and bestowed a fake smile our way. Just the way she impatiently raked her French manicured fingers thru that shoulder length, back combed mushroom hairdo of hers that was dyed light brown screamed, *hurry up and get your asses outta that car and into this house so you can put a cool ten-thousand in my pocket!*

Fuck her and her time. I hadn't been to one single class in almost two weeks, I'd wasted five hours at Arnetta's and sixty dollars plus three more hours taking all that weave out of my head so I could re-do it because I'd started wondering if that hairdo had been the green light that had made Ellington come on to me--he hadn't tried anything like that *before* I got my hair done like that and Craig *had said* it made me look like a hoochie.

Add to that the fact that I was operating on the four hours of sleep from the night I slept on the couch when Craig came in late and I was watching *Light the Red Lantern* and the two catnaps from the times my body shut down from exhaustion.

Right now it felt like some cruel, opposing force was chopping my life into tiny pieces waiting to see how I'd put it all back together.

Looking at a house was the last thing on my mind. The first time we were supposed to look at it, it didn't work out. She was the one that had the flat tire but we had to call her--even though *she* was the one that was going to be making money off *us*!

This house was out. No if's ands or buts about it. There was no way I could be happy here. We could just stay in the apartment for a few more months. We'd been living there all this time anyway. "Craig, let's look at the house objectively okay, sweetie. It's only the first one. I'm sure there are a lot of other ones we need to check out, k?"

Craig leaned over to give me a kiss. "Baby. We makin' dis dacision tagether. If you not down, ain't no signatures goin' down... I know dis week been crazy fa you." His eyes held that same soft look that had captured me in the first place. "In uh minute, we gon' be able ta put all dis shit behind us an' chill in our new crib. We ain't gon' have shit ta worry 'bout 'cept uh whole bunch uh Walkers runnin' 'round da house." Craig smiled. He turned back to the windshield and looked straight ahead into a world of his own. "We gon' have uh whole lodda steamy assed love makin' sessions," he added rubbing my hand on his dick outside his pants.

"I'm serious. I don't want us to rush into anything." I pulled my hand away. I was *not* trying to befriend Dick at the present moment.

"Okay, got'chu. Come on, git out." He got out, came around to the passengers side and helped me out.

"Hiiii," the real estate lady crooned like a moaning sports commentator with a serious case of throat cancer.

166

"So *you're* the lucky lady," she cooed, still not appeasing me. She reminded me of those hybrid Craisins "fruit" snacks--something that just sounded like it wasn't right.

And the way Craig tried to impress her? It was disgusting! He always knew how to charm the pants off the ladies--how to "play the game," as he called it which always ended with them eating out of the palm of his hands...or licking his balls!

I was impressed the minute she opened the flowered white iron security front door everybody and their mama in Detroit had to try to halt the ever prominent thieves in the hood.

The heavy wooden arched doorway reminded me of church ceilings. There was a section that had tons of closet space and mirrors on the double closet doors when you first entered the house, another polished wooden door filled with small glass squares opened to a generously spacious living and dining room. A chandelier accented the dining room, hardwood floors, natural wood trim around the doors and windows, there was a built in curio made out of wood and glass, four recessed lights across from the picture window in the living room with brand new gray carpet *and* a fireplace. The kitchen was newly remodeled white on white completed by a dishwasher and a couple of glass cabinet, a built in wine rack finishing it off with a breakfast nook that was tucked away into the rear of the kitchen. You could look out of the nook's bay window and see the backyard. The screened-in back porch would be perfect for Pharaoh and Mauri...there was a two-car garage and a long backyard.

As if *that* wasn't enough, upstairs there were four bedrooms with ample closet space, a freshly painted bathroom with a brand new tub and a marble floor, there was another bathroom in the master bedroom and a half bath downstairs. The basement had walls that were knotty pine--the real stuff, not that fake drawn on looking paneling looking crap. The floor was tiled, which made for a perfectly finished basement. There was an area that could easily be converted into another bathroom. I could see turning the basement into a den or a TV room until Pharaoh got older and wanted the downstairs for his bedroom so he could feel like he had his own spot like Sherra's brother Tommy did when he turned fourteen and wanted more space to "chill" in. Besides, after Pharaoh graduated from high school, he'd be off to college and we'd have our basement back.

Considering that the house was brick, the price was excellent. The older couple that owned it were retiring and moving to a condo in the suburbs.

I loved the Seven Mile/Outer Drive area. It was right off 696, close to Northland and Fairlane Mall, it wasn't too far from Southfield and the school in Farmington Hills Darren and I planned to put Pharaoh in.

There were tons of salons *and* churches (surely I would overcome my fear and, in time, join another one, right?) and it was only a few minutes away from downtown. Perfect.

Craig was right. A house like this one wasn't going to be on the market for long. I had to live here. I could just see myself sipping on a glass of freshly squeezed lemonade while I studied on the back porch. I could even see having more children in the near future—just no more Mauri's! She was his first so maybe he wouldn't act the same way with the rest of our kids in the future.

Too bad all this crap just went down with church. It would have been the perfect place for a fancy-smancy dinner party with salad and entrée forks, fine china, vintage wine and Billy Holiday buzzing in the background. Even though the city has a bad rep, there are older, well-built houses like this one that are absolutely beautiful.

"Baby, whas wrong wit'chu? Why you breathin' all hard an' breakin' uh sweat? You lookin' like you got rabies or some shit! You ain't 'bout ta attack me, is you? It's jus uh house, bae…I ain't gon' force you ta like it—*I* thank it's off da chains but we 'bout ta check out da otha ones our list. If somebody else make uh offer an' git it, den it wasn't meant for us, aright?" He held my hand and probed my eyes with his.

Yes, this house, dammit! I wasn't even tripping about staying in the city anymore.

"Whad up, bae?" He pulled me closer to him. Meanwhile Craisins threw another one of those 'give me your money' smiles our way.

"I *do not* like her. Feels like she's rushing us or something." *Buythishouse! Buythishouse! Butthishouse, dammit! You're the man! Pick this house!* I bit my lip so hard it started tingling.

"Baby, chill. You wont uh house *or what*?"

I didn't say anything the whole ride to the next house we were about to look at.

Next door to the house we were about to view there was Big Mama Whew-Woo in a tired, faded army green, sleeveless moo-moo with ankles so swollen they looked like tree stumps. She moved lethargically slow on her porch unfazed by the October wind, like it was a scorching summer's day. I already knew how this was going to be. If this hair sticking up thing, moving around like a broken down vehicle, with all those layers of juicy, fat tire rolls like a Michelin Man, block club gossiper was the neighbor, I wasn't about to live next door.

Just like the other one two miles away, this one was brick with four bedrooms but the owners were asking seven thousand dollars less than the previous house and there was only one bathroom and a half one in the basement. There was no chandelier, no breakfast nook, the carpet was old, the basement wasn't finished and it reeked like a slew of old people bathed in a potion of mustard greens, Vicks Vapor Rub and A and D ointment had rolled all over the basement floor before they moved out.

I immediately shook my head no before Craig had a chance to ask what I thought.

"You kinda picky fa uh person still livin' in uh lil' ass apartment wit'out uh dishwasher or uh garbage disposal." He chuckled.

The third house was also brick and looked well taken care of from the outside. Inside, though, was another story. The owners hadn't moved out and it was real junky, the walls looked slimy and were in need of a serious paint job. It didn't help that the owners were there while we looked at it.

When we looked in the bedrooms, the husband, with his loud, I-splashed-myself-in-shit-to-cover-up-my-strange-odor Avon cologne that clogged up my nose hairs, followed us like we were going to steal some of his wife's gaudy dollar store knick-knacks that should have been dusted five years ago.

This time Craig looked at me, shook his head no and turned up his lips in that street manner of his when the owners weren't looking. At least we were both on the same page on this one.

The final house was a mixture of the last two we'd just seen. It was ten minutes away and around the corner from Eight Mile in a seemingly nice neighborhood. None of the neighboring houses were vacant, burned up or vandalized and it seemed like the owners kept their properties up; my guess was that there weren't too many renters on the block. Renters versus homeowners made all the difference on how a neighborhood would be in a couple of years in Detroit.

All the houses on this street were the bungalows—one big bedroom in the attic, two on the main floor kind of homes. The street was lined with trees and little kids barreling down the street in red and yellow Wal-Mart Big Wheels and tons of boys between eleven to thirteen wearing long, shiny black doo rags that flapped against the back of their scrawny gingerbread and wheat colored necks. They circled the middle of the street, oblivious to the cars zipping by missing them only by an inch as they played a game of basketball with a crate rim at the top of a pole.

To me, they were the future hoodlums who'd soon be breaking into my house once they reached sixteen and needed the latest gear or pair of Jordans.

My mother's house had been broken into twice but we got hit three times all together when I was growing up. Each time we knew it was Ahdre and his gang.

"Bae, look. Could you stop trippin' fa *one* second? Damn! I been on da grind, tryin' ta make sho' you an' ma kids git us uh crib. All *you* doin' is complainin'! I know you goin' thru yo' shit but, you gon' have ta chill. You startin' ta git on ma nerves, fa real, Leigh." There he goes again, talking to somebody like they're some kind of bottom feeder. "*I* used ta be one of da lil' homies, shootin' hoops, not worryin' 'bout shit but dem new Jordans." Um-hm. I bet...and he went to *juvie*, too. "You beein' 'bout as prejudiced as dem ole White ladies dat be thankin' evry youn' cat from da hood gon' try ta gank 'em. Why you even wit me if *dis* how you gon' be? Hell, why 'on't chu find you some wack ass White dude dat's gon' rock some tight assed GAP jeans wit chu, shave off his mustache an' move you up ta Rodchester Hills somewhere so yo' ass can be 'bout as disconnected from da hood as Tiger Woods? You already be funny actin' 'bout rentin' apartments ta da young cats dat be tryin' git in da building!" He retorted after I voiced my concerns.

The way he said it, they way he yelled made my eyes burn. But as usual, I didn't argue with him. It wasn't going to do shit but make everything worse and turn into a fight that lasted two days with one of us sleeping on the couch.

I swear sometimes Craig could say things in such a way that I felt torn down or flat the fuck out wrong for saying shit to him. I was going to have to be smarter about what I said and how I said it.

He might not have understood my point but *I* knew what I was talking about.

Ahdre and his sisters lived next door to us. He was tall and handsome with his wavy hair and banana colored skin. Although his sisters were like three and five years older than I was, they played hoola hoop, double dutch, jump rope and Uno cards in the yard with me and they always brought their cat Fluffy over since my mother wouldn't let me have anything but boring gold fish that you couldn't even tell whether they were sleeping or dead.

Sometimes mom would let me and Tamika toast marshmallows and Ahdre'd make the fire for us in the front yard and T and I would camp out on the closed-in front porch and make up stories while the crickets chirped and we'd trade Garbage Pail Kids cards and play with our Cabbage Patch dolls and they'd come over and tell scary stories.

There was this one year we had everybody on the block come over to help pick our apple, pear and plum trees. That was like the best day ever growing up. Ahdre and all the other boys climbed up the pear tree since it was the tallest. They shook the limbs to get the pears down while everybody got apples and plums from the other two trees. It was like a fruit picking festival in our very own backyard.

Ahdre's sister were absolutely gorgeous. Dee Dee, with her freckles and asymmetrical styled red hair, always smelled like warm cocoa or baby powder. Rela was a maple brown tone, had long, curly lashes and had one of the curviest shapes I'd ever seen a twelve year old have. I used to wish I looked like her.

By the time Dee Dee hit thirteen and Rela was fifteen, they were in the alley letting guys do a lot more than feel on them in exchange for five-dollar bags of weed. Ahdre solicited customers for them. He was fourteen at the time and the ringleader of a gang that terrorized the then Black, Polish, Ugoslovic and Arabic mixed neighborhood with robberies and unnecessary shoot-outs. Crack hadn't hit Detroit yet otherwise, they probably would have been into that, too.

The first time his crew hit our house, they stole my mother's thousand-dollar camera, lifted up the mattress and found her three-thousand and some odd dollar savings, took our color TV along with the nineteen inch black and white one in my room. And as if that wasn't enough, they busted holes in our living room walls and knocked out all our windows in the dinning room.

The second time they robbed us, they stole all my mother's leather skirts and tore up the only pictures she had of herself as a little girl down south with her father. Later that month some dude tried to sell her one of her own skirts out of his trunk.

The third and final time we got hit by them, grandma, Tamika and uncle Mylo, were over for our usual Friday night family get-together. Later on that evening, when uncle Mylo went to mow the lawn he couldn't find the lawn mower in the garage and mom's first brand new car, a red Ford Tempo, was gone.

Before that they were the big kids I loved playing with and considered my play brother and sisters.

Their mother was off somewhere in LA pursuing some kind of Hollywood career while they lived with their alcoholic grandfather who beat up their baggy mouthed, toothless grandmother who, although still looked younger than her years, kept black eyes and casts on her arms.

They were the reason I never tried weed.

They were beautiful and smart young girls and had schooled me on everything from how to "cuss" (even though at that time I didn't know what curse words were), they showed me how to pop gum so loud a person across the street could hear it snap and how to walk and sway my hips in a way that would get all the boys in the neighborhood's attention. And before he joined that gang, Ahdre had helped me learn my times tables. Eventually they moved farther to the east side but the damage they'd done from Chene all the way to Gratiot remained. My old neighborhood had turned into empty lots where houses once stood or abandoned houses that had long since been vacated by their rightful owners who were tired of being easy prey. Most of the people who'd lived in the once quaint neighborhood ran for cover to Hamtramck or to suburbs far, far away from the city in order to find relief from types like Ahdre's crew who forever changed the street that was once a place to watch beautiful rainbows from living room bay windows and a place where you could walk to the corner store for bread from the small, Yugoslavian owned bakery where the flies got into the glass cabinets but everyone—because Janetta, the Arabic girl everybody on the block loved who lived up the street's parents owned it-- still bought cinnamon rolls there anyway that was next door to the Tru Value hardware store where all the workers knew you by first and last name and where you could buy a Barbie doll for only three dollars and get a free lollipop to go along with a purchase.

The area was now marred with prostitutes who handled business in the raggedy houses like it was their office space. A slaughter house that kept its lot full of trucks loaded with squealing pigs minutes away from death and a bacon breakfast fate opened on the corner of Chene and St. Aubin while a massive garbage incinerator was built near I-94, leaving nearby streets smelling like dead rodents.

All the memories of watching *Mr. Dressup* on the Canadian station, *Three's Company*, *Mama's Family*, *Family Feud*, *Out of This World* (with Evie), Molly Ringwald movies, re-runs of *The Jeffersons*, *What's Happening* and *The Golden Girls*, eating mom's baked cookies after summer school, Hop-Scotch, having coloring contests upstairs in the huge attic with Tamika and playing outside pretending the enormous tree in the front yard was a dinosaur (dinosaurs were a big deal back then) were now forever tainted.

My mother spotted Dee Dee begging in front of a grocery store supposedly for money for diapers for the snot nosed, dirt smudged, clothes-less baby on her hip. Grandma'd been a teacher's aid in the middle school Rela barely attended.

Years ago grandma turned the news on and made me watch as the news anchor went into detail when Rela's naked and severely burned body was been found in an alley, filled with crushed glass that had been intentionally infused into her skin and vagina, only five years after they left the street mom and I moved off.

"See. Dis what happen ta fas girls like Rela. Pretty don't mean nothin' when ya fas an' ain't tryin ta get nutin' in ya' brain. Don't chu try ta start no mess like dis, ya' hear me? If you git inta some mess like dat, I promise you *I* ain't gon' be up in no funeral.

"I ain't git all tha education y'all got tha chance ta git nowadays... Grew up on my daddy's farm in Mississippi—yes Lawd! Had ta pick cotton. Had ta quit school come fifth grade; had ta help ma mama an' daddy out in dem fields. But I came here an' got uh chance ta git my GED. Ma mama an' daddy had twenty kids, 'cluding me an' most of dem lil' niggas wudden't up ta no good no how. Dat's why I ain't have no whole bunch uh kids ta shame me when dey grew up. But you two? Y'all godda lodda promise. 'Memba dat, Sweet T an' Leigh! If y'all *eva* git inta somin' like dis here Greener gal went an' did, I won't even 'memba y'all names!" She sat in her rocking chair, quickly fanning herself in the air condition-less August heat when the news segment on Rela Greener's death ended. That was twelve years ago; I was twelve, Tamika was ten.

Last year in an English class, we had to read 'Tralalah' by Hubert Selby. It grossed me out so bad I almost threw up at the end of the story. The first thing that came to mind after I read it was Rela.

Things like that kept me in church and trying to stay close to the Lord and away from shit like what Niquie was into.

The way things stood now, even though I hadn't been viciously raped and killed by some John, Grandma still wouldn't have showed up at my funeral. Tamika's behind was so wild, it was a wonder grandma hadn't kicked he out yet but *I* was the one she was ignoring, not Tamika.

I spent all this time trying to do the right thing and look at how my life was turning out; I didn't even have a church to go to. When you listened to church on the radio the first thing they asked you was what church you went to. If you said you didn't go to church, they'd tell you to find one and start making suggestions. Greater Mount Zion was always on their list.

"Baby? Baby?" Craig asked snapping me out of my thoughts.

"I know what I'm talking about Craig. And I *don't* appreciate that lil' comment about me finding a White dude *or* when you said I'm trying to avoid my own people. When I was little we kept getting robbed by some 'lil homies' I grew up playing with... Now. If somebody wants to rob a bank or the government on some white-collar, money laundering stuff, they can do their thing--in my book the government's the biggest thug around anyway and they can afford to take a loss. But when a person robs his brother and sister next door who're struggling to make it just like he is, I don't respect that...That's a bully, 'cause they don't have the balls ta steal from the ones that mess the system up."

"Damn, girl. See. Dis why I fell in love wit cho' ass. Wha'chu know 'bout white-collar crime an' infiltration? You ain't up on no shit like dat! Come on. Les go check dis house out. We gon' make it da last one fa tanight. I know you need ta chill. Da las week an' uh half been crazy, bae. I'm sorry. But I think dis is what we need—uh fresh start."

Yeah, we needed a fresh new start all right. But for some odd reason, nothing felt right even though I *did* like the first house. And I kept seeing flashes of Craig dressed like Ahdre used to be dressed back in the day with gold chains around his neck and Kango's, breaking into people's homes.

"Bae, you cryin'? Aright, fa git it. We 'bouta go home. I ain't tryin' ta make you depressed an' shit."

"I'm straight." I stepped out of Craig's car.

I wasn't ready to go back to the apartment.

"Okay." Craisins smacked her lips and was ready to get down to business. "The owners are here at this one, too. The husband is about to retire. They're moving to North Carolina. It's a nice little deal. Only a hundred-thousand. So far, they've only gotten one offer. It was way below asking price, though. So let's see what you both think!" Oh the enthusiasm! We might as well all join arms and cut a jig along the sidewalk!

"Hi," a light brown skinned lady with a short wave curl and hips so wide they were unhidden even in the loose tracksuit she was wearing.

Craig threw on the charm while I checked out their house. They had a slightly older people décor of teal, peach and cream wallpaper borders going on but the hardwood floors looked like they'd been newly refurbished. The kitchen was white and black and had new appliances that the couple was leaving behind.

Craig chatted enthusiastically with the husband while I lagged behind. An entertainment show on the television in the living room caught my attention. The show's host was talking about Madonna. Why was Madonna's birthday August sixteenth—the same day as Mauri's! I don't believe in astrology. It stems from The Enemy but it was weird. The host had some guy on talking about how Madonna went to church in a fur and didn't wear anything under it and how they used to makeout in church. This was definitely a sign. When she was old enough, Mauri was going to Sunday School ASAP.

"You like da house or not?" Craig pulled me with him to look around upstairs.

"It's nice. We'll talk later," I whispered back. "Baby, you said we were making this decision together. We haven't even looked at a lot of houses yet and I--I don't like this one," I stated rather plainly after buckling my seatbelt after we got back in the car. I was about to go for it but I had to play it off. "The first house we saw--I thought *it* was an excellent deal. What do you think, sweetheart?"

"Man, bae, I think dat first house is dat deal. If we ain't even look at no moe houses, dat'uh be it."

"Well, I think we should make an offer on it. But the decision is ultimately up to you, baby. I trust you...you're handling your business, you know."

"Man, Leigh, you know how ta make uh nigga feel good, you know? I was startin' ta worry dat I ain't makin' you happy. Uh real man *godda* be able ta make his woman happy. Here. Hit Donna up. Jus press TALK." He handed me his Nextel.

"Y*ess*," she answered as we turned the corner behind her car.

"Donna, start dat paperwork up, Ma. We gettin' dat first house," he informed her on speakerphone.

"*Ooo*kay. Excellent choice. Follow me. We'll head to the office right away, then! I'm going Lodge." I hated it when people left out simple words like The and On. What she should have said was, I'm GETTING ON THE Lodge. Uggh! Hated to be giving her a commission. Usually I wasn't this mean to people. But I just didn't like her.

The whole ride there, Craig had a huge ass grin on his face and kept talking about how our life was going to be from now on.

We went into the office on Nine Mile and Greenfield. Craig filled out the paperwork and called himself explaining the process to me so, for his sake, I faked like I didn't know what was going on. I had already asked Scott tons of questions about the whole purchasing process after I found out he was an agent and he'd given me a book that explained everything from current mortgage rates to purchasing options and Michigan laws along with websites to check out. Personal Rule # 3--something I learned from Darren: Never go into something with "uneducated blinders" on— that was one of his favorite mottos.

Now, not to say that I couldn't ever just be happy for once but, even with all the excitement going on, I *was* paying attention to the fact that Craig was *not* putting my name on anything--nada, zilch, once we reached the office. I felt a little offended and a little—oh, what would the word be? Shafted. Yes...shafted like a muthafuka. He was forgetting *all* about his better half! His wifey! What the fuck?

"Hole'on Donna. I godda talk ta ma girl right quick." He led me out into the hallway out of Donna's earshot. "Baby. Whad up? Why you lookin' like dat?"

"To start, I didn't sign anything. This obviously won't be my house, hunh?" My eyes were cutting my eyelids. This was all wrong. What if we didn't get married right away? So much had happened, the plans were all up in the air right now. I could just see this heading in the wrong direction.

175

"You trus me, Leigh?"

"Why are you asking me that *now*?"

Donna was trying to steal a peek. We were standing only a few feet away from the door of her office suite.

"You 'on't trus me? Look me in da eyes!" I couldn't. Come to think of it, we'd never discussed whether or not we were going to sign joint for the house. Not even after we started looking. "Leigh. Look me in da eyes right nah. You trus me?" He pulled me close to him and tilted my head. "You trus me, yes or no?"

"...I...yeah."

"Aright...." That very second he looked and sounded like a member of the mafia yet, oddly enough, I felt a certain peacefulness come over me. I knew my man. My inner soul knew he wouldn't try to pull one over on me.

We went back into her office. Craig asked questions about locking in a mortgage rate and they finished completing the documents for the offer. "Nah, baby. Jus 'cause we put in uh offer don't mean we gon' git it but, we still gon' celebrate!"

He got carryout from the Fishbones downtown and drove back to the apartment after I talked him out of picking up the kids from Sherra's.

"Damn. I fagot ta run ta da stoe." He started his car up again and pulled around the corner to the liquor store.

"Come on Craig. No alcohol this time. Please."

"You really don't like fa me ta drink, hunh?"

"Not tonight. *Please*."

"Aright, *bae*, aright. You know whad? Dis uh new start fa us. I ain't gon' have ta be up in da place you slept wit Darren at. We can both wash da slate clean an' git our family tagetha, youknowhaImean?"

After we ate he turned the stereo up and kicked off his black Cole Haan shoes. "Come on." He jitted to a mix that was on 98. One thing about Craig--he could dance. He put my legs around his waist, pulled me in the air and moved like a dancer. Moving like this, with a hundred and twenty extra pounds wrapped around him, he might get baby number three real soon. "Come on, soul train line time," he said smiling and stomping on the living room floor.

I started clapping all loud. "No, it's only the two of us. Let's do the New Dance Show. Way more fun." We joked around doing old school dances and copying off of dancers that used to be on the low budget Detroit rendition of Soul Train. "Hey! You wanna go to River Rock?" I suggested. The only clubs we'd ever gone to together were more soul food joints than clubs.

"What! Hee*ell*, naw! You? Go ta da River Rock? Since when?" He laughed. "Yeah. Les go."

"Wait. I godda change."

"You goin' fa real?"

"Yeah, why not?"

"Jus weird, dat's all. Aright. Hurry up an' go git dressed, den."

I jumped out of the shower and put on a pair of True Religion jeans that loved my butt and hips with the matching jacket, a thin, low cut crème see thru knitted sweater for underneath, pulled out a pair of brown leather Jimmy Choo ankle boots, my Vuitton Monogram Ambre purse along with a crème fedora knit hat. Thirty minutes later, after slightly waving my hair with the crimping irons, a hint of Michael perfume mixed with Victoria's Vanilla and some gloss and lip liner, I had a sexy classy meets chic look going on and was ready to go.

I actually felt good for a change.

Normally Craig would have complained about a forty-five minute wait but he was on his cell with a guy from work, not paying me any attention until we got ready to get in the truck.

"Leigh? Whad da fuck? I mean, couldn't you uh worn sumthen uh lot *less* sexy? Damn. Uh brotha gon' have ta fight tonight. We ain't goin' ta River Rock. We bout to hit up Networks."

"That's cool with me. I haven't been to a club since what, since we hooked up? Really not since before Pharaoh. Let's go." I poked out my lips, tilted my head from side to side, made up a beat and rocked to it.

"Hell naw." Craig laughed as I gripped the steering wheel. "Naw, I'ma drive. Move over. An' baby. Jus sit dere, don't dance."

"*You* are crazy," I retorted.

We pulled up and did valet. Right off the bat Craig ran into some fellas he knew. When he introduced me as his wife he kept his arms tightly wrapped around my waist and wouldn't let them shake my hand.

"I *can* drink here, right?"

"Virgin Sprite," I chirped, swaying to Lil Kim's latest song.

"Come on, bae. Jus one. We got uh lot ta celebrate. An' don't be up in here dancin' like dat. I 'on't wont chu lookin' like one uh dem ghetto bitches. Do like you usually do, act all feminine an' shit--look like uh model, baby."

"Like you said, we don't know for sure that we've got the house yet. You drink, I dance on the dance floor by *myself*--ghetto as I wanna be." I threw my hands up in the air, twisted my lips and bobbed to the music like I was a rapper or something.

"Aright, aright. Drinks off!"

"Yep. Thought so." I pulled him out onto the dance floor. The crowd was cool. Lots of couples in their late twenties. Immediately the females started eyeing us. The fellas looked my way but were more polite than the ladies. You could smell the jealousy of the cheap weaves continually tossing Craig 'when she go to the bathroom, come get my number' looks. We always had that kind of effect on people. Hell, we looked damn good together.

When Craig and I took a break from the dance floor, a few guys he worked with came over. "Man, I *see* why you wanna marry her," this one so-so looking guy complimented Craig.

"Yeah, man, she bad," another one added. I thought Craig was going to get pissed and demand to leave but, instead, he didn't drink the rest of the night and we continued having a good time.

"BABY."

"...What?"

"We got da house! Donna said anotha couple had put in uh offer but it was three thousand dollars less than ours! WE GOT DA HOUSE! Git dressed. I'm gittin' off early!" Craig shouted waking me up out of my sleep.

"Umm—yaay, that's hot."

"Git dressed. I'm 'bout ta be dere in uh hour." He hung up.

I rolled over and went back to sleep.

"LEIGH! LEIGH, BABY I *tole* you ta be dressed when I got in! Lately you be takin' all day jus ta throw on some clothes an' shit."

"...Um-hm...Um-hm...I'm getting up..."

"Call whatever da fuck yo' girl name is, we gittin' da kids."

"...Yeah..."

"Leigh! Git up, baby! Baby? You aright?"

"...Five more minutes..."

"Git up! Leigh? Wake da fuck up!" Craig thrusted the house phone in my face barely missing my forehead. "We gittin' da kids. Baby. Come on! Wake up!"

I dragged myself into the bathroom and washed up—which was totally against self-policy. I always, always took either a shower or a bath. But I didn't feel well. What I felt like was a wad of phlegm.

I threw on the velvet pink Juicy outfit my mother'd stitched a fancy L on the front of and followed Craig out the door.

"You sure dat's what you wanna be in when you git married?" Craig asked as I handed him the keys to my truck. He sure was taking to driving *my ride* much more than necessary these days.

"Why don't we just take your car? Wait a minute. What? Get married. *What*?" My face unintentionally scrunched up. Surely I hadn't heard him right!

"We gittin' da kids 'cause, one: I want my kids back home an' two: dey need ta witness dey mama an' daddy say 'I do'!"

"Okay. What? Discussion please. This is becoming a *big* problem. Last time I checked, there were *two* of us in this relationship. If you're gonna do something that involves me, let *ME* know ahead of time. So *WE* can discuss it! How tha hell you gon' just up and tell me WE GETTING MARRIED TA'DAY! WHAT KINDA SHIT YOU SMOKIN'? I WANT MY MOTHER AT MY CEREMONY! AND MY FRIENDS AND FLOWERS AND BRIDESMAIDS! AND LOOK AT ALL THE SHIT THAT'S GOING ON RIGHT NOW! CAN WE JUST *CHILL* FOR A MINUTE?" I huffed not caring if the tenants heard. I got out the Explorer, slammed the door and ran to the entrance of the apartment but I had left my purse in the truck and didn't have my keys on me.

I walked back to the passenger's side breathing hard, my whole body shaking a hula dancer's hips.

"Baby... Calm down, would you?" Craig stated calmly looking at me more than a little confused.

I couldn't stop trembling the whole way to Sherra's house even after she brought the kids out.

Pharaoh had gotten a much needed haircut. Tommy must have taken him to the barbershop with him. "Mommy! Crai—"

"--Dad—Pharaoh. Whud I tell you 'bout dat, boy. Daddy," Craig corrected him while locking Mauri in her carseat.

"Call me." Sherra's eyebrows were furrowed as Craig rushed off and headed downtown.

"Wait, wait, wait. Before we go to the justice of the peace, we need to talk." I couldn't believe this shit.

Craig halted in the middle of Gratiot screeching the tires. "Nah whad? You 'ont wanna marry me, Leigh?"

"That's not—that's *not* it!"

"Aright, den. If you 'ont wanna do dis shit nah, you gon' at least git dat tattoo, RIGHT NAH!"

"...Would you just chill for a minute! What's the rush? We're together. We just *got* a *house*. We need to wait to see how all this pans out first. Besides. You said you wanted me to get the tattoo as a birthday gift *next year*. Why—"

"—I KNOW WHEN MY MUHFUCKIN' BIRTHDAY IS! WHAT DA FUCK YO' ASS NEED TA WAIT FOE, HUNGH? YOU KNOW WHAT? *YO'* ASS IS *CRAZY*! WHAT? YOU THANK YOU TOO

GOOD ALLA UH SUDDEN? YOU ALWAYS GODDA HAVE SHIT
YO' WAY ALL DA MUHFUCKIN' TIME!"

"CR*AI*G! YOU JUST SPRUNG ALL OF THIS—"

"--Tell me sumen. When I went ta da ressroom, what happened
las night? You git Bop's number or some shit 'cause yo' ass started actin'
real funny afta dat? You ain't even wanna dance no moe? YOU BEDDA
START TALKIN'! WHAD DA FUCK IS *REALLY UP*?"

"NO, YOU KNOW WHAT? *YO' ASS IS* CRAZY! DAT'S
WHAT'S REALLY UP! YOU DON'T JUST *TELL* SOMEBODY YOU
GON' MARRY DEM RIGHT NOW LIKE THIS!" You just like, 'We
gon' git married in ten minutes.'" I copied off his voice. Who did he think
he was? God? President of the world? Martin Luther King? Naomi
Campbell or some shit?

"YOU KNOW WHAD? FUCK YOU! STUPID ASS BI*IACH*H!"
He reached over from the driver's seat, opened the passenger's side of my
truck and pushed me smack dab on my knees into the middle of Gratiot
and Seven Mile's busy intersection and sped off. Cars hissed and blew at
me like I was a bum looking to get hit on purpose for a lawsuit. It was
worse than embarrassing. My grandma stayed right around the corner.
What if Tamika was driving her somewhere and they saw me out here like
this. My eyes were so cloudy I couldn't even see where I was going. I
made it past the stoplight without getting hit but I didn't have my purse or
my phone or any money on me. I couldn't even call anybody unless I
called Tamika collect. Nope--Sherra. There was no way I wanted my mom
hearing about this. She'd probably say it was all my own fault anyway.

Then again, maybe it was. I *did* want to marry Craig. It's just that
I had it all planned out in my head the way I wanted it to be. And he was
acting like a marriage ceremony was nothing.

My dumb ass. I was always fucking up. I should have just gone
with it. Now I was standing here looking stupid as hell standing in front of
a graffitied phone in front of McDonalds parking lot. And Sherra's phone
didn't accept collect calls. It was cold, I didn't have on a jacket...

I sat on one of the yellow parking lot car cement blocks in front of
the phone and tried to tell myself that I wasn't freezing and that none of
this was happening.

It must have been a half-day because I was surrounded by high
schoolers. A couple of girls were pushing babies in strollers and walking
towards the bus stop. A chick in an orange, 2 fa $50, sherling pointed my
way and laughed. Another girl that looked like she was straight up retarded
with a conical, flat shaped head and a pin-curled ponytail joined her.

"Leigh! Leigh? Cum'on. Git in da truck." I heard his voice behind
me.

The diamond bezel and pink Gucci crocodile band watch Darren had given me for my birthday clearly stated that it was now twenty-seven minutes later.

As I walked back to the truck thoughts ran across the gray and white cement specks of sidewalk like credits at the end of a morbid movie.

"...I'ma havta take dis truck inta da shop—I thank da tire godda titty in it..."

"...*What?*"

"...A titty in da tire—you know, one uh dem bubbles you git when you hit uh curb or some shit..."

Part II
Trash

CHAPTER 11

"MA! MOM-MEE?" Pharaoh climbed into the bed with me. "I love you."

"...I love you too, sweetie."

"Mom?"

"Hmmm?" I rolled over and looked at him.

"If you get mad at us again, please don't make us go to Tamika's...I like Sherra's house bedder."

"Why, sweetie?"

"'Cause."

"Because of what?"

"She got the Cat Lady over there. And I don't like her. She pull on my ears when grandma and Tamika not lookin' and scratches me. She don't—doesn't like Mauri either. She hit Mauri on da face. And Tamika don't—doeesn't? Doesn't give us any food. Only grandma. And grandma talks about you real mean, mommy. And granny don't like you, too."

"You think I sent you over Tamika's because I was mad at you?"

"Um-hum."

"Nooo. No, honey. Oh, you're making mommy really feel bad. No. I just...you know what. There will never be a time when I leave you with Tamika again if she's being mean to you and not treating you or Mauri fairly. And if you go over Sherra's house, it's not because I'm mad at you. I love you and Mauri very, very, *very* much." I rubbed the back of his head.

"But you always say Mauri is cuttin' up and that you 'on't—"

"—Don't."

"Don't like the way she acts like."

"—The way she behaves sometimes. Well...Mauri is still a baby and your--your—Craig and I have to train her. That's all."

"Mauri loves you mom. And I love her and you...but not Craig no more. He's scary. You gonna tell him?"

"What! No, no." I reached over and put him in my arms. "So Tamika has a cat now?"

"No. It's a girl. Her name is Rainy. And she looks like cats. And she scratches. And she says meow a lot. I don't like 'er. And Tamika won't feed me or Mauri. And Cat Lady hits Mauri!"

"Wait. So when you went over to Tamika's house, she gave you a spanking when you acted up? Granny, T and Grandma give you whoopins?"

"No. Only Cat Lady. Granny and big ma don't be—"

"—Are not—"

"--Are not there anymore. Only T and the Cat Lady and some boys that be real big. I hate them. I told Cat Lady my mom will beat her ass if she hit Mauri one more time."

"Aright. Aright, sweetie. You don't have to worry about a cat lady anymore. And don't use that word, ass, anymore either. But you *are* right about one thing--when mommy see's her *she is* gone kick ha ass. Don't say that word, though. Craig and I shouldn't be using that kind of language."

"Yeah. You should pay me a quarter every time you say the bad words. That's what Sherra does when Dina says 'em." (This was way before *Girlfriends* came out and Mya started that with her son mind you).

"Deal. A quarter." I scooted him over and got out of bed and rushed to the bathroom to brush my teeth.

"Mom?" Pharaoh called from the other side of the door.

"What?"

"You goin' somewhere?"

"Shh! I'll be out in a minute." Pharaoh missed me. I hated shushing him. He and Mauri usually sat next to the bathroom door whenever I took a bath or shower unless they were watching T.V. and anytime I washed dishes Pharaoh and Mauri were right there running trucks over my feet. Anywhere I went they were right next to me or either crying if they couldn't find me. Craig was home from work snoring on the couch. I guess he called himself monitoring me. After that little stunt of his yesterday it was just a matter of time before I changed the locks on his ass. Now was not the time for Pharaoh to be shouting a million questions thru the door. I was on a mission. Today might very well be the day Tamika got her assed kicked by yours truly. Hell, I was mad enough to kick my own ass for leaving them with her if what Pharaoh said was true.

Five minutes later I was about to slip out of the back door in the kitchen to Tamika's. "Shh. Come on. You can put your on shoes in the hallway—"

"—Leigh? Leigh? Where da fuck you thank you goin'?" Craig darted into the kitchen.

"We aren't cool. I'm still not talking ta yo' ass." I pushed Pharaoh into the hallway.

"Look. You mad and I'm mad. Both uh us bein mad ain't gon' git us nowhere. Tamorrow we closin' on da house. Les jus chill taday. I done already tole chu I'm sorry for da way I acted, bae--stop holdin' dat shit over my head!"

"Oh you really think it's that easy don't chu? Fuck you. Besides, I got other things to think about, I just heard that Tamika was abusing my kids. Pharaoh's scared to death to go back over there and he's saying something about a cat or a cat lady that was knocking Mauri upside the head." I knew that would pull on his heartstrings and make him leave me the fuck alone.

"Aright. I'll ride wit chu."

"No."

"Why not?"

"I'm getting my hair done after that."

"I thought you said you cain't take no kids up ta dat spot."

"I don't have to explain shit ta yo' ass. Peace out!" I snapped back. Damn, Craig really did have a good memory.

"So where you goin'? Come on baby, stop bullshittin. I'm sorry. Whad? I gotta git on my hands an' knees ta apologize?"

Where was this nigga coming from? He *almost* looked sincere-- almost being the operative word. After you get shoved out of your own truck onto pavement rolling past your face, you just can't trust someone who'd do something like that to you anymore. "I godda go. I'm 'bout ta whip Tamika's ass for not feeding my kids."

Craig grabbed his dark brown leather coat along with Mauri's and was in his car before I was. "Hole up." He got out of the car and called somebody on his phone. That was weird. Why'd he have to get out the car?

Neither one of us had a word to say the whole way over there, the radio filled in the silence.

"Stay in the car," I commanded ready to see the white meat of Tamika's head if I had an inkling that Pharaoh hadn't been exaggerating. If he was right, she was about to be officially written off my list as far as family was concerned.

"Damn, baby! Why you knockin' like you da muhfuckin' po-po's?" A tall, heavy set, gorilla faced boy in a black, raggedy looking leather coat agitatedly questioned after opening the door. I had a key but with my grandmother not speaking to me and all, it seemed more appropriate to knock.

"Who *the fuck* are *you*?" I asked pushing him out of my way. "Tamika? Tamika, get yo' ass out here! *Grrrandddma? Grand-ma!*"

"Yo' T! You bedda git yo' ass down here quick. I 'on't know who dis bougie-ass broad thank she is steppin' up in here like so but, she 'bout to get smacked!" gorilla face shouted. His words spat on my cheeks.

I pushed Gorilla face in the chest, almost knocking him to the floor. He was messing with the wrong one. Thanks to Brother Farston, Demetrius Gray, Ellington and Craig, I already had enough anger brewing in me to snap his neck off and I came prepared: Vaseline slicked on my face, thick silver rings I had gotten from the African festival on all my fingers—and a couple of 'em were sharp and pointy.

You could tell something was wrong just from looking around grandma's house. It was a mess. Too many forty-ounce beer bottles on the dining room table to count. Ashtrays all over the place--there was even a bag of weed left out on the coffee table. Garbage littered the floors like carpet. It was colder inside the house than it was outside and the place reeked. The whole house smelled like rotten meat. Gnats looking to hatch a fresh batch of babies clustered in the kitchen and lit on dishes laden with food probably from weeks ago. Greasy stained, white and gray moldy plates covered the counters waiting for the day they'd one day meet dishwashing liquid and bleach. Grandma was a neat freak. She'd never let her house go like this.

There was another guy I didn't recognize in the kitchen raiding what little food was in the gnat-infested refrigerator. "Hey, sexy," he didn't take his eyes away from the fridge.

I walked back into the living room to see Tamika finally traipsing her sorry ass downstairs. She kept her head bent low. "Whad up?" Her eyes were heavy with thick, darkened bags underneath and her bottom lip was split.

"Where's grandma?"

"She at yo' mama house."

"Good. 'Cause I'm bout ta *whip* yo' *busted lookin' ass*! How you gon' not feed *my kids*. And you got some *bitch* smackin' Mauri? All you had ta do was *tell* me you couldn't keep 'em! You offered! Remember? I got enough shit of my own ta deal with!" Before I realized what I was doing, I punched her in the stomach and she doubled over. She didn't even attempt to fight back which really pissed me off. "Oh! Oh, *nooow* you can't fight, right? You dog out my kids but you won't fight woman to woman, hungh?" The pastor's face, flashed before my eyes right before I swung on her again. This time I got her in the jaw. Right side.

"You such a self-absorbed, spoiled assed brat. Fuck you! *Fuck yo' stupid ass*!" She struggled between sobs. The gorilla-faced bastard I had knocked down came over and tried to help her up.

"Yo', T! I done aready tole chu! I 'on't believe in hittin' no woman but I'm 'bout ta swing on dis bitch, right here!" he yelled.

"Naw, it's cool. Fuck tha bitch. She ain't my cousin no how! Get out! Go find anotha Reverend dick ta suck!"

That was it.

I started bashing her face in with my fists, I scraped my nails up against her forehead, which left slithers of her skin curled under my nails and I punched her in the eye three good times and cocked her in the mouth so hard her face contorted to the right for a minute--for all the times she said she was prettier than me back in the day.

I punched her in the face again, this time a little harder. Her jawbone thudded against my knuckles and clicked. She slumped down in the corner next to the stairs and scooted into a ball like she didn't know how to fight. So I smashed her ribs a couple of times with my Adidas and grabbed a fistful of her raggedy braids and I snatched and yanked 'em until blood started trickling from her scalp. And she *still* wasn't fighting back! So I kept beating that ass. And it felt good.

Craig came in and lifted me in the air in right before I swung on her again. "*Y'all* need ta talk," Craig stated raising his eyebrows at me. "Yo' T, I on't know what's up, but dese dudes godda chill somewhere while y'all talk fa uh few," he added. "Y'all s'posed to be beddar dan dis." He'd always been cool with Tamika.

"You thank you da shit!" Tamika huffed. "All you do is sit around while niggas pay fa shit. Yo' mama spoiled yo' ass rotten. You godda man worshipin' da ground yo' ass walk on but all yo' ass know ha ta do is complain! Nah, you tryin' ta *boss* yo' Debo ass up in *my* shit? We ain't gotsta *eva* speak again far as I'm concerned! We ain't really related no how!" Her front teeth were bright red.

"Oh, I see. You wont cho' *ass* whipped again, hungh?"

"See, you so FUCKIN SELF-ABSORBED! You ain't even heard shit I jus said!"

"Ain't shit else fa me ta hear. You didn't take care of my kids and you're messing over grandma.

"Just look at how nasty this house is! *You* the one thas spoiled. You never got whipped for shit uh day in yo' life. Maybe thas what's wrong with you right now. It might be too late fa grandma ta knock some sense inta yo' head but I don't have no problem showing you whas up again! Ta da white meat, *Bitch*! *Ta-da-white-meat*!" If she was finally ready to go toe to toe, I still had plenty of energy. I wasn't hearing *shit* she had to say. She had basically tortured my kids and from the looks of it, she wasn't taking care of herself very well either. You wouldn't catch me or my house looking like that no matter what was going on.

"You's uh silly bitch, fa real. It's all about yo' hair an' yo' nails gittin' did evry week an' bein' uh nurse. You stuck in uh fake world. You'uh thank bein' kicked outta Mt. Zion woulda taught yo' ass something. Like I said, we ain't related no how." She paused. We both took the time to catch our breath. "My mother came over here uh month ago--some snobby ass, Pilipino chic. CEO accountant at GM an' shit. She came over here talkin' 'bout, *she couldn't keep me 'cause her parents woulda killed her.*

"She was in college when she got pregnant wit me...say my real father tole her he couldn't help her so she was on her own—so she claim, people always puttin' shit on anotha muhfucka. She said they was away at school—that's how dey met. She gave me his number...say he uh doctor." Tamika nodded her head back and forth. I couldn't tell if it was from the beat down she just got or if it was from this story she was now rambling on and on about. "So she gave me ta yo' uncle Mylo right after I was born. When she was in labor he was at tha hospital wit her an' evrythang. She say she told Mylo I was his kid an' he believed her..." She shook her head again. I didn't say anything. My thoughts of Tamika were still jaundiced from how she had treated Mauri and Pharaoh. "She said he tried ta marry her but her parents wudden't 'bout ta let her marry no Black man. An' guess what? Yo' lovely lil' grand*mother* knew 'bout alla dis! She say she contacted yo' grandma right after she heard Mylo got killed. But ain't body ever tole me...I got four brothas an' sisters all together--and no body ever told me not one thang! ...All dese years...since Mylo been shot...it's jus been me...an' ain't no body never tole me tha truth." She broke down into loud sobs. "I called you three times...three times Leigh. An' you know what? You was too busy. Every *mutha-fuck-in'* time. So 'cuse me if I 'on't count you as my number one cuz no moe. Hell, *Craig* talked to me when I first found out. Dat's moe dan I can say fa yo' ass."

I squatted down next to her at the bottom of the stairs not knowing what to say. "So you let some chick hit Mauri 'cause you were mad at me? And *where is this bitch*, anyway?" I still needed to know what that was about. Why'd she agree to keep my kids in the first place if all of this was going on? If she wanted to pay me back she should have tried to do that instead of taking it out on Mauri and Pharaoh.

"I apologize fa dat shit. It wasn't cool. But it wasn't me. I be havin' uh lot uh my peep's up in here. Dey da only muthafuckas I got. Evrybody else wanna lie an' shit. Shit, yo' mama knew Karen was tryin' ta contact me uh long time ago!"

"So, what, you feel like since we supposedly aren't related you ain't have ta feed my kids? I 'on't give a fuck what you think! We been like sisters. You *are* family! And why isn't grandma here?"

"I *was* feeding them. They just eat too damn much. It was only one day when I was high that...look, I'm sorry. Fa real. I'm sorry 'bout that. But it wudden't on purpose. I can see why you heated over it." She paused and looked me in the eyes. She seemed sincerely sorry. But she was still high or something. "Yo' grandma ain't here 'cause dis was Mylo's house. In his will, fifty percent of evrythang he left was s'posed to be mine. Yo' grandma didn't gimme none uh da money he had in da bank or shit else. He might uh been uh street gambler but he always kept money in da bank. So you know what? Dis house is mine! Shit! Whad else I got? Hunh?

What else I got? A fucked up situation, that's what! And don't no body give uh fuck!

"That bitch that's s'posed to be ma real mama act like she scared ta fuckin' hug me an' shit. She all prissy like yo' ass wit her red BMW. Came over here wit some lil' White boy looked like he my age flauntin' him around talkin 'bout he her boyfriend an' shit. An' you know what? Da bitch got uh dog--uh lil' bitty muthafucka she was carryin' 'round in her purse dat she treat bedder dan my ass!"

"Look, you always have me--always. I'm not down for Mauri getting hit...but all that's over...I'm here for you. My bad, T." I grabbed her and hugged her. Once again I had fucked up. "Let's get you cleaned up—"

"--Nah. Ungh-uh. I'm tight. I ain't some lil' ass kid. I'm good."

"...Why don't you get dressed and go with me to KD's. We can get our hair done and go to Ilya's for massages."

"Leigh? You cain't fix me. We ain't tha same type uh people. Give you uh new outfit an' you all good. Me, ma shit gon' always be fucked up..." This was not the same person I knew and loved, the girl that used to talk to only the finest guys and made them pay for her hair to get done and always had guys taking her shopping. This person was dark beyond the extra rings I had added to her eyes. Tamika was corroding in misery and needed me.

"Come on T. Come with me. I'm not leaving you here like this."

"I *said* NO! I'm good." She stared off into space.

"Okay, okay. But we need to sit down and talk. My mom, grandmother, *your* mother, you—even your father. Maybe you can confront them about the whole thing and let them know how you feel about the situation." That's what I'd want to do if I were her. If I could confront my father right now I would. Problem is, I don't even know his last name or any details about him; any man walking down the street could be my father for all I know. My mother never told me anything about him except that he said I wasn't his.

Tamika still didn't respond.

"If grandmother and my mother really *did* know and didn't tell you, you should confront them. You can't just sit in the house and get high and drunk all day. You're better than—"

"--Leigh! Shut da hell up! You ain't got shit ta say 'bout ma life! If you cared, you woulda been dere when I was *callin* you! Could chu leave?"

"Look, T. I'm sorry. I should have been there for you but, you godda remember, I've been going thru a lot myself. But I'm here for you— from now on. Why don't come over on Saturday?"

"...What? I'ma come over and get my ass kicked again?" She let out a seriously exhausted sigh.

"T? No, come on now. I already feel bad about—about all l of this. You know my mother and grandma aren't speaking to me either. We both have to look out for each other."

"...Yeah, whatever. I been had cho' back an' I'm done. I ain't got shit else ta say ta you."

"Well...alright. There's nothing I can do say or do so to show you I care so...I guess I'll see you then."

Craig came out of the dining room, hugged Tamika and whispered something in her ear, probably trying to get her to makeup with me.

"I think I need to call her or stop by here tomorrow. I'm gonna call my mom when I come from the salon and spa. I *can't believe* they did that to Tamika," I said wiping the blood off the sides of my brand new Adidas.

"Why 'on't you call 'em nah?"

"I already feel bad. I don't want them bringing me down any worse... Why didn't you tell me all this was going on with T? And since when did *you two* get *all* tight?" I asked taking off the rings and stuffing them in my purse before putting my engagement ring back on.

"So nah it's *my* fault you beat da girl's ass?"

"She shoulda said something up front! How come she didn't say anything about it when she got the kids? How was I supposed to know? You know what? FUCK YOU! WHAT, YOU GONNA PUT ME OUT THE CAR AGAIN? I mean, it is *YOUR* CAR YOUR DRIVING THIS TIME?" I shouted so loud, the kids woke up and Mauri started crying.

Yeah, I *was* wrong for beating Tamika down like that but I didn't play when it came to my kids. And yes, a lot of this was my fault. I shouldn't have left them over there. But if Craig was in on it, why'd he let the kids stay with her in the first place? It looked like what grandma used to call a flophouse and it definitely wasn't they type of environment you wanted your kids in.

Craig pulled the car over and stared at me for a minute. One minute can seem very long when one is just sitting there motionless and staring at you with a blank expression on their face. He was making me uncomfortable. Instead of going off on him, I had an urge to just grab his face and smash it against the dashboard of his Mustang.

"Baby. We got too much drama goin' on. Life ain't s'posed ta be like dis." He grabbed my hand. "I was on some bogus ass shit yestaday but I ain't gon' clown on you like dat no moe--you got ma word on dat. But chu took dat shit wit T too far. Das yo' cousin, Leigh. She need you right nah. One thing she got right, she *did* called you over an' over. You was too

190

fucked up over dat shit wit da church ta talk ta her...I'ma git her ta come over. Git y'all on speakin' terms again."

"Yeah, whatever...You're heading the wrong way. You might as well take Eight mile to Evergreen. KD's on Eleven and Evergreen."

"You still goin' ta da salon *after alla dat*?"

"AHH--YEAH! Do you know how long it's been since I've been up there?"

"You crazy...too superficial, Leigh...besides, I 'on't wanna drive all the way out there. Why on't chu just get yo' hair did at Ilya's."

"How *you* know about *that* spot?"

"You told Sherra you was gittin' uh massage dere yesterday...an' uh lodda girls at work be goin' up dere ta get dey hair did—"

"—Done. I hate it when you say that. It's done—not did!"

He laughed.

"No, I'm going to *KD's* for my hair."

He made a swift and dangerous U-turn on Seven Mile and headed to KD's.

"Mommy? I'm hungry," Pharaoh informed me.

"McDonalds," Mauri chimed in.

"Whad, Mauri? Pharaoh turned you on to Mickey D's?" I turned around and looked at her as she kicked her feet in her car seat.

"Nope. DaDa."

"Daddy—Mauri—Daddy! I hate it when you say DaDa—"

"—You so fuckin critical, Leigh—"

"--A quarter mom! And you owe me three more." Pharaoh didn't miss a beat.

"Quarter!" Mauri added mimicking Pharaoh. She may not have known what he was talking about but she was not one to be left out.

"Alright you two," I retorted back. I gave Craig a stiff look and turned up the radio to 92.3. Luther's "A House Is Not A Home" was playing. He wasn't lying. Tamika might have claimed grandma's house but it wasn't a home anymore.

"Wha'chu wont?" Craig asked pulling into the driveway.

"Can you just go inside? I don't trust drive-thrus. Just fries--well, make it a Big Mac combo. Get them hamburger Happy Meals." Hopefully I'd get on his nerves and he'd drop me off. I didn't want him to be waiting for me in the parking lot like I knew he planned on doing.

He sighed and got out the car. "I know what ma kids eat, Leigh." Les go inside."

The kids got all excited when he took them to the indoor playhouse. I never allowed them to play in those things. One time on the news they did a test that showed all the nasty bacteria harboring all over

191

those jungle gym things. "All it takes is one kid with meningitis in that playhouse Craig and they're sick."

"Leigh, would you stop bein' so goddamn anal? You *need ta be* thankin' 'bout how you jus clowned yo' cousin..."

"...I feel bad about the Tamika thing," I defended.

"...Yeah. So, whad you gon' do?"

"...I don't know," I sighed. Life was starting to feel a lot heavier. Felt like I had sumo wrestlers sitting on my shoulders.

"Jus talk ta her, Leigh..." He shook his head in disdain at me.

IN SOUTHFIELD, KD'S WAS thumpin' even though it was only Wednesday evening. The parking lot was filled the SUV's of ballers that didn't go anywhere else to get their waves tapered and fro's faded. The top notch only came here or to Ilya's.

At KD's you could catch up on what was going on in the city and check out the who's who of the metro area. Darren put me up on this spot a couple of months after Pharaoh was born. He was a twice a week regular himself.

"I'ma chill foe uh few at ma mama's house. Call me when you 'bouta be done." Good. I needed a break away from his crazy ass. "Bae, don't be gettin' no crazy ass hairdos. I 'on't like all dat hood shit on you." He was the exact opposite of Darren. While Darren required his woman or baby's mother to look good at all times and expected any female in his life to live in clothing boutiques and Somerset, to relish designer e-accounts, spas and upscale salons, Craig didn't want me to look anything closed to polished. He preferred it when I did my own hair and acted like pedicures and massages were the very thing that held the Black race down. He was always going on and on about how Black America spent the most money in an economy that didn't even give us proper respect.

At first I bought into it. Now I believed it was his way of ensuring himself a homely looking woman he wouldn't have to spend too much money on.

When I pushed the glass doors open and entered the lobby I felt like a bum thanks to the old pair of Sears jeans and an out of style fuzzy, baby blue TJ Maxx sweater I had on. Nevertheless all eyes were *definitely* on me when I stepped in the place and it wasn't those "Harlot/Jezebel" glares Mt. Zion members tossed my way when they spotted me out and about. This was *the* look--the 'That's Darren's Baby Mama' look. I took a second to let the smell of Affirm relaxers, Marcel curling irons and Finisheen waft into me. The aroma made me as giddy as a kid sniffing white out and glue.

"No! Ungh-uh, Sweetie. You *ain't about ta* wait in no lobby, we ain't seen you for a whole month! Get cho' hot butt in here!" Beat, KD's assistant, ushered me away from the receptionist and hurried to the back of the salon. "Even though you *are* dressed like a crackhead, you look still absolutely gorgeous darling!" he gushed. He claimed to have a girlfriend but, it was very obvious that he and KD were either bi or just flat out homo. They had grown up in church but Lord knows they only acted like they were saved whenever they had problems with the law.

"You should get some light brown contacts and some blonde highlights. You'd be breakin 'em dowwwwn, forreal Leigh." Beat talked so fast and flung his hands every which way, it was sometimes hard to keep up with him. Skinny and very, very dark, he looked like he could have very well been Seal's handsome younger brother.

"So what's been up?" he chirped, massaging my scalp, "You shoulda got your massage at Ilya's first. Now you have ta be careful you don't mess your hair up."

"Well, school's going great—I can't wait until I become a nurse." Ha! What a far cry from the truth. I'd just missed two and a half weeks of school and was about to beg all my instructors to let me makeup all the assignments since I couldn't afford to lose any credits this semester. But you never let anybody see you sweat. Like they say, fake it till you make it.

As Beat concurrently blow dried my hair and watched the fashion show on the huge, flat television next to KD's station, I took in the scene.

Every girl in the place looked like money. All light skinned, longhaired chicks, pale, half-White looking females. Almost all of them were either real skinny or had huge butts. Other than the short haired, Nia Long look-a-like who was cinnamon skinned, petite and exceptionally pretty who KD was micro curling, I was the only brown skinned client in the place. You could be light skinned and average looking and still get in on a dough boy. But if you were on the brown side, you had to damn near be a model or have some hellified game.

The hustlers' girls talked in whispers and moved their hands with precise limp movements like preprogrammed girly robots. You could tell they were all stuck up and either the wives or girlfriends of the *true* hustlers of the city. The careless expressions on their faces only made them looked snootier.

One pretty pale faced, grey-eyed chick had a black eye she'd almost covered well with makeup. Her eyes stayed down the whole time SaySay, a tall dark skinned, raunchy mouthed top Detroit stylist flat ironed her long, ashy brown waves bone straight. The girl stared off at nothing in particular as she sat in SaySay's chair. She was so still she looked dead. I couldn't see what she was wearing since her stylist cape was covering her outfit and her hands were hidden underneath it.

Then there was Pamela, a tan skinned girl who couldn't have been older than nineteen. She never cracked a smile the entire time I was there and looked like a zombie. She had two huge diamond rings on her dainty, thin French manicured hand, a diamond necklace that was no less than ten g's, two diamond tennis bracelets that were definitely not those pencil mark, cluster diamonds. On top of that, the rounds gracing her ears were way bigger than mine. That shit was ridiculous. *She* had the multicolor Speedy Vuitton purse I had wanted Craig to get for my birthday but he didn't, a pair of tan, skinny heeled Timberland boots to die for *and* a soft bone colored cashmere sweater and pant ensemble! I almost felt jealous. But I knew the real deal. When one knows the real deal, they can't envy poignant heartache.

All of us had '*the look*' the money players liked. We were the ones they wanted at home to cook and clean and be good girls and mommies while they were out in the streets doing whatever the hell they wanted to do. I'd read the same story so many times.

In high school, my guilty pleasure after reading a few chapters of the bible was a good, smut filled, ghetto, shoot 'em up, drug-dealin', sex laden, hood book. In the end, whether it was the good girl turned bad or the bad girl who'd escaped the streets all thanks due to a hustlin' boyfriend who put her up real nice while he made the money type of scenario, their fate was always the same. They always ended up being the victim of some nigga. Or the victim of society. Or the victim of the government.

Pretty, size three wearing, long, 'good' hair having, freaks in the bed for their man, kind of victims.

"You okay, darling?" Beat questioned looking into my eyes. My vision was becoming blurry.

"Yeah. My allergies are acting up."

"Nah, I know you ain't allergic to no salon? That the reason you took so long ta come back?" he teased. We both laughed.

"No. For real." I closed my eyes signaling that today was not going to be one of our catch up on Leigh's life days and sat back and enjoyed the scalp massage he was giving.

"Get up, Sweetie, KD is readily awaiting you!" He clasped his hands and curtsied after I tipped him thirty dollars.

"And get that gum out of your mouth! You look like a cow!" he snapped handing me a piece of paper towel as I walked over to KD's remote controlled chair. It was on a platform for everybody up in the salon to take note. If you stepped a foot on his platform, you were at least coming out of one-fifty—no excuses.

"What do you need, Leigh?" KD's voice sounded like it was dripping with green snot. He always acted like he was doing you a favor by doing your hair. But I knew he liked me. Otherwise, I wouldn't be in his chair.

"Just a simple flat iron," I answered, flipping open a book Craig had placed in my purse entitled *The Mis-Education of the Negro*. It had a woman with a lock placed on top of her head. Typical Craig! I wouldn't have minded--if he knew how to act. How was he going to try to *groom* me into Perfect Afrocentric Woman when he wasn't even on point? I shoved the book back into my purse and was about to summon Beat over so he could hand me the latest *In Style* magazine but I was distracted by a handsome, Butterfinger candy bar skinned guy who's goatee Chez, the barber, was precisely fine-tuning.

At that very moment, I swear, I swear, I swear! My heart stopped. I felt nervous and delightfully delighted at the same time. My feet started tingling. My heart started dancing. I couldn't take my eyes off him. The man was simply divine.

He was very slim--slimmer than Craig, it looked like he might be a tad bit shorter than Craig too--he was sitting down so I couldn't tell. His face was finely chiseled. Everything about him, his nose, his dark eyes, his lips, *everything* about the man was beautiful. He had a certain clean-cut quality about him and his aura seemed to be one of wisdom. My eyes couldn't take in enough of him. And then, it happened.

He winked at me.

Suddenly, right before my very eyes, I could see myself having his twins. I wanted him. Bad. Both of us in the room together with R Kelly's 12 Play playing softly in the background would be lethal. He wouldn't even have to go in half--I'd be willing to do *all* the work.

I slid my hand under the cape KD had just placed on me to hide my ring. *Bad girl, Bad Leigh!* I tried to stop looking at him. *You are supposed to be a woman of the Lord!*

--But how far has that really gotten you, hung Your man's one step from kickin' your ass. He didn't let you sign on the offer for the house.. How do you know he's gonna let you sign at closing, hmm? AND, need I remind you, he kicked you out of the truck Darren bought--for you! Craig runs you and you let him. You woulda been better off with Darren, he's too uppity to waste time fighting the way this one does. Darren would have just tuned you out if you said something he didn't like... Or he would have simply given you his credit card to go shopping...

Something was doing a good job of possessing me and muffling all my reasoning and functioning faculties. I had to stop, I had to annihilate the thing inside me.

Cut it out! You are: honest, faithful, loyal...

"Beat? Could you please grab the *In Style* magazine, Sweetie?" There. That would keep my mind off this ungodliness.

But he beat Beat to it. "I got it." Yes. *Yes* he *did* have it...and I wanted him to *give it* to me! Umm...

Do you have a girl and if so, does she give it to you like you want it, like a pro? If tha answer ta either question is no, here's my number, I really want you, oh, you got my body feeling like whoa...

He got out of Chez's chair, went over to the coffee table where all the magazines were sprawled out, walked over and placed the latest copies of *In Style*, *Black Men* and *Essence* in my right hand.

"Looked like your type of reads." The smell of Issey Miyake wafted in the air as he sat back in the barber's chair directly across from me. Chez smiled my way and gave a knowing look.

Our eyes flirted with each other the rest of his mustache line up. After he pulled out a huge knot and paid Chez, he discreetly slipped his number in my purse and left. You would have had to zoom in to catch it, one blink of the eye and you wouldn't have noticed the number drop. He was smooth. Good thing. Chez was Darren's barber too.

"WHY YOU STANDIN' OUTSIDE? Whad? Dey got uh rule, after you git cho' hair did you cain't stay in dere no moe?" Craig fussed as I hopped in the car hoping no one peeped the not so new Mustang—not that I was embarrassed about it. I just didn't want Darren getting more ammunition.

"No."

"Hey mom, looking goot!" Pharaoh commented with Mauri trying to repeat after him. He had this thing going on lately where his d's sounded more like t's.

"Thanks. Did you all have fun at grandma's house?" I asked.

"...Yes," Pharaoh replied. He was lying. I knew how it really was for him. Craig's mom probably gushed all over Mauri and left him out of the Walker Love Reunion.

"Yeah, ma mama was happy ta see 'em. You still goin' ta dat spa?"

"Yep. I already missed two appointments."

"Aright." He sighed non-approvingly but resigned to saying anything more.

"It's owned by Ethiopians--isn't that nice? Why don't you and the kids do dinner there while I get my massage? They have a salon, a spa *and* a café in there."

"Naw, I'm straight. Dat place too bougie fa me. I'ma head ta da crib."

"It's funny how Africans and other foreigners come over here and go from nothing to rich...You'd think Black Americans would try to do the same thing... We're too busy talkin' 'bout *The Man* holdin' us back."

"It's easier fa foreigners. An' I ain't gon' be all up on no African's tip noway. Dey 'ont like Black muhfukas; dey da ones dat sold dey own inta slavery an' Africans usually be tryin' ta act White an' shit. Dey 'ont give uh fuck about da Black experience... Make sure you hurry yo' ass back. After dat massage, Ima need one too..." He tried to put my hand on the zipper of his jeans. I snatched my hand back.

"*That's* three quarters. I'm gonna be rich," Pharaoh quipped.

"Craig, quit cursing in front of them." He kissed me on the cheek as I got into my truck. "Call me when you git dere." In other words, *I wanna make sure you're where you're supposed to be.*

"Yeah, yeah, yeah." I shut the door and dialed my mother's number the minute I pulled from in front of the apartment. "Hey mom. Mom? I saw T today—"

"--You *and* Tamika! Don't call my house *no moe*! Y'all gon' have ta get it together with the Lord. Hope it's sooner than later!" CALL ENDED flashed on the screen of my cell.

"THAT'S IT!" I shouted getting the Lodge Freeway ramp on Glendale to head downtown. "FUCK 'EM! YEAH, I SAID IT, FUCK MA *AND* GRANDMA!" I turned this one new rap song I liked up. "BIA-BIA"...yeah, I knew a lot of 'em right now.

I tried to call Tamika but her phone was disconnected. This family was a live circus.

The valet dude took my keys and parked my truck in the lot near the Gem Theater. The minute I was in Spa Ilya, nothing my mother, Craig or anybody else had said or done was on my mind. The café was becoming more of a swanky nightclub—especially since they stayed open until four in the morning. Nothing in Detroit usually stayed open that long. Tonight an up and coming saxophonist was being featured. I'd heard some of his music on the public radio station a couple of times and loved it. His music was drifting into the lobby.

The lobby is very pretty. There's a waterfall that runs along the wall next to the café, marble floors that are always gleaming and soft recessed lights...

"Appoint-ament with ZZZada?" the Somalian receptionist inquired from behind a desk so high, until I went up the stairs all I could see was her Miss Africa pageant looking face and long neck. She has a really, really thick accent that is sometimes hard to understand and if you ask her to repeat something, she acts like she's deaf. She acts prissier than anyone I've ever met and always wears a butt length black weave. She reminded me of the type that was always saying "In *my* country, deese is bedder dan what chu Americans blah, blah, blah..."

The salon is on the second floor and attracts a well to do clientele. News anchors, the mayor's wife, old money and the social elite not necessarily directly linked to drug money come here to get their hair done and for makeovers and spa retreats.

The third level is where the famous spa can be found and it is absolutely breathtaking. Elegant chandeliers in the waiting area, crème plush carpet, fresh orchids and calla lily arrangements throughout. Every other month they changed the wallpaper that covers the wall of the waiting area. They've been featured in a couple of magazines, *Elle, Essence, Black Entreprise* and *Ebony*.

Must be nice to have a family that can cooperate well enough to own such a lucrative company.

With the exception of the French masseuse, Lana, all the estheticians and nail techs are very proper speaking Blacks who're always holding conversations about the bible amongst themselves or Ethiopians related to the Ilya's.

Jahla and Jazada are my girls. La runs the salon, Zada manages the spa. Jahla is more of the quiet type but she's seventeen, just graduated from high school this summer and drives an Escalade. I don't talk to her as much since she's younger but girl is together and cool peeps. Zada is one of the *only* people I trust telling anything to.

After I signed in at the desk, a man in a butler's uniform lifted the lid from the silver platter of chocolates. "Soup de jour?" he asked handing me a menu to choose a complimentary soup from.

"I'll have the clam chowder, thank you."

"Hey, Leigh. Have a seat. Z's gonna be out in a sec. I love your hair," Zada's best friend greeted.

"Thanks. Your hair looks good too. You look like a model as always." She had a boyish, 360 degree waved haircut that was freshly tapered and suited her well. Kiona's very pretty and has the right kind of head shape for that sort of look.

"Oh, whatever. I'm good. So what's been up with you?" she asked giving a warm smile.

"Ggggirl! Don't even ask. Drama."

"Well, things'll work out. Just pray or meditate and you'll figure everything out."

"Thank you. That's the nicest thing I've heard all day. And how have you been? Last I heard you'd decided to go to U of M."

What I wouldn't do to be like her and Zada. *They* have it made. Zada's nineteen and drives a pearly white Cadillac DeVille *and* she has a boyfriend she's been with since high school who's at University of California and one of the top players in college basketball right now. Anytime she tells me something she makes me swear not to spread any of her business—something about her parents being extra nosey. But I think it's also because she doesn't want to mess up her play with the fellas and, if I was in her shoes, I wouldn't either. You can tell she's a heartbreaker.

"School's good. I won an award that'll let me to get in more galleries and I made the basketball team. I'm happy," Kiona chirped.

"That's hot. You paint?"

"No. Photography major."

Zada came out. "Heyyy Leigh." She hugged me and flashed those gorgeous deep-set dimples of hers. Her hair is really thick, long and jet-black. She kind of looks like Essence Atkins or a slightly browner Salma Hayek with her round eyes and oval face. "Let's get you in the room."

There were vanilla candles lined up against the wall, sage on the oil burner, a beautifully framed collage of pressed lavender flowers hung on the other wall while a fancy written passage from the book of Psalms encased in a silver frame covered another wall.

"You know I love vanilla, right?"

"That's why I made sure we had some in here."

"Bye, Leigh. Zada?" Kiona called from the couch still flipping thru *Blindspot* magazine.

"Yep?"

"I'll stick around til you get off. We're still goin' out, right?"

"Yep." Zada called back before slipping out so I could undress.

Zada hadn't made three footsteps back into room and I was already telling her too much. You weren't supposed to talk during a massage but this evening I couldn't help it. I told her about the church thing and my fear of getting married. She was a good listener. When Kiona came in to offer me a cup of chamomile tea, I let her in on everything too.

"Leigh. You have a *lot* going on. But I think you're being too hard on yourself. You started out with your own place and went to school. You're smart. As long as you don't mess up with your classes you're good, girl. Don't let anyone take that away from you—especially not some *guy*. You can get dressed—unless you want to take advantage of our special on a Brazillian?" Zada asked after Kiona left.

"Yeah, but it's gonna hurt like hell. Oh, the pains of being a lady. Go ahead and clean my girl up. Leave a strip, though—I'm not trying to look underage, nah."

"You know what Leigh? You need to have fun more often, that's all. Why don't you hang out with me and Kiona sometime?" she asked matter factly, as if she wasn't about to rip all the hair off my pussy.

"Yeah. I will. That sounds like a good idea."

"We're going to that Eryka Badu/Floetry concert at the Fox next month, why don't you go with us."

She wanted to hang out with *me*? Her family was rich. *Rich* rich. Maybe I wasn't such a bad person after all. She and her sister are the type that'll be featured in *Ebony* when they get married.

"That wasn't that bad, was it? Don't hurt 'em." Zada laughed once she was done.

I paid her the two hundred dollar fee, tipped her well and headed back home.

Home. One thought of the word and the sumo's were back on my shoulders.

I should have turned around and hung out with Zada and Kiona tonight—that's what I wanted to do. ...But I had responsibilities. And homework I still hadn't done. Add to that the house signing was scheduled for tomorrow... I hadn't spent any quality time with the kids... Responsibilities.

I pulled in my parking spot behind the building and just sat there not wanting to go inside. I backed the car out, drove around the corner to Ponchatrain and pulled out the tiny square of paper.

I need that
313-333-7105
Kevin

Before I had enough time to change my mind, I dialed the number but ended up hanging up before it rung. What was I doing? I'd just met the man! He was going to think I was desperate. That's what I would have thought if I gave a dude my number and he called me a few hours later. I slipped the number in my bra and headed back to the apartment.

"Hey, bae. Dese kids funny! Mauri an' Pharaoh been dancin'. Pharaoh thank he got skills!"

"That's because he *does*!" I gave my son a kiss.

"What we gon' eat?" Craig asked ignoring the fact that I was tired.

"You're hungry *again*?"

"We only ate one time taday, what'chu talkin' 'bout?"

"Carry out it is. What do you all want?" Nothing around here delivered.

"FoFo's." The minute he replied, Mauri and Pharaoh started chanting "FoFo" over and over all weird like they were in some kind of kiddy cult.

"Aye you two! Simmer down! Put on your quiet voices."

"I wont dey catfish."

"Alright. Hurry up so we can get back."

"What? Why 'on't you jus go?"

I gave him a look.

"Aright, aright. Git in da car y'all."

"See. *This* is what I'm talking about. Why should I have to leave back out to get something for you to eat when you have a car and two hands and two feet? You've been home for two hours. You could've gotten something from the café earlier! Or at least called me before I got all the way home."

"I wasn't hungry den. But guess what?" He leaned over next to my ear and whispered, "I love you. You gon' gimme some tonight?"

"Unbelievable! Un-be-fuckin'-lievable! You know what? How 'bout you just sleep on the couch tonight—better yet, the floor."

"Man, whatever. Here." He handed me thirty dollars. I went into FoFo's and, of all people, ran into Pastor Ellington but before any words were exchanged, Craig was putting his hand in mine.

"Well, well, well." Pastor looked back and forth from me to Craig. "Long time no see."

"Oh, you got balls nah, hungh? You wudden't sayin' nutin' when I was knockin' you upside cho' muthafuckin' head," Craig stated. His nostrils were flared.

"Can't wait to see you in court. Can't wait."

"Yep. You *need* ta spend some time wit cho' own woman an' stop tryin' ta git wit evrybody else's."

"Yep. Can't wait til next month's trial. See you. Find da Lord sometime soon. Maybe he'll keep you outta jail." He gave a hearty, grotesque sounding laugh, grabbed his food off the counter and left. He looked nothing like the man I'd spent years listening to on the pulpit. The sight of him made the marrow in my bones grow ice cold.

"Come on baby, don't worry 'bout dat sick ass muthafucka." Since we'd called the order in we didn't have to wait.

"I saw him dat's why I came in."

"Yeah. Good lookin' out."

I didn't have an appetite and didn't care when Craig ate most of my food. No point in wasting a chicken wing, candied yam and collard green dinner. Fried chicken doesn't taste the same after you warm it up or put it in the refrigerator. And Craig was eating more and more lately. Like his stomach had been replaced with a pregnant woman's.

After the kids ate I played with them and let them stay up a little longer.

"Come on, when you commin' ta bed?"

"I'll be there...*Coming to America* is on. I just wanna see my favorite part."

"Aright." He ran his hands across my nipples. Like *that* was gonna turn me on. He'd drunk enough beers to get a buzz. In a few minutes he's be knocked out and I'd be able to fall asleep peacefully on the couch.

Everything was wrong. Nothing made sense. I loved Craig, no doubt about it. But I wasn't happy. Something between us was bitterly different and my eyebrow twitched every time I asked myself if I had taken him back too quickly.

I tried calling Tamika again, as if calling her this time would rewind the day back to the time I believed Craig was all mine and I was all his.

The phone was still just as disconnected as it was earlier.

I drifted off to sleep still thinking about her. Grandma and mom were wrong if they'd really found out Tamika wasn't Mylo's biological daughter and hadn't told her her mother had been looking for her.

Uncle Mylo was killed when T was eleven by grandma's brother—my great and alcoholic uncle Richard--over a crap game and it had jacked Tamika up for a minute. She had to go to the counselor the rest of sixth grade. Mylo was a good father. He always made time for T even though he liked to party in the streets; he was always around when Tamika's teeth were missing and the Tooth Fairy needed to show up and at every parent-teacher conference before his death—he even came to mine when mom couldn't make it.

But just like that, he was killed by his own uncle and out of Tamika's life for good.

THE NEXT MORNING CRAIG called off work again. He was ready to get the show on the road and ready to close on the house. "Hurry up and get dressed baby, and *damn*! Turn dat muthafukin' radio down. You got it loud as hell up in here."

"Tom Joyner's got Gabrielle Union on."

"Nah ain't da time. I godda get back ta work dis afternoon--I only called off fa dis morning. Dis girl up in human resources lookin' out fa me."

"Always a girl..." my voice trailed off.

"Baby? Who I'm buyin' dis house fo'? You. So stop actin' like dat an' show uh brotha some love?" His head was tilted to the side and his eyebrows were raised. Either he was trying to check me on the sly or wanted me to be as excited about the house as he was. Either way, I didn't care.

"Whatever..." I didn't feel well. It felt like needles were pricking the lining of my stomach.

After three minutes of scanning the closet and dresser drawers, I put on a fuzzy off-white fitted sweater, some wide legged suit pants the same color and a long Versace sweater-coat with dark brown and off-white fur trim around the collar that grazed my ankles, the Versace watch I bought right after I found out Craig had been cheating with that Angela Bitch, lip gloss was a must and some mascara. I threw my freshly flat-ironed hair into a sloppy runway twist, my favorite pair of chocolate brown Jimmy Choo boots and a mist of Carolina Herrera perfume. Who could argue? I looked and smelled good.

"Damn, girl, come here." Craig tried to get in on a little tongue action. I let his tongue enter my lips but did little in return.

"Ugh. Why is your mouth so sticky? Gross." Instead of getting horny I started thinking about all the germs that were probably loaded in his saliva and esophagus.

"Les go." He patted my butt and we were all off in my truck once again. Was Craig pimping me? If that was the case, he'd be asking me to sign for the house by myself. But I didn't have enough income to do that... Then again he was paying his dues in this relationship as well.

"You know what, baby? I think I want another truck...a Lexus or a Mountaineer is nice if you wanna go lower end... "

"Yeah, dat's uh plan. But dis time, keep Darren out of it. I mean, git his discount but he ain't signing on yo' shit no moe."

Good. He *wasn't* trying to live off Darren but little did he know. Darren *paid* for my car up front—there was never a note although I lead him to believe there was one and that it was covered in child support arrangements.

"Aight Lil' Mama an' Man, git ready, we 'bouta go put money down on our house. You ready Man, you an' Ma can make uh club-house in da backyard next summer... Y'all gon' have y'all own rooms. Gimme five!"

"Yeah!" Pharaoh and Mauri squealed in delight.

"Look you two, when we go in this place I don't want any cutting up. If I have to tell either one of you to be quiet, you're getting popped. You hear me?" I got two yeses that chanted the word over and over the rest of the way and didn't stop until we got to the parking lot of Craisins office.

There were four people sitting spaced out around a long oval conference table in the other room in her office suite. Papers and black binders were spread out and arranged on the conference table.

"Why hello little one!" Craisins gushed over Mauri. "She is *really* a doll. And what have we here? Oh! A little gentleman," she stated looking down at Pharaoh before making her way to the heavy set Black guy in a well-tailored, pricey looking suit who was sitting at the end of the table. The room was filled with smoke and fingernails stained brown from the habit.

Craig carefully read over all the documents before signing and handed over a check for five thousand. Just like Scott said our mortgage would be for thirty years and, if we paid the house off within three years, we would be penalized. It was ridiculous! Why did a person get penalized for paying off their own shit? The government was a trip!

You spend six months out of the year working just to give Uncle Sam all your earnings and then waited for them to give you a tax refund like they're really doing something when it was your money in the first place! I could go on and on. Humans made life harder than it needed to be. If I had the money, I would have paid cash for the house and called it a day. All that interest we were going to wind up owing was bull. But Craig *did* get a good fixed rate for us so I guess it would all somehow balanced out in the end.

He got the keys and made more small talk with Craisins and one of the guys in the office. You couldn't help but notice the excitement in his face when he spoke. "Les go check it out right quick! We *godda* check it out! Then I'ma head ta work. We got us uh crib, baby!" He leaned over and kissed me before he pulled off. He dialed his mother and a couple of his homies up to tell them what happened at the closing over speakerphone. He was the first person in his family and among his boys to buy a house.

The sun was shining like a good omen, the leaves were doing their fancy red, orange, brown autumn colored thing, the air was crisp and the house looked really nice when we pulled into the driveway. It looked nicer than I'd remembered.

"Tad-dah!" he shouted opening the door. The kids ran inside.

Watching his face made me smile. Craig was so animated.

"Come here! Gimme uh kiss bae. You know what we godda do? We gon' hafta break dis bad boy *in*! It's gon' be some pussy lickin,' dick strokin' lovemakin' goin' on real soon up in dis joint, right here in front of da fireplace. Start packin' taday. Make sure you git some boxes from Farmer Jack. I wanna move on Sunday--I'ma hit up all da fellas. Oh yeah, call Budget an' make da reservations fa da truck, baby. I wanna get all dis tagether so you 'on't have ta worry 'bout shit."

"Yeah, but remember. I've got to run to the school to talk to my instructors. And since my mother isn't speaking to me and me and Tamika're on the outs, I don't have a babysitter. I need to see if Dina'll watch them 'til I figure something out. Would you mind if we move three Sundays from now? I mean, we can start packing things and taking stuff over but I have to wait until Rick finds a replacement for me *and* I've got to catch up on classes. We can get it all done by Thanksgiving—be moved in and settled in by then. What do you think?"

"We 'on't even celebrate Thanksgiving. How da hell you gon' celebrate takin' some land from da Natives 'cause some Europeans needed it? We 'bouta move way bafoe dat—prob'ly by next Sunday. You can manage da place after we move til dey git somebody."

"...Yeah... Well, the house *is* beautiful."

"It's our house, bae."

We walked around the place discussing what type of furniture we wanted for each room. "Yeah, you good at decoratin' an' hookin thangs up, I *will* say dat 'bout cho' ass. Go head, do yo' thang, baby--jus don't be pickin' out no hotel lookin' shit." He laughed.

Pharaoh picked the room he wanted between the other three bedrooms, we had the master suite while Craig chose Mauri's room from the other two bedrooms. I'd already decided the fourth bedroom would be the guest room and a playroom for the kids. I was going to find two bookshelves that matched the maple colored wood throughout the house for the living room and the basement was going to be a den. I was getting as excited as Craig already was!

We headed back to the car sad to be leaving the house so soon. Craig and I talked non-stop, crazy-excited the whole ride to the apartment. Coming back to the apartment was a big let down. It seemed so small and cramped in comparison to the house. Kind of like having a good dream only to wake up and realize you were late for work.

Maybe we wouldn't argue as much in the new house. If he got on my nerves, I could just go to another room and not have to look at his face. I could read and get caught up on all my work without dealing with tenants. I could even study on the back porch. That would be nice...with the ozone layer being so fucked up lately, you could have a couple of nice, sixty-degree days in November.

I kissed Craig good-bye and switched to the drivers seat, pulled off and headed to school.

I finally had a few seconds to call Sherra. I whipped my phone out of the eight hundred-dollar soft leather purse that matched my boots perfectly. I absolutely loved this purse. I'd seen Kimora Lee on E! with one just like it. Darren bought it after I quit speaking to him because of that "Project muthafuka" comment.

"Hey girl. I *have* to tell you WHAT *happened* yesterday," I started. My right hand flew into the air as I got ready to bring her up to date with all the latest news. Whenever I got this excited I started talking so fast the words started stringing together in valley girl fashion.

"--*Girrrrrllll*. Wait! Lemme tell *you*! You know what Pharaoh said happened when he was at Tami—"

"—*That's what* I'm *tryin ta tell you* about!" I went into the whole shebang of how I'd beaten T's ass and how I felt bad after the fact.

"Wait a minute. I got more fa you. Wha'chu 'bouta do?"

"I've got to go to school to talk to my teachers. This semester's been *so* fucked up—"

"--We need ta talk! Why 'on't you stop by ma house? I'll ride wit chu so I can fill you in. After that we can go eat somewhere. Floods?"

"Yeah, can Dina watch the kids?"

"Girl, yeah! She ain't doing nothin' but watchin' old re-runs of *In Living Color* on cable as usual."

I took the Lodge to 94 and flew over to the eastside where Sherra stayed glad to at least have *one* real female friend. Craig was cool to talk to but there are times when a girl needs to talk *about* her man to a homegirl! As long as it's the right one, though. Too many females will soak it all in and use it as ammunition to hook up with your man behind your back. Sherra wasn't like that.

When she climbed in the truck, her face looked more than upset. Her dark, arched eyebrows were raised like she'd just witnessed a murder and her eyes held a, 'you'll never believe this!' look. She waited impatiently as Dina got the kids out of the car shaking her head back and forth and breathing heavily.

"What's wrong?" Uh-oh. It was something major.

"Finish telling me what happened wit Tamika," her voice was seriously eerie.

I went into detail about the Mylo/real mother thing pulling into the school parking lot as I finished. "So what's the deal with you?" I asked curious as to why she hadn't been shedding the 411. Even thought I'd rambled on, she normally would have cut in and said her piece by now.

"I'll wait 'til you finish. You gon' have ta sit down for *dis* one," she stated still looking like she just heard somebody'd killed her dog.

I went to one my classes just as it was ending. "Where you been?" Lamar asked. His boys were standing next to him.

"Yeah, lookin' all good up in here, Mrs. Walker." Durrell added. That was just in case Craig was around and to see if we were still together.

"Man, you bedda be in class next week." Lamar was very cute. He and Craig used to work together before Craig started working at GM. "We miss lookin' at chu. Syke, naw," Lamar added. "Where Craig at?"

"Work."

A couple of the females walked by while the guys from class were talking to me and rolled their eyes.

"Hello Ms. Anderson. How nice of you to finally decide to show up." Mr. Lohligan was pissed.

I explained to him that I had been under serious duress as I had encountered a family emergency and that I honesty did enjoy having him as an instructor (all truth, I wasn't sucking up) and that, if he let me make up all the work I had missed, I promised I'd be the student I was three weeks ago.

He agreed and told me that he knew I was a good student and had been waiting for an explanation.

I'd gotten lucky and had him last semester for microbiology. He was excellent. He always took time to break down theories students didn't understand unlike some of the instructors who simply breezed thru textbooks and flunked most of the class indifferently. I couldn't afford to drop this Human Anatomy and Physiology II course. Thank God he agreed to let me makeup the work. One down, three more to go.

Only one other instructor was in her office. Mrs. Kennedy was rather understanding and gave me all the required readings and was allowing me make up the quizzes by doing take home test for the Intro to Nutrition course. "I don't let more than three absences slide, Leigh. Make sure you don't abuse this allowance. I want the packet completed by Tuesday. That gives you the whole weekend."

That worked. I thanked her and Father God once again afterwards and left out of the school with Sherra who was completely silent at this point.

We parked in the Casino like we had done way back three, four years ago in that old hooptie of mine and headed for Floods with Dominique.

As much as I chit-chatted about my massage at Ilya's and promised to treat her the next time I went, she still acted somber. If it was something *that* juicy why didn't she just come out with it already? Making me wait on major info was never her style.

"Okay. Hold up. Are you gonna tell me what's going on or what?"

"Okay. Let's go in the casino right quick." She moved away from the elevator that led to the outside and went inside Greek Town casino instead. Her movements were jerky and clumsy and she looked at her shoes without blinking and avoided my questioning eyes the entire three-floor elevator ride.

Sherra plunked down onto one of the stools in front of a slot machine and motioned for me to do the same once we flashed our ID's and walked past the restrooms.

"Girl, dis chick named Angela--and I know she wudden't lying 'cause when we talked two weeks ago I 'member you said Craig had cheated on you wit uh bitch named Angela—she goin' 'round talkin' 'bout she pregnant by uh nigga named Craig dat work at dat GM Detroit-Hamtramck plant in da office. She's uh janitor at my job--and she's uh *raggedy bitch*, too--look like da kinda female dat'uh go on *Maury Povich* talkin' 'bout 'Who's Da Daddy.'"

Disdain curled in her lips as she continued, "She always wear cheap lookin' blonde weaves even though she darker than me and she built real funny—you know, big shoulders and big titties wit no ass and no hips, like uh female football player. She said he won't take her calls no more and he talkin' 'bout she'd bedder shut dat shit up or else she askin' fa trouble. She plottin' ta have her brothas jump Craig by November. She said dat she was faithful ta him and dat he cousins wit her girl Tamika. She said she called him four months ago and some chick answered tha phone when she had tried to hit him up on da number he had called her from. She said she was pissed at first but was gon' give him a second chance but he tripped out on her and stopped kickin' it wit her after dat.

"So she tried to git Tamika ta git him ta call her but Tamika said he had started kickin' it with some chick from his job," she whispered, slamming her left hand against the machine. "I hate ta be tha bearer of bad news but you needed ta hear about *dis* shit...I know it's been uh lot uh drama goin' on but..." She shook her head. "You need ta know about dis shit right here..."

"...Okay, okay, okay. Repeat this." I placed my hands on the temples of my forehead, looked her dead in the mouth and paid attention to every single syllable coming out to make *sure* I wasn't going deaf, that I wasn't hearing things and that I wasn't in some foggy nightmare of a dream. My eyebrows were raised so high they felt like they about to fly off.

I rested an elbow on the machine. Three slots away somebody's grandma was screaming all kinds of Hallelujah and praises as three cherries popped in front of her face.

"Dat *girl*. Angela. She pregnant wit Craig's baby *and* she cool wit Tamika! But she said Tamika don't know she plannin' on havin' him put in tha hospital. She said she ain't gon' git uh hit put out on him 'cause he her babby daddy but--if ya ask me, she ain't got no pull like dat ta be orderin' no hit out on nobody--dat part is just talk. Whenever I be 'bout ta git off work, she be doin' trash rounds. She so stupid and talk so much, I jus play dumb and let her talk.

"Leigh, I gotta say. It 'on't sound like she makin' all dis up. She 'on't even mention yo' name and she 'on't know we tight—I 'on't talk ta her all like dat.

"But I know one thing. She said she gon' catch him real soon an' she said she just found out two days ago he be goin' out ta lunch at Floods wit Tamika an' his new bitch almost every day. But she usually be workin' durin' dat time, plus her brothas ain't gon' jump him up in dere. You know how security up in Flood's be..." She paused and tried to read my face. Her heavy chest heaved in and out. "I think, rather than me telling you, you need ta keep goin' up ta Floods ta check to see if you see him in there...prove it ta *yourself*..." she added since I still hadn't said anything.

A long time ago—well--who am I fooling—three weeks ago, I would have fainted.

Six months ago, I would have been crushed, devastated, disturbed, fasting, calling Evangelist First Lady Ellington, undergoing crying spells and screaming 'Why God, Why?' up and down the place right about now.

But today was different. I snorted, a partial, "Hmm" and looked around. People were laughing, winning and losing at the slots. This had been my first time even being up in the place outside of the restaurants--neither Sherra nor I believed in gambling.

Life was going on as usual. Casino cocktail girls—some heavy, some disgustingly bone thin of various races--in their playboy bunny 'wanna be' red and black corsets uniforms with black panties and sheer stockings walking around giving patrons drinks.

And what was I doing while all this living was going on around me? Wasting my life on someone who was doing a good job of proving that he'd never love me the way I needed him to love me back? Being somebody's fool time after time?

Even Darren wasn't as bad as Craig! *And* he had money! *And* he had asked me to marry him--in a fucked up way, yes, but I would have been in a house a long time ago--a much bigger and better one!

I should have gone away to college like Darren said on our first date...could have met a nice, family oriented guy whose parents were professionals and had been married for twenty-five years. Instead, I was living out a rap song.

"Let's go over there right nah," I drawled in a deep, unlike me sounding voice. "I believe you, but I wanna see. I wanna see if his ass is over there. Yeah, and didn't I just tell you 'bout how *cool* him and Tamika've been lately? He probably fuckin' dat rat, too. I wanna see...I wanna see dis shit... Um-hmm...I wanna see..."

"Leigh, try to get yourself together, nah. You scarin' me. I know dis is some deep stuff but...um...let's sit here for uh minute. Yo' eyes lookin' real crazy right nah." She talked nervously as her hands trembled. "I had ta tell you. I couldn't let you go out like dat."

"Crazy? I ain't crazy...I know what's up. Dis muthafuka on some bullshid, that's whad! Signin' fa uh house in only his name and—"

"—He *whattt!*" her voice shot up and her words sprung in the air like a frisbee. "You ain't tell me dat part! What'chu gon' do, Leigh?"

"I'll figure that one out in a lil bit, but right about nah, we 'bouta walk up in Floods, I'ma play it real cool and we gon' see what's really good. We gon' see..." I couldn't stop shaking my head up and down. "...We gon' see if Craig is, in fact, there wit-a-bitch!" I looked at my Versace watch. Two-thirteen. "Let's go," I commanded.

The zing of the shiny silver and lemon and cherry fruit slot machines, the smokers blowing non-cognizant circles in the air, the chubby Irish looking red headed male bartender now laughing with a heavy set dude tapping on his bottle of Miller Lite with his thumb, my mother, my grandmother, Craig, Tamika—all of them had something in common. None of them cared about me, none of them gave a shit!

I crossed the street in a blur. Blue Cross Blue Shield workers were milling about in front of the building, some laughing, some on cell phones. The walk seemed like forever to Floods. We slinked our way in since there was no cover during lunch and scanned the room for a head of curly black hair that looked like Craig's. I moved swiftly and chose a table near the kitchen and restroom with a perfect view of the entry and exit door. That way there would be no escape routes available for these muthafuckas.

Lo and behold, who did we have laughing it up so hard, they didn't even see us step foot inside?

There they were. Near the stage as the jazz band played. The lead singer was smiling as hard as the tall looking bitch Craig had his arm wrapped all around. And guess who was next to the happy couple?

Tamika, black eyes and all.

Now, the bitch who was playing in the same silky mustache my daughter usually played with was one *odd* looking spectacle. I wanted to get closer to see what the fuck she really was. I squinted and still couldn't tell.

"Wait, Leigh!" Sherra grabbed my sleeve. "We should just leave. We got some conformation. We can slip out da back door or you can just watch 'em for uh minutes and go. *Please* don't do nothin' crazy. You scarin' me, fa real, nah."

"Naw. I'm good. You did what you was supposed ta do--let me know and let me see fa myself. I'm walkin' over there." Of all the days for me *not* to carry my knife and mace!

"Why hello there, husband to be." The drawl returned. Instantly Craig's neck hung like one of those cheap silvery brown wire hangers from the dry cleaners. His arm was still around this—this thing. And she really was a sight to see. Her eyes were huge and almond shaped--I swear they were bigger than Niquie's eyes. They reminded me of the aliens they put on National Inquirer covers under captions like 'Aliens Raise Human Baby' that you couldn't help *but* notice while standing in line at the grocery store.

Her face was shaped exactly like a heart with a widow's peak, high, hard cheekbones and a chin so pointy, she could use it to carve a turkey. A couple of shades lighter than me, she had a large bottom lip with a thin line of a top lip that was now forced into a tight pucker.

She wore a white poet's sleeved blouse that was buttoned all the way up to her neck, carmel stir-up pants and dark riding boots. An olive green trench coat draped over chair. She looked like a Spiegel's 1992 catalog ad. Really, who dressed like that nowadays?

"Hey baby, dis is Raina--Lorraina." He laughed, a short and sour sounding, "Heh, heh." "Donna? You know? Da real estate agent. Dat's her mother. Sit down. Chill wit us. I was jus tellin' her how much you love our new house." He couldn't get the words out fast enough and wore a goofy, smiley expression that, along with Tamika's scared eyes and gapped open mouth, said it all.

"How dare you not speak to your favorite cousin, Tamika." Oh how the sarcasm dripped in my voice. I gave the side of her head a nice little push to the right. "And you my dear. Rushing to work only to hang out at Floods, hmm?" I yanked on Craig's ear so hard, I left a red mark.

Then, before I could get to the Raina bitch, she did the strangest thing that answered all the questions I had had.

She purred. Like a real, live, cat! This was some out of this world shit. She looked like a human alien, Siamese cat, person!

"So *you're* the bitch that likes to hit my daughter, hmm?" And without a second thought, I took her steak knife and with intended precision slid it against her cheek, down the right side of her face leaving a slither opened to red perfection trailing down her face.

She sat there releasing curls of smoke from her tiny triangular nostrils. After thirty good seconds she finally responded. "Whaad? No need to gitchur pan-dies all in a knod, kee-deen" I guess that was supposed to be kitten. "Must you be so mean? I know not whaad you speak of?" She had a weird accent but sounded a bit like Craisins. Her hair, although it was long, black and combed to the back, was that same 'I tried to press it myself but it got fuzzy' texture as the real estate agent's and even though she was sitting down, I could tell she was taller than me.

She kept fluttering her eyes. Was this bitch high on something? Who acted like this for real—in public? I was glad Sherra stepped up behind me to witness this strangeness.

"Baby, that's mean. Here. Come sit down. Let me get you a seat," Craig rushed.

"No-No!" I abruptly shouted putting my hand up in protest. Twelve empty alcoholic beverage glasses sat cluttered on the table and each one of them had something clear on the rocks in front of them.

I put my face close to the cat bitch that'd been hitting my daughter and breathed, "You can have him, I'm done with him now." I picked up her fork faking a jab to her eye. She didn't move or flinch and it was enough to make me to think about actually poking her eye out but, on second thought, the pain she'd suffer from Craig would suffice.

It was Tamika's turn. "You know you're right? We aren't the same kind of people. But just remember this: I...know...where...*you live*. Expect a visit *real soon*," I whispered.

Then, I stated to Craig, "See ya later tonight when you come to get your belongings, hmm? Oh yes, I have *plans for* you, *dahr-ling*." I took his plate of catfish, macaroni, red beans and rice and slammed it with all my might against his face, making sure I didn't get anything on my outfit then walked off with Sherra steps behind. Security was running behind her. But I didn't run, I walked my normal pace. Maybe it was enough that we were leaving or that I was a familiar face to the Heavy D look alike bouncer. Whatever the case was, they didn't bother following us out of the door. I could still feel the thud of the ceramic plate against Craig's forehead within my fingertips. This wasn't some phony episode of *Cheaters* with bad actors and elementary storylines and crummy little infomercials stuck in between. This reality show was my life.

"I'll drive," Sherra rushed, stealing the keys out of my hand. "I'm worried 'bout chu. You beatin' up bitches and shit and you look crazy right nah. I almost wish I wouldn'ta tole you. Um, let's pray—"

"Fuck a prayer. There *is no* God." My lips hardened. "All these years--trying to be a faithful Christian, look where it's gotten me...no mother to talk to, a grandmother who won't speak to me and both of them are quote unquote *saved!* A preacher that wanted to get all up in my vaginal walls. A piece of shit fiance, a cousin so fucking jealous it was as easy for her to stab me in the back as it was for her to cut up that steak she had sitting in front of her...there's no such thing as a God. "

"You can't blame the Lord for that no good bastard!"

"Are you friend or foe, Sherra?"

"*Leiigghh*? I'm your friend! And please! Stop talking like dat! Let's go talk ta someone. I'm takin' off work tonight ta make sure you're okay. You wanna go to a counselor? You could go ta Receiving Hospital or—"

"--You sound like foe ta me. I'm okay. I just have to make plans, that's all. Change some locks. Cut some balls off—you know, the usual for situations like these. I'm good. Hungry, though. Let's go somewhere to eat. You know what I have a taste for? Outback!"

"I ain't got no money ta be goin' out ta eat right na—"

"--Nonsense! I've got you."

"Noooo! We goin' ta my house. Dina cooked las night. There's plenty of—"

"--No, sweetie. I'm going home--after I get something to eat. Do you think Dina can watch the kids a bit longer?"

"You ain't got no choice on dat one. I ain't lettin them go home witchu actin' like dis!"

I began to laugh, really loud and hard. I don't know why, or what was so funny. Suddenly it just felt good to laugh and I couldn't stop laughing until my stomach started hurting and I had to gasp for air.

Sherra parked in Receiving Hospital's parking structure and was now pulling on my arm trying to get me out of the passengers seat. "Hey! Hey! That's Versace you're tugging on! Stop. Get back in the car. I'm--I'm fine. I just need something in my stomach. You know what the good part to all of this is?"

"What?" She looked me up and down all cockeyed with her hand on her phone like it was a gun resting on her side.

"I didn't sign with him for that house!"

"Yes, yes...that was...that was good..." She still hadn't closed my door.

"And you know why all of this is all my fault?"

"It is *not* your fault!" She shouted it like I had called her an obscene name.

"Yeah, it *is*! I kept feeling like something wasn't right but my stupid ass kept getting deeper and deeper in it. That real estate agent didn't sit well with me from day one. I felt like Craig was rushing and too pressed to get back with me. We spent all our time arguing when we were together. And lately he's been drinking like he was bred by a sailor and a fish...

"I just kept getting that feeling in my gut...from the second night after I took him back... If he likes that gray skinned, alien, cat lady—moe power to 'em! Pharaoh ain't miss the mark with his nickname fa ha ass!"

She slammed my door, got back in the driver's seat and started biting her nails and spitting them shits all over the interior of my truck. Ugh. Until now she had been doing a good job of growing out of that bad habit for the last few months.

"Let's get carry out and go back to your place. You need ta hurry up and change da locks."

"Oh, I know..."

"...I thought you was gon' pull something out cho' purse and stab all of 'em."

"Good thing I switched purses today or else I would've!"

"See, I told you, there *is* a God. Then yo' ass would've ended up in jail for three murders. And fa what? Pieces of shit?"

"You can shut that God shit up right nah!"

"Leigh, you been my best friend fa seven years, nah. I'ma be here fa you. Dis too much shit fa one person ta have ta deal wit alone...you'll be okay in time."

"I'm okay, *NOW*! A little hurt and disappointed but..." I suddenly didn't feel like talking anymore. Mya's song, "Movin' On" came in on the satellite station. I blasted the radio and sung along.

"Well...one thing fa sure...she sounds good singin' even when she's goin' crazy..." Sherra commented to herself.

When that went off, I pulled out my I-Pod and played the song again. Then it was "Hey Ladies" by Destiny's Child. Then a mix song that repeated lyrics about beating a bitch with a bat over and over. Some Mary songs. Brandy's "Learn the Hard Way" and "Almost Doesn't Count" ...Music could really dig into your soul. One day I was gonna have to meet Mya and Brandy and tell them how their songs sung out to the woe that was my love life.

"*What is* dat thing?" Sherra asked. She had been eyeing it for a while.

"An I-Pod. It just came out. You can buy songs online and download 'em on here. Darren bought it for me and told me what website to go to to get the songs from. He even gave me the password to his account," I answered after we got some food and went back to my place.

Even though I wasn't looking forward to the pain in the ass it was going to be I called a locksmith. I was going to have to give all eight residents in my section of the building new keys for the front and back doors. There were twenty-four units all together but the building was divided into three sections and each had their own separate entry. Good thing I didn't have to get keys for the other sixteen tenants in the other two sections of the building.

I didn't bother packing all his clothes and shit up like I had the last time. I didn't peep a word of it to Sherra but my plan was to get the bitch back. I was going to use his ass, like he had used me. I was about to get paid off this one! I would make him feel so guilty and make him give me as much money as he made a week. *And* I was going to call that Kevin dude and set something real nice up with him. Maybe a dinner date. He looked like he had it going on. I didn't know if her was a big time baller just yet but he had to be *something* to be up in Chez's chair.

When I got tired of using and abusing Craig, I would drop him like an oversized formulation of feces.

It was apparent that he didn't want a woman who'd treat his ass right. He was one of those people--like most in this world--that respected the muthafuckas that dogged them out but dogged the very people that had their back and really loved them.

"YOU KNOW HE AIN'T gon' change," Sherra commented flicking thru channels with the remote. She'd spent the night and was giving me no signs of a coming departure, which was beginning to irk me. I wanted to call that guy.

"Girl, I ain't thinkin' about Craig all like that anymore," I stated snapping the bubble wrap from a package Darren had sent for Pharaoh. There was something wonderful about bubble wrap. The way it squished against your fingertips...the sound as the bubble popped. Yeah, bubble wrap was one of those small things that made the world a better place. I'd seen pink bubble wrap, blue, purple...I wondered if they had yellow or red--or if you could purchase it somewhere? I imagined wrapping myself up in bubbly wrap and rolling all over the floor popping myself away. "I thought we were made for each other—neither one of us have middle names." I laughed. "...In the end, whatever happens, happens..." I added, finalizing my thoughts on The Gamer.

"What you gon' do, Leigh? Once you take them back after they do stuff like this, they 'on't ever change. You shoulda told somebody uh long time ago about how he was actin'. I'm glad we talked the other day or else I probably wouldn't have even thought twice about what she was saying."

I wanted to say, *how tha hell you got so much expertise on my situation? When was the last time yo' ass had a boyfriend? You ain't even felt a dick inside you yet...*But her heart was in the right place. Instead I pretended to care about the words that continued coming out of her mouth. "Yeah, Sherra, I'll figure everything out. Don't let me hold you up. I gotta contact those other two teachers so I can catch up. And I know you got stuff to do...I appreciate all that you've done, girl. I owe you big time."

"I 'on't feel right about leaving you here...why on't chu come ta my place for a while? Craig is crazy. You on't need ta be here by yo'self when he try ta come back over. He's got all his stuff here--eventually he's *gonna* come back!"

"Sher*rrrraaa*! I will *be okay*! Girl, go ta work. Ple*assse*. You already got the kids. I'll be fine..."

"...Well...you sound like you want me ta leave...I got a bad feeling about leaving you here, dough...You sure you gonna be okay goin' up ta Detroit Community today? Ain't no body up there on Fridays. Maybe you should go another day. You should email all your teachers and wait ta go back...switch campuses next semester or sumthen."

Eventually I convinced her I was okay and dropped her off at her job. She gave me her work number for "just in case I needed it," as she put it. Had she been there when I whipped Tamika's ass, she'd have known there was nothing to be worried about. With all the shit I just went thru, I knew how to take care of myself.

The first thing I did before I got out of the car after I dropped her off was hit Kevy, Kev up. He answered on the first ring. "Hello." His voice was full of rich, sexy flavor.

"Hey, Kevin. This is Lisa, the girl from KD's."

"Whassup, Ma? I been waiting for you to hit me up."

"...Well, I did."

"You got a brotha over here smiling. What's the deal? You married?"

"—Noo!" I offered all too quickly. He laughed.

"Well, I'm a straight up kinda dude. I kick it with a few. But I liked you and yo' vibe. I'd like to take you out to dinner. How's tomorrow?"

"Aaaah...it would have to be around like...nine?"

"Alright. It's all up to you. Sweet Georgia Brown, Southern Fires, East Franklins, Fishbones?"

I'd just gone to Southern Fires with Craig two weeks ago and Sweet Georgia Brown was one of Darren's Detroit favorites so that was out. "Fishbones would be nice." We could do East Franklin's another night.

"Aright. Can I hit you up in an hour? I got some business to take care of—money to make."

I put on the sexiest, babiest voice I could. "Yeah, baby. Handle your business."

"Damn, make that forty minutes."

I drove over to Somerset mall to look for something for our date. On the way there, I called to check up on the kids and found out Pharaoh had a crush on Dina and had asked her to marry him when he turned four and that Mauri had been crying for "milk from mommy" and wouldn't accept a bottle or regular food. My milk was basically drying out. With everything that had happened, the kids'd spent more time away from home than with me and Craig. But what could I do? I couldn't bring them home until I spoke to Craig and figured out exactly how to handle him; this time it wasn't about my own feelings, it was all about safety.

"Hey, baby. What you up to?" Kevin asked as I picked up a pink gypsy halter-top from Nordstrom with silver stitched filigree and sequences on it that accentuated the tons of cleavage I had going on.

"Shopping. I look like I'm talking to myself with this earpiece in my ear."

He laughed. "Next time let me know how much you need before you go."

Oh yeah. This friends with benefits thing was going to work. When had Craig *ever* offered to give me any shopping money before we had started fucking? Hell, before he moved in, I had paid for his lunch a couple of times before he had asked me out on our first real date!

"Aww. You're so sweet." The baby voice was doing its job.

"You play tennis or swim?"

"No. Why?"

"Aright. Well, you about to learn sometime soon. We gotta get you some gear for some sports. What do you usually do for fun?"

"I'm a mother. I take care of my kids and go to school."

"Aright, aright, I respect that but I godda make sure you're getting all you can outta life. A woman as fine as you should be doing some things... I think you're gonna enjoy hanging out with me."

We talked for an hour and eventually got past casual conversation but I still hadn't found out what he did for a living or where he lived. But it didn't matter. I liked him. He was blunt, a bit more seasoned than any guys I'd ever dated, very fond of phone sex, more of a listener and not as talkative as I would have preferred however he did laugh at my jokes and was as much of a Jerry Seinfield fan as I was which, in my book, made him a keeper.

I purchased a pair of Seven boot-cut jeans that rested nicely in the crack of the roundness of my behind and made my butt look more than inviting, the Vuitton purse I had been dreaming about, a bottle of Michael perfume and the sexiest swimming suit I could find from a boutique that specialized in handcrafted lingerie and one of a kind swimwear from Italy. I grabbed a salad from Cosi for lunch/dinner and dreadfully headed back to the apartment.

The only calls I got the entire night were from Sherra and the kids but I still couldn't fall asleep. Every faint creek, every uncertain thump in the wall, every chirp of a car alarm, anytime a resident entered the building and creaked the heavy metal doors my heart raced and my stomach was ready to give up its lining. Paranoia was getting the best of me. I put on that song Kelis screams "I Hate You So Much Right Now!" and Gwen Stefani's "Sunday Morning" and played them over and over to cover up the strange noises.

To my relief, the next morning came and went with no sign of Craig. I needed a gun. To avoid soliciting Darren's help, I'd have to look online and research Michigan's permit laws...

AFTER STUDYING ALL DAY and still not catching up on homework, going to spend time with the kids and caving in to Mauri's demand for breasts milk—which turned into me holding her and reading *The Three Billy Goats Gruff* to her instead thanks to the lack of milk, at a quarter to seven I was able to get back to the apartment and take a relaxing, 'make sure my body smelled right' soak in the tub and left to meet Kevin at the restaurant.

When I entered he stood up and greeted me with a sexy ass smile. The brother was fine. He wore a soft, black leather pea coat, a tee shirt underneath a casual black lambs wool sweater that revealed strong, angular shoulders of which I later found out was Burberry along with a pair of slightly slimmer fitting jeans than what most fellas in the hood wore and a black wool Ventair Kangol that sat on top of his freshly shaved haircut.

His chocolate skin was so smooth--like a candy bar in the flesh, compelling enough to lean over and lick his cheeks but I somehow managed to maintain my composure. All of his features, from his deep-set, dark eyes to his perfect nose and goatee were well defined and chiseled to deliver this impeccably handsome man. Whoever said Black was ugly lied!

He had reserved a table near the waterfall that connected to the Athenaeum hotel. As I ate my favorite Fishbone's dish of crab cakes, stuffed mushrooms and spicy Creole rice, I enjoyed his laidback style and approach to life. He wasn't trying to school me like Craig had and he didn't try to show off like Darren. Instead he did Richard Pryor impressions, we talked about growing up in the D and high school since we'd both gone to King and the conversation was good.

"I got a room upstairs…you down?" he asked. I replied by licking my lips and sliding my hand in his.

"You know I took a risk taking you out, right? You godda be somebody's wife or *some*body's baby mama. I bet he'd try to kill us both if they knew what *we* were about to *do*…"

"Maybe, maybe not." I chuckled rubbing my breasts against his elbow.

When we entered the room, I did all I could to make sure my mouth didn't drop to the floor. The bathroom had an isolated toilet that was separated by a wall from the Jacuzzi. Both the bathroom and the living room and had skylights. There was a flat-screened television that fit across a large expanse of the wall in the living room with a fireplace underneath it. White candles sat on top of the nightstands next to the king sized bed waiting to be lit and, streets over, there was a nice view of the Detroit River.

A bottle of Dom was on ice next to the sterling silver plate sitting underneath two glasses along with a dozen pink roses. "You said you were wearing pink tonight so…" He smiled sensually at me.

"They're *beauuuutiful*." I played off my excitement by *not* jumping up and down and squealing in delight like a contestant on *Wheel of Fortune* who'd just won the final prize. I had NEVER gotten roses from any man—not on Valentine's day in high school even though every nerd in the school professed to have a major crush on me, not on Sweetest Day, not on Mother's Day, not on my birthday--NEVER! Yeah, yeah, yeah--cards, too many teddy bears to keep, balloons, singing telegrams from Craig…but before this night, the rose bouquet category remained null and void.

Kevin didn't get mad when I refused the champagne. He just sat on the living room sofa, lit a blunt and chilled with me. Then, we made our way to the Jacuzzi. Of course I brought that black newly purchased swimming suit *thang*. Its crisscross straps went around my body, it was cut very, very low and showed off the 32DD twins that'd grown thanks to the two kids and had a circular cut-out that revealed my belly button. The sides were cut so high, my hips felt more than naked and the g-string part in the back didn't cover my behind any better. I loved it! With a body like this I'd never have a case of low self-esteem!

"Damn, you thick in tha thighs and got that lil' bitty waist…you work-out?"

"Nope. Just blessed."

"Fa sho. I knew females that ran track and didn't have legs close to what you got. They don't make 'em like you anymore. Come here, baby girl." He put the roach (end of the blunt) in the ashtray and pulled me close thru the bubbles. Slowly and carefully he slid his tongue in my mouth. Within minutes that lovely swimming *thang* was on the floor next to us along with his navy pin striped boxing shorts. And, with the way he slid his finger against my second tongue, teasingly and enticingly wickedly, my inner walls were wetter than the Jacuzzi's water.

In the flickering candlelight, we took turns impressing each other mimicking love wildly, cruelly and insanely, like we were the last two human species on earth with only one day left to live. He was thicker than what I could take but gentle, nevertheless--with my ankles near my ears-- he pushed me past my limits and I was more than willing to receive his surging deepness. "A lil' pain is good for the soul," he breathed continuing. It hurt so good, I couldn't protest. And it suited his fancy.

I gazed up at the skylight as he dozed off not even concerned about our condom-less episode. Something about him felt...familiar. Maybe there was such a thing as past lives. He was easy to be around and didn't leave me feeling lacking...or uncomfortable. I rested my head on his left shoulder and watched him sleep. Lightly...lightly, light-*ly* then he breathed out, each time was the exact same.

His side profile was perfect. Not one feature on his golden brown face had an imperfection.

His cell phone rung interrupting the high I was getting just from looking at him. It beeped only once before he snatched it off the nightstand on his side of the bed. "Yeah? Aright...aright. Gimme twenty." He swiftly picked up his clothes from the chair next to the nightstand, went into the bathroom and came out a few minutes later. "I'm gonna have to run, baby girl. I'll hit you up soon—real soon." He kissed me on my forehead, slapped something on the nightstand and was less than a shadow in the doorway seconds later.

Yep, instinct deemed that I had fallen into the likes of a street healer.

I fell asleep against the silkiness of the sheets where his scent lingered on. Here I was safe.

Part of me wished to never step foot onto 1 Merton Road again. They always said dreams could come true. Somewhere not far from reach, a new life awaited...

CHAPTER 12

I WOKE UP FEELING better than I had in a long time. It was almost twelve. I threw my clothes on and got ready to leave, taking in the whole scene in. I looked like a replica of a dorkie spring fresh dish detergent ad or something. Before grabbing my hot pink leather pea coat, I noticed the bills laid out on the nightstand. My eyes bucked. One thousand dollars? One *thousand* dollars! This time I *did* jump up and down like a little kid.

"Hey, girl. You look nice," out of no where a dark skinned guy in a T-shirt and a black Detroit hat flipped to the back stated, walking up beside me as I left the Athenaeum.

My hair was a wild mess. I had pinned the back up since the water from the late night Jacuzzi duet had taken its toll on my do and was wearing the spaghetti strapped undershirt I'd worn yesterday under my halter as a top and I was sans bra. It was so warm, I hadn't even put my coat on.

"Thanks." I paid him no attention and waited to cross the street to the Casino parking structure. I had to get my ticket validated, go check on the kids, check on a call I'd gotten from Mr. Moses who lived right over me, school—too much shit to do.

"You get it all the time, you don't even care about a compliment anymore, hungh?" he asked smiling. "I'm only a valet guy, I know. But doesn't it still count?"

"*What*?" I asked rather annoyed until I actually took the time to look at him.

He was fine as hell! Very, very black, like a smooth skinned African and well built. Probably had a big ding-a-ling—the tall, dark and slender ones always did. A college boy, too proper sounding to be from here—I assessed him right off the bat, working while in school. "You don't sound like you're from here," I stated deciding against crossing the street and ignoring him.

"I'm from Hawaii but I go to Wayne State. Premed."

"From *Hawaii*?"

"Yeah, there are Black people there, *too*." He laughed, reading my thoughts. "Ricco," he extended his hand to shake mine. "...I've got to go throw my uniform on, my shift starts in a second. But, *you* are pretty and I love your smile--I had to tell you. I even like the way you walk," he complimented.

Yeah, the pink ankle gator boots I had on did give me that extra feminine sway but what was really good? A sista could get used to this kind of treatment! See what happened when you mentally dumped Trash! "You're cute too, but *waaay* too young for me. And I have kids."

"If a man really likes you, he'll accept your kids—remember that." He switched from the seriousness of his last statement, "I'm too young, huh? Oh, well. You should still give me your number. We can hang out sometime."

"No. I've got someone. But if I'm ever in the area and see you, I'll stop by and say hello." This could be a test administered by Mr. Kev.

"All right, that's cool. Looks like it's gonna rain really bad today. Check out the clouds." He pointed. "They're pretty heavy." We watched as clouds parted into cotton puffballs and quickly veiled the sun. In seconds, the sky went from sunny and blue to the ugliest, smoggiest shade of white-gray I'd ever seen.

"Be safe. Be safe, alright?" He stuck his hand out once more and gave me an old school five with some dap before going on about his business. Something about the way he hadn't hounded me and that good boy thing he had going on made me wish I *had* gotten his number. It would have been nice to have a guy friend. But then again, that was how I'd gotten in trouble with you know who: T-r-a-s-h. He hadn't had anything either. Just a dude in school. No thanks. If I was gonna have a 'friend' you best believe I was gonna 'benefit'! I wasn't about to be on the short end of the stick EVER again.

I ran by to see the kids but no one was there. I went back to the apartment and tried to get the rest of my homework done. I was getting real fidgety. I called Sherra. She texted me on my cell that they were at church.

I called my mother again. Still no answer.

I tried harder and still couldn't focus.

I turned on the television and flipped thru the channels. There was a VH1 *Driven* show on Beyonce that was pretty interesting. Just as I got comfortable on the couch the bell rang. I looked out the window. It was Trash. Sure, I had a plan but I was still nervous. Rehearsal isn't the same as the actual Showtime.

I stepped into the small entrance area. "Yep?" I couldn't bring myself to look at him.

Across the street a guy was walking with a forty ounce in his hand and a dog leash in the other. Only thing was there was no dog. It looked odd.

"Hey... I need ta talk ta you..."

"Umm-hm. What's up? Where's Meow Meow and Back-Stabbin'-Ika?"

"Leigh, I ain't come here ta argue. *Please.* Can I come in? I jus wanna talk ta you an' explain evrythang. It's not what you thankin'."

"Well *please* step in. I'd like to hear this one. What excuse is it this time?" I held the door open. "And you know *Angela* is pregnant by you, right? Remember how you *claimed* you didn't really do anything with her? ...Um-hmm." I added once he was sitting on the couch. I stood against the wall next to the dining room.

"I know." He looked down at his shoes. "Dat's what she say. But Leigh, it *ain't* ma kid. I know dat fa sho'. Look. I know you thank I'm sleepin' wit Raina but it ain't like dat. She be lookin' out fa me when I be late an' shit. You know how dey eager ta push uh new nigga out. Yeah, I know she like me but I ain't wit it. She know we 'bout ta be married. An'...I'm jus bein' real wit chu bae, Tamika need uh job so, I been tryin' ta git Raina ta look out foe her. She can move her paperwork real quick. I understan' if you mad an' shit. Dat's why I gave you yo' space."

The house phone rang. "Just a second, I've got to take this." Normally I would have ignored Darren's call but he'd left four urgent voicemail messages on my cell this morning for me to hit him back. Blowing up somebody's phone was definitely *not* his style. Something had to be wrong.

"Hey. What's going on?" I asked, disregarding Craig's major attitude. He stretched out on the couch, swaying his legs back and forth, his lower jaw flexing and throbbing in anger.

"Look. My boy said he saw you at Fishbones with that Calvin muhfuka. If hangin' out wit whack ass drug niggas is what you wanna do then you 'on't need to be the guardian of *my* child. Cut dat shit out, Leigh. I'm warnin' you. I 'on't send you my money fa you to be out enjoyin' uh night out on town wit some hoe ass, hot muhfuka. It's only uh matter of seconds before the game gets 'im. What happens if you get shot ridin' wit 'im, hung? And I bet you didn't know he got a wife out in Minnesota. You playin' ya'self, baby and makin' me look bad in tha process. If you all horney like that--and you not gettin' it from that busted-ass Craig muhfuka you never had any business gettin' wit in the first goddamn place--you got my number, use it. People know you have a son by me. Don't be *doin'* that shit again. Understood?"

"Don't you have a girlfriend?" He must have lost his mind talking to me like I was his property!

"Do we have an understanding?" he asked, ignoring the question the same way I was ignoring Craig's malevolent glare.

"...Yeah..." I reluctantly agreed. How could I not? I had too much to lose. Uncertain d-i-c-k and possible hood rich dollars were not the same as a big, *legal* bird in the hand...although it *had been* fun! Kevin and I would definitely have to play it more low-key next time around, even though he was the kind of brotha you *did* wanna be seen with.

"I'm serious. Squash dat shit. We'll talk. I want you to help with my birthday party. I'll give you the details later. Peace, baby."

"Peace."

"I love how you ignoring uh nigga. I'm over here tryin' ta pour out ma heart out ta yo' ass but you too busy chit-chattin' wit *dat* muhafuka. Come here, I wanna talk ta you."

"I'm good. Whatever you have to say, say it." I stayed posted against the wall, cool and calm as could be.

"Leigh, cum on." He got up and walked over to me. I scooted away, making sure to maintain a healthy distance between us. Otherwise I'd be trying to kill him. And that wouldn't be good for my plan. I needed him to be around so I could use his ass.

"Craig...I love you but I know what I saw. That shit—that whole scene the other day was just flat the fuck out wrong. You were supposed to be at work! You lied. Just like you lying about dat Angela bitch. Why don't you get the baby tested to see if it's yours when she drops it? That'll prove some shit right there! And as far as that Lorraina shit goes—you wrong for that one. How you gon' fuck wit uh bitch that's physically abusing *your* child? I thought you were better than that! I've been thinkin' something was up for a long time. But you know me—*always giving you the benefit of the doubt.* And you had the nerve to have me all up in yo' hoe's mama's face lookin' for a house? Oh you *really do* think I'm stupid, don't you?"

"Baby! That ain't my kid! I swear, baby. I 'on't need no test *ta tell* me *shit!* Baby! Bae?" He dropped to his knees, wrapped his arms tightly around my legs and started sobbing profusely against my brand new jeans.

"Ugh, don't be gettin' snot on me!" I tried to shove him away.

"Baby, I'm *sorry.* Why you actin' like dis? Why? You 'on't love me no moe? You 'on't love me?" He repeated his tired, sorrowful song like it really meant something.

"Get up! You on some serious bullshit. You just keep *fuckin' up*. If you *really* sorry, stop doin' tha same thing over and over. Chance after chance I give you and what do I get in return?"

"Baby, I'm sorry. I'm sorry, baby." Repetitive crap. "I know you, Leigh. You ain't got dat love fa me in yo' eyes no moe. You 'on't love me no moe do you? Jus say it!"

Okay. He could really cut the dramatic shit out. It was peculiar behavior and downright scary. What woman wants to see the man she used to be madly in love with, resort to a pitiful, loathsome mucous ridden loser?

"In time, maybe you'll get your shit together... Don't expect me to just up and move in that house with you right now, though. You been playin' me from day one... Threw me out tha truck the other day... You know what? I don't really know you Craig. Only time'll tell what'll happen with us."

"Come on, don't say you 'on't want da house, baby. Don't tell me dat! I got it fa you! I got it fa *yoooou*! Come on, baby. Les move next week. Please, Leigh, please. It ain't like what you thankin'. Come on, Leigh. I love you baby. I love you. I'uh give ma life fa you an' you *know* it. Come on, jus say you gon' move in da house wit me. Das all I'm askin'. Stay wit me, bae--you my *life*. I cain't make it wit'out chu!" He rubbed his face against my thighs. As he rocked back and forth looking up at me he reminded me of a drugged monk.

I kept my eyes on him and reached for the phone. "Oh, I almost forgot to call about the kids. I'm supposed to be picking them up in a few minutes," I lied.

He lurched upward and snatched the phone out of my hand. "WHAT DA HELL YOU DOIN' DAT SHIT FOE, HUNGH? WHAT DA HELL YOU TRYIN' TA DO!" He was in my face like an angry drill sergeant, so close a tear on the tip of his nose trailed onto my upper lip. Within seconds he grabbed me by my hair and pushed my face into the wall. "ANSWER DA QUESTION, *BITCH*!" Everything faded, first silver dots then into complete darkness.

His thumb pressed into my neck so deep, it hurt when I gasped for air. I used my elbow to jab him in his leg and was able to get back on my feet. But then the hardwood floor swirled under me as he carried me to the bedroom. I pounded on his face with my fists. "WHAT THA HELL IS WRONG WITH YOU!" With the exception of his eyebrows that furrowed into two separate angry triangles connecting in the middle, his face was vacant. "I LOVE YOU! STOP ACTIN' LIKE THIS! STOP!" I screamed as he slammed me between the corner of the wall and bed so hard, I could feel the wire of the springs prickle against my ribcage. Everything...faded...

...into outer space...

...into a silvery blackness...

I think...

I think I saw the moon...I swear I saw the moon.

"You 'on't love me no moe. I know you, Leigh. And you 'ON'T love me no moe." His voice was now much lower. Eyes fully black, red and blazing, eyebrows full of malice, officially possessed.

His normally tanned skin held a greenish tint and his voice sounded like teeth being scraped against a chalkboard. His fingers, they were a million freshly sharpened needles infecting my soul. Every time his breath touched my skin, I shuddered in disgust.

He squished me underneath him and looked into my eyes with such revolting, debased passion, I threw up in his face and on my chest.

Rather than letting me grab a tissue off the nightstand, he continued holding me in a constraining embrace as he gazed at me with the most hideous, far away glare.

Remnants of custard colored vomit continued sliding down my chin onto my throat.

And the song started. A thousand men in that chain gang chanting their jungle chant from decade's yore. *A-who-da-hey, A-who-da-heem.* His breath was in synch with every syllable.

The song beat and pounded ferociously in my head. As if it were on repeat as this crazy thing scraped at my collarbone with his stinging flickering, purpled tongue.

I pushed him away, pulled the lamp off the nightstand and knocked it against his face. A small crack of blood appeared. He stumbled away from me, looked down as I scurried off the bed and, with one swift movement, pulled me back by my leg and I was once again underneath him.

"Stop fightin' me baby. Why you keep fightin' me? Why you keep givin' my love away? If you woulda stopped sleepin' wit Darren, I wudden't uh never had ta do dis, I wuddn't uh did nothin'. But you wudden't listen. Yo' ass WUDDEN'T LISTEN!" He smacked my face with the back of his hand. "I kept beggin' you ta stop fuckin' him, Leigh." He turned his head and started crying again. "But you wudden't... You love Darren, don't chu? Don't chu? Yeah, you love dat muhfuka...that's the nigga you wont." He ripped open my halter top and exposed my breasts. I winced as he stuffed first one, then both nipples into his mouth like a greedy cannibal.

I yanked the curls of his jet-black hair and pounded his forehead against the alarm clock. He chuckled and continued the feast sliding down my body tearing away all my clothing as he sniffed my goose bumped skin. He stopped at my crotch. "You 'on't smell like me no moe..."

"STOP, PLEASE! IF YOU LOVE ME, STOP ACTIN' LIKE THIS!" Maybe if I could appeal to the sense he once had he'd realize what he was doing and wake up out of his demonic trance.

Pastor Ellington's face appeared, *"God showed me that his heart is like stone right now! God showed me that his heart is like stone right now!"*

Look, Pastor is unzipping his pants!

See that? Craig's coming in the door right now with Mauri in his arms. Give him the phone!

Why is this hoodrat on yo' phone?

Look: there he is in the computer lab! Ignore him, you've got class in a few minutes...A date? Why, sure! Let's hang out again! What time are you taking lunch? I'll meet you after class...

He says I have a sweet smile! He says I have the most innocent eyes! He says I'm fine! He says I am what he has always wanted! He says he says he says he says he says he says
he
says
He likes me!

It all ran across the ceiling in a clear, icy blur as Craig pulled my jeans down and forced my legs apart, still filling himself with my breasts.

"STOOOOPPP! STOOOOPPP!" I screamed to no avail. It only excited him more. His eyes bubbled, flooded with ill satisfaction.

Okay, you're strong Leigh, fight this crazy ass bastard off! Fight! You've got to fight! Get him off you! Call 911! Fight! I used my legs to push the bitch off the bed. He snatched the cordless phone and threw it into the hallway laughing. "You ain't godda love me, but I'ma still love you Leigh--I'ma still love you." He laughed in a sing-song vice before biting my nipple. I thought it was torn off. Excruciating pain surged thru my whole body mixed with a warm coolness as I bled.

He pushed my arms up above my head so hard I heard my elbow crack like a breaking pretzel and whenever I tried to move it felt like torture because of the way he now had my hands squeezed and fixed in the metal leaf design on top of the bed frame. Quickly he moved about making multiple knots with the sheets to tie around my wrists. He climbed back on top of me still laughing as he unzipped his pants. His blood stained lips made him look more satanically insane. His dick was already hard but he stroked it against my face and pushed the tip into my left eye. "Let's see you suck it fa real dis time." He shoved it in my mouth and warned, "Be good, baby...be good." He took a few seconds to look down at me before his eyes rolled back in pleasure. His lips were tucked into his mouth and his cheeks now looked as though they were puffed with fat instead of manly and square.

After what seemed like infinite eternities of time with me laying on the pillow pinned down, I tasted the most rancid, unloving wad of vinegar-like acid crawl against my throat. I choked it up and spit it onto the pillow. That only angered him. He took the engagement ring off the nightstand and forced it in my mouth then he reached over and struggled with one arm for something in between the mattresses and pulled out a silver gun with a silencer on the tip. "I bet you 'on't be cryin' when Darren do it." He laughed as he slid in and out of me like a light skinned, merciless Boa Constrictor.

He held the gun on the bridge of my nose between my eyes with his free hand. "Jus remember, all you had ta do was move in wit me--I *got dat* house fa yo' ass. An' da ring." When he smiled the gun went off. I closed my eyes even tighter expecting everything to once again fade, waiting for whatever it is that happens when you get your head blown off to happen. "I wanted ta marry you. Whad? I'm not good enough *fa you* 'cause I ain't got *Darren's money*? You glad you got Pharaoh ain't 'chu? He yo' lil' money boy. But you on' like Mauri, do you? DO YOU?" The way he started screaming, "HEY! HEY!" he sounded like a dog barking the words. "I asked you a question, goddamn it! ANSWER THE MUHFUCKIN' QUESTION BITCH!" he hacked and spit on my face. "You wish you ain't neva had her, DON'T CHU?" I stayed silent. There was a second shot, this time it hit the spot in the wall right above my head. "Why I have ta fall in love wit'chu? Why? *Why*? You 'on't even wont me no moe, do you?

"You jus like Dalaina an' you jus like my mama. You know what ma used to say? She *wished she ain't* have me! She wished she ain't have me! Maybe daddy woulda stayed...he was in jail fa tryin' ta git moe money fa his family... If she wudden'ta got knocked up wit me, maybe he wudden'ta got caught up... An' you know whas crazy? Even dough she said dat, I still love her—an' I still love you, Leigh. I love da hell outta you!"

"You're crazy. You don't love me. And I'll never be in love with you again. You need help," I growled as he drained himself into me.

"Oh, oh, you 'on't love me, hungh? You 'ont *love me*? Aright. Das aright 'cause you ain't gon' love no body else...you ain't gon' love no body else...you ain't givin' my pussy ta no-muthafukin'-body else, eva again," he taunted so many times, I tuned him out by reminding myself it would eventually be over.

It would have been better for him to gouge my eyes out; it would have been better for him to shut me in a coffin loaded with a hundred over-grown hungry rats ready to dine on a breathing carcass.

Oh look! It's grandma, ma and T... at K-Mart—the one on Sherwood and Outer Drive.
We're gonna shop until it gets dark outside.
The day is so beautiful. It is sunny and there are a million suns dancing in the sky.
It is warm. Very warm.

We want to pull out the water hose and play in it but Grandma is rushing us in the car.

"Aw, man. Grandma is always mean! Grown-ups ain't no fun!"

"T let's ask grandma to get us those Cocokey slush drinks!"

"It's Coco Cola Silly Billy!"

"My name is not Silly! It's Leigh! Pee Pee, Tee Tee!"

"Ya'll keep it up an' y'all ain't gon' get NO toys taday! Y'all hear me? I 'on't wanna hear all dat mess taday!"

"Yes mom!"

"T?"

"Yes, Auntie,"

Grandma is going off on mom about all the money she owes her. It's funny when mom gets yelled at by Grand.

Me and T are walking behind them cracking up.

We are home now. We want to play with our new Barbie's and the brand new Easy Bake Oven but we are tired...so tired we both fall asleep on the bunk beds without putting our sleeping clothes on. We don't even take off our blue and silver gelly shoes...

Why was he taking so long? He could slit my throat, suffocate me, the gunshot to the head thing'd be rather easy...a nice way out...he could take my body as long as I kept my soul.

The wrestling, this war of opposing forces continued ruthlessly prolonging the fight. But the invasion was not Craig...

> *It* was a wicked spirit force that had lived many centuries before within the charcoal, gates of burnt dreams stuck in the realms of abomination only ones like him could understand.

> *It* was an external gray revolting monster with shiny, lovelacking serpentine eyes internally filled with filthy decomposed blood...

> *It* seeked pleasure by inflicting circles of encumbering pain...

> *It* enslaved purity's spirit and vigilantly persecuted its prisoners souls...

> *It* stuck sharpened grief into every soft space left in the world...

> *It* had never been given wholesome, sacred love...

> The serpent had rotted before *it* even hatched.

He turned and whispered to the wall before embracing me tightly, "I have to." Surges of ill intent raced inside too many times to count, too many afflictions to survive. It is one of the worse things that can happen between man and woman. But at least it was the end.

LISTEN TO THEM:

Sangin'—not singing
'cause dis here is uh fanga numbin'
cotton field frum centuries layin' still.

An' on dis here low sangin' day,
dere wuddn't no sun hangin' way up high
but it was sho' bright out—Lawd,
it was sho' bright,
look like da sky wudden't nothin'
but sum great big ole white light!

Dey was gon' hang ha
an' by dat time (wit dey cups uh moonshine)
da crowd had started carin' less and less
'cause she wudden't fit fa da sharecroppin' grind
an' fa ha uh life wid'out 'im uh sho nuff be best…

*Can somebody please wash me away? Can somebody please wash
me away…*

Can somebody please washmeaway? Can somebody please wash me away...

Can somebody please wash me away? Can somebody please wash me away...

Can somebodyplease washmeaway? Can somebody please wash me away...

Can somebody please wash me away? Can somebody please wash me away...

Can somebodyplease washmeaway? Can somebody please wash me away...

Can somebody please wash me away? Can somebody please wash me away...

Can somebodyplease washmeaway? Can somebody please wash me away...

Can

Somebody

Please

Wash

Me

Away?

CHAPTER 13

BRIGHT WHITE LIGHTS INTERRUPTED the serenity of the swirling drabness circling and lifting my soul.

Something wasn't right.

The White chick in the burgundy scrubs like the ones you wore when you were interning, she's the nurse. Emergency room? Yeah. No...wait, it's Henry Ford hospital...

"Get tha fuck out." I tried to shout it but the words wouldn't come out right. My throat was tight and scorched everything into a whisper.

Get Well Soon balloons. A card sitting in the middle of that ugly purple and dandelion looking flower medley. All of it from him—the Cat That Swallowed the Canary sitting in the chair next to my bed looking all sad eyed and concerned.

I pressed the red button on the side of the bed. When the nurse came in I pointed his way. "I'm not dead? ...He did this."

"Okay, hon. Just lay back and try to get some rest--I know you're upset. You're gonna be okay."

"I want him to leave."

She looked at him and they exchanged sympathetic looks before she said anything else. "You're gonna be fine. You've just undergone surgery, sweetie. In a little bit they're gonna take some more X-rays. Good thing your fiancé found you and brought you here."

"No. No... *He did* this."

"Leigh, because of the severity of the event you survived, some damage occurred. You were stabbed in the introitus—the opening of the vagina. You're being monitored and checked for any possible ruptures or punctures that may have affected your bladder." She placed her cold hand on top of mine. "You're a survivor. You lost some blood and suffered from shock but you made it, hon. Once you recover you'll have a chance to speak with a counselor. K?"

"I want him OUT of this room." The IV slid over and yanked me back into the bed. I couldn't move even if I wanted to anyway, everything from the waist down was numb. It actually felt like I didn't have any legs.

"Calm down, sweetie! Please! You're probably hallucinating right now. Get some rest. Lemme know if you need anything."

"I JUST TOLD YOU! I NEED FA YOU TA GET HIM OUTTA HERE! I DON'T EVER WANNA SEE HIS FACE AGAIN! CAN YOU GET THE POLICE UP IN HERE OR WHAT? ARE YOU SLOW? I'M TRYIN' TA TELL YOU, HE DID THIS! GET HIM OUTTA HERE! AND DON'T BRING SHIT UP IN HERE THAT'S MALE—DON'T

GIMME NO MALE DOCTOR! DON'T TAKE ME TA NO MALE RADIOLOGIST! DON'T EVEN BRING A MALE COP TA DIS ROOM! YOU GOT ME OR YOU 'ON'T UNDERSTAND ENGLISH?"

"MS. ANDERSON! You're fiancé told me you're in school for nur—"

"—He is NOT my fiancé! He DID THIS TO ME!" I took the ring off my finger and threw it in his face. He'd put this shit right back on my finger. I was pissed but shout as I might, everything was coming out slurred and my heart was racing and fluttering.

"OKAY MS. ANDERSON. You have to get some rest. I understand your upset, it's normal after situations like yours. It's not your fault.

"If you want him out, I'm sure he'll leave but he's only here to..." Blah, Blah, Blah...the rest of what this bitch was saying really didn't matter. Fuckin' cunt. As usual he'd showered the whole staff with his sparkling, cunning charm. This motherfuka right here was the Ted Bundy of Detroit!

Weren't there rules for shit like this? Didn't the patients have a say in who visited them? Damn I wish I hadn't been missing school, I'd know a lot more about patient's rights.

Two other nurses entered the room and started fussing with the IV in my arm.

"STTTTOOOP!" My whole body shook with all nine syllables. "GETHIMOUTTA HERE! AAAAAHHH! I WANT HIM OUT!" It felt like I was going insane.

"Pu-lease-cam-dow!" an Asian nurse with a round face and almost non-existent eyebrows insisted while the other nurses, the one that was buddy-buddy with the Devil and a heavy set Black grandma looking nurse with a Jherri curl continued acting like backup.

...Vaguely...I could see his hands sliding me into the bathtub...*washing me away*...the orange juice he wanted me to drink, he kept making me drink...just a little toothpaste, "*Come on bae...*"

...*Can somebody please*...

He got up and stood over to me. There were no scars on his face from that lamp I broke over his head.

I closed my eyes. "You been thru uh lot, Leigh an' I'm--I'm—I'm sorry, bae. We gon' be aright, dough. We in dis tagetha. No matter whad went down, you know I love you. I still godda go ta court fa dat shit wit cho' Pastor an' evrythang—but...jus--jus git bedder, bae an'...whatever you wont, whatever you wont you gon' git it." He paused. "I ain't perfect—but chu ain't eitha." When he took my hand and sandwiched it between his, my heart began racing so fast the heart monitor started beeping and flashing 250 over 180. "I love you Leigh." He kissed me on the forehead and sat back down in the chair next to the bed.

"Craig? LEAVE!" Undying hate for every male species resided deep within the walls of every cell in my soul.

"Aright. But first I wanna make sure you aright. Cain't I jus sit here wit chu? I godda go back ta work in uh few hours anyway--I'ma be outta yo' way. I'ma give you yo' space, fa real. I'm. jus..I'm sorry," he whispered leaning over me as his eyes filled with tears.

All right. On to plan B. "Alright then. Could you rub my feet?" I was about to play the role. There was no other way to get this crazy ass bastard out of my room.

"Yeah bae, anythang you say." He rubbed my feet for all of three minutes while I faked like I was falling asleep. Actually I was tired as hell and really did need to go to sleep but I had to hold out a little longer.

He sat back down but this time he scooted his chair away from the bed, picked up the remote and flicked thru the channels.

Zing! I woke back up. "Craig. I hate you. You should go jump off a bridge or something but could you rub my feet like I asked?" I gave him a 'hurry yo' ass up and hop to it' look, snapped my fingers and pointed at my feet.

"Yeah, ma bad." He went ta rubbin' away. And just like that—I zonked out again and back to the television he went.

"Craig! Chop-Chop! The feet, bitch! The feet!" I clapped my hands a couple of times--the heavily sedated pop up doll was back in action right after he had tuned in to a rerun of the *Jamie Foxx Show* and laughed a couple of those hearty laughs of his.

He sighed, "Aright." He wanted to give me that 'cut-this-shit-out' look something awful, but couldn't.

Then it was a cramp in my hand that needed to be rubbed away. Then I was thirsty but I needed a different brand of water from the one they had in the vending machines down the hallway and in the cafeteria. Then I had to have a chicken strip meal from KFC...

Within an hour, the bitch couldn't take it and left and I zonked out for real this time but Craig's presence lingered on. When I went to sleep I swear I heard his voice lurking around in my dream.

"...Whatever went down wit me an' you, stay between me an' you..."

When we first met I didn't know it but there was an unmistakable connection between us. Now the thick, magical coil joining us together had thinned to nothingness. Craig'd only allowed my love to coat the surface of his inner being as it is with chemisorptions and spirits born broken.

But no matter how hard you fight it or what your mind tells you, no matter how thin the coil of love may become, it doesn't just disappear or evaporate away. There are still those raggedy broken wire bits left to remind you. You can stay away from a guy, breakup with him, make a point to never see him again and move on but your heart will never let you forget.

Think with your head and not your heart: we've all heard it as many times as people call on God when they're scared. Yet human nature dictates the heart will win the fight against the head almost every time.

The heart does not know shame nor pride but the mind does and, this time around, I wasn't about to be embarrassed again.

A WEEK HAD PASSED and I was still in the hospital. More lab tests, x-rays and examinations by faces I hoped to one day forget. Faces that tried not to stare. Faces that repeated, "It's not your fault," after looking over my chart even though I'd never said it was.

I continued refusing to speak with the counselor and decided against talking to the cops. I had worked here--I knew how it was. The doctors, nurses and the janitors all had their own gossip networks and 'Patient Hall of Shame' discussions. Sometimes cases came in that were being covered by the news, which made every employee in the hospital a journalist for The Henry Ford Primetime Drama of the day.

With all the mess going on with Pastor Ellington and Mt. Zion, who was really going to believe me anyway? I couldn't even begin to imagine going to court against Craig for this shit. What if, in some odd twist of fate, he and Pastor hooked up against me? Then what? How many people besides Sherra were going to believe me? My mother had believed Ellington's story over mine.

There was this nice guy named Shawn who worked on the same floor I was on but in a different unit. Whenever he was working he stopped by my room when Craig wasn't around which was cool. He was always making me laugh.

I was bored and depressed and hoping he stopped by tonight. He was the only thing that made being here not so bad. But he had already come by my room twice today.

"Hey, Leigh. Whassup?" Shawn came in, putting his coat on the chair and sat at the foot of my bed.

"I'm glad you came. I thought you went home already."

"You know I don't leave without coming to see you--I just got off. The other guy was late coming in What's wrong?"

"It's Friday and I'm here. You do the math."

"I know how to cheer you up." He brought a couple of his boys who worked in the cafeteria to the room. They cracked jokes on each other, brought me food from the diner across the street and turned my room into a party—well, not really but it was much better than being stuck watching re-runs on cable all by myself.

One of the dudes was cute and kept staring at me like he wanted to holla but he didn't--male bashing was a very good deterrent.

After they left Shawn sat on the edge of the bed and turned the television off then turned it back on. "Leigh?"

"Yep."

"When you get your Get Out of Jail Free Card, I hope you don't forget about me."

"Course not."

"I wanna take you out---somewhere nice."

"You're over there looking all serious."

He chuckled.

To start, Shawn had a grotesque patch of hair missing in the back of his head that looked like a permanent tetanus spot. It was pink and brown and ugh! Just looking at it made me shudder. And his head was shaped like a box. His mustache was lined up too thin and left a slightly green cast underneath his nose on his philtrum and his lips were bright pink soup coolers like a caricature straight off one of those racist coon cartoons they used to draw of Black people. And he was only five seven with puny shoulders.

Yes he had a bachelors and at twenty-six lived alone in one of those sharp ass Riverplace townhouse apartments downtown but I wasn't looking for anybody. *Nothing* like him. He needed to put concealer on that tetanus bald spot and a tube of black lipstick. A little metrosexuality wouldn't hurt in his case.

"Shawn, you know I have somebody but, you know you're my boy. You're good people." I was sincere. I'd call him sometime. He was sweet...but he was downright mean on the eyes. The way he looked, one of his parents had to be a blowfish or a turtle.

Besides, I had a lot of other things on my mind. Something about this incident with me and Craig was all too familiar.

I knew—or at least I hoped, I wasn't crazy but...I knew this'd happened before. Each time, right before I fell asleep, I could see her. The thin, brown girl with the golden and sun colored hair just like Mauri's. She had the prettiest smile—when she did smile, which was very seldom.

She was in fields filling baskets with dandelions and loved to frolic in the fields at dawn every chance she got. Being alone underneath the sky, it was her only pleasure until he came looking.

237

No matter how far she'd go, he'd always find her and ruin everything. When he showed up, the sky was no longer a white tableau with decorations painted up there just for her. But that was how it was. Work and never-ending backaches on the plantation—a place were dreams were not allowed to exist.

And since nothing mattered, she jumped over the broom and married him. Square shoulders and black curly hair--everybody in town said he was the most handsomest they'd ever seen. But she had never noticed. She'd never noticed him nor the White boy who came and kept coming with letters and all those coins. It was rude, her not accepting the plantation owner's son and all. She kept begging and pleading, pleading and begging but he was getting tired. All those lovely letters took time to think up and she still wasn't budging. So he did what any other right-minded gent pushed to his limit uh do, took her right before the roosters started crowing—yes lawd--deep inside the wheat fields and he promised no one would know, he promised she'd come around and nobody'd ever know.

But somebody did see and somebody did tell and he kept promising he'd stop but he couldn't, he just couldn't, she was sho sweet,— a waste made niggra, let 'im tell ya'! An' why couldn't dem niggas jus keep dey floppy lipped mouths shut? A hundred pennies he'd promised 'em.

Good Lawd! when the family found out. No room to be shamed by no nigga cropper, no sir-ee! Pulled her plum out' the shanty, its tin shutters barely hanging to the windows, black curly haired babies lying on the floor inside crying like they knew soon their mother'd be dying, the brown paper dress sagging in the middle, they couldn't care. No kinda shame like that be circling 'round they good name. People talked and rumors walked, ya' see.

Ain't no help gon' evr 'gain mess an' mix wit dey blue blood--nigga sharecroppa she was! Good for da hangin'!

Nobody else said uh word of it 'til da sun sat up 'gainst the horizon.

And maybe...maybe it was the best thing.

That husband of hers, handsome as he was, had sucked ha dry from the time she was eleven—had his eye on ha when dey both was seven. First night after they'd hopped over da broom he'd showed her how it was gon' be. Yes, he be da one always stumblin' in with da moonshine tucked up tight 'gainst his chest--da one wit all dem other lil' seeds whad kept croppin' up —his squared off jaw line sho' nuff markin' each an' every one of 'em. An' nuthin' uh make 'im tell ha da truth. So it was, in dat way, all right ta 'im. Fa her, his love was purplin' fists; fa her, his love was broken wrists, uh floor full uh babies who cried an' cried whenever she wasn't in sight. Some will tell you babies dat lil' don't know but if you wudda seen dem babies, you'd uh knowed uh whole lot bedder.

Him, as fine as dey still say he was, he made it easier for the White boy—she was already used to that kind of pushing and shoving.

Twenty hate-filled lashes of the horsewhip the husband gave her when her he found out and after that, she was doomed to sleep alongside the shack without even the threadbare patches of that ragged dress, body out, free to be taunted by anyone passing. He wouldn't even give her the tattered blanket her mother'd sewn for the babies before she fell dead in the middle of the fields.

For him, it was as simple as he was. So what if the White boy took her, shouldn't have looked his way when he came to collect, shouldn't have been so what they called pretty. So nice. That's what everybody in town said—that she was nice.

What a shame. There had been so many other suitors, so many suitors with softer hands but just as strong. Hands that would have known how to love her. Such a task shouldn't have been so hard. She'd always been eager to please.

At least with the hanging she wouldn't be his anymore.

And when he finally realized, when the moonshine finally left him, he stood there begging and pleading and pleading and begging as they lifted her up in the tree, after it was much too late…

"…Leigh? Leigh?" Shawn's face was foggy. "What's wrong?" A concerned look crossed his face.

"Can you stay with me? *Please*?"

"Yeah. You're shaking. You okay?"

"Yeah." Because Shawn made Laila Hathman go away…for a while at least.

Whenever Craig came to visit, repeating how much he loved me over and over and with those long apologies of his, she sat in the corner of the room with those two pitiful lackluster eyes of hers looking dead into me.

And, the minute Craig left, I'd call Shawn's work extension praying he was working.

THE KIDS CAME ALMOST every day, which temporarily lifted my spirits but seeing them was tricky. I had to make sure they came during the times Craig was supposed (supposed being the operative word) to be at work. He wanted to keep them while I was "recuperating" as he called it, since his mother was supposedly offering to watch them when he was working. He claimed he was staying with her since he was waiting on me to move into the new house with him.

Sherra never asked what happened and I still hadn't told her. Whenever she came to visit, her eyes were sad. I could tell she figured Craig had something to do it. She tried not to look it but I could tell she was disappointed. "Girl, you should talk ta that counselor. This was part of tha problem with tha whole church thing—you didn't tell anyone when everything first started happening. You have ta say *sumthen*!" she always advised at the end of her visits.

There was no way I was going to speak to a counselor here--plain and simple. This was where I was supposed to be interning soon and on top of that, a couple of people I knew worked here. It was beyond embarrassing. Just the way the nurses looked at you—all extra, *extra* sympathetic—fumbling for the right words when they spoke. It was disgusting and they weren't going to do anything except put all the stuff I said in the medical records and everybody'd be all up in my business. It was already bad enough I'd be working here one day and have to face working in a place where people had access to this incident. Even worse, if anybody at Mount Zion heard about it, they'd be eating it up. No thank you. I had a HAP health care plan, if I wanted to talk to someone later on I could. But it wouldn't be here.

The real dilemma was getting the bi-polar, schizo motherfucka that had put me in here, out of my life.

CHAPTER 14

I GOT RELEASED LATER that week on Thursday with the damages limited to the opening muscles of the vagina, tons of stitches and a prescription for Vicoden. Sherra pulled up her car the hospital's back driveway and pushed me in a wheelchair so I wouldn't have to walk. Thank goodness Trash'd quit insisting on coming to get me. He finally backed down when I said he was probably going to lose his job from all of his absences. No matter how much he fucked Meow, my bet was she could only cover up so many excuses—unless she was sexing up the CEO's too. She looked she'd be in on the dominatrix scene or some other too 'weird-for-Black-people' shit that suited CEO types well.

But later for all of them. Inside I felt like pink, torn, unwanted cardboard. I felt so much I felt nothing.

The wind snapped against my face as I left behind the dreary life as a patient/victim and stepped into another plateau of depression.

So long for this semester of classes, it was a lost 'cause at this point.

"Okay, where you want me ta take you?" Sherra asked not really wanting to hear the answer.

"My place. I need some time alone. It's been too many muthafuka's in my face for ten days."

"Okay." She sighed, full of resignation and switched the subject. "Those kids are *fuun*-nee! Mauri done made up dis dance. She be up dere rockin' her shoulders from side ta side... Ma did her hair real cute the otha day. Evrybody up in church was talkin' 'bout how pretty her hair is. An' she already don't like no other girls, girl! When Marsa brought Ajia over and tried ta get dem ta play together, she jus sucked on her thumb and stared at Jia den when Jia tried to play wit 'im, she gon' walk over dere and push Pharaoh away from Jia! She possessive of her brotha and she *love* Tommy. She be following him around wit her hands up in da air talking 'bout *'pleeeese'* in dat lil' bitty voice of hers 'til he pick her up and carry her evywhere. He took her ta Chucky Cheese yesterday wit Marsa an 'Jia. Pharaoh wanted ta stay home wit Dina--sometime he act like uh grown man, I tell you. Don't let Dina boyfriend call, girl. One time Pharaoh hung up on 'im." Sherra tossed her head back and gave a hearty, throaty laugh that reminded me of hanging out summer nights at Belle Isle, high school picnics--a time when hood didn't mean hoodrat and worry free-days back in the fifth grade when I used to go to Chrysler.

For a second I was jealous. I couldn't remember the last time I laughed for real like that. "Yeah. I'm gonna get them...tomorrow...maybe the weekend... Then you won't have to be bothered anymore. You know I'ma hook y'all up on the money tip. Is two good?"

"Two *what*?"

"Thousand. If not just say the word and we can stop at the bank."

"Girl, naw! You need to be savin' *all* yo' money an' plannin' yo' escape from that source of Satan named Cra--"

"--Trash. We don't call him by that anymore." I snickered.

"It ain't funny. *He is* trash and it's a shame too. I used to think he was *soooooooooo* fine for uh light skinned guy—but not in that way, you know--he is—well, he *was* yo' man"

"Yeah, it's always the fine ones that end up being crazy."

"Don't say dat! I been prayin' ma husband be fine! An' dat's what I'ma get--uh fine, man dat *ain't* crazy, okay!"

"I hope so..."

"...Jus give Dina like...two...two hundred 'cause those kids can sho' eat!"

"Nah, stop by the bank. Y'all had them for what--a month on and off?"

"Look. You're ma girl. Don't worry 'bout it. If you need us ta keep 'em, dat's cool, they *are* my godchildren. Jus git yo'self together. Dat's what's wrong in tha Black community—we 'ont support each other and thas why we 'on't have a sense of community no more. In old world countries, they be big on community. Jus 'cause you need ta take care uh some things doesn't make you uh bad mother.

"Pharaoh do be having dem nights where he be asking uh hundred questions 'bout chu, though. An' don't forget ta put 'Lord bless Leigh' in uh prayer! He'll shout it in there, nah! Lord bless my mommy, Leigh Anderson." She copied off his voice, laughed and shook her head then paused for a couple of minutes. "Leigh? What chu gon' do?" she asked quietly as she pulled in front of my place.

"Well. The locks are changed. I won't be letting him in...I'm still trying to figure everything else out."

"I *know* he had something ta do with you being in tha hospital...something's wrong wit *his* crazy ass. Did chu see how he was lookin' dat day at Floods? His eyes ain't look right. I cain't tell you what ta do 'bout him--that's yo' business--but it ain't goin' right..."

"...Thanks, girl. I'll let you know what day I'm coming for the kids..."

"Aright..." She shut the door and drove off. I checked the mailbox but it was empty. Instead, all the mail was neatly stacked on the dinning room table in a pile. There was a new bed and mattress in the bedroom. I called the locksmith immediately and had the locks changed a second time.

There were three letters from the owners of the apartment, Rick and his wife, stating that there was reason to believe I wasn't in compliance with agreement of employment I signed when I was initially given the job. I hadn't returned six tenants calls, I'd been reported for being absent more than I was at home which made it hard for residents to contact me and fighting and noise violations complaints had been made from tenants against me on more than three occasions.

Rick wanted me to move out by the second week of November. That was in less than two weeks! I picked up the phone to call them immediately. My voicemail was full on both phones—the house phone and my cell. My cell! Damn. Craig hadn't brought it with him to the hospital. Did the nurse take it? She'd taken my clothing and put it in that rape kit— or whatever she'd called it—for tests but I had refused it since I wasn't about to let go of a brand new four hundred dollar outfit and it would have been a waste anyway. I didn't have the same clothes on during the incident that I had on when I came to the hospital. Craig had changed them.

Never mind. My cell was on the top of the table. Good thing I always kept it locked. With Craig being so anti-Darren and all, I hadn't had a choice.

I tried to use a previously good rapport to convince Rick to let me keep my job, but that wasn't working so I resorted to begging to keep the only job I had. The final deal was, if I proved myself for two months and kept up my end of my contract, I could keep the position. Otherwise, they had some middle-aged couple that were ready and willing to live rent-free.

Kevin/Calvin'd left three messages on the voicemail. An invitation to go swimming somewhere in Troy, another one asking me if I wanted to go shopping and an invitation to go to New York with him—to hang out and look pretty while he took care of some business. I was pissed. How would I look calling him back now? I had tons of doctors visits scheduled and wasn't going to be able to do anything that smelled like sex until further notice and doctor's approval and there was no way I could be around him without wanting it.

Then Craig started blowing up my phone. "Hey bae. You feelin' bedder?"

"Craig? You know how you said you would give me anything I asked for, right, once I came home?"

"Yeah, I know what I said…"

"Well, what I'm asking you for right now is ta be left tha hell alone." I hung up. Thank goodness he didn't call back.

I hadn't cooked in so long...eating a home cooked meal would be nice. There were two Cornish hens in the freezer that I took down and thawed in the microwave while I started the rice and string beans on the stove. When I took the chicken out one dropped and made a strange sound like it'd cracked.

Cleaning the cavity out, removing the tiny little heart and liver out and throwing them in the garbage, I thought about how similar we were, me and this chicken... I was scraping the insides the same way the doctors had scraped and scraped looking for clues and traces of semen that had been washed away by the very perpetrator.

What guy would want me now? And what if I couldn't have any more children because of this shit? I was only twenty-four—I wanted to have another kid later on down the road. Yeah, the doctors had said I was lucky since the damages were limited to three inches but what if they'd just been saying that, what if they were wrong? What if I was never going to be the same after this? *How* could I be the same after any of this?

And what if I *didn't* stay with Craig? All he was going to do was move on to another female who'd take his shit and then I'd be alone, looking stupid just like I was looking stupid right now for not being with Darren. He had some new on again off again chick that was getting way more money than what he sent me even though they didn't have a child together.

As many arguments as me and Darren had, he never once called me a bitch or even attempted to hit me. He'd simply catch a dry ass tone and tell me to call him when I wasn't as upset. Or send a gift. Don't get me wrong, he had gotten pissed at me plenty of times before but he channeled his anger differently.

Everything turned wavy as I sat on the kitchen floor and cried. I didn't make any noise. I didn't want to hear it. I was stupid. I couldn't do shit right. I was always saying the wrong thing...

Craig probably wouldn't have even taken things that far that day if I wouldn't have talked to Darren while he was over here trying to talk things out.

...What if I *was* crazy? Usually, when a person is mentally off they're the last one to know—if they ever figure it out.

Or maybe I had done something evil in a past life and I was reaping what I'd sowed.

Could be that I was just a hoe. That would explain why men were always trying to hook up with me for a quick fuck and it would explain why they cheated and never really wanted to be with me. Maybe in a past life I had been forced to be a courtesan or a concubine or maybe I hadn't even been forced to do it, maybe in another time and place I was a harlot and I still had that kind of energy on me. No one likes that type of woman. Not back then, not now. That's why no man ever wasted their time loving me. I wasn't worth it.

I couldn't even be mad at my father. He was smart. He knew I wouldn't have done anything except mess up his life if he would have stuck around.

I was evil and I had turned Craig into an evil person too. He'd kicked me in the stomach and in the ribs with his boots... If I wouldn't have been getting money from Darren, Craig wouldn't have been trippin' so hard. If the shoe was on the other foot and some chick was giving Craig money every month, I would have been pissed too.

I ran to the bathroom and tried to look at myself in the vanity mirror but I couldn't look the whore in the face. I hated the reflection of the person trying to stare back at me...

The cute, tiny upturned nose. The innocent almond eyes. The sweet smile--that's what everyone always said. That's why *she* thought she was so muthafuckin' cute. *She* tried to be a goody two shoes but she kept fucking up. That's what happened when you were evil, wrong guys, wrong choices, wrong everything...

I'd fix her ass. I'd make sure nobody ever wanted her again—one way or the other. That way I could be left alone. I could just take care of my kids and never have to worry about shit again.

I snatched Craig's clippers off the shelf in the medicine cabinet, turned them on and let the buzz pace back and forth against my scalp like a lawn mower zigzagging designs on overgrown grass. It felt cool and relaxing against all the hot, angry bubbling thoughts. I put the clippers next to my wrist but, quickly, an invisible supernatural-like force knocked them right out of my hands and onto the floor. I shook so hard I plummeted onto the cold hardness of the floor and cried myself to sleep.

When I woke up the apartment was filled with smoke and the stench of charcoaled green beans and ashy granite pellets of rice. I opened the porch door and as many windows as I could since some of them were swollen shut from the radiator. It was a miracle a fire hadn't started.

When I looked in the mirror, a third of my hair on the right side of my head was shaved completely off. The uneven choppiness of this new do made me look like a furry animal with tortured eyes.

I was scared. So scared, I picked up the phone and called Shawn—who else did I have? It seemed like I was always disappointing Sherra and if she came she would have been judging me.

Shawn took off work and within thirty minutes, he was sitting on the couch listening as I told him everything, how I met Darren #1, Darren

#2, Craig, what happened with me and the pastor—everything except that Craig was the reason I'd been in the hospital.

He just listened. He didn't push a bible in my face, didn't tell me to go to a counselor and he didn't tell me I looked crazy with a third of my hair in this new partial G.I. Jane cut (I hadn't thought to cover it up—it wasn't like I was trying to impress anybody anyhow).

The whole time he was over he hadn't tried anything—not even testing me for a kiss. He simply listened, slept on the couch and left in the morning for work even though he'd only gotten an hour of sleep.

DARREN CALLED ON SUNDAY insisting that I host his birthday party. I knew it was to make it look like everything was a bed of roses. No doubt his inner circle and cronies had heard about me going out with Kevin/Calvin. One thing he hated was to look bad or, in his words, to look be a "laughing stock." He said his girlfriend wasn't going to be there so I'd be the only host. Pharaoh was coming and they'd both be wearing the same thing: navy blazers, Diesel jeans and gymies, and white button down shirts with navy hats.

The chef and servers were already booked. All I had to do basically was look good--sexy not slutty, laugh when appropriate, smile and keep my mouth shut--unless I was agreeing with something he said and I needed to make sure Pharaoh went to bed after dinner so as to be put away for the real party. Well. At least Pharaoh would get a chance to sleep in his bedroom over there. So far he'd only slept there five times.

I didn't know what to tell Darren. I didn't feel like doing anything except sleep. My hair looked terrible and, one thing for sure, Darren hated weave. He wasn't about to be okay with me showing up with anything he detected was fake. I mulled it over and finally decided to call KD.

"Leigh, what's wrong with you? You done lost your fuckin' mind calling me on Sunday unless this is an emergency, sweetie. I was getting filled up with the Holy Ghost! *I'M AT PERFECTING! AND THA CHOIR IS OFF-THA-CHAINS! WHAT THA HELL YOU WANT?* And make it quick!" Even as he snapped he still overly pronounced every syllable, which gave him an extra proper, squawkish tone.

"KD! IT *IS* AN EMERGENCY! I need your help. I'm suffering from a major hair accident!"

"If you've tried to do your hair yourself or if you went to someone else, *I'mmm not* bailing you out--you're back to square one!" Although he was known for snatching up females with 'wrong hair do's' at the mall or any other public place with a hair offender milling about and he'd demand the chosen Hair No-No follow him to his salon right that moment, one thing he did not do was fix one of his regulars after they had insulted him by going to another stylist or a homemade hair mishap.

"No, no—it's nothing like that! I had to have a test and they had to cut some of my hair!"

"Hhhmm...is it really bad?" He was excited instead of sympathetic.

"Terrible. I look like an abused animal off *Animal Cops*!"

"Okay, darling. Don't worry, I'll hook you up. We'll do you tomorrow—that way no one will be in to see you looking a hot mess! You can't be walking around *NOT* looking like the princess you are! Be there at twelve. If you aren't, it's your ass! Chow."

I felt a little bit better—KD had the power to make my hair issue less of an issue but I was still depressed.

Shawn called a few hours later and asked me to do dinner with him. Any other time I wouldn't have even considered it but the way I was feeling right about now, I jumped at the opportunity. I chose a place no one in Darren's click would be snooping around: Denny's. Denny's in Roseville. And it was far away from Craig's neck of the woods too.

I met up with him instead of agreeing to let him pick me up wearing a hat cocked to the right. I tried to play off the missing locks by parting my hair down the middle. I had thrown on some old, before Pharaoh's time jeans, an ugly gray sweater with paint spots that I usually only wore when I cleaned up the building, no lip gloss--even though my lips were peeling and in serious need of some chapstick and my nails were crying out for a manicure and some serious cuticle TLC .

"You look better than ever," he complimented smiling.

"Whatever. Ya' *lying* and you know it," I stated shoving a spoonful of hash browns in my mouth like I didn't have table manners.

"No seriously. You look as beautiful as you did when I first saw you." I continued chewing. He continued talking. "I passed your room...you were flicking thru channels, not even paying any attention. I kept walking by trying to check you out. You kept tapping your fingers against the remote. And your hair was in a ponytail way up on top of your head...but even if you took the looks away, you'd be beautiful. You've got a stellar personality."

I was about to tell him he should let his mustache grow in more but the last part of what he said caught me off guard. "Stellar?" I laughed at his choice of words.

"Yes. Stellar..." he confirmed, still staring at me.

"...How do *you* know?" The bacon was delicious. It was like I was tasting turkey for the first time--I couldn't stop hogging everything down. It was the first time I had had anything to eat since I'd left the hospital.

"I spent a whole week and a half studying you, talking to you and hanging out with you. I can tell...observation is an excellent means of figuring lots of things out—especially people. You grew up sheltered even though you saw a lot. You ran into a bunch of idiots that never loved themselves and weren't able to really love you because of it... If you focus on yourself, in time, you'll be alright and you'll stop letting losers take advantage of you. You've got a lot of love to give to the right man.

"Classy with a lil' hood going on, a heart-melting smile and a *very* spiritual soul—I'd say you're real wife material."

I wondered what he observed about Craig.

"Shawn? Don't call my kids fathers losers, alright?" I pointed my fork his way.

"I didn't specifically say—"

"—Well that's what it sounded like."

"I'm sorry, alright? I wasn't trying to be offensive. My bad." He looked down briefly at his untouched plate.

"Um-hm." I kept stuffing my face like a pig. Umh! Even the eggs were on point—not too salty and just the right amount of pepper!

He wasn't saying anything. I looked up at him for the first time, "...So what's your story? What makes Shawn tick? What makes you laugh?" He was kindhearted but I didn't know much else about him although we'd spent hours talking on the phone for the last couple of days. I'd been the one doing all the talking for the most part but he didn't seem irritated by my incessant chatter.

Listening for a change, I learned that he had five brothers and sisters, was the middle child and that his parents were still happily married and lived in North Carolina. Everyone in his family went to college. He and his mother'd gone at the same time and finished the same year from different schools. She hadn't been able to finish when she was younger. Once she got married and his sibling came along it was impossible even though his father had a degree in education and taught at an elementary school, she was preoccupied as a homemaker and a seamstress who worked from home. Since it was a much talked about dream of hers, his father saw to it that she finished even though she was uncertain about going back at first.

He believed in God but wasn't a church fanatic, hated reading but made himself read the newspaper every day. Likes: playing cards, science, going to the movies and football. He was interesting enough.

We continued talking for hours, this time making it an equal exchange. When we parted ways and got into our cars, he called my cell and we talked until I, in his words, "Made it home safely."

Craig had left message after message on the house phone. I erased them all and headed for bed.

I slept on the opposite end of the mattress, at the foot with my feet resting on the newly purchased headboard. I couldn't stand being in the bedroom. It made me itch. And I couldn't sleep on the couch either; Craig always sat on it and it smelled like him.

"OOOOOOOH *GIRRRRRRRRRRRRL!* It is bad! Thank *Gawd* they didn't have to shave it all off! You'd be lookin' like a pussy!" Beat declared.

"Umph-hm!" KD added in. I broke into tears.

"Oh, now, now. It's not that bad. We'll figure something out. You know Darren doesn't like weave but we'll play it off."

I shot upright in overly erect posture in the chair at KD's words. "What? What!"

"You can be real with us, Leigh. We know you're Darren's child's mother—everybody knows. In fact, he asked when was the last time you came in. I t*ole* him it's been a minute—that was before your visit two weeks ago—anyway, *he* tole *meee* to make sure I got you in here, pronto--he said he'd even pay for it! And sweetie, you do look bad! You don't have to worry about this one, we're taking him up on his offer. You know he loves you, Leigh... Are you still with that other dude?"

"KD! IT IS ALL OFF LIMITS! *OFF LIMITS!* UNDERSTAND?"

"*Okkkay.* Well, all *right!* Sounds like there are some smoldering flames goin' on somewhere for somebody ta *meee!* And I ain't mad at chu! Not only is Darren fine with those beautiful light green, twinkling eyes of his--boy is *paid* out his *mind!* Have you picked up a Crain's lately?" he zipped more to Beat than me.

"Glad to know you're still on the Diva list. You had us worried for a minute!" Beat patted me on the back.

"Well, you should consider your shit gold. Golden pussy makes golden babies. Your child is *bbblllessed*, chile! Do you know how many pretty, *pretty* bitches up in Michigan want to be with Darren—let alone have a baby by him? Huh, to have him still sniffing after you, you had to've put it on 'em!" KD exclaimed.

I started crying again.

"Leigh, cheer up! Now that is *NOT* something to cry over! Your hair? That's a different story—but Darren, that's a reason to celebrate.

Here, try this," Beat offered me something white and powdery he pulled out a vial hanging around his neck that looked like a cross.

"Whaaatt!" I couldn't believe what was going on right before my very eyes as he and KD filled their noses to satisfaction.

"It can be your best friend. Especially in times like these." He laughed.

"No, un-ungh, I'm straight."

"Well—the more the merrier! Don't mind me. Everybody's got their issues. For you it's your hair...and this is *MINE*." He threw a pouty smile to me then Beat.

I ended up with a slightly wavy, jet black weave that was way longer than my own long tresses which naturally reached the middle of my back--except on the shaved off side. The do stopped short only an inch above my butt. KD had wrapped all my hair up as a base and held it in place with tons and tons of globby, brown, cement glue-like gel for the side that was zilcho and kaput. He managed to somehow leave enough scalp out to give me a center part complete with the edges of my hair blending in well enough with the weave to make anyone who didn't know me think it was real. I looked in the mirror still hating the girl that blinked back but loving her look, nevertheless. It was definitely a model look.

"Okay, you have *got* to be in my hair show. Looking like *this*? You are *wayyy* too much for the D. You'd better move yo' ass to Beverly Hills before you get stalked!" KD fussed. "This way, we can tell Darren you had to get it for a hair show so he won't be mad."

"No—no. We'll tell him the truth. It was for a hospital test." That way I wouldn't owe them anything extra, they wouldn't have anything on me and, if he received any billing information there would be no questions and blanks needing to be filled in about the extended hospital stay.

THEN TUESDAY CAME AND depression invited itself over to stay like an old friend who was homeless. I put Billie Holiday's song "Good Morning Heartache" on repeat and played it the rest of the morning.

I had to go and drop all my classes since almost all of my teachers had emailed instructing me to do so. The only instructor who hadn't was Mrs. Kennedy and I was too embarrassed to turn in the work she'd allowed me to makeup. I hadn't even completed it. Now I would be a semester behind. It was bad enough nursing classes were intensive. I had been doing really well before when school first started. All that hard work in September down the drain. Back in the day the lowest GPA I'd ever gotten at Detroit Community was a 3.7. I'd done better than this when I was pregnant with Pharaoh and even when I had skipped two weeks of high school back in the day.

I slept thru four whole days. I only got up for appointments with tenants to set up maintenance requests. I didn't brush my teeth, take a morning shower or take the usual nightly bath and I didn't answer any calls outside of stuff regarding the apartment. But they all kept calling. Sherra, Shawn, Beat, Darren and of course, of course, of fucking course: Trash. His court date was coming up and he needed me there, still wanted me to move in the house with him, wanted to start over.

He said the same shit in every voicemail message. The sound of his voice always called for a lil' Vico, as I nicknamed them.

I laid down to go to sleep. A plethora of kaleidoscope colors abundantly looped and circled into their own world of existence. Flashes, blobs, jellyfish-like torrents in vivid and varying hues of royal blues began to rush onto the ceiling like a million people running nowhere in particular. A few streams of the color slid off the ceiling to rest next to me.

"*We are blue! And here for you! We shall protect you from all the happiness you have never known!*" they repeated happily as their faces smiled in merriment. Swirling eddies of misery swung around and loomed over me as they bared cold, bitter smiles and wouldn't stop circling the bed. They bumped all the happy blue faces away and started staring at me as tears dropped from their cartoon-like faces...

Her once beautiful cinnamon face is now crinkled and withered. Her eyes hang above the bags and dark circles holding multitudes of sorrow, enough for generations to come.

She is bent over in the back yard. A new mule. No one notices she is human, a woman. No one would care anyway. She is smart but has thrown it all away for simple pleasures. She bends over, clothes-less, revealing the womanly portions of herself for the masses to see, to view even though she knows they do not see the value. They will soon be branding her. Her black hair sways past her shoulders in the wind. She turns to view each one of her torturers. Two are women, a grandmother and granddaughter preparing the burning iron that will soon meld onto her ass. To them she is nothing but a mule. They cannot see she is a woman or that she is crying. But she is too strong or shall we say, she has been tortured too long to feel the pain. She cannot cry out any more. For this reason her mouth stays open, agape in permanent horror.

She gains courage, from out of nowhere it seems but it is Orisha. Orisha gives her the strength to ask. "Please, do not let the men whip me. You can brand me—only the two of you, but not the men. Please." They agree but to them, head touching her feet, womanly openings open to the world, she is a mule

they cannot see

251

> *do not wish to see*
> *do not care*
> *that she is a woman...*

I woke up in a cold sweat and tried to scream but something was wrong; my teeth were covered in hair. Tons and tons of hair protruded from my mouth making it difficult to speak. A brown bundled hairweft was wrapped around my wisdom teeth. I tried to shout, to yell to scream for help but the hair--it had taken over my mouth!

I shot out of bed not able to make any sense out of it. I rushed to the bathroom and looked in the mirror.

There was no hair in my mouth. I looked regular. And I could talk.

That dream scared the shit out of me. It was way too real and too weird. I looked for my purse and got ready to go to Sherra's. *"It wasn't no dream, bitch. It was YOU! You's a stupid bitch, bitch!"* The sinister voice taunted and taunted and wouldn't stop.

I turned and tried to locate the Thing but there was nothing, just my stupid ass jumping around the apartment like a psycho with Billie Holiday's voice singing in the background. I turned the stereo off and turned all the lights on in the apartment just like I used to do when I was six and had nightmares after watching E.T.

This was the kind of shit you couldn't tell anybody.

And I couldn't stop shaking.

Did I really look as bad as that woman mule thing in real life? Had I been a whore? Had I done something to make Craig act like that? Had I really corrupted the Pastor?

It had to be my fault; had it just been Craig, then I could write it off. But the Pastor? He was a man of God!

And Craig *did* love me. He loved me. I remember when things were really good between us. We barely argued at first. Maybe I should have waited to have Mauri; maybe then he would have loved Pharaoh the same way he loved his own child.

I couldn't live like this. What was the point? Nobody cared about anyone except themselves. Where was my mother when I needed her? Tamika had helped Craig cheat on me and was probably sleeping with him herself. She always talked on and on about how fine he was every chance she got! Back in the day Tamika was more than just my cousin, she was my best friend.

There was no point. I wasn't about to be a nurse anytime soon and, with a fucked up pussy, how was I gonna be able to please a man? I'd been kicked out of church. No one believed my story and deep down I knew Craig wasn't completely buying what I told him. I was a terrible mother. My kids hadn't been home in almost two months. Mauri was being potty trained by someone else…

That was it. It was settled. Today was the day Leigh No Middle Name Anderson died. The end of a fucked up story. When something isn't working you have to leave it alone. Death *had* to be better than this.

I left out of the apartment and walked around the corner to a ran-down Arabic owned store on Six Mile to get one of Craig's favorite vodka's--Belvedere. A few guys sitting on the rooftop of a four family-flat behind the yellow and red paint-peeling bum infested, broken glass filled parking lot of the store howled and shouted for me to come over so that I, "Lil Mama", could let them "Tweak this here pussy."

Ignoring them I walked back to the crib, swallowed ten Vico's, gulped down the nasty, clear liquid that felt like a flame trickling down my throat and kept swallowing and swallowing until everything went blank. It would all soon be over…

Oooh, look at those clouds. They sure are pretty. There is a silver one, a baby blue one, a pink one. Oooh. Just float. Float… See how much fun it is. And look behind you—over to your right, The Care Bears are over there.

Let's laugh. We can laugh, it's okay. Come here. Look. You can see any city, any place you want from up here. Just don't float too far or you'll bump into the cotton candy and forget to look down at all the beautiful places. Yes, yes, those places are beautiful but up here, you can always smile and dance and laugh and play…

Oh, what's that you say? You don't believe me? No? Well, there is more. There is more I tell you! There are other places here you will like. Give me your hand…please? Please? I won't hurt you. I promise. Okay, see, that wasn't hard. You can trust me.

Listen to the harps, they are playing a song just for you! Relax, for it is your special song. Look, look! There are pillars! Ten pillars of gold. You came here long, long, ago, ancient years of the past. But then you left. Everyone has missed your smile. Look at the men. They are all waiting for you. Go! It's okay. Go! They await you. Ohh, their arms are outstretched. They are waiting for you. They wish to hug you—to let you know that all will be okay. Where are the women? They are in the other room. Go on, hug the one waiting for you, shortly you will meet everyone. They are eager to see you again.

For there is a certain slumber that falls upon all of us…there are varying sections of time…each one is meant to be filled. But there are different planets, different streams of time. The sad spaces and woes are over now. Do not worry about any of that, shhh…

Look. There he is. He is handsome. He is...he is...well, you know him. He is your king. He wishes to dance. Don't worry, you will soon learn the language and I will leave you be. But hurry, he is telling you he wants to dance. That is it. Good! You're good. See how light you travel. He is lifting you. No? You are not a burden! You speak such human nonsense sometimes! You are never a burden! Let's take that word away, okay? Okay? Wait!

Wait! Don't look that way! Stop! Pay no attention to him! For that is Qualimar—he—he wait!

The snake speaks like unnerving chalky teeth against grayness, against a gray wall...teeth grating against the concrete of the sidewalk. OOOH, YES! He is full of venom and he will bite. No matter how nice you are, he will one day bite, for he would not be Qualimar if he did not follow his true nature.

Wait—wait—if you just get past him—there is more—there is better! Wait! Your king shall fade!

(But she could not wait! There were two faces. She called them Mauri and Pharaoh--more human speech some say). Look at how they beg for her. They are confused. "Yes! Yes! She is here! Mommy!" They chant each night before falling asleep. It is so sad. So sad for such a bosom buddy. She guessed but never really knew. It is sad. So sad for them all. It is sad. The children are confused. Look at their faces. They do not know. No one knew. But the children? Who will care for the children?

They do not know...

They do not know...

They do not know...they cannot understand...

I opened my eyes. Images of Mauri and Pharaoh filled my head like oversized, block letters crammed into befuddling thoughts. I couldn't move. I wanted so badly to move but I couldn't. My mouth was numb and I was drooling uncontrollably. I could feel it slowly sliding down my cheek and into my left ear.

Please God! Yes, you! God! If—if you let me make it...just let me make it. If you do, please, if you care about me, please let me make it. Let me be okay. The kids, my children, please! Please, let someone come! Let them help me!

"Don't be ashamed this time!" I didn't have time to question where the voice was coming from.

Okay, I promise. Help me! Please. Somebody! Help!

"Fool, can't no body hear you! Ya' mouth is numb, remember?"

It felt like forever. Not being able to move, barely being able to see. Then, there was a sparkle…a shimmer. Hope? Hope! Would my prayers be answered? Please!

I was finally able to lift my arm a little after a long period of struggling. It had to be God, I was weak and could barely feel anything. I tried until I finally touched the nightstand. Usually the cordless was there but I couldn't feel it. I kept feeling around--it wasn't there. *Quick! What else can you do, Leigh? Think! Think faster! Come on! You're losing it! Hurry up, bitch! You're losing it!*

"Okay, look. You can do it! Do it. Reach. There is something! Now touch it!" the voice coached.

It was my cell--already opened instead of flipped shut. I fumbled for the buttons and reached the one on the left that felt bigger than the other buttons. *That should be Talk…okay, keep talking, keep thinking— you've got to! Keep going. It's the only way your gonna make it! Keep talking! You're gonna make it…you can! Just stay up! Don't fall asleep! Don't!*

What seemed like another eternity but was actually only a little more than twenty minutes passed before the EMS showed up, walked into my apartment and put me on the gurney.

The last person I'd called on my cell had been Darren earlier that day. When I pressed the Talk button it dialed him. He thought I had been fighting with Craig or something and said he'd heard me choking and sensed something was wrong and since he'd called a few times and both phones went straight to voicemail, he contacted the police who came in and found me drooling with my eyes rolled in the back of my head and everything on the nightstand and rushed the paramedics over.

When I got to Receiving Hospital Darren had taken off work and was already there. He was the last person I wanted privy to all *this* shit.

This hospital thing was played. I didn't know which visit was worse. I had to swallow a blackish purple, thick, nasty, repulsive chalky mixture that crept slowly down my throat like a liquid beast. My arms and legs were locked onto the hospital bed since I was on 'suicide watch'. The only time I wasn't locked to the bedpost was when I had to go to the restroom and the only restroom available to suicidals was door-less. There were too many crazy looking and acting men in the area for me to bring myself to pee for the audience. And I had to stay and complete the treatment session. I wouldn't get out until after the doctors monitored my progress and determined whether or not it was okay to release me. I was weak. I'd lost twenty pounds knocking me down to an even hundred and making my five foot four frame look sickly. My eyes had thick, greenish bags underneath them and my throat hurt like something was roasting in it.

Darren wasn't happy at all. He made them switch me to Bon Secours Cottage Hospital in Gross Pointe for treatment and didn't leave until I was admitted. Since I was worried about the situation with Rick and the apartment, he called Rick. After Darren talked to him, there was no problem with my leave of absence.

Darren even called to check up on me everyday.

This place was weird but a relief. Five women were in my group. There was Kim the Dateless Prom Valedictorian and with her it was always, "Fuck what you heard, she wasn't no nerd!" and constant crying about her curse of ugliness--the three reasons she'd tried unsuccessfully to diminish her time on earth by breaking her glasses and using the lenses to try to slit her throat. Stupid, nerd. If she would have used a knife, I wouldn't have been forced to wake up every morning to the sound of her static-like tears--she was my roommate. Then there was Contessa who, at thirty-four, was the soon to be ex-homemaking wife of a judge. She found out he'd been cheating on her for three years with her younger sister, couldn't handle the divorce and was allergic to working outside of her home and anything that sounded like minimum wage. Then there was Sheila a forty-five year old, afro sporting lawyer who was funny and cool as hell. How and why she'd tried to shorten her God-given life sentence remained a mystery since she never, ever talked about it in any of the group therapy meetings. And, oh yes, Elaine. The Middle Eastern Indian who, in my opinion, was crying wolf just to stay away from those five badass kids of hers and her cheap husband. She was always talking about "One day she was going to'doit!" and had been sent by her husband who was a doctor and probably tired of hearing her wolf cries. "Dees is reee-li such a beau-t-ful fa-cil-li-tie," she stated everyday as though it had been her first. Seemed like it was as close to a spa resort as she was gonna get with that penny pinching husband of hers.

All things considered I only had a few problems with the place. You couldn't sleep more than eight hours or the nurses would be in your room interrogating you like they were the police.

Kim wasn't allowed to wear her glasses (and what a shame. It would have been nice for her to have been allowed shades. She was cockeyed and, being such, maintaining eye contact with her messed with my stomach. Mentally afflicted *and* my roommate, ignoring her pleas for conversation was out--unless I wanted to worry about being cut in the esophagus with saved up pieces of glass come early morning). She constantly bumped into people or you'd find her talking to the wall thinking it was someone in our group.

Contessa, whose head, I noticed, had begun to tremble uncontrollably within my short arrival, was always staring and squinting at everyone in the group unless medicated. But, truly, I didn't mind. I'd secretly wanted to find the guts to unremittingly stare at people myself. After all, it was kind of sad that there were so many different looking people on earth but looking or staring at a person was somehow deemed rude.

Side Note: Our therapist was a small White woman originally named Cheryl who wore feathered dream catchers and shapeless dresses of colorful vertical arrangements that made it look as though she'd stolen her wardrobe from the Native American sections of a museum. At her request we called her Luna. Behind her back Sheila and I called her La Lunatic. She deemed herself a "Healer" instead of a counselor and claimed to work with the angels.

Once I noticed the extent in which she fancied and encouraged my "gift" of visions, I utilized her ridiculousness to get more sleep time since she felt I was receiving more "messages." The trade off was being her favorite, which entailed being summoned to sit near her during aura readings and meditation time and being constantly harassed about what my "energy field" had picked up on. Unfortunately or fortunately, under her guidance, I became rather good at identifying auras.

Still, overall, in the words of Elaine Menew Pajdir Patel, it really wasn't a bad place.

We started the day with mental exercises that consisted of writing in our journals then Yoga, which was my favorite. It was my first time trying it since that pastor had preached about it being based in false religion. Even though I made fun of the treatment clinic for including Yoga, it made me feel better. We were even encouraged to pray or meditate and given positive affirmations according to our own personal issues.

But the strangest thing continued to occur after we were done with the various stretches and did our meditations. I kept seeing myself near a fireplace with a faceless man with Mauri and Pharaoh sitting next to us.

Now, considering all that had happened this year since August and the fact that Craig's house had a fireplace, right about now, I was NOT trying to be worried about a man. I was finally, as encouraged here at Cottage, only worried about my health and my future. So I tried with all my might to block it out. For all I knew, it was another one of those visions that would be encouraging me to go off on the deep end again. After that last episode and this new mental spa resort, I wasn't about to try anything like suicide again!

Here is where I ran a major problem: Talking to that counselor was mandatory.

After avoiding him as long as I could, my time had come. He was young, Jewish and fulfilled the stereotype Craig and I had created about psychologists. Telling this dude all my business was about as classy as sitting on a toilet in a public restroom without covering it with tissue first, in my book.

"You look like Ross from *Friends*," I stated slumping down in the seat across his from him.

"You look like a very attractive young lady who should be happy with herself," he retorted.

"Is it legal for you to talk to me in such a manner?" He was pissing me off yet humoring.

"Is there a reason you avoided me for three days?"

"Maybe I don't like Jewish guys."

"Maybe I don't like smart mouthed young ladies who try to act harder than they really are." His deeply creased hooded dark brown eyes were actually kind and sympathetic and gave the impression of recreational drug use.

"...I think I like you. You passed the test."

"Oh, thanks." He was sarcastic. "It means a lot. No seriously. I *am* glad you're here. Let's be real—"

"—What? Since when do guys like *you* do Ebonics? You can speak to me without all that. It's offensive."

"All right. Sorry..." He just sat there staring at me. In another environment, I would have been attracted to him but...when you are in a crazy ward, you don't try things like that with the psych dude...who is on drugs.

"...So?"

"...Leigh. What's your deal? Seems like you really do need to talk."

"I thought you were a psychologist, not a psychic."

"Oh, you've got jokes, huh?" he spat back calmly. We sat there for twenty minutes with me pulling on my hospital gown and him staring back and forth from the clock to me.

Then, finally, it was, am I a hoe? I had began really enjoying sex until all of this and-- (okay, off that 'cause he might write down that I *was* in fact a hoe and, being that he probably was in Darren's circle, I didn't want him thinking I *was* like Niquie after all).

So? Okay...well, doc, I did have this one incident in the seventh grade where Richard Phillips grabbed me by my breasts and shoved me into the gymnasium after school when I went in there looking for Tamika because she was in art club and I wanted to join the club for the afternoon since mom was running late.

And oh, how he tugged on the 32C's and yes, I remembered the taste of that turnipy kiss and yes he was popular and oh how I was disgusted but no, I did not tell and he was so popular no one would've believed me anyway and yes I saw him everyday and no I still never told anyone about it until today and then I wore loose baggy clothes and everyone thought I was simply the biggest TLC fan but deep down inside I was disgusted that I had the biggest breasts in seventh, eighth and the entire ninth grade and damn, I hoped another guy'd never ever noticed until I met Domonique and yes she was my girl and oh she was sexy and always wilin' out and had made me want to dress sexy and then the dudes I met, some of the D's most wanted and let me shut up on Darren 'cause you're probably in his click, then Trash and yada, yada church shit yada, then on to this one song that was my life with all the Bitches watching and hatin' on me that I wished would just SHUT UP and yes I was a bad mother and I had abandoned my kids like my mom'd recently abandoned me and a little bit more about my childhood and up to the girl that was a mule and had bags like the one I now had under my eyes and yuck! yes, damn skippy I hated Leigh aka The Dumb Ass & Shit Starter that Should Have Been Much Smarter! And please don't think all Black people grow up daddy-less, have children out of wed-lock and get raped by the love of their life—whoops, it was someone I knew by not my ex-fiancé, no...never him.

Kind Eyes responded by saying, "Actually, none of this is your fault. But you do need to learn from these experiences. You are very intelligent...you merely need to extricate yourself from your negative environment. I mean, you can't escape running into church members you used to associate with. Based on their behaviors, consider yourself lucky to no longer be involved with them.

"...You need a plan—like an affirmation to build your self-esteem and to get your self-projection up to par... Another thing: you really need to rid yourself of that relationship. Tomorrow? Same time?"

So the Dumb Ass & Shit Starter said, "Yes" like it was a major business appointment and left. Dumb Ass wasn't *that* dumb. If she didn't play along, they might start saying she was an unfit mother and try to take her kids away...

Finally, after much hesitation, I called Sherra and told her where I was and I called Shawn and talked to him everyday for at least an hour. I was even honest with him about the whole ordeal. He was happy I was still in existence on planet earth but made a point of letting me know how majorly upset he was about the whole thing and promised to take me somewhere fun once I went home.

CHAPTER 15

SELF-HELP AND FEMINIST BOOKS in tow recommended by Kind Eyes himself, along with the promises of enrolling back in electric violin and yoga classes and continuing my sessions with the lady he'd referred, I was allowed to go home two weeks later.

"Hey." I smiled at Darren. He smelled nice. He always smelled nice.

"How do you feel?" His sincere eyes awaited a response.

"Much better. Listen, Darren...I have to thank you. You saved my life. I was really going thru some shit... You don't know the half of it. It was crazy. But I do feel better..." I could tell I'd caught him off guard. He rarely showed emotion. To him it was distasteful coming from a man.

He reached over to the passenger's seat of the Benz SUV and hugged me tightly as he rubbed my back. "I'm glad you're aright." For a second, I thought I saw a tear about to make a debut. He held me a good minute and sighed after letting go. "I need to ask you a favor," he blurted out.

"Wha-what?" I was already taken back by his behavior. What kind of favor was he going to want?

"Insteada staying at yo' apartment, can you stay at my place? I already talked to Rick. They said some lady that lives in your building—you know a Debra?"

"Yeah, my neighbor."

"Well, they said she'd be willing to fill your spot for the next month. I know how you don't wanna let your place go so... I think it would be good for you to hang out at my house—just for a while. ...Get Pharaoh."

"Okay...Wait. What about Mauri?"

"...Yeah. Bring yo' kids or see if your previous babysitting arrangements'll still work. I don't want you at your place by yourself. I already had your car taken to my place... You talked to that other muthafuka?"

"...Cool... No, I haven't talked to Tra--him since--since before coming here."

"Well. You know he placed a missing people's report on you... He went to court on *some* shit against your pastor but somehow his slick ass got out of it... He's on probation, though--John told me." Leave it to one of Darren's connects to let him know how anything and everything was going down in Michigan. "But dat nigga shut up after a while. Make sure you change your number—*that's the* problem right there...I 'on't know why you chose *him*...why 'on't you let him keep the girl?"

"The girl is *my daughter*! *HELL* NO!"

"Aright, aright, calm down. What you gonna do about the kids?"

"…Well, can you drive me by there to see them? Then, I'll chill for a few days and get them…"

"You can get them tomorrow if you'd like. I'll have Lanette give me a reference for a nanny that'll help you out with 'em. I don't want Pharaoh thinking his parents aren't there for him." All this time and he hadn't seen Pharaoh; I guess this incident had really gotten to him.

"Okay."

"KD is doing your hair tomorrow, too. Hit that spa up. I'll hang out with you…go shopping and get some things, if you'd need to." His words were like magic until I remembered the current condition of my scalp. I made arrangements to just get my nails done and to take care of the weave at another pre-arranged afterhours time.

The kids were gone when we got there so we waited for Tommy to bring them back but Darren wouldn't come in with me. Then we went by the apartment so I could get some of my things. I was grateful to have Darren with me since the place freaked me out. There were pills scattered next to the bed. That bottle of Belvedere stood on the nightstand frozen in time, waiting to welcome me back into my own private world of misery.

He kept conversation going the whole ride to his home sensing the onset of anxiety I wasn't doing well to hide. Craig left both the cell and the house voicemail filled with messages. Tons of drunken, under the influence pleas to call him, threats—he even mailed me three letters asking if I had moved, to please move in the house with him along with his promises to go to counseling. I didn't want to think about him.

It was crazy but I still loved him. I hated to admit it. I just wasn't *in* love with him anymore. Not after all of this. And he was going to be a problem. I already knew that. He was accustomed to walking all over me, treating me like shit and knowing he could make a big comeback. It was going to be hard to get rid of him now that that sort of pattern had been set.

Stepping out the truck and into Darren's newly purchased million dollar plus, mansion in Oakland Township was overwhelming—a nice change of pace—but definitely overwhelming. The entrance was grand and regal. The pavement of the noir semi-circular driveway was as smooth as icing. The neighborhood was lined with newly built houses spaced far apart from each other, some hidden behind black iron gates. The air was fresh, clean and so pure it was almost as if you were on another planet. There were six bedrooms—the master suite alone was as big as my apartment's living room, dining room and kitchen combined. There were five and a half bathrooms, the home theatre he'd always wanted, a great room, a built in stainless steel oven and fridge completed the kitchen along with pots hanging over the counter of the island and hardwood floors. And even with all that room, there was still a huge breakfast nook with sparkling bay windows. Add to that a family room, a library that doubled as Darren's home office, a bridge-like foyer with a sofa table and flowers and a mirror framed in square glass on the landing of the steps all overlooked the living room...an *in*door pool with a really high logwood ceiling? Yes, yes I *could* stay here for a while!

Every room was completed with the proper, expensive, traditional and classic yet boring furnishings with the exception of Pharaoh's bedroom.

Pharaoh's room had a full sized race car bed with toys neatly lined up on one wall. There were pictures of him when he was six months, a year and a picture of him on his second birthday sitting on top of the dresser and the dresser was packed with clothes that were his current size. There was a picture of me holding him at the hospital the day he was born on the wall and another picture of him, me and Darren right before I'd taken Pharaoh home from the hospital that had been blown up and was hanging next to the door...my mother had insisted on taking that picture.

When I went back downstairs, he took me into the kitchen and introduced me to his housekeeper, Ms. Lanette, an older Black lady with her hair dyed so dark and so greased up it looked like she had strings of ink colored yarn sitting on top of her head. Her blackened smokers lips tightened. For some reason, I didn't like her off rip. "Hi." Her greeting was chilly as she looked me up and down and sized me up. I didn't respond. "Oh, yeah, Ezrina, come meet da girl," she added giving my hair a good glancing over as she tried to figure out whether or not it was weave.

"Oh, yeah. Hi you?" The lady who was supposed to become the nanny of my kids rushed into the kitchen from the hallway and asked. Her words held over and ran together like the remnants of a southern accent. And her eyes were too close together, giving her an eerie appearance. She looked like a rehabilitated, older, female version of that crackhead man in Receiving who was also schizophrenic. When she reached out to hug me, I could just feel the fakeness. My stomach flutter.

"Darren? Darren?" I rushed up the circular stairs after him, leaving those two behind in the kitchen. "Something's up with that lady, that Ezrin lady—and your housekeeper! Please don't think I'm crazy but—but—Ross, I mean my counselor from—you know--the place—he told me to trust my intuition--he said it's very strong. I—I am not leaving Pharaoh and Mauri with either of them!" Either Ross was right or Luna'd put a curse on me for secretly believing her to be a witch.

"Whoa! Slow down. Ms. Lanette's been here since I moved here and everything's been straight. She shows up on time, cleans my place and

CHAPTER 16

DARREN LEFT TO TAKE care of last minute business since we were scheduled to leave for our flight to Florida tomorrow morning. He walked with an extra pep in his step and kissed me for a good minute before leaving out.

I did what I should have done months ago and I could finally say I was happy.

I waited until Darren's car pulled out of the garage to dial Shawn's number. The way Shawn was, he'd be thinking something terrible happened if I didn't call him sometime soon

"He*yyyy* you." He laughed. "I was worried about you. I didn't know what the deal was. You didn't tell me where you were so it wasn't like I could visit. You feelin' better?"

"Yes—much--but it wasn't so bad, really. I learned about myself and the unhealthy patterns I've gotten used to repeating that I have to break and I'm *really* into Yoga now! Oh my gosh Shawn I love it!"

"That's good… Wanna go for a movie? Think you feel up to it?"

"No, I've got the kids and I'm about to take the babysitter home."

"…Oh…well, you can bring them. Or, I can pay for the babysitter to keep 'em a little longer?" he offered.

"Ahh…let me check with her first." I put the phone on mute and called Dina from out of the guest bedroom.

"Girrrrlll, yeah. If you payin', I'm stayin'! Besides, uh sista can get used ta bein' up in here! How come you ain't tell no body yo' baby diddy was paid fa real, fa real! You lucky! Whaad, I need ta be a size three ta get it like you got it? Girl, Craig was fine, but Darren look uh lil' bit finer wit all dis bread he stackin'. Huh! I'll stay! You need me ta stay tamorrow, too?"

I laughed. "No, we're going to Miami… Thanks for staying. I shouldn't be that long."

"*AAA*nytime. I'm 'bout ta go watch dis movie dat's 'bout ta come on. Mauri an' Pharaoh both knocked out! I made 'em play hard dan a mug' las night so they'll quit wakin' up so freakin' early." We both laughed.

"Yeah, Shawn, I'll go. Let me see if Sherra wants to come—"

"--Well, I kinda had a surprise for you--just us is cool."

"…Oh. Okay. I'll be leaving in like an hour. Matterfact, make that two hours. Star Theatre—my bad—make that the AMC across from Oakland Mall." Nobody went there. That place was always practically empty except for White couples that looked like they listened to Incubus and seniors from the area. I wasn't about to have Darren's crew spotting me out with a dude. There was no way he was going to believe we were just friends.

"That long?" He laughed. "Alright."

I dressed down in a pair of Jeans from Saks, a pair of black leather ankle boots and a fluffy black turtlenecked loose fitting sweater, pulled my weave into a ponytail and no makeup--only a dab of lip gloss. I wasn't about to be giving Shawn the wrong impression. I was picking up on the fact that he was starting to like me a little more than he needed to but I was going to have to switch it up and make it clear that the only thing going down between us was f-r-i-e-n-d-s-h-i-p. He was too cool for me to just quit hanging with. After all, he *had* been there for me when I was going thru all that mess.

As crazy as it sounded I wanted to stop by the apartment. I drove over, parked in the back and went looking for my I-Pod I'd forgotten to get.

The doorbell rang. I looked out of the porch window. An old lady with a raggedy white *Madea* looking wig and a walker stood at the front door. I went to the entrance to see what she wanted. "Can I help you?" At the last second I decided not to open my porch door.

"Yeah, bay'beh, I called 'bout dat vacant 'partment."

"Ah..." Maybe she'd spoken to Debra earlier. I didn't have anything available at the present time unless Debra had forgotten to give me a move-out notice. I stepped into the hallway and walked to the door but before I got a chance to open it, I caught the eyes thru the grid of the bars on the window next to the building's front door. Those hard, beady little eyes, the barely there mustache--both belonged to a man! A man pretending to be an old, bent over, decrepit lady!

It turned sideways to try to block me from getting a closer view. There was a running car with tinted windows in the alley across the street. I rushed back into my apartment and called the police.

Thank you, thank you, thank you! Somebody was looking out for me... The saltshaker I'd used to season the Cornish hens I'd planned on eating on that almost fateful afternoon fell off the counter. I hadn't touched it and it for damn sure wasn't close enough to the edge of the counter to simply fall on it's own.

Although sitting in that apartment almost made me lose two whole weeks worth of recovery, I didn't leave until the police arrived to escort me to my car. I prayed for that same protecting force to stick around until the cops came.

I completed a report and gave them the name of the number one suspect. Trash.

When I called Shawn and relayed the whole story to him, he politely went off on me for going there by myself. "Leigh, you *know* you have to take safety precautions," he continued after I arrived at the low-key theater. I should have gone back to Darren's but I knew I wouldn't be seeing Shawn for a while with the trip and out of respect for Darren.

While Shawn was in line getting my nachos, I switched my cell from vibrate to silent because of an Unavailable number that kept calling back to back even though I wasn't answering. On second thought, it could have been Dina or my mother--finally.

I went ahead and pressed Talk. "LEIGH! IT'S ME---WAIT! DON'T HANG UP! DESE MUHFUKAS JUS JACKED ME! I JUS BOUGHT CHU DAT NEW TRUCK YOU SAID YOU WONTED—UH MOUNTAINEER—TA SURPRISE YOU WIT! An' *outta nowhere,* dese muhfuckas ganked me when I pulled up at cho' place ta see if you had came back! Dey *TRIIIEEED* TA SHOOT--" I hung up on his ass and turned the phone off. He was pathetic--resorting to that kind of a bullshit ass lie to cover up the major set up he just tried to pull on me. Sick....really sick and twisted.

I was positive Shawn was tired of hearing about all my drama so I kept the newest recent craziness to myself.

"What's the matter?" he turned and asked ten minutes into the flick.

"What? Nothing."

"No. What's wrong? You don't wanna be here? You wanna go somewhere else? We can see another movie if you want? Whada you wanna do?"

I sighed. "*Nooo*--I'm *fine.*" I sounded grumpy but I was actually paranoid and thinking about never going back to that apartment again. Leaving whatever was in there, there.

I thought about it more and more. I heard Sherra's voice, "*She plannin' on havin' her brothers jump him in November. She plannin' on havin' her brothers jump him in November. She planning on havin' her brothers jump him in November...*" Was it that Angela thang?

No. Couldn't be!

But the glimmer that sparkled after this new revelation gave me my answer. "I'm fine." I smiled, sat back and enjoyed the rest of the comedy.

"Are you hungry?" he asked as we left.

"Um, *yea.*"

"I shouldn't have even asked. 'Member that time you sent me and Tyron to Mama's Kitchen two times in the same day for the gumbo special?"

"Yeah, I can't believe y'all snuck out to get it for me. Ty was pissed at me, boy. You coulda got fired for that." I chuckled thinking back to that day when I was in Henry Ford about as famished as a kid on one of those Feed The Needy commercials with flies buzzing all around and landing on their eyes.

"I wasn't worried about it. You know I'd do anything for you... Ty was trying to hook up with you, that's the only reason he went. But he gave up--you were always doggin' men."

"Yeah...that was back then. Hey—let's do lunch another time, okay? I've got some news to tell you." What was I thinking? I needed to quickly break the Darren situation to him in a nice, 'I still wanna be your friend, your buddy, your ace, but I'm taken—it can never happen' kind of speech. Then, I'd go buy something so Darren would think I'd been out shopping and take my ass home. Lunch with my boy was out.

"Wait. It can't be as important as what I've got to tell you. You sure you don't wanna have lunch? Big Fish is right up the street—or we can do whatever you want? I hate that we went to Denny's the first time we ever went out."

"Yeah, see that's the thing. I've got something to tell you, too, and—"

"—Leigh. Look, I *really need* to talk to you. Can we go sit somewhere?"

"...Alright." I followed him to his car. I already didn't like the sound of this.

"You riding with me?"

"No. Just tell me what's up. I've got to go home—"

"—Well, see that's just what it's about. I love you--from the time I first laid eyes on you, I *loved* you. You're beautiful, you've got the personality a man dreams of. I've never felt this close to a woman before. Back in the day I registered on this one dating site...none of them went past first dates, though--but it wasn't a big deal, you know?

"It's always been like that. I used to hate Valentines Day when I was a kid. All the girls were all up on the pretty boys and the thugs and wouldn't give me the time of day. I was starting to think love might not happen for me, maybe it was just one of those things in life, you know. I have everything else I want. But then I met you and-- "

"--Wait! Wait, wait, wait, wait, wait! *Shawnnnn*, stop! You *can't* be in love with me! We've only known—*barely* known each--other for a month! I'm not gonna lie, I can't see *not* having you in my life but you're my boy. Let's not mess up our friendship."

"I know! But hear me out! You're absolutely beautiful--but, even if you weren't, I would still love you, Leigh." His eyes begged me to listen and for the first time in a long time tears were welling up in someone else's eyes instead of mine. I had to block his words from sinking into my calcifying heart. And I was disgusted. At myself. At his tears. I couldn't like him the way he wanted me to. I was already in love. And falling out of love with someone else. And trying to fall back in love with *myself*...

"...After I got out of the psych clinic, my son's father picked me up. Remember when I told you he was the one I was blessed enough to reach that one day? Well, he helped get the EMS and—and...I've been staying with him ever since. He *loves me* Shawn. *He loves* me. I've known him since I was twenty/twenty-one. He's been making a lot of sacrifices lately to make sure I recover—"

"--Leigh, *Leigh*?" The way he said my name, you would have thought I was torturing him. "Please tell me you're not hooking up with *him*--the guy you said treated you like a sex toy from day one? Why is it women never want the men that'll really love them and care about them, hunh, why is that? You all fall in love with the ones that won't *ever* respect you then you all turn around and say all men do is dog women out. You all don't want good men!

"You don't think you deserve to be loved? Is that what it is? Or is it because he's got money? If that's it, then I can accept it--if you're choosing money over love, I can accept that. Love is almost never certain. But I *promise* you my love for you is..."

"...Shawn—Shawn? You're going to make someone a wonderful—"

"—Leigh! It could be YOU—not *some*one! You! Bring the kids, move in with me, we'll get married, I'll get a bigger place. I'll take care of you. I make around forty a year--that's nothing like what you're used to but I can take care of you while you finish school. Everything I have is good as yours. I'd love you *and* your kids. You won't have to worry about anything—it'uh never be hard for me to love you—never! There's no other woman for me. Ever since I first laid eyes on you I've felt like this. I could never understand why you went thru the shit you went thru with guys— you aren't hard to love at all." I couldn't take it. I rushed to open the car door. "Hold up, I'm not trying to scare you." He reached for my arm. "Look. 'Member that night we slept on the floor in your living room and you held my hand 'til you fell asleep? Just—just try something. If you really don't have any feelings for me, if I'm just getting the wires mixed up and we really don't have anything, we'll both know. Just—just kiss me."

I sat twisted in the opposite direction with my legs hanging out of the ajar door. I wanted to. To prove that I wasn't feeling anything for him. Or I could just run like hell, jump in my truck and never see him again.

I turned towards him and let him cradle my face in his hands. The way he touched my cheek, the way he lightly caressed my skin so gently, my heart fluttered for a second. The moment we kissed, nothing else mattered. I could feel everything in him pull me into him but it wasn't enough. I wanted more. I tasted the side of his neck while he traced my ear with his lips. My hand slid under his coat onto his chest as his hand teased the nape of my neck. And then I felt a twinge of disgust. "We can't." I could barely whisper the words. His eyes were putting up a good fight, searching and probing for the real answer.

I ran to my truck. There was no way it could work. I loved Darren. I already had a son with him. He loved me, I could tell. We were going to Miami tomorrow. There was just no way I could be with Shawn. I sped off like a maniac and drove to Somerset, parked on the Nordstrom's side of the parking structure and just sat there with no energy to get out and go inside the mall.

It was just that simple. I'd proved it to him. I didn't like him the way he liked me. I wasn't all into Craig or Darren at first but I hadn't gotten disgusted the first time we kissed either.

But if it was all so simple, why did it feel so terrible? He wouldn't want to be cool with me now, not after this. Loosing him as a friend was like taking two bullets in the chest.

I went to Steve Madden's to see if they had finally received those cream and gold gator boots in my size from the other store. As sharp as they were, I wasn't even excited. I didn't want them anymore but I bought them anyway. I needed an excuse for why I had been gone so long.

I got back into the truck, turned the radio off, zipped on 75 North and made it home. Everything was like miasma until I opened the door with the key Darren had given me this morning.

The kids were running around and driving Dina bananas. They all rushed to greet me when I came in. Darren's eyes twinkled in their famous fashion. He gave me a hug and smiled that sexy smile of his. But after Tommy picked Dina up, Darren didn't forget to ask where I'd been. I told him about the apartment thing and lied about going to the mall to meet up with some old girlfriends I hadn't seen in a while.

"What? You went by that apartment *again*?"

"I know…I—"

"--Did you give Craig your new number?"

"NO! I--I just—I still have my old phone…Look! I know, I know it was stupid, but he's gonna be going crazy over Mauri soon and—"

"—Where's the phone?" I pulled it out of my purse and handed it over. He threw it in the trash outside. "In order to get better, you've got to learn how to let go, Leigh." And there were no more questions.

274

We packed and got ready for the trip. I was ecstatic. This would be my first time on a plane—although I wasn't going to tell Darren that.

I fixed fillet mignon, string bean casserole and twice baked potatoes for dinner. The kids refused the fillet mignon but ate the other two options. I was pleased with how well Mauri was behaving. Being over Sherra's had gotten her in check. She even squeaked out her version of "Thank you" when I put her plate in front of her.

We talked and took a bath together after I put the kids in bed. Darren kissed me on the cheek before I fell asleep curled in his arms between the crème satin sheets. Everything was the way it was supposed to be and I was excited to be going to Miami tomorrow.

BEING IN METRO AIRPORT felt weird. Seeing all those dolphin-looking planes slowly but surely shooting up in the air was not my idea of fun. The idea of flying without the help of Vicoden was nice but, planes? No. Now, I wanted to turn around and take the kids and myself back home. What if something happened? That one child was the only survivor of that plane crash way back in 1985. Her mother had covered her with her body. How was I going to be able to protect both of these kids at the same time?

And who was I going to pray to if the plane went down or if we got hi-jacked? I mean, yeah, now I believed there was something greater out there after everything I'd just gone thru ...but was it *really* Jesus? What if there were other higher powers that I didn't know anything about yet? Would they still help if something happened? It would probably be best to simply ask for protection without worrying about calling on a specific name.

"Darren, if the plane starts crashing, cover Pharaoh with your body, okay?" I asked after passing thru security and showing something to the blonde, frizzy haired, White ticket-person lady.

"I promise, Leigh. He started smiling and chuckling. "Baby, calm down, aright? We're taking the jet. It's private. It shouldn't be that bad, aright?"

"You never told me you owned a jet," I stated frowning as I following him onto the ramp. He was rolling both of our Louis Vuitton suitcases with his left hand and wheeling Mauri's Winnie the Pooh suitcase and carrying my Vuitton bag with my cosmetics and hair stuff in it in his right hand and his laptop bag was barely hanging on his shoulder. Pharaoh was rolling his own suitcase while I remained hands free with the exception of Mauri and my purse.

"I don't, it's like a timeshare."

"Oh." I knew we were staying in one of his timeshares once we got there, I just didn't know they did the same thing for planes.

He sat quietly reading a non-fiction book about the Great Depression while I flicked thru one of my Ross reads. The children were glued to *Lion King* above them on the flat screen.

Three smooth plane riding, sunny sky gazing hours later, we were in Miami and all I wanted to do was hit the water. It was seventy-three degrees.

"Let's wait on the beach, aright baby? It'll be warmer a little later and I've got some business ta take care of. Why don't you take the kids to the Art Deco District and check out the architecture tour they got runnin' today? I got the tickets already in case you wanted to check it out."

"...Hm...that might be fun." Art, yes. Architecture? I don't think so. But he was trying.

"You going?"

"Yeah, I guess."

There was a World War II and Deco Underworld tour showing but—kids and all, I had to skip them and Darren hadn't gotten the tickets for them anyway. I probably would have liked that Underworld one. I had always secretly admired gangsters like Al Capone. Next to *The Sound of Music* my favorite movie was *Scarface*.

Instead we did the Deco of MiMo tour, which was supposed to be all about the historical and tropically inspired buildings. I couldn't have cared less, all that mattered was that it was the paradise that is Miami and Darren had his own personal Metro Cars driver drive me and the kids to all the places he listed on the itinerary.

After going to Parrot Jungle Island downtown, I was tired and ready to get something that wasn't in the bird family to eat. We went to a restaurant the driver said had excellent lobster right off Ocean Drive before going back to the beach house.

There were no words to describe how beautiful the house was. The outside of the three story home was very modern, white rectangles-- like those places you always saw on television shows that took place in California and looked like real-life, glass houses with barely anything but windows showing from the outside. The kitchen was black, stainless steel and white—everything in the house except the artwork was either extra, extra white or black or brushed silver and meticulously clean like a ten person cleaning crew visited on a daily basis. I almost felt like that girl out on that first date with Darren again. This was much more than what I could have ever dreamed of.

I was tired and dozed off to sleep while the kids busied themselves with Nickelodeon. Hours later I woke up to Darren trying to slide in me.

I screamed like Hitler and a dozen colonists were touching me. I did *not* want to be touched down there! I had even started wearing panties! Next week I had an appointment with the Gyn at Henry Ford, until then that area was off limits—probably even longer regardless of what the doctor said—huh! And, thus, the bloodcurdling scream to *convey* the point!

Pharaoh knocked on the door like he was the police.

"Aright, aright. I'm sorry, *damn* why you godda do all that? All you had to do was--"

"--JUST DON'T, Okay? Pharaoh, I'm okay--"

"—Ma?" Darren opened the door feeling his son's need to be convinced. He actually picked him up and hugged him. Pharaoh kept his eyes on me the whole time as I sat up in the bed. His eyebrows were furrowed as he bit his bottom lip and continued watching me. Finally convinced I was okay, he went back to Nickelodeon.

"Leigh?"

"Yes?"

"My bad..."

"...Whatever..."

"Let's go out on the balcony."

I sighed.

"Come on, baby."

I just wanted to lay in bed but I got up anyway. "Darren?"

"Yeah, babe."

"...Look at the water...it's so, clear, so blue and beautiful. Why can't life always be like this...stress-free without all the extra drama?"

"It can be...if you're with me." He handed me a glass of bubbly. Normally I didn't but I accepted--I needed something to calm my nerves since they'd taken away my little Vico's. "It's your call...I'd never force you to get into something you didn't want, Leigh. You had me from day one." He stared off into the sky that was now a palette of varying red, orange, blue and white brush strokes against the sky.

Before either of us could utter another word, I was in his lap, loving him, loving my new perfect life and making him happy as best I could under the current conditions. On the balcony, in plain view of beach strollers I gave him all of me—everything I had.

"...That's a good girl, Leigh," he could barely get the words as he throbbed with pleasure within my mouth. "That's a good girl...Ssshit-Ahh, that's it...*that's it*, baby... Damn, you good..."

It turned me on more than anything ever had. I was all down for being respected as a woman and all that jazz but, as far as not needing a man? That feminist male hatin' shit was out. The house never said it wanted to be like the car. The snake never tried to turn into a fly. I liked being a woman. I wasn't about to try to be like no man. People were way too confused nowadays. That was part of the problem with the world. Everybody wanted to be independent. Everybody wanted to go around shouting *they ain't need nobody* when in actuality we were made for each other. A man needs a woman just as much as a woman needs a man. You don't think so? Try to conceive a baby without the opposite sex. You've got to have the egg and some sperm...

And right now what I needed was to feel and taste the fluidity that made him a man. Had I known giving head could be like this, I would have been one for living in his lap a long time ago.

Afterwards he pulled me on top of him. I rested my head against his hard chest. "I think I've finally figured Darren Pewter out."

"What?"

"You love me for real."

Biting on his lower lip, he looked down into my eyes and smiled, solidifying the answer. I felt like a little girl safe in the arms of a big, strong papa bear...well...a slim, yet, strapping papa bear.

THE NEXT MORNING I was on a spree that could only be dubbed a shopper's paradise. I decided to call Darren to see if he wanted to do lunch. My stomach was growling. Two days into the trip and I was already tired of his disappearing acts. I thought he said the point of this trip was so we could spend time together.

"Oh, my bad baby, me and the guys are having lunch and checkin' out dis strip joint. We'll do dinner tonight," he stated like it was as simple as two plus two. I didn't like the sound of the music coming thru the phone; sounded like every other word was pussy!

"What!" I slammed shut my phone, dropped the two hundred and fifty dollar dress I was about to get for Mauri with his card and asked the driver to take us back to the house. Why would he do some shit like *that*? What, I wasn't good enough? I was so angry I couldn't even think.

I called Sherra but she didn't pick up. I wanted to call Shawn but I couldn't--that was trouble if you ever wanted to ask for it. He was such a pushover he'd probably try to get me to come back and move in with him all over again. But I needed to call somebody for a second opinion on this shit cause the way I was feeling, I was ready to pop Darren's head off!

Then there was Kevin/Calvin. He was definitely someone to keep for "just in case" instances like these and silly, silly me! I hadn't even given him my new number yet and it wasn't like I could call him anyway. It was still a bit risky. Later for that one. Then, the more I thought about it, it all boiled down to one thing: either I was going to be with Darren or I wasn't. In times like these, getting mad was not the answer. But getting even sure as hell was!

The minute he got in, I was dressed and, in the words of Lawanda off *In Living Color*, "Rets ta go!"

"Hey, Darren. Watch the kids please." I slid past him and opened the door.

"What? *Fa what*?" He was indignant.

"Plans," I stated rather simply while making sure my keys were in my white ruffled clutch purse that matched the fitted, icy white Dior pants suit I was wearing baring nothing under the blazer except a diamond necklace that sunk into a ton of cleavage like a dazzling suit tie.

He pulled me close to him and looked me sternly in the eyes licking his lips. "Where you goin', baby?"

"Oh…nowhere in particular. I met this really nice girl when I was shopping and she asked me to go see the Chippendales with her tonight. They're in town…it should be fun…" I had to force myself not to blink. Otherwise my black kohl rimmed eyes and mascara'd be all messed up— I'd put four coats on--my lashes still weren't dry. And I'd spent thirty minutes on my face and the slick bun that was way too tight and now pulling my eyes upward like a chick from a subtitled Asian flick.

"Well, cancel. We're going out to dinner. I'm glad you're dressed. I already made the reservation."

"No…sorry, I can't. I don't wanna stand Shelly up. Besides, I need to do *some*thing fun while I'm here. This *is* Miami, you know!"

He pulled me close to him. His tongue, filled with desire, slid between my parted lips and fed my body melding fervor…I couldn't even breathe.

We ended up going to a Miami Heat versus The Wizards game at the American Airlines Arena. We sat only two rows behind the coaches and players on the bench. Even though Mauri was scared of all the commotion at first, it was wonderful--my life was becoming wonderful. They even caught her smiling on the screen during halftime. She made me proud by waving for the cameras when I asked her to.

The rest of our vacation, I didn't call Darren during his absenteeism and in turn, the kids and I went shopping, hit the beaches, aquariums and the zoo and enjoyed ourselves and Darren did breakfast and dinner with us and every evening it was family time.

WHEN WE GOT BACK to Michigan, I thought I'd get a chance to kick back, catch up on some reading and prepare for the next semester by going over old class work and registering but it didn't go like that.

Even though there was a new cleaning crew (two older Mexican women who were the only ones Darren and I agreed on out of nine interviewees) being the future Mrs. Pewter was very demanding. On Monday's there were movies at the DIA that we just *had* to go view after I did my weekly rendezvous hair appointment with KD--one of Darren's buddies was over the program at the Institute of Arts. Tuesday's I had to wake up at six to jog with him before violin and voice lessons which took up the rest of the day if you included practicing before and after classes, Wednesday it was jogging at six, then yoga, then the counseling session, then dinner as a family—that I had to make from scratch each and every time since Darren claimed I could throw down in the kitchen, Thursday jog at six, have something done for lunch since he came home for the afternoon massage. Some chick from Ilya's that, thank goodness wasn't Zada's beautiful ass, came and gave us both hour and a half Swedish's, Friday's he did boys night out but I had to make sure all the merciless tons of laundry were completed, the clothes were picked up from the cleaners and I had to plan a weekly menu and go grocery shopping, Saturday I could sleep in after I fixed his breakfast but while he was gone I had to stay home unless I went shopping and had the receipts to prove my whereabouts but after three, when he got off work, it was whatever he decided he wanted to do as a family. Sunday was the official Sleep-In, Porno-Watching day (which I didn't mind--especially when he pulled out a video and Mr. Marcus' sexy ass was involved. Now that brotha? Umph...that's all I can say). On Sunday's after that, I got the rest of the day to myself. Dina would come and take the kids off my hands while Darren usually chilled around the house and did his own thing in the basement and played pool down there with Mike in the evening.

I WENT TO WHAT I was hoping would be the last follow-up Gyn appointment and then decided to visit Shawn before I left the hospital. Usually he was scheduled for days except on Fridays and Saturday nights when he worked second shift.

I had called him once when I was in Miami but he hadn't answered and, truthfully speaking, I could see why not. But, maybe if I saw him in person and talked to him, maybe we could move past that and still be friends. Next to Sherra, he was my only other friend.

"Yes, is Shawn Meyers in today?" I asked the brown skinned, freckled face girl sitting behind the desk with mauve scrubs on and that same ole, plain flat-ironed wrap that you could still see the comb marks in like every other chick in Detroit was sporting. That was one hairstyle I still couldn't understand—it looked like those pageboy's and mushroom do's like what Nell and Addie used to wear on *Gimme A Break*. All the chicks with thinning hair were wearing a wrap swooped onto the sides of their faces. Ugh.

"Ahm…" she paused for what seemed like a whole century before adding, "Ahm sorry but—ahm--he was killed two Wensdese ago in uh car accident. He got hit by uh drunk driva." Wetness lingered in the corner of her eyes. "He was so nice, he ain't neva did nothin' ta nobody. I'm sure he up in heaven somewhere. Dat was my boy. His funeral was on Mondie. We wearin' blue ribbons ta remember him. You can git one." She pointed to the opposite end of the counter. "…Blue was his favorite color. Evrybody up in here wearin' one."

I stood there, at the counter with my arms folded across my chest. "What?" I said it so calmly, like I couldn't even feel the three bullets puncturing my heart.

"…Yeah, two weeks ago he was on his way home after he had dropped Ty off and dey said dis drunk lady had hit him an' she had tried ta run but den dey caught her."

From that point on I couldn't remember anything except someone handing me a peach Kleenex and everything turning blurry-white.

"YOU OKAY?" DARREN ASKED that night over dinner. The doctor said it would be okay for me to proceed with normal activities—finally. And after weeks of waiting to hear it, now it was the furthest thing from my mind.

Shawn? Dead? I loved him. He had always been there whenever I needed him…and now I couldn't even go visit his site. He'd been buried back home in North Carolina.

What other guy had ever accepted me, jacked up hair, bags under my eyes, no weave, no designer shit, nothing?

Death is as permanent as it gets and nothing can fix it; the person is gone—you can't find them anywhere. Why couldn't a drunk driver have hit Craig's crazy ass instead? Well—I was wrong for that one…but…

"Yeah." I tried to crack a smile.

Darren was being as patient as a man like him could be. He could have been getting it from anywhere he wanted yet he was waiting on me. And here I was, sitting in the lap of luxury feeling terrible. Why was it always like this, why was something always happening to make my life miserable? I finally had someone wonderful in my life yet and still, I couldn't stop thinking about Shawn being dead, how I missed the funeral, remembering the kiss, remembering Denny's and the way he'd called my personality "stellar." And I kept wondering if we would have been on speaking terms if we would have talked or hung out the day he got into the accident and if maybe it wouldn't have happened. Those mean 'what if's' kept making me replay that one Sunday afternoon over again and again.

Shawn never would have left me to go to the strip club like Darren had and would probably continue to do until he got so old he couldn't go. Even if Darren was a paraplegic or had brain damage and became a vegetable, he'd still be up in a strip club. He probably had it written in his Do Not Resuscitate/Resuscitation instructions...he'd have somebody wheel his vegetable ass to the joint even if he was blind.

But. I had to remind myself that I'd made the right decision, being with Darren. I hadn't liked Shawn like that—no matter how nice he was. If we would have gotten together, I probably would have ended up cheating on him and making him miserable. And he was so weak when it came to me, he probably wouldn't have left. He didn't deserve any of that.

But. If I hadn't liked him like that, why was my heart so heavy right now? Why was I wishing I would have met his family, known his mother, his father, his brothers and sisters—people I could share memories of him with?

I don't know, maybe it could have worked; maybe he would have been the one.

All of this was making me realize a lot of things. You never know when your time on this earth will be over. You can wish you're dead all you want, when someone close to you is gone and you can never have another conversation with them again, it makes you appreciate being able to see, to hear, dance and love--the things that are really priceless that us humans overlook; the beauties of life us humans do not think about when minor inconveniences and temporary veneers of pain come our way.

Each moment in life only happens once.

I needed to stop thinking about what it would have been like to have been with Shawn. I could have been with him but that wasn't the path I chose. Why was I even thinking about being with another man when I had Darren? Darren was slowly but surely letting his guards down and making room for me. Shawn had been my friend and, yes it was okay to miss him, but wrong to compare him to the man I now loved unconditionally.

"...Yeah, I'm okay." Fake it 'til you make it. Besides, I couldn't talk to Darren about anything like this.

"Good. I got tickets for the game at the Palace tonight. It's Piston's versus the Bulls."

"Yaaah!" Pharaoh cheered as he and his father exchanged fives.

The bulls? Cool. That Tyson Chandler was one of the finest things around on the NBA court. Seven-one? There are many, many things a girl can do with something of that stature.

"See if Dina can keep, the baby. If you call her now she'll be able to make it over here in time," Darren stated after another sip of his glass of Grey Goose. He was always getting drunk during dinner and falling asleep right after he ate. If it wasn't for his strict workout regiment he'd have a gut the size of a woman's eleven months pregnant stomach.

"What? Mauri can go!" I fumed. It was always something with him at dinnertime about Mauri.

"Well...just call Dina to see," he stated nonchalantly as he continued enjoying the homemade lasagna I'd cut all the vegetables up from scratch to make. As down as I was over Shawn, I still managed to cook. I'd even made apple pie for dessert. I had to. Darren would have tripped if he came home to carryout or a meal without dessert since I had gotten him spoiled. And *I* was barely able to enjoy any of it since *he* seemed to prefer the new, fifteen pounds less look I'd acquired thanks to being hospitalized from the Craig thing and being depressed 24/7. How the hell was he gonna just take it upon himself to conveniently leave *my* baby out?

"Darren? She's going or you can forget about the news from the doctor." He understood what I meant. He looked at me and continued eating as if I hadn't said anything but all four of us went to the game. Huh.

Afterwards, Dina watched the kids so we could go to the Piston's after party at a sports bar in Pontiac.

This was a scene I had never been a part of. There were strippers on the dance floor completely nude, swaying over the players—a few of whom were totally smashed already. The music was so loud you would have thought *Rap City* was having a concert up in the place starring Big Tymers and Juvenille and the dimly lit club was filled with LaLa smoke that messed with my eyes the whole night and even though underneath my white floor length fur I was wearing a winter white ensemble consisting of a long sleeved mid-drift sweater, a Siman Tu necklace and bracelet set, a cute curve hugging mini skirt and a pair of suede wedge platform Marc Jacobs boots that came up to my thighs, I was the most *overdressed* female up in the spot.

Blonde White chicks that I could have sworn I saw behind cash registers at Somerset, the kind that looked like they'd gone to Catholic school from kindergarten to the twelfth grade flooded the place on the hunt for available players to pull on the dance floor. Black chicks that looked like White Victoria Secret's models guided some of the ballers to stalls in the restrooms. I found that out the first and only time I went to the restroom that night when I saw a shadow with three heads in the stall next to me. I rushed out as they moaned and giggled and spotted this one chick flat out snuffing that Beat shit over the sink. This was not my kind of scene.

When I went back to where Darren was sitting, a puppet looking, too tanned for her own health and for anyone's eyesight coming into contact with her, White brunette was sitting across from him. Her breast were completely uncovered as her bikini top hid underneath her sized FF Fucking Fake tits.

"Leigh, this is Barbie," he instantly introduced us. "Barbie, this is my girl."

"So *youuuu're* the lucky chick? You need to win an award for snagging *him*! Everybody's tried--be*lieve* me! You're pretty. Very pretty. I know you aren't a dancer if you're out with Darren," she stated giving Darren knowing eyes. "You sing?"

"Yes."

"Have I heard any of your stuff?"

"No!"

"Wanna dance?"

"No!" I retorted without hesitation. After she left, every barracuda up in there was up on my man—in front of me if they hadn't hooked up with one of the teammates! And these broads were asking *me* could *we* all go somewhere!

"Ohhh, No! Take me home! *Now*!" I growled at Darren when we were finally alone at our table.

"Aright, gimme a second. I still haven't kicked it with Marvin." He got up to look for his boy.

"Hey? Want some company?" A guy I recognized from the team but couldn't recall the name of asked sitting down next to me after Darren had been gone for a good amount of seconds that were turning into countless minutes.

"If you're not crazy. This is *not* my kind of scene! I'd rather be at home baking cookies or reading," I huffed, wondering if Darren was somewhere in a restroom stall doing some shit that would have made me a very unhappy camper.

"I feel you." He laughed. "If it weren't for—well you know—we *did* win—I'd be at the crib chilling playing video games." At that moment, since he wasn't Ty Chandler, it didn't matter if he was a star player or a bench warmer, I wanted to know where the hell Darren was but B-Ball kept talking, like I cared.

Finally when I spotted Darren making his way to the table, I laughed and acted as though whatever What's His Face was saying was seriously funny. I put my hand on top of his, giving him the green light, suggested I was here with my cousin and surely, just as planned, Ball Player asked for my number. We talked a bit more before he gave me his cell...he lived in Oakland Township too--whatever, whatever...more conversation and a final aright, he'd call.

Darren was observing and definitely not happy. Good. That's what he deserved. After he left, Darren came and squished next to me.

"Let's go." Ooooh he was pissed!

"Other than my mother, no one except you has *ever* had the key to *any* of my cribs, Leigh. Don't pull that TaLia shit." After he spoke his piece, neither one of us uttered a word the whole ride home.

I called myself going to sleep on the couch but Darren grabbed my wrist and gave me a look that let me know he wasn't having it. And since he wasn't about to head for the couch either, I rolled up like a mummy in the sheets and locked my legs in that 'you ain't getting' none tonight' position. The words of that valet guy from the Athenaeum echoed, *"If a man really likes you, he will accept your kids—remember that. I'm too young, hung?"* and an image of a hand reaching out at all the wrong things flashed behind the close-lidded darkness before I dozed off.

THE NEXT DAY I called my house phone voicemail checking for wishful messages from my mother, which was--of course--a major wish.

But there was something about Craig's voice and his messages that bothered me beyond the empty promises and pleas for me to be with him. I could barely make out anything he said. His speech was slurred and a sloppy mess on all four day's worth of messages but on the last one he asked me to meet him at his job to talk. For the most part, meeting him there seemed safe. It wasn't like he was going to act crazy at work. But I was an emotional wreck. Part of me feared not going to meet him; part of me hated myself for even thinking about going to see him. And as terrible as it sounded, even after all that had gone down with us, a small envelope of love sat tucked in the corner of my heart for him. Outside of Mauri and Pharaoh, though, Darren had taken up the rest of the space.

Long after Darren was gone, I got the kids dressed and headed to Hamtramck, dialed *67 and hit Craig up to let him know I was on my way.

When we got there, I parked by the security station and insisted on meeting him at my truck and made him stand outside with the window only cracked an inch.

Craig's flannel, red and black shirt and black jeans were ironed and clean, but he looked terrible. His eyes were bloodshot, his face had a thick cut that ran all the way in the middle of his face from the temple of his forehead past his goatee from when he had gotten carjacked and robbed

285

and he was holding onto a bottle of Everclear orange juice like it was a forty. "Hey, bae. I miss you. Uh mink, hunh? You look good—different, but'chu looked good...somebody cashin' out, hunh?" His eyes were filled with shimmering wavy tears. "The court case was cra...azy. Dey had uh whole bunch uh dem...dem...muthafuckas dere ta testify 'gainst me an' shit. Wudden't none uh dem even up in dere when all da action was goin' down. But it was cool, dough. I wished you woulda been dere. How long you been up to everythang? Oh, yeah. Um. Dem muthafuckas, man, dat carjackin' was on some crazy shit. Crazy. I had ta fight. Dey was tryin'. But dey ain't get shit but yo' truck. You know I—I--I had godd'it fa you. You know dat. I know. I'm sorry Leigh. Sorry azz hell. You mean da world ta me. I 'ont know. It's like you just mean everything. An' some...sometime I cain't thank 'bout it--but when dey jacked me, dat shit was wild. You woulda been proud of uh nigga, dough. I handled ma business. Fa sho'. But dat house ain't right widdout'chu up in dere. It ain't--itwassupposedtabefoeus, youknow? Youknow? An' I missyou. Icantgo'onwiddout'chu." His eyes were unfocused. I'd been at Receiving long enough to know what the crazy eye looked like and this was it. Something was wrong. His thoughts were choppy and at times so incoherent I had to keep asking him to repeat what he was saying.

"Hey--hey? Lemme foe uh minute. Can I? ...Come on, I needta hold da baby."

"Craig...we've got to go."

"You be like...yeah, yeah."

"What? Look, I better get going."

"Please? Look at me this way. Come on, nah, baby. Aye! Lemme hol' her. You s'possed ta love me, 'member?"

As hard as it was for me to keep him from his child, I couldn't. This was going to have to be good enough. "Bye, Craig."

"Come on! I cain't even hold you? I been comin' almost everyday lookin' fa y'all. I cain't even hold you? Her?" His eyebrows were furrowed and he started coughing and choking. "Aight, aight. We'll den at least promise me you gon' call. You gon' at least do dat," he stated, finally catching his breath.

"...I'll try to."

"Naw, I said promise. *Promise*, Leigh."

"...Yeah, I'll...I'll call."

"Promise dat on ev-er-y-thang, bae." He placed his hand on the window. We stared at each other without blinking for a few seconds before I pulled off with his greasy handprint smeared on the window.

Even if we could go back and erase everything, it wouldn't ever be like it was when I was blinded by what I then thought was love. He looked as terrible as this whole situation was. What the hell was going on with him anyway? Was Karma like *that* on a nigga?

I prayed to Jesus and the powers that be to have mercy on Craig, after all, he was still my daughter's father and even though I would never ever be with him again, it was hard for me to completely hate him. It's hard to hate someone when you understand where they've come from and why.

I took the long way, driving around the city for a second to think and to try to clear my mind, taking in familiar streets loaded with memories *and* dealing with Mauri kicking and screaming, acting the way she used to behave. Passing I-94 as I drove past Hamtramck I remembered one of the most perfect days of my life when me and my mother went to what was then Farmer Jacks but had all now turned into Food Basics a few streets over the first day it opened. A beautiful slate gray-blue sky without a cloud to be found. The sun was somewhere around but you could look straight up at the sky without burning your eyes and it reminded me of the way I had always imagined the earth looking when Noah opened the doors of the ark right before the rainbow. That one day was like paradise. Everything inside was clean and crisp and brand new from the freshly baked glazed doughnuts to the gleaming, shiny floor to the jazz playing over the speakers; it was more like a gourmet market instead of a grocery store.

I had just started high school and mom and I talked about my first week of school the whole time. The way she looked at me, proud that I was growing up and already thinking about college, made me wish I could go back to that day.

As I passed Northern high school trying to block out Mauri's yelling, I remembered the pre-high school days I spent globbing my hair into gelled up ponytails, listening to LL Cool J wising I could get a weave ponytail so I could be a 'Round the Way Girl', going to D'Mongo's to get my hair relaxed and curled into that asymmetrical mushroom with the tail that came down to the middle of my back I used to sport thinking I was 'sweet' back in the day. I'd listen to Troop while I wrapped my hair for the night and painted my toes. Back then, being thirteen, I spent rainy days in front of the mirror, wishing I was grown, daydreaming about boys on the football team, going to the roller rink on Sundays with the homies from church wearing my gold herringbone necklace and that nugget ring my mother'd bought one Christmas from Finger Hut.

And I always thought I was the "junk" as we used to say, when I wore those Used and Damaged Jeans ma'd finally gotten out of the layaway. My only worries back then were which pair of pants to wear to school, not stuttering around Jamal, the dude on the football team I had a major crush on and getting my drivers permit when I turned fifteen.

Driving down Davison Freeway, I glanced over at that strange hill that looked like aluminum and granite crumbs along Livernois and the service drive. For years, every time I pass it, I've always wondered what it is and why it's there.

Being near my apartment, I wanted to stop by but had finally learned my lesson. Weird as it seemed, I missed my old life a bit—when Craig and I had been on better terms...back when the very sight of him didn't freak me out. I missed being able to just go to school and be a mother. Now, everything I did I had to look glamorous. I had to play the perfect role--like I was an eternal actress in the film of Darren's life.

"Mom?"

"Yes, sweetie?" I looked up at Pharaoh's reflection in the rearview mirror.

"How come you're not talkin'? I like it when you make funny voices and let me read the stop signs...you don't do it anymore."

"Sorry, hon. Mommy's just thinking. On the way home, you can read all the signs *and* you can tell me 'Go' when the light turns--what?"

"GREEN!"

"Yep"

"Yes!" He threw his hands up in excitement. "Can we get a car at the store mom?"

"Yes, sweetie. If they have a car buggy, I'll make sure we get one, okay?"

"Yaay!"

At least he could still enjoy the simple things in life. I couldn't remember the last time I'd been able to do the same. I decided, since I needed to get groceries anyway, to go to the store in the old hood. Besides, the Meijers near Darren didn't have certain things the hood was a sure bet for, like turkey necks. As I pulled into the Food Basics on Woodward in Highland Park, Mauri was still at it. I picked her up and held her in my arms and tried to shush her.

I shouldn't have taken the kids when I went to see Craig. Already I had to make sure Pharaoh didn't bring it up—he might have known to keep quiet when Craig asked him questions but when it came to his father he was different--he was willing to tell it all. And Mauri was talking pretty well to not even be two yet. All this made me feel like I was back in time during that break up over that Angela bitch when I had to cover up every thing I did.

I was tired. I hadn't gotten in until four-thirty in the morning and, as usual, I had to wake up at six with Darren. After he left for work I was only able to steal two hours of much needed sleep afterwards.

I shouldn't have cancelled with Dina. All this kicking me in my stomach and screaming for DaDa Mauri action was enough to push me over the edge. And Pharaoh wasn't too pleased when we couldn't find one of those kiddy car buggies, either. I tried to put him in the back of a regular cart but he kindly informed me that he was big enough to walk and to help get the groceries instead.

Being in the familiar isles felt nice, though. Seeing collard greens in the fresh produce section made my day. Where Darren lived, you could forget about finding a Dark & Lovely perm in the haircare section, finding weave at the various chain beauty supplies or getting Black Opal makeup from Walgreen's *or* seeing more than one or two Black people. And if and when you did spot another Black constituent, they avoided contact and didn't smile back.

But what took the cake was when Mauri stood up next to my mink coat that was laying next to her in the front seat of the shopping cart, slid down the side, landed on the floor on her hands and knees and ran off after kicking me in the ankle interrupting the debate I was having on which fish to get for tonight's dinner.

"Pharaoh, stay here and watch my purse!" I was furious. She had the speed of an African Olympic runner from Kenya. A guy caught her right before she rammed into a whole shelf of Prego spaghetti sauce bottles.

"Hey, lil' girl. Why you runnin' from your mom's? You don't wanna get snatched up by a bad guy now, do you? You're too cute to be acting like that. Come on, let's let your mom wipe your face. What's your name?"

"Mmmaritania." She looked up at him and smiled.

"Mauritania," I added, "We call her Mauri." My voice was very unfriendly.

"Oh, like the African country?" he asked looking like he was thinking about something for a second. "That's hot that you thought of a name like that." His voice was fairly deep and held a slight New York-ish accent.

"Thanks." I grabbed her and stuffed her back into the buggy. She was way too comfortable all up in his arms. I could see how this was going to be. I needed to spend more time with her so she wouldn't be starting out early. Even if Darren spent a little time with her, maybe she wouldn't have a need to be so into the fellas.

Pharaoh pulled up with the shopping cart. "Alright, thanks." I held onto the front bar for support. This little girl had given me a good one in the right ankle with those Timberland boots of hers--you would have thought they were baby steel toes.

"What's your name, man?" he asked Pharaoh. Little man responded and smiled.

"You need any help?" The guy raised his eyebrows and partially smiled at me. No wonder Mauri'd allowed him to pick her up. His curiously magnetic presence had a gravitational effect. I had to fight the urge to stare into his eyes. They were like two moons holding much needed secrets mankind had been waiting centuries to receive.

"No, I'm good." I faked a quick smile as I rubbed my boot.

"Well...aright." He must not have been convinced because he continued walking next to me as I shopped.

Oh boy here we go again. "Thanks for your help." I gave him a look signaling that his work as the Baby Catcher was done here.

"...Yeah, you already thanked me..." His eyes caught mine and wouldn't let go.

"She'll be okay. Really. Don't let us hold you up." I thought about it for a second and started to turn my lips up into duckbills, hold my wrist up like it was limp and shout in a rather retarded voice, "O-thay! Thank-ooh," so he'd go away but then again, that'd be ignorant. And plus I didn't want one of my kids to wind up seriously talking like that.

Although he now had Mauri as calm and as happy as she could be, I had somebody. And the dude was clearly *not* my type.

He wasn't obese but he was a big guy with big, broad shoulders and he was real tall—like around six-four. His skin was real smooth and the telltale shade of brown that hinted that one of his parents was probably lighter and one was dark. He had short locks that, from a distance, almost looked like a fro and faded into a taper around his ears and neckline and his line-up was clean--like he'd just stepped out of the barbershop. His sleepy eyes sort of glittered and when he blinked both his top and bottom eyelids closed and only parted enough for his dark brown pupils to smile thru. His teeth were extra white and the top ones were perfectly straight but kind of big while his bottom teeth were crooked in the front. Darren and even *Trash* had perfectly straight teeth. *Two* rows of nice, sparkling white teeth were requirements. I couldn't remember anything about Shawn's--at first I couldn't bare looking at him then, after I got past his face, I was too stuck on the soup coolers to notice anything else.

This guy wasn't hard on the eyes. He was actually really cute. He had one of those defined but slightly flattened noses that could have come from a Native American heritage. Problem was he was chubby, he had a babyface and didn't have a mustache or goatee—it looked like he couldn't even grow facial hair. Off rip you could definitely tell he was younger than me. Gross.

I'd been thinking about a friend for when Darren chose not to act right but it was already a wrap. I needed no more drama and Kevin/Calvin was that deal. Shit, he had rocked the pussy ri-ta-ti-ti-tight, for real! *And* he was a hustler? Oh, yeah. Why should a girl settle for such an average baby-boy-of-a-fellow when she could get as many true ballers as her little heart desired?

I ignored him but he continued walking next to me and watching me like he was studying me or something. "So you enjoying this crazy weather? I mean, it was like seventy sumthen two days ago. Now it's five below. Ozone's really messed up, hungh?"

"…Probably." I reached for a box of Tide on the top shelf.

"I got it." He smiled and chuckled like he was containing something real funny. "Cold weather's okay, I guess…it gives us something to appreciate when summer hits, right?"

"…Probably." I scanned over the brands of cheese that were on sale. I could hook up some homemade macaroni. We hadn't had that in a while and it was Mauri's favorite. "Look, Ma-Ma. Mommy's gonna make some mac and cheese!" I smiled in her face. She turned her attention from ole boy for a second to clap and gave me a kiss.

"Oh, that's somebody's favorite, hungh?" The blue-collar, hip-hop head smiled back at her. Mauri reached her arms out for him to pick her up.

I gave her my best evil eye. "Stop, Ma."

"It's cool. She's just being a doll." He smiled at her.

I was itching to tell him I had someone but just in case he was simply being nice, I didn't. I didn't want to come off all rude and, on top of that, I had already been called stuck-up and cursed out in situations like these by too many guys. One time this guy in a pimped out burgundy Intrepid with those gaudy-ass spinning gold rims rolled down his window and threw a chunk of cement at my truck when I was at the stop sign after I brushed him and his honking horn off. He barely missed my head and ended up shattering the back window behind me on the driver's side. To this day I'm still trying to figure out what he was doing with a piece of *cement* in his car.

"You know what? I like skunks…*and* the way they smell." I shook my head affirming my statement, stared up at the isle 9A sign and smiled. There. That would *definitely* make him go away. One thing about Black men, they won't mess with no crazy woman. And actually, I did like skunks—it all started with Peppy LePew. Back at Cottage, Elaine and I had

291

gotten into a conversation on off beat likes. She had a thing for El Debarge. Who knew his music had made it all the way over to the Middle East? When I told her about my skunk admiration, even *she* thought that was strange and *she* wanted to live in the crazy ward.

"Hey, they Black, right? Me personally, I like lizards. I had one back in the day."

Okay, now seriously. What the hell was wrong with *him*? I had been around a lot of crazy people recently—myself included—and even *I* had to say his response was abnormal.

Change in plans. Time to go back to ignoring him. I looked over my list and made sure to get a carton of soy milk (both Pharaoh and I are lactose intolerant) and a few other items I had almost forgot to get.

"Hey. Don't worry about standing in line--I got you," he stated as I approached the checkout line after grabbing a jug of Pharaoh's favorite Juicy Juice. Now *that* was more than a pleasant sentiment of chivalry! I grabbed my coat, took Mauri and Pharaoh and sat on the bench in front of the baggers. He was staring at me. I avoided all eye contact and put pressure on my foot with my hand to try to make the throbbing stop. I couldn't wait to get into the car and take my boot off. Out of my peripheral vision, I could see him still smirking like he could tell I was avoiding looking his way on purpose. When it was time to pay, I walked to the cashier with the credit card Darren had signed me on wondering just who this dude was. As much as I wanted to feel weirded out by him, I didn't.

"Hey, Lil' Man, can you push the buggy while I help your motha out?" Pharaoh, being the three year old gent he was, acted like buggy pushing with Mauri in the kiddy seat was a badge of honor even though he had to practically lift his arms up over his head to reach the handle bar. "It's too icy for you to try to walk on that foot in those boots," he stated, lifting me into his arms.

The guy *carried* me to my car! *Carried* me! Good thing I'd parked in front.

People looked on. Old ladies with heads as shaky as Contessa's smiled. Older men with untamed fro's and centered bald spots gave him compliments and mad respect. It was really funny, a sight to see.

"Click your doors open." He helped me slide into the drivers seat and opened the back door for the kids and put the groceries in the back as I put Mauri in her car seat. "Here's my card. I'm Smiley. Well—that's my nickname. My ma says my eyes always look like they're smiling and—anyway--it's my last name...First name's Malik. But you can call me Smiley. What's your name?"

"...Leigh..."

"...Leigh." He slowly nodded his head up and down like he was in some kind of deep thought. "Call me sometime, if you ever need any plumbing assistance. Or if you just wanna talk...or go out to dinner...I didn't see a ring on your finger...and you never said—well...call me sometime." Before I checked him for talking dirty, I looked at his business card and noted the badge on his navy Carhartt jacket. Inside the small white square, *Smiley Plumbing* was stitched in navy cursive letters across the left side of the lapel.

"...Thanks—tha...thanks." I lingered in the door fiddling with the diamond solitaire on my platinum necklace. My mink blew in the harsh winter's wind as he walked away. I didn't want him to leave just yet. I wanted to steal another glance at that space between his nose and his upper lip--something about it was absolutely adorable and oddly inviting.

He stopped in his tracks and turned around and caught me watching him.

I felt like I'd been caught doing something naughty when he smirked back. I closed the door feeling my cheeks grow warm against the cold air. There was something about him...

But hell, what did I know? Lately every guy I met I was saying, *there's something about him; he was special; he was fine...*

I started the car, turned the radio to 92.3 and tossed his card out the window once he was out of sight.

Now Darren? There was something about *him*. Plenty! What I *needed* to do was go home and cook for my man and show him just how much I loved him. Maybe I'd dress up for him tonight... I had just bought a hot lil' number ...

But—even more importantly, I needed to find a church to join. I was seriously slipping and not appreciating what I had. I'd been receiving too many blessings lately to not to be thinking about God; that wasn't right. Yoga relaxed me but spirituality I was seriously suffering. Before the Pastor thing, life had been much better. Maybe Perfecting Church would be cool. Hopefully Darren would want to go.

I called Sherra to see if she was up to coming with me on Sunday. "Girl, I haven't seen you and those kids in a minute. Stop by. Mama just made some tacos. You know Pharaoh be mashin' them mug's." She was trying to check up on me on the sly. It was also the anniversary of her father's death. He died three years ago from Sickle Cell. She usually looked at the family photo albums and recalled memories from when he was alive around this time. It was tradition for me to come over and talk about it with the family.

The kids were happy to see her and her mom. Dina and Tommy were both gone. We sat downstairs in the basement and caught up.

"Girl, I'm glad you finally deciding ta leave Craig alone! *He* is *crazy*. I'm almost positive dat was one of Angela's brothers. I wonder why dey came ta yo' crib, though?" When she stopped to ponder the question she sucked on her bottom lip and frowned. "I'ma find out tamorrow when I see her."

Darren called interrupting our conversation. "Hey, sweetie what's up? You miss me?"

"...Where you at?"

"I'm over Sherra's. Why? What's wrong?"

"Nothing. I called home but I didn't get you... Aren't you supposed to be fixing dinner?"

"Well, *yeah* but I haven't seen Sherra in—"

"—Leigh, make sure dinner is ready on time, aright."

"...Alright." I sighed. "I'll be leaving in a second. I Love you."

"Aright." He hung up. He was always worried about me and trying to make sure I stayed out of harms way.

"Girl, I'd better be getting home. You need to come over one day. All this time and you haven't been over..." I felt bad leaving so early. We hadn't even gotten a chance to talk about her dad yet. She never talked about it unless it was this time of the year.

"Girl, dis new job promotion is a trip. I be tired when I get off work. Not only do they work me, dem people work my nerves! Dey so stuck up! I work around a lot of quote unquote artists. Girl, dey so freakin' eccentric and bougie. But, it's cool, though. I'm learning a lot about editing and layouts." She walked us out to the car and kissed the kids on the forehead. They waved at her until we reached the end of the block.

I wished I could have stayed and spent the night like usual.

But one thing I didn't feel bad about was the way my life was changing. It really wasn't that bad now. It was time for me to forget about Mr. Kevin/Calvin. Not only did I want to be in the warm comfort of Darren's lair, it was where I was supposed to be.

AFTER I PUT THE kids to bed, I was ready to give Darren the seduction of a lifetime. The candles were lit, I had bought a sexy, sheer pink nightgown with tons of ruffles in the front and a pair of clear stripper heels from Priscilla's and was ready to please my man.

Instead of jumping right into everything Darren surprised me with a trip down memory lane back to the days when he used to come over to visit when Pharaoh was a baby and he was scared to hold him and Pharaoh's past three birthday parties. "You know, Leigh I'm really glad you're here," he whispered pulling me onto his lap. "I'm willing to give you a lot...but...you've gotta cut tha immature shit out."

"*What*?" Here I was trying to give him some and he was taking it upon himself to call *me* immature? I needed to understand this!

"Did you erase that number from last night outta your phone?"

"Wait a minute. *What*?"

"Don't play dumb, Leigh...did you or didn't you? It's not gonna work if you're gonna still be hangin' around tha hood in Highland Park grocery shopping an' shit an' getting otha niggas numbers. You throw out ole boy's number from last night?

"Who, Raquon Nelson?"

"You know what I'm talking 'bout...either you want this, or you don't. What's it gonna be?"

I was confused. How did he know exactly which location I went to? There was a Farmer Jacks/Food Basics right around the corner here. Had that Smiley guy been a decoy? I decided not to say anything. I wasn't about to give up any unnecessary information. And why was he so worried about Raquon?

"...Yeah, I saw the receipt. You went to the grocery store over there. Why? You still talking to Craig?"

"No..." I was dumbfounded.

"Aright. This is it. Either you want this or you don't. Like I told you before, it's your call. The past is the past here on out."

I slid my tongue in his mouth after gazing into his eyes. "I *know* what I want. Do *you*?"

"You gon' have ta get on birth control, baby. These condoms ain't what it is," he answered, grinning before he proceeded to make me very happy for the next hour and a half. We released into each other's arms and fell into peaceful slumber.

UNLIKE CRAIG, DARREN FLAT out refused to go to church with me like most of the other 'intellectual erudite.' Problem was I wasn't ready to go by myself. After all that had happened, the thought of stepping foot into *any* church still made me queasy.

Instead, on Sundays we ended up doing matinees, going to the Detroit Institute of Arts and every cultural thing under the sun, which didn't leave room for a church sermon.

Still, life was good. We did Thanksgiving at his parent's new home that was only two houses from the mayor's mansion downtown across from Indian Village. But his parents were a bit too nosey for my taste. Being around them was like going to sleep in makeup—something you hated to do but it sometimes it had to happen. I caught them glaring at Mauri as if she was a peach skinned demon-leper baby. But it was still nice to be involved in a big family gathering. I hadn't had a Thanksgiving like this one since I was little.

As if we hadn't done Thanksgiving in grand fashion, Darren decided to go all out for Christmas this year at his house.

He wanted to treat his parents to a Christmas in Hawaii but since the auto show gala was coming up and, being so heavily involved in arrangements with his dealership, he was extremely stressed and nixed the vacation until a later date.

We took the kids to see the Nutcracker, ice-skating at Hart Plaza and sledding at Bloomer Park with Jim from the dealership and his White wife and mulatto kid-family. (I didn't have a problem with them until Jim's wife kept asking questions about what to do about her three daughters "frizzy, spongy" hair. Nothing looked wrong with the two ponytailed hairdo's they were wearing to me. And what did she expect with a husband with beady bee chest hairs peeking thru the top two unbuttoned buttons of his shirts?).

Darren and I also went to see the Detroit Symphony Orchestra and hit up the Opera House to see *Anoush*—this Armenian play about a girl in love with this Shepard boy who ends up being killed by her brother. And *Carmen*—which I absolutely loved! Not that I was opposed to it but, who would have *ever thought* I'd like opera!

Then there was the dealership company bash that was going to be held at Cobo Hall.

There were too many to do's but it was fun. In the end, all the shopping for the perfect garments and waking up early to run errands for Darren always paid off when we actually attended the events.

I didn't have a problem with him being in the limelight. You can't have two stars in a relationship. That's why a lot of celebrity marriages don't work out. Being in the background and taking some of the load off his shoulder was just fine, after all, Darren was The Man and I, being his woman, always reaped the rewards. There were always too many compliments to count and we always had a good time.

He purchased a huge tree that stood next to the fireplace. His parents and sisters came over to help decorate which I found out was a Pewter family ritual.

Pharaoh was excited and was always following Darren around and, of course, Darren blatantly enjoyed the admiration.

This was the first time in a long, long time I actually felt the spirit of the holiday season. I didn't even want a gift. It had already been granted

CHAPTER 17

I WOKE UP AFTER sleeping in until nine feeling good on this day of January twentieth. Or should I say exhilarated! Nine o'clock compared to six? Ah, yeah.

I got up ready to take a hot, steamy shower and noticed Darren's phone on top of the armoire. I reached up and grabbed it. As tempting as it was to look thru his calls, I resisted and slid into the shower. Turning the water on, I kept thinking about it. There wasn't any harm in simply *looking,* he was always checking up on me and making sure *I* was on the up and up...

I went back and grabbed it dripping water and soap all over the floor. It was locked. Hmmm...I tried a few likely codes before pressing in 1112, his birthday month and day and bingo! it unlocked.

Three calls to the office, a call to Danielle, a call to a number I didn't recognized. I dialed it—just to see. A chick that sounded like that puppet thing from the Piston's party answered. When I disguised my voice as a man, she quickly reminded me that she was Barbie and asked if I had a cold and needed her to soothe it away like she had a week ago.

Next I checked his voicemail. There was a saved message from Danielle. She was asking him what was taking him so long. It was the night before Christmas and I remember that night because he and I were curled up in bed watching movies after the kids fell asleep and he kept kissing me on the forehead and telling me how fine I was.

He had sent her four text messages in reply. The last one?

4.
Hey baby i miss u 2
can.t do 2nite, c u
soon tho i.ll call
2morrow wear sumthn
sexy n play w/ it 4 me

Another voicemail message from some chick named Simone. She couldn't wait for him to eat her pussy again like he had the other day. Then a dude named Ron asking Darren if he wanted to come to an orgy at his crib. That was a week ago—the same night Darren said he had to go check up on his sister because she was upset about an argument she had with her boyfriend.

Lies. All lies. He'd been lying like a muthafucka to me! Why didn't he just say, *"I want an open relationship, Leigh."* Then, I could have made an informed choice!

I was enraged. I called Syra, Mike's fiancee. Darren had encouraged a friendship between us and seemed to favor Syra much more than Sherra.

"Hey, Leigh!" she chirped. She was always way too chirpy for my taste but cool nevertheless.

"Syra, I am *soooo* upset!" I shouted thru vicious sobs.

"Oh, no, hon! What's the prob?"

"I just found out that Darren's *still* sleeping with Danielle! And he's—he's seeing that bitch I told you about from the Piston's afterparty! And he was out with some Simone bitch and fuckin' in orgies! I am *soooooo* hurt! I loved him! I thought we were a couple! I thought—"

"--Hold on, hon. Now calm down. Did he breakup with ya'?"

"No—but I—"

"—Did he ever talk about getting engaged or married to ya'?"

"Well, yeah but now I CAN'T trust him and—"

"—Leigh! Calm down. You'll get over it. Mike does the same stuff. You have to just learn how to deal with it. You get everything you want, I don't see Darren taking any of *those* bitches anywhere and he always talks about how wonderful *you* are. *Mike* says *Darren* says you're the one! He's gonna settle down with ya'! Fuck the small shit--that's what I say. I have everything I could *ever* want. I don't have to work, I just got my boobs done. Oh, yeah, I almost forgot to tell you," her voice slowed down and got really, really low, "for Mike's b-day, we're going to...*The Hamptons!"* she shouted making me pull the phone away from my ears for a second. "And Darren's going too, so you'll be going! Isn't that *hot?*"

Fuck what she was talking about. Mike's birthday? Who cared. "I can't believe Darren! He's always checking my phone, the bills—everything! When I exchanged numbers with Raquon Nelson at that party, he made sure I deleted *his* number!"

"Oooh, jeez... Ra *Nelson* tried to talk to you? *Wow*—that's hot...well...that's just the luck of the draw. We don't make the money so we can't play like the boys...and every guy in the world is gonna do it--even the broke ones...me and you are lucky—we've got cutie pie's that are rolling in the dough...why don't we go shopping? That'll cheer you up!"

"No, Syra! I'm pissed!"

"Want me to come over?"

"NO!"

"Well...sitting over there pouting and feeling bad isn't gonna change things. If ya' love Darren, you just have to accept him the way he is. You're better off with him than Ra. How d'you know If Raquon's already got a wifey or not? *You're Darren's* woman. That means a lot. Just don't stress out over it. I'm here if you wanna go to Somerset. I'll check up on you later. I've got to go workout. Mike says I look like I'm trying to turn into the Good Year Blimp! Toodles, hon!" She was almost six feet and skinnier than Kate Moss when she was on drugs. This airhead obviously wasn't going to be any help. Mike could kill her and she'd be okay with it as long as she was put in a designer casket and had a MAC makeup artist hook her up for the funeral. *Well, you gotta go sometime*, she'd probably say! She was going to be a loon ball like Contessa when Mike got tired of her and traded her in for a newer model.

While chauvinistic philosophy might have worked for her, *I* wasn't buying it. I wanted someone I could trust and love for real who'd love me back just the same. That's all I've ever wanted and longed for. The only reason I had crept with Kevin--or whatever his name was, was because I found out Craig was a trashy piece of shit.

I was tired of shit like this. All I wanted was a good, strong monogamous relationship, to know I was loved…to be married to Darren and to live a nice, peaceful life. I didn't even have to be a nurse. I liked being at home taking care of my family while my man made the big bucks. I liked being a woman and having a man. I had skipped registering for classes this semester since Darren didn't want me going to Detroit Community and I didn't have time for school anyway. I was more than willing to do whatever Darren wanted. But not if he was going to forever cheat on me! Why did men constantly do whatever the hell they wanted but they couldn't take it when a woman did half the shit they did?

Women are the progenitors of life, we hold new generations within our wombs yet we continually get treated like pigeon tits no matter the decade nor a new century; it's always this Women on the Bottom shit. Women are tricked time and time again into submitting to a class much less than their real worth. King David had so many wives he couldn't even spend two whole days with each one of them within a year and he *still* went after Bathsheba. King Solomon had three hundred wives and like seven hundred concubines and had all his male attendants castrated so as to keep his harem on lock for his very own gluttonous penis. Now let's be real--one thousand women? That's just wrong. They had to be lesbians or asexual or sexually retarded. There was no way he could have possibly satisfied all of them on a monthly basis. If the bible was going to glorify his surplus of seven hundred women, why wasn't polyandry glorified, too? All those lonely concubines and wives had to be getting it from somewhere else on the side.

Why is it always okay for men to do women wrong but unacceptable for women to rub a hair the wrong way on a man by societal standards? If a woman does the same thing men do to women then they're hoes and shit.

Men are greedy and selfish. What they don't realize is that they can have a woman who is willing to do anything they want her to do—within reason, a woman who'll love them and who'll be willing to do everything to make her man happy. All they have to do is know how to treat her. A real man doesn't have to use force, he doesn't have to yell or cheat to get what he wants out of a woman. All he has to do is be a good man—what I've never had.

There was no way I was about to deal with this shit right here!

I picked up the phone off the nightstand to call Sherra but I was startled when Darren walked in. He was supposed to be at work.

"Why you call Craig two times in November and *one* time in December, Leigh?" He waved the cell phone bill in the air.

"Oh! We playin' *Jeopardy* now, are we? *Why are you* still fucking Danielle? And Barbie? And Simone? And orgies wit'cha boy Ron? Hungh? ANSWER THAT!" I waved his cell in the air.

"Yeah, I came home for that." He snatched his phone out of my hands and continued, "But then I looked at the bill after getting the mail and saw this shit! If you want Craig, you need to get yo' shit right now and step. I didn't get you that Lexus truck for Christmas fa you to be creepin' on the side with that muthafucka!"

"It's the pot calling the kettle black—only I wasn't *fucking* Craig—or anybody else. I only called him because we had business to discuss. He's trying to get full custody of Mauri!"

"Hell! Let 'em! That's *his* child! That'll be the first time he stood up and acted like a man! He was living off the money I sent you and Pharaoh for the longest!"

"Let him take *my* child? That's *my* child!"

"The girl *is bad*, Leigh! I'm one step away from lighting a fire on that ass the next time she tears up one of Pharaoh's toys. I paid some nice ass dollars for that corvette of his she was trying to break on purpose after you spanked her for chewing up my monthly report and I caught her pouring water on the computer—*on ma mutha'fukin' Apple laptop*! I'm holding you down and planning on marrying you one day. You ain't got shit ta say about what I do in my personal time. We aren't married yet! Besides--I spend every night in the bed with *you*! You, Leigh! I 'on't wanna hear dis shit. You got one more time to call Craig and that bedda be ta tell him ta get his muthafuckin' ass hell raiser! End of discussion." He always said what he meant. If he wanted Mauri gone, that's what was going to go down.

"You know what Darren? FUCK YOU! *FUCK YOU!* Yeah, I said it. You ain't abouta make me chose between you and my child. I'm *not* leavin' her with that crazy ass bastard—"

"—*You* was the one that hooked up with him! You coulda been with me a long time ago. You wouldn'uh even had ta deal wit all dat dumb shit—yo' ass getting' *raped* an' shit! You so fuckin' stupid! *You* da one dat hooked up wit dat bitch ass nigga. When you gon' start actin' like you got some sense? We gon' have more kids one day anyway. I on't know why you actin' like it's so hard to do! Let *dat nigga* deal wit dat shit."

"If you don't want Mauri here, I'M NOT STAYING! I'm not gon' just turn my daughter over to *him*! She's *my* baby. What, you think you can just erase her or something? Even if you *aren't* in the picture tamorrow, *that's* still *ma* child! Got tha nerve ta say, 'I 'on't see why *it's* so hard ta do!" I mimicked his voice. "Here I am loving you with every fiber of my soul and you out here getting' yo' whistle wet wit every high-class hooker in da metro area! Fuck you! I was willing to love you unconditionally--UNCONDITONALLY! But if you're not gonna accept my child--and if you not gon' stop being uh hoe I ain't 'bouta waste *my* time. LIKE I SAID, *FUCK YO'* ASS! I'ma love *myself* even if you *don't*-- TRIFLIN' ASS M*UTHAFUCK*A!"

"Where you gon' go? Back to that shabby ass apartment? You gon' hook back up with Craig? Where? Who's gonna put the world in the palm of yo' ungrateful hands like I do? When I met yo' ass, you ain't have shit but uh raggedy car! Call that nigga an' make the arrangements--like *I* said. You oughtta be happy ta get that thing off yo' hands. I done seen her pop you upside yo' head uh coupla times--"

"--Hell NO!"

"Aright. Peace. Be out by the time I get back tonight." He gave an sinister smirk before taking the keys to my new truck off my key ring and walking out of the bedroom door. "Let's see how long it take you ta make tha *right decision* for uh muthafuckin' change! ...You got back wit *that bitch* after he cheated on yo' ass and *you* took *his* shit! He ain't do half uh what I do fa yo' ass!" he shouted from downstairs before slamming the garage door and pulling off.

AS USUAL, SHERRA WAS there for the rescue. I packed as many of my belongings and the kid's clothes as I could into her Camry, crying hysterically the whole time.

I stayed with her family for a month in their two family flat before I finally went back to the apartment. I didn't want to go back there but it wasn't like I had a choice. I didn't want to wear out my welcome in Sherra's house and it was time to do *something*. I had to make a life for myself. A life free and clear of Craig *and* Darren.

Darren stopped paying for my counseling sessions and had even stopped giving me money for Pharaoh and still hadn't given me the truck back. Still, I had made up my mind. There was no way. The words of that valet guy played in my head over and over like a scratched up cd. If he wasn't going to accept my child, I was *not* going to be with him—flat out.

But Darren calling every other day to see if I'd changed my mind on the Mauri issue and if I'd gotten over his "personal activities" didn't make it any easier. I was hoping that by calmly talking to him when he called he would at least give me the truck back but, after a week of being back in that still eerie apartment and having no funds outside of three hundred dollars in the bank, he wasn't caving on anything—not even the Lexus.

I had to wait until March before I'd get a check from the apartment owners since Debra'd taken care of February's duties.

Twice I thought about going to the welfare or Family Independency Agency to get food stamps and Medicaid but I decided to hold out to see how things turned out. I never grew up on that low-budget, lazy people shit and didn't want to start a habit of it. But soon, I'd have to do something about insurance, at least for Pharaoh since Darren had canceled the plan he had for both of us. Only Mauri had insurance and that was thru Craig's job.

Most of the food in the apartment was spoiled so I had to throw it out. After I cooked everything in the freezer that wasn't freezer-burned, I broke down and caught the bus to go to the bank.

The bus stop was cattycorner from the apartment, which although convenient, was worse than embarrassing. Two of the tenants in my building passed me and drove back around to ask if I needed a ride. I thanked them and hurried up and ushered them away. I felt like a gold fish thrown out of the sea into an empty sink.

How was I gonna be able to take care of myself and two other little people depending on me? I was supposed to be their provider but I didn't have shit to provide them with and the situation was beginning to look very glum. No wonder people got mixed up in selling drugs and illegal activities. Working a minimum wage gig full-time wasn't going to get me anywhere near close to the way I was accustomed to living. But it wasn't like I was about to be a hustler out on the streets anytime soon—I wasn't capable of doing stuff like that. And I had kids. Now being a hustler's *wife*? I could pull that off as long as he accepted the kids as part of the package and kept everything away from home. If I laid off on the Langston Hughes, Zora Neal Hurston and poli-sci conversations, didn't let it seep out that I'd grown up on Sweet Valley and Judy Blume and halted some of the cultural activities I liked that made guys in the hood say I acted too White, it could work.

Darren was a hustler too, but legal and liked Cultured Leigh but wasn't about to accept my other kid. The hood type of hustler wouldn't be as stuck up and would be much more likely to deal with the two little extras.

It was humiliating getting on the pollution filled, overcrowded, sticky floored bus as what seemed like a hundred ratty eyes eyeballed me and my kids like we were scalawags and rightfully belonged to their hoodrat troop.

"It's three dolas, ma'am! Lessen you wont uh transfa," the bus driver screeched as I searched in my wallet for change.

"—Um—um, my bad. I thought I had a ten in here—"

"--Unghhhuh. Dat's whad dey all say." She didn't have any sympathy. Having to stand there while she talked to me like that made me even more disgusted at my new lot in life. I was flat-out broke. There wasn't any way around that fact. I hadn't even been this poor before I had Pharaoh! I searched my jean pockets and still couldn't find enough money for the fare. I know I remember putting a five and a ten in my wallet.

We were now approaching the fourth block and I still hadn't coughed up the three dollars.

"I got ha," an old man in a faded blue, grimy mud-ridden snowsuit came forward and stuffed the dollars into the feeder thingy.

"Thank you," I managed, too embarrassed to look his way thereafter. He was missing teeth two front teeth and his gray hair reminded me of Grady from *Sandford and Son*.

This is the best you could do, I reminded myself as we came to a jerking halt at the stoplight. It wasn't like I could've called a cab. Darren had taken all my credit cards.

During the ride I learned that Tone loved Axle and SES was going to be in jail until 2016 and for this reason everyone should say "Fuck The Police" all thanks due to writers who chose the window ledge to advertise their works.

I almost missed the stop because I forgot to pull the silver cord to let Madame Bus Driver know my time with her was up. I stepped off the bus pushing the kids ahead of me.

"Mauri! Watch it!" I lifted her up into my arms and walked into the Credit Union on Seven Mile and Livernois after she almost stepped into a glob of yellow spit on the way in.

The credit union was packed. I stood in line praying, hoping and wishing not to run into anyone I knew. I took all but five dollars out of my account. As I walked off the parking lot to cross the street and headed to Food Basics I heard a familiar voice calling my name frantically like it was the end of the world or something.

I turned around and, head hanging out of the driver's window of a navy Benz, there sat Dominique. Of all people to run into! She was all smiles. I only had two choices: A-keep walking and ignore her or B-bite the bullet and speak like wasn't shit wrong.

She got out of her car and headed my way, frantically waving and smiling like a nut leaving me with choice B.

"Hh*hheeeeyyyyy*, Leigh!" she crooned. "Gosh, it's been forever!" She circled herself around me in a smothering embrace.

"You've got k*iddddds*?" she marveled, finally letting me go.

"Yes. Pharaoh and Mauritania," I stated matter factly praying that within seconds she would evaporate. I had on raggedy scuff marked, once white but now gray and black bulky ass Sketcher gymshoes that I usually only wore when cleaning tenants apartments, a Sears pea coat-- seeing as how a fur would be mighty inappropriate for a bus adventure, jeans from when I was pregnant with Pharaoh and my hair hadn't been done in over a month so I had done my best to cover the problem with a hat, once again cocked to the right side as cover up. I had a five-carat ring on my right hand that anyone seeing me in this disheveled mess would no doubt believe to be the finest cubic zirconium had to offer. But at least the kids looked decent.

"OOOh! They're gorgeous! How old are you two," she bent down to asked them. Pharaoh smiled and answered for Mauri too since Mauri just looked up at me. "I'm married now," she gushed, like I couldn't tell from that sparkly thing that glowed like a celestial light on her left ring finger.

I wanted to be like, *"I was engaged once and about to marry the guy you stopped speaking to me over! So there!"* Instead, I threw her a plastered smile.

"I'm Mrs. Gregory Attwater, now, Leigh. So much has changed…"

I didn't hear shit else she said. Gregory ATTWATER? The mayor of Southfield? Hell, naw!

"The mayor, right?" I asked to make sure we were both talking about the same man.

"Yes. He's the love of my life. It'll be a year in a minute…Leigh…so much has changed…I'm researching information on Egyptian, Zen and Yoruba beliefs right now," she offered. "…Girl, I used to be a lost soul. Here…here's my number. Call me sometimes. You should visit my church sometime soon. I know it's different from what you're used to but…well. It made me free. I've gotten rid of a lot of my past demons, Leigh…if you…if you ever want to talk or…or stop by to visit my church—feel free." She was smiling ear to ear like somebody's little retarded sister. But she *did* have on a tasteful business suit and looked polished. Her hair was still poofy like a porn star's and she still had on makeup but...she looked different. Niquie, in a non-revealing suit? Married? To a mayor? Who'd have guessed. I guess after the sheep-cloning thing and with Whitney Houston marrying Bobby, anything in life was possible these days.

"...Yeah, sure. Thanks." I was thankful she wrote it down instead of waiting for me to pull out a cell. Darren had taken my phone. "Alright," I added along with another fake smile and walked towards Food Basics angry as hell.

This is what you're gonna have to deal with. You can't be with Darren unless he changes. You know he isn't going to change so what can you do? You made the right decision... Coaching yourself was hard as hell.

Darren and Craig, although on two different ends of the spectrum, were one and the same. No matter how I had to struggle, I was making the right decision.

They didn't lie when they said doing the right thing wasn't easy but God why did it have to be this hard? Why couldn't Darren have been faithful? Why couldn't he just accept my child?

I was so angry and hurt, I almost ran over an older lady with my buggy. I couldn't think. My chest was burning inside. I grimmed a bagger so hard when he smiled at me, I wouldn't even blame him if he was scared to smile at any other Black woman for the next couple of years.

I wasn't even twenty-five yet and had gone from a regular life, to riches, all the way down to ultimate rags. This wasn't how the rags to riches storyline was supposed to go. I couldn't even afford a cheap ass bottle of clearance priced bubble bath from Avon and that shit was only sixty-seven cents! The way things were right about now, I couldn't afford the basic shit I needed--shit like bubble bath wasn't no necessity!

Looking at prices with new, budget-mindful eyes let me know what I was going to have to do within the next week. There was no way I was about to make it thru the next ten days before getting that shanty of a five hundred dollar check. I was going to have to get food stamps, that was all to it. I thought about calling Kevin but that thought was immediately thrown out the window. My hair was a hot mess.

And going to KD's was definitely out and Arnetta, whose prices I adored, was nowhere near an option. My best bet would be to shave the rest of my hair off--at least then it would be even.

After making the most savvy purchases, choosing generic brands and only putting bargains deals in the shopping cart, I was now left with two hundred and fifteen dollars.

Last month alone I'd spent more than four thousand in one hour.

Pharaoh and I struggled with the bags until we got to the Seven Mile bus stop, sat on the bench and rested our arms by putting everything on the ground. Mauri cooperated by walking ahead of us and understanding that mommy couldn't hold her hand.

After almost thirty minutes in the cold, wondering when the bus was going to make an appearance and hoping every far away white truck or white van was that white and green bus that would take us home, a white company van made a U turn, pulled up and stopped in front of us.

"Hey, Leigh. What's up? You never called..."

It was that young ass, Eye Smiling dude. Was there any mercy for me to be found on earth? I looked like a bad rendition of a Supreme wearing a cheap wig because of the way my hair was filleted to the side (Fa-laid. Yes, I made that word up. If you could see the way my hair was looking, combed over to the side thus so, you'd understand!). Now that's a shame--when your own hair looks like a synthetic wig!

I rolled my eyes and didn't say shit to him. Hopefully he'd get the hint and cease and desist. This was not the time for a brotha to be trying to run some weak ass game.

"Whassup? Where you tryin' to go? I got a few minutes before my next appointment, I can take you."

I thought about it a good minute before deciding to take the ride. It wasn't like I'd gotten any strange vibes from him and the weather *was* bone chillingly cold. We'd been standing outside waiting on the bus for the last half an hour. I needed to get the kids home. Not having to struggle on a treacherous bus with a bunch of bags of groceries was more than appealing.

He drove the kind of van that only seated two people--the kind with the back compartment sectioned off. Both of the kids were squished on my lap while all the grocery bags crowded around my feet but he made conversation that eased my awkwardness and even made me laugh a couple times. "Aright. Hit me up tonight. I've been waiting to hear from you," he stated and handed me another one of his business cards after he finished bringing all the groceries up to the front door of the building.

That evening I cleaned up the place, fixed spaghetti and salad for dinner, put the kids to bed and cried until the next morning.

THIS WAS THE DAY I had to go to The Agency.

We all got on the bus more accustomed to the ride and got off at the Welfare Palace on Glendale.

There was a young girl sitting in there with half her head braided taking down the rest of her hair. There were guys in what Darren called

"Gas Station Gear" since, in warmer months, bootleg clothiers sold cheap renditions of Burberry, Gucci and the like in front of gas stations.

The greasy gray stained, grimey dirt filled chairs were so unfit for human bodies to sit and mingle on, had I not brought the kids, I wouldn't have sat down (I was one step away from putting paper towel from the restroom down on the chairs). Then you had to take a number and give all your personal information to the intake worker who looked like she'd done well to finish tenth grade. She talked extremely loud like everyone was deaf, had maroon oval shaped fake nails, maroon lipstick on, maroon hair and her Wal-Mart outfit reminded me of Barney--if he ever decided to change the color of his suit to maroon.

And of course, Pharaoh had to use the restroom. When we went into the restroom—if you could call it that—people'd written their frustrations all over the walls, a few of the scribbles warning future patrons about the workers who had bitchy attitudes and were assholes.

When my name was finally called an hour later, I walked to the back and was greeted by another intake worker, this time a man who was dressed like MC Hammer from back in the day. I could have sworn he cleaned out every Shoppers World in 1990--and what a shame because I really did like the real Hammer; this poor guy, who looked like his manifesto was "Aw shucks," and probably wore a raccoon hat with the tail still on the hide 'cause, in his likely words, "Dis Michigan, fa sho'--you 'ont neva know if'n snow uh rain gon' crop up, baaaybeh!" was insulting the lovely and talented Hammer with his faithfully cheap imitation. His neck was loaded with low budget gold plated ropes and meaningless medallions and: 'I'm frontin' like they real' diamonds that were encrusted and glued on top of aluminum pieces. To make matters worse he had way too much mystery product in his hair that gunked together to form a flaky, dandruffy, oily mess that was eleven times out of ten the reason for the white acne hills and circly black 'busted it' marks branching onto his forehead and I had to tell *him* all my personal business? Hell no!

But he was nice, nonetheless, and he ignored Mauri who was now preoccupied with sticking her tongue out like a dehydrated animal and making a loud, "BLLLAHGH," sound every few seconds without cracking a smile. Pharaoh was cracking up at her shenanigans but it worried me. When Hammer left, I whispered in her ear that she was gonna get it if she didn't quit it but it didn't make her stop the odd performance. I guess this was the sequel to her nose digging, finger residue licking phase from last week that I had halted by popping those little pumpkined hands on four different occasions.

307

"Hi, I'm Mrs. Dotson. I'll be your case worker," she stated taking a seat across from me at her desk. She looked like a good-hearted person. I didn't get any bad vibes from her.

Within seconds, after moving Mauri and Pharaoh to a cubicle across from us where they were still in view and Mauri was still at her new antic, I was telling her everything from when I first met Craig to why I was now in my current predicament. She listened and shook her head in empathy. "Girl. I had an ex-husband that was like that last baby daddy of yours. Once they think they got'chu, they don't ever act right again. Good thing you got away from him. I applaud you on that one. Just think about what cho' life would have been like if you stayed with him. Have you tried going to another church? Maybe that'll help. Here, I'll give you my Pastor's number. She's a woman so that might make you feel comfortable with our ministry."

By the end of my appointment with her, I felt a little better and would be receiving emergency stamps that went into effect the next day, cash assistance of three hundred dollars, Medicaid for myself and both the kids—in case Craig took Mauri off—a monthly childcare stipend based on the fact that I did have a job but was actually a hookup and a voucher to get fifty percent off a car from the auction on Five Mile in Redford.

That was much better than nothing. Much better.

After leaving the welfare office, I purchased packages of Sage and Nag Champa incense from a man posted in front of the gas station next to the bus stop. I hadn't bought incense since back in the day.

This time the bus ride home didn't seem so bad. At least I would be getting a car soon. I stared right back at as many faces as I could. My findings were that people really didn't like it—even if you looked at them with an unreadable expression.

I put the kids in the tub the minute we entered the apartment and played with them for a while afterwards before they fell asleep. Today Oprah's show was about healing from old wounds and caught my attention. Then *Divorce Court* came on with a case that pissed me off all over again and, at the end of the evening after pouring my heart out to Sherra and blasting Dominique, I still felt lonely and disgusted with my life.

Adding insult to injury, Darren called and asked to speak with Pharaoh. I refused to speak to him since the kids were already asleep and I didn't want Pharaoh to talking about how much he missed his dad all over again. Since I couldn't use my new staring tactic via telephone, I remained silent for so long Darren started trying real hard "Damn, Leigh. Why you gotta be actin' like this? A man can't just call to check up on his kid and his woman?"

Silence.

Then, finally "Darren, if *I* was your woman, you wouldn't have been out there with any and everything professing to have a coochie between the legs and Mauri would have never been a problem. Whatever." After I hung the phone up in his ear he called back and left a voicemail message.

"It doesn't have to go like this. We need to talk. Call me when you're ready to act like an adult." ...Erased it.

Syra called next in what was at best an obvious set up. I'd never given her this number. "Hey, Leigh. What's the deal? Darren is, like, really shook up about your sudden departure. He really loves you, Leigh. You shouldn't act like this. Nobody's perfect--*especially* not a man. Don't you miss 'em?"

"...Sy, let me just put it to you this way. If he's gonna be a cheater and if he's going to try to make me kick my daughter out of my life, it's not gonna work."

"Well...just talk to 'em. Maybe you two can come to some sort of agreement. Don't make me come over there and knock some sense into your head, chick. You know I don't know *anything* about Detroit but I'll come out there!" she teased.

"Girl, *you* in *Detroit.* Hmph. That'uh be like my *grand*mother hangin' out in a strip club on *Sun*day morning! You wouldn't dare."

"...Well, probably not. Darren says your neighborhood's really bad... Well, I'm gonna call you tomorrow to see how everything's goin'. Just talk to 'em alright?"

"...Yeah." I could tell Darren was sitting in on the three-way call because she didn't say anything about Mike getting on her nerves and she didn't brag about how much she'd spent on her latest shopping jaunt. Who *really* needed to act like an adult?

Once again, I couldn't go to sleep. I sat there staring off into space wondering if my life was really worth living. Had it not have been for those two babies in the other room, I probably would have gone past another attempt and been laying in the ground next week without any remorse. I envied the dead. They didn't have the plague of dealing with feelings and hurt and unyielding pain. Yeah, sure, there were days life was really worth living but honestly, at this point, it seemed like the con's I was constantly dealing with were outweighing the pro's.

Sitting in the dark my mind starting playing tricks on me. I started thinking about the girl again. Even though she hadn't appeared lately, her memory still lurked around. She was the side effect of Craig busting my head against the wall I guess. From the corner of my eye I saw a shadow flicker past the porch window but it didn't freak me out. I jut felt calm, like there was nothing to fear. I closed my eyes and felt energy rush into me. When I opened my eyes again, the shadow faded into a shimmery figure that completely disappeared. Shawn.

I got up, lit a few sticks of sage and just sat there, enjoying this feeling of calmness, of tranquility. I hadn't felt this relaxed since around my birthday.

Man, I wished Shawn was around. We'd probably be playing cards all night and cracking up at any and everything. He'd taught me how to play 21, poker and some game I was good at and kept beating him at that I think he called Crazy 8.

He cared about me, selflessly. Darren didn't. All those Playboy magazines Darren looked at right in front of me while asking me to jack him off while he flipped thru the pages, the porno collection I'd found in the basement that he insisted on watching with or without me every Sunday only to talk about how he'd love to "fuck" the starring females right around the kids, the way he always gawked when an attractive woman passed and whispered in my ear whether or not he thought the chick had a "juicy" ass or not... Everyone said it was normal male activity for a guy like Darren. But, no matter how you tossed the dice and rolled it, it still stung. I kept hoping he'd really care and stop one day but I guess that day was never really gonna come. With Darren it was all for show. I was a 'sensible' choice--one that made his family semi-proud, although they didn't approve of my daughter. If you took Mauri away, I'd probably make the family completely proud. Add to that the fact that I'd finally sucked his dick like it was a golden caramel covered rod and, oh yes, he was happy with his choice--for the most part. Problem was, even though he knew I wanted to be with him and would do whatever he wanted, I wasn't about to add females in our bedroom scene and I wasn't gonna agree to let him kick it with other females without me either and I wasn't gonna agree to put Mauri out like she was an unwanted pet!

Thinking about Darren made the dreariness come back. I turned on the stereo to 107.5 hoping to catch Jill Scott or India Arie playing or some jazz--something to take my mind off things. The only thing on was one of those damn, I'm a Fuckin' Forlorn Woman songs that droned on and on and was enough to make me go hug the toilet until I puked breakfast, lunch and dinner up.

I wondered what the Smiley dude was like. He seemed cool enough. But he could never fix the fucked up baby daddy situations going on right now.

I searched my purse for his number and decided against calling.

Why was it whenever something went wrong I was always looking to a man to make me feel better? You might as well say Black men are prejudiced against women because they treat us the same way a colonist would treat a slave. Why look for another one to go thru all this mess with again?

Sherra'd recently talked to Angela and apparently Craig had taken Angela out in my old Explorer and she remembered the license plate and followed him to my place one time. Her brothers went on the hunt for Craig and, after carjacking that Mountaineer and beating him down, her brothers were happy with their semi-success and were leaving matters alone.

But knowing Angela's crew wasn't planning on showing up at my place again still didn't mean life was about to turn into a bowl of plucky ducky little cherries.

Then Craig called and left a message I didn't waste time listening to.

I broke down.

Maybe this Eye Smiling dude would be all right. I couldn't expect Sherra to be available every time I was depressed or going crazy over some monkey-assed fool.

"Hey, it's Leigh," I stated after finding that card. He'd seen me at my worst and still tried to holla and since calling Kevin was out and memorizing Raquon Nelson's number was unrealistic, I decided to see what was up with this guy.

"Whad? Whad? She finally called!" he teased. "I'm glad I spotted you yestaday otherwise I guess I woulda still been checking my phone every hour. Whassup?"

"...A lot." That sounded stupid and made it seem like I was dripping in drama. But I couldn't think of anything in particular to talk about. It wasn't like I was about to go into what was really going on like I could've with Shawn.

"Like what? You don't strike me as the quiet type..."

"...How *you* figure?"

"You look like the type of woman who knows what she wants and gets it."

"...Yeah, well...I like skunks..."

"And I like lizards." We both busted out laughing. "Walruses cool, too—they brown skinned so technically, they Black."

"Yeah, well, that's true." From that point on we were talking like we'd known each other forever, watching *Comic View,* playing 'Name That Silk, Stephanie Mills, Keith Sweat and Gerald Levert Tune', we swapped lyrics from old school rappers like Queen Latifa, YoYo, Digable Planets and Slick Rick since we'd both grown up in the eighties and nineties. We laughed so many times, I spent half the time on the phone unable to breath and started getting stomach cramps. Even the way he said "Bananas" instead of crazy was funny.

We didn't get off the phone until a quarter to five in the morning. "If I didn't have ta be on an appointment at eight, I wouldn't even be tryin' ta hang up."

"No. Go ahead. Handle your business." One thing I was not going to do was tell a working man to skip out on business on *my* behalf!

"Well, I should be done with all my jobs by three, I can take you up to tha auction--they have one at six. If we get there early you can check out tha cars first before they run 'em. You might even be able ta get one before it hits the line," he offered.

"Are you sure you can take me?"

"Yeah, otherwise I wouldn't offer."

"...Well...okay."

"Aright, then. See you at four-thirty. Same place I dropped you off yesterday?"

"Yep."

"Bet."

THE REST OF THE day felt light and airy and different. I did a few yoga stretches while the kids were sleeping and meditated on my life like I'd learned in The Program only instead of raising my energy and all that crap, I focused on what I wanted to see manifest in my life soon.

1. I will get my truck back
2. I will get my hair done-- real soon
3. I will enroll in classes
4. I will be truly happy forever
5. I will have a good, emotionally mature man that will be faithful and not put me thru any of this crap I have already visited
6. I will find a good church
7. I will find a way to mend the relationship with my mother.

"You want it, you got it and much more than that!"

Ever since that thing with Craig and I went down, I had been seriously tripping. I needed to make an appointment to go for more counseling sessions--real soon, sooner than a hair appointment. *There are no voices, it's just this apartment. As soon as you can, you need to move. You will be fine,* I silently repeated until I forgot about The Voice.

I know God talked to Moses but…schizophrenics heard voices too. I know 'cause even though I wasn't there for that long, I saw *a whole bunch* of those crazy fuckers up in Receiving smiling at the wall, laughing at nothing and listening to conversations they had going on with themselves. One guy said he had cartoons playing in his head and I did my best--*did my best* to stay the hell away from that mothafucker. I was glad we had on restraints. Who knows what one of them crazy voices might have told him to do to me? His bed was right next to mine. Well…I could at least be grateful Darren found me in the nick of time and took me out of *that* place.

Yeah, we were gonna have to nip the voice thing in the bud.

So then I called to check on the status of my aid. Sure enough, just like Mrs. Dotson said the funds were on my card. I dialed up KD to set another Monday appointment up and scheduled doctor and dental appointments for the kids.

With me, good luck always seemed to break even with a terrible strike of the bad. Like Craig's latest voicemail trying to threaten somebody. If I didn't talk to him by the time he got off work, he claimed he was "Gon' sit in front uh da 'partment 'til I got home or find out where Darren lived an' bust some caps in his windows." Another wrench thrown in my mix.

So.

I called him back and *politely* stated…that I was getting an Order of Protection against his ass. And that he would be going to jail tonight if he stepped anywhere he even *thought* I might be—especially since he had just made the mistake of harassing me on tape. That, plus the fact that I told him Darren had recently gotten me a gun--a lie, yes--but it squashed the threats on his end.

Dina came over to watch the kids since I didn't want them around Smiley. "Girl, I 'on't know whas wrong wit chu! *You* need ta find yo' way *back ta* Darren's crib! *And* you payin' me way less? Ungh-uh, Leigh. Somethin' gotsta ta be wrong wit chu!" she declared outraged that I had left some "good money."

I ignored her comments. She had, after all, come over on short notice. I could finally afford to pay her something be it much less than what I had been giving her and I didn't want my kids getting used to seeing men come and go. Growing up my mother had kept her dates away from me and set a good moral example. The kids didn't need to be around him, Smiley was just going to be a friend.

HE ARRIVED ON TIME in a burgundy Yukon this time instead of the company van. During our ride, I found out Smiley was two years younger than me and would turn twenty-three May the sixth—the day after Pharaoh's birthday. He finished his bachelors in business a year ago from U of D and now owned the plumbing business his father started years ago and just retired from. Everyone in his family pitched in and helped him with the company making it a true family business. We definitely needed more Black families like his around--Smiley Plumbing even did contractual work for the city every now and again. I was impressed.

"You know I forgot ta get what I went to tha store for after we met?" he asked as the jazz rendition of Stevie Wonder's song "All I Do" by Kirk Whalum and some chick with a good voice ended. I was noticing how he was playing a CD loaded with love songs even though I'd done a good job of emphasizing the just FRIENDS—no benefits thing last night when we talked. And while I didn't mind Ms. Badu's duet with Mr. Wyclef "In Love With You," the final freakin' straw was when Whitney Houston's "Lover For Life" came on and he got all quiet.

"...Really?" I asked, responding to his question extra late. "Mind if I turn the radio on?" I was sure, him being a hip-hop head and all, he had a stash of A Tribe Called Quest, some Nas-- *something* else to play. Where the hell was it already?

He looked over at me and chuckled. "...Go 'head..." I flipped thru the stations and stopped on a 702 song I liked. As the background vocalist dude continuously repeated, "*I still love you*," I was reminded of something I *really* did *not* want to think about.

This was me and Darren's song—well--had been our song. One time, he hurt my feelings so bad, he called and requested it on 98. Dedicating a song via radio was definitely not Darren's style--too pauper-ish for his taste, he claimed. He especially hated it when callers got all excited over winning ninety-eight dollars. But he had called in anyway to try ease his way out of the doghouse.

I immediately flipped to 102.7. The second I got comfortable in the passengers seat, "That Woman" came on. "Ughck! I hate this song." I rolled my eyes in disgust as I tapped thru the stations set on his radio again. "I used to like it--who doesn't like the Isley Brothers? But, then who wants to hear a man tell a woman 'just do what I say?' *Not my* ass! You can do everything a man asks you to and they *still* won't care or appreciate it!"

"It's like *that*? What if you had a good man? If he catered to you, you wouldn't be willing to reciprocate?" He laughed as I ignored his question. I settled on 101.9. They always had old-school jazz on around this time.

"Aw yeah. This is the man right here!" He snapped his fingers to a Miles Davis song. When the following number came on, he bobbed his head and added his rough voice along with the singer's.

"You sound like a rapper."

"Yeah. I been on the scene. Got a few hooks up..."

I could already see how that probably went. He was probably one of those dudes who spent a lot of time dreaming about becoming a platinum selling, hardcore rapper but wasn't about to get anywhere outside of amateur nights at Club 2000 and church plays. I kept my *Don't quit your day job* comment to myself considering he was pretty decent.

"Hey? You know that one song...dang, I can't remember who sings it... It was at the end of that movie that just came out not too long ago...Mya! That's it. Something about being free and single..." He turned the radio all the way down.

"I know what song you're talking about. 'Free'."

"How does it go? I only heard it once..."

"It starts off like—" I copied off the halting sound the record intro's with before she starts singing and slid my hand in one swift, circular like dj scratching a record.

He started cracking up. "Aright, aright. You know tha rest?"

"Yeah." I sung the first verse and got all into it like I was the main act on *Show Time at the Apollo*.

"Damn, girl. You got skills. You need ta do something with that."

"Oh, so you tricked me?" The more I thought about the lyrics, the more I saw what he was doing. He looked over at me and grinned.

When we got to the auction, Smiley took charge checking out the best deals, starting up cars to see what they sounded like and within an hour had compiled a list of my top five choices. The first was a red Honda Accord that, at two thousand, was quite frankly...out of my budget. The second was a gold Malibu with a cracked windshield that, even at fifteen hundred, was...out of my measly budget. If the prices didn't by chance drop during the auction, it looked like my best bet was the four-year old black Stratus going for eight zero zero. It was clean and it seemed like it would drive okay even though it was well over 100,000 miles. "Let's hope for the best," he stated when the cars started rolling out.

I didn't have a chance on getting the Honda or the Malibu since the bidders up-ed the price over the original asking prices for both cars. Then, the Stratus stopped driving in the middle of the line.

"That's three out," Smiley whispered. Finally, the last car on his list rolled out. It was an old school, hatch back, gray Ford Escort. They started the bid at one hundred dollars. There were no takers until Smiley raised his hand.

"Naw, ungh-uh! I don't want that piece of crap!" He was crazy. How was I gonna go from a brand new Explorer to the latest Lex to a ragamuffin *monstrosity* of a ride like that? It wasn't like *Pimp My Ride* took candidates from Michigan! And without some kind of drastic car makeover, that was *not* about to work! "That's not my style!" I folded my arms across my chest and snapped my neck it so hard it should have popped right off.

"And *sold* to the nice young man on my left!" the auction guy stated, pointing at Smiley.

"Leigh, when I tested it, it sounded good, it had less miles than that Stratus that didn't even make it down the isle, it'll be good on gas and easy to repair. It's a sensible choice for right now. Besides, I'm paying for it. With the buyers fee's, it's gonna be three hundred dollars. The buyer's fees cost more than your car! Now *that's* what I call a deal!"

I could have wiped the smile off his sensible, thrifty face. When he put it on his list I thought he was joking with me—*joshing me for real*.

I needed to hurry up and get my hair done so I could hook back up with Kevin. That way I'd have enough money to get something worth riding in for a minute.

"Dang, I can't even get a thank you? It's only temporary. I 'on't know what happened to ya' truck but at least this way you won't have to be on the bus. Let's go get the money order so you can drive it home tonight. They've got the auto Insurance people sitting next to the cashier's window--we can hook that up, too."

I hadn't known him long enough to expect him to splurge but...he wasn't driving no hatch back from the eighties ride. "It's not my style but thanks. You really don't have to pay for it. I'll just come back tomorrow and take care of it," I stated flatly. That way, I could see if I could come up with more money and get something else at their Saturday auction. Forget that--I was saving my voucher. He'd only be saving fifty dollars, anyway—that was basically wasting the damn discount.

"It's cool. I figure, if you woulda called me when we first met, I would have taken you out at least fifteen times by now. Yo' car is costing me less than what I woulda spent taking you out to dinner and whatnot. I like you and you've got kids. You don't need to be on a bus--you know how they run in Detroit...and we still got cold weather... It's cool."

After he paid the five hundred twenty five dollars to get everything taken care of including my temporary plates from the Secretary of State since they stayed open later on Wednesdays, I followed him to my hideout of a choice: Denny's in Southfield on Telegraph since he was so insistent we "go out to celebrate." I'd have preferred celebrating kissing a monkey's stinky, hairy, pink pissy ass.

We sat far in the back, tucked away from the rest of the dining room. I still needed to be careful with the Darren issue especially now. I was going to have to use the fact that he wanted me back to get my *Lex* back.

"So? How did it drive?" he asked smiling from ear to ear, all proud. He called it a "smart buy," I called it CHEAPNESS.

"It rode rather well...the tape player" (swallowing hard) "looks like it works. Amazingly the radio has a little bump to it." Well...that was the truth. But the last time I had a cassette player in my car was during my pre-Darren days. A cassette player. That just sounded like something from Anno Domini times.

"See, I told you. It was pretty clean on the inside, too. Whoever had it before obviously took good care of it. Looks like they kept it waxed."

When a car was flat gray, what good was a *waxing* gonna do? This guy obviously did not know what kind of woman I was. The rest of the dinner I faked like all was good, wondering what it all meant. I wasn't about to *sleep* with *him*. He was nice and, yes, I wanted to hang out with him sometime. But if he thought giving me a raggedy, out-of-date-car was good game and a sure bet for a one-night stand, he had me twisted. He was *too* young...dumb ass muthafucka...

What I *needed* to do was take a time out for some serious thinking. Maybe Syra *was* right. All men cheat. All men treat women like shit one way or another. Maybe being with someone who was financially secure and doling out the funds was as good as it got for a woman. I bet this smiling ass muthafucka was a cheater. His good yet cheap impression wasn't gonna do anything but eventually flip the scrip, too, just like Darren and Craig.

I peeped him. Three decent females walked by with nice shapes. He didn't look up one time. He just kept talking like he was all into me. He talked about spirituality, his life goals and about how he wanted a family. When the bill came he didn't hesitate like Craig had on our first couple of dates--like he was expecting to go dutch or something. But this was only Denny's where I'd only scarfed down a simple slice of cheesecake minus the syrupy cherry shit while he took advantage of the $5.99 swiss bacon and mushroom melt combo and strawberry lemonade refills. So what? Yeah, he was acting okay now, but he was still a man. At some point he was going to show his ass—and it was probably hairy, too.

A man's definition of love? Sex and a good chase or challenge. Once you give 'em sex, they change and stop acting like they care; once you quit giving them a good chase or stop being a challenge, they just move on to the next chic that either isn't interested in their ass or one smart enough to know how to keep the upper hand in the game.

Men don't love women. Nope. They don't even see us as equal counterparts. That's why it's so easy for them to act like women don't have the same color blood as theirs.

"Here, you might need this." He handed me two tens.

"For?" What the hell could I possibly do with twenty dollars? Could that voice please come back and tell me? Twenty dollars?

"For gas. Prices been mad high. It's a lil' something--should fill you up. Come, on. I'll put some gas in it before you ride home." We went to the BP gas station across the street. He paid for the fill up and we headed home in opposite directions.

I still didn't know where he lived. He was so cheap, my bet was he posted down in mommy and daddy's basement.

"Girl, what is that *you just* pulled up *in*?" Dina asked the moment I opened the door. That was the same question I'd been asking myself the whole time I rode in that thing.

"*Girrrll*, I don't even know," was all I could muster up to say. "At least it runs." I stated as she was leaving.

That night Malik called just as I drifted off to sleep. "Hello?"

"Whad up, Leigh—I like saying ya' name... Just calling to see if you made it in aright. I'm mad tired. I'll hit you up when I get a chance tomorrow."

I don't remember whether or not I said goodbye. All I remember is waking up and still not having the keys to my brand new truck.

Chapter 18

It was now well into March and, after a week of dealing with angry tenants and only having four dollars and thirty-three cents to my name, I finally received a check, which meant I could finally afford to go to KD's. But it wasn't going to be like when I was with Darren and I could get my hair done every week—with two bags of bohemian hair totaling a hundred and sixty dollars and KD charging me four hundred, my hair was gonna *have to last* the rest of the month.

I had Dina drive me to KD's so he and Beat wouldn't get a glimpse of the eyesore I had to drive.

Looking the way I was supposed to, I was now officially ready to reconnect with Kevin. I called his phone only to find out his number was disconnected. I was *so* pissed! *Now* what was I supposed to do? I was looking all good and for what?

My phone rang. Yes, unfortunately I had gotten a pay as you go Go Phone since, driving in something like this, you never knew when you were going to have to call a towing service. It was Smiley. "Hey. I know you on your minutes so I'm not gonna hold you up—I just wanted to let chu know there's gonna be an event at this place tomorrow night and I'd really dig it if you went with me. Would you be able to make it?"

"Sure. Where?"

"It's right around the corner from you. Black Madonna Unity Center. Program starts at seven. Bring the kids too, if you can."

"Black Madonna *Unity Center*? ...I don't know. What denomination is that 'cause I'm Christian and I heard they okay homosexuality and all that other crap in those Unity Centers. I'm not down for *anything* like—"

"—Leigh? Come. Please."

"...Um...I don't know. Let me call you when I get home, okay?"

He was a nice guy. A really, *really* nice guy and he reminded me of Shawn--only he was much more of a looker--not saying Shawn was ugly or anything. Shawn's heart made a lot of pretty boys and so called handsome thugs look like garbage wrapped in pretty packages. But going to a church I'd always been told was wrong made me uncomfortable. I didn't want to hurt Smiley's feelings or look like an unholy bitch but I wasn't about to step into a place like that.

Now taking *him* to the church my worker had told me about wasn't a bad idea.

I went to get the kids from Dina and started thinking about how much better life was with Smiley around. He called when he said he would *and* he called everyday--usually afternoon-ish and then again in the evening. He wasn't boring to talk to and our conversations always ended on a positive note.

I was still thinking about Smiley and that Black Unity Center thing about to pull into my parking space behind the building when I noticed a hunter green Mountaineer posted in my spot.

It was for damn sure him. Qualimar. Craig's side profile showed in the driver's window. He'd left tons of messages talking about how he got "my truck" back.

I turned into the alley, drove off and called the police. I'd gotten a protection order against him yesterday but it hadn't been served yet. They said the process took a couple of day. I guess if a woman got killed in between it was just too bad.

I drove over to my mother's house but either she wasn't there or just didn't answer. I couldn't tell since she always parked in the garage.

I called Smiley and began telling him a few bits of the million pieces to the story that was the history of Leigh and Craig. I was panicking and talking so fast I could barely breathe.

"You can stop by where I'm at right now and wait 'til I'm done. I'll ride back with you to your place."

"Where are you?"

"On Seven Mile and Outer Dri—"

"—No! That's not gonna work. Never mind." That was too close to Craig's to be sitting and waiting for who knew how long. Where was I going to go? Craig's first guess would be Sherra's.

"Aright. You can ride out to my place and chill 'til I get there."

"How long you think you'll be? I've got my kids."

"I'll give you my keys."

"Your keys?" Was he *crazy*?

"Yeah, I trust you. And I know where you live if you try something," he chuckled and gave me the address to the location he was working at. When I showed up he stepped outside. "Make sure you turn the key to the left--it gets kinda stuck. Take the Lodge and come up on Northwestern Highway. Take that to Thirteen Mile—you're gonna have to do a turn around after the light. Call me when you get there." He motioned for me to give him my keychain and placed two keys on it.

This cat lived in Farmington Hills? In a house? And he trusted me enough to hand over his keys? I called Sherra and told her, within limited minutes, about it.

"Ggggirl. Be careful on that. Dese men nowadays be crazy. Don't *no man* jus offer you tha keys ta his place like dat! You might get over there and he be done killed you and ate you fa dinner or sumthen. You can come by here if you wont to."

I took a deep breath and asked myself if I could trust him. My stomach didn't flutter, I didn't get any weird feelings about it. I felt okay going there. "Well, here's his address if you don't hear from me in an hour. And if I call and say I'm Fine twice—that means call the police."

"Well...alright, Leigh. I hope you know what you're doing..."

I called Craig's mother after I drove down the freeway ramp to tell her to tell her *son* to stop harassing me if he liked his freedom. Maybe she could talk some sense into him. "Hello? Hello?" My phone got staticicky for a few seconds before it cleared up.

"Yeah! I musta made uh mistake an' hung ya' up, honey. Like I was sayin' dat boy ain't right no kinda way! He got anotha baby on da way by some gurl stay 'round da corna an' he wont even say nothin' ta *dat* po' gurl. An' he *still ain't* tryin' ta take care uh dat six year ole eryboday know hiz—an' dat's uh cute lil' ole boy, too, it's uh shame. Da chile stay right 'cross da street. Den he got dat Angela hussy callin' my phone talkin' 'bout her son hiz but he still out dere chasin' afta dat bougie ass Leila, Lee-Lee--whatever dat thang's name be. Nah I *cain't stand ha*! He go crazy over *dat thang*--like she gold uh sum shit! Seem like he like ha da most but she sho' is da most *stuckest up* one out uh all dem trolls! Well...least he finally came clean wit me 'bout tryin' dat ole crack. I found dat shit out when I wuz cleanin' up his room uh long time 'go. Dat's why I had put his triflin' azz out! Den he moved his azz in wit dat Leila 'steada gittin' clean from dat shit.

"Nah, I'ma tel'you--dat chile need help! He ain't neva been right no how! I done gave up on 'em. I mean, if he try ta git right, I'ma be here but--let 'im tell it—evrythang he do ma fault! Dat's why I 'on't try ta help 'em out no moe. Hmmph! Bessie, I tell ya! I'm so sick uh no good niggas! An' dey be ya' own goddamn chilren too!"

I hung up. "Thank you, God! Thank you, Jesus!" That was three minutes worth my time.

"What mommy?" Pharaoh asked.

"God just told mommy some things she needed to know, that's all sweetie."

"Oh...God tells me a lot too, mom."

"Really? Like what?"

"...Um...like you feel sad. And you miss dad. And you don't like this car. I don't like it either mommy—it's not tall like the truck ...Ma? ...I miss daddy. When are we going to see him?"

"Hopefully soon, sweetie. But you know what?"

"What?"

"Isn't this better than taking the bus?"

"The bus was fun."

"*What*? Why?"

"'Cause."

"'Cause what, sweetie?"

"We got to see a lot of people. Like those twins. That was my second time seeing two twins. Dina taught me that word, mom. Twins." He sniffed his nose hard and shook his head like he was a sage of an old man and had just kicked out a pound of knowledge.

"That's good, sweetheart. We're about to go somewhere that is going to be fun, too. But we can't tell people about it, okay. When we get in here, I don't want you or Mauri touching anything. Stay by me and don't touch anything. Got it?" I warned pulling in front of the address Smiley had given me.

"Yep. No problemo, mom."

"Well...unbuckle your seatbelt." I pulled into Smiley's driveway. He stayed in a well kept, light brick ranch in an older and seemingly quiet subdivision.

I sighed and asked myself if I was sure about going in. No bad feelings...well, alright. I went in thru the side door.

"Wipe your shoes off...Mauri? I said wipe your shoes off!"

"Take 'em off, mommy?"

"No, keep them on for now."

I looked around the kitchen. There were a multitude of dishes in the sink although he had a dishwasher. The small lightwood and white table looked as though it could barely accommodate a party of three and didn't come close to matching the dark wooded cabinetry that matched the dark wooden trim of the rest of the house. It was filled with mail, newspapers and a few plates with yellow crumbs stuck on them. The ceiling fan was still running with the light on.

The completely barren off white, carpeted living room only had a large family picture hanging over the fireplace but the den made up for the living room's lack of furniture. It had a hunter green leather couch and recliner with a flat screen television against the wall. There was a large stereo that sat on the floor underneath the TV. On the end tables near the sliding doors that led to the patio were six pictures, him with Dougie Fresh, Rakim, Outcast, Musiq, Nas and Kelis and there was a bag of weed sitting next to a picture of him and Luducris.

Being every bit of nosey as I was cautious, I roamed around a bit more. The house had three bedrooms—the master bedroom was the only one that wasn't empty. He had a king sized bed without a headboard and an armoire with a television in it and a box set DVD collection of *Def*

Comedy Jam, *The Matrix* and four movies on quantum physics. In his closet although he had a decent amount of business suits there were too many Moschino and other weird named jeans to count and tons of boots. Looked like he lived up to true Hip Hop gear code.

There were two bathrooms—one up stairs and one in the basement. Both of them had shiny wallpaper that looked like something from the set of *The Jeffersons*. In the hallway that let to the front door there were four pictures. One of Bob Marley another of Malcolm X, a drawing of a nude Black woman in a sensual pose, the fourth was a picture of Al Paccino from a scene in *Scarface*.

The finished basement was obviously makeshift office space. An oversized calendar filled with penciled in appointments sat on top of a desk. The walls were knotty pine and natural colored Berber carpeted the floors. Clothes begging to be washed piled up against the floor near the washing machine and dryer. He needed a woman around to hook his place up. It had tons of potential with the right decorative touch.

I called Sherra and assured her that all was well and that I would call her back in half an hour.

"Darren, I'm dealing with a serious problem right now. I need your help," I proposed as I loaded the dishwasher. I had called him *67 from Smiley's phone.

"Yeah, I *know* you got a serious problem. You need to rethink what you want in life," he snapped.

"No. Seriously. When I went home, Craig was waiting for me. I don't feel safe. Can you see if John can do something to rush that PPO I just got on him? It still hasn't been served. Can they take it to him on his job or something?"

"See. This is what I'm talking about. You need to figure out what you want. I'm not gonna be bailing you out every time you make a fucked up decision. It's on *you*. Either we talk like two civilized adults on Saturday and you move back over here or you leave me outta yo' bullshit."

I hung up on him and dialed another number so Smiley wouldn't see it if he pressed redial.

Darren was right, I couldn't expect him to look out for me—if I *could* count on him, we'd still be together. I pondered on what I needed to do about Craig in the future as I cleaned up the rest of the kitchen and looked in Smiley's refrigerator for something to cook. There was hardly anything in there except Styrofoam carry out orders and tons of Hearty Man frozen dinners in the freezer.

After lucking up and finding a package of Perdue chicken wings that weren't frozen, I seasoned and baked them, put on some mac and cheese from out of the box, hooked it up with shredded cheese as best as I could considering he didn't have the stuff I needed to make the homemade kind, warmed up some rolls and put on a pot of frozen peas. While dinner cooked, I washed his clothes, glad he obviously only wore boxers and hadn't had any moose tracks or tighty-whitey's in the pile. Keeping busy took my mind off things and, truthfully, I kind of felt bad for Smiley. He needed to hire a housekeeper or something.

"Hey. I almost forgot to call you once I got in. My bad." I called Malik almost two hours later.

"Yeah, I'm on the way there now."

"Okay. I'll see you in a few."

"Aright. Peace."

I called Sherra back. "Girl, everything's still cool. We'll talk later." I'd seen her number on the caller ID a couple of times. I didn't want her thinking something went awry the way she worried.

"What's up, Smiley?" I smiled as he opened the door. "You've got a nice place. You need a lil' help on the decoration tip, but it's cool. We'll work on that later."

"Damn, look at you. You cleaned up around here? I hope you ain't go thru my shit." He gave me a hug.

"No, I didn't. I just straightened up the kitchen and helped you out in the laundry department. Dinner's almost ready. Why don't you sit down?"

"Bet. Keep this up and I *will* be letting you decorate my crib."

"This is your house?"

"Yeah. I bought it last year."

"Oh…well…you're different from a lot of brothas out here--that's for sure."

Pharaoh asked Smiley a couple of questions about trucks and cars while Mauri ate her food and clapped every time Pharaoh said 'Macaroni'. Dinner was a whole lot of laughing and talking.

Afterwards he and I sat on the living room floor. The kids were in the den watching cartoons on Nickelodeon.

"Smiley, I'm really glad you came into my life. I've been thru a lot and…" I sighed and I could have sworn he said something that sounded like, "I know" under his breath but he didn't say anything else. He stared deep into me letting me know he wanted me to finish saying what *I myself* wasn't sure I needed to tell him. "…I don't know how to say what I want to say to you… I've—I've just learned over the years not to trust anyone. Life is hard and I'm tired of always having to fight—these days everything is a fight… It's like there's always gonna be someone trying to take advantage of you if they think you're nice or a good person… After everything I've been thru, there's almost nothing else that can happen that would be as bad as what I've already dealt with. I'm just—I'm just *sick* of everything—especially relationships and guys. I know I'm babbling on and on like a crazy person but…" I shook my heads at my sudden loss of words. "…You're probably like 'Why's she all up in my crib if she doesn't trust anybody and whatnot?' But…I don't know. I just—I kinda feel like I can trust you—I asked myself before I even opened the door whether or not I was making a mistake coming over here… But I didn't get any bad vibes from you. It's probably like way too soon for me to say that but…"

"…I feel where you're coming from. You been dealing with some real lame ass muthafuckas… It ain't crazy. You just on a higher level and vibration than what most of the people surroundin' you on and you're startin' ta be more conscious of the Spirit and oneness inside you."

It was weird how he put it but, okay. "What makes me think you can trust me—I mean, like for you to let me come to your house all like this? "

"…Well. From day one, it was like this: The day we met I was meditating all morning on how I want my life to be, right. I had an hour before my next appointment so I went ta get one of those Italian subs for lunch--we do a lodda residential work in Sherwood Forest—but, they didn't have any subs at the one on Seven Mile so I went to the one in Highland Park."

"…I know how that is, when you really have a taste for something, you don't want anything else."

"Exactly and they subs be off the chains. So I was thinking about all my options. Then, I started thinking about what kind of woman I want. I already did the strip clubs and the dating scene. I definitely know what I don't want off rip—oh, I learned that shit! I mean, females try ta holla all the time, especially when they find out uh brotha got his own hustle goin' on an' shit. But cute faces and easy access stopped doing it fa me a long time ago. I ain't need no more young ass girls I was gonna have ta argue with all the time 'cause they not on my level. A lodda them weren't doing nothing but taking up space on earth and wasting time. I'm not about that. What I wanted was that perfect fit like how my moms and pops are.

"So I was like, Mother and Father, *you* show to me who I'm supposed ta be with--I already know *how* I wanna live. I trust you enough to know you'll give me tha best—exactly what I'm supposed to have. Right after that Mauri flew by, right, and I caught her and I saw you.

"I was like, her. I want *her*. This is the one. This is the one Mother and Father want me to have. Everything about your *energy* just *felt* right. But I was like, it's gonna take time. Mother and Father let me know up front, 'Yo', she's got some scars. She's gonna have to heal on her own first. But she's the one you need—she'll make you happy'." He nodded his head in accordance with his words. "When I saw you that second time at the bus stop, I was like 'I godda *get her*.' I *godda* let her know I'm for real, man.' I knew it was gonna be hard 'cause a lodda brothas ain't got they shit together nowadays. I wanted to take my time and show you I ain't in that category..."

"...Wait. What do your mother and father—*the Mother and Father*--what do they have to do with anything?" He was confusing me. When we first met I hadn't seen him with anybody else.

"God and the Goddess--you know."

"No. I believe in Jesus. For a minute, I almost lost my faith but...a situation occurred in my life that made me believe again."

"Well...I believe in Jesus, too, but I feel he's God's son. And since masculine energy alone can't procreate, there's got to be feminine energy as well. It's not a new school of thought, though. A lodda old world religions believed in God as well as the Goddess. That's why Egyptians created the Onk. The vertical part represents male force, the circle is feminine force. You know how Mary gets pregnant with Jesus? She's what? Jesus mother. Newer religions left women out of the picture to fulfill otha goals in order to further male dominance and shit. With tha exception of Catholicism, a lodda religions make Mary a minuscule part of his existence. But I'm not all into Catholic beliefs either. They've been involved in too many wars and mind control over concentrated populations—in my opinion. But what a lodda religions do is exclude the female energy and only promote belief in The Father, The Son and The Holy Spirit. That's why I'm not any particular religion. I believe *we are* created in God's image. A man and woman are needed in order to bring forth human life onto earth, so, in my opinion, our Creators are male and female Spirits as well. I try to maintain a spiritual center in my life with Oneness but I'm not out here searching for somebody to tell me what the Creators want me to do. *They*—God and Goddess--tell me in their own time and it works for me."

"...Hmmm...that's definitely a new thought...How old are you again? Are you sure you're twenty-two? You seem so—so I don't know--"

"—Old. Like I've been here before? Yeah. I'm an old soul. This definitely isn't my first time around... Your Spirit and soul are younger, though. You've probably only been here once or twice before. Maybe that's why we connect so well...to balance each other out."

"I've only been here once? ...That sounds like an insult." I frowned. "Besides. It would be twice." That Laila chick was definitely me somewhere back in time.

"Is being new to this world an insult?"

"...I don't know."

"There's pro's and con's to everything…" Okay, I'd say this guy had me baffled yet *very* interested but he definitely had unorthodox beliefs.

We sat in the lingering silence, drifting into our own private thoughts for a while before I opened back up. Within two hours, he knew everything I'd ever wished for, everything I'd been thru--the pain, the disintegration of my life, how I'd never truly been loved by any man. I even told him the truth about the Craig thing, the girl *and* the visions.

Until today, I'd never met another Black person who shared my belief in past lives. I was like a volcano that had been waiting for years to explode this very night. I had promised myself not to be real with any other man—ever--but I didn't feel stupid for telling him anything. The way he listened and didn't judge me and my mistakes, it was all unreal. And when he hugged me it was over. I couldn't stop crying which *did* make me feel stupid. He kissed me on the forehead and held me close against his chest. "You're tuning into Spirit. You'll be okay. You were already headed for a higher plane. You just got thrown off your path for a minute, that's all. At least you woke up. A lodda people never get a chance to be anything otha than a walking carcasses on this planet." His words comforted me as he nuzzled my forehead with his chin. His energy was massive. And reassuring.

I'd asked for a good man.

He was a mixture of Darren's best qualities--hardworking and able to build towards wealth along with Craig's best assets--Afrocentric, with a street edge and he was nice looking the major difference was his heart was good just like Shawn's.

When I was ready for a relationship, if I ever wanted one later on down the road, he could no doubt be the one.

"…It's getting late, I'd better be getting home." I wiped my face with the tissue he'd just gotten from the bathroom. I wasn't about to give him the wrong idea by staying the night. "…Um…"

"What? What's wrong?"

"…Nothing."

"Naw, say whatever's on ya's mind."

"…Just… Never mind. Darren's right. I can't keep involving other men in the affairs of the other men in my life—if that make any sense."

Smiley sat back down on the floor with me, held out his hand, reached for mine and tilted my chin towards him. His eyes were doing a good job of letting me know I didn't need to avoid them.

"…I don't feel comfortable going back to my place. I…I need that Order of Protection on him like pronto, otherwise…"

"Aright. Let's put the kids in the car. I'll trail you to the precinct on Eleven Mile. That muthafuka'uh get dem papers tomorrow, watch... How you feel about getting a gun?"

Once we got to the station, we spoke with an officer who agreed to make sure Trash was served in the morning at work. Smiley pulled an officer to the side and said something to him and I ended up being escorted home by a patrol car.

"MOMMY?"

"Yes, dear?"

"You like Smiley, don't you?"

"Well...yes, he's my friend."

"Me and Mauri like him too," Pharaoh commented shaking his head up and down as I helped him fix his shirt he'd put on inside out.

"That's good to know, sweetie. You put on your shirt *and* helped your sister with hers. Now *that* was nice. I'm proud of you. Okay, when you see this tag, try to make sure you put it on like this." I took another shirt and demonstrated. "Give mommy a kiss for doing such a good job."

"Mom?"

"Um-hm?"

"I love you."

"I love you, too"

I was still a bit nervous about going to this Center thing and taking the kids but, since it seemed to mean so much to Smiley, I agreed to go.

After filing my nails and a coat of clear polish--since I couldn't afford to get a French manicure set anymore, curling my weave and carefully pulling my hair in an upsweep, putting on some lipgloss, a pair of three thousand dollar Mikimoto pearls and the matching ring Darren had given me when we were in Miami, a white Dolce Gabbana button down blouse that tied into a huge ruffled bow in front under my neck, my favorite Escada wide legged twill pants, a pair of black suede Dior ankle boots and grabbing my black suede clutch purse and light brown fox shawl, I was ready to meet him.

It was only two blocks away but the entire ride I wanted to turn around and go home. *"Well, well, well, what have we here? Look who's trying to go to chuuurch!"* The way the evil resonated in every syllable of the word church made every hair on my body raise. *"You know you're not ready for chuuurch. Huh! It's some weird ass shit anyhow—Mother and Father! Who ever heard of such nonsense! Whatever message you need, you can get it at home. The last thing you need right about now is somebody feeding you some more bull. That's all it is, you know. Now turn around and go home, Dumb Ass!"* the wicked, convicting inner voice taunted.

I had to force myself to go. Getting into the car and driving was like pushing a mountain the size of the earth ahead of me. I was already dressed and looking good—I had to go. *I have to go*, I ended the debate as I pulled into the last parking space left on the church lot.

Smiley stood with one hand in his pocket waiting for us in the hallway surprising me with that dapper looking black suit of his completed with a pair of cuff links and a tie that coincidentally matched my slacks. For a minute there I felt underdressed—I could have at least worn a dress and put Pharoah in a blazer.

"Hey, Leigh. You look nice...*real* nice," he complimented while picking up Mauri. "This is my boy, G," he introduced. The guy in the fitted navy suit that looked like he'd donned it from a Temptation's sixties wardrobe rack, with his head tilted back wearing a pair of those old schooled Sly Stone looking sunglasses, with his head shaved really low and a curly-q filigree design shaved on the entire right side of his head who was standing next to Smiley was fine as hell. He smelled really nice, too. He was doing this thing with his mouth, like he had an invisible toothpick in his mouth or something. He reminded me of that one dude from the Neptunes—a group Smiley'd put me up on the other night when I was at his house. Matter of fact, he looked exactly like that dude. Smooth, kinda cocky, slightly street and definitely ahead of his time, the brother had the kind of style that made you want to know more about him. And he was three years older than Smiley. This was definitely something for Sherra to meet and greet and look into some time soon although he was a bit lighter than what she normally went for. Naah. On second thought, she liked guys that were a lot more ghetto than his type and since he didn't look like he was going to be buying a pair of gators anytime soon or like he knew all the latest Hustles or ballroom danced to the latest R&B songs or carried a bible next to a gat in his belt for those "jus in case instances," that blind date was a no-go.

"Whassup, Leigh. Heard a lodda 'bout chu. All good, all good. Good to finally meet." He bit his lower lip, sandwiched my hand in both of his and shook it before putting his hands back in his pockets and looking away. A rather boney, light carmel skinned guy, you could immediately tell he was the type that was always thinking and always on the go. Probably a skateboarder, too.

People moved hurriedly about to and fro. Light taps of earthy perfume oils bounced about in the air. Women dressed in yellow, red, purple and other colorfully designed, loose fitting African garments that still did nothing to hide the thickness of their curves, greeted each other with smiles and met in warm embraces.

On a calendar on the wall across from where Smiley was standing activities were listed for the current week's schedule of yoga, sewing, ballroom dance lessons and senior activities.

There was a sign up sheet for soup kitchen volunteers near a mural of Malcolm X, Martin Luther King Jr. and Marcus Garvey on a wall leading to the basement.

On the wall across from the auditorium was a painting of a Black, lock wearing Jesus and on the wall that led to the restrooms was a painting of a beautiful dark skinned woman with a head-wrap as tall as the ones Erykah Badu wore adorned in silver bangles with a tear in one of her luminous brown eyes as she looked down at the world she held loosely in the palm of her elegant hand. Behind her on a throne sat a lighter skinned Black man with light encircling him. For some reason I studied the paintings without blinking until Smiley reached for my hand and led me to the auditorium.

A woman who looked like her name would be something like TeTula, wearing an orange pointy triangular Egyptian hat, with a crinkly neck like the mother off *Good Times*, who had a voice range that was out of this world stood on the stage. She dropped from soprano to alto so smoothly had I not have been there to witness it myself I would have thought there were two other people on the platform with her singing the Negroe spiritual. When she finished they introduced the guest speaker-- some petite, fragile-looking lady with a head wrap so high it looked like a rectangle reaching for the sky perched on top of her head. Sister Shahrya.

Apparently she was a big shot around here. Everyone stood up and clapped until she finally broke her tight smile and began speaking. "Brothers and Sisters, I am so glad to be here tonight. You all look beautiful! Just beautiful! I'm seeing mothers and fathers holding hands. Beautiful brown babies, young men and women...my, my, my! My people are some beautiful people! Forget all that negative stuff they try to say about us darker people--we are beautiful y'all!" Everyone clapped like clapping was about to go out of style but I didn't see the big deal. I started thinking of ways I could possibly get my truck back. If I agreed to move back in with Darren, couldn't I move right back out and roll with my ride? No, what was I thinking--that wouldn't work. He'd *really* be pissed with me then and definitely take it back and who knows what else.

Next possible plan...hmm...the more I put him off and ignored him it seemed like the harder he tried to get back together. It was just like that after I had Pharaoh. He wasn't doing anything but the same stuff all over again... If I completely ignored him, I could get that damn Lex back--

God, I looked good in my truck! It rode so smooth…and that tan leather interior was soo soft…the waxed crème paint…the gold customized cursive letters: L-e-x-u-s…that brand new luxury vehicle smell…

Yep, thata be how I'd get my shit back. Plus, I still had clothes at Darren's house and I wanted all of my outfits and Pharaoh's clothes were gonna be too small soon--might as well get all his clothes, too--he could at least wear them before he outgrew them. Those baby Diesel jeans were the cutest and he had at least six pair at Darren's. Hm! This plan *could* just work. Go over there lookin' real sexy, play hard to get, make him think I was considering moving back in…and leave his ass—with my Lexus.

Just as Adina's "T-Shirt & Panties" started playing in my head, this Sister Somebody's words caught me off guard. "…and that is why Black women are out here struggling in the system after the man—or should I say, *boy*--they think they're so in love with leaves them. They are crying and hurt when they know he didn't treat them right in the first place! And why? Lack of love for self—a vicious cycle! Sisters, how many of y'all just knew the dude y'all met wasn't gon' act right the first time y'all laid eyes on 'im but ya' kept talkin' to him anyway? Talkin' 'bout he look *good*." She put her finger in her mouth and made a face that made her nose crinkle. "I know I met 'em at da club an' he got dem otha three girlz'z numba's but—he look *goooooooooood* an' he had on sum Armoni!" The crowd roared in laughter. "Don't laugh, 'cause it ain't funny. Some of y'all still gon' do it again come Saturday night up at—at—what's the name of that club we passed downtown?" A couple of people called out names of a few clubs. "Club *Networks*! Thank you. *Um-hmmh*! See I know you be up in there!" She continued to talk but I couldn't hear anything past the words she'd just uttered that had latched on to me and wouldn't let go.

When I first met Darren there was something him--about his aura that I hadn't liked off rip.

With Craig, my first thought was *he looks like a player, don't pay him any attention just get the paper and go to class…*

I listened on. "So now you are all depressed, thinking no brotha will ever really love you. A young beautiful Black woman ready to give up on herself and the whole race of Black men." She began talking faster, "You're tired of feeling like everybody else has it better than you do and now…" Abruptly her words turned into a whisper, "You're thinking of ways to end it all. You're ready to die." She gave a long, dramatic pause. *"Am I speaking to somebody out there*! Some of y'all may have only come here a few times, for some of y'all this may be your first time, but I'm here today—sorry brothas, y'all gon' get y'all chance soon—*today*, Mother and Father told me to come here and speak to these sistas! But look brothas! I need y'all to stay seated. I need y'all here because the current situation of our young, Black women is directly linked to you and your futures and the futures of your sons and daughters.

"Sistas, when you live with a soul filled and violated with low self esteem, when you accept all the negativity the world tries to shoot your way, you kill that beautiful Black Spirit. That beautiful Black soul? It dies. You become a walking carcass! Oh yeah, I know it's hard. It's hard to always be on guard, to be strong. To keep that self esteem high..."

Had Smiley told this lady my business? "How do you know her?" I whispered in his ear as he shifted Mauri, who was comfortably sleeping in his arms, onto his left leg.

"I don't—not personally. She's from Atlanta. She's active in the neo-movement in Georgia."

"Oh."

For the next hour she broke down the issues Black women in America face and hit too close to home. At the end of her sermon or speech—whatever they called it around here—she admonished every woman to stand up and repeat this thing about praying, loving oneself and healing from old garbage. Then she mentioned her website and asked us to visit it for meditations, healing prayers and positive mantras.

The event turned out to be a lot better than I'd imagined. When it ended I still had so many questions, though. Her sermon felt like spiritual medicine sent specifically for my soul. I wanted to know more about this movement she was a part of and this whole Black Unity thing--Madonna Center--whatever it was.

"She won't have time to speak to you. She's a speaker, this is what she is paid to do--tell you shit to get you all excited so you'll purchase her book. She's a business lady, that's all. Save your bucks for something at that boutique at Somerset. She's rich enough. Don't give her your last ten, Dumb Ass!"

"No, I want that book," I countered not realizing I was talking out loud.

Smiley heard. "What? You dug Sister Shahyra's address, hunh? Let's go meet her. I'll get you a copy."

I stood in line so eager to meet her, I felt like an imbecilic idiot. When my time finally came I stumbled over the words and completely embarrassed myself by breaking into tears. "It's like you were speaking to me! I—I'm at that point in my life right now and—I-I-don't know—"

She interrupted my struggle with a real, real warm embracing hug. "You are going to be okay. You've got love in your heart. And you fought to come here today—that's what the Mother and the Father are telling me right now. But they love you. You're gonna be okay and you're gonna live a rich, fulfilling life. But you have *got* to start listening to the message the

Makers give you--not negativity." She was a tiny woman but her words and her voice would make you think she was a six foot, plus sized sista. "Email me and let me know your thoughts on my book," she said after signing a page and handing me her card.

After the crying saga ended, I stood near the wall with the mural waiting for Smiley to finish conversing with Gabe.

"*Ohhh*-my-goodness! It looks like the universe *does* want us to reconnect!" I was getting tapped on the shoulders by the one and only: Dominique. Next to her stood the slender brown skinned, fro sporting mayor of Southfield looking like he was straight from a Black exploitation flick.

"Honey, *this* is one of the girls I was telling you about--one of my best friends--Leigh!"

I just couldn't get away from this girl. At least today I was looking good. "Hi. Nice to see you," I lied.

"Ooh my goodness! It's s*ooo* funny! Here I was hoping you would call so I could invite you to my church. And here you are! I'm s*oooo* excited. Was Sister Shahyra on point or what?"

"This is *your* church?" I was more than shocked.

"Yeah," she responded, then shouted—yes, *shouted*, "Hey, Smiley!" as he walked over.

"Whassup?" He hugged her and gave the mayor an old-school handshake.

"Mal-*liiik*," she crooned. "You never told me you knew my best friend. We go wa*aay* back!" She went on. "Leigh, he's like my little brother. Are you two dating?"

First of all, she could keep the lil' bro comment. I could have been like, *your husband looks more like your dad 'cause he's sho' past forty and pushin' fifty*! And why was she trying to be all up in *my* business? We were *not* best friends and we for damn sure weren't cordial associates. Not anymore.

I gave another one of my fake smiles and nudged Smiley in his side.

"We're good friends. I'm hoping to date her," he answered honestly.

"Uh-oh, Leigh." She raised her eyebrows, sucked in her cheeks and nudged me. "Call me. I'd love for you to stop by this weekend."

"Okay." I smiled, relieved to be parting from the likes of Mrs. Now We Gon' Do Right' Dom-A-Neeky.

Smiley came over to my place afterwards. This was the first time he had come inside. "I didn't know you knew Dominique. That's my homegirl."

"Hmmph. You sure you didn't hook up with her back in the day--*before* Mr. Attwater?"

"I neva *hooked up* wit ha. Why you asked me *that*?"

"*That* girl used to be *the biggest hoe*! She quit speaking to me 'cause of Pharaoh's dad! *That's* the one I told you about!"

"Oh, yeah...well...people change. She's cool and she's got her stuff together. Her husband be hooking me up with jobs. I don't wanna know all about her past... We all do stupid shit when we're young or don't know better."

I switched the subject as I lit a stick of incense and a candle on the coffee table. He took off his suit jacket and I changed into a tank top and loose legged sweat pants and we laid back on the couch and enjoyed chilling to a Bob Marley CD he'd brought in with him.

I found out a few more things about him. He grew up in New York. His family came here when he was fifteen, hence the accent that came and went. He went in depth about which songs on the album were his favorite and why.

After an hour or so he got up to leave. "I gotta get up early. Appointments. I'll hit you up tomorrow, Leigh." And just like that he was gone, not even an attempted kiss.

THE REST OF THE week was excellent. I finished reading Sister Shahyra's book and was working on a meditation for inner peace and healing. Every morning while the kids were sleeping I would get up, make tea infusions from herbs I got at the Eastern Market and visualize myself in an euphoric state of true happiness. I imagined being on a beach walking alone the shore letting the water touch my feet. Each time, I would eventually float towards a yellow and white sky. For some reason I was always wearing something white and fluttery that covered my body from head to toe and made me look like a woman from an old world country. I saw all my current worries with Craig float into an orange and red abyss and sink underneath the sand beneath me as I flew towards the sky. The people from Mt. Zion turned into ants and crept away becoming invisible.

When I told Smiley about it, he simply said, "Beautiful."

I KEPT THINKING ABOUT calling Dominique but every time I got ready to dial her number, I'd change my mind. *She* was the one who had acted nasty towards *me*. I had x-ed her out of my life a long time ago. Sherra and I both agreed that life without her was just fine.

"You can call her if *you wont to* but the bible says, a leopard *cannot* change its spots, *okay*?" After Sherra's comment I threw her number away along with the thought of reconnecting with her.

The next day Smiley called asking if I had contacted her yet. "She's waiting to hear from you. I think you need to talk ta ha. But, I'ma stay outta the business. Here's her number in case you need it--you know it's 'bouta be ha birthday." I went ahead and wrote it down but I wasn't about to call that heifer.

On Friday, I drove the kids to Dina's since Smiley was taking me to the movies and out to dinner—some place a buddy of his played the piano at.

I was actually real excited about it. I rushed back home to get dressed. When I jumped out of my car I thought about how Smiley was going to flash that cute smile of his and say, "That's whassup" when I told him I wanted to go to church with him on Sunday.

Before going to that Center place, I was certain after my Kevin/Calvin excursion my name had been etched on the inevitable list of the red ones who were fire bound head first. Much to my relief, there were no hour-long sermons on hell--only options to help one find his or her own spiritual plan and tons of open discussions that focused on the theory of humans being energy and matter and always a part of the universe once created. They were even having an open discussion on Sister Shahyra's speech. Now, I could deal with that even though Sister Shahyra wouldn't be there this Sunday. I could handle a church like this.

The humming and sinner-redemption thing was played. I was starting to see the traditional church as one of the problems within the Black community. Go on Sunday, blame the devil for behaving badly or either miss out on enjoying this life hopin' an' uh wishin' fa dem pearly gates. And—oh, yes, everyone—no matter how terrible they might be—*everyone* is going to heaven. There wasn't one time I'd gone to a funeral where the preacher didn't say the person in the casket was heaven-bound. "Gon' be lookin' down on us frum above"—even if the person had been a drug dealer or a murderer. Why many of us Black folks—no matter how much education we attained didn't seemed to have a problem with this ideology, I just couldn't understand.

I reached to turn the knob of the entrance door smiling and thinking about what Smiley'd say when I repeated my new, erudite philosophy but a hand pulled me back and grabbed my wrist tightly.

I stood as still as a statue, tense and unprepared for what might come next. At least the kids weren't here to see their mother get blown to ashes or kidnapped.

Whatever happens just let it go fast. Please.

"We need ta talk." Rather than show fear, I turned around to face Darren. The way his trench coat hung over his shoulders like a cape and, with that lethally serious expression on his face, I wanted to laugh. For some reason he reminded me of Dark Wing Duck. "Leigh. I've done a lot of thinking lately and... I know you love me... I never intended to give my heart completely to anyone. I made that promise to myself years ago—way before I met you.

"But I love you and--and I can't imagine another night without you sleeping next to me. I'm ready to settle down. I need you. If you're willing to forgive me, I'm willing to get on my knees right now and give you this ring. I'm willing to change." He pulled out a ring with a round so huge I thought I'd lose my eyesight from the glare. "Please Leigh, will you marry me?"

"*WHAT*! Have you lost your mind? You—" I still hadn't forgotten about that 'you ain't have shit but a raggedy car when I met you' comment of his.

"—Nah. Your truck is waitin' in tha front." He raised his eyebrows and looked back at the Escort I'd just popped out of. "...I'm serious...on our first date, you wore a pink and white top with Black cartoon chicks on the front. You kept kicking my foot 'cause you thought it was part of the table... You hadn't even had liquor before.

"And you turned me on like—like--I 'on't know. Like no other female ever had. You know when you *really* impressed me?" I was too out done to respond. "When I tried to get you to give me some head and you grabbed me and slid me on top of you instead. Mad game. I was on top of females tryin' ta get me caught up. Why you think Pharaoh's the only one I've got out here?"

"...I remember it differently. I remember how you didn't even *open the door for me* after you drove me back to my car..."

He shook his head in disagreement. "It wasn't even like that. You did something to me--I didn't know how to deal with it. I ain't wanna be all on somebody like that.

"What I *wanted* was for you to spend the night with me, I wanted you to wake up next to me... You know, you've always been different. Most females? They hound me and shit—hell, I had my share of stalkers-- money does something to females. But you weren't phased. You didn't try ta get shit out of me—not even while you were pregnant.

"When Pharaoh was born I had a lodda shit going on. TaLia was always mad at me over stupid shit, moving out and moving back in. My dad was in the hospital sick. Work was crazy 'cause we had to fire a coupla salespeople...I had uh lot goin' on. But you didn't bring uh whole lodda drama ta me. That made me love you uh whole lot more, Leigh. I was fa real when I asked you ta marry me that day we went to look at houses but...I had ta play it off, just in case it wasn't what you was tryin' ta do…but, Leigh, I'm not on the games anymore. I need ta know, will you marry me?"

I thought back to my wish. A good, emotionally mature man who would be faithful, a man that wouldn't put me thru unnecessary drama.

…If you let something go and it came back to you, didn't that mean it was yours to keep?

Was this it? Was this my chance, my shot at true happiness?

I had been thru a lot with Darren and, no, he wasn't perfect. But he *was* my child's father. I had known him way longer than I'd known Smiley. For all I knew, Smiley was running game--twenty times out of ten he was running game. I was thinking that from day one after we started kicking it… Besides we were just cool anyway.

I looked in Darren's eyes and searched for truth. "I'm serious, Leigh." He got down on the ground, on both knees between his truck and a tenant's clunky white topped burnt-orange, old school Thunderbird with the headlight falling out of its socket.

"Da*aaarrre*n! What about—what about Danielle and Barbie and all the other females on your list? How am I supposed to know the next time we go on a trip that you won't be off somewhere double timing with another female or—or if you say you're going to the office—how am I supposed to know whether or not you're lying? And what about the Mauri issue? You don't—"

"--Well. She *is* your child. I'm gonna have to learn to love her the way I love Pharaoh. I love you, Leigh." He held out the ring, still waiting for me to give him the go ahead before he slid it on my finger. "No prenup, nothing. I'm giving you my heart—everything I have is yours, Leigh."

"N-ao, no—ah—yeah?...Yes? Yes!"

He picked me up and flung me into his arms. A tear fell down his face accompanying his sly smile. I felt it on his cheek when he kissed me on my nose. He still had that weird infatuation with my nose. "Let's celebrate," Darren said following me into the apartment. After I changed clothes I called Dina and asked her to keep the kids the rest of the night.

We went to a restaurant at the top of the Renaissance. After that we went to his parents place, then to Mike's and Syra's to tell them the news before we headed back to his house.

That night we made love in so many positions, I was sure we'd set a record two gymnasts couldn't break.

"Leigh, baby?" He laid on top of me, held my face and looked directly in my eyes. I love you. I'ma always love you."

I WOKE UP EXPECTING to be waking up out of a dream but the moonlit silhouette snoring rather loudly next to me with his strong arm still wrapped around my waist let me know it was real...all of it was real.

CHAPTER 19

"DID YOU CONTACT RICK yet and tell him you're gonna be quittin'?" Darren asked as I flipped thru bridal magazines. He was doing much better at asking rather than demanding these days.

"No...no, but I will...I can't decide on what kind of dress I want. I wanted something with sleeves but then I saw this *sharp* fitted, sleeveless dress—hold on. Lemme find it so I can show it to you...but I kinda had my mind set on something poufy at the bottom with lots of tulle... Oooh! *Babe*, look at this one--it's gorgeous!" There were so many styles to choose from, I'd have to go into the boutique to try them all on before I could even think about narrowing my choices down.

"Yeah, Vera Wang? That's hot. You've got the body for that one right there. I'm glad you finally quit insisting on having Sherra's mother make your dress. This is our wedding, baby, not some mammy made sew off. You'll see what I'm talking about once we get the pictures back."

Yeah, that had been a major argument between us. "...How come you haven't called Rick yet?" he asked as he debated over which salad dressing he wanted out of the three I left out on the counter next to the chicken salad I fixed for lunch.

"...I don't know, babe. Don't worry, I'll call." Truth was, as bad as it sounded, I wasn't ready to let go of my apartment just yet. So much had happened backup was a necessity nowadays. Track records were starting to make me think, when it came to a relationship with a man, everything goes good until he realizes the woman really does love him. After that, once the hunt is over and he's got the prey is in his hands, it's a wrap. He's not gonna ever act right again.

"Oh, yeah, another thing--before I forget, I wanna get some new furniture in here...this Old English, corporate office scheme you've got going on is driving me crazy. Feels like I'm in an office environment instead of at home."

"Aright, aright, baby, do it, then. Why don't you check out some stuff from a coupla magazines and show me my choices. Sy did that for Mike's crib. Why don't you take her with you? She's up on all that." He came up to the tall chair I was sitting in with my elbows leaning on the island's countertop and untied my red satin robe for a quickie before leaving for the dealership.

Within seconds that long brown friend of his was causing a much-welcomed commotion within my body. Afterwards, he sensually pulled on my lips with his and handed me all my credit cards back. "You sure you haven't dabbled in no plastic surgery? Yo' titties look like two big ass, brown mountain tops," he chuckled touching my braless chest. His eyes were glued to them as they responded with a few bounces to his touch.

"Nope. All natural, baby."

"Damn, girl." He gave me another kiss. "I'll be back by five. Love you."

"Love you, too." I waved to the side door. My eyes were now stuck on a pearly, off white satin sleeveless number.

Four days into April and life was now finally worry and stress free.

"MMMmmom! I'm up!" Pharaoh yelled rushing into my legs and hugging them.

I picked him up, "Gimme a kiss." He puckered his lips like an old man, "Ugh. Don't give mommy a sloppy, wet one," I joked. His little handsome face held my nose and eyes but otherwise he was the splitting image of his father right down to his golden brown tone--he even had Darren's slender physique and was already quite muscular for a three year old. Pharoah was definitely going to be athletic like Darren.

Darren played tennis, was on a baseball team he and his buddies started and he'd been on the soccer team in high school and in college. I'd never even known a Black American who was into *soccer* until Darren. And he was fanatical about winning; winning meant everything. Sometimes—like when he lost—he scared me. But it was that same competitive drive that made him successful at work and made those six figures.

We played, just Pharaoh and I, for a while before Dina showed up, happy to be back in elite babysitter status. I got dressed and left to do a little window shopping for wedding ideas.

The ceremony was going to be held at Reviving Spirit on Grand River since Darren's parents were members while our reception was to be held at Cobo Hall. Five hundred guests—tons of A-listers that hung in Darren's circle were expected to show. Someone had contacted him and made plans for our picture to be in *Ebony*. I was especially excited about that.

I went to the apartment, took care of business, threw the four letters Malik sent in the trash, erased his messages off the voicemail along with Craig's and left.

I went to Detroit Community ready to finally register for spring classes but ended up taking the class schedule with me. I was going to have to wait the semester out and do late summer classes in July since the wedding was in June and I needed three weeks off since Darren'd booked our honeymoon for two weeks in the Bahamas.

Sherra met up with me in Rochester Hills after she got off work so we could go to the bridal shop to look at dresses. "Leigh? All this time and you *still* don't know what color scheme you gon' go with? Picking a dress is easy. What you *need* ta do is decide on yo' wedding colors," Sherra advised.

Finally we came up with silver and black. The bridesmaids would wear silver, Darren and his boys would wear black and the decorations were going to be clear and silver.

We went to a place on Ten Mile and Van Dyke to look at decorations and gushed over millions of fancy options just for fun--I didn't have to worry about decorating. Darren had someone taking care of centerpieces already and all the other minute details.

Then we drove to Oakland mall to eat at Olga's--our spot back in the day and caught up on each other's lives.

"Leigh? Dat *is* dat bitch! Leigh! I been lookin' fa yo' ass evrywhere! Baby, it's almost ma birthday an' I still ain't heard shit from you. You doin' me dirty!" Craig was now making his way from Sam Goody's near the entrance of the mall to our booth, which was out in the open and near the atrium of the mall. There was a brown-skinned girl and a little boy with him. The chick slowed down with the kid, turned around and went into Sam Goody's while he slid in the booth next to me and stared at Sherra. "I need ta talk ta her foe uh second," he stated like he was God.

Sherra just sat there looking at me.

"Whatever you need to say, you can say it right now--nobody's leaving." I continued drinking my vanilla milkshake. I eyed his arm as it tainted my shoulder until he got the hint and rested his arm on top of the booth instead.

He finally realized I wasn't about to bow down to his command and make Sherra move. "You know why I'm here? 'Cause I been at cho' place foe uh hour—even dough I could git put up in jail fa dat shit since you gon' go git uh PPO out on'me! I been *waitin'* on yo' ass ta pop up. Been lookin' fa you fa da las week. Wudden'ta even found yo' ass if I wuddn't out here lookin' fa somin ta git Mauri!

"You know it's 'bout ta be ma birthday! And you *know* yo' *Black ass* ain't right! ...But look! Take uh look at dis!" He slammed the thin sheet of pink paper on the table. "I ain't da father uh dat bitch's baby, Leigh..." he sounded like he was on stage on a Mauri Povich show.

"Well--*good* for you. But I'm sure *there are* quite a few other women our there walkin' around with *Walkers* besides *me*. You know what? On the ninth, instead of having a birthday party, you should make it

'Meet Cho' Daddy Day'!" I cracked up. "Now *that*, would be funny--but don't invite Angela. Ungh-uh. She's *so ugly*, she'll make all the kids cry."

"You on some serious ass bullshit!"

"...Security! Security?" I joked scanning the mall for an officer. With that Craig shuffled his sorry ass away.

"Fuck yo' ass, den. You 'on't know da true meanin' uh love no how!" He hissed the words and walked away in a stride that made it look as though his shoulders were swaying side to side.

"Security!" I joked—last one for the road.

"I'm glad he left. I thought I was gon' have ta pull out my pepper spray!" Sherra shook her head and took her hand out of her purse. "My *goodness*! *That* was *crazy*!"

"And *he* looks *crazy*! Did you look at his eyes?"

"Looked like a mad dog wit a evil spirit possessing 'im!"

"*Okay*!" We both shook our heads to that. "Nah, that's my baby's daddy and I used to love him but *be* with *him* again? Ungh-uh! NEVER!" I'd done a good job of hiding my fear. They always said dogs could smell it. Thank goodness he walked away without trying to pull another stunt.

We did manage to plan a few things for the ceremony before I headed back home. Sherra had given me a book on wedding planning but since Darren had gotten a coordinator I didn't really need it—this whole wedding thing wasn't stressful at all.

I was very, very, very, very, very, *verrry* excited.

Sherra was going to be the maid of honor and I'd be a married woman by the end of June. We would have done it in May but then our anniversary would have collided with Pharaoh's birthday.

LATER THAT WEEK, I went back to my place to meet with maintenance about the furnace. Tenants had been complaining about the sweltering temperatures of their apartments and since many of the windows were either swollen or painted shut, they were upset about their electricity bills being high from using fans around the clock. Even my place felt like a sauna.

While I was waiting for maintenance to arrive, Lavonne from #8 who was moving out stopped by to drop off her keys. "*Girl, some guy* keep stoppin' by here ta see *you*. He askin' evrybody questions 'bout chu," she informed me as she filled out her paperwork with the forwarding address. I automatically assumed it was one of Craig's boys coming over to try to talk to me for him since I had a PPO on his ass. "Naw, girl. It was dis real cute, tall ass muthafuka. I ain't know who he was so I ain't say shit. But Craig be by here all da time, too. Dey probly gon' run inta each otha *sometime soon*..." The way she was licking the pages of the paperwork was disgusting me. Couldn't she just flip thru the pages without going thru all of that? And those red and purple designs and dangling fake gold trinkets on the whites of her french manicured acrylic nails--some people just didn't know when to stop.

"Thanks, Lavonne." I pursed my lips so I wouldn't say the wrong thing or mention anything about Craig. She was a gossip if I ever knew one.

Of course, maintenance also had to remind me that Smiley had been snooping around looking for me. I needed to call him and give him that car back. I wouldn't feel right about taking it to the junkyard. That was how you reaped some bad karma. He could take it back to the auction and sell it. Who would buy it? I did not have an answer for that question but at least it would be off my hands.

I rushed out, taking as many things in suitcases and garment bags as I could. It was now time to let this place go. It had starting bearing nothing but bad memories a long time ago anyway.

I was more paranoid than a weedhead getting in the truck. I expected Malik to pop up out of the bushes any minute like a ninja.

I was relieved once I got on 696 and headed home. He was the last person I needed to see. I was going to mail him the keys and tell him to pick that ragamuffin of a car up--better yet there was no time like the present. I drove to the post office, slid the keys off my chain, took the insurance papers out of my wallet and mailed everything to him without a return address or a note. He was smart—he'd get the hint.

"DAMN, GIRL," DARREN PATTED me on my butt. "It's getting' fatter. You gon' have ta start jogging with me again. Do that dress right June fifteenth."

"You know I like to eat, baby."

"Thick now, fat later—and I 'on't like fat...I got a surprise for you. Elaina's fixing dinner so you don't have to cook. Dina's got the kids. It's just us. Why 'ont we enjoy a candlelight dinner? We're gonna check out a movie afterwards. I didn't get the tickets yet since you're always hollerin' about me always trying to make all the decisions and shit. It's up to you—whatever you wanna see. See? I'm learning, baby." He leaned towards me and planted a kiss on my lips.

"And I'm proud of you."

We sat in the dining room and enjoyed a spring green salad with freshly made lemon and olive oil dressing, wild rice, wild mushrooms and lobster. It was good but I know I could have hooked up it a lot better—the portions were extra small and not seasoned well. Still, we enjoyed dinner in true five-star ambiance with Floetry softly playing in the background.

He reached for my hand and stared at me for a while without speaking. "...I wanna make you as happy as you make me, Leigh."

After dinner I showered and threw on a fitted pair of jeans, a white tee shirt with "Pretty" stitched in pink across the front I'd gotten from a boutique in Birmingham and a pair of black gator $2,500 ankle boots Darren had gotten me last Christmas.

"Mike and Sy are hangin' with us so I thought we'd meet up with 'em in Southfield City," he stated as I climbed in his truck. "*Damn*, girl. You even look good in jeans!"

I was smiling--like always these days. "Cool. I haven't seen Syra in a minute. I need to fill her in on all the details. I wonder how she's going to feel about wearing silver?"

"That's female shit. All me and Mike plan on doing is showing up, the rest is up to you." He chuckled shaking his head. Darren and I cracked jokes on Mike and Sy the whole ride to the Star Theater. They were funny. Whether or not it was on purpose, Sy sure did live up to that blonde haired, blue-eyed stereotype.

"Oh-My-God! Leigh? *You* (extended emphasis and pause) are...*gettingfat!* (the words all run together here). We have got to pay Jenny Craig a visit, pronto, hon! Pronto! We can't have you *looking* like a *whale* on *your* wedding day! You need to cut back on salt—matterfact, just don't eat! Just do fruit juice. You have a juicer?" Sy exclaimed right after we walked in and spotted them.

"I've *only gained* ten pounds!" I gritted my teeth. Before, being in and out of the hospital, I was fifteen pounds heavier than what I was right now and I looked fine. I even missed having that slight jiggle to my behind.

She was just jealous. She'd been engaged to Mike for over two years and he still hadn't given her a date. My deal was sealed.

"*God.*" She rolled her eyes. I didn't mean it like that, but I'll workout with you! K?"

"Yeah, whatever..." She was already getting on my nerves. Maybe we could just have Darren's sisters and Sherra in the wedding. But it was just a wishful thought. Darren wasn't going to let me kick her out of the bridal party.

He and Mike stood in line laughing and exchanging what I was sure were fiancée stories. Sy kept talking and talking to me like I cared. Tonight she was really killing every nerve in my nervous system slowly but surely, one by one every time she opened her mouth.

As we walked to the theatre our movie was showing in, I heard someone call my name. I turned around and choked so hard on the lemonade Darren'd just handed me, some of it spewed out of my nose.

It was Smiley! Right there. Standing against the wall next to a framed 'Coming Soon' ad near a red bench far away on the opposite end of the atrium.

First my heart stopped. Completely.

Then, before it began palpitating ferociously--like I was being thrown off a cliff, my vision blurred and everything in sight turned into rolling somersaults that pitter-pattered at the end of every heartbeat.

I ignored him and walked in the theater.

"Who was that?" Darren asked frowning indignantly.

"Nobody--just a guy from my old church," I replied walking as normally as I could towards the row of seats all the way in the back at top of the theater where Mike was already sitting.

"Oh." He bought it, his face calmed down and it was business as usual when the movie trailers started.

But I couldn't concentrate. Who was that bitch he was with? Sure, she was tall and pretty... no...ugh. On second thought, she wasn't all *that* cute. She was a few shades lighter than me and much, much chunkier with black-framed glasses pushed all the way up on the bridge of her nose like she was trying to make them blend in with her eyebrows or something. I had a ceramic piggy bank once that looked like her—with circular white glasses perched at the top of it's nose.

Whatever. We'd never even kissed on the lips. He was a free agent. He could do whatever the hell he wanted. All I could do was hope she made him happy.

Then I had to use it. I had to go so bad, the cooch started getting hotter by the minute. I sat there squeezing my legs so tight I thought I was about to fly away but I just couldn't bring myself to go out there.

Thirty minutes later the choice came down to two things. Go on myself or go to the restroom. I asked and practically begged Sy to come along but she was too caught up in the movie or either too scared to leave Mike's side for a minute.

I made it to the restroom just in time to *not* have a self-induced water accident. The way I was checking around the corner of the restroom entrance before I left out to make sure the coast was clear enough to walk back to the theater without running into him, it looked like I was doing a *007* scene.

Mailing those keys was the best thing I'd done all day.

While the three musketeers chatted on incessantly about their favorite parts of the movie afterwards, I was thinking about how Smiley and I met. It was weird—the way he just popped into my life.

All this running into a nigga stuff made me want to move out of the country. Right about now, Canada'd be a real good option.

We split the foursome into a twosome and walked to Darren's truck. My heart fluttered again! He was parked next to a burgundy Yukon—of all the muthafuckin' vehicles in Southfield! ZKZ 005, yep, that was his license plate.

"Darren? Can we hurry up and get home? I'm tired." No one was in Smiley's truck but what if the movie he'd gone to was about to end? And Darren was taking forever to pull off! Mike had just called him on his cell. Damn! Hadn't they spent enough time talking already? He sat there going on and on like he and Mike were having a meeting. I couldn't take it. "Baby, you two are acting like girls! Can we like seriously go home? I want to get in the pool for a second before we go to bed." I tried to conceal my annoyance. Finally he pulled off.

When we got back, I put on a swimming suit and met Darren at the pool. He wanted to teach me how to do a basic stroke but it was no use. Instead, he tried to teach me how to float on my back. I thought I was really doing something once I made it from one end of the pool to the other. He got a few good laughs off me before he started showing off doing the Butterfly and a whole bunch of other fancy strokes I wasn't worried about learning. A sista was *not* about to get the weave wet, okay!

"Come on, babe. If you learn how to swim, we can skip the morning jog. We'll do laps instead."

"You're serious. No more jogging?"

"Yep. And wear this swimming suit again—*please*. Nah *that's* some sexy ass shit." He popped the g-string. Same thing Mr. Kevy/ Kev had said about this lil' number...um hm...

"Bet. I'll meet you here six sharp." I'd have to invest in a good swimming cap real soon.

"...Baby? Since when you start saying, '*bet*'?"

"I don't know. I've always said that, haven't I?"

"Since *when*? ...It sounds weird."

"Shut-up!"

"Well! I'm just saying!" he yelled chasing me up the stairs. We met in the Jacuzzi of the master bathroom in our bedroom. He picked me up and pretended to throw me into the water before he slid in pulling me on top of him.

THE NEXT MORNING I called and gave Rick my two-week notice. He wasn't angry at all. He said something about knowing it was coming and hoping to get an invitation to the wedding. It felt like five elephants had just been lifted off my neck after I got off the phone with him.

Mona, the wedding coordinator, came over to discuss our color scheme and to make sure I'd made the appointment with the boutique for my dress. We'd already found a bakery for our cake—Darren's mother recommended the place and it was going to be absolutely gorgeous. It was a pearly, silk material-looking vanilla/lemon cake with actual edible pearls set into the filigree of the icing. Since Cobo was handling the food, we were pretty much set. Darren and the fellas had already taken care of their tuxes.

Getting the bridesmaids together? Now that was another story. Sy claimed she didn't want to be fitted yet since she was still losing weight--where the weight was that needed to be shedded, nobody on earth would ever know. Then there was the issue of Darren's two sisters. Christina and Samantha. Two very, very, *very* uncooperative little blank blank's. Whenever I tried to tell Darren to talk to them, they'd fake like they were going for their scheduled fittings, then, the next day after each appointment, it never failed, the seamstress would call and notify me that they had missed yet another slot she'd blocked out for them. She was annoyed and I was ready to kill 'em!

Had it not been for Darren's desire to do the big whooptie-do wedding thing, I would have said sayonara, left the circus behind, gone on a cruise and gotten married on the ship.

After Mona left, I met Sy at the gym to begin my session with the personal trainer she supposedly set up. I knew Darren was the mastermind behind the idea when the buff ass female drill sergeant came out. He wasn't about to let me workout with some sexy masculine piece of work--which was quite all right with me. He did take care of his body and had muscles going on in all the right places. Just thinking about it made me wet...

After an hour of feeling like my body was on fire, getting yelled at and having to deal with spit jumping out of the workout sergeant's mouth onto my cheeks and her terrible lisp that made "sit-ups" sound like "thit-upths," the persecution ended.

"If you keep at it, it'll be fun in no time!" Sy chirped.

"Sy? If you don't wanna lose your two front teeth, shut tha hell up! K?" I gave her a mock smile.

"*Leeeigh*! You are so*oo* mean... God, I was only trying to *heelllp*!" She tried to peep her head in my shower.

"You got one more time," I warned sliding the shower curtain shut.

When I got in my truck, I was so drained and sore, I reclined the seat all the way back and just listened to jazz on 107.5. Once I got home, I meditated--it had been a minute and I needed to clear my head. I only had

347

thirty minutes before I had to pick up the kids. After that, 'Me Time' would be officially over.

I put some organic honey in my mug of Black Eye Susan tealeaves, lit a few sage sticks—which Darren hated—and sat next to the pool on top of my yoga mat. Closing my eyes I imagined positive energy surrounding me just like Sister Shahyra recommended in her book. I sat imagining my wedding going smoothly but each time I tried, I'd start thinking about something else--like why old people liked gardening or who invented high heeled shoes then I'd start wondering how Smiley met that chick he had taken to the movies and why he had acted like he was all into to me if he was getting mucho pussy-o already. That explained why he hadn't tried to get any. Whenever a man tried to sell you on that 'I just want to get to know you' shit, it always meant: *I got other pussy on lock so if I don't get it from you, I'm still good*!

Just thinking about it pissed me off.

"Call Dominique." There was that voice again. Now why, of all people, would I call *Dominique*? She was friends with that Smiley muthafucka—not me!

I gazed at the water. That usually always calmed my nerves. I began my repeating, "I am happy. I am loved. I—"

AND BACK TO A SCREETCHING *HALT!*

There was Smiley's face again surrounded by a halo of beaming violet and white light, head tilted against the back of the couch, in his own world with his eyes closed as he listened to Marley.

"Okay. Spirit and Etheric body, what are you trying to tell me? Talk to me. I am listening and ready to receive." I'd learned about charkas, auras, the spiritual body and how to ask the Creators and the angels for help from reading Sister Shahyra's book and looking up info on the net. The way she explained spiritual plane interactions was easier to understand than Luna's 'lets all hold hands and feel the wind' crazy methodology.

"Baby? What *tha hell* are you doin'?" I saw Smiley's face for a second but it was Darren in real life peering in the glass doorway with a look of utter confusion contorting his face.

"Babe. Come here. Sit down. Look at this." I placed the book on his lap.

"...Leigh, that's that metaphysical crap. Throw that shit out—if you'd like. That's the problem right there. How long have you been inta *that* shit?"

"It's not like what you think. Here. Try it. Close your eyes. Now. Imagine—" he snatched his hand away. "Baby. I don't have time for this shit. If I wanna relax, I swim or pick up an educational book, go to a movie--*normal* recreational activities. And you don't have time for da voodoo either!

"I heard you still haven't decided on the entrée for the reception. Now *that's* what you need to be thinking 'bout. Come on." He helped me up. "Let's go get the kids. I'm not gonna tell you to throw that shit out but…well…it's up to you. Just don't be doing that around the kids. They might tell people you talk to yourself or something."

"If I can't talk to myself, then who can I talk to?" I gave him a kooky smile and messed with him. When we got in his truck I started singing that song, "*I talk to myself 'cause there is no one to talk to, people ask me why, why I do what I dooo.*"

"Leigh? CUT THAT SHIT OUT!" That was the third time I'd ever *really* heard him yell. I was freaking him out.

"Baby, I'm just playing with you. I didn't think *you* got scared-- now *that's* funny. But I'm keeping the book. I like it. It's not what you think."

He gave me a weird side glance and turned the radio up.

When we got off 94 there was a major accident delaying traffic on Chalmers. A white van had been rammed into a tree in the middle of the grassy island that divided the street's north and south directions. A few feet away a burgundy Yukon was turned over stuck in between the island of grass and part of the street.

A news anchor stood in front of the Yukon while channel 7 and channel 4's cameramen covered the story. EMS workers rushed about like a swarm of bees sliding a body onto a gurney. Large pools of bright red blood stained the lane closest to the island of grass like spilled red paint. Old men in overalls with pipes hanging out of their mouths and mothers with babies on their hips stood on their porches, people got out of cars to get a closer look--it was terrible.

"OH MY GOD! SMILEY! SMILEY!" I opened my door. "Darren! Turn! I've got to go over there! I've got—"

"--Hell naw. *You* need to calm *down*. Look at all that glass. I'm not about to roll my tires thru that shit!"

"I've got to go over there! I've got to!" I opened my door, jumped out and zoomed over to an EMS worker. "SIR! EXCUSE ME--*SIR*! WHAT'S THE NAME? WHAT IS THE NAME!"

"Ma'am. You're gonna have to step back." I couldn't move. "Please, ma'am!"

"Okay, okay! But just tell me, is the guy's name Malik? Is one the drivers involved named Malik Smiley? Was one of the passengers last name Smiley? SAY SOMETHING, PLEASE!" I begged. I was a second away from shaking the EMS guy by the stiff collar of his blue uniform.

"No! The Yukon is a lady. The guy from the van was a man. I don't think I heard them say Smile or Malcolm."

"Is one of the drivers named *Malik*?"

"Ma'am? You're in the way." He closed the doors. I watched as they sped off. I had to try to get in touch with Smiley. What if it *was* him?

Darren stayed on the service drive pulling up as close to Chalmers as he was going to get still complaining about rolling in glass. "I thought it was my cousin. He drives a van. I'm sorry. I had to make sure," I explained buckling my seat belt once I got back into the truck.

"...You okay?"

"Yeah...NO! They didn't really say whether or not it was him! I miss—I miss my family."

"I know...soon we're gonna have our own family..."

"Yeah? I really love you, Darren... When you see something like that it makes you think, doesn't it?"

"...Yeah...I love you, too. Turn the news on—950—on AM. See if they mention a name."

I did. But that wasn't good enough. I wanted to *follow* that EMS truck. This was torture. Especially after what happened to Shawn...

THE MINUTE I GOT home I shot into the den, turned on the news and waited for a name praying and hoping it wasn't Malik Smiley. It was weird how I'd bumped into him yesterday and then kept seeing him today in those foggy dreams when I was trying to meditate...premonitions!

Coverage on the story was taking too damn long! If that bitch or girlfriend of his had been driving and hurt that man, I was going to find her ass and make sure she felt some form of vengeful wrath.

A half an hour passed before they stated any details on the accident. It didn't sound like Smiley'd been in it but I needed to call him to be sure. I slipped out of the room and went into the basement brushing past the bar and the guest bedroom and locked the bathroom door to call him. "Smiley? Are you okay? I've been feeling weird all day...and then I saw this accident. It's all over the news. When you get a chance, call me and let me know if—if you're okay--even if you you're not okay, just call me—if you can--*please*. This is Leigh--this is my new number." I sat on the top of the toilet seat praying over and over that he was all right. Waiting was like being strangled for hours. Pharaoh was calling my name and searching for me. Mauri was crying. I deleted the number and turned my phone off knowing how Darren would sometimes take it upon himself to answer my phone and look thru my calls.

After helping Mauri find her stuffed Sponge Bob, I went back to the bathroom in the basement, turned my phone back on and checked the new messages. Still no Smiley. I had to call him again. I had to. "Oh my God! You answered! You had me worried *ta death*! I saw this accident and—and I thought—'cause it looked like your truck--and I panicked and I just--I wanted to know, to make sure you were okay! Are you okay? *Please* tell me you're alright 'cause--"

"—LEIGH? Baby, calm down. I'm fine, I'm fine! I'm on my way home. Yeah, I heard about that accident. But *you* the one that had *me* worried. I been calling you. Where are you? Can I come over? I saw you yesterday and I—"

"—Smiley, I've godda go. I can't talk right now. But I'm glad you're okay." I could barely breathe. I would have gone crazy if I wouldn't have heard his voice.

"LEIGH? LEIGH! WAIT! *DON'T* HANG UP!"

But I had to. I couldn't talk to him. My question had been answered, he was okay. That was all that mattered.

A QUARTER PAST FOUR I got up to use the bathroom and on instinct grabbed my phone, turned it on and checked the voicemail. There were three new messages:

10:01PM
1. Hey Leigh, it's me... I don't know *whas up* wit chu... I saw you holding *some* dude's hand yesterday. I hope that's not one of ya' kids fathers...not 'cause I'm jealous but—well I'm lying. I *was* jealous--I love you--you know that. But I hope you not wit one of them muthafuckas fa ya' own sanity... Why 'on't you call me, Leigh? Much love. Peace.

10:29PM
2. Something's wrong, Leigh. I 'on't know what's up but, my inner spirit ain't lettin' me rest. I godda talk ta you... Call me.

1:46AM
3. Leigh, look. I 'on't want anotha man's wife. But I want you. Are you married now or sumthen? What's tha deal? We godda talk, fa real. I 'on't think tha universe would bring you inta my life justa tear you away like this... I'm up. Call me. I 'on't even know if you're aright--c'mon, nah. You could at least pick up ya' phone...

I listened to the messages over and over before finally erasing them.

Then I couldn't go back to sleep, I couldn't focus long enough to meditate and I couldn't stop thinking about Smiley. I didn't know what to do. All I knew was that I wasn't about to fuck my life up. I shouldn't have called him.

I got back in the bed and slid close to Darren. He was handsome. And he was beginning to learn how to give and receive love—he was finally what I had always wanted him to be. Maybe the reason everything happened the way it did was to make me appreciate him more, to make me appreciate my life and everything I'd been given. There was definitely a reason he'd been the one to find me that day and there had to be a reason I met him almost four years ago at Hart Plaza. When we first met he hadn't been ready for me and, as naïve as I was back then, I definitely wasn't ready for him. But we were both ready for each other now. This was what God had in store for me but the devil always had a way of interrupting things.

Fuck this religious freedom shit. It wasn't working.

"Darren? Darren?"

"What! Did I oversleep?" He popped up.

"No. No, you've got another hour and a half... Baby?" I tapped him on the shoulder. "I need to ask you something. Can we go to church on Sunday?"

"Damn it, Leigh, I'm sleeping!" He pulled his pillow over his face.

I laid in the bed staring at the ceiling. *"Call Smiley! Do it! Call him now!"* I rushed back to the bathroom in the basement with my phone and locked the door behind me dialing the digits so fast I called the wrong number twice. His number wasn't in my phonebook.

"LEIGH?" He answered before the phone completed the first ring.

"It's like four-thirty in the morning! What are you doing up?" I whispered.

"I told you—well—if you listened to my messages. I'm guessing you did? I can't go to sleep. I was sitting here praying on us. Praying for an answer and I *swear* I *just* asked, 'If she's really fa me, make her call. Like today, man! Sooner than uh muthafucka!' I can't function like this! Can we meet up? We godda talk."

"...I can't..." I could hear him still breathing on the other end but other than that, the phone went dead. As much as I wanted to, I couldn't bring myself to hang up on him. ".........It'll have to be at ten," I finally whispered.

"At night?"

"No. In the morning--I can't meet any other time."

"Bet. Where?"

"I don't—I don't know—"

"---My place. I'ma cancel my morning appointments. Leigh, don't forget."

"I Promise."

"Fa sho." We both hung up.

I WAS SO ANTSY I drove Darren absolutely bonkers during my first swimming lesson. My nerves were tying into knots and twirling about in a wild frenzy. He tried to hide his irritation, "Baby, go back to bed. We'll start over tomorrow, okay?" he kissed me on the forehead.

"Sorry."

"You don't have ta apologize. But you might wanna lay off the coffee today. You're acting weird. Did you find out if it was your cousin or not?"

"Yeah...it wasn't."

"Aright. I'll call you later. I think Samantha went to get fitted. She left a message."

"Good."

WHEN DINA FINALLY CAME over at nine-fifteen, I practically leaped over her and jumped in my truck. My weave was pulled back into a ponytail. I had on a navy, silver and white BeBe sweat suit with a sports bra underneath it ready to meet with Smiley before I hit the gym for my twelve o'clock workout.

I had to stop getting myself caught up! I needed to go back to being faithful and Godly like I used to be. Craig—Trash started this. He was the one that made me feel like no matter what I did, no matter how much I loved any man, he wasn't going to do anything but lie and cheat and expect me to deal with his shit like it wasn't nothing. Darren'd scared me a couple of times but at least he had finally grown up. Garbage Fiend wasn't ever going to change.

When I got to Smiley's crib, the wooden side door was already open but the white storm door was locked. His ceiling fan was on along with the light. What was it with him and that fan? I rang the bell. He appeared in the kitchen within seconds, flung the door open, took me in his arms and held me like he wasn't ever going to let go. He smelled like soap and all my favorite things...like a warm day on a beach. He smelled like looking at the stars and falling asleep underneath the sky. He smelled like the way I felt after I read Pharaoh and Mauri a bedtime story and tucked them in.

He lifted me off the ground and deeper into his arms.

Our colors matched. He had on a gray T-shirt and a pair of navy and white Nike track pants and a pair of white socks and Nike flip-flops.

When he finally put me down, he motioned for me to come in. The pain in his eyes was slowly peeling away.

I walked into the living room. Since there wasn't any furniture in there I couldn't get too comfortable. We sat there on the floor warming up to each other, waiting to see who would be the bravest.

"I saw you the other day...I called your name...you started walking faster. I sent you numerous letters, Leigh... What did I do to hurt you?"

"...I saw you, too. You were with *some* chick..."

"I was with my sister and my brother. Look behind you." He nodded his head backwards. "That's Nonndaye on the left... I'm happy you're here." Still leaning back on his hands, he scooted closer towards me, not taking his eyes away one second. His gaze was so overwhelming I couldn't look him in the face. I kept searching the carpet for the right words, the right time to say what I had to say, what needed to be said. "Can I hold you?" The softness in his eyes made me continue cleaning the dirt underneath my nails.

I scooted farther away and sat cross-legged. "Smiley, I went thru something like this before and I have to tell you. I'm engaged. I'm getting married June fifteenth... I don't know you all like that." I don't know why I said that last part but I did. All I could do was go with it now. I continued staring at my hands as my legs continued flapping. "You don't know me all like that either. I'm not some naïve, little virgin chick that's a goody two shoes like what you're probably looking for. I've been thru a lot and I'm—I'm not the one for you. If we were meant to be, we would have been in a relationship a long time ago. I—I'm sorry." I started fidgeting with my ring. "Even though it's kinda soon, I *do* love you and I have feelings for you but--"

He reached his arm out and touched my face. I stopped playing with the ring and closed my eyes so I could remember the feeling, to savor it. He reminded me of magic.

He rested his leg against my knee as my legs rocked up and down in nervousness. The material of his track pants made a soft, leaf rustling noise against my right leg. "I waited for you for two hours that Friday evening, Leigh..." I couldn't look at anything but his fingers. The good thing about his fingernails was that they didn't have that white lunate part above the cuticles. "...Let me tell you sumthen off rip. I'm not the kind of brotha to be waiting around, gettin' stood up on uh date, goin' home hurt than uh muhfucka an' shit. I kept wondering if you were okay. Wondering if that crazy ass Craig muhafucka had done something to you. Wondering if the kids were okay. Anybody else? I woulda straight up charged it to the game and been like fuck it. But I couldn't forget you, Leigh.

"So? I called. No answer. I went by there everyday. Some female named Lashawn--Yvonne—something like that--came to the door in a robe and tried to get me to come up to her apartment one time when I stopped by.

"Then the thought ran thru my head, 'Yo, what if I run into her and she's with anotha dude? I can't keep coming by here like this.' And I ran into one of them muthafuckas, too. He was ringing yo' bell like he was outta his muthafuckin' mind, yo'. I got back in my ride and drove off. I was thinking maybe that was why you weren't there.

"Can I ask you something?" He didn't wait for me to reply, "Were you engaged when we first met?" I shook my head no. "What about when I saw you at the bus stop?" I shook my head no again. He scooted closer leaving no gaps between us this time. Lightly he touched my hand and traced the baby fingernail on my right hand with his index finger. "*It's this--this* connection right here! I haven't been able to think straight since that Friday. All I want is you. Look at me. Look! Do I look like I'm aright?" His eyes turned watery as he chuckled. "You got this *effect* on me--for a reason." He lifted my hands from the carpet and hugged me without asking this time. I had to let him touch me. He felt like cuddling up against a familiar quilt. I nuzzled his chin with my forehead as he caressed my back.

But Darren. One flash of Darren's face and I pulled back abruptly.

"Leigh, I love you and I *know* you feelin' me the same way. What's goin' on?"

"I just told you. I'm engaged. I can't even say I *trust* you or anything but with Darren, we've—we've been thru so much together and we know each other—" He covered my lips with his finger and drew me to him until our lips sealed the deal. He traced my lips against his tongue and softly sucked them between the moistness of his own lips before his tongue melted into mine.

At that moment, that very moment, I was on another planet in another time.

His face shifted into complete agony when I pulled away yet again. Strain and confusion swept over him. His eyes became glazed over. "Leigh? Why are you fighting us? You know you're supposed to be with me--we both know it." After he said it a warm breeze flowed throughout me into the core of my soul like a centrifugal force, something that was linked in a bond stronger than love even. Along with that kiss, I'd given him my life force. I scooted away, hoping to once again feel like I was among the breathing here on earth.

"What is it you need, hunh?" He tilted my face upwards, forcing me to look into his eyes. "What?" I couldn't say anything. "I'd be lying if I said as long as he made you happy I'd be cool wit it 'cause I know *I'M* what you need Leigh!"

I shot up ready to leave. I couldn't keep listening to this shit! "SO-SO WHAT AM I SUPPOSED TO DO? I'M SUPPOSED TO JUST HURT—TO HURT SOMEONE WHO LOVES ME *WAY MORE* THAN YOU *DO*—SOMEONE WHO'S KNOWN ME ALL THIS TIME AND *STILL* LOVES ME? HE'S BEEN THERE FOR ME! I CAN'T JUST UP AND DO THAT TO HIM! IF *THAT'S* WHAT YOU EXPECT, YOU GOT IT TWISTED! IF ALL THIS 'IT'S MEANT TO BE' SHIT IS REALLY WHAT'S UP WE WOULDA MET A LONG TIME AGO! IT DOESN'T WORK LIKE THAT IN THE REAL WORLD SMILEY! LIVE A COUPLE MORE YEARS! *GOD* I WISH I WOULDA *NEVER* TOLD YOU ANYTHING ABOUT MY PAST RELATIONSHIPS!"

"You just mad 'cause you want me, too. *You* want *me* as much as I want and *need you*! We both know he 'on't love you as much as I do! I woulda never had you out on the streets in the cold with two kids. I bet he was the one that had you out there like that, wasn't he?" I straight up started walking to the door. "Wait a minute, Leigh! Listen ta me." He stood in front of me holding both of my hands. "If you can really just up and leave and forget all about me, look me in the eyes and tell me. Say it. Say you don't want me. Say you don't need me. Tell me ole boy'll give you what you *want* and what you *need*. He might be able ta hook you up wit uh Lexus an' shit but he ain't me an' you know it.

"Every time I meditate, every single time, I see yo' face! Higher powers ain't cruel like that. If *we weren't meant to be* and if you *didn't* love me, you woulda never called yesterday *or* early this morning."

I snatched my hands out of his grip.

Everything felt like scribble scrabble. I couldn't even stand up. Somehow I ended up on the floor with my face in my hands. This was like that day in Shawn's car...all that time I spent regretting, thinking about all the what ifs. But Smiley wasn't Shawn.

I closed my eyes and asked the questions that would end everything. *God, Jesus, Mother, Father, angels, Universe—whatever—help me! Is this man standing before me the one for me? Is this who I'm supposed to be with? Is he the one who'll be different from the rest? The one like that valet guy said who'll love both of my children as his own? What if we hook up? Will he be right? Or will he be out cheatin' while I sit around waiting on him hand and foot like a fool? TELL ME 'cause I'm confused--I don't know which way to turn!*

"I have already given you the answer, dear child. It is now up to you, dear one..." With that, the voice floated away.

"I'ma tell you what's up. You prayin' about what to do. You askin' fa guidance. You wanna know if I'm really the one. How I know? 'Cause our *souls* are *tied* to each other spiritually, far beyond the physical plane, Leigh. Even if you wouldn'ta told me shit about you in the past, I woulda still felt dat shit!" He nodded his head in agreement with his own statement.

I went to the bathroom and rinsed my face, walked to the side door and walked out.

"Why are you so scared of *this*? Of *us*? I understand you been thru some shit but it's *me*, Leigh." He tapped emphatically on his chest with both hands. "Tell me you're gonna be happy and I'll--I'll..." He shook his head in dismay and his voice quieted. "As much as it would kill me, I'd leave you alone..." He bit his top lip really hard and took a deep, deep breath. I saw a man standing in front of the World Trade Center building make the exact same face on 9-11 right after he found out his wife had been killed.

Smiley breathed so heavily, I could see his chest rise and fall with every heartbeat. His bright red eyes stared at me pensively from the corner of his side-glance as he leaned against the frame of the doorway and propped the storm door open with his foot.

I stood against my truck looking right back at him and at those crimson eyes. "...I'll be happy."

His head dropped and he rubbed his chin shaking his head up and down as though he was trying to make the words that had just come out of my mouth feel okay. As he tried to look at me, right at that moment, I felt my heart beat in the same swift rhythm of his.

"...I'll be here tomorrow in the morning with the kids...what time are you waking up?"

"Six." Still breathing heavy, he looked up.

"I'll be here then."

I FOLLOWED THE NORMAL routine and went for the work out knowing I was making the right decision.

After all that had happened over the last five years—even before my children had been born, I knew now more than ever what I wanted out of life. Shawn had shown me the way I deserved to be treated but Smiley was the man assigned to me all along... I hadn't been ready. Not until after Shawn and Darren and Craig—the good, the bad and the dangerously ugly.

I let Syra ramble on and on, I even smiled at a few of her ridiculously rude comments about my shape.

357

When I got back to Darren's place, I packed some of my things and the kids things and sent Dina home after paying her for the rest of the day.

I called Darren but he didn't answer so I wrote him a letter.

Dear Darren,

I love you tremendously but I now know this will never work. There is someone else for you just as there is someone else for me. I hope, if not just for the sake of being, at least for that of our son's, we will remain true friends.

Sincerely,

Leigh

I rolled it up, slid the letter inside the engagement ring and placed all four of his credit cards on the counter and took the kids back to the apartment.

The three logs tucked underneath my arms and the last sumo on my shoulder all went away leaving me without any regrets.

SIX HOURS LATER DARREN called yelling into the phone. "LEIGH, BABY! WHERE ARE YOU? I'M SORRY BABY! I SWEAR I WAS GONNA END THAT SHIT WITH DANIELLE! I SWEAR TA YOU, BABY! IT WAS JUST THAT ONE MUTHAFUCKIN' TIME, BABY! *DAMN*! I *KNEW* SHE WAS GON' CALL YOU! I'M SORRY, BABY! I KNOW I FUCKED UP! JUST—"

"—Darren? Darren, look. You don't have to explain. It's okay. It's best we both just move on. I'll give you your truck back. As a matterfact, Sherra's about to get off work so I can drive it up there—"

"—Naw, come on, nah Leigh!" In the midst of panic, he started crying. Darren? Crying? What was next, talking elephants and a live circus showing up at my door? "Bay-*bee*, come on nah, I 'on't love Danielle. I *LOVE* you. But she kept coming up to my job and—I—come on, nah, Leigh. We're engaged. We're about to be married! You know we're good together! You know that! Bay-*bee*, I won't have a bachelor's party, I won't—"

"—Darren, we can't get married--"

"--LEIGH! How we look calling everything off? What is everybody gonna think? LOOK, BABY, IT WAS JUST THAT ONE TIME--"

"—Hopefully--" Every time I tried to say something he would interrupt and talk all fast and ramble every kind of apology imaginable so I started talking over him, "WE'LL REMAIN FRIENDS. BUT," once he quieted down I stopped shouting, "--but we're *not* meant for each other--"

"—WAIT! WAIT!"

"Darren? I have to go."

"Baby, keep the truck, I'll give you time to think about what you doin', we can put the wedding on hold or—or--or we can do it earlier--I fucked up but I *love you*! I'ma change, baby! I'm not gon' do dat shit no moe, Leigh, I promise! I didn't—"

"—*BYE* Darren. I'm dropping your car off a little later." He had a meeting tonight that he couldn't miss. He'd be leaving around eight.

"—NO! Listen, Leigh! LEIGH I'M COMIN' OVER THERE RIGHT NA--"

"--Don't even think about it."

"BABY—"

I hung up on him.

Most of the things in the apartment were packed. The kids were busy playing a game Pharaoh'd made up. I sat on the couch, closed my eyes and listened as their giggles echoed against the apartment walls. They were happy, innocent and completely unaware of the new direction their young lives would soon be headed in.

...There she is, the little ball of color we shall call Pink. Oh, look...Pink is very happy these days singing among the flowers, taking some of their beauty along with her. Soon, she will share all she has found with the ones destined to join her in the joyful song. She is Pink, she is — the apartment bell buzzed me awake.

It was Sherra. "Leigh, wha'chu 'bout to do *dis* time? You *sure* you wanna give up yo' truck. You was talkin' 'bout it all while you and Darren had broke up... You sure about all dis? Why 'on't you jus wait and take some time and think everything over?"

"I'm as sure as I'm ever gonna be, girl. And you know what's funny? After I left, he called and told on himself. *Why* was he still messing with Danielle? I have the universe on my side, girl. Even if he woulda cleaned up his act fa real, he's not who's been assigned to me."

"...*Men*! I tell you!" She shook her head, finally convinced. "But it's God that's lookin' out fa you—not no universe. Ever since that hospital thing, you been on some weird stuff."

When we got to Darren's house, I parked the truck in the driveway, opened the door and left the keys along with his cell phone on the counter, locked the door and left. It was eight thirty. He probably didn't think I was really gonna do it.

When he came in he'd find his belongings.

I drove Sherra back to her place since she was letting me borrow her car tomorrow.

That night, even in that apartment, even though I had to disconnect the phone because of Darren's back to back drunken calls, I slept peacefully, without a care in the world with Mauri and Pharaoh next to me.

CHAPTER 20

"YESTERDAY. Around seven in the evening. What were you up to? Did anything happen a lil' out of the ordinary?" I asked as Smiley pulled out the all the luggage I had crammed in the trunk.

"Nope. I was meditating, smoking' some herb...some pink shit started poppin' up but it wasn't no outta tha ordinary shit." He laughed. "Pink reps love. I was thinking about you all day. Why?" I pushed the luggage out of his hand. "Damn, ma! What's up wi-"

I grabbed him and kissed him all over his face while we stood in the middle of the driveway. "I fell asleep and I had this dream. There were Pink stars floating all around. Yesterday! Around seven! Something *told me* to ask you!"

"Kinda strong—don't you think. You just grabbed the neck of a man that's six-four like some kinda iron lady. You jump up when I blinked or something?" He laughed. "I told you, baby: soul tie. That's how you explain that." He leaned down and looked into my face. "...You still like skunks?"

"Yep. You still like lizards?"

He drew me closer and kissed me. It was a long, body altering, knee quaking kind of experience.

After he got everything out of Sherra's car, he placed a sleeping bag over Mauri and Pharaoh who were fast asleep on the couch and sat across from me at the kitchen table.

"Leigh. I know our relationship hasn't fit the official dating bill but I wanna ask you to marry me. I wanna spend the rest of my life with you. But I know you need some You time. So, if you're down, I'll move in with my peeps for the time being and let you do you for a while. I'm more than willin' ta go with your flow. Leigh, will you?"

I had never had sex with him, I didn't know if IT was way too big or gravely petite in size and structure or if IT could satisfy the middle, I hadn't met his family... But I knew like never before. This was the one who was supposed to be my man and I was honored to know I'd one day be his wife. I nodded yes as he reached across the table and slid the gold band on the same finger I'd just removed a burden from only hours ago.

"I got it yesterday. It's only temporary, baby--I had to get something so you'd know I'm fa real. You can pick the one you want for the ceremony. Can I hold you?" he asked right before biting his bottom lip. I slid to his side of the tiny table and sat in his lap. "I love you, Leigh. It doesn't matter what you did in the past. I'm just glad you came into my life and that you're here right now with me. I was dying without you...a man can't really survive without a good woman by his side.

"When I first saw you, I was like, man, she's beautiful. It was just something about you. But the thing I love the most about you is yo' heart. You sealed the deal when you fixed dinner *and* washed my clothes that one time. You ain't have ta do all that—no other woman has ever taken care of me like that. I know, fa sho', you're an extension of me—that female counterpart I needed. That's why, right now, right here I'm promising to give you everything you need and want.

"My dad and my brother help out with the business but I'm makin' contacts and moves so it'll grow into something even bigger one of these days. Pop started off without even graduating from high school and he did it. It's time for me to pick up where he left off. Some of the seeds I planted are beginning to pop up. I know it's gonna take a lil' time. But I'ma make sure you ain't ever godda worry about having food on the table or being loved again, you got my word on that.

"Ever since the day we met, the second thing I do when I wake up in the morning is ask the Mother and Father to let me be the man you deserve--right after I thank them for meeting another day. I wanna make you happy, baby..." I couldn't do anything but listen. I still couldn't believe I'd lucked up and met a man like him. "I'm serious."

"...As long as you don't start acting crazy, you got me."

"You had me day one. Now that I've had a taste of what life's like *with* you, I'm not trying to lose you on some ill shit," he stated cradling my face in his hands after wiping away a years worth of solid tears from my eyes with his thumb.

He kept talking but I was distracted by what I was feeling in those black Nike track pants. Nice. Very promising in size...felt like it had some sort of curve going on and it was time to find out what was really good.

"Umm..." I giggled licking the side of his face, "...You know, there's whip cream and strawberries in the fridge..." I put my finger in my mouth and traced my lips with my pinky as I looked up at him.

"Wai-wai-wait! Hold up, baby, hol'up! I—I ain't--lift up for a minute." He slid me off him and smoothed out his track pants. "Matterfact, can you sit in the otha chair? As hard as this is for me--and it's more than hard right about now!" He rubbed his face in frustration. "I think we need to wait on that. Oh, I want it a*ariigh*t--and I'm probably gonna have to call you for a phone hook up *every* night but, like I said, you need some You time for a minute. I 'ont wanna rush it. I mean OH YEAH! IT'S GONNA GO DOWN!" He sighed like he was in pain. "My feelings for you alone could make me bust. And I 'on't wanna embarrass myself shootin' all over the place after three seconds. Let's do us both a favor." He placed a hand on his eyebrow. It looked like he was seriously hurting. "My dad's covering some of the morning appointments—that's why the van's not here. The kids are probably gonna be hungry. What do you wanna eat?"

I was hungry but for something else at the present moment. Yeah, that was all fine and dandy but could he at least *show it* to me? I had never, ever kicked it with any guy who was 'willing to wait.' Even though I had taken my time with Craig and he had pretended to go along with it, he kept trying me and started getting pissed when he realized I was sticking to my guns... He'd joke about getting it from somebody else. Sad part was I didn't realize he wasn't joking.

"Yeah, what's around here?"

"There's a Coney Island off Evergreen. I don't wanna wake up the kids or else we could go. I'll go pick something up. What do you all want?"

"Just turkey bacon and hash browns for the kids. The same thing with a hard boiled egg for me."

"That's it? No pancakes or sausage or anything else?"

"No, that's it."

"I'm telling you this right now--your kids are my kids, no matter what. I respect the other dudes but, from here on out, they're my mine too. I don't want you to feel like it's you and them and me and you. It's us. We're about to be a family, baby." I couldn't believe him. I rushed over to hug him before he left. "NO! Stay right there! I can't have you touching me right now. I'd be like BBBBBBBang-bang-bang PPPPPPOW-PPP-POW!" We both laughed as he made a motion with his hand like his dick was a gun shooting all over the place. "You already got me sprung, I can't handle nothing else right now. I'd be sick and up in an emergency room if you forgot ta call an' shit."

When he got back we ate breakfast and made arrangements for the Salvation Army to pick the rest of the things up from the apartment on Monday. I didn't even want the kids brand new bunk bed that was there.

"Tomorrow, around seven, if you won't be busy, I wanna to take you to meet the rest of the family. They've heard a lot about you. It's time for you all to meet." I smiled. It would be nice to meet the people who'd raised such a good man. "Well, I'll stop by here tonight after I finish my appointments. Here." He placed the keys to the Yukon in my hand along with fifty dollars before driving off in the Escort. He still hadn't mentioned the enveloped car key thing.

The rest of the day I found myself staring at my ring. It was the most valuable piece of jewelry I'd ever gotten.

Tommy drove Sherra over to pick up her car that afternoon since he had a half-day and she'd just gotten out of class.

"Girl, how you always be gettin' guys wit money? Dis uh nice house."

"Girl, forget the house. I'm in love, Sherra. Do you know he wants to *wait* on *sex*? I can't even begin to explain the way I feel about him--it's like I'm finally complete. But I wouldn't mind getting some, though!"

"Girl, you bedda watch it! You sure he ain't gay or got somebody on tha side? Didn't you say you saw him at the movies wit uh female?"

"That was his sister."

"Hmmh...that's what dey all say." She cut her eyes and looked at me like I was the most 'ignorant*est*' thang she'd ever seen.

"No, seriously. It's the same girl from the picture in the living room. But I want you to meet him. You're gonna love him, girl. I'm telling you, it was fate. I'm just glad I finally started paying attention to the signs the Makers were giving me."

"It was *Jesus*—not no goddamn '*makers*,'--as long as this new guy ain't crazy. *You* need ta remember Christ. The devil wanted yo' life but you still here. God's been blessin' you—remember that."

"Thanks for everything Sherra. Will you be my maid of honor?"

"...Yeah." She gave me a hug and joined T-Man with the kids in the den and played with them for a while before they left. "I'll call you tomorrow."

"YOU LOOK GOOD." Smiley smiled after coming in and sitting down on the couch in the den. I'd just put Mauri in bed. Pharaoh was up trying to play a game on Play Station.

"I wanna ask you--what kind of wedding do you want? Or do you wanna hold off on a date for now."

"No, I know what I want. I'd like a small wedding. It doesn't have to be a big fanfare." I didn't know what he could afford so whatever was fine with me. All I knew was that I wanted to marry him. For sure, without any trace of doubt in my mind, I wanted to be Mrs. Smiley.

"Well. What about if we got married in Hawaii? My parents are planning on going in December around the holidays. A brotha from the center can do the ceremony, if that's cool with you... How many bridesmaids you gonna have?"

"Just one."

"That's ain't bad. We can pay for Sherra then."

"Hawaii? Ohmygoodness! I've never been! It's perfect!"

"So what do you wanna do till then?"

"What do you mean?"

"What do you wanna do with your life, baby?"

"…Well…I wanted to register for spring/summer classes--I already missed two semesters. I'm a year behind now and I *really do* want my degree. But…" My heart started feeling heavy.

"But what?"

"…Well…" I walked over to the sliding patio doors and twirled the clear stick that maneuvered the vertical blinds back and forth between my fingers. I'd never noticed how hard a skinny piece of plastic could be until now.

The mere thought of being a nurse or being near a trauma unit made me uncomfortable. He sensed that I didn't want to be hugged or touched and stayed on the couch. "Can we go in the living room?" I finally asked, nodding at Pharaoh who was busy losing yet having a blast. I sat propped against the bottom ledge of the fireplace across from where he was spread out on the floor. "I don't know if I wanna be a nurse anymore-- not after Craig."

"…Well. Take some time to think about it. Do a semester. Take a couple otha classes you need to take anyway and go check out say, Wayne State or Oakland, see how many of the credits you already have can be applied to anotha major later on down the road. You said you wanted to get your bachelors, right?"

"…Yeah." I moved next to him and rested my head against his shoulder. The only other thing I could see myself doing was shop. Hmmm, maybe I could be a personal shopper? But did you even need a degree to do that?

When Pharaoh fell asleep Smiley left and called me once he made it to his parents place in Southfield.

The next morning Smiley stopped by and gave me some money to get my hair done before he went to his first appointment.

I wasn't about to go back to KD's. He was a part of a life I wasn't looking back on anymore.

Dina came over to watch the kids while I was at Ilya's Spa.

"YOU DON'T HAVE TO be embarrassed about your hair, Leigh. This is why we have private booths," Jahla reminded me.

I ended up with another long weave that was parted down the middle and looked just as good as the job KD'd done although she hadn't loaded my hair down with gel like KD always did.

I got a manicure and pedicure by this older Black lady that kept her I-Pod earplugs on the entire time, which I thought was a bit rude.

"What's wrong with her?" I asked Zada.

"Oh, Karen? She's listening to the bible. She puts the CD version on her I-Pod. She's new."

Zada and I chit chatted for a few although she didn't act like her usual calm, happy-go-lucky self. She was antsy and looked exhausted.

"Girl, I hope some guy hasn't finally gotten to you and jacked you up."

"No, it's not that. I'm just tired and I got into an argument with Ki."

"Girl, you and Kiona'll make up. You know how it is with best friends. Sometimes you need a break from each other."

"Yeah, that's what everybody says. What's up with you? You look different."

"I know. The hair."

"No, you look like you're glowing," she snickered. "You know what they say *does* that."

"Girl. I'm in love--for real this time. Craig is history. And I left Darren."

"You WHAAT!" Her mouth dropped to the floor right before she began to tell me about all the different females Darren had charging their services to his account for the last three years—including the time during of our short engagement. Of course Barbie was on the list!

"I tried to warn you without violating company policy." She shook her head lamentably. "I'm happy for you. Darren didn't seem like your type." She crinkled her nose. "My dad didn't allow me to service him. He was kinda creepy and—until I got my dad on him—he tried to talk all condescending and stuff to everybody. He's upper-class trash. I've been around men with *way* more money than what he has and they don't act like that." Look at this cute lil' chick trying to talk like she knew something. But her family was rich. She wasn't lying when she said she'd been exposed to *some real money*.

I WAS LOOKING FOR something to wear after I got the kids dressed but none of the clothes on my side of the closet hanging next to Smiley's stuff looked right anymore and it wasn't like my wardrobe was out of style.

Finally I decided to wear a pair of casual and somewhat loose fitting 'Your Son's Not Marrying A Slut' suede beige pants, a red boat neck fitted sweater—so as to still look like I had 'a little style and grace' and a nice shape and I wore a pair of tan and white of skinny heeled, cowgirl Steve Madden boots with a gold pair of dangly gypsy earrings, Michael Kors perfume and five gold bangles to help show off my ring.

When Smiley came in he clutched his chest Fred Sanford style and faked a heart attack on the kitchen floor looking like a huge fish flipping out of water. "Baby, I'ma be keepin' you on tha phone. I'ma be out on appointments jackin' up jobs 'cause I'ma be tired from being up all night." He said coding up the phone sex thing. Pharaoh and I cracked up. "You see how Ma looks? *This* is what a real lady is supposed to look like," he schooled Pharaoh who looked up at me and smiled extra hard.

Smiley picked Mauri up and put her in the car seat. "No!" she screamed not wanting to be locked up again. "I know, I know—you 'on't wanna get put in jail again, hunh? We're about to go meet some people who really wanna meet chu. You want them to see you with your face screwed up like this?" He did an impression of Mauri that made her laugh. "They even got some macaroni and cheese over there. Aright. See. I knew you were a good girl." One minute flat and she was all good. She loved her some Smiley, I tell you.

His parent's house was a brick colonial style home topped with white aluminum siding. It looked a little like Craig's house.

Smiley rang the bell before opening the door with his key. When we came in everybody was sitting in the living room except Smiley's mother and his cousin Katrina. He'd already told me his parents had adopted Trina after his aunt passed away five years ago. The two of them were busy in the kitchen.

"Ma, this is Leigh, my fiancee," he said proudly. She was a heavy-set high yellow woman, stood around five-nine, she had a gap between her two front teeth and her head was wrapped in a multi-colored scarf with dangling fringes on it.

She looked at me over the rim of her glasses and twisted her mouth and scrunched her eyebrows in disapproval like she recognized me from a Most Wanted flyer in the post office. "Aright, help us set the table," was her only response along with a sigh. She handed me napkins and pointed at the glasses. "Don't touch the rim. Set six out there." She nodded her head towards the dining room. You would have thought I was the hired help.

"So *you're* the *one* that had my cousin all *upset*," Katrina muttered, moving her head and her eyes like a snake as she placed the baked chicken in the center of the table and monitored my glass handling skills. I smiled back at her silently wishing Smiley would step back into the room. That's a shame when a twelve year old can make you so nervous your armpits start getting extra hot.

Prayer was real, real long. Smiley's father was mumbling and going all in depth about what? I really didn't care to know. But there was this non-fiction book I read a long time ago and had it not have been for what was going on right now, I wouldn't have remembered anything about it.

The author had this whole theory of humans having imaginary tails. It even suggested being out somewhere and testing your capabilities by *'tapping'* your *'tail'* on someone's shoulder. He said they'd more than likely feel it and make eye contact with you unless they were purposely blocking your energy. Yes, *that* was when I refunded the book and got my money back. However, the electrocuting glare I now felt continually burning against my face was turning me into a 'tail tapping' believer. When I opened my eyes Smiley's mother and Katrina were grimming the mess out of me. You would have thought I had *Devil's Daughter* and three 6's neatly carved into my forehead. Looked like they were planning on staring at me long enough to make me evaporate away from the dinner table and out of Smiley's life forever.

His brother Chad wasn't too friendly either. "So...how you get my brotha ta move outta his *own* house?" he asked during an equally uncomfortable dessert of peach cobbler. My heart stopped. While they all watched me seriously waiting for a response I focused on the four elbows of macaroni sitting idly on my plate. I shouldn't have eaten *anything* they'd cooked.

"Hold up! What's wrong with you? Yo', dude! You *can't* talk ta her like that. *I* moved out for a second. By choice. And I'm grown, son. I don't have to explain my actions to you." Malik was looking at Chad like Chad had lost his mind.

"Son, ya' brother's just concerned," his father defended. He was a thin, dark and Native American looking Black man with small eyes that made him look like he was always squinting.

I caught him glancing over Pharaoh and Mauri more than a couple of times during that awful cobbler. I've never been a fan of any kind of cobbler. It looked like raw eggs covered in syrup...uck. I could tell they thought I was trying to be snooty since I wasn't gobbling it up.

When Nonndaye came in from class she walked up to Smiley and asked him to come down to the basement with her. When he came back he was heated. He motioned for me to step into the hallway. "Look. I'm not a fan of how my family is acting right now. If I woulda known they were gonna show-out like this, I'da neva brought you over here. Let's get the kids. We're abouta go. But I need ta talk ta them for a second. Wait for me in tha truck."

On the way out I heard part of the conversation. "Boy, she got two kids aready—look like two different daddies *ta me*--and she fa damn sho' look older *dan you* boy! Nah dat's uh sack chaser if I ever laid uh eye on one. Don't you be brangin' no snooty, bougie, wit-ha-mouth-all-sucked-in, old as dirt woman up in *my* crib!

"Daye said she da one you saw at da movies cheatin' on you! How you look marryin' somethin' like ta had you goin' crazy, missin' appointments an' layin' 'round listenin' ta dem damn love song all day?

You done certainly lost yo' damn mind! Ain't no 'mounta looks worth da heartache an' money *dat one right dere* gon' cost you! Ya' bedda have 'nuff sense left ta know not ta be whipped ova some hussified bedroom action!

"What happened ta dat nice lil' Candace girl? Now *that's* da type you need ta be lookin' at! She was spiritual an' cul'chud—ain't have *no nail-on-hair* tacked onta ha head *an'* she still crazy 'bout chu! Candy called Daye da otha day ta see how everybody was. *Like I keep tryin' ta tell yo' hard headed ass, dat's* da type uh young lady ya' need ta be wit right dere!" I wanted to listen to the rest of what he was saying but I didn't want the kids to hear all the commotion.

"Mommy? Why are you crying? You didn't like those people?" Pharaoh asked frowning.

"Ohh. I'll be alright, sweetie...mommy'll be alright."

"I'm sorry baby," Smiley apologized after getting in the truck. "Come here." He reached over to hug me.

"No."

"No? No, what?"

"You know what? They're right. I'm older than you *and* I've got kids. I'm not about to come between you and them like that. I know what it's like to not have a good relationship with your family. I'll see if I can stay with Sherra for a--"

"—Whoa! Whoa! Leigh, you love me?"

"Yeah--of course but I—"

"—*Aright, then.* I asked you to marry me 'cause I love you and I wanna spend the rest of my life with you. End of Discussion. If they 'ont wanna accept our relationship, their loss. Nobody wanted my moms ta marry pop. She was in college while he was working on his GED but she married him anyway. They been togetha twenty-five years and they raised me well. I can't believe they acted like that! They didn't even try ta get ta know you." He shook his head in disgust. "We'll just have to change some of our plans, that's all...Unless I get an apartment, I'm gonna have to stay at the crib with you all... I 'on't know if I can afford to get an apartment *and* do Hawaii...with the way they actin', they may *not even be* at *the ceremony*...and I'm *definitely not* gonna be able to live with you and hold out that long... G! I'ma hit Gabe up and see what's the deal wit him."

"...Well...yeah, I still need to get some things together but, seriously, I want to marry you, Smiley. We could do it in May. You can stay in the house and not even have to stay with G."

"...I 'on't know, baby... I think I'ma still see what G's on. I wanna make sure you—"

369

"---WHAT? YOU WHAT? Since you think I'm so fucked up, why you even wanna marry me, then?" I threw my hands up like it was a street fight and went from ladylike to a growling ganstress in seconds and flung my arm his way.

"Baby? You need ta chill. It's not like that. We'll talk about it when we get back to—"

"—Nope. YOU CAN SAY IT *NOW*! Say whatever tha FUCK you *tryin' ta say*!" Mauri started crying. "*SHUT IT* UP! I'm not tryin' ta hear all-uh-dat right now!" I turned around from my seat and held up my brush. "Keep on crying and watch me tear them legs up!"

He grabbed my arm in mid air and pulled into an isolated corner of a strip mall at the end of the block. "Leigh. Can you step outside for a minute?" he asked getting out of the drivers side. He stood in the back of the truck waiting for me to join him.

I was heated. "Sounds like YOU got some last minute booty you need ta take care of ta me! Or like you havin' doubts! If you was gonna be doubting *'US'*, you shouldn'ta started all this *'soulmate'* shit. My life was just fine before you carried me outta tha damn grocery store!"

"Baby, listen. Listen. This is all I'm trying to say: You've been thru uh lodda shit and it hasn't even been uh year. I 'on't wanna rush tha process. We know we're supposed ta be tagetha. *That's* why I gave you *this* ring." He reached for my left hand. Snatching myself from his grip, I hit him by mistake in the jaw so hard, it echoed. His eyes closed and his mouth shifted to the side. He rubbed his jaw and looked over his right shoulder avoiding eye contact with me.

I gasped. "I'm sorry. I—I didn't mean...Smiley? ...Your family hates me--and I can understand why. I've got a lot of *shit* still wrong with me... I understand. You don't wanna fuck. Okay, I can understand that, too. So LEAVE ME THA HELL ALONE, THEN! Go back to your normal, drama-free life! Tomorrow, I'm out. Fuck niggas. All y'all do is try ta bully somebody, cheat and lie all the muthafuckin' time anyway!" I stomped off slamming my heels against the tar pavement with each step and went inside Rite Aid totally forgetting the kids were in the truck.

I slid down on the bench underneath the pharmacy's window, put my face in my hands and closed my eyes, oblivious to the people walking by looking at me like I was crazy. A couple of minutes later I felt the heat of a big, secure arm wrapping itself around me. "Come on, baby. Let's go home." I looked out of the passenger's window the rest of the ten-minute ride.

"I said I love you. I said I'ma be here. Ain't shit you can do ta change that, Leigh. I'm willing to shut my peeps down if I have to. I already know how my dad is, if he tries ta trip on me with the company, fuck it. I'll just have to start up Smiley Two or some shit. I'll be able ta make it 'til somethin' else pops off.

"But it's not what you thinking. There ain't no pussy no where out in tha streets I'm chasing afta. Baby, please don't take this the wrong way but you've been raped by two different bastards and you been thru *a lodda* shit… After all that *and* that Darren muthafucka you need some time to heal. Otherwise all that negative energy's gonna continue to haunt you and transfer into the next life. That's what God and the Goddess are telling me right now. When *they* give me the go ahead, it's curtains—you and me can go down in the books and make history. We'll be that real-deal fairytale *fa sho'*, youknowwhatImean? I'm hoping ta be with you the next time around, too… You get where I'm coming from?" he asked pulling me on his lap as he sat on the edge of the bed once we were at the house.

"…Yeah…Smiley?"

"Yeah, babe?"

"…I'm sorry."

Malik cupped my face in his massive hands and looked me square in the eyes for a minute without blinking like he was doing some sort of telepathic ritual. "I know it wasn't on purpose but don't ever hit me again. I've never hit you and I'm *not* gon' hit you. Gimme tha same respect… All I want you to do right now is worry about Leigh and chill." His face was serious. He didn't say anything or do anything else except let me know thru that fixed stare of his not to wile out like that again. Did this man know how to handle me and my insecurities or what? Now *that* was the biggest turn on ever.

I leaned against him and sung a few lines of this song I'd made up then I started feeling shy and stopped in the middle of the chorus. He held my hand and fixed gentle kisses on me until I warmed back up and finished the rest of the song as I ran my fingers thru his locks. "Sing something else ta me." He placed my hand back in his hair and closed his eyes. "Thas some sexy ass shit you got going on. If I ever get real mad at you, all you godda do is sing sumthen in my ear just like that and you'll be straight. Can you sing that last part to me one more time." I pulled him close enough to lay my cheek against the smoothness of his forehead and softly let the words roll away. "Baby? You singing it like you really mean it…" I laid the back of my hand against the mocha of his cheeks and kissed his thick, silky eyebrows. That night we slept wrapped in the royalty of each other arms. Just snuggling next to him was more than enough.

CHAPTER 21

THE FUZZY PINK LITTLE BOP
--the one with the diamond
on top,

she lives on the glass stage
flitting over high's and low's
with her satin toes

not noticing
the spiked ball
rolling wicked circles
big and small
coming,
coming to poke
and smoke
her magic away

the one who is gray,
wearing spikes everyday
knows—
pain left unattended
how perfectly it grows,
and also how to tie
perfect misery bows

                                            ...cornea copula
to this so-called world when the pink fades...
                        (reality can sometimes be a motha
when you on to something)...

There was Mrs. Maddox with her nosy ass, peering thru her patio doors at me. By now you'd think she'd be used to seeing me out here meditating on the yoga mat. Later for her, I was waiting for Smiley to finish his second appointment so he could call me back and I could tell him about the vision I had--I had already called him three times and it wasn't even ten o'clock yet. Being around the house with nothing to do after *the Golden Girls* and *Mama's Family* went off was driving me crazy. I could tell he was trying not let me know I was irritating him. He was probably even happier than I was that my classes started today.

"Whoa! You talkin' bout fight tha power na, hungh?" Dina joked when she came in.

I was wearing a pair of cream shorts and a cream knitted sleeveless turtleneck, brown wedged heeled sandals and a brown head wrap tied in a ball in the back. I needed to get my hair done but since Pharaoh and Malik's birthdays were on Thursday and Friday, I was trying to wait. "No, I just need to get my hair done. I need a touch up on these edges," I said patting my scarf.

"Yeah, 'cause that is *not* yo' style. Next Smiley gon' turn into uh Rasta and y'all gon' be wearin' camouflage all the time.

"When you was wit Darren he kept you laced. Don't be fallin' off, nah. You ain't never go around lookin' like no Ant Jemima fa as long as I done known you--you know you ma girl, I godda let'chu know!"

"Smiley would make a sexy Rasta, I don't know what you talkin' 'bout!" I retorted as she laughed.

I pulled into the northwest campus on Greenfield and parked the Yukon in the only spot I could find that didn't have broken glass all over the place, grabbed my Vuitton ready for a new semester. When I opened the entrance door it smelled bad—like burnt elementary school cafeteria burgers and, with all the eighteen/nineteen year olds horse-playing around, I felt like I *was* in elementary school. Then this girl with two toddlers straddling behind her bumped me out of the way while I was checking the board for my classroom numbers. She looked almost just like this one girl who used to sit next to me in an algebra class two semesters ago that had pulled a pomegranate out of a Farmer's Jack bag and cut it with a steak knife and started chewing on the seeds and spitting them back into the shopping bag the whole first half of class. I stepped aside and let her and her kids get in front of me. The back of her tattered red notebook was covered with greasy fingerprints.

After I found out which room my nutrition class was going to be held in, I was ready to get back in the truck. It was the same MF-in' room I was sitting in that one night when Darren called and invited me to TGIFriday's. I went straight to the registrar's office and dropped it.

I went to the library and, to kill time, pulled a book out of my bag I had been reading about using the positive energy available in our universe to get what you needed and wanted out of life. According to the author, words held power and humans could receive positive things if they were willing to ask the Godly spirit realm. Smiley was the only person I'd shown the book to. Most people choose not to think outside the 'given' box and don't want to understand stuff like this and most of the time, when people don't understand something, instead of checking it out, they start judging and labeling those more willing to look into "higher vibrations," as

Smiley calls it. Whether or not there was truth to the author's hypothesis, I liked the concept. I had already read it once before.

Sometimes, when you go thru a lot of negative situations you need to hear something upbuilding—something that'll make you feel good. Maybe that's why so many Black folks like church. Even if you're poor church'll make you feel good--the hope of heaven and whatnot. I guess the opposite alternatives are alcohol and drugs and shit...seems like humans are a lot weaker and a lot stronger than what most people have been taught to believe. Maybe those who are addicted to drugs and alcohol aren't necessarily weak per se, maybe they are looking for life alternatives but have gotten hooked on the wrong ones. I used to think people who committed suicide were cowards--that's what Ellington always said. But lately I'd changed my perspective on it. Take Sylvia Plath for instance. She seemed like one of those people who simply wasn't able to deal with all the sadness and injustice of this world. Now crazy fuckers like Jim Jones don't count. *That* MF was just crazy. I saw a documentary on him last week and it was so eerie, I went to sleep with all the lights on that night.

Two hours later I went to my next class and when I saw Mr. Lohligan behind the desk, I turned around and walked out of the building. Before, I had been, in his words, "a top notch student." But when I emailed him back in October about the classes I had missed, he didn't even respond. I bet he thought I was just like all those other students who fell asleep in class.

I turned the key in the ignition but the truck didn't do anything. When I tried cranking it up again it still didn't do anything. Dead battery. I had left the lights on. I was always messing *something* up. Already I had locked the keys in the car twice.

"Don't worry 'bout it, baby. I can't make it down there to give you a jump right now but hold on--let me hit G up, he should be able to get over there. He's off today," Smiley reassured me after I called AAA and got a two-hour roadside assistance wait-time.

School didn't feel right anymore. Just being in the parking lot was irritating. Who would've thought the day would come when I'd hate being at school? Being at Detroit Community had given me a good start and helped me learn a lot about African and Black history. All the time I spent in public school, I'd never learned anything about Malcolm X or Marcus Garvey or anything. All we did was sing a song for Martin Luther King's birthday in elementary school, Martin Luther King plays in middle school and test on the founding fathers in high school. I was very grateful to Detroit Community for offering African and African American Studies courses. A lot of Blacks don't know how rich their history is or understand the real struggle our people endured prior to the sixties. But, even though it wasn't going to be easy, it was time for me to move on from Detroit Community and time to let go of the past.

No matter how bad memories and people from the past were or are, it's not always easy to just accept the things that have happened and move on. It's even harder to move on and accept that a particular time is over when the past memory is a good one—especially when a present situation is not as wonderful. The future is always uncertain. The only thing I guess we really have is the present. Right now I was being given a fresh start with a promising future. I wasn't about to fuck that up too. I'd love to still be cool with Tylil and RayRay but, things would never be like when we were twelve and playing Hide N' Go Seek in the forest at church picnics. Whatever the past might have been, I'm positive everything is happening right now for a reason.

...At least I knew I didn't have AIDS or any other STD. After the incident I had to have regular checkups. And after finding out from Zada that Danielle had recently gotten Chlamydia from Darren, I was even happier that I wasn't still with him. But as happy as I was with Smiley, I still needed to come to grips with the past. I needed to feel like a real person again. So much had happened. I wanted to know I'd be okay one day... That the diamond that'd been taken away would one day come back. How long was it going to take?

"Yo' Leigh, whad up? Pop your trunk, lady."

I opened my eyes in the middle of my request to be made whole again. It was Gabe in a hunter green T-shirt with a white Long John shirt underneath. I stepped out of the truck. "Whad up, Leigh? Good to see, good to see." He raised up from under the hood to give me a hug. "You know, I gotta say. You make my mans real happy and shit. I've known him since I was a senior in high school—he liked to hang with us older cats.

"I've *never* seen ole boy like this. After he graduated, he stepped it up a notch in college--got real serious about his hustle—dig what I'm sayin'? Dude's always had the ladies chasing but he's different with you, ma. It's like you two complete the puzzle for each other and shit. Y'all got me thinkin' like lemme find my soul mate right about now." He talked so fast his words sounded like one quick buzzing song.

G's sleepy-eyed, handsome, light caramel face slyly smiled at me as he made sure the battery was charged. We stared at each other a few seconds before quickly looking away. With his freshly lined up haircut he was fine...and it just looked like, inside those jeans that hung perfectly from his slim frame he'd have a big dick—the kind that could make an addict out of a sista. Gabe was that bad good boy/intellectual but hood type every sista needed in her life: true blue husband material.

But I wasn't really fazed. Smiley was the finest man on earth to me. Every time I looked into his eyes I could feel how much he loved me. He handled his business, was loyal than a muthafucka and left none of my needs unmet. Well…except on the sexual tip. He was still on that 'Leigh you need ta heal' shit.

I sat in the truck for a while after G drove off and on a whim drove to the center. Around this time they were usually doing the soup kitchen and activities for seniors. I was always telling Smiley I was going to go help out and still hadn't gone yet. Might as well go today since I didn't have anything else better to do and Dina was already watching the kids.

The minute I got there I spotted Dominique's ass and of course she had to walk up and say something. "Hey, Leigh—I mean, Lovely." She laughed like she was in the audience at *Comic View*. She was wearing a low cut, short-sleeved kentae cloth shirt that fit and had a ruffle at the bottom of it, black slacks and a pair of black pumps. Her hair was piled mile high on top of her head and just as curly as usual. But her makeup was laid! I had to give her that.

"What?" I tried not to be annoyed.

"Lovely. That's what Smiley calls you, right?"

Ludacris "Hoe" started playing in my head. *Stank-Stank, that's what me and Sherra call you!* Her bubbly ass demeanor was disgusting. And what the hell was she talking about anyway? Smiley never called me '*Lovely.*' "I'm here to help with lunch services."

"Great! I'm the coordinator," she beamed. Oh, really. Could someone please get a horn for her to toot? A nice big shiny one. "Leigh, you *look great*, but then again, you've always been pretty." She handed me a pair of clear plastic gloves and motioned for me to stand next to her. "Soon, it's gonna be crowded in here. So what have you been up to? I hear there are *wedding bells ringing in the air*!"

I was so happy when the patrons came in I didn't know what to do! This girl was determined to patch up a torn friendship. No amount of big willy stitch work was going to do the trick…trick, hmmm…

I watched her and, as much as I hated to admit it, she didn't seem like the same person I knew way back when. She was gracious to the people in line. She knew a lot of them by name and a lot of people came and hugged her before they even got in line. When the seniors came in for lunch she sat down and chatted with them. "Look at this." She pulled a partially sewn shirt out of her bag. "I know it's messed up but, I'm trying Sister Westwood. Tomorrow can you help me with my pattern?"

Well, maybe she isn't that bad, I thought as I grabbed my purse to leave after the program switched to the Seniors Stitching It Up.

"Wait! Would you mind sticking around? I'm leaving in thirty minutes. I've been dying to catch up with you." Her eyes eagerly awaited a response. She still had some big eyes, boy. And she was still very pretty—another fact I hated to admit.

"...Yeah, I guess." AAAAHH! Why did get myself into this!

"Well, great. We can go for coffee or something."

As I waited for her, I tried calling my mother again. I just couldn't imagine her missing her Baby King's birthday. And I really wanted her to meet Smiley--she didn't even know anything about him yet.

"Hello?" she answered.

"Hi, mom it's me! Pharaoh's birthday is coming up. I really want you to come, ma. He'd die if you didn't. And he can't stop talking about you, either. I—we miss you." Click. A few seconds later Smiley, Pharaoh and Mauri were all smiling back at me on my phone's picture screensaver.

The only reason she'd answered in the first place was because she didn't recognize my new number. Not speaking to her was like being cut really deep only to have the wound doused with salt and vinegar.

The way she was acting, I wished something would haunt her and throw pictures of her two grandchildren at her every night. But constantly thinking about the way things now were with her and getting angry about it wasn't going to do anything to change the situation. I actually felt sorry for her--Ellington wouldn't be half as loyal if she'd done something to one of *his* kids. I was going to have to do one of those Oprah psychologists moves on her and find a way to forgive her—write her a letter and tear it up or something.

How could she be like this towards her own daughter? She hadn't even given me a chance to tell her my side of the story. Maybe I should have told her what happened before the Mt. Zion cult had a chance to infuse Ellington's story in her first but she probably still wouldn't have believed what I said over her pastor's story anyway. As much as it hurt, I wasn't going to be able to continue stalking her and hoping for that one day to come when we'd be on speaking terms again.

Religion is sometimes a beast. I don't see how something that can divide families and nations can be considered Godly. Right now there are countries right next to each other that hate each other even though the inhabitants look just alike and sometimes even speak the same language—all because of religion. Christians don't like Muslims, Catholics don't agree with Christianity, a lot of people hate Jews, Christians don't like Buddhists; a lot of confusion would end if people just believed in God and got rid of the whole concept of religion or at least learned how to respect other people's beliefs.

"Okay. Ready?" Dominique walked up.

I stood up but got jerked back and almost fell. The end of my head wrap was stuck on the wooden prong of the chair's backing. When I stood up it completely unwrapped. The shaved down part of my hair had grown a whopping three inches--I looked like a misguided, lopsided Mohawk and a few of the seniors and Niquie had gotten a good view of the unsightly mess. I wrapped my head back up as quickly as possible and followed Dominique, who pretended not to notice, up the stairs.

We ended up at Starbucks in Southfield. "Leigh...I miss you and Sherra. You two were the only girlfriends I ever had," she started over a cup of hot cocoa. I didn't respond, I didn't have anything to add. As she tapped her French manicured nails against the paper cup, I remembered how she used to hold whiskey and cognac on the rocks in that exact, almost limp finger pose right before she got drunk. Sherra and I had to help her walk to the car every time we all went out and the whole time she'd be begging us to let her leave with some dude she'd just met.

"I'll never forget the day my life changed. It was three years ago in January. I was high on X, drunk and with some guy I had just met. He needed to make a run so he locked me in his basement. 'Until he got back'—he said." She rolled her eyes in repulsion. "I was so fucked up I couldn't even think. I waited and waited, then, I sobered up and pulled out my phone to try to call you but it was dead--and it was like a year almost since we had talked... So I stayed locked down there and tried to make the best out of it. Two days had gone by and I hadn't heard shit from him, I didn't have my phone charger--nothin'. I was scanning the channels on cable. There wasn't shit on to watch and for some reason--you know that channel that tells you what's on? It was blurry. So...I reached on top of the television for the TV guide and—there were a whole bunch of papers and mail piled on top so I started looking thru it checking for his last name and stuff. When I was flipping thru the papers I found this one lab result document. The guy was HIV positive and he hadn't told me shit. We had messed around and stuff, but something had made me pull out a condom even though he got real pissed about it and tried to take it off.

"I sat there trippin'. I couldn't believe it. And I needed somebody to come get me. But I couldn't do anything but wait. So...finally, like three days later—he was a baller and had been on runs or whatever—he finally came back. I had been waiting in his basement for *five* days. No food...nothing! The only reason I had water was because he had a shower and a sink down there.

"When he walked in, he had brought four guys that he wanted me to to um-hook up with. He was like, 'dis trick bitch right here finer dan uh muhafuka, an' since it ain't no fun if da homies cain't have none, get in where y'all fit in.' They were all laughing. They were drunk and obviously on some other stuff... Me? I was sober and in my *right* mind at this point. So I refused...and...well...I'll spare you the details--but it wasn't good. I fought. I had to fight them off with everything I had. Mother and Father protected me, girl. I felt a strength that was beyond my own. They raped me, yeah...but...it could have been so much worse. I just knew they were gonna kill me that afternoon. And in a way, they kinda did.

"When they finally let me go, I got in my car and drove to the nearest park and cried for hours. I felt disgusted...real disgusted... Before I went home, I realized I needed gas in my car or I was gonna be stranded so I went to a station on Grand River and Greenfield. This lady was in there just smiling all crazy. She had her head wrapped and stuff. She was looking at me when I walked up to the cashier and she smiled. I was still crying and I was about to cuss her out. I thought she was laughing at me or something. But instead, she told me that God and the Goddess had a plan for me that was so much greater than what I'd ever imagined. Then she just up and hugged me outta the blue. She gave me her number and asked me to come to her church that night. So I did. When I got there I knew it was my answer. I was about to go home that night and blow my head off. All I had ever been to anybody--Harold, to the ballers I'd dated—to the two players off the NFL I had kicked it with, to the niggas off the block—all I ever was ta any of 'em was some quick ass, nothing else—not even human.

"They'll say it's not true but that's the way a lot of guys see women. Meat for a quick fix—that's how I felt everyday, all day. Whenever I'd meet a guy I really liked, they weren't trying to be serious with me. Whether it was a one-night stand or I was dating somebody it always ended up the same way. But that incident was my breaking point.

"I—I wanted it all to end. Hell, I figured nobody'd care anyway. I hadn't talked to my mother since I had moved out of her house...

"But that lady—Sister Smith, helped save my life. The next day I went to the hospital and got checked and reported everything. Before I went to the Center that night, I was just going to let it all slide and take it out on myself. Some of the workshops they had at The Center taught me how to develop my own relationship with my makers—I mean, everybody doesn't need a church—that's not what I'm saying. I'm just saying the people there had a really positive impact on me. I started learning about Egypt and other old world cultures... It wasn't like I had to come and give up all my money to some preacher or like I had to go somewhere and listen to somebody tell me I was a heathen...

"So, anyway, Sister Smith helped me get a job working at the Southfield library as a receptionist. I moved, changed my cell number and left the past in the past. That's why I started volunteering for the soup kitchen—I couldn't just sit back without giving something back.

"And you know what? The people who came to the soup kitchen, they accepted me. They talked to me like I was human. They listened to my story. Some of them were junkies, or had lost their jobs, a few people had gotten divorced or lost in society while a few of them had made conscious decisions to drop out of society--but each one of them helped turn my life around...

"Then I met Greg. I was at the car wash waiting for my car." She smiled. "He was the first guy to ever take me out without trying to get some first and he was the first guy to ever asked what my real name was, too. Everybody always called me Niquie or Geneva--my street alias--I got it from a font I used to use when I sent out emails... Where was I? Oh, yeah. So we started dating and—I figured he was gonna eventually dump me when I told him about my past—but, instead he made an appointment for me to see a counselor. Can you believe that, girl?

"So, after I came to grips with my life, my past and all of that—he asked me to marry him and I didn't know what to say. At first I was like, 'No.' I didn't want to *ever* be with another man again. I had even started dating a few females. One of them was alright...but—well, you know—I always liked the dick—I mean men...

"But, Greg was real patient with me. He stuck around even though we weren't intimate and, when I was ready, he proposed again, girl but I waited for Spirit to guide me. When I got my answer, I told him yes, besides, I was in love with him from the get go anyway but, I was scared. And—"

At this point my weak ass was already crying. It was like she had taken a page out of my journal and added a little more to it. "Leigh, you don't have to cry for me—trust me—I did enough of that myself. But—"

"—No, girl. I feel you. I've been thru some stuff that would blow your mind and--" I stopped short feeling bad for cutting her off. "Go on, I'm listening."

"Well, *would* I have done things differently? I *wish* I could've but it didn't work out that way. I didn't know any better. I was out in tha streets lookin' for a brotha to love me but all I was getting was high ass hooker status and my bills paid. Every holiday I was by myself while they'd be at home with their wives or their girlfriends—the ones they so-call 'respected.' I coulda pointed out where almost any baller in the hood was posted at, I had an account this one guy that played for the Lions put money into every month and even then, every holiday, I was alone. No phone calls, nothing.

"But I wasn't jealous of the women they were with—ungh-uh. They're still gettin' cheated on and treated like property, too. That was the whole reason I started being like 'I gotta get paid' in the first place. The wife, the fiancee, the girlfriend, the hoe, the mistress--all of them suffer in relationships like that.

"So, then, after I had gotten my life together and I was feeling way, *way better* about who I was and after I was finally able to look in the mirror and actually *like* the person looking back at me, I got tested *something awful*, girl.

"After finding out I was HIV negative—and trust me I prayed that away *real hard*--I finally felt like I had a real reason to live. I didn't want my time to be up at that point.

"But then, this guy offered me a leading role in a movie he was about to shoot in LA for Video Tech. Now you know that was a test! They're the biggest company in Black porn—the upscale stuff.

"...I'd be lying if I told you I wasn't about to do it—I was even gonna use my alias as my industry name. They were offering me three hundred K a year. My housing was gonna be covered if I did x amount of movies *and everything*. And—truth be told—I was good at fucking. I liked it. Hell, I lived for ana--my bad. I shouldn't be talking like this to—"

"—Dominique! It's not even like that. Be real. Girl, I ain't as *innocent* as you *think*."

She smiled and continued, "But when I meditated I kept seeing that HIV confirmation that dude had on top of the television.

"I was planning on leaving without telling Greg and going out there even after everything that had happened. Do you know one of the guys that raped me shot me? On purpose? I mean, he grazed me and—thankfully, it wasn't real serious--but, look," she pulled her sleeve up and exposed a scar that looked like a tiny gash. "For weeks I could still hear the way they were laughing and the gunshot after he fired at me ringing in my head. They had the nerve to give me three G's when they finally shoved me out of the side door... And I was still gonna go to Cali... I was beyond lost, girl.

"I was at Metro airport, bound for LAX when I decided my life needed to change once and for all. Evil forces wanted my spirit, Leigh. I mean, I'm not hating on no porn stars, I still like India *and* Dee myself—I'm just being real, sorry."

"Girl, India is that deal, she don't be looking all raggedy *and* girl is banking. What?" We slapped fives and had to laugh at ourselves afterwards.

"What I meant to say is that it wasn't my destiny. I probably woulda gotten strung out on something worse and wound up dead. I *know* I wouldn't be alive right now. I was too wild and didn't know when to stop. But..." She sighed before taking another sip of her latte. "I was blessed to meet Sister Smith that day in the gas station. She's like my surrogate mother now.

"And Greg? I don't care what they say about Black men. There *are* some good ones out there. If a man really loves you, you'll know by the way he treats you. I mean, we have our arguments and stuff—who doesn't—but, I *know* he loves me.

"...After those guys raped me and *whipped my ass*, I can't have kids. Having kids meant everything to Greg since he doesn't have any but he *still* married me... We're about to adopt... It's not the same as having your own—well, maybe I shouldn't say that. Maybe there's a child out there that needs us as badly as we need him or her. I'm excited about it. I know, I *know* I ran my mouth and probably told you way *too* much but, Leigh, I really miss you and Sherra and... I *know* I wasn't always a good friend but, I...I want you to understand where I was coming from and where I've been. I didn't have a mother like yours and--trust me--my life wasn't no bed uh roses growing up. When I was little, Barbara'd lock me in the basement for hours when she wanted to go out—that's part of why I was always truant from school—it's a miracle I even graduated from elementary. I remember one time I asked her for something to eat--I had to be like four. She slammed my head into the toilet and made me drink water out of it... I think she had really fallen for my father but she was too young to know how to deal with the situation.

"One time she told me that she had ran into his wife and kids when she had gone to his gas station to ask him for some money. You should have seen the look in her eyes... I know for a fact he paid my grandmother off so she wouldn't press charges.

"I've forgiven them but I don't deal with Barbara or her family. She's only with Harold 'cause he takes care of her financially. She's not about to leave him any time soon. And my grandmother had abused her the same way...used to beat her with bullwhips, make her stand outside in the winter without a coat and she broke Barbara's arm one time...

"I'm just glad I finally received a wake up call. Otherwise I'd probably be repeating--" Dominique stopped short for a few seconds and stared out of the window. Shaking her head, she sighed. "Being pretty was the only thing I had going for myself and even then—that same prettiness was gonna be the death of me... But, there comes a time when you can't go around blaming other people for your problems. You've gotta face the demons lurking around in your mind and grow into something better." This was as real as Dominique had ever been with me.

I reached over and squeezed her hand. We talked until Starbucks closed.

"I WAS WONDERING WHERE you were," Smiley tried to fuss when I came in. Dina was long gone leaving him with the kids. He looked back and forth from Dominique to me and started smiling like he was on a Kool Aid commercial. "Well, I'm 'bout to head off to G's. I'm tired and I needta be up at five."

"Baby, can you stick around for a second? I wanna talk to you," I asked as he grabbed his coat.

"Don't mind me, Malik. I'm about to leave anyway," Dominique protested laughing.

"Naah. Y'all need ta do tha girls night thing. And *I* godda make *that* money. How else are we gonna make it to Hawaii? Peace out, baby. I'll hit you up before I go to sleep." Um hm. For phone sex.

Dom and I stayed up the whole night. I filled her in up to the present day on my life, we cracked up at our own mishaps, ate popcorn and acted like we were sixteen again.

Chapter 22

It was twelve in the after noon and Darren'd already emailed me five times. "What?" I huffed after calling him back on private. He wasn't about to get my new cell number and I didn't have time for his begging today. I still needed to get all the plans together for Smiley and Pharaoh's birthday parties.

"Baby—"

"--One more time and *I'm hanging up*, Darren."

"Sorry. You know I still love you, bab—Leigh--I can't help it... I wanna have Pharaoh's party at the crib—I already scheduled the caterers."

"That won't be necessary. Next year is your turn. We already rented the Jeepers in Auburn Hills for a couple of hours. It starts at six o'clock. See you then."

"WAIT! Leigh! I—I had a major surprise for you. Oh yeah--I put some money in your account and I been waiting for you to pick your truck back up. Why you actin' like this? Can you just stop by here tomorrow? *Please*?"

"Keep your truck. See you Thursday at six. Peace." I hung up. I didn't need shit from him except for him to show up and spend time with his son at his party. And if he couldn't comply with that, it was cool. Smiley was more than willing to adopt both of the kids in the event the opportunity arose.

Before going to choose a cake from the bakery from the plaza up the street, I called and set up counseling sessions with a new therapist that was unaffiliated with Darren and his crew. I set up voice and violin lessons at the Southfield Cultural Center. When I had moved back to the apartment I didn't have the money for the sessions. Otherwise I wouldn't have stopped the classes. It was nice to actually feeling like you were good at *something*.

Smiley called catching me before I left out and we caught up on phone sex since Dominique had spent the night. "I'm not going back to school. After yesterday, I just don't think I want to go back," I informed him after I told him about the vision I had yesterday.

"I mean, if you wanna be a homemaker, I'm straight with that but make sure it's what *you* wanna do. I don't want you blaming me for not helping you reach your full potential twenty years from now. YouknowwhatImean? Figure out what your purpose in life is. If it's not school, fine but I godda feeling you got a dream you need to go tor. If you want Leigh, you can really contribute something to the world."

"You're always way too deep for your own good, you know that? 'Contribute something to the world'? Somebody's got some mighty ostentatious dreams for me, hungh?"

"Nah. You can really be something—*for yourself*, not to impress me or nobody else. The potential is in you and if you use it, you're gonna be helping a lot of otha people out. I ain't tryin' ta share you but the world needs sistas like you to stand up, baby."

"Okay, whatever, Smiley. Have a good day baby. I love you."

"Um-hm."

"Um-hm? Um-hm. Aright. I see how you are."

"Well, promise me you gonna think about what I said."

"...Yeah...I will."

"You know I love you. I'm just speakin' truth, baby."

"WHAD UP, MA?" Smiley came in earlier than I was expecting. I ran out of the kitchen to the bathroom and searched underneath the sink in the basket with all my hair stuff in it for a scarf to cover my hair up. Good thing he'd only caught a glimpse of me from the left. "Aye, why you running when I come to in? What's up?" He tapped on the locked bathroom door. Until now I had done a very good job of *never* letting him see my real hair condition.

"Hold on, I'm abouta come out." I wrapped my hair and slid an auburn satin scarf on.

"What's wrong wit ya' head?" he quizzed.

"Nothing... How was your day--oh, yeah, I been meaning to ask you what you wanna do for your birthday? You never told me. All you said was that you wanted to hit up that reggae club on Woodward. What else?"

"Naah. Back up. What's the problem? Why can't I see ya' hair?" He put his hand on his chin and started looking at me sideways.

"...Nothing, baby." Okay. I was starting to get real uncomfortable. He was looking at me like I'd just told him I was a man or something. What if he made me show him my hair and then wasn't attracted to me anymore? Wasn't shit cute about having a three-inched, antipodal strip running down the right side of your cranium.

"Aright...take ya' scarf off for uh minute, then."

"Why?"

"I just wanna see." He wasn't about to let up.

"No." I wasn't about to back down either. I wasn't about to lose him. Not now. He made an attempt to pull my scarf off. "I saaaaaaaaaaaaid, NO!" I got loud and was ready to get 'Bout-it, Bout-it' on him all over again. Who did he think he was trying to take something off *my* head?

"Aright. You itchin' for an argument and *I ain't* about to argue wit chu." He left out of the side door. Seconds later when he came back in he threw a CD into the stereo system. Some song about loving yourself and being a Black woman. "Nah...I'ma ask you one more time. Can you *please* take-the-scarf-off?" He tilted his head to the side and stared thru me relentlessly as he bit his bottom lip.

Oh goodness. "And I'ma tell *you* one more time. NO!" I walked back into the kitchen and finished loading the dishes into the dishwasher. The kids had made a sloppy mess on their plates with the turkey chilli I'd fixed.

"What's wrong wit ya' hair?"

"I need a perm, that's all."

"First of all, do you know what they put in that shit? It's not good for *your hair* or *your body*. When you relax your hair, it's like you sayin' 'I wasn't created good enough.' And then, on top of that, you can't get some of the messages, God and Goddess send you. Hair is like an antenna for humans--like an extension into the universe. No woman in my family's ever put that *conk* coon shit on their hair." His face turned into repulsion when he spit out the word conk.

"Trina and Daye *both* had bone straight ass hairstyles *when I saw 'em.*"

"They get their hair pressed or eitha they wear braids."

"Yeah, well, I'm not ya' mama, ya' sister or ya' cousin. Marry one of them, then," I stated flatly as the song continued blasting.

"Leigh. Look at me. You be lookin' good when you get all hooked up—fa sho'. But I love *you* for who *you* are. Nappy, bald headed—it doesn't matta. I'm about ta play this song again. But this time I want you to listen to it." He guided me into the den and sat down on the couch pulling me on his lap with him. After the song ended, he sat there staring off into space. I scooted off his lap and sat next to him as he played with a lock on top of his head like he was in a trance--like he was picking up one of those hair antennae messages he was just talking about. Ten good minutes passed before I finally gave in. Partially to see how he would take it, partially to free myself.

Shawn had seen my accident right after it was freshly shaved off and he *still wanted me*. If Smiley didn't... I'd just have to find a way to get over him...eventually. And then I'd be single. For a long, long, long, long, *long* time. I wasn't about to go thru all this relationship shit again. Relationships could be draining. One minute everything'd be fine then, seconds later the shit was fucked up—you never knew which way the pendulum was going to swing. That was how it had always been with

Craig *and* Darren. My relationship with Smiley hadn't reached bi-polar status just yet but, if and when it did, I was prepared.

"Alright, alright. Look." I pulled the scarf off feeling like a first time science fair experiment. "I did this to myself--after I came back from the hospital. It was a bad time. I shouldn't have gone back to that apartment. And I almost slit my wrist with the clippers, too. So, now that you officially think I'm crazy, what?" I felt way too exposed, internally and externally.

"...We're supposed to be one, Leigh. If you feel better walking around with it on, fine. But if you can walk around without covering your head up when I'm not here then you don't have to do it when I'm around eitha. I love you. No matter what. I'm just glad you didn't end up taking yourself outta this world. Then who would I have? I woulda had to live my whole life without my soulmate." He put his hand in my hair. And I let him for a minute. Then I put my scarf back on. It was nice—actually wonderful to know he accepted me no matter how I looked but I wasn't about to be walking around the house looking crazy when he came home from work. I wasn't stupid. I'd seen a couple of his female clients and they didn't look raggedy.

"Hey?" I had a sudden impulse.

"Yeah?"

I took his hand and led him into the bedroom. The kids were busy running in circles in the living room and making enough noise to make any sane person look into permanent earplugs.

I locked the door behind us, threw him onto the bed and slid up against the thickness of his body. After unzipping his pants I took off my T-shirt and showed off my hardened nipples. He was already trembling uncontrollably, which thrilled me. I placed his hands on the fullness of my breasts and talked dirtier than I ever had during our phone sessions. Gingerly, I took him in my hands and jacked him off like a pro paying attention to the moves that did the most to him, repeated them when he wasn't expecting it with spit subbing for lube. I guess a little belly and no ass made for one promising future sex life. It was longer than Darren's-- *way* thicker and it curved upward. Felt like I was holding a slippery, bonefied letter J in my hands. The hook *and* girth made me kinda curious—I'd never seen one of those before.

And he did his part. I had always been a fan of nipple action but the twins had *never* gotten the attention they deserved until Mr. Malik Smiley. He tweaked, lightly pinched, teased, rubbed and sucked my D's good enough to make me cum. "I told you it was only gonna be a few seconds... And that was only a hand job." He shook his head in dismay as he wiped my hand off with tissue.

"Well... It was *eight minutes*--I should know. My hand started getting tired. But it was fun. You took care of my girls *and* you just satisfied a woman in minutes—nah, *that's what I'm talking 'bout.*" I gave him a devilish grin. This was *my man.* I at least needed to feel it in my hands if nothing else. A sister needed something while she was on pause.

"But I don't know..." My voice trailed off.

"...What?" All of a sudden he wasn't looking too happy.

"...Ah... I don't know if all of *that* is gonna fit!"

He laughed. "For every problem, there's a solution..."

"Umm, I already like the way that sounds--oh, yeah--one more thing. You're gonna need to put a pole in the basement."

"Umm-hmm—yeah, God and Goddess knew what they were doing. I definitely got that freak in tha bed I needed... And I asked for that, too." He gave me a knowing look and chuckled.

We laid there communicating without words for a while before he finally spoke. "You wanna get married next month? I been thinking..."

"Baby? I thought you'd never ask. I'd love to."

"SINCE YOU'RE NOT DOING a touch up, why don't we try something different and cut it even? Besides, it's about to get really hot and you're gonna get tired of all this hair you have *already* being trapped under a weave—especially since you joined Bally's and all." Jahla stared at me thru her station mirror. She was a lot taller than Zada, wore black cat-eye glasses and had a slightly rounder face and a much smaller chest. She'd traded her mid-back length curls for a cute, bouncy chin length retro fro.

Jahla's just as gorgeous as her older sister. Jahzada could easily become a petite sized model while Jahla could do runway.

Jahla ran her dainty fingers thru my brittle, damaged, glue-bonded tresses. "You really do have some nice hair—it's thick and with a little mouse—who knows?"

"...I don't know." I was apprehensive. All my life I'd gotten compliments on the length of my hair. And my texture wasn't the same as hers. Within no time her hair would be down her back again. Who knew if my hair'd ever grow back again? I'd already been waiting forever for the little fuzz that had finally cropped up.

"You have a nice head shape and face for it... We could do something that would give you a spunky sophisticated look. And I'd leave it long enough to curl and play around with... And, hey! If you wanted, you could even get ponytails and stuff, too." She was doing well to sell her preference.

One thing for sure, I was tired of feeling lopsided every time I took my scarf off. "…Well, let's go for it. I guess I should trust you…"

"Girl, I am *not* going to mess you up. I promise you're gonna like it. I've been thinking about a cut for you for a minute."

"Alright, look," she announced twirling my chair around to face the mirror two hours later. I knew I was going to start balling if it was ugly. Already I'd started feeling sick when I saw fifteen inched strands of my hair splayed onto the marble floor beneath me.

"Oh, my goodness! It looks *gooooood*! I can't *be-lieeeeeeeee-ve* it!" I looked different, like a totally different person. Definitely more sophisticated.

"Girl you look like a bad you know what…" Jahla didn't curse.

"A bad Bitch? Girl, I know! What did you do to the color?"

"I added a bit of warmth to your hair to bring out your skin tone and to get you ready for summer." The brownish auburn tint made me look like a Hollywood star along with the cut. My slightly waved hair was flattened against my head but spiked a bit on top. The edges near my ear came to a fine point and there was enough overall length to try other styles in the future. I couldn't stop staring at myself. "And see? We didn't even relax it. I don't know why KD was giving you relaxers in the first place. All you need to do is put mouse on it when it's wet and tie it down with strips like these. You can get 'em at the beauty supply for like a dollar.

"You'll probably need to come in every week for a trim unless you wanna line yourself up and just come in twice a month. It shouldn't be that bad, though--we didn't give you a shaved taper. If it grows out a lil', you'll be able to play it off. Oh yeah, use this shampoo. It's really good for our hair," she advised.

From the minute I stepped out onto the streets, I got noticed. Cars honked; a few fellas who worked at thirty-sixth district court walked up and started a casual conversation while I waited for valet to pull up with my car.

Each step I took, my hips, my behind and my legs all staked their claim in a confident, sexy swagger that made my stride lethal. No one could tell me anything! *I* was the shit! I'd gotten three different offers for lunch by the time I tipped the valet--the most compliments I'd ever gotten strictly on face. Usually it was a flat out "you're fine" or "that body." This time it was all about "the girl with that beautiful face."

At stoplights, guys rolled down their windows and asked me to pull over. I'm talking 'bout businessmen in suits, B-Boys, the thugs—all kinds of fine men. I enjoyed the attention but always made a point to hold up my ring and let them know I was unavailable, much to their disappointment. Poor things.

Dina's mouth fell open when I entered the house. "Girl you look gorgeous! You look something like that new girl—that model that always be on the cover of *King* magazine and on those Maybeline commercials.

Pharaoh looked confused for a second before starting another game on Playstation.

"Mommy?" Mauri asked looking up and scrunching her eyebrows. "Yes, sweetie, it's mommy." I picked her up and let her pat my hair. It was first time in months I'd let her touch my hair.

"Your plate's in the microwave and salad's in the fridge," I informed Smiley as he slid his work boots off.

He stood speechless for a few seconds thereafter. "DAMN, BABY!" He pulled me into the bedroom and couldn't stop kissing me and feeling on my butt. "Yeah, we *godda get* married soon. But I wanna do it the right way--so you know I'm for real and ta set an example fa tha kids. I ain't tryin' ta do you like them otha muthafuckas." We both walked out of the room breathing *real* heavy.

"...Hey?" He looked up from the baked fish, alfredo pasta and the spring green salad I'd fixed. "...Why you been workin' out so much lately?"

"...Well, I read in Sister Shahyra's book that we as Black Americans don't always take the best care of our health, our country has a high obesity rate *and*... I feel better after I work out..." I turned away from straightening the cluttered cabinets to face him.

"...You want me to lose weight?" His eyes were suspicious.

"What? No... Why'd you ask me *that*?"

"Well...you aren't nowhere near fat and you've been cooking like you on some otha shit lately."

"Baby." I sat on his lap. "You know how you told me you'd love me no matter how *my* hair looked? I feel the same way about you in every way. If you get heavier or skinnier, I don't care as long as you continue loving me the way you do. But, I *will* say this: we need to cut out some of the processed foods we eat and we need to stop going to Coney Island all the time. It's not healthy and I'm not gonna be feeding my body junk and I'm definitely *not* about to be fixing *my* man food that's gonna slowly kill him either. After meeting something like you, I'm not ready to be a widow anytime soon." Being that I could read his thoughts, I also knew what else he was hinting at. "Just because I got this hair cut and finally got rid of low hair-esteem, doesn't mean I'm about to start thinking I'm too good for you—or that I'm going to want somebody else. I've never felt anything this strong for *any* man in the world. I love you, Smiley." He looked up and took my hand from his face and kissed it. Our eyes met and, with his eyes, he smiled back at mine.

I know it's terrible and I hate to admit it but, at first, I just knew I was out of Shawn *and* Malik's league but, actually, both of them were better people than the kind of person I'd started turning into for a minute there.

"What you thinkin' 'bout? You lookin' all serious."

"Nothing. Hey, you wanna go to the Southfield library with us tonight? The kids're getting addicted to the telie and I know it's *my* fault. I got so used to being depressed, I was always pushing them off on Nickelodeon. Tonight they have a children's storyteller coming—it's every Wednesday. I think I'm gonna make it one of their weekly activities."

I was still sitting on his lap. He pulled me closer to him, "Damn, girl. You getting it together over night, hungh? I'm proud of you. Yeah, let's go. There's some books I been meaning to pick up anyway. Promise me something, though?"

"Hmm?"

"You won't loose this bubble." He popped my butt. "These thighs." He rubbed my legs and squinted his eyes and sucked in his breath, "And that smile. It always does something to me. That's why you need my last name." I shook my head and tried not to smile back. I loved it when he twisted his lips like that--my baby definitely had a lil' hood in him.

"You need ta stop--that's what you need to do!"

"Can't take it, can you?" I tried to laugh without smiling. "Aaahh—yep. There it goes," he teased as I broke into a toothy grin.

We had a good time. When story time ended, Smiley ordered two hot cocoas at the library's café for us and apple juice for the kids. We sat by the fireplace as he read another children's book to Mauri and Pharaoh who weren't quite ready to leave. He was so animated they couldn't stop laughing. I just sat back and watched in sheer admiration.

"We need more Black families like y'all," an older, salt and pepper haired man commented as he walked by.

"I GOT THE GO ahead earlier this week, baby. You have a particular day in mind?" he asked from the driver's seat of the van. It was getting harder and harder to see him leave each night. I couldn't wait til I could sleep next to Smiley. There was nothing like the one night we'd fallen asleep in each other's arms. I needed that feeling every night.

"June eighth?"

"Aright. I'll start shopping for flight deals. I think I already found a place to stay at—it's a resort. I'll give you the info so you can check it out online and see if you like it. I'ma see if the travel agent Greg uses'll hook us up."

Plying myself away after he kissed me good night was absolutely awful. It felt like he was going off to war or something else just as bad.

CHAPTER 23

PHARAOH MADE IT VERY clear that it was his big day by getting up at five thirty in the morning and acting like he'd had two gallons of sugar for breakfast.

At five o'clock, Sherra and her family showed up at Jeepers to help set up. She'd invited a few of her little cousins along with Tommy's girlfriend's daughter since they were the only other kids Pharaoh and Mauri played with and I didn't have any other kids to invite.

"Girl! You look good!" Sherra's mother grabbed me and hugged me after planting a kiss and red lipstick on my cheek. The minute she stepped in the door Pharaoh was stuck to her.

"No, Mama Harris, *you* look good." I swear this was one lady who just wasn't aging. Her short height and twenty something looking skin only made her look younger.

"What I tell you 'bout that, chile? It's mama ta you—not no Mama Harris." She smiled.

"Whad up, LeeLee. Don't start tryin' ta think you cute." Tommy, with his fresh ceasar, wave haircut sportin' self, came over and playfully patted me on the head. Marsa smiled. She was a cute, babyfaced brown skinned girl and was doing exceptionally well in high school being a teenage mother. I gave her a hug and caught up on the colleges she was interested in going to.

Niquie called for directions and rushed over.

"What chu invite *dat* hoe for?" Sherra complained out of Niquie's earshot.

"Sher, don't start. You need to talk to her. Tonight, after the party, we're all going out. And don't try to back out."

"Hmph…whatever." She cut her eyes at me and finished setting napkins on the table next to the cake.

"Hey, girl. You look good!" Niquie complimented.

"So do you." She had her hair pulled back into a slick, long ponytail and was wearing a yellow baby doll top with a pair of Seven jeans and a pair of strappy, four inched heel sandals with crystal butterflys on them that were to die for. Her outfit kind of matched mine.

I had on a short, pink baby doll top with a white midriff jean jacket, my favorite pair of Seven jeans and a pair of pink and white shell toe Adidas. Mauri was in a pink baby doll dress and had on pink and white baby Adidas while Smiley and Pharaoh were both wearing white Adidas tee's, matching navy and white Adidas track pants and gymshoes. The only difference was Smiley was wearing an Adidas visor but he'd found a navy hat with the number four on the front for Pharaoh.

"Girl, look." Niquie tugged on her Tiffany's chain with the dangling heart and matching bracelet. I had on the exact same set. And we both had round diamond earrings on. We busted out laughing. "How'd you get your eye shadow like that? It's hot," she inquired.

"It's Estee's new trio. I put the pink on first and added a little brown in the crease," I responded before being thrown off by her sudden grimace. I turned around only to see Darren entering with Mike and Syra.

Niquie quickly regained her composure but Darren looked like he was going to have a heart attack when he spotted me. He was walking all fast like he was George Jefferson. "Hey, bab-" I gave him a look that cut him off. "I—I mean, Leigh. Come here, can I talk to you for a second? Please."

"Sure."

He took a second look at Niquie like it was déjà vu before pulling me to the side. "I know I fucked up. But I wanna let you know I'm sorry-- for real. I miss you and I—and I need you back in my life. When I said I loved you, I was serious. I meant what I said... And *damn*, why you gotta be looking so good? You sportin' a lil' washboard now, huh?" He attempted to touch my stomach after tapping me on the nose.

I jerked away and, before I had a chance to say anything, I felt Smiley's arm around my waist. "This is my fiancé, Smiley," I introduced them as Malik stuck his available hand out for a shake. Darren looked as if he'd just been attacked by a hundred E.T.'s and brought back down to earth. Finally, when he started breathing again, he shook his head in disbelief. I didn't know what exactly was about to go down but it didn't look too good.

"Well, man... I really love this woman. I know I fucked up but I really love this one. She's definitely a keeper," he stated in a sincerely regretful tone.

"Yeah, I'm blessed to have her in my life."

"Hold up. You said your name's Smiley?"

"Yeah."

"You heard of Smiley plumbing?"

Malik curved those sexy ass weed-smoking lips of his into a proud grin. "Yeah, that's me and my peeps."

"Oh, yeah? I heard about your company. So *you're* that young dude everybody's talkin' 'bout. They say your company's taking off, fa sho'. My boy—you know, the mayor of Detroit, right? He put us up on you."

"Oh, yeah? Sometimes Detroit visits my church. Well, I'm trying. I've definitely got a vision."

"Yeah…well. Keep puttin' in the time and, with the way everybody's talking, you definitely gon' be on the come-up, stackin'." Darren actually sounded genuine.

"It's nice meeting you, man," Smiley stated before walking over to help Pharaoh who was calling Smiley over to lift him into one of the rides.

"Leigh… I wish it was still us… But—well I'm happy you aren't with that project rat. I'll give it to you, this one's got potential. But if he ever fucks up, you know how to reach me. You gon' always have ma heart, baby." A tear formed in the corner of his eye. The photographer came over and snapped a picture of the scene. Darren gave me one more glancing over, shook his head and walked over to join Pharaoh and Smiley.

I went over to where Niquie was standing all by herself. Sy was rolling her blues at Niq and watching Mike as though her life depended on it.

"Girl, I used to have *major* beef with that one right there." Niquie nodded towards Sy before laughing it off. "I had a thing running with Michelangelo back in the day. She used to be a dancer. And *boy* was she sweating him," she whispered.

"*That's* his real name? Michelangelo—*uuggh!*" I laughed. Mike definitely didn't fit his name.

"Hey." Sy stepped towards me under the pretense of starting conversation. "Something smells in here. Must be the trash…" she alluded looking towards Niquie. Niquie walked away and was cut off by Mauri who was now waving her arms in the air to be picked up.

"Oh, I'm sorry. I forgot to introduce you to one of my best friends. That's Mrs. Gregory *Attwater*—you know—the mayor of Southfield? That's *his* wife… Did you check out that ring she's wearing?" I widened my eyes for emphasize. I wasn't about to let her think she'd gotten one up on Dominique. Sy's mouth promptly hit the floor.

"I think Mike and I are about to head out, we're on the way to the Yacht Club—they're having an exclusive party and we're VIP. Nice seeing you." Try as she might, she couldn't conceal her anger. Her face was completely red. She went over and harassed Mike in efforts of getting him to leave but he was too busy drooling over Niquie like she was a lobster feast.

And of all people, Darren's parents showed up frontin' like they spent quality time with Pharaoh. Pharaoh wasn't even interested in talking to them. He waited politely while they made small talk and then raced back over to where Sherra's mother was following the cameraman once they all left. Mama Harris had been on the photographer's heels making sure he got as many pictures his roll of film could take.

"Oh, my gosh, girl. This little girl's won my heart. She's so *adorable*! If you ever need a babysitter just give me a holler," Niquie gushed while holding Mauri who, amazingly, was quite comfortable in her arms. I guess she had gotten tired of competing for Tommy's attention with Marsa's daughter Jia.

"You want a goddaughter?"

"Oh, my gosh! You wouldn't?"

"Consider it done."

"Besides, Sherra's got Pharaoh. It's your turn."

"Auntie Di-*na*? Dina?" I looked around and smiled as Pharaoh called Dina over to help him pour the juice into his cup. I guess he had gotten over his crush after all.

Everything I needed was right here standing before me at Jeepers; my family was here and this had very well turned into one of the best days of my life.

After we cleaned up I pulled Sherra to the side. "Okay, make sure you tell them, you're spending the night at my place. I'm taking you home tomorrow. We're about to go out. And watch that carping tongue of yours."

"Aright, aright. Gosh. You sure you not *in* da mafia?" she joked, yanking her arm back. She was well aware of the *Scarface*, *Godfather*, *Casino* fetish.

Dina and Tommy took the kids with them since tomorrow was Smiley's birthday. He still hadn't really said what he wanted to do but he'd told me not to worry too much about making plans.

Smiley walked out with G who had stopped by for the party and headed to his crib while Sherra, Niquie and I went to Starbucks. The ride there was so tense, even good reggae wasn't shaking the stiffness going on.

"Okay. Here's the deal. Sherra we were all cool before. Life changes. We've had our moments good and bad. It's time to squash tha beef. You two need to talk so I'm gonna go sit over there. Deal?"

"Not like I have a choice!" Sherra folded her arms and twisted her lips to the side.

"Exactly." I went on the other side of the coffee shop and ran today's events over in my head. I still couldn't believe Darren took everything so well. There had to be a catch. Seemed like he was going to try something before everything was said and done. But I didn't want to think about any of that. Instead I sat quietly thinking about the wedding and then opened this Andy Warhol book that was funny as hell and finished reading a chapter.

A while later I looked over there and saw Sherra's finger all up in Niquie's face. Well, they couldn't go anywhere. I stole Niq's keys out of her purse when they first sat down and Sherra'd rode with me.

I walked over to them ready to call a truce or the EMS only to find both of them cracking up talking about a pair of cheap shoes I had way back when from Rainbow. The heel broke the second we went inside Legends nightclub so I had to sit down the whole night. "That's not funny. You two're supposed to be making up, not making fun of me!"

"Oh come on. You know dat shit was funny as hell. You was dancing like crazy in that chair. 'Member how you was standin' on your tippy-toe when we left out," Niq interjected before getting up and copying off how ridiculous I had looked walking out of the club—even I had to laugh.

"And you tried ta wear those shoes *again* when we went out ta Captains!" Sherra added shaking her head.

"You wanna talk about somebody? Aright. *Well*, what about that time that guy was trying to *rob you* at tha bus stop and—"

"—You ain't have nothin' but some pennies and nickels on you and dude threw tha change in yo' face and was like, 'I cain't even buy uh pint uh liquor wit dis shit here!' " Niquie finished my sentence, lighting into Sherra.

"Um-hm. Evrybody told yo' ass ta stop working dem late shifts at Burger King! But you wudden't tryin' ta listen. All you was thinking about was: *Joe* and *that prom*." I added

All Sherra could do was bust out laughing right along with us. "He was like, 'How you gon' pay da bus fare?' I just showed him my student bus card and he walked off." Sherra chuckled.

CHAPTER 24

I WANTED TO DO more but Smiley insisted on a 'come as you are' type of dinner thing downtown at Fishbones. His family was there along with G, an Israeli guy everybody called Yogurt who Smiley'd known since elementary school and Hakeem--a dude from the center.

I felt four hundred percent better after Sherra, Dina, Dominique and Greg showed up—otherwise it would have been a very unpretty event. When they finished dinner even though everyone else was having dessert, his family gave him his presents and left and Smiley's mother made sure to give me an 'I still don't like yo' triflin' behind' look as they left out.

They weren't trying to push him out of the family business but they were non-vocally standing their ground on not liking my ass. The way he was handling it surprised me, though. He kept them at a distance since they were refusing to come to our wedding and he brought me with him whenever they invited him over. His reasoning was since we were getting married, we were about to be one; at some point they were going to have to respect that. But no matter how much they wanted to hate me, I made up my mind to be respectful towards them as long as they didn't try anything with me like talking about me in my face. All things considered, they *had* done an excellent job raising my man.

I was surprised Greg came with us to the reggae spot. You could tell he was really fond of Malik. Although Greg had a gray stripe of hair that ran across the front of his head, he looked better with the low fade he was wearing than he had with that long side-burned fro. He seemed like he had a good sense of humor and actually looked more than decent in his white, button down shirt, jeans and casual black shoes. Niq had her hair pulled into a regal fifty-ish bun with a white summer blouse, jeans the same color as Greg's, huge sparkly princess cut earrings on her ears and a pair of white snake skin six inched sandals on her freshly French pedicured feet. And her makeup was flawless as usual.

Pulling out her chair every time she got up and with his subtle affectionate touches and glances it was easy to see that he treated Niq like royalty. Together they looked like a ritzy couple.

I wore a casual form fitting white strapless ruffled dress Craig never allowed me to wear that was just long enough to not be *too* short and did well to show off my legs. A pair of one carat diamonds graced my ears, a heavy tennis bracelet on my wrist, a short natural French manicure on my fingernails and toes and, with my favorite nine hundred dollar mink silver Valentina heels, I was simple classy chic.

Smiley wore the Bob Marley T-shirt I'd gotten him for his birthday over another tee shirt and some extra baggy jeans that hung just right on him along with his favorite Timb's.

The minute we entered the smoke filled, dimly lit green, red and black club, it seemed like every Rasta up in the joint came up to greet him.

A few sistas checked me out like they had been planning on landing Smiley and wanted to peep the competition to see if they still had a chance.

The place was off the hook and crowded with faces that got even more live after Malik entered. He said his "whassups," and pulled me onto the dance floor and we did our thing for a few songs. I was real tempted to wind my hips and do some of them Patra reggae *thangs* on the dance floor but me and Niq just exchanged looks and kept rocking to the beats in respectable, rhythmic fashion with our men. The whole time I was thinking about how I was going to break into the real deal and slow wind all night long for my baby after this wedding. Looked like Niq was going to be doing *that* later tonight.

Smiley was smiling as wide as humanly possible and we were making up some crazy moves that had Dina cracking up. "Psspt. Look," Niq nudged me. Sherra and G were standing against the wall talking. "Now, *that*? That would be funny!" she added. I nodded my head in agreement secretly hoping something would come out of it.

Then we went to another spot—some new club that opened last week. "Ma main man, whassup, whassup," the doorman greeted Smiley and gave him an old school shake. "They got drinks for you and whole ya' crew if y'all want 'em, all night--all night, partna." The two level loft-like club was packed shoulder to shoulder with young Black professionals and the hip-hop, extra Afrocentric type which was an odd mix; there were even a few rave looking White kids in there and it was cool. I notice Sherra stopped clutching the side of her purse with the mace sticking up in it after a couple of minutes. She'd probably smuggled it in between her chest.

When Smiley went to the bar this really pretty brunette haired White girl was flirting with him while he was waiting for his boy who was the bartender to get him a beer. Then some dark skinned chick sidled up next to him. She had a jet-black layered weave like Rachel from *Friends*, ample breasts and hips that looked like they measured up to something in the forties arena. I watched as she rested her hand on top of his. He didn't even do anything about it. A third chick—some flat-chested, without a bra, light skinned, skinny girl with neat, skinny brown shoulder length locks wearing a cute halter top and a pair of cargo pants slid in on the other side of him and sat on top of the stool at the bar just a-gigglin' on his every word. She was of those natural types that didn't believe in wearing makeup. The thang couldn't have been a day older than twenty.

I couldn't believe his ass. He started looking around and shit. If he was gonna act like this he could've just done his birthday with his boys.

I slipped my ass even further into the crowd. He left the bar and started walking towards the dance floor and stopped to flirt with a few other females. It was like every bitch up in the spot knew he had a big dick. Hell, looked like a few of 'em knew more about IT than I did, which was fine. If he was some kind of player who was known all over town that was cool. Bump fighting over a nigga. Bump trying to staying with a nigga that wasn't gonna be right. And no. I wasn't about to lose my mind all over again over some triflin' ass, monkey brained clown—nah, ungh-uh. I was just gon' call *every motherfuckin' thang off*!

I walked right past the line of chicks in the restroom and went into the stall when a female walked out of one. I was dialing Sherra's phone to tell her we were about to leave but my phone vibrated interrupting the call. "Hey baby, where are you? I been lookin' fa you." He wasn't doing shit but pulling a Craig--keeping tabs on *me* so *he* could do whatever he wanted now that he thought he had me. Nope. Not tonight, not *ever* again. Fuck that.

"I'm in the restroom." No point in going off on him. Might as well just play it cool. And bounce.

"Oh. Aright."

I stayed in the stall few a more minutes. My heart was racing. Well, when I came out and looked in the mirror, one thing was for damn sure: I *was* pretty--even *I* had to give myself that. Even with just a little bit of the bronzer on my cheeks, lip-gloss and mascara on. I could play the game right back if I wanted to... But. Why? What was the point in that? Do all of that for what? Still get hurt in the long run after going thru all the shenanigans. I was just gonna leave him alone. And I'd be all right.

He grabbed my arm and stuffed me into a hug in the hallway when I left out of the restroom.

"Whoa!" I shrieked. You scared me."

"My bad. Dang girl, what was taking you so long? You had to do the do?" he joked.

"No, I don't *do* that in public."

"Umm-hm. Come here. I want you ta meet this girl I used to kick it wit so she'll know whassup. Oh yeah--my ex is here. I wanna make sure she meets you, too."

The light skinned, skinny, lock headed, bra-disbelieving girl was his ex, Candace. She and the other girl at the bar looked at me with their eyes so cross, I needed a bulletproof vest after Smiley introduced me as his fiancée.

He handed me a Safe Sex On the Beach and led the way to the dance floor. The DJ asked him to come up on stage and help with the tracks in the booth. I moved to the side of the dance floor next to Hakeem since Sherra was nowhere to be found and the rest of the crew was off doing their own thing upstairs in VIP.

"I'm stayin' posted down here. There's ain't enough ladies upstairs fa me," Hakeem stated. He was trying to make small talk but I wasn't listening to anything he was saying. There were two girls standing next to a high-topped table with their backs turned to Hakeem having a conversation I wanted to hear.

"Girl, *Malik's* the one I was tellin' you about!" It was that dark skinned girl with the weave. I turned my back so they wouldn't see me standing behind them. Hakeem was tall--a good obstruction.

"The *best sex* you ever had?" The Loudmouth asked The Weave thru an old-school Aaron Hall song.

"Girl, *YES*! He had me cumin' for ten minutes *every, single time*—I kid you not! I was feining so hard, I couldn't stop hittin' ole boy up. I'd just *think* about him and get wet. *And* he bankin', too!"

"Hmph! You bedda get on dat tanight—you know how *we* do!"

"He changed his number way back last year...started actin' all funny an' shit—you know how niggas be flippin' da script and it wudden't like I knew where he stayed at--I couldn't find him. This the first time I seen him out in *long* time."

"Um-hum. That bitch prob'ly put her foot down or sumthen."

"Um-hm. But I tole him I ain't have a problem sharin'--shit, still don't!"

"Okay!" They swapped fives and busted out laughing.

"I think I see Niq—I'm going over there," I stated to Hakeem, pointing across the room. I'd heard enough. He followed me and, after spotting a girl he stated was his type, he stayed back and flirted.

"Today is ma man's birthday, y'all. Make some *noiiiiiissssseee*! We 'bout ta get him on the mike and let him do his thing!" The DJ shouted. Everybody shouted back and clapped like crazy just as I was walking in the center of the dance floor. Seconds later, a Malik Smiley I'd never seen before stood center stage and took over the place commanding attention with this real hot lyrical flow. He free styled for a couple of minutes, randomly throwing in my name. His words were like poetry. Then he moved on from a flow about love to this flow about Black men in the hood in some smooth assed Jamaican patois. He was obviously known for this song. He broke that shit *down* and added flavor to the performance by moving his feet to the beat after he finished one of his verses. His head was moving like a rhythmic gnat high on hip-hop and his eyes had that telltale glaze that comes from hitting the trees. When he turned the mic towards the audience, they shouted back the chorus line like a bunch of barracudas and before I knew anything, he was pulling me on stage and introducing me as the woman who completed his life: His soon to be wife and The LoveLeighest thing on earth. He moved the mic away from his mouth, "Help me hook this shit up. Repeat this line." He whispered it in my ear. "You hear that track Eric's playing? Do sumthen wit it."

I repeated the chorus line whenever he looked at me and gave me the cue even though I was a little shy. I hadn't sung in front of a crowd in a long time.

"Baby! You were phenomenal!" I gushed once we got off the stage. My baby was certainly a loveable character.

Sherra came up and smiled. "G*irrrlll, you be getting 'em.* You shoulda seen these females up in here. They was like, 'they give it three months 'cause Smiley ain't gon' be able ta shut down all the you-know-what dat be in his face.' An' that light skinned girl over there—wit tha locks—you see tha one I'm talkin' 'bout?" I nodded yes. "I heard her say his sister told her he'uh be here tonight. She was pissed talkin' 'bout he ain't neva let her up on no stage when they was together even though she can flow. *Talk about tha haters*!"

"...Aye, how's that Gabe dude?" I asked her switching the subject as Smiley went to chill with Yogurt, Gabe and a group of other fellas he knew.

"...That *skinny boy*? Girl, I 'on't like *him*. He's weird and he talk too fast."

"Oh." I sighed ready to give up on her. Niq was on the floor slow dancing to a R Kelly song with her husband. Her eyes were closed as she rested her head upon his shoulder. She looked like she was in a fairytale she never wanted to wake up from and Greg was holding her like she was a delicate moonbeam he wanted to forever keep in his arms. It seemed like he was real protective of her emotions but he didn't strike me as the overbearing type. Being around them tonight, I could understand why she'd fallen for him. Dina was kicking it with a Rasta dude in full-fledged army gear on the other side of the dance floor. And here was Sherra. "Let's go dance," I suggested when a new song came on.

"*Girl...* Smiley gon' be cool wit that?" I rolled my eyes and hauled her butt on the dance floor with me. After a guy came up behind her and started dancing, I spaced myself away from them and did my own thing the next song. "Girl, I'm saved. I ain't 'bout ta be lettin' no fool paw his grimy mitts on me on *nobody's* dance floor. Hmh!" Sherra said frowning her eyebrows like an angry *Sesame Street* puppet when she came up beside me to dance.

We rolled out before the club shut down and went our separate ways after the fellas wished Malik another good year.

I hugged Niq and Sherra and invited them over for dinner next week. "Oh, yeah, you two. Don't make any plans for the week of June eighth. You're gonna be in a wedding in Hawaii," I casually announced. "Oh Ma Good-ness! Oh Ma *Good-ness*!" Dom and Sher started walking around all crazy acting like Shanae-Nae. They walked back over to the truck and squeezed me into a tight hug and started singing some song about getting married way off key and out of tune on purpose.

"Um—what about me?" Dina questioned.

"Oh...oops"

"I'm just playing, I'm just playing! Y'all go ahead and do y'all thang. But you coulda thought about uh sista, dough." She smiled. "And I still wanna be paid for that week!" she hollered behind her as she climbed in the car. I gave her a look. "Okay, okay. You 'on't havta pay me, *dang*! Look at how you be treatin' yo' lil' sister!"

The whole ride home I kept making him do some of his other songs. "I should be mad at you for hiding all this talent from me," I joked. "You heard me. I see you over there trying not to blush, acting all hard."

"...You know what G said when I asked him what he thought about Sherra?" Malik asked opening my car door.

"You asked him about Sherra? Get outta here!" I pushed him.

"Aright, baby? Don't do that. You know how you got them iron hands? My stomach can't handle all that."

"My bad. I'm just trippin'! *I* asked *her* what *she* thought about *Gabe*! Okay! So out with it! What did he say?"

"Well, I was tryin' ta look out for uh brotha. He's so reserved the ladies always think he's real arrogant but he's one of the coolest dudes on the planet."

"Okay, okay! Whatdidhesay? Whatdidhesay?"

"He didn't like her. He said she's regular and she talks too slow."

I almost pushed him again and stopped myself. "GUESS WHAT? *She* said *she* didn't like *him*. And get this--she said he was weird and talked too fast!" We both stopped in the middle of the doorway, looked at each other and busted out laughing.

"Baby?"

"Yeah?" I looked up at him.

"Let's sleep in the backyard tonight. I got uh tent in the basement. You down?"

403

"Yeah, that'll be fun. Lemme go change. Last one outside is a crack head!" I ran into the bedroom.

"Why you gon' do that to yo' self? You know I 'on't like junkies."

"Hmm. Bet I beat you, White Lips."

It ended up being a tie.

"Oh, yeah. Thanks for my I-Pod. A brotha could use this bad boy. I already bought thirty songs off I-tunes today," he said plugging it into the mini speaker and rotating the menu to his jazz playlist.

"Happy birthday, baby." I leaned in to taste his sexy lips. "Your lips *and* your eyes have *always* turned me on," I whispered rolling over onto my sleeping bag.

"Why *you* godda be so sexy, hungh?" he asked, laying on his back and rolling a blunt. I'd never seen him smoke before. The way he twirled the brown paper between the pad of his fingertips and his thumbs was sexy. "...You know what?"

"What?" I looked over at him and smiled faintly.

"I'ma wait on this. I 'on't feel right doing it in front of you."

"...I don't care, baby."

"Would you ever smoke?"

"No. I made that decision years ago—you know that. Why?"

"So, I shouldn't do it in front of you then, that's all. I don't wanna disrespect you... 'Member when we first met and you wouldn't look me in the eyes?" I hid my smiled in the flap of my sleeping bag. Tonight as we camped out underneath the stars, I felt a bond I'd never fathomed possible to share one human to another. With our heads sticking out of the tent, we counted as many stars as we could glittering in the sky. "Baby." He pulled my sleeping bag closer to him, melting my body against the side of his as he ran his fingers against the freeness of my hair. "You have a level of class that—I godda say, is mad impressive. Anotha woman couldn't hold a candle next ta you. You're my real angel, you know that?"

"Well...you're my King in real life...my first, my only and my friend..." I murmured drifting off to sleep on the euphoria that was his chest. Lying on his chest was like resting on crystal feathered butterfly wings riding on a trip to heaven.

CHAPTER 25

I WAS SO EXCITED about the wedding I couldn't think about anything else--nothing else! Two more weeks to go before I'd finally be *Mrs. Leigh...SMILEY!!!!!!!*

Last week we'd gone to pick my ring. All together it was six carats, a row of clear round diamonds and a swirl of round black and white pave diamonds that met together eternity style and held the three carat marquis inside the very center of the ring like it was on display.

Smiley'd gotten a deal from one of his clients who owned a jewelry store in Rodchester Hills which cut the price to a fourth of what was on the tag. I couldn't believe it when he laid down the total for my ring in cash on the glass counter the day I got it. He hated using credit and usually paid cash up front whenever he purchased anything but, even with the discount, it wasn't like the ring was cheap.

Everywhere I went people asked to look at it, which sometimes made me uncomfortable. I wasn't trying to get robbed. And it *was too* pretty! A sista had to stay on top of manicures to do it justice. But I still wore the first ring he proposed with on my right hand. Sentimental value couldn't be purchased.

I was so excited I started redecorating the house so I'd have something else to do besides count down the days and even that was fun—especially with Niq and Sher helping. Smiley'd given me a nice budget to work with. There were so many things to get...furniture, plates, vases, rugs, drapes for the living room, wooden blinds, lamps. The Mikasa store had the perfect chinaware, TJ Maxx was good for knick knacks, The H Gallery--a high end houseware store in Birmingham that had everything I didn't even know I wanted and Yogurt knew a South African furniture maker who'd sent us a wholesale catalog.

On the way to meet Dom and Sherra to help with the soup kitchen, I stopped by the Family Independency Agency. When Mrs. Dotson came out to meet me at the counter I placed a thank you envelope in her hands and gave her a huge hug.

"Girl, you look *good*! But go back ta school, sweetie. Make sure you get some kinda degree. The way you had talked about yo' classes, you need to be in *somebody's* college. And thank you. I appreciate it. No body's ever given me uh card—come to think of it, nobody's ever even told me 'thank you.' Anytime you want to, call me. Here's my cell and ma house number. I wanna hear from you, nah. And I want pictures of that wedding."

"Alright. Bye Mrs. Dotson." When I left out I couldn't help but remember that one day I was standing across the street at the bus stop. Just when you thought you knew what was ahead of you, a new unexpected curveball came flying your way.

I clicked the door to the Yukon open and drove off of Glendale. Funny thing about the Yukon was, even though it was only two years old, Smiley'd gotten it from the auction. It looked almost just like the new ones out on the market only there wasn't a car note on it.

Driving in the city you could feel summer swaying among the trees. Everything looked fresh and bright and new and for a minute. I felt like I was down in the Delta or driving along the countryside.

Summertime was in the teenagers strolling down the streets yelling and horse-playing with each other. Summertime was in the middle of sidewalks next to barbeque grills where storefront churches fixed dinners and offered car washes for money for their youth programs summer trips. Summertime sat on top of women as they flaunted the kind of freshly done hairstyles that had men pulling over and dangling out of car windows. Summertime circled children heading home with only one day of school left. Summertime sat and watched basketball courts filled with diasporas of browns talking smack and occasionally backing it all up with wanna be Jordan shots.

I was about to pass Six Mile and couldn't resist looking at the old apartment as I drove by. It was like driving past a loved one's tombstone.

When I reached BMUC, I parked next to Gabe's black and white nineteen sixty something Cadillac convertible. This summer he planned to drive it in the Woodward Dream Cruise. He loved that car. But during the winter he drove a black Grand Am. All this time of knowing him and I still didn't know what that he did for a living. I could never get it out of Smiley... I wonder if he even knew?

"Hey, Lil' Bit. Whad up?" Speaking of the devil. He was wearing a Jimmy Hendrix T-shirt with another tee shirt under it, Banana Republic jeans along with a short silver necklace that looked like something a Goth kid would wear, a pair of black sixties glasses—I guessed to match his car--and a pair of black closed toe sandals. I noticed a tattoo written sideways on his left wrist but couldn't make it out. I didn't ask since I didn't want him to think I was extra concerned.

"Hey, G. What are you doing here? When and *where* do you work?" I laughed but I was seriously waiting for the answer.

"Nice to see you, too. Today, I'm helping serve." He gave me a fake punch in the shoulder as we walked down the stairs. He had a way of talking to you yet looking past you as though a thought had just rolled by that he needed to chase after. And his eyes always looked as if he had just hit that Mary Jane.

"I'm starting to think we got a Tommy from *Martin* on our hands," I whispered to Sherra as I waited for Linda Sims to pass in line.

"No, he's a cartoonist," she answered matter factly.

"How *you* know?"

"His office is right across from my cubicle--hey Ms. Sims, how you enjoyin' summer so far?" She cut our conversation short. She should have told me that a long time ago!

"Hey, I need to make a run on the Boulevard before we go to the mall," Niq said in the church parking lot after we were done with the soup kitchen.

"Well, we could just go another day. I have to practice violin tonight for class tomorrow."

"No, it won't take that long. Plus I wanna go to the Great Indoors with you. Greg's not letting me redecorate again anytime soon--last year he said I went crazy. That's probably why 'Lik gave you a budget."

"...Well, alright."

I followed Niq while Sherra followed me to some strange place on West Grand Boulevard near 75. Niq rolled down her window and spoke extra long to a guard who finally opened the gate and let us in. The area was deserted and, with my ring, I wasn't ready to be jacked so I pulled in the lot after her. This was right around the corner from where the Piquette market used to be. Something about that meat market was weird. It always smelled funny. But now that it'd burned down I kinda missed it. Most of the people working there couldn't pronounce it right and called it Pie-kwet and it'd been surrounded by desolate shanty-like factories that made you feel like you were in a devastated part of Russia--or any other place that was always cloudy. Every holiday my grandmother'd go there and we'd come out with tons of meat for only forty dollars. Across the parking lot from where Piquette had been, there used to be a flea market you could get anything from a brand new pair of Chef's pants for only a dollar to brand new queen sized mattresses for twenty-five dollars. Detroit could be ghetto like that sometimes. That was one of the reasons you had to love the D.

After fifteen minutes of waiting in my car for Niq, I called Sher on her phone. "I'm leaving. I've got a lot ta do today, dig?"

"Leigh. Please. It's cool when Smiley says 'yo' and 'dig', but it's not ya' style, sweetie. You 'on't sound right. I know you love ole boy but leave tha New York slang ta him, okay?"

"Whatever, shut up. I'm out, she's taking too long."

"Hold on. Come ta my car right quick."

I rolled my eyes remembering back in the day how slow Niq could be. I guess some things never changed. But maybe I could use the time to pry more information on G from Sherra. He was definitely a character, that was for sure.

"Yeah?" I asked. She got out of her car and grabbed me real tight by the arm. Her eyes looked weird. "What da hell? *Sherra*? Sherra, what's going on?" She didn't say shit. She rushed me in the same warehouse-looking building Dominique had disappeared into. Sherra's face looked angry and her grip on my arm was too strong for me to slip away from her. I couldn't believe I was about to have to defend myself against her and Dominique. But when shit is about to go down, you don't have time to think, you have to defend yourself. "WHAT DA HELL IS YO' MUTHAFUKIN' PROBLEM? I'ma give yo' ass *one* second ta get da fuck up off me 'fore I beat cho' ass!" I wasn't fast enough. She grabbed my arms and pulled them real tight behind my back like I was under arrested. "Fire! Fire!" I screamed as loud as I could as she shoved my head close to my chest and pushed me ahead of her up a dark, dreary stairwell. I'd learned in a women's studies class to never yell "help." People weren't too quick to rush into a crime scene. I kicked her in the knee and continued screaming at the top of my lunges. I didn't know what she was about to do but I guess I was about to find out.

A brown wooded door flew open.

"SUR*PPPPPPPPPPPPPPPPPPPPRI*SE!" The whole crew screamed.

"Aw! MAN, FUCK Y'ALL! SERIOUSLY! DON'T YOU *EVER* DO SOME SHIT LIKE THIS TA ME AGAIN! You *know* I *hate* surprises!" My heart wouldn't stop thudding even after I found out they'd arranged a Jack and Jill shower for me and Smiley.

Everybody was cracking up laughing at my ass.

"Yo', babe? What was dat 'fire' shit about?" Smiley almost couldn't stop laughing to ask.

All I could do was shake my head.

"It was hard for me to keep a straight face. But look. If you *ever* kick me like that again, yo' ass is dead." Sherra was still smiling. "You are *the hardest* person to surprise. You ask too many questions. But I had to take you 'cause I couldn't figure out another way ta get you ta go in. Niq had to make sure G was here and that he had brought the food in. Plus I had ta make sure Tommy remembered he was supposed ta watch the kids so Dina could come."

G's loft was an out of this world, spectacular work of art in itself. He had the entire third floor, which made for a humongously spacious pad. Track lights hung from the high ceilings. The exposed brick walls were covered with paintings and sketches--drawings that showed off tremendous talent; abstracts, cartoons, picture-like and minimalist styles. There was a swing underneath a skylight that Niq was now using to lift herself into the air. Next to the skylight right next to the swing was a corner that looked like a mini greenhouse filled with a small forest of plants, some as tall as small trees. Bjork played right before one of Jamiroquai's albums blasted over the sound system. Old fashion records hung on pegs along the wall. When I asked G how he came up with the concept, he simply stated, "So I could find 'em," and kept walking towards the refrigerator. There was a huge silver Mac laptop on a glass desk next to an easel. Posted on the wall across from the funny looking wooden futon that was draped with a fuzzy black blanket he had the same flat screen TV Malik had. In the bedroom a huge oversized bed that looked much larger than king size rested on the floor underneath the huge window void of curtains and blinds. A vintage nightstand held an old school, from the twenties kind of phone with the circular receiver and triangular earpiece you had to hold. There was a shiny metallic bookshelf filled with tons books on Malcolm X, books on the dark continent, movies, art books and a ton of his portfolios.

Being nosey and touring his place I missed Detroit's wife come in. The mayor's wife was a cute dark skinned sister with locks that were so tiny from far away you couldn't even tell they were locks.

"Hey, girl, I heard about that ring!" She smiled. "It is *too* sharp. I'm about to harass D to get me another one." We both laughed. At first I had been real distant towards her since Darren hung real tough with her husband but she and I had gotten cool since we seemed to always end up sitting near each other at the center on Sundays. She was too busy with her own hectic life to be worried about my personal affairs and she adored Malik and--I found out from Niq--she wasn't at all a Darren fan. She and Niq had a pretty good rapport since they were often at many of the same events. Sherra liked her because she was dark skinned.

Sherra's mother and a perfumed oil smelling, army camouflage baggy pant wearing Dina came over along with a few more of Smiley's Rasta friends and Yogurt, officially starting the party.

The fellas stood in a corner of the huge living room kicking their feet in some jumpy dance Smiley was good at while swapping lyrics and challenging each other's freestyle abilities. The only thing missing was a bong. But that was out anyway. He usually only indulged on weekends with his boys.

I called Mrs. Dotson and invited her hoping she'd be able to make it on such a short notice.

"Could somebody *pul-lease*, change the music up in here?" Ma complained thru a Zap Mama song. G shook his head and threw on an Anita Baker CD. Then it was Luther and Motown for the rest of the party.

After the Pizza Papalis deep-dish vegetarian pizza, Dina's chicken wings that were fried to perfection, red beans and rice, and plantain, it was gift time. When she got off work, Mrs. Dotson came over and joined the party bringing a white lacy nightgown everybody tried to embarrass Smiley and me about. Instead we kissed until they begged us to stop. "Man, I ain't tryin' ta see all that," G shook his head. "Nevertheless, I'm happy for y'all two gay ass love birds."

"Well, what do you buy the couple that already has everything? Nothing. Here you two go." Sherra handed me a gold envelope. Everybody else seemed to be on the same tip. Greg couldn't make it but he and Niq did a good job of hooking a brotha and sista up. We ended up with almost five g's, which, as Smiley whispered in my ear when we were alone in the kitchen, "Was quite a*rrrit*e."

"Honeymoon, here we come!" I said reading his mind and swapping fives with him. "Now I see why you wanted to chill with G. It's amazing in here," I added.

He smiled. "Well, soon we'll be living together so...hangin' wit him for now is cool."

"Ummh, hmm. I bet."

I walked past the bedroom and noticed Sherra and G standing in there spaced far, far apart—just the two of them. I stood near the doorway and eavesdropped—she would have certainly done it to me.

"I don't like you," she stated blandly. If she kept this up, she was *never* going to get any! Next, she was gonna stop shaving her armpits and waxing her eyebrows or--in the event she began growing a beard—she would be one of those types who didn't even attempt laser hair removal treatments. If and when some kind of Feminist Acerbity did occur, I was going to kidnap her and force her to let go of that virginity one way or the other—even if it meant I had to hook her up with a male escort. And if she didn't comply, I'd blackmail her with that weed-smoking incident--*she was just curious my behind*!

"Yeah... I don't like you either," he responded rather nonchalantly as he walked over to his alarm clock and tinkered with it. "Gotta wake up early tomorrow..." he added, saying it more to himself than her.

"So? I didn't ask... You spilled that punch on me on purpose."

"...Get over it... That was last year. And it blended in with that red shirt you had on." He yawned. She was right, G did talk kind of fast. I stole a peek, surprised they hadn't caught me yet. I was able to make out the tattoo: Freedom, written in thick black antique-looking letters.

"Hmm… You're an oreo," Sherra assessed and walked out of the room. I played it off and acted like I'd just walked out of the bathroom. I couldn't wait to tell Niq.

"Chemistry if you ask me," she whispered covering her mouth.

"Girl, she'd beat poor G's behind everyday. He'd be an abused husband coming out with his story years later after he hired a bodyguard. You shoulda seen her man-handle me earlier!"

"Fire! Fire!" Niq mimicked walking out of the kitchen cracking up.

We partied until well after ten even though it was a work night. Mrs. Dotson was very impressed by Smiley and wanted to hook her niece up with Gabe.

"That was cool. I'm glad they came thru with something since I ain't havin' uh bachelor party--I 'ont need ta pay no stripper. I already got what I need and *I'm good*…as long as you promise ta hook a brotha up immediately, promptly, fa sho', with no delays, right after the 'I do' part!"

"Oh, I do." I held up my hand like I was under oath, looked him up and down and licked my lips.

Malik tilted his head back and smirked in that sexy stance of his, licked his lips and planted a soft kiss on mine before he watched me pull out of the gate.

"NO, LET'S WAIT ON putting the drapes up. Smiley's gonna have to drill 'em in place, besides—you know how he likes to feel all 'involved' and whatnot… Doesn't it look out-cold in here?" I asked in awe of the living room's new look. Sherra was busy trying to open the box for the drapes that had just gotten delivered anyway.

"The furniture makes it much, much cozier," Niquie assessed before going to the kitchen to pour another glass of the vanilla shake Sherra'd made that was on point. Lately she had been testing out a multitude of recipes on us like we were lab rats.

"What? Is that a better way of saying 'makes it look smaller'?" I shouted after her.

"Can you *ever* just take a compliment?" she called back.

"Huh! All day long," Sherra quipped twisting her mouth and raising an eyebrow my way.

Dom and Sher saved me from making the mistake of choosing overly modern furniture that—although it would have looked sharp for the moment—would have been outdated in a couple of years. Instead, with their help, I decided on a somewhat classic scheme and made it trendy with accent pieces. A pearlized crème and gray sofa and loveseat, a glass oval coffee table and end tables that matched the wood throughout the house. G painted a few separately framed abstracts that together made one piece. We placed them near the sofa. With a few vases and exotic brushed silver floor lamps to match.

I only added a glass table for the stereo and two bookshelves in the den and left it alone since Smiley had done a pretty decent job with it.

We had the cabinets redone to update the kitchen and we hooked the dinning room up by lifting the carpet to reveal a gorgeous hardwood floor, a tan-ish marble table that helped blend the furniture in the den with the living room, padded fabric chairs, a chandelier, a wide brushed silver framed mirror for the wall and an all glass curio that showed off the chinaware and hand dipped candles and fancy glassware.

For Mauri's room we chose a white bedroom suite with a canopied bed Dom said Mauri kept pointing at. We put a cute girly border up around the top of her bedroom walls, added accessories from Macy's, a lavender comforter with tons of square and circular deco pillows trimmed in iridescent sequins and we organized the closet with shelves--Dominique had already gotten her too many clothes.

Pharaoh picked out a red and black racecar bed that was just like the one he had at Darren's for his room along with a desk and a kiddy armoire.

For me and Smiley's room, I chose a mattress that was so soft, it felt like laying on a king sized pillow filled with feathers, a grand, noir leather quilted headboard and bed-frame, matching black wooden nightstands and a dresser with a huge mirror to stand over it. Along the wall next to our closet was a framed drawing of the African continent in simulated gold.

We took down the shiny wallpaper in both bathrooms but (of course) Smiley wasn't too keen on paying painters. He, G and Hakeem did a really good paint job instead. One was a pastel yellow and white while the other was painted white and cotton candy lavender. A mini, old-fashioned chandelier was placed in the front bathroom while recessed lighting replaced the lights over the mirror in the other bathroom. Decorative towels, mats, matching flower paintings, beautifully ornate towel holders and candles and the bathrooms were done.

Smiley got a new desk with a chair that massaged the back, a new and much faster running computer. *Scarface* and some of his other keepsake pictures hung on the wall and another wall was put up to divide the laundry area while a play area for the kids—for use only when he wasn't working in his office—took up the extra space. Oh yes. And we put a shiny gold pole in the basement for our very own, after kiddy hours spot...

The three of us sat in the dining room, sipping our shakes and admiring each room like we were on a Black version of a Martha Stewart show as a Sade CD played on the stereo when Smiley came in making a ruckus. "Aye, babe! Babe? Where you at? Aye! Aye! I GOT THAT EXTENDED CONTRACT WITH THE CITY! WE GOT IT! WE GOT IT BABY! Do you *know* what *this* means?" He swooped me into the air, swung me around and kissed me. Smiley Plumbing was going commercial. My baby was about to be making some big time loot. The company's expansion meant he was going to have to hire a team of employees.

"Okay, call everybody up. I'm 'bouta cook. We're celebrating. What do y'all wanna eat? I could do uh roast?" Sherra grabbed her purse to go to the store.

"NO!" Smiley, Niq and I all shouted in unison.

"Ah, ah, lets--lets do fish...fish and chips," Smiley quickly added so as to not hurt her feelings. Some things she could hook up... Some dishes she could fuck up.

"Yeah, that perch you fried last Friday was the bomb—but we need to cut all this fried stuff down... I'm doing a salad," I added.

"And I can eat it," Niq chimed in. She did not cook. Good thing we were cool again. I was sure Greg appreciated getting invited over for home cooked meals on a regular basis.

"Oh, yeah—y'all did y'all thang and hooked this crib up--that's fa sho'." Smiley was pleased.

CHAPTER 26

THE BALMY KAUAI BREEZE blew its blessings upon me and fluttered against the white scarf on my head. The sheer shawl wrapped around my shoulders, raised against my back and traveled in the wind like a kite still connecting me to the sandy earth below. It made me remember the vision I had what now seemed like a long, long time ago, the vision Smiley had simply regarded as, "Beautiful".

I was a queen in the white dress Mama Harris had sewn for me. It dipped low in the back and was long and fitted. I had chosen the loosely wrapped head covering instead of a regular tiara-crowned veil and was now a new woman from a world of old. I was about to give the King of my dreams a newly wrapped present to treasure into an infinite and timeless forever.

Dominique, Sherra, Greg, G, Dina, Pharaoh and Mauri all smiled against nature's green, blue, and brown backdrop as I walked past them and stood next to Smiley. He reached for my hand as Mauri waved at us.

At that moment, when my hand slid into his, I felt as though I'd finally made it to the lulling tranquility some call heaven. The twinkles of joy that emitted from his eyes, Malik Smiley, who like I, had no middle name, made the solitary cloud in the sky that lingered about in it's very own lonely corner, over the blue Po'ipu gem-like waters, fade into a palm tree next to where Brother Davis was standing. When I looked into Smiley's eyes again the cloud completely disappeared.

As we exchanged declaration of intentions we'd written to one another, I let the energy of his words invoke themselves into me; twinkles, shimmers, glitters of happiness. This feeling could be compared to nothing other than Spirit's ethereal bliss.

Malik's smooth brown skin delighted the sun against the blackness of his tuxedo. "Leigh, you are the spirit of honey that has mixed within the blood of my veins--the only mother of the dark continent who's energy was able to balance my very own. I promise to love you, to respect you, to cherish and protect you and to loyally and faithfully share my entire being with you and you alone no matter the tribulations that may come our way. May we complete the journey of our lives together forever as one, until death do us part." He placed the marquis upon my finger after I switched the bouquet of calla lilies into my right hand. His smile poured rays of satisfying energy throughout my entirety as his was the only real nourishment my spirit had ever truly craved.

"I, Leigh Anderson, stand before you today, recognizing you as the one Father God and Mother Goddess sent forth to me. I promise to love you, to believe in you, to trust you, to encourage you and to give you,

Malik Smiley, all the components of my soul, my spirit and my heart. For there is no other walking the earth for me. No matter what forces of destruction may cross our path, I promise you loyalty and faithfulness until death do us part." I placed the white gold band on his finger.

Beneath the palm trees, Smiley held me delicately against his soul and lit his lips upon mine to light a flame that would continue to burn a million years and more, taking me to my very own promised land.

Dominique's eyes filled with tears right before Greg reached over to hold her hand.

"I now pronounce you, Husband and Wife." Brother Davis finished our ceremony smiling long and hard before hugging us both.

I hugged everyone, ready to break away and share my soul with Smiley. I wanted everything to be just right, to be as perfect as Smiley was. I looked around and took in Kauai. No wonder they called it the Garden Island. It was paradise with jewel-like emerald-topped mountains, luscious green grass, and the medley of flowers in their endless variations and colors. No place on earth should be so beautiful. But it was.

"Well. Our condo is on the other side of the island so, we won't be seeing you two until you get back. Besides, we're leaving Wednesday anyway—so I've got to enjoy as much of my second honeymoon as I can, see you." Dominique hugged me. "I'm happy for you, Leigh...for us. Look at how we've grown." She smiled.

"I'm proud of you. It was beautiful." Sherra added in. "Well, we've got to go."

"I thought you were gonna stay for a few days and leave when Niq leaves?"

"Nah, I'm leaving tomorrow night." She smiled. I felt bad. Had it been me, I wouldn't have wanted to stay all alone on the island while my two best friends were enjoying a romantic getaway, either. But in my heart I knew she would one day find her king as well. She was so unselfish, she hadn't even allowed us to pay her way. "I love you," I said hugging her again.

"I know. I love you, too—even Smiley." The elegant upsweep she wore her hair in revealed her pretty dark brown face in a way that made her look different.

Dina and the kids waved as my husband and I walked towards our condo. I took my heels off and allowed my feet to flop within the silkiness of the sand. My toes curled around a couple of small sea shells. "Baby, this place is wonderful. I'm glad you picked it. It's way more personal and special than if we would have stayed in a hotel... I love you, Smiley." The scenery, the beaches the waterfalls of the Regan Resort, the villa-like condo—it was enough to make you want to live here forever.

"I'm glad you like it. Although, I don't think you're gonna be seeing too much of it for the next three days." He smiled grabbing my waist. "Good thing we got a secluded spot. I'm 'bout ta learn every inch of this sexy body from head ta toe."

"So? We've got two weeks. I'm thinkin' bedroom first, then on that balcony."

"Yeah, I'ma have you on the beach and—wait uh minute. What happened to G? I didn't see him leave. He came up to me and said 'I did 'im proud' and straight up vanished."

"You know, he didn't even hug me? I just thought about that... I feel bad for him and Sherra. How long is he staying?"

"He didn't say but...I think I need to call him or something. I mean, I know he doesn't have anything against you. He's just like that sometimes. But when I was staying over there I picked up on how he had started talking about wantin' what we had."

Smiley pulled out his phone after walking up the steps to the condo and sat on the top step. "Once I hear from him, I'm turning this phone off til' we get back," he stated looking at me and licking his lips solidifying both of our thoughts. "Hey G, you need ta answer yo' phone, man. I'm on ma honeymoon lookin' fa yo' ass. Where you at? Hit uh brotha back--real quick, real quick, son, serious business. "Call Dom and see if she knows what's up," he added after ending his message on G's voicemail.

I called her three times before she finally answered, "Yeah?" She sounded out of breath like she had been running or something. "I didn't think you'd have any problems knowing what to do! You already *have* two kids! Girl, I'm about to get some—I *THOUGHT* THAT'S WHAT YOU'D BE TRYIN' TA DO, RIGHT ABOUT NOW. *WHAT*????"

"Yeah, yeah, yeah--look. We didn't see G leave and he didn't even say anything to me after the ceremony. You know if he's okay? That's not like him."

"...Well...alright. I'll call him and see what's up. Peace out! You need to be doin' what I'm 'bout ta do!"

"Oh, *trust me*, as soon as I find G, I'ma kill 'im fa holdin' uh sista up. And then I'ma get down ta tha real deal wit *ma* man. Talk to you in two weeks." I pressed End and slid off my veil.

"Call Sherra and see if she knows what's up. I can't take it. I'm 'bout ta go in and start getting ready for that promise you made. 'Member? No bachelor's party as long as—"

"—Oh, I already know. Blame ya' boy, *not me*."

Sherra answered the third time I called on the fourth ring. She sounded grumpy. "Sher? I didn't see G leave and 'Lik's worried. You know where he is? He's holding up our honeymoon. He didn't even say anything to me--that's not like him."

"Yeah, he's right here. We were both 'bouta go eat dinner."

"...Well." I was about to hate myself for this one but, both of them seemed really down in spirits. "Alright, why don't you two stop by real quick?"

She sighed, "...*Leigh*?" and then she sighed again, "It's no big deal. I'll see you when you come home. How *you* look? You supposed ta be getting' sum."

"*Please*? He didn't even say anything to me..."

"Alright, alright. Here. Talk to 'im." She handed G the phone.

"Yeah?" He was so nonchalant it wasn't even funny anymore.

"What's the deal? You didn't even say bye or anything..."

"Oh, no offense. By the way, you got Mauri's bag? Dina can't find it."

"Oooh. Wait a minute. Lemme check." I ran inside only to see the bag on the top of the counter. "Hey, baby. Hold on a sec. They need Mauri's bag." Smiley was already in the bedroom under the covers making a tent with...well--with himself and now giving me a tortured look. "Yeah, it's here. Hurry up. And don't bring the kids. I don't want them crying to stay with us again--usually they cry to *stay* with Dina but I guess they wanna stay in paradise too, hunh? HURRY UP!"

"Yeah, yeah, yeah, *aright*."

When G and Sherra walked up, the expression both of their faces was dismal.

"G? You were wrong for just walking off like that, I thought we were family. How come you didn't even say anything to me after the ceremony." Maybe he *didn't* really like me.

"Oh, come on now." He grabbed me and gave me a big hug.

I handed Sherra the bag. "Here. Smile you two. Hang out tonight or something." Sherra had already started walking off. This wasn't like her at all. She was acting flat out jealous—which I could semi-understand. My wedding *was* all the stuff fairy tales were made of. But I was basically her sister. She wasn't allowed to get jealous.

I pulled her arm and noticed a smear. Makeup? She was covering up a tattoo on her upper arm. I grabbed her and rubbed the rest of the cover up off! "WHAD DA HELL!" **GABE H.**

"Well, you're the one who insisted on having us wearing these sleeveless dresses." She chuckled. I snatched both of them by their arms and pulled them inside with me.

"BABY! YOU'VE GOT TO COME OUT HERE AND SEE THIS! GABE AND SHERRA ARE HERE, BABY!"

417

He came out in a silk robe that did nothing to hide his future plans. "DIS SHIT BEDDA BE *IMPORTANT* THAN *UH MUTHAFUCKA*!"

"Look!" I thrusted Sherra his way.

"What tha FUCK!" He looked like he still wanted to be upset about the delay going on with the bedroom show but couldn't.

Gabe just stood there looking bored as ever. "Your place is set up same as ours," he noted more to himself than anyone else as he looked around.

"I've *godda* call Dom for this one." I went to the breakfast bar to pick up my cell.

"She already knows. She caught us kissing in the Center's parking lot the day y'all had the shower," Sherra interjected. I couldn't believe this. "He was only acting funny because he didn't wanna ruin you guys' shine. We're really happy for you two—you know—with all the drama y'all had goin' on and whatnot. We didn't wanna to tell you until later... We got married earlier that day."

"YOU WHAT!?!" Smiley and I both shouted dropping our mouths to the floor.

"Yeah, justice of the peace. We couldn't decide on a church. She wanted Baptist. I wanted the Center."

"Aright you two. We'll see you later. We have our own honeymoon to attend to," Sherra said reaching for the doorknob getting ready to walk out.

"Wait a minute! How come Dom didn't say anything? MARRIED? HOW COME YOU TWO DIDN'T JUST TELL US?"

"Well...it's really no big deal," Sherra stated as G simply shrugged. They were acting like holy matrimony was the equivalent of rolling up to a Burger King intercom and ordering a Junior Whopper value meal.

"You've got a *tattoo* of G's *name* on your *arm*! It is a big deal! It's a very, very, big, *humongous* deal!"

"Whatever. I've got her name on me, too." He cut his eyes like I was irking the only nerve he had left and lifted the right sleeve of his tux to reveal:

SHERRA H, MY LOVE

written on his outer lower arm in the same block letters as the Freedom tattoo on the inner part of his left forearm.

"That explains the long sleeves... So *that* explains the long sleeves... I swear It was like ninety-degrees the other day and you had on a freakin' sweater!" I pushed G completely out of the doorway and yelled at Sherra. "And *that's* why you reminded me to get that pole in the basement—I had completely forgot about it but *you remembered*! That explains it! You two make me sick! Get out! You'd think you'd tell your best friend when you lose your much-cherished virginity in marriage! Is *G* the '*person*' you smoked with on lunch last year? Um-hm, you know you two do kinda smell like pot right now." When they first walked up, I had sniffed it on them. I was gonna let it slide but she was flat-out wrong for withholding all this info from *me* of all people. She knew every last drop of my business. "Yeah, I'm right, hungh?" She rushed out of the entrance with a priceless look of embarrassment scrawled all over her face. "That's right! Run! You've got all those years of not getting any to make up for!"

"So *that's* why it started taking him a long time to open up when I came to crash at the crib...unh-hunh, *that's* the one from work!" Smiley shook his head and broke into a huge grin. "Thanks for remembering that pole, Sher!" he called out after them. G grinned back and continued walking down the steps. He reached for Sherra's hand as I closed the door.

I sat down at the kitchen table and shook my head. Just when you thought you had seen it all, something new was always awaiting you in another bag. They had definitely tricked us all right.

"Aye, baby? Can we have that meeting in the bedroom? I already nutted twice on GP (general principal) just from waiting!" He threw his hands up in the air in frustration, walked over to where I was sitting at the kitchen breakfast bar and started unzipping the back of my dress real fast.

"Wait! I godda go change. I want everything to be *just* right. Hold on, baby." I ran into the other bedroom to get my bag I'd placed everything I needed for this moment.

"*Arrrrgh*! Leigh! L*eeeeeiiiiigggh*! Come on! G's probably getting more action than me right about nah!" he yelled after me as I went into the bathroom and locked the door.

I'd waited for this. I wanted everything to be just like it had been over and over again in my dreams. I slid my bridal dress off and picked up the long silk and lace, beaded white nightgown. In the front, lace appliqué slightly covered my breasts. A long split showed off the sun kissed glimmer that now browned my legs, the split running into the sheer form fitted material that laid against my upper stomach and revealed the lower portion of my chest as though it had been custom made.

I slid my French manicured toes into the lace heels, my heart beating madly as if it was the very first time when I dabbed the jasmine oil on. ...In a sense I *was* a virgin. I was *his* virgin and he, too, was mine.

Appreciating the healing powers of time, I was ready to give myself to the man I'd been created for the soul purposes of loving, the only man I was supposed to love completely, wholeheartedly and unconditionally.

Between the sheets in the room next to me, the only man entitled to me would soon be receiving my soul and it felt as though gossamer wings had been fastened upon the entirety of my back.

I entered the doorway of the bedroom and lifted my gaze upon him. He stared into me, taking in the rebirth of my now unsullied spirit.

In his nakedness, he stood up and reached for me, to receive me, holding my body close to his chest the way the sky now closely held the slow setting sun as I gazed out the open double balcony doors...

...Loosely, gingerly, delicately, tenderly, naturally, the way forces that know nothing of constricting physical bounds intertwine together. He looked into me, understanding who I had forever been and our souls fell upon each other, locked in a fervent embrace that spoke more words than either one of us had ever spoken our whole lives upon this earth.

I found a protective hiding space away from the rest of the world underneath his chest. As he slid against me tenderly tracing my face the same way he had months ago when I had tried to deny the reality of his love, I promised, with my eyes, never to resist him again.

My body trembled in the same manner the evening breeze now affected the balcony curtains as he delicately touched me with adoring fingers. When I could no longer take his melding touch, his eyes looked into mine knowing I was completely ready to allow him to become a part of me. Seconds later, I endured a brief twinge of virgin-like sharpness and a tear of pleasure tricked down my face. My gaze eased the concern from his and...

> our souls began
> singing in harmony,
> responding to touches
> of tactile and intangible ecstasy,
> exploring new and familiar spaces...

EVEN IF YOU DON'T...

I HAD BEEN STANDING in the doorway of Pharaoh's bedroom so long I lost track of time.

Watching him as he sleeps, I can see why he's been stealing all the fifth grade girls' hearts. He is quite handsome, that straight-A, lil' captain of the football team son of ours.

Any minute the Sherra and Gabe Hill tribe will be here to take the kids to Tommy's football game at MSU. (You know I had to ask and, yes, she *did* wait until she got married--which is probably why they now have FIVE absolutely gorgeous, healthy and happy kids. Good thing they purchased G's building. They certainly need the room! Sher's got her own column in the paper and G now works from home. You can learn *two* hundred and one things about *their* relationship from that Sunday comic strip of his—humorous but it's all love. They have just released the first volume of their Dada, feminist ranting and experimental art-filled magazine, entitled BlackShoeGrind by Hill).

Mauri is as pretty as can be but has inherited Craig's eyebrows (speaking of whom is in rehab, unable to get/maintain a job even within the fast food sector and has been known to insist upon calling every female he comes in contact with Leigh). I am currently working on convincing Smiley to allow her to get them waxed. My hypothesis as to why she is the third grade bully has narrowed down to the middle brow connection. As a mother, I hate to see my gorgeous eight-year-old baby doll looking as though she is always angry strictly on GP. Other than that, she plays the drums like she was born to be in a rock and roll African band and has organized a softball team Smiley coaches which consists of her brother, Niq and Greg's son Aiden (the adoption process went smoothly, thank goodness. She couldn't wait to bring that boy home and totally has her hands full--Greg being re-elected into office and all) and some of Sher and G's kids—I don't feel like remembering all my nieces and nephews' names right now. But I *have* to say this: they named their second son—the one right after Gabriel Junior, they named him Jupiter! ...Yeah. Then again, my kids get teased all the time because of their names. But, as I always tell them, their names have true meanings.

Like Sunrise Maleika Smiley, the three year old little one (who is now taking violin lessons after bugging a straight year, all when she was two about it. She wakes up every morning smiling and is the only one in the house with a middle name). She gave Smiley a major scare during her labor. They said the way he flipped out had them worried the entire four hours I was in critical condition but after the Caesarean she and I and Smiley were just fine. All I remember is waking up to him holding my hand as the sun was rising. Everyone, including Mama Harris and Mrs. Dotson (who is truly my aunt) came in from the waiting room where they'd been waiting the whole time. Darren even popped up to make sure I was okay—who called and told him I was going thru complications, I don't know.

(What I do know is one time he made the mistake of stating that he wanted me to carry his next child but would not *dare* slip up and say anything else close to anything like that again. Besides, even though the date has been on 'To Be Announced' status for the past two years, he is now engaged to Syra after Mike dumped her and married a sista who's a math teacher, has him on an eleven PM curfew *and* has him doing professional swing dancing competitions with her. Two weeks after he broke up with Sy, he was married to TaShena).

As for Smiley and me? We have everyday problems just like anyone else but, at the end of the day, he is my best friend. And...there is much to be said about a wonderful man and the magical powers of a hook (Think back to the letter J and you'll know). But I'm not going to get all into the details--after all, he *is my husband*! And, yes, he *is* perfect. For anyone out there who begs to differ, you, too—even if you don't believe at first—you too will change your mind once you meet your very own dream.

Smiley's family finally accepted our marriage after Maleika was born. (I guess they *finally* realized I wasn't going anywhere and wanted to be in Sunrise's life—she *is* his parent's first grandchild and they are doing a very good job of spoiling or, should I say, loving her). My mother and grandmother, unfortunately, still do not wish to have anything to do with me.

But. I can truly say that I am happy. I am now a psychologist (a year and counting *and* setting my own hours--three days a week with clients, one day for research, thank you very much). Specializing in women's issues, I conduct ongoing workshops at the Center and hold statewide seminars on various themes of self-love, self-esteem and domestic violence.

The day after we got back from our honeymoon Smiley talked me into going to Wayne State to register.

How could I not love the man!

Thank You's

Thanks to my parents M. William Adufutse and Annie Adufutse; thanks to my uncle Keith H. Taylor for the good mix of common sense and foresight and for understanding another artist.

A thank you to Burton International and the summer writing workshops there and all my early teachers from the fourth grade to the eighth who made learning fun and for the Writer's Circle and workshops -- I would definitely not be a writer were it not for your encouragement. Another thank you to Cass Technical (the best high school in the world!) and my teachers there and the Michigan Youth Arts and the creative writing course I took way back when; Ferris State for their Governor's Leadership Seminar of which pushed me to pursue much more than I'd previously deemed possible; Wayne State University for having such good instructors in the Sociology and African American studies departments and Columbia College Chicago for helping me grow and become a better writer.

More thank you's to Lakeyla M. for believing in this book when hardly anyone else did and for reading all the revisions, to Dorothy J. for the moral support and Tamika for showing up and supporting. Thank to Alysyn C. for her help in the beginning phase and a big shout out to Asia/Nozomi Live for being there on the graphics tip with the new cover—thanks Maisha H. for introducing us; a huge thank you to Vanessa Nieson for looking out on the editing tip and for being a good person from the fourth grade up to now. Another thank you for that one person who always pushed me to work on the manuscript and to see it to fruition, a thank you to all the people who have helped me along the way and to all the people who said I'd never do it — you all were nothing but motivational forces!

Last but never, never least, one big huge thanks to my I-book, my baby, with all the keys all scratched off from all the time spent typing, mommy loves you!

Printed in the United States
146368LV00001B/1/P

9 781604 022735

Дневной
Дозор